JONATHAN KELLERMAN

TWO COMPLETE ALEX DELAWARE NOVELS

DEVIL'S WALTZ

Bad Love

WINGS BOOKS
NEW YORK

This 2003 edition is published by Wings Books®, an imprint of Random House Value Publishing, a division of Random House, Inc., New York, by arrangement with Ballantine, a division of Random House, Inc.

Wings Books® and colophon are trademarks of Random House, Inc.

Random House
New York • Toronto • London • Sydney • Auckland
www.randomhouse.com

Printed and bound in the United States of America

A catalog record for this title is available from the Library of Congress.

ISBN 0-517-22196-9

10 9 8 7 6 5 4 3

Contents

DEVIL'S WALTZ

To my son, Jesse,
a gentleman and a scholar

———————

Special thanks to Reuben Eagle,
Allan Marder, Yuki Novick, Michael Samet,
Dennis Payne, and Harry Weisman, M.D.

Ring out old shapes of foul disease;
Ring out the narrowing lust of gold.

—ALFRED, LORD TENNYSON

1

It was a place of fear and myth, home of miracles and the worst kind of failure.

I'd spent a quarter of my life there, learning to deal with the rhythm, the madness, the starched *whiteness* of it all.

Five years' absence had turned me into a stranger, and as I entered the lobby anxiety tickled my belly.

Glass doors, black granite floors, high, concave travertine walls advertising the names of dead benefactors.

Glossy depot for an unguided tour of uncertainty.

Spring, outside, but in here time had a different meaning.

A group of surgical interns—God, they were taking them young—slouched by on paper-soled scrub slippers, humbled by double shifts. My own shoes were leather-bottomed and they clacked on the granite.

Ice-slick floors. I'd just started my internship when they'd been installed. I remembered the protests. Petitions against the illogic of polished stone in a place where children ran and walked and limped and wheeled. But some philanthropist had liked the look. Back in the days when philanthropists had been easy to come by.

Not much granite visible this morning; a crush of humanity filled the lobby, most of it dark-skinned and cheaply dressed, queued up at the glassed-in booths, waiting for the favors of stone-faced clerks. The clerks avoided eye contact and worshipped paper. The lines didn't seem to be moving.

Babies wailed and suckled; women sagged; men swallowed curses and stared at the floor. Strangers bumped against one another and sought refuge in the placebo of banter. Some of the children—those who still looked like children—twisted and bounced and struggled against weary adult arms, breaking away for precious seconds of freedom before being snagged and reeled back in. Others—pale, thin, sunken, bald, painted in unnatural colors—stood there silently, heartbreakingly compliant. Sharp words in foreign tongues crackled above the drone of the paging operators. An occasional smile or bit of cheer brightened the inertial gloom, only to go out like a spark from a wet flint.

As I got closer I smelled it.

Rubbing alcohol, antibiotic bitters, the sticky-ripe liqueur of elixir and affliction.

Eau de Hospital. Some things never changed. But I had; my hands were cold.

I eased my way through the crowd. Just as I got to the elevators, a heavyset man in a navy-blue rent-a-cop uniform stepped out of nowhere and blocked my way. Blond-gray crewcut and a shave so close his skin looked wet-sanded. Black-frame glasses over a triangular face.

"Can I help you, sir?"

"I'm Dr. Delaware. I have an appointment with Dr. Eves."

"I need to see some ID, sir."

Surprised, I fished a five-year-old clip-on badge out of my pocket. He took it and studied it as if it were a clue to something. Looked up at me, then back at the ten-year-old black-and-white photo. There was a walkie-talkie in his hand. Holstered pistol on his belt.

I said, "Looks like things have tightened up a bit since I was last here."

"This is expired," he said. "You still on staff, sir?"

"Yes."

He frowned and pocketed the badge.

I said, "Is there some kind of problem?"

"New badges required, sir. If you go right past the chapel, over to Security, they can shoot your picture and fix you up." He touched the badge on his lapel. Color photograph, ten-digit ID number.

"How long will that take?" I said.

"Depends, sir." He looked past me, as if suddenly bored.

"On what?"

"How many are ahead of you. Whether your paperwork's current."

I said, "Listen, my appointment with Dr. Eves is in just a couple of minutes. I'll take care of the badge on my way out."

" 'Fraid not, sir," he said, still focused somewhere else. He folded his arms across his chest. "Regulations."

"Is this something recent?"

"Letters were sent to the medical staff last summer."

"Must have missed that one." Must have dropped it in the trash, unopened, like most of my hospital mail.

He didn't answer.

"I'm really pressed for time," I said. "How about if I get a visitor's badge to tide me over?"

"Visitor's badges are for visitors, sir."

"I'm visiting Dr. Eves."

He swung his eyes back to me. Another frown—darker, contemplative. He inspected the pattern on my tie. Touched his belt on the holster side.

"Visitor's badges are over at Registration," he said, hooking a thumb at one of the dense queues.

He crossed his arms again.

I smiled. "No way around it, huh?"

"No, sir."

"Just past the chapel?"

"Just past and turn right."

"Been having crime problems?" I said.

"I don't make the rules, sir. I just enforce them."

He waited a moment before moving aside, followed my exit with his squint. I turned the corner, half expecting to see him trailing, but the corridor was empty and silent.

The door marked SECURITY SERVICES was twenty paces down. A sign hung from the knob: BACK IN above a printed clock with movable hands set at 9:30 A.M. My watch said 9:10. I knocked anyway. No answer. I looked back. No rent-a-cop. Remembering a staff elevator just past Nuclear Medicine, I continued down the hall.

Nuclear Medicine was now COMMUNITY RESOURCES. Another closed door. The elevator was still there but the buttons were missing; the machine had been switched to key-operated. I was looking for the nearest stairway when a couple of orderlies appeared, wheeling an empty gurney. Both were young, tall, black, sporting geometrically carved hip-hop hairstyles. Talking earnestly about the Raiders game. One of them produced a key, inserted it into the lock, and turned. The elevator doors opened on walls covered with padded batting. Junk-food wrappers and a piece of dirty-looking gauze littered the floor. The orderlies pushed the gurney in. I followed.

General Pediatrics occupied the eastern end of the fourth floor, separated from the Newborn Ward by a swinging wooden door. I knew the outpatient clinic had been open for only fifteen minutes but the small waiting room was already overflowing. Sneezes and coughs, glazed looks and hyperactivity. Tight maternal hands gripped babes and toddlers, paperwork, and the magic plastic of Medi-Cal cards. To the right of the reception window was a set of double doors marked PATIENTS REGISTER FIRST over a Spanish translation of same.

I pushed through and walked past a long white corridor tacked with safety and nutrition posters, county health bulletins, and bilingual exhortations to nurture, vaccinate, and abstain from alcohol and dope. A dozen or so examining rooms were in use, their chart-racks brimming over. Cat-cries and the sounds of comfort seeped from under the doors. Across the hall were files, supply cabinets, and a refrigerator marked with a red cross. A secretary tapped a computer keyboard. Nurses hustled between the cabinets and the exam rooms. Residents spoke into chin-cradled phones and trailed after fast-stepping attending physicians.

The wall right-angled to a shorter hallway lined with doctors' offices. Stephanie Eves's open door was the third in a set of seven.

The room was ten by twelve, with institutional-beige walls relieved by bracket shelves filled with books and journals, a couple of Miró posters, and one cloudy window with an eastern view. Beyond the glint of car-tops, the peaks of the Hollywood hills seemed to be dissolving into a broth of billboards and smog.

The desk was standard hospital-issue phony walnut and chrome, pushed up against one wall. A hard-looking chrome and orange-cloth chair competed for space with a scuffed brown Naugahyde recliner. Between the chairs a thrift-shop end table supported a coffee maker and a struggling philodendron in a blue ceramic pot.

Stephanie sat at the desk, wearing a long white coat over a wine-and-gray dress, writing on an outpatient intake form. A chin-high stack of charts shadowed her writing arm. When I stepped into the room she looked up, put down her pen, smiled, and stood.

"Alex."

She'd turned into a good-looking woman. The dull-brown hair, once worn shoulder-length, limp, and barretted, was short, frosted at the tips, and feathered. Contact lenses had replaced granny glasses, revealing amber eyes I'd never noticed before. Her bone structure seemed stronger, more sculpted. She'd never been heavy; now she was thin. Time hadn't ignored her as she entered the dark side of thirty; a mesh of feathers gathered at the corners of her eyes and there was some hardness at the mouth. Makeup handled all of it well.

"Good to see you," she said, taking my hand.

"Good to see you, Steph."

We hugged briefly.

"Can I get you something?" She pointed to the coffee machine, arm jangling. Gold vermeil bracelets looped her wrist. Gold watch on the other arm. No rings. "Plain old coffee or real *café au lait*? This little guy actually steams the milk."

I said no thanks and looked at the machine. Small, squat, black matte and brushed steel, logo of a German manufacturer. The carafe was tiny—two cups' worth. Next to it sat a petite copper pitcher.

"Cute, huh?" she said. "Gift from a friend. Gotta do something to bring a little style into this place."

She smiled. Style was something she'd never cared about. I smiled back and settled in the recliner. A leatherbound book sat on a nearby table. I picked it up. Collected poems of Byron. Bookmark from a store named Browsers—up on Los Feliz, just above Holly-wood. Dusty and crowded, with an emphasis on verse. Lots of junk, a few treasures. I'd gone there as an intern, during lunch hour.

Stephanie said, "He's some writer. I'm trying to expand my interests."

I put the book down. She sat in her desk chair and wheeled around facing me, legs crossed. Pale-gray stockings and suede pumps matched her dress.

"You look great," I said.

Another smile, casual but full, as if she'd expected the compliment but was still pleased by it. "You, too, Alex. Thanks for coming on such short notice."

"You piqued my interest."

"Did I?"

"Sure. All those hints of high intrigue."

She half turned toward the desk, removed a chart from the stack, let it rest in her lap but didn't open it.

"Yup," she said, "it's a challenging one, that's for sure."

Standing suddenly, she walked to the door, closed it, and sat back down.

"So," she said, "how does it feel to be back?"

"Almost got busted on the way in."

I told her about my encounter with the security guard.

"Fascist," she said cheerfully, and my memory banks reactivated: grievance committees over which she'd presided. White coat disdained for jeans, sandals, bleached cotton blouses. *Stephanie, not Doctor. Titles are exclusionary devices of the power elite. . . .*

I said, "Yeah, it was kind of paramilitary," but she just gazed at the chart in her lap.

"High intrigue," she said. "What we've got is a whodunit, howdunit—a *did-anyone-do-it*. Only this is no Agatha Christie thing, Alex. This is a real-life mess. I don't know if you can help, but I'm not sure what else to do."

Voices from the corridor filtered in, squalls and scolding and fleeing footsteps. Then a child's cry of terror pierced the plaster.

"This place is a zoo," she said. "Let's get out of here."

2

A door at the rear of the clinic opened to a stairway. We descended to
the first basement level. Stephanie moved fast, almost jogging down
the steps.

The cafeteria was nearly empty—one orange-topped table occupied by a male intern reading the sports section, two others shared by
slumping couples who looked as if they'd slept in their clothes.
Parents spending the night. Something we'd fought for.

Empty trays and dirty dishes cluttered some of the other tables.
A hair-netted orderly circulated slowly, filling salt shakers.

On the eastern wall was the door to the doctors' dining room:
polished teak panels, finely etched brass nameplate. Some philanthropist with a nautical bent. Stephanie bypassed it and led me to a booth
at the far end of the main room.

"Sure you don't want coffee?" she said.

Remembering the hospital mud, I said, "Already filled my
caffeine quota."

"I know what you mean."

She ran her hand through her hair and we sat.

"Okay," she said. "What we've got is a twenty-one-month-old white female, full-term pregnancy, normal delivery, APGAR of nine. The only significant historical factor is that just before this child was born, a male sib died of sudden infant death syndrome at age one year."

"Any other children?" I said, taking out a note pad and pen.

"No, there's just Cassie. Who looked fine until she was three months old, at which time her mother reported going in at night to check on her and finding her not breathing."

"Checking because she was nervous about SIDS?"

"Exactly. When she wasn't able to rouse the baby, she administered CPR, got her going. Then they brought her into the E.R. By the time I arrived she looked fine, nothing remarkable on exam. I admitted her for observation, did all the usual tests. Nothing. After discharge we set the family up with a sleep monitor and an alarm. Over the next few months the bell went off a few times but they were always false positives—the baby was breathing fine. The graphs show some tracings that could be very brief apnea but there are also lots of movement artifacts—the baby thrashing around. I figured maybe she was just restless—those alarms aren't foolproof—and put down the first episode to some quirky thing. But I did have the pulmonologists look at her because of her brother's SIDS. Negative. So we decided just to keep a close eye on her during the high-risk period for crib death."

"A year?"

She nodded. "I played it safe—fifteen months. Started with weekly outpatient checkups, tapered off so that by nine months I was willing to let them go till the one-year exam. Two days after the nine-month checkup they're back at E.R., middle-of-the-night respiratory problems—the baby woke up gasping, with a croupy bark. More CPR by mom and they bring her in."

"Isn't CPR kind of extreme for croup? Did the baby actually pass out?"

"No, she never lost consciousness, just gasped a lot. Mom may have been overreacting, but with her losing the first child, who could blame her? By the time I got to the E.R., the baby looked fine, no fever, no distress. No surprise, either. Cool night air can clear up croup. I ran a chest X-ray and bloodwork, all normal. Prescribed decongestants, fluids, and rest and was ready to send them home but the mother asked me to admit her. She was convinced there was something serious going on. I was almost certain there wasn't, but we'd been seeing some scary respiratory things recently, so I admitted her, ordered daily bloodwork. Her counts were normal and after a couple of days of getting stuck, she was going hysterical at the sight of a white coat. I discharged her, went back to weekly outpatient follow-up, during which the baby would have nothing to do with me. Minute I walk into the exam room she screams."

"The fun part of being a doctor," I said.

She gave a sad smile, glanced over at the food servers. "They're closing up. Want anything?"

"No thanks."

"If you don't mind, I haven't had breakfast yet."

"Sure, go ahead."

She walked briskly to the metal counters and came back with half a grapefruit on a plate and a cup of coffee. She took a sip of the coffee and grimaced.

"Maybe it needs some steamed milk," I said.

She wiped her mouth with a napkin. "Nothing can save this."

"Least it doesn't cost anything."

"Says who?"

"What? No more free coffee for the docs?"

"Them days are gone, Alex."

"Another tradition bites the dust," I said. "The old budgetary blues?"

"What else? Coffee and tea are forty-nine cents a cup now. Wonder how many cups it'll take to balance the books."

She ate some grapefruit. I fiddled with my pen and said, "I remember how hard you guys fought to get the interns and residents in on the freebie."

She shook her head. "Amazing what seemed important back then."

"Money problems worse than usual?"

"Afraid so." She frowned, put her spoon down and pushed the grapefruit away. "Anyway, back to the case. Where was I?"

"The baby screaming at you."

"Right. Okay, again things start to look good, so again I taper off and terminate, set up an appointment in two months. Three days later, back in the E.R., two A.M. Another croup thing. Only this time the mother says the kid *did* pass out—actually turned blue. More CPR."

"Three days after you terminated," I said, making a note. "Last time it was two."

"Interesting, huh? Okay, I do an E.R. checkup. The baby's blood pressure is up a bit and she's breathing rapidly. But getting plenty of oxygen in. No wheeze, but I was thinking either acute asthma or some sort of anxiety reaction."

"Panic at being back in the hospital again?"

"That, or just the mother's distress rubbing off on her."

"Was the mother showing a lot of overt distress?"

"Not really, but you know how it is with mothers and kids—the vibes. On the other hand, I wasn't ready to rule out something physical. A baby passing out is something to take seriously."

"Sure," I said, "but it could also have been a tantrum gone too far. Some kids learn young how to hold their breath and pass out."

"I know, but this happened in the middle of the night, Alex, not after some power struggle. So I admit her again, order allergy tests, complete pulmonary functions—no asthma. I also start thinking of rarer stuff: membrane problems, an idiopathic brain thing, an enzyme disorder. They're up on Five for a week, real merry-go-round, consults by every specialty in the house, lots of poking and probing. Poor little thing's freaking out as soon as the door to her room opens, no one's coming up with a diagnosis, and the whole time she's in, there are no breathing difficulties. Reinforcing my anxiety theory. I discharge them and the next time I see them in the office, I do nothing but try to play with her. But she still won't have anything to do with me. So I gently raise the anxiety issue with mom but she's not buying."

"How'd she take that?" I said.

"No anger—that's not this lady's style. She just said she couldn't see it, the baby being so young. I told her phobias could occur at any age, but I clearly wasn't getting through. So I backed off, sent them home, gave her some time to think about it. Hoping that as the baby approached one year and the SIDS risk dropped, mom's fears would diminish and the baby would start to relax too. Four days later they were back in the E.R., croup, gasping, mom's in tears, *begging* for an admit. I put the baby in but ordered no tests. Nothing even remotely invasive, just observation. And the baby looked perfect—not even a sniffle. At that point I took the mom aside and leaned more heavily on the psychological angle. Still no sale."

"Did you ever bring up the first child's death?"

She shook her head. "No. I thought of it but at the time it just didn't seem right, Alex. Overloading the lady. I figured I had a good feel for her—I was the attending doc when they brought the first child in dead. Handled the whole post-mortem . . . I carried him to the morgue, Alex."

She closed her eyes, opened them but focused away from me.

"What hell," I said.

"Yeah—and it was a chance thing. They were Rita's private patients, but she was out of town and I was on call. I didn't know them from Adam but I got stuck doing the death conference, too. I tried to do some basic counseling, gave them referrals to grief groups, but they weren't interested. When they came back a year and a half later, wanting me to take care of the *new* baby, I was really surprised."

"Why?"

"I would have predicted they'd associate me with the tragedy, a kill-the-messenger kind of thing. When they didn't, I figured I'd handled them well."

"I'm sure you did."

She shrugged.

I said, "How'd Rita react to your taking over?"

"What choice did she have? She wasn't around when they needed her. She was going through her own problems at the time. Her husband—you know who she was married to, don't you?"

"Otto Kohler."

"The famous conductor—that's how she used to refer to him: 'My husband, the famous conductor.' "

"He died recently, didn't he?"

"Few months ago. He'd been sick for a while, series of strokes. Since then, Rita's been gone even more than usual and the rest of us have been picking up a lot of the slack. Mostly, she attends conventions and presents old papers. She's actually going to retire." Embarrassed smile. "I've been considering applying for her position, Alex. Do you see me as a division head?"

"Sure."

"Really?"

"Sure, Steph. Why not?"

"I don't know. The position's kind of . . . inherently authoritarian."

"To some extent," I said. "But I'd imagine the position can adapt to different styles of leadership."

"Well," she said, "I'm not sure I'd make a good leader. I don't really like telling people what to do. . . . Anyway, enough about that. I'm getting off track. There were two more passing-out episodes before I brought up the psych thing again."

"Two more," I said, looking at my notes. "I've got a total of five."

"Correct."

"How old's the baby by now?"

"Just under a year. And a hospital veteran. Two more admits, negative for everything. At that point I sat mom down and *strongly* recommended a psych consult. To which she reacted with . . . here, let me give you the exact quote."

She opened the chart and read softly: " 'I know that makes sense, Dr. Eves, but I just *know* Cassie's sick. If you'd only seen her—lying there, cyanotic.' End of quote."

"She phrased it that way? 'Cyanotic'?"

"Yup. She has a medical background. Studied to be a respiratory tech."

"And both her kids stop breathing. Interesting."

"Yes." Hard smile. "At the time I didn't realize how interesting. I was still caught up in the puzzle—trying to arrive at a diagnosis, worrying when the next crisis was going to be and if I'd be able to do anything about it. To my surprise it didn't happen for a while."

She looked at the chart again. "A month passes, two, three, still no sign of them. I'm happy the baby's okay but I'm also starting to wonder if maybe they've just found themselves another doc. So I called the home, talked to mom. Everything's fine. Then I realized that in the heat of everything, the baby had never had her one-year exam. I schedule it, find everything intact, with the exception that she's a little slow vocally and verbally."

"How slow?"

"No retardation or anything like that. She just made very few sounds—in fact I didn't hear anything from her at all, and mom said she was pretty quiet at home, too. I tried to do a Bailey test, but couldn't because the baby wouldn't cooperate. My guesstimate was about a two-month lag, but you know at that age it doesn't take much to tip the scales, and given all the stress the poor thing's been through, no big deal. But brilliant me. Bringing up language development got mom worried about *that*. So I sent them over to ENT and Speech and Hearing, who found her ears and laryngeal structure one hundred percent normal and concurred with my assessment: possible mild delay in reaction to medical trauma. I gave the mom suggestions about stimulating speech and didn't hear from them for another two months."

"Baby's fourteen months old," I said, writing.

"And back in the E.R., four days later. But not with breathing probs. This time she's spiking a temp—a hundred and five. Flushed and dry, and breathing fast. To be honest, Alex, I was almost *happy* to see the fever—at least I had something organic to work with. Then the white count came back normal, nothing viral or bacterial. So I ran a toxicology. Clean. Still, lab tests aren't perfect—even our error rates are running ten to twenty percent. And that spike was real—I took the temp myself. We bathed her and Tylenoled her down to a hundred and two, admitted her with a fever-of-unknown-origin diagnosis, pushed fluids, put her through some real hell: spinal tap to rule out meningitis, even though her ears were clear and her neck was supple, because for all we knew she had one heck of a headache she couldn't tell us about. Plus twice-daily bloodwork—she went bananas, had to be held down. Even with that, she managed to dislodge the needle a couple of times."

She exhaled and pushed the grapefruit farther away. Her forehead had moistened. Swabbing it with a napkin, she said, "First time I've told it like this from the beginning."

"You haven't had any case conferences?"

"No, we don't do much of that anymore. Rita's basically use-less."

I said, "How did the mother react to all the procedures?"

"Some tears, but basically she stayed composed. Able to comfort the baby, cuddling her when it was over. I made sure she never was involved in holding the baby down—integrity of the mother-child bond. See, your lectures stuck, Alex. Of course the *rest* of us felt like Nazis."

She wiped her brow again. "Anyway, the blood tests kept coming back normal but I held off discharge until she'd had no fever for four days running."

Sighing, she burrowed her fingers through her hair and flipped through her chart.

"Next fever spike: the kid's fifteen months old, mother claims a hundred and six."

"Dangerous."

"You bet. E.R. doc records a hundred and four and a half, bathes and doses it down to a hundred and one and a half. And mom reports new symptoms: retching, projectile vomiting, diarrhea. And black *stools.*"

"Internal bleeding?"

"Sounds like it. That made *everyone* sit up. The diaper she had on did show some evidence of diarrhea, but no blood. Mom said she threw the bloody one out, would try to retrieve it. On exam, the kid's rectal area was a little red, some irritation at the external edges of the sphincter. But no bowel distension that I can palpate—her belly's nice and soft, maybe a bit tender to the touch. But that's hard to gauge 'cause she's freaking out, nonstop, at being examined."

"Raw rectum," I said. "Any scarring?"

"No, no, nothing like that. Just mild irritation, consistent with diarrhea. Obstruction or appendicitis needed to be ruled out. I called in a surgeon, Joe Leibowitz—you know how thorough he is. He examined her, said there was nothing that justified cutting her open but we should admit her and watch her for a while. We put an I.V. in—*great* fun—did a complete panel, and this time there was a slightly elevated white count. But still within normal limits, nothing that would jibe with a hundred and four and a half. Next day she was down to one hundred. Day after that, ninety-nine point two, and her tummy didn't seem to hurt. Joe said definitely no appendicitis, call in GI. I got a consult from Tony Franks and he evaluated her for early signs of irritable bowel syndrome, Crohn's disease, liver problems. Negative. Another tox panel, a careful diet history. I called in Allergy and Immunology again, to test her for some weird hypersensitivity to something."

"Was she on formula?"

"Nope, a breast-fed baby, though by that time she was totally on solids. After a week she was looking perfect. Thank God we didn't cut her open."

"Fifteen months old," I said. "Just past the high-risk period for SIDS. So the respiratory system quiets and the gut starts acting up?"

Stephanie gave me a long, searching look. "Want to hazard a diagnosis?"

"Is that all of it?"

"Un-uh. There were two other GI crises. At sixteen months—four days after an appointment with Tony in Gastro clinic—and a month and a half later, following his final appointment with them."

"Same symptoms?"

"Right. But both those times, mom actually brought in bloody diapers and we worked them over for every possible pathogen—I mean we're talking typhoid, cholera, tropical maladies that have never been seen on this continent. Some sort of environmental toxin—lead, heavy metals, you name it. But all we found was a little healthy blood."

"Are the parents in some sort of work that would expose the child to weird pollutants?"

"Hardly. She's a full-time mom and he's a college professor."

"Biology?"

"Sociology. But before we get off on the family structure, there's more. Another type of crisis. Six weeks ago. Bye-bye gut, hello new organ system. Want to take a guess which one?"

I thought for a moment. "Neurological?"

"Bingo." She reached over and touched my arm. "I feel so vindicated calling you in."

"Seizures?"

"Middle of the night. Grand mal, according to the parents, right down to the frothing at the mouth. The EEG showed no abnormal wave activity and the kid had all her reflexes, but we put her through a CAT scan, another spinal, and all the high-tech neuro-radiology video games, on the chance she had some kind of brain tumor. That *really* scared me, Alex, because when I thought about it I realized a tumor could have caused *everything* that had been happening, right from the beginning. A growth impinging on different brain centers, causing different symptoms as it grew."

She shook her head. "Wouldn't *that* have been a happy situation? Me talking psychosomatic and there's an astrocytoma or something growing inside her? Thank God all her scans were totally clean."

"Did she look post-seizural when you saw her in the E.R.?"

"In terms of being drowsy and listless, she did. But that's also consistent with a little kid being dragged to the hospital in the middle of the night and put through the wringer. Still, it scared me—that there could be something organic I was missing. I asked Neurology to follow up. They did for a month, found nothing, terminated. Two weeks later—*two days ago*—another seizure. And I really need your help, Alex. They're up in Five West, right now. And that's the whole kaboodle, history-wise. Ready to give me some wisdom now?"

I scanned my notes.

Recurrent, unexplained illnesses. Multiple hospitalizations.

Shifting organ systems.

Discrepancies between symptoms and lab tests.

Female child showing panic at being treated or handled.

Mother with a paramedical training.

Nice mother.

Nice mother who might just be a monster. Scripting, choreographing, and directing a Grand Guignol, and casting her own child as unwitting star.

Rare diagnosis, but the facts fit. Up until twenty years ago nobody had heard of it.

"Munchausen syndrome by proxy," I said, putting my notes down. "Sounds like a textbook case."

Her eyes narrowed. "Yes, it does. When you hear it all strung together like this. But when you're right in the middle of it . . . even now I can't be sure."

"You're still considering something organic?"

"I have to until I can prove otherwise. There was another case—last year, over at County. *Twenty-five* consecutive admits for recurrent weird infections during a six-month period. Also a female child, attentive mother who looked too calm for the staff's peace of mind. *That* baby was really going downhill and they were just about ready to call in the authorities when it turned out to be a rare immunodeficiency—three documented cases in the literature, special tests that had to be done at NIH. Moment I heard about it, I had Cassie tested for the same thing. Negative. But that doesn't mean there isn't some other factor I haven't caught. New stuff keeps popping up—I can barely keep up with the journals."

She moved her spoon around in her coffee.

"Or maybe I'm just denying—trying to make myself feel better for not seeing the Munchausen thing sooner. Which is why I called you in—I need some direction, Alex. Tell me which way to go with this."

I thought for a while.

Munchausen syndrome.

A.k.a. *pseudologia fantastica.*

A.k.a. factitious illness disorder.

An especially grotesque form of pathological lying, named after Baron von Munchausen, the world-class prevaricator.

Munchausen is hypochondriasis gone mad. Patients fabricating disease by mutilating and poisoning themselves, or just lying. Playing mind games with physicians and nurses—with the health-care system itself.

Adult Munchausen patients manage to get hospitalized repeatedly, medicated needlessly, even cut open on the operating table.

Pitiful, masochistic, and perplexing—a twist of the psyche that still defies comprehension.

But what we were considering here was beyond pity. It was an evil variant:

Munchausen by proxy.

Parents—mothers, invariably—faking illness in their own offspring. Using their children—especially daughters—as crucibles for a hideous concoction of lies, pain, and disease.

I said, "So much of it fits, Steph. Right from the beginning.

The apnea and passing out could be due to smothering—those movement artifacts on the monitor could mean she was struggling."

She winced. "God, yes. I just did some reading, found a case in England where movement artifacts tipped them off to the baby being smothered."

"Plus, with mom being a respiratory tech, breathing could be the first system she'd choose to mess with. What about the intestinal stuff? Some kind of poisoning?"

"Most likely, but it's nothing the tox panel could come up with when they tested."

"Maybe she used something short-acting."

"Or an inert irritant that activated the bowel mechanically, but passed right through."

"And the seizures?"

"Same thing, I guess. I don't *know*, Alex. I really don't *know*." She squeezed my arm again. "I've got no evidence at all and what if I'm wrong? I need you to be objective. Give Cassie's mom the benefit of the doubt—maybe I'm misjudging her. Try to get into her head."

"I can't promise a miracle, Steph."

"I know. But *anything* you can do will be helpful. Things could get really messy with this one."

"Did you tell the mother I'd be consulting?"

She nodded.

"Is she more amenable to a psych consult now?"

"I wouldn't say amenable, but she agreed. I think I convinced her by backing away from any suggestion that stress was *causing* Cassie's problems. Far as she's concerned, *I* think the seizures are bona fide organic. But I did press the need for helping Cassie adjust to the trauma of hospitalization. Told her epilepsy would mean Cassie can expect to see a lot more of this place and we're going to have to help her deal with it. I said you were an expert on medical trauma, might be able to do some hypnosis thing to relax Cassie during procedures. That sound reasonable?"

I nodded.

"Meanwhile," she said, "you can be analyzing the mother. See if she's a psychopath."

"If it is Munchausen by proxy, we may not be looking for a psychopath."

"What then? What kind of nut does this to her own kid?"

"No one really knows," I said. "It's been a while since I looked at the literature, but the best guess used to be some kind of mixed personality disorder. The problem is, documented cases are so rare, there really isn't a good data base."

"It's still that way, Alex. I looked up sources over at the med school and came up with very little."

"I'd like to borrow the articles."

"I read them there, didn't check them out," she said. "But I think I still have the references written down somewhere. And I think I remember that mixed personality business—whatever that means."

"It means we don't know, so we're fudging. Part of the problem is that psychologists and psychiatrists depend on information we get from the patient. And taking a history from a Munchausen means relying upon a habitual liar. But the stories they tell, once you expose them, *do* seem to be fairly consistent: early experience with serious physical illness or trauma, families that overemphasized disease and health, child abuse, sometimes incest. Leading to very poor self-esteem, problems with relationships, and a pathological need for attention. Illness becomes the arena in which they act out that need—that's why so many of them enter health professions. But lots of people with those same histories *don't* become Munchausens. And the same history applies both to Munchausens who abuse themselves and the proxies who torment their kids. In fact, there's some suggestion that Munchausen-by-proxy parents start out as self-abusers and switch, at some point, to using their kids. But as for why and when that happens, no one knows."

"Weird," she said, shaking her head. "It's like a dance. I feel I'm waltzing around with her, but she's leading."

"Devil's waltz," I said.

She shuddered. "I know we're not talking hard science, Alex, but if you could just dig your way in there, tell me if you think she's doing it. . . ."

"Sure. But I am a bit curious why you didn't call in the hospital Psych department."

"Never liked the hospital Psych department," she said. "Too Freudian. Hardesty wanted to put everyone on the couch. It's a moot point, anyway. There is no Psych department."

"What do you mean?"

"They were all fired."

"The whole department? When?"

"Few months ago. Don't you read your staff newsletter?"

"Not very often."

"Obviously. Well, Psych's dissolved. Hardesty's county contract was canceled and he never wrote any grants, so there was no financial backup. The board decided not to pick up the cost."

"What about Hardesty's tenure? The others—weren't Greiler and Pantissa tenured, too?"

"Probably. But tenure, as it turns out, comes from the med school, not the hospital. So they've still got their titles. Salaries are a whole other story. Quite a revelation for those of us who thought we had job security. Not that anyone fought for Hardesty. Everyone thought he and his guys were deadwood."

"No more Psych department," I said. "No more free coffee. What else?"

"Oh, plenty. Does it affect you, there being no Psych department—in terms of your staff privileges, I mean?"

"No, my appointment's in pediatrics. Oncology, actually, though it's been years since I've seen any cancer patients."

"Good," she said. "Then there won't be any procedural hassles. Any more questions before we go up?"

"Just a couple of observations. If it is Munchausen by proxy, there's some time pressure—the usual picture is an escalating pattern. Sometimes kids die, Steph."

"I know," she said miserably, pressing her fingertips to her temples. "I know I may need to confront the mother. That's why I have to be sure."

"The other thing is the first child—the boy. I assume you're considering him a possible homicide."

"Oh, God, yes. That's really been eating at me. When my suspicions about the mother started to gel, I pulled his chart and went over it with a fine-tooth comb. But there was nothing iffy. Rita's ongoing notes were good—he was perfectly healthy before he died and the autopsy was inconclusive, as so many of them are. Now here I am with a living, breathing child and I can't do a thing to help *her*."

"Sounds like you're doing everything you can."

"Trying, but it's so damned frustrating."

I said, "What about the father? We haven't talked about him."

"I don't really have a good feel for him. Mother's clearly the primary caretaker and it's her I've been dealing with most of the time. Once I started to think of it as a possible Munchausen by proxy, she seemed especially important to focus on, because aren't mothers always the ones?"

"Yes," I said, "but in some cases the father turns out to be a passive accomplice. Any sign he suspects something?"

"If he has, he hasn't told me. He doesn't seem especially passive—nice enough. So is she, for that matter. They're both nice, Alex. That's one of the things that makes it so difficult."

"Typical Munchausen scenario. The nurses probably love them."

She nodded.

"What's the other?" I said.

"The other what?"

"Thing that makes it so difficult."

She closed her eyes and rubbed them and took a long time to answer.

"The other thing," she said, "and this may sound horribly cold-hearted and political, is who they *are*. Socially. Politically. The child's full name is Cassie Brooks *Jones*—set off any buzzers?"

"No," I said. "Jones isn't exactly memorable."

"Jones, as in Charles L. Junior. Hotshot financier? The hospital's primary money manager?"

"Don't know him."

"That's right—you don't read your newsletters. Well, as of eight months ago he's also chairman of the board. There was a big shake-up."

"The budget?"

"What else. Anyway, here's the genealogy: Charles Junior's only son is Charles the Third—like royalty. He goes by *Chip*—Cassie's daddy. The mom is Cindy. The dead son was Chad—Charles the Fourth."

"All *C*s," I said. "Sounds like they like order."

"Whatever. The main thing is, Cassie is Charles Junior's only *grandchild*. Isn't that wonderful, Alex? Here I am with a potential Munchausen by proxy that could explode in everyone's face, and the patient's the only grandchild of the guy who took away the free coffee."

3

We got up from the table and she said, "If you don't mind, we can take the stairs up."

"Morning aerobics? Sure."

"You hit thirty-five," she said, smoothing her dress and buttoning her white coat, "and the old basal metabolism goes to hell. Got to work hard not to be lumpy. Plus, the elevators still move on Valium Standard Time."

We walked toward the cafeteria's main exit. The tables were completely empty now. A brown-uniformed maintenance worker was wet-mopping the floor, and we had to step gingerly to maintain traction.

I said, "The elevator I took to your office was converted to key lock. Why the need for all the security?"

"The official line is crime prevention," she said. "Keeping all the street craziness out of here. Which to some extent is valid—there *have* been increased problems, mostly during the night shift. But can you remember a time when East Hollywood didn't get bad after dark?"

We reached the door. Another maintenance man was locking it and when he saw us, he gave a world-weary look and held it open for us.

Stephanie said, "Reduced hours—another budget cut."

Out in the hallway, things had gotten frantic. Doctors blew past in boisterous groups, filling the air with fast talk. Families traipsed through, wheeling doll-sized veteran journeyors to and from the ordeals wrought by science.

A silent crowd was assembled at the elevator doors, clumped like human droplets, waiting for any of three lifts that had settled simultaneously on the third floor. Waiting, always the waiting . . .

Stephanie moved through deftly, nodding at familiar faces but never stopping. I followed close behind, avoiding collision with I.V. poles.

When we entered the basement stairwell, I said, "What kind of crime problems have there been?"

"The usual, but more so," she said, climbing. "Car thefts, vandalism, purse snatchings. Some muggings out on Sunset. And a couple of nurses were assaulted in the parking lot across the street a few months ago."

"Sexual assaults?" I said, taking two steps at a time in order to keep up.

"That was never made clear. Neither of them came back to talk about it. They were night-shift floats, not regular staff. What I *heard* was that they were beaten up pretty badly and had their purses stolen. The police sent a community relations officer who gave us the usual personal safety lecture and admitted that, bottom line, there was little anyone could do to guarantee safety unless the hospital was turned into an armed camp. The women on the staff screamed a lot and the administration promised to have Security patrol more regularly."

"Any follow-through?"

"Guess so—you see more uniforms in the lots and there've been no attacks since then. But the protection came with a whole bunch of other stuff no one asked for. Robocops on campus, new badges, frequent hassles like the one you just went through. Personally, I think we played right into the administration's hands—gave them an excuse for exercising more control. And once they get it, they'll never relinquish it."

"C students getting revenge?"

She stopped climbing and looked down at me over her shoulder, smiling sheepishly. "You *remember* that?"

"Vividly."

"Pretty mouthy back then, wasn't I?"

"The fire of youth," I said. "And they deserved it—talking down to you in front of everyone, that 'Dr. *Ms.*' stuff."

"Yeah, they *were* a pretty cheeky bunch, weren't they." She resumed the climb, but more slowly. "Banker's hours, martini lunches, sitting around shmoozing in the caf and sending *us* memos about increasing efficiency and cutting costs."

A few steps later she stopped again. "C students—I can't believe I actually said that." Her cheeks were aflame. "I *was* obnoxious, wasn't I?"

"Inspired, Steph."

"More like *per*spired. Those were crazy times, Alex. Totally crazy."

"Sure were," I said. "But don't dismiss what we accomplished: equal pay for female staff, parents rooming in, the playrooms."

"And let us not forget free coffee for the house staff."

A few steps later: "Even so, Alex, so much of what we obsessed on seems so misdirected. We focused on personalities but the problem was the system. One bunch of C students leaves, another arrives, and the same old problems go on. Sometimes I wonder if I've stayed here too long. Look at you—away from it for all these years and you look better than ever."

"So do you," I said, thinking of what she'd just told me about trying for the division-head position.

"Me?" She smiled. "Well, you're *gallant* to say so, but in my case, it's not due to personal fulfillment. Just clean living."

The fifth floor housed children aged one to eleven who were not in need of high-tech care. The hundred beds in the east ward took up two thirds of the floor space.

The remaining third was set aside for a twenty-bed private unit on the west side, separated from the ward by teak doors lettered THE HANNAH CHAPELL SPECIAL UNIT in brass.

Chappy Ward. Off limits to the hoi polloi and trainees, maintained by endowments, private insurance, and personal checks; not a Medi-Cal form in sight.

Private meant Muzak flowing from concealed ceiling speakers, carpeted floors instead of linoleum, one patient per room in place of three or more, TVs that worked almost all the time, though they were still black-and-white antiques.

This morning, nearly all twenty rooms were empty. A trio of bored-looking R.N.'s stood behind the counter at the nursing station. A few feet away a unit clerk filed her nails.

"Morning, Dr. Eves," said one of the nurses, addressing Stephanie but watching me and looking none too friendly. I wondered why and smiled at her anyway. She turned away. Early fifties, short, chunky, grainy-skinned, long-jawed, sprayed blond hair. Powder-blue uniform trimmed with white. Atop the stiff hair, a starched cap; I hadn't seen one of those in a long time.

The two other nurses, Filipinas in their twenties, glanced at each other and moved away as if spurred by a silent code.

Stephanie said, "Morning, Vicki. How's our girl doing?"

"So far so good." Reaching over, the blond nurse pulled a chart out of the slot marked 505 W and handed it to Stephanie. Her nails were stubby and gnawed. Her gaze settled on me again. The old charm was still not working.

"This is Dr. Alex Delaware," said Stephanie, thumbing through the chart, "our consulting psychologist. Dr. Delaware, Vicki Bottomley, Cassie's primary care nurse."

"Cindy said you'd be coming by," said the nurse, making it sound like bad news. Stephanie kept reading.

"Pleased to meet you," I said.

"Pleased to meet *you*." A challenging sullenness in her voice made Stephanie look up.

"Everything okay, Vicki?"

"Peachy," said the nurse, flashing a smile as jovial as a slap across the face. "Everything's fine. She held down most of her breakfast, fluids and P/O meds—"

"What meds?"

"Just Tylenol. An hour ago. Cindy said she had a headache—"

"Tylenol One?"

"Yes, Dr. Eves, just the kid stuff, liquid, one teaspoon—it's all in there." She pointed to the chart.

"Yes, I see," said Stephanie, reading. "Well, that's all right for today, Vicki, but next time no meds—not even OTC stuff—without my approval. I need to authorize *everything,* other than food and beverage, that passes between this child's lips. Okay?"

"Sure," said Bottomley, smiling again. "No problem. I just thought—"

"No harm done, Vicki," said Stephanie, reaching over and patting the nurse's shoulder. "I'm sure I would have okayed Tylenol. It's just that with this kid's history we've got to be super-careful to tease out drug reactions."

"Yes, Dr. Eves. Is there anything else?"

Stephanie read more of the chart, then closed it and handed it back. "No, not at the moment, unless there's something you want to report."

Bottomley shook her head.

"Okay, then. I'm going to go in and introduce Dr. Delaware. Anything about Cassie you want to share?"

Bottomley removed a bobby pin from her hair and stuck it back in, fastening blond strands to the cap. Her eyes were wide-set and long-lashed, a soft, pretty blue in the tense, gritty terrain of her face.

She said, "Like what?"

"Anything Dr. Delaware should know, to help Cassie and her parents, Vicki."

Bottomley stared at Stephanie for a moment, then turned to me, glaring. "There's nothing wrong with them. They're just regular people."

I said, "I hear Cassie gets pretty anxious about medical procedures."

Bottomley put her hands on her hips. "Wouldn't *you,* if you got stuck as much as she does?"

Stephanie said, "Vicki—"

"Sure," I said, smiling. "It's a perfectly normal reaction, but sometimes normal anxiety can be helped by behavioral treatment."

Bottomley gave a small, tight laugh. "Maybe so. Good luck."

Stephanie started to say something. I touched her arm and said, "Why don't we get going?"

"Sure." To Bottomley: "Remember, nothing P/O except food and drink."

Bottomley held on to her smile. "Yes, Doctor. Now, if it's all right with you, I'd like to leave the floor for a few minutes."

Stephanie looked at her watch. "Break time?"

"No. Just wanted to go down to the gift shop and get Cassie a LuvBunny—you know those stuffed bunnies, the cartoons on TV? She's crazy about them. I figure with you people in there, she should be fine for a few minutes."

Stephanie looked at me. Bottomley followed her glance with what seemed to be satisfaction, gave another tight laugh, and left. Her walk was a brisk waddle. The starched cap floated along the empty corridor like a kite caught in a tailwind.

Stephanie took my arm and steered me away from the station.

"Sorry, Alex. I've never seen her like that."

"Has she been Cassie's nurse before?"

"Several times—almost from the beginning. She and Cindy have developed a good rapport and Cassie seems to like her too. When Cassie comes in, they ask for her."

"She seems to have gotten pretty possessive."

"She does have a tendency to get involved, but I've always looked at that as a positive thing. Families love her—she's one of the most committed nurses I've ever worked with. With morale the way it is, commitment's hard to find."

"Does her commitment extend to home visits?"

"Not as far as I know. The only home things were a couple I did, with one of the residents, at the very beginning, to set up the sleep monitor—" She touched her mouth. "You're not suggesting she had something to do with—"

"I'm not suggesting anything," I said, wondering if I was, because Bottomley had chapped my hide. "Just throwing out ideas."

"Hmm . . . well, that's some idea. Munchausen nurse? I guess the medical background fits."

"There've been cases," I said. "Nurses and doctors looking for attention, and usually they're the really possessive ones. But if Cassie's problems have always started at home and resolved in the hospital, that would rule her out, unless Vicki's a permanent resident at the Jones household."

"She isn't. At least not as far as I know. No, of course she isn't—I'd know if she was."

She looked unsure. Beaten down. I realized what a toll the case was taking.

"I would like to know why she was so hostile to me," I said. "Not for personal reasons but in terms of the dynamics of this family. If Vicki and the mother are tight and Vicki doesn't like me, that could sour my consult."

"Good point . . . I don't know *what*'s eating at her."

"I assume you haven't discussed your suspicion of Cindy with her?"

"No. You're really the first person I've talked to about it. That's why I phrased my no-meds instructions in terms of drug reactions. Cindy's also been asked not to bring food from home for the same reason. Vicki and the nurses on the other shifts are supposed to log everything Cassie eats." She frowned. "Of course if Vicki's overstepping her bounds, she might not be following through. Want me to have her transferred? Nursing Ad would give me hell, but I suppose I could swing it pretty quickly."

"Not on my account. Let's keep things stable for the time being."

We walked behind the station. Stephanie retrieved the chart and studied it again.

"Everything looks okay," she said finally. "But I'll have a talk with her anyway."

I said, "Let me have a look."

She gave me the chart. Her usual neat handwriting and detailed notes. They included a family-structure chart that I spent some time on.

"No grandparents on the mother's side?"

She shook her head. "Cindy lost her parents young. Chip lost his mom, too, when he was a teenager. Old Chuck's the only grandparent left."

"Does he get up here much to visit?"

"From time to time. He's a busy man."

I continued reading. "Cindy's only twenty-six . . . maybe Vicki's a mother figure for her."

"Maybe," she said. "Whatever it is, I'll keep a tight leash on her."

"Don't come down too hard right now, Steph. I don't want to be seen by Vicki—or Cindy—as someone who makes anyone's life harder. Give me a chance to get to know Vicki. She could turn out to be an ally."

"Okay," she said. "This human relations stuff is your area. But let me know if she continues to be difficult. I don't want *anything* getting in the way of solving this thing."

The room was inundated with LuvBunnies—on the windowsill, nightstand, the bed tray, atop the TV. A bucktoothed, rainbow-hued welcoming party.

The rails of the bed were lowered. A beautiful child lay sleeping—a tiny bundle barely swelling the covers.

Her heart-face was turned to one side; her rosebud mouth, pink and parted. Buttermilk skin, chubby cheeks, nubbin nose. Her hair was sleek, straight, and black and trickled onto her shoulders. The bangs were moist and they stuck to her forehead. A ring of lace collar was visible above the blanket hem. One hand was concealed; the other, dimpled and clenched, gathered the fabric. Its thumb was the size of a lima bean.

The sleeper sofa by the window was unfolded to a single bed that had been made up. Military corners, pillow smooth as eggshell. A flowered vinyl overnight bag sat on the floor next to an empty food tray.

A young woman sat cross-legged on the edge of the mattress, reading *TV Guide*. As soon as she saw us she put down the magazine and got up.

Five five, firm figure, slightly long-waisted. Same shiny dark hair as her daughter's, parted in the middle, tied back loosely and gathered in a thick braid that nearly reached her waist. Same facial cast as Cassie's, too, stretched by maturity to something just barely longer than the perfect oval. Fine nose; straight, wide, unpainted mouth with naturally dark lips. Big brown eyes. Bloodshot.

No makeup, scrubbed complexion. A girlish woman. Twenty-six but she could easily have passed for a college student.

From the bed came a soft, breathy sound. Cassie sighing. All of us looked over at her. Her eyelids remained closed but they fluttered. Threads of lavender vein were visible beneath the skin. She rolled over, facing away from us.

I thought of a bisque doll.

All around us, the LuvBunnies leered.

Cindy Jones looked down at her daughter, reached over and smoothed hair out of the child's eyes.

Turning back to us, she ran her hands over her clothes, hurriedly, as if searching for unfastened buttons. The clothes were simple—plaid cotton shirt over faded jeans and medium-heeled sandals. A pink plastic Swatch watch. Not the post-deb, VIP daughter-in-law I'd expected.

"Well," whispered Stephanie, "looks like someone's snoozing away. Get any sleep yourself, Cindy?"

"A little." Soft voice, pleasant. She didn't have to whisper.

"Our mattresses have a way to go, don't they?"

"I'm fine, Dr. Eves." Her smile was tired. "Actually, Cassie slept great. She woke once, around five, and needed a cuddle. I held her and sang to her for a while and finally she fell back around seven. Guess that's why she's still out."

"Vicki said she had a headache."

"Yes, when she woke. Vicki gave her some liquid Tylenol and that seemed to work."

"Tylenol was the right thing to give her, Cindy. But in the future all medications—even over-the-counter stuff—will have to be approved by me. Just to play it safe."

The brown eyes opened wide. "Oh. Sure. I'm sorry."

Stephanie smiled. "No big deal. I just want to be careful. Cindy, this is Dr. Delaware, the psychologist we spoke about."

"Hello, Dr. Delaware."

"Hello, Mrs. Jones."

"Cindy." She extended a narrow hand and smiled shyly. Likable. I knew my job wasn't going to be easy.

Stephanie said, "As I told you, Dr. Delaware's an expert on

anxiety in children. If anyone can help Cassie cope, he can. He'd like to talk with you right now, if this is a good time."

"Oh . . . sure. This is fine." Cindy touched her braid and looked worried.

"Terrific," said Stephanie. "If there's nothing you need from me, I'll be going."

"Nothing I can think of right now, Dr. Eves. I was just wondering if you'd . . . come up with anything?"

"Not yet, Cindy. Yesterday's EEG was totally normal. But, as we've discussed, with children this age that's not always conclusive. The nurses haven't charted any seizurelike behavior. Have you noticed anything?"

"No . . . not really."

"Not really?" Stephanie took a step closer. She was only an inch taller than the other woman but seemed much larger.

Cindy Jones passed her upper lip under her top teeth, then released it. "Nothing—it's probably not important."

"It's okay, Cindy. Tell me anything, even if you think it's irrelevant."

"Well, I'm sure it's nothing, but sometimes I wonder if she's tuning out—not listening when I talk to her? Kind of staring off into space—like a petit mal? I'm sure it's nothing and I'm just seeing it because I'm looking for things now."

"When did you start noticing this?"

"Yesterday, after we were admitted."

"You never saw it at home?"

"I . . . no. But it could have been happening and I just didn't notice. Or maybe it's nothing. It probably is nothing—I don't know."

The pretty face began to buckle.

Stephanie patted her and Cindy moved toward the gesture, almost imperceptibly, as if to gain more comfort from it.

Stephanie stepped back, breaking contact. "How often have these staring episodes been occurring?"

"Maybe a couple of times a day. It's probably nothing—just her concentrating. She's always been good at concentrating—when she plays at home she concentrates really well."

"Well, that's good—the fact that she's got a good attention span."

Cindy nodded but she didn't look reassured.

Stephanie drew an appointment book out of a coat pocket, ripped out a back page and handed it to Cindy. "Tell you what, next time you see this staring, make a record of the exact time and call in Vicki or whoever's on duty to have a look, okay?"

"Okay. But it doesn't last long, Dr. Eves. Just a few seconds."

"Just do the best you can," said Stephanie. "In the meantime, I'll leave you and Dr. Delaware to get acquainted."

Pausing for a moment to look at the sleeping child, she smiled at both of us and left.

When the door closed, Cindy looked down at the bed. "I'll fold this up so you'll have somewhere to sit." There were delicate lavender veins under her skin, too. At the temples, throbbing.

"Let's do it together," I said.

That seemed to startle her. "No, that's okay."

Bending, she took hold of the mattress and lifted. I did likewise and the two of us turned the bed back into a sofa.

She smoothed the cushions, stood back, and said, "Please."

Feeling as if I were in a geisha house, I complied.

She walked over to the green chair and removed the LuvBunnies. Placing them on the nightstand, she pulled the chair opposite the couch and sat, feet flat on the floor, a hand on each slender thigh.

I reached over, took one of the stuffed animals from the window ledge, and stroked it. Through the glass the treetops of Griffith Park were green-black and cloudlike.

"Cute," I said. "Gifts?"

"Some of them are. Some we brought from home. We wanted Cassie to feel at home here."

"The hospital's become a second home, hasn't it?"

She stared at me. Tears filled the brown eyes, magnifying them. A look of shame spread across her face.

Shame? Or guilt?

Her hands shot up quickly to conceal it.

She cried silently for a while.

I got a tissue from the box on the bed table and waited.

4

She uncovered her face. "Sorry."

"No need to be," I said. "There aren't too many things more stressful than having a sick child."

She nodded. "The worst thing is not knowing—watching her suffer and not knowing . . . If only someone could figure it out."

"The other symptoms resolved. Maybe this will too."

Looping her braid over one shoulder, she fingered the ends. "I sure hope so. But . . ."

I smiled but said nothing.

She said, "The other things were more . . . typical. Normal—if that makes any sense."

"Normal childhood diseases," I said.

"Yes—croup, diarrhea. Other kids have them. Maybe not as severe, but they have them, so you can understand those kinds of things. But seizures . . . that's just not *normal*."

"Sometimes," I said, "kids have seizures after a high fever. One or two episodes and then it never recurs."

"Yes, I know. Dr. Eves told me about that. But Cassie wasn't spiking a temp when she had hers. The other times—when she had gastrointestinal problems—there were fevers. She was burning up, then. A hundred and *six*." She tugged the braid. "And then that went away and I thought we were going to be okay, and then the seizures just came out of nowhere—it was really frightening. I heard something in her room—like a knocking. I went in and she was shaking so hard the crib was rattling."

Her lips began to quiver. She stilled them with a hand. Crushed the tissue I'd given her with the other.

I said, "Scary."

"*Terrifying*," she said, looking me in the eye. "But the worst thing was watching her suffer and not being able to do anything. The helplessness—it's the worst thing. I knew better than to pick her up, but still . . . Do you have children?"

"No."

Her eyes left my face, as if she'd suddenly lost interest. Sighing, she got up and walked to the bed, still carrying the crumpled tissue. She bent, tucked the blanket higher around the little girl's neck, and kissed Cassie's cheek. Cassie's breathing quickened for a second, then slowed. Cindy remained at the bedside, watching her sleep.

"She's beautiful," I said.

"She's my *pudding* pie."

She reached down, touched Cassie's forehead, then drew back her arm and let it drop to her side. After gazing down for several more seconds, she returned to the chair.

I said, "In terms of her suffering, there's no evidence seizures are painful."

"That's what Dr. Eves says," she said doubtfully. "I sure hope so . . . but if you'd have seen her afterwards—she was just *drained*."

She turned and stared out the window. I waited a while, then said, "Except for the headache, how's she doing today?"

"Okay. For the little she's been up."

"And the headache occurred at five this morning?"

"Yes. She woke up with it."

"Vicki was already on shift by then?"

Nod. "She's pulling a double—came on last night for the eleven-to-seven and stayed for the seven-to-three."

"Pretty dedicated."

"She is. She's a big help. We're lucky to have her."

"Does she ever come out to the house?"

That surprised her. "Just a couple of times—not to help, just to visit. She brought Cassie her first LuvBunny, and now Cassie's in love with them."

The look of surprise remained on her face. Rather than deal with it, I said, "How did Cassie let you know her head hurt?"

"By pointing to it and crying. She didn't tell me, if that's what you mean. She only has a few words. *Daw* for dog, *bah-bah* for bottle, and even with those, sometimes she still points. Dr. Eves says she's a few months behind in her language development."

"It's not unusual for children who've been hospitalized a lot to lag a bit. It's not permanent."

"I try to work with her at home—talking to her as much as I can. I read to her when she'll let me."

"Good."

"Sometimes she likes it but sometimes she's really jumpy—especially after a bad night."

"Are there a lot of bad nights?"

"Not a lot, but they're hard on her."

"What happens?"

"She wakes up as if she's having a bad dream. Tossing and turning and crying. I hold her and sometimes she falls back to sleep. But sometimes she's up for a long time—kind of weepy. The morning after, she's usually jumpy."

"Jumpy in what way?"

"Has trouble concentrating. Other times she can concentrate on something for a long time—an hour or more. I look for those times, try to read to her, talk to her. So that her speech will pick up. Any other suggestions?"

"Sounds like you're on the right track," I said.

"Sometimes I get the feeling she doesn't talk because she doesn't have to. I guess I can tell what she wants, and I give it to her before she has to talk."

"Was that what happened with the headache?"

"Exactly. She woke up crying and tossing around. First thing I did was touch her forehead to see if she was warm. Cool as a cucumber. Which didn't surprise me—it wasn't a scared cry. More of a pain cry.

By now I can tell the difference. So I started asking her what hurt and she finally touched her head. I know it doesn't sound scientific, but you just kind of develop a feel for a child—almost like radar."

Glance at the bed. "If her CAT scan hadn't come back normal that same afternoon, I would have really been scared."

"Because of the headache?"

"After you're here long enough, you see things. Start thinking of the worst things that can happen. It still scares me when she cries out at night—I never know what's going to happen."

She broke into tears again and dabbed at her eyes with the crumpled tissue. I gave her a fresh one.

"I'm really sorry, Dr. Delaware. I just can't stand to see her hurt."

"Of course," I said. "And the irony is that the very things that are being done to help her—the tests and procedures—are causing her the most pain."

She took a deep breath and nodded.

I said, "That's why Dr. Eves asked me to see you. There are psychological techniques that can help children deal with procedural anxiety and, sometimes, even reduce the pain itself."

"Techniques," she said, echoing the way Vicki Bottomley had, but with none of the nurse's sarcasm. "That would be great—I'd sure appreciate anything you could do. Watching her go through her bloodwork is like . . . It's just horrible."

I remembered what Stephanie had said about her composure during procedures.

As if reading me, she said, "Every time someone walks in that door with a needle, I just freeze inside, even though I keep smiling. My smiles are for Cassie. I try really hard not to get upset in front of her but I know she's got to feel it."

"The radar."

"We're so close—she's my one and only. She just looks at me and she knows. I'm not helping her but what can I do? I can't just leave her alone with them."

"Dr. Eves thinks you're doing great."

Something in the brown eyes. A momentary hardening? Then a tired smile.

"Dr. Eves is wonderful. We . . . She was the . . . She's really been wonderful with Cassie, even though Cassie won't have anything more to do with her. I know all these illnesses have been horrible for her, too. Every time the E.R. calls her, I feel bad about putting *her* through it again."

"It's her job," I said.

She looked as if I'd struck her. "I'm sure with her it's more than just a job."

"Yes, it is." I realized the LuvBunny was still in my hand. I was squeezing it.

Fluffing its tummy, I put it back on the ledge. Cindy watched me, stroking her braid.

"I didn't mean to snap," she said, "but what you just said— about Dr. Eves doing her job—it made me think about *my* job. Being a mother. I don't seem to be pulling that off too well, do I? No one *trains* you for that."

She looked away.

"Cindy," I said, leaning forward, "this is a tough thing to go through. Not exactly business as usual."

A smile danced across her lips for just an instant. Sad madonna smile.

Madonna-monster?

Stephanie had asked me to keep an open mind but I knew I was using her suspicions as a point of departure.

Guilty till proven innocent?

What Milo would call limited thinking. I resolved to concentrate on what I actually observed.

Nothing grossly pathologic, so far. No obvious signs of emotional imbalance, no overt histrionics or pathologic attention-seeking. Yet I wondered if she hadn't succeeded—in her own quiet way—in keeping the focus squarely on herself. Starting off talking about Cassie but ending with her maternal failings.

Then again, hadn't I elicited confession? Using shrink looks, shrink pauses and phrases to open her up?

I thought of the way she presented herself—the rope of braid that served as her worry beads, the lack of makeup, conspicuously plain clothes on a woman of her social rank.

All of it could be seen as reverse drama. In a room full of socialites she'd be noticed.

Other things clogged my analytical sieve as I tried to fit her to a Munchausen-by-proxy profile.

The easy usage of hospital jargon: *Spiking temps . . . pulling a double.*

Cyanotic . . .

Leftovers from her respiratory-tech training? Or evidence of an untoward attraction to things medical?

Or maybe nothing more ominous than too many hours spent in this place. During my years on the wards I'd met plumbers and housewives and teamsters and accountants—parents of chronically ill kids who slept and ate and lived at the hospital and ended up sounding like first-year residents.

None of them had poisoned their kids.

Cindy touched her braid and looked back at me.

I smiled, trying to look reassuring, wondering about her certainty that Cassie and she were able to communicate on a near-telepathic level.

Blurred ego boundaries?

The kind of pathologic overidentification that feeds into child abuse?

Then again, what mother didn't claim—often correctly—a radarlike link with her baby? Why suspect this mother of anything more than good bonding?

Because this mother's babies didn't lead healthy, happy lives.

Cindy was still looking at me. I knew I couldn't go on weighing every nuance and still come across as genuine.

I glanced over at the child in the bed, as perfect as a bisque doll.

Her mother's voodoo doll?

"You're doing your best," I said. "That's all anyone can ask."

I hoped it sounded more sincere than I felt. Before Cindy could respond, Cassie opened her eyes, yawned, rubbed her lids and sat up groggily. Both hands were out from under the covers now. The one that had been concealed was puffy and bore needle bruises and yellow Betadine stains.

Cindy rushed over to her and held her. "Good *morning*, baby." New music in her voice. She kissed Cassie's cheek.

Cassie gazed up at her and let her head rest against Cindy's abdomen. Cindy stroked her hair and held her close. Yawning again,

Cassie looked around until her eyes settled on the LuvBunnies on the nightstand.

Pointing to the stuffed animals, she began making urgent whining noises:

"Eh, eh."

Cindy reached over and snagged a pink animal. "Here you go, baby. It's *Funny*Bunny and he's saying, 'Good *morning*, Miss Cassie Jones. Did you have a good *dream*?' "

Talking softly, slowly, in the goofy, eager-to-please voice of a kiddy-show host.

Cassie snatched the doll. Holding it to her chest, she closed her eyes and swayed, and for a moment I thought she'd fall back asleep. But a moment later the eyes opened and stayed that way. Big and brown, just like her mother's.

Her big-eyed gaze jumped around the room once more, swinging in my direction and stopping.

We made eye contact.

I smiled.

She screamed.

5

Cindy held her and rocked her and said, "It's okay. He's our friend."

Cassie threw the LuvBunny on the floor, then began sobbing for it.

I picked it up and held it out to her. She shrank back and clung to her mother. I gave Cindy the doll, took a yellow bunny from the shelf, and sat back down.

I began to play with the animal, manipulating its arms, chatting nonsense. Cassie continued crying and Cindy kept up a quiet, comforting patter, too soft to hear. I stayed with the bunny. After a minute or so, Cassie's volume dropped a notch.

Cindy said, "Look, honey—you see? Dr. Delaware likes the bunnies, too."

Cassie gulped, gasped, and let out a wail.

"No, he's not going to hurt you, honey. He's our friend."

I stared at the doll's overbite and shook one of its paws. A white heart on its belly bore yellow letters: *SillyBunny* and the trademark ®. A tag near its crotch said MADE IN TAIWAN.

Cassie paused for breath.

Cindy said, "It's okay, honey, everything's okay."

Whimper and sniff from the bed.

"How 'bout a story, baby, okay? Once upon a time there was a princess named Cassandra who lived in a great big castle and had wonderful dreams about candy and whipped-cream clouds. . . ."

Cassie stared up. Her bruised hand touched her lips.

I placed the yellow bunny on the floor, opened my briefcase, and took out a notebook and a pencil. Cindy stopped talking for a moment, then resumed her story. Cassie was calm now, caught up in another world.

I started to draw. A bunny. I hoped.

A few minutes later it was clear the Disney folk had nothing to worry about, but I thought the end product managed to be cute and sufficiently rabbitlike. I added a hat and a bow tie, reached into the case again, and found the box of colored markers I kept there along with other tools of the trade.

I began coloring. The markers squeaked. Rustles came from the bed. Cindy stopped telling her story.

"Oh, look, honey, Dr. Delaware's *drawing*. What are you drawing, Dr. Delaware?"

Before I could answer, the word *doctor* precipitated another tearstorm.

Again, maternal comfort squelched it.

I held up my masterpiece.

"Oh, look, honey, it's a *bunny*. And he's wearing a hat. And a bow tie—isn't that *silly*?"

Silence.

"Well, *I* think it's silly. Do you think he's one of the LuvBunnies, Cass?"

Silence.

"Did Dr. Delaware draw a LuvBunny?"

Whimper.

"C'mon, Cass, there's nothing to worry about. Dr. Delaware won't do anything to hurt you. He's the kind of doctor who never gives shots."

Bleats. It took a while for Cindy to calm her down. Finally she was able to resume her story. Princess Cassandra riding a white horse . . .

I drew a companion for Mr. HatBunny. Same rodent face but short ears, polka-dot dress—Ms. Squirrel. I added an amorphous-looking acorn, pulled the page out of the notebook, reached over and placed it on the bed near Cassie's feet.

She whipped her head around just as I got back to my seat.

Cindy said, "Oh, look, he's done a . . . *prairie* dog, too. And she's a *girl,* Cass—look at her dress. Isn't that *funny?* And she's got big *dots* all over her dress, Cass. That's so *funny*—a prairie dog in a dress!"

Warm, womanly laughter. At the tail end, a child's giggle.

"So *silly.* I wonder if she's going to a *party* with that dress . . . or maybe she's going to go *shopping* or something, huh? Wouldn't that be silly, a prairie dog going shopping at the *mall?* Going with her friend Mr. Bunny, and he's got that silly hat on—the two of them are really dressed up silly. Maybe they'll go to Toys "Я" Us and get their *own* dolls—wouldn't *that* be something, Cass? Yeah, that would be silly. *Boy,* Dr. Delaware sure makes silly pictures—wonder what he's going to do now!"

I smiled and lifted my pencil. Something easy: hippopotamus . . . just a bathtub with legs . . .

"What's your bunny's name, Dr. Delaware?"

"Benny."

"Benny *Bunny*—that's *ridiculous*!"

I smiled, concealing my artistic struggle. The bathtub was looking too fierce. . . . The problem was the grin . . . too aggressive—more like a dehorned rhino . . . What would Freud say about that?

I performed reconstructive surgery on the critter's mouth.

"Benny the *Hat* Bunny—didja *hear* that, Cass?"

High-pitched, little-kid laughter.

"And what about the prairie dog, Dr. Delaware? What's *her* name?"

"Priscilla . . ." Working away. The hippo finally hippolike, but still something wrong . . . the grin venal—the greasy smirk of a carny barker . . . Maybe a dog would have been easier . . .

"*Pris*ci*l*la the prairie dog! Do you believe *that*!"

"*Pilla!*"

"Yes, Priscilla!"

"*Pilla!*"

"Very *good*, Cass! That's excellent! Pris*ci*lla. Can you say that again?"

Silence.

"Pris*ci*lla—*Pri-scil-la.* You just said it. Here, watch my mouth, Cass."

Silence.

"Okay, you don't have to if you don't want to. Let's get back to Princess Cassandra Silversparkle, riding Snowflake up into the Shiny Country . . ."

The hippo was finally done. Scarred by smudges and eraser abrasions, but at least it didn't look as if it had a rap sheet. I placed it on top of the bedcovers.

"Oh, look, Cass. We know what this is, don't we? A *hippopotamus*—and he's holding a . . ."

"A yo-yo," I said.

"A *yo*-yo! A hippo with a *yo*-yo—that is *really* silly. You know what I think, Cass? I think Dr. Delaware can be pretty silly when he wants to, even though he's a doctor. What do *you* think?"

I faced the little girl. Our eyes locked once more. Hers flickered. The rosebud mouth began to pout, lower lip curling. Hard to imagine anyone being capable of hurting her.

I said, "Would you like me to draw some more?"

She looked at her mother and grabbed Cindy's sleeve.

"Sure," said Cindy. "Let's see what other silly things Dr. Delaware can draw, okay?"

Minuscule nod from Cassie. She buried her head in Cindy's blouse.

Back to the drawing board.

A mangy hound, a cross-eyed duck, and a spavined horse later, she was tolerating my presence.

I edged the chair closer to the bed, gradually. Chatted with Cindy about games and toys and favorite foods. When Cassie seemed to be taking me for granted, I pushed right up against the mattress and taught Cindy a drawing game—the two of us alternating turning squiggles into objects. Child analyst's technique for building rapport and getting to the unconscious in a nonthreatening way.

Using Cindy as a go-between even as I studied her.

Investigated her.

I drew an angular squiggle and handed the paper to her. She and Cassie were snuggled together; they could have been a poster for National Bonding Week. Cindy turned the squiggle into a house and handed the paper back, saying, "Not very good, but . . ."

Cassie's lips turned up a bit. Then down. Her eyes closed and she pressed her face against Cindy's blouse. Grabbed a breast and squeezed. Cindy lowered the hand gently and placed it in her own lap. I saw the puncture marks on Cassie's flesh. Black dots, like snakebites.

Cindy made easy, cooing sounds. Cassie nuzzled, shifted position, and gathered a handful of blouse.

Sleepy again. Cindy kissed the top of her head.

I'd been trained to heal, trained to believe in the open, honest therapeutic relationship. Being in this room made me feel like a con man.

Then I thought about raging fevers and bloody diarrhea and convulsions so intense they rattled the crib, remembered a little baby boy who'd died in his crib, and my self-doubts turned stale and crumbled.

By 10:45, I'd been there for more than half an hour, mostly watching Cassie lie in Cindy's arms. But she seemed more comfortable with me, even smiling once or twice. Time to pack up and declare success.

I stood. Cassie started to fuss.

Cindy sniffed the air, wrinkled her nose, and said, "Uh-oh."

Gently, she rolled Cassie onto her back and changed the little girl's diaper.

Powdered, patted, and reclothed, Cassie remained restless. Pointing at the floor, she said, "Ah! Ah! Ah! Ah!"

"Out?"

Emphatic nod. *"Ahd!"*

She got on her knees and tried to stand on the bed, wobbling on the soft mattress. Cindy held her under the arms, lifted her off, and placed her on the floor. "You want to walk around? Let's get some slippers on you." The two of them walked to the closet. Cassie's pajama bottoms were too long for her and they dragged on the floor. Standing, she looked even tinier. But sturdy. Good steady walk, good sense of balance.

I picked up my briefcase.

Kneeling, Cindy put fuzzy pink bunny slippers on Cassie's feet. These rodents had clear plastic eyes with movable black beads for pupils and each time Cassie moved, her feet hissed.

She tried to jump, barely got off the ground.

Cindy said, "Good jump, Cass."

The door opened and a man came in.

He looked to be in his late thirties. Six two or so, and very slim. His hair was dark-brown, wavy, and thick, combed straight back and left long enough to curl over his collar. He had a full face at odds with the lanky physique, rounded further by a bushy, cropped brown beard flecked with gray. His features were soft and pleasant. A gold stud pierced his left earlobe. The clothes he had on were loose-fitting but well cut: blue-and-white striped button-down shirt under a gray tweed sport coat; baggy, pleated black cords; black running shoes that looked brand-new.

A coffee cup was in one hand.

"It's Daddy!" said Cindy.

Cassie held out her arms.

The tall man put the cup down and said, "Morning, ladies." Kissing Cindy's cheek, he scooped Cassie up.

The little girl squealed as he held her aloft. He brought her close with one swift, descending motion.

"How's my baby?" he said, pressing her to his beard. His nose disappeared under her hair and she giggled. "How's the little *grande dame* of the diaper set?"

Cassie put both of her hands in *his* hair and pulled.

"Ouch!"

Giggle. Yank.

"Double ouch!"

Baby-guffaw.

"Ouch-a-*roo*!"

They played a bit longer; then he pulled away and said, "Whew. You're too rough for me, Spike!"

Cindy said, "This is Dr. Delaware, honey. The psychologist? Doctor, Cassie's dad."

The man turned toward me, holding on to Cassie, and extended his free hand. "Chip Jones. Good to meet you."

His grip was strong. Cassie was still yanking on his hair, messing it. He seemed impervious.

"I minored in psych," he said, smiling. "Forgot most of it." To Cindy: "How's everything?"

" 'Bout the same."

He frowned. Looked at his wrist. Another Swatch.

Cindy said, "On the run?"

"Unfortunately. Just wanted to see your faces." He picked up the coffee cup and held it out to her.

"No, thanks."

"You're sure?"

"Nah, I'm fine."

"Stomach?"

She touched her abdomen and said, "Just feeling a little woozy. How long can you stay?"

"In and out," he said. "Got a twelve o'clock class, then meetings for the rest of the day—probably dumb to drive all the way over, but I missed you guys."

Cindy smiled.

Chip kissed her, then Cassie.

Cindy said, "Daddy can't stay, Cass. Bummer, huh?"

"Dah-dee."

Chip gave Cassie's chin a gentle tweak. She continued playing with his beard. "I'll try to kick by later this evening. Stay as long as you need me."

"Great," said Cindy.

"*Dah-dee.*"

"Dah-dee," said Chip. "Dah-dee love you. You cute." To Cindy: "Not a good idea at all, coming for two minutes. Now I'm really gonna miss you."

"We miss you too, Daddy."

"I was in the neighborhood," he said. "So to speak—this side of the hill, at least."

"The U?"

"Yup. Library duty." He turned to me: "I teach over at West Valley C.C. New campus, not much in terms of reference resources. So when I have some serious research to do, I go over to the university."

"My alma mater," I said.

"That so? I went to school back east." He tickled Cassie's belly. "Get any sleep at all, Cin?"

"Plenty."

"Sure?"

"Uh-huh."

"Want some herb tea? I think I've got some chamomile in the car."

"No, thanks, hon. Dr. Delaware has some techniques to help Cassie deal with the p-a-i-n."

Chip looked at me while stroking Cassie's arm. "That would be terrific. This has been an incredible ordeal." His eyes were slate-blue with a slight droop, very deep-set.

"I know it has," I said.

Chip and Cindy looked at each other, then at me.

"Well," I said, "I'll be shoving off now. Come by to see you tomorrow morning."

I bent and whispered goodbye to Cassie. She batted her lashes and turned away.

Chip laughed. "What a flirt. It's inborn, isn't it?"

Cindy said, "Your techniques. When can we talk about that?"

"Soon," I said. "First I need to get a rapport with Cassie. I think we did pretty well today."

"Oh. Sure. We did great. Didn't we, pudding?"

"Is ten o'clock a good time for you?"

"Sure," said Cindy. "We're not going anywhere."

Chip looked at her and said, "Dr. Eves didn't say anything about discharge?"

"Not yet. She wants to keep observing."

He sighed. "Okay."

I walked to the door.

Chip said, "I've got to be running, myself, Doctor. If you can hold on for one sec, I'll walk out with you."

"Sure."

He took his wife's hand.

I closed the door, walked to the nursing station, and went behind the desk. Vicki Bottomley was back from the gift shop, sitting in the unit clerk's chair, reading *RN*. No one else was around. A box wrapped with Western Peds gift-shop paper sat on the counter, next to a coil of catheter tubing and a stack of insurance forms.

She didn't look up as I lifted Cassie's chart from the rack and began leafing through. I skimmed through the medical history and came upon Stephanie's psychosocial history. Wondering about the age difference between Chip and Cindy, I looked up his biographical data.

Charles L. Jones III. Age: 38. Educational level: Master's degree. Occupation: College professor.

Sensing someone looking at me, I lowered the chart and saw Vicki whipping her head back toward her magazine.

"So," I said, "how were things down in the gift shop?"

She lowered the journal. "Is there something specific you need from me?"

"Anything that would help me work with Cassie's anxiety."

Her pretty eyes narrowed. "Dr. Eves already asked me that. You were right here."

"Just wondering if something occurred to you in the meantime."

"Nothing *occurred*," she said, "I don't know anything—I'm just the nurse."

"The nurse often knows more than anybody."

"Tell it to the salary committee." She lifted the magazine high, concealing her face.

I was considering my response when I heard my name called. Chip Jones strode toward me.

"Thanks for waiting."

The sound of his voice made Vicki stop reading. She straightened her cap and said, "Hi, Dr. Jones." A sweet smile spread across her face, honey on stale bread.

Chip leaned on the counter, grinned, and shook his head. "There

you go again, Vicki, trying to promote me." To me: "I'm A.B.D.—
that's 'all but dissertation,' Vicki—but generous Ms. Bottomley here
keeps trying to graduate me before I earn it."

Vicki managed to work up another dirt-eating smile. "Degree
or not, what's the difference?"

"Well," said Chip, "it might make quite a difference to someone
like Dr. Delaware here, who genuinely earned his."

"I'm sure it *does*."

He heard the acid in her voice and gave her a quizzical look. She
got flustered and looked away.

He noticed the gift box. "Vicki. Again?"

"It's just a little something."

"That's very sweet of you, Vicki, but totally unnecessary."

"I wanted to, Dr. Jones. She's such an angel."

"That she is, Vicki." He smiled. "Another bunny?"

"Well, she likes them, Dr. Jones."

"*Mister,* Vicki—if you insist on using a title, how about Herr
Professor? It has a nice classical ring to it, wouldn't you agree, Dr.
Delaware?"

"Absolutely."

He said, "I'm prattling—this place addles me. Thank you
again, Vicki. You're very sweet."

Bottomley went scarlet.

Chip turned to me. "Ready if you are, Doctor."

We walked through the teak doors into the hustle of Five East. A
child being wheeled somewhere was crying, a little boy hooked to an
I.V. and turbaned with bandages. Chip took it in, frowning but not
talking.

As we approached the elevators he shook his head and said,
"Good old Vicki. What a shameless brown-noser. But she got kind of
uppity with you back there, didn't she?"

"I'm not her favorite person."

"Why?"

"I don't know."

"Ever have any hassles with her before?"

"Nope. Never met her before."

He shook his head. "Well, I'm sorry for you, but she seems to be taking really good care of Cassie. And Cindy likes her. I think she reminds Cindy of her aunt—she had an aunt who raised her. Also a nurse, real tough egg."

After we passed a gaggle of dazed-looking medical students, he said, "It's probably territorial—Vicki's reaction to you. Some kind of turf battle, wouldn't you say?"

"Could be."

"I notice a lot of that kind of thing around here. Possessiveness over patients. As if they're commodities."

"Have you experienced that personally?"

"Oh, sure. Plus, our situation heightens the tension. People think that we're worth kissing up to, because we've got some sort of direct line to the power structure. I assume you know who my dad is."

I nodded.

He said, "It rubs me the wrong way, being treated differently. I worry about it leading to substandard care for Cassie."

"In what way?"

"I don't know, nothing specific—I guess I'm just not comfortable with being an exception. I don't want anyone missing something important because they hung back or broke routine out of fear of offending our family. Not that Dr. Eves isn't great—I have nothing but respect for her. It's more the whole system—a feeling I get when I'm here."

He slowed his pace. "Maybe I'm just talking through my hat. The frustration. Cassie's been sick with one thing or another for virtually her whole life and no one's figured out what's wrong yet, and we also . . . What I'm saying is that this hospital's a highly formalized structure and whenever the rules change in a formalized structure, you run the risk of structural cracks. That's my field of interest: Formal Org—Formal Organizations. And let me tell you, this is some organization."

We reached the elevators. He punched the button and said, "I hope you can help Cassie with the shots—she's gone through an absolute nightmare. Cindy, too. She's a fantastic mother, but with this kind of thing, self-doubts are inevitable."

"Is she blaming herself?" I said.

"Sometimes. Even though it's totally unjustified. I try to tell her, but . . ."

He shook his head and put his hands together. The knuckles were white. Reaching up, he rotated his earring.

"The strain on her's been incredible."

"Must be rough on you, too," I said.

"It hasn't been fun, that's for sure. But the worst of it falls on Cindy. To be honest, we've got your basic, traditional, sex role—stereotyped marriage—I work; she takes care of things at home. It's by mutual choice—what *Cindy* really wanted. I'm involved at home to some extent—probably not as much as I should be—but child rearing's really Cindy's domain. God knows she's a hell of a lot better at it than I am. So when something goes wrong in that sphere, she takes all the responsibility on her shoulders."

He stroked his beard and shook his head. "Now, *that* was an impressive bit of defensive pedantry, wasn't it? Yes, sure, it's been *damned* rough on me. Seeing someone you love . . . I assume you know about Chad—our first baby?"

I nodded.

"We hit *bottom* with that, Dr. Delaware. There's just no way to . . ." Closing his eyes, he shook his head again. Hard, as if trying to dislodge mental burrs.

"Let's just say it wasn't anything I'd wish on my worst enemy."

He jabbed the elevator button, glanced at his watch. "Looks like we caught the local, Doctor. Anyway, we were just coming out of it—Cindy and I. Pulling ourselves together and starting to enjoy Cassie when *this* mess hit the fan . . . Unbelievable."

The elevator arrived. Two candy-stripers and a doctor exited, and we stepped in. Chip pushed the ground-floor button and settled with his back against the compartment's rear wall.

"You just never know what life's going to throw you," he said. "I've always been stubborn. Probably to a fault—an obnoxious individualist. Probably because a lot of conformity was shoved down my throat at an early age. But I've come to realize I'm pretty conservative. Buying into the basic values: Live your life according to the rules and things will eventually work out. Hopelessly naïve, of course. But you get into a certain mode of thinking and it feels right, so you keep doing it. That's as good a definition of faith as any, I guess. But I'm fast losing mine."

The elevator stopped at four. A Hispanic woman in her fifties and a boy of around ten got on. The boy was short, stocky, bespectacled. His blunt face bore the unmistakable cast of Down's syndrome. Chip smiled at them. The boy didn't appear to notice him. The woman looked very tired. No one talked. The two of them got off at three.

When the door closed, Chip kept staring at it. As we resumed our descent he said, "Take that poor woman. She didn't expect that—child of her old age and now she has to take care of him forever. Something like that'll shake up your entire worldview. That's what's happened to me—the whole child-rearing thing. No more assumptions about happy endings."

He turned to me. The slate eyes were fierce. "I really hope you can help Cassandra. As long as she has to go through this shit, let her be spared some of the pain."

The elevator landed. The moment the door opened, he was out and gone.

When I got back to the General Peds clinic, Stephanie was in one of the exam rooms. I waited outside until she came out a few minutes later, followed by a huge black woman and a girl of around five. The girl wore a red polka-dot dress and had coal-black skin, cornrows, and beautiful African features. One of her hands gripped Stephanie's; the other held a lollipop. A tear stream striped her cheek, lacquer on ebony. A round pink Band-Aid dotted the crook of one arm.

Stephanie was saying, "You did great, Tonya." She saw me and mouthed, "My office," before returning her attention to the girl.

I went to her consult room. The Byron book was back on the shelf, its gilded spine conspicuous among the texts.

I thumbed through a recent copy of *Pediatrics*. Not long after, Stephanie came in, closed the door, and sank into her desk chair.

"So," she said, "how'd it go?"

"Fine, outside of Ms. Bottomley's continuing antagonism."

"She get in the way?"

"No, just more of the same." I told her about the scene with the nurse and Chip. "Trying to get on his good side but it probably backfired. He sees her as a shameless ass-kisser, though he does think she takes good care of Cassie. And his analysis of why she resents me is probably right-on: competing for the attentions of the VIP patient."

"Attention seeking, huh? There's a bit of Munchausen symptomology."

"Yup. In addition, she did visit the home. But only a couple of times, a while back. So it still doesn't seem likely she could have caused anything. But let's keep our eyes on her."

"I already started, Alex. Asked around about her. The nursing office thinks she's tops. She gets consistently good ratings, no complaints. And as far as I can tell there's been no unusual pattern of illness in any of her patients. But my offer's still open—she causes too much hassle, she's transferred."

"Let me see if I can work things out with her. Cindy and Chip like her."

"Even though she's an ass-kisser."

"Even though. Incidentally, he feels that way about the entire hospital. Doesn't like getting special treatment."

"In what way?"

"No specific complaints, and he made a point of saying he likes *you*. He's just got a general concern that something could be missed because of who his father is. More than anything, he looks weary. They both do."

"Aren't we all," she said. "So what's your initial take on mama?"

"She wasn't what I expected—neither of them was. They seem more health-food restaurant than country club. And they're also different from each other. She's very . . . I guess the best word for it is *basic*. Unsophisticated. Especially for a honcho's daughter-in-law. I can see Chip growing up rich, but he's not exactly corporate son."

"The earring?"

"The earring, his choice of profession, his general demeanor. He talked about getting conformity shoved at him throughout childhood and rebelling. Maybe marrying Cindy was part of it. There's a twelve-year difference between them. Was she his student?"

"Could be, I don't know. Is that relevant in terms of Munchausen?"

"Not really. I'm just getting my feet wet. In terms of a Munchausen profile, it's too early to tell much about her. She does toss some jargon into her speech and she's highly identified with Cassie—feels the two of them have an almost telepathic link. The physical resemblance between them is strong—Cassie's like a miniature of her. That could enhance the identification, I suppose."

"Meaning if Cindy hates herself she could be projecting it on to Cassie?"

"It's possible," I said. "But I'm a long way off from interpretation. Did Chad also resemble her?"

"I saw him dead, Alex." She covered her face, rubbed her eyes, looked up. "All I remember was that he was a pretty little boy. Gray, like one of those cherub statues you put in a garden. Tell the truth, I tried *not* to look at him."

She picked up a demitasse cup, looked ready to throw it.

"God, what a nightmare. Carrying him down to the morgue. The staff elevator was jammed. I was just standing around, holding this *bundle*. Waiting. People passing right by me, gabbing—I wanted to scream. Finally I walked over to the public elevators, rode down with a bunch of other people. Patients, parents. Trying not to look at *them*. So they wouldn't know what I was carrying."

We sat for a while. Then she said, "Espresso," leaned over toward the little black machine and turned it on. A red light glowed. "Loaded and ready to go. Let's caffeine our troubles away. Oh, let me give you those references."

She took a piece of paper from the desk and handed it to me. List of ten articles.

"Thanks."

"Notice anything else," she said, "about Cindy?"

"No *belle indifférence* or dramatic attention seeking, so far. On the contrary, she seemed very low-key. Chip did mention that the aunt who raised her was a nurse, so we've got a possible early exposure to health-related issues, on top of her being a respiratory tech. But that's really pretty thin, by itself. Her child-rearing skills seem good—exemplary, even."

"What about the relationship with her husband? Pick up any stress there?"

"No. Have you?"

She shook her head. Smiled. "But I thought you guys had tricks."

"Didn't bring my bag this morning. Actually, they seem to get along pretty well."

"One big happy family," she said. "Have you ever seen a case like this before?"

"Never," I said. "Munchausens avoid psychologists and psychiatrists like the plague because we're proof no one's taking their diseases seriously. The closest I've come are doctor-hoppers—parents convinced something's wrong with their kids, running from specialist to specialist even though no one can find any real symptoms. When I was in practice I used to get referrals from doctors driven crazy by them. But I never treated them for long. When they showed up at all, they tended to be pretty hostile and almost always dropped out quickly."

"Doctor-hoppers," she said. "Never thought of them as mini-Munchausens."

"Could be the same dynamic at a milder level. Obsession with health, seeking attention from authority figures while dancing around with them."

"The waltz," she said. "What about Cassie? How's she functioning?"

"Exactly as you described—she freaked out when she saw me, but calmed down eventually."

"Then you're doing better than I am."

"I don't stick her with needles, Steph."

She gave a sour smile. "Maybe I went into the wrong field. Anything else you can tell me about her?"

"No major pathology, maybe some minor language delay. If her speech doesn't get better in the next six months, I'd have it checked out with a full psych battery, including neuropsych testing."

She began ordering the piles on her desk. Swiveled and faced me.

"Six months," she said. "If she's still alive by then."

6

The waiting room was hot with bodies and impatience. Several of the mothers flashed hopeful looks at Stephanie as she walked me out. She smiled, said, "Soon," and ushered me into the hall.

A group of men—three white-coated doctors and one business suit in gray flannel—was heading our way. The lead white-coat noticed us and called out, "Dr. Eves!"

Stephanie grimaced. "Wonderful."

She stopped and the men came abreast. The white-coats were all in their fifties and had the well-fed, well-shaven look of senior attending physicians with established practices.

Business-suit was younger—mid-thirties—and hefty. Six feet, 230 or so, big round shoulders padded with fat under a broad columnar head. He had short dishwater hair and bland features, except for a nose that had been broken and reset imperfectly. A wispy narrow mustache failed to give the face any depth. He looked like an ex-jock playing the corporate game. He stood behind the others, too far away for me to read his badge.

The lead doctor was also thickset, and very tall. He had wide razor-edge lips and thinning curly hair the color of silver plate that he wore longish and winged at the sides. A heavy, outthrusting chin gave his face the illusion of forward movement. His eyes were quick and brown, his skin pinkish and gleaming as if fresh from the sauna. The two doctors flanking him were medium-sized, gray-haired, and bespectacled. In one case, the hair was a toupee.

Chin said, "How're things in the trenches, Dr. Eves?" in a deep, adenoidal voice.

Stephanie said, "Trenchlike."

He turned to me and did some eyebrow calisthenics.

Stephanie said, "This is Dr. Delaware, a member of our staff."

He shot his hand out. "Don't believe it's been my pleasure. George Plumb."

"Pleased to meet you, Dr. Plumb."

Vise-grip handshake. "Delaware," he said. "What division are you with, Doctor?"

"I'm a psychologist."

"Ah."

The two gray-haired men looked at me but didn't talk or move. Suit seemed to be counting the holes in the acoustical ceiling.

"He's with pediatrics," said Stephanie. "Serving as a consultant on the Cassie Jones case—helping the family cope with the stress."

Plumb swung his eyes back to her. "Ah. Very good." He touched her arm lightly. She endured it for a moment, then backed away.

He renewed his smile. "You and I need to confer, Stephanie. I'll have my girl call yours and set it up."

"I don't have a girl, George. The five of us share one *woman* secretary."

The gray twins looked at her as if she were floating in a jar. Suit was somewhere else.

Plumb kept smiling. "Yes, the ever-changing nomenclature. Well, then my *girl* will call your *woman*. Be well, Stephanie."

He led his entourage away, stopped several yards down the hall, and ran his eyes up and down a wall, as if measuring.

"What are you going to dismantle now, boys?" said Stephanie under her breath.

Plumb resumed walking and the group disappeared around a corner.

I said, "What was that all about?"

"That was about *Doctor* Plumb, our new chief administrator and CEO. Papa Jones's boy—Mr. Bottom Line."

"M.D. administrator?"

She laughed. "What, the coat? No, he's no doc. Just some kind of asinine Ph.D. or something—" She stopped, colored. "Jeez, I'm sorry."

I had to laugh. "Don't worry about it."

"I'm *really* sorry, Alex. You know how I feel about psychologists—"

"Forget it." I put my arm over her shoulder. She slipped hers around my waist.

"My mind is going," she said softly. "I am definitely falling apart."

"What's Plumb's degree in?"

"Business or management, something like that. He uses it to the hilt—insists on being called Doctor, wears a white coat. Most of his lackeys have doctorates, too—like Frick and Frack over there: Roberts and Novak, his numbers crunchers. They all love to traipse into the doctors' dining room and take over a table. Show up at medical meetings and rounds for no apparent reason, walking around staring and measuring and taking notes. Like the way Plumb just stopped and sized up that wall. I wouldn't be surprised if the carpenters show up soon. Dividing three offices into six, turning clinical space into administrative offices. And now he wants to *confer* with me—there's something to look forward to."

"Are you vulnerable?"

"Everyone is, but General Peds is at the bottom of the barrel. We've got no fancy technology or heroics to make headlines. Most of what we do's outpatient, so our reimbursement level's the lowest in the hospital. Since Psych's gone." She smiled.

"Even technology doesn't seem immune," I said. "This morning, when I was looking for an elevator, I went by where Nuclear Medicine used to be and the suite had been given over to something called Community Services."

"Another of Plumb's coups. But don't worry about the Nukers— they're okay. Moved upstairs to Two, same square footage, though patients have trouble finding them. But some of the other divisions have had real problems—Nephrology, Rheumatology, your buddies in Oncology. They're stuck in trailers across the street."

"Trailers?"

"As in Winnebago."

"Those are major divisions, Steph. Why do they put up with it?"

"No choice, Alex. They signed away their rights. They were supposed to be housed in the old Hollywood Lutheran Tower— Western Peds bought it a couple of years ago, after Lutheran had to divest because of *their* budget problems. The board promised to build fantastic suites for anyone who moved over there. Construction was supposed to start last year. The divisions that agreed were moved to the trailers and their old space was given to someone else. Then they discovered—*Plumb* discovered—that even though enough money had been raised to make a down payment on the tower and do some of the remodeling, insufficient funds had been allocated to do the rest and to *maintain* it. Trifling matter of thirteen million dollars. Try raising that in this climate—heroes are already in short supply because we've got a charity hospital image and no one wants their name on a bunch of doctors' offices."

"Trailers," I said. "Melendez-Lynch must be overjoyed."

"Melendez-Lynch went *adios,* last year."

"You're kidding. Raoul *lived* here."

"Not anymore. Miami. Some hospital offered him chief of staff, and he took it. I hear he's getting triple the salary and half the headaches."

"It *has* been a long time," I said. "Raoul had all those research grants. How'd they let him get away?"

"Research doesn't matter to these people, Alex. They don't want to pay the overhead. It's a whole new game." She let her arm fall from my waist. We began walking.

"Who's the other guy?" I said. "Mr. Gray Suit."

"Oh, him." She looked unnerved. "That's Huenengarth— *Presley* Huenengarth. Head of security."

"He looks like an enforcer," I said. "Muscle for those who don't pay their bills?"

She laughed. "That wouldn't be so terrible. The hospital's bad debt is over eighty percent. No, he doesn't seem to do much of anything, except follow Plumb around and *lurk*. Some of the staff think he's spooky."

"In what way?"

She didn't answer for a moment. "His manner, I guess."

"You have any bad experiences with him?"

"Me? No. Why?"

"You look a little antsy talking about him."

"No," she said. "It's nothing personal—just the way he acts to everyone. Showing up when you're not expecting him. Materializing around corners. You'll come out of a patient's room and he'll just *be* there."

"Sounds charming."

"*Très*. But what's a *girl* to do? Call Security?"

I rode down to the ground floor alone, found Security open, endured a uniformed guard's five-minute interrogation, and finally earned the right to have a full-color badge made.

The picture came out looking like a mug shot. I snapped the badge onto my lapel and took the stairs down to the sub-basement level, heading for the hospital library, ready to check out Stephanie's references.

The door was locked. An undated memorandum taped to the door said new library hours were three to five P.M., Monday through Wednesday.

I checked the adjoining reading room. Open but unoccupied. I stepped into another world: oiled paneling, tufted leather chester-fields and wing chairs, worn but good Persian rugs over a shoe-buffed herringbone oak floor.

Hollywood seemed planets away.

Once the study of a Cotswolds manor house, the entire room had been donated years ago—before I'd arrived as an intern—transported across the Atlantic and reconstructed under the financial guidance of an Anglophile patron who felt doctors need to relax in high style. A patron who'd never spent time with a Western Peds doctor.

I strode across the room and tried the connecting door to the library. Open.

The windowless room was pitch-dark and I turned on the lights.

Most of the shelves were empty; a few bore thin stacks of mismatched journals. Careless piles of books sat on the floor. The rear wall was bare.

The computer I'd used to run Medline searches was nowhere in sight. Neither was the golden-oak card catalogue with its hand-lettered parchment labels. The only furniture was a gray metal table. Taped to the top was a piece of paper. An inter-hospital memo, dated three months ago.

TO: Professional Staff
FROM: G. H. Plumb, MBA, DBA, Chief Executive Officer
SUBJECT: Library Restructure

In accordance with repeated requests by the Professional Staff and a subsequent confirmatory decision by the Research Committee, the Board of Directors in General Assembly, and the Finance Subcommittee of the Executive Board, the Medical Library reference index will be converted to a fully computerized system utilizing Orion and Melvyl-type standard library data search programs. The contract for this conversion has been put out to competitive bid and, after careful deliberation and cost/benefit computation, has been awarded to BIO-DAT, Inc., of Pittsburgh, Pennsylvania, a concern specializing in medical and scientific research probe systems and health-care workstation integration. BIO-DAT officials have informed us that the entire process should take approximately three weeks, once they are in full receipt of all relevant data. Accordingly, the library's current card files will be shipped to BIO-DAT headquarters in Pittsburgh for the duration of the conversion process, and returned to Los Angeles for purposes of storage and archival activity, once the conversion has been terminated. Your cooperation and forbearance during the conversion period is solicited.

Three weeks had stretched to three months.

I ran my finger along the metal table and ended up with a dust-blackened tip.

Turning off the light, I left the room.

*   *   *

Sunset Boulevard was a bouillabaisse of rage and squalor mixed with immigrant hope and livened by the spice of easy felony.

I drove past the flesh clubs, the new-music caverns, titanic show-biz billboards, and the anorexically oriented boutiques of the Strip, crossed Doheny and slipped into the dollar-shrines of Beverly Hills. Passing my turnoff at Beverly Glen, I headed for a place where serious research could always be done. The place where Chip Jones had done his.

The Biomed library was filled with the inquisitive and the obligated. Sitting at one of the monitors was someone I recognized.

Gamine face, intense eyes, dangling earrings, and a double pierce on the right ear. The tawny bob had grown out to a shoulder-length wedge. A line of white collar showed over a navy-blue crew-neck.

When had I last seen her? Three years or so. Making her twenty.

I wondered if she'd gotten her Ph.D. yet.

She was tapping the keys rapidly, bringing data to the screen. As I neared I saw that the text was in German. The word *neuropeptide* kept popping out.

"Hi, Jennifer."

She spun around. "Alex!" Big smile. She gave me a kiss on the cheek and got off her stool.

"Is it Dr. Leavitt yet?" I said.

"This June," she said. "Wrapping up my dissertation."

"Congratulations. Neuroanatomy?"

"Neurochemistry—much more practical, right?"

"Still planning on going to med school?"

"Next fall. Stanford."

"Psychiatry?"

"I don't know," she said. "Maybe something a bit more . . . concrete. No offense. I'm going to take my time and see what appeals to me."

"Well, there's certainly no hurry—what are you, twelve years old?"

"Twenty! I'll be twenty-one next month."

"A veritable crone."

"Weren't you young, too, when you finished?"

"Not that young. I was shaving."

She laughed again. "It's great to see you. Hear from Jamey at all?"

"I got a postcard at Christmas. From New Hampshire. He's renting a farm there. Writing poetry."

"Is he . . . all right?"

"He's better. There was no return address on the card and he wasn't listed. So I called the psychiatrist who treated him up in Carmel and she said he'd been maintaining pretty well on medication. Apparently he's got someone to take care of him. One of the nurses who worked with him up there."

"Well, that's good," she said. "Poor guy. He had so much going for and against him."

"Good way to put it. Have you had any contact with the other people in the group?"

The group. *Project 160.* As in IQ. Accelerated academics for kids with genius intellects. A grand experiment; one of its members ended up accused of serial murder. I'd gotten involved, taken a joyride into hatred and corruption. . . .

". . . is at Harvard Law and working for a judge, Felicia's studying math at Columbia, and David dropped out of U. of Chicago med school after one semester and became a commodities trader. In the pits. He always was kind of an eighties guy. Anyway, the project's defunct—Dr. Flowers didn't renew the grant."

"Health problems?"

"That was part of it. And of course the publicity about Jamey didn't help. She moved to Hawaii. I think she wanted to minimize her stress—because of the M.S."

Catching up with the past for the second time today, I realized how many loose ends I'd let dangle.

"So," she said, "what brings you here?"

"Looking up some case material."

"Anything interesting?"

"Munchausen syndrome by proxy. Familiar with it?"

"I've heard of Munchausen—people abusing their bodies to fake disease, right? But what's the proxy part?"

"People faking disease in their children."

"Well, *that's* certainly hideous. What kinds of illnesses?"

"Almost anything. The most common symptoms are breathing problems, bleeding disorders, fevers, infections, pseudoseizures."

"By *proxy*," she said. "The *word* is unnerving—so calculated, like some sort of business deal. Are you actually working with a family like that?"

"I'm evaluating a family to see if that's what's going on. It's still in the differential diagnosis stage. I have some preliminary references, thought I'd review the literature."

She smiled. "Card-file, or have you become computer-friendly?"

"Computer. If the screen talks English."

"Do you have a faculty account for SAP?"

"No. What's that?"

" 'Search and Print.' New system. Journals on file—complete texts scanned and entered. You can actually call up entire articles and have them printed. Faculty only, if you're willing to pay. My chairman got me a temporary lectureship and an account of my own. He expects me to publish my results and put his name on it. Unfortunately, foreign journals haven't been entered into the system yet, so I've got to locate those the old-fashioned way."

She pointed to the screen. "The master tongue. Don't you just love these sixty-letter words and umlauts? The grammar's nuts, but my mother helps me with the tough passages."

I remembered her mother. Heavyset and pleasant, fragrant of dough and sugar. Blue numbers on a soft white arm.

"Get an SAP card," she said. "It's a kick."

"Don't know if I'd qualify. My appointment's across town."

"I think you would. Just show them your faculty card and pay a fee. It takes about a week to process."

"I'll do it later, then. Can't wait that long."

"No, of course not. Listen, I've got plenty of time left on my account. My chairman wants me to use all of it up so he can ask for a bigger computer budget next year. If you want me to run you a search, just let me finish up with this, and we'll find all there is to know about people who *proxy* their kids."

*　　*　　*

We rode up to the SAP room at the top of the stacks. The search system looked no different from the terminals we'd just left: computers arranged in rows of partitioned cubicles. We found a free station and Jennifer searched for Munchausen-by-proxy references. The screen filled quickly. The list included all the articles Stephanie had given me, and more.

"Looks like the earliest one that comes up is 1977," she said. "*Lancet*. Meadow, R. 'Munchausen syndrome by proxy: The hinterland of child abuse.' "

"That's the seminal article," I said. "Meadow's the British pediatrician who recognized the syndrome and named it."

"The hinterland . . . that's ominous too. And here's a list of related topics: Munchausen syndrome, child abuse, incest, dissociative reactions."

"Try dissociative reactions first."

For the next hour we sifted through hundreds of references, distilling a dozen more articles that seemed to be relevant. When we were through, Jennifer saved the file and typed in a code.

"That'll link us to the printing system," she said.

The printers were housed behind blue panels that lined two walls of the adjoining room. Each contained a small screen, a card slot, a keyboard, and a mesh catch-bin under a foot-wide horizontal slit that reminded me of George Plumb's mouth. Two of the terminals weren't in use. One was marked OUT OF ORDER.

Jennifer activated the operative screen by inserting a plastic card in the slot, then typing in a letter-number code, followed by the call letters of the first and last articles we'd retrieved. Seconds later the bin began to fill with paper.

Jennifer said, "Automatically collated. Pretty nifty, huh?"

I said, "Melvyl and Orion—those are basic programs, right?"

"*Neanderthal*. One step above cards."

"If a hospital wanted to convert to computerized search and had a limited budget, could it go beyond that?"

"Sure. Way beyond. There are tons of new software programs. Even an office practitioner could go beyond that."

"Ever hear of a company called BIO-DAT?"

"No, can't say that I have, but that doesn't mean anything—

I'm no computer person. For me it's just a tool. Why? What do they do?"

"They're computerizing the library at Western Pediatric Hospital. Converting reference cards to Melvyl and Orion. Supposed to be a three-week job but they've been at it for three months."

"Is it a huge library?"

"No, quite a small one, actually."

"If all they're doing is probe and search, with a print-scanner it could be done in a couple of days."

"What if they don't have a scanner?"

"Then they're Stone Age. That would mean hand-transfer. Actually typing in each reference. But why would you hire a company with such a primitive setup when— Ah, it's finished."

A thick sheaf of papers filled the bin.

"Presto-gizmo, all the gain, none of the pain," she said. "One day they'll probably be able to program the stapling."

I thanked her, wished her well, and drove home with the fat bundle of documents on the passenger seat. After checking in with my service, going through the mail, and feeding the fish—the koi who'd survived infancy were thriving—I gulped down half a roast beef sandwich left over from last night's supper, swigged a beer, and started in on my homework.

People who proxied their kids . . .

Three hours later, I felt scummy. Even the dry prose of medical journals had failed to dim the horror.

Devil's waltz . . .

Poisoning by salt, sugar, alcohol, narcotics, expectorants, laxatives, emetics, even feces and pus used to create "bacteriologically battered babies."

Infants and toddlers subjected to a staggering list of torments that brought to mind Nazi "experiments." Case after case of children in whom a frighteningly wide range of phony diseases had been induced—virtually every pathology, it seemed, could be faked.

Mothers most frequently the culprits.

Daughters, almost always the victims.

The criminal profile: model mommy, often charming and personable, with a background in medicine or a paramedical field. Unusual calmness in the face of disaster—blunted affect masquerading as good coping. A hovering, protective nature—one specialist even warned doctors to look out for "overly caring" mothers.

Whatever that meant.

I remembered how Cindy Jones's tears had dried the moment Cassie had awakened. How she'd taken charge, with cuddles, fairy tales, the maternal breast.

Good child rearing or something evil?

Something else fit too.

Another *Lancet* article by Dr. Roy Meadow, the pioneer researcher. A discovery, in 1984, after examining the backgrounds of thirty-two children with manufactured epilepsy:

Seven siblings, dead and buried.

All expired from crib death.

7

I read some more until seven, then worked on the galley proofs of a monograph I'd just gotten accepted for publication: the emotional adjustment of a school full of children targeted by a sniper a year ago. The school's principal had become a friend of mine, then more. Then she went back to Texas to attend to a sick father. He died and she never returned.

Loose ends . . .

I reached Robin at her studio. She'd told me she was elbow-deep in a trying project—building four matching Stealth bomber-shaped guitars for a heavy metal band with neither budget nor self-control—and I wasn't surprised to hear the strain in her voice.

"Bad time?"

"No, no, it's good talking to someone who isn't drunk."

Shouts in the background. I said, "Is that the boys?"

"Being boys. I keep booting them out and they keep coming back. Like mildew. You'd think they'd have something to keep them busy—trashing their hotel suite, maybe—but— Uh-oh, hold on. *Lucas,* get *away* from there! You may need your fingers some day.

Sorry, Alex. He was drumming near the circular saw." Her voice softened: "Listen, I've got to go. How about Friday night—if that's okay with you?"

"It's okay. Mine or yours?"

"I'm not sure exactly when I'll be ready, Alex, so let me come by and get you. I promise no later than nine, okay?"

"Okay."

We said our goodbyes and I sat thinking about how independent she'd become.

I took out my old Martin guitar and finger-picked for a while. Then I went back into my study and reread the Munchausen articles a couple of times over, hoping to pick up something—some clinical cue— that I might have missed. But no insights were forthcoming; all I could think of was Cassie Jones's chubby face turned into something gray and sepulchral.

I wondered if it was even a question of science—if all the medical wisdom in the world was going to take me where I needed to go.

Maybe time for a different kind of specialist.

I phoned a West Hollywood number. A sultry female voice said, "You've reached Blue Investigations. Our office is closed. If you wish to leave a nonemergency message, do so after the first tone. In an emergency, wait until two tones have sounded."

After the second beep, I said, "It's Alex, Milo. Call me at home," and picked up my guitar again.

I'd played ten bars of "Windy and Warm" when the phone rang.

A voice that sounded far away said, "What's the emergency, pal?"

"*Blue* Investigations?"

"As in cop."

"Ah."

"Too abstract?" he said. "Do you get a porno connotation?"

"No, it's fine—very L.A. Whose voice is on the message?"

"Rick's sister."

"The dentist?"

"Yeah. Good pipes, huh?"

"Terrific. She sounds like Peggy Lee."

"Gives you fever when she drills your molars."

"When'd you go private?"

"Yeah, well, you know how it is—the lure of the dollar. Just a little moonlighting, actually. Long as the department keeps force-feeding me tedium during the day, might as well get paid well for it on the off hours."

"Not loving your computers yet?"

"Hey, I love 'em but they don't love me. 'Course, now they're saying the goddam things give off bad vibes—literally. Electromagnetic crap, probably slowly destroying this perfect body." A burst of static washed over the tail end of the sentence.

"Where are you calling from?" I said.

"Car phone. Wrapping up a job."

"Rick's car?"

"*Mine*. My phone too. It's a new age, Doctor. Rapid communication and even faster decay. Anyway, what's up?"

"I wanted to ask your advice on something—a case I'm working on—"

"Say no more—"

"I—"

"I mean it, Alex. *Say. No. More.* Cellular and privacy don't mix. Anyone can listen in. Hold tight."

He cut the line. My doorbell rang twenty minutes later.

"I was close," he said, tramping into my kitchen. "Wilshire near Barrington, paranoid lover surveillance."

In his left hand was an LAPD note pad and a black mobile phone the size of a bar of soap. He was dressed for undercover work: navy-blue Members Only jacket over a shirt of the same color, gray twill pants, brown desert boots. Maybe five pounds lighter than the last time I'd seen him—but that still added up to at least 250 of them distributed unevenly over 75 inches: long thin legs, protruberant gut, jowls surrendering to gravity and crowding his collar.

His hair had been recently cut—clipped short at back and sides, left full at the top. The black thatch hanging over his forehead showed a few strands of white. His sideburns reached the bottom of his ear lobes, a good inch longer than department regulations—but that was the least of the department's problems with him.

Milo was oblivious to fashion. He'd had the same look since I'd known him. Now Melrose trendies were adopting it; I doubted he'd noticed.

His big, pockmarked face was night-shift pale. But his startling green eyes seemed clearer than usual.

He said, "*You* look wired."

Opening the refrigerator, he bypassed the bottles of Grolsch, removed an unopened quart jar of grapefruit juice, and uncapped it with a quick twist of two thick fingers.

I handed him a glass. He filled it, drained it, filled again and drank.

"Vitamin C, free enterprise, snappy-sounding business title— you're moving too fast for me, Milo."

Putting the glass down, he licked his lips. "Actually," he said, "*Blue*'s an acronym. Big Lug's Uneasy Enterprise—Rick's idea of wit. Though I admit it was accurate at the time—jumping into the private sector wasn't exactly your smooth transition. But I'm glad I did it, because of the bread. I've become serious about financial security in my old age."

"What do you charge?"

"Fifty to eighty per hour, depending. Not as good as a shrink, but I'm not complaining. City wants to waste what it taught me, have me sit in front of a screen all day, it's their loss. By night, I'm getting my detective exercise."

"Any interesting cases?"

"Nah, mostly petty bullshit surveillance to keep the paranoids happy. But at least it gets me out on the street."

He poured more juice and drank. "I don't know how long I can take it—the day job."

He rubbed his face, as if washing without water. Suddenly, he looked worn, stripped of entrepreneurial cheer.

I thought of all he'd been through during the last year. Breaking the jaw of a superior who'd put his life in danger. Doing it on live television. The police department settling with him because going public could have proved embarrassing. No charges pressed, six months' unpaid leave, then a return to West L.A. Robbery/Homicide with a one-notch demotion to Detective II. Finding out, six months later, that no detective jobs were open at West L.A., or any other division, due to "unforeseen" budget cuts.

They shunted him—"temporarily"—to a data-processing job at Parker Center, where he was put under the tutelage of a flagrantly effeminate civilian instructor and taught how to play with computers. The department's not-so-subtle reminder that assault was one thing, but what he did in bed was neither forgotten nor forgiven.

"Still thinking of going to court?" I said.

"I don't know. Rick wants me to fight to the death. Says the way they reneged proves they'll never give me a break. But I know if I take it to court, that's it for me in the department. Even if I win."

He removed his jacket and tossed it on the counter. "Enough bullshit self-pity. What can I do for *you*?"

I told him about Cassie Jones, gave him a mini-lecture on Munchausen syndrome. He drank and made no comment. Looked almost as if he were tuning out.

I said, "Have you heard of this before?"

"No. Why?"

"Most people react a little more strongly."

"Just taking it all in . . . Actually, it reminded me of something. Several years ago. There was this guy came into the E.R. at Cedars. Bleeding ulcer. Rick saw him, asked him about stress. Guy says he's been hitting the bottle very heavy 'cause he's guilty about being a murderer and getting away with it. Seems he'd been with a call girl, gotten mad and cut her up. Badly—real psycho slasher thing. Rick nodded and said uh-huh; then he got the hell out of there and called Security—then me. The murder had taken place in Westwood. At the time I was in a car with Del Hardy, working on some robberies over in Pico-Robertson, and the two of us bopped over right away, Mirandized him, and listened to what he had to say.

"The turkey was *overjoyed* to see us. *Vomiting* out details like we were his salvation. Names, addresses, dates, weapon. He denied any other murders and came up clean for wants and warrants. A real middle-of-the-road type of guy, even owned his own business— carpet cleaning, I think. We booked him, had him repeat his confession on tape, and figured we'd picked up a dream solve. Then we proceeded to round up verifying details and found nothing. No crime, no physical evidence of any murder at that particular date and place; no hooker had ever lived at that address or anywhere nearby. No hooker fitting the name and description he'd given us had ever existed *anywhere* in L.A. So we checked unidentified victims, but none of the Jane Does in the morgue fit, and no moniker in Vice's files matched the one he said his girl used. We even ran checks in other cities, contacted the FBI, figuring maybe he got disoriented—some kind of psycho thing—and mixed up his locale. *He* kept insisting it had happened exactly the way he was telling it. Kept saying he wanted to be punished.

"After three straight days of this: *nada*. Guy's got a court-appointed attorney against his will, and the lawyer's screaming at us to make a case or let his client go. Our lieutenant is putting the pressure on—put up or shut up. So we keep digging. Zilch.

"At this point we begin to suspect we've been had, and confront the guy. He denies it. Really convincing—De Niro could have taken lessons. So we go over it *again*. Backtracking, double-checking, driving ourselves crazy. And still come up empty. Finally, we're convinced it's a scam, get overtly pissed off at the guy—major league bad-cop/bad-cop. *He* reacts by getting pissed off, too. But it's an embarrassed kind of anger. Slimy. Like he knows he's been found out and is being extra-indignant in order to put us on the defensive."

He shook his head and hummed the *Twilight Zone* theme.

"What happened?" I said.

"What could happen? We let him walk out and never heard from the asshole again. We could have busted him for filing a false report, but that would have bought us lots of paperwork and court time, and for what? Lecture and a fine on a first offense knocked down to a misdemeanor? No, thank you. We were really steamed, Alex. I've never *seen* Del so mad. It had been a heavy week, plenty of real crimes, very few solutions. And *this* bastard yanks our chains with total *bullshit*."

Remembered anger colored his face.

"Confessors," he said. "Attention-seeking, jerking everyone around. Doesn't that sound like your Munchausen losers?"

"Sounds a lot like them," I said. "Never thought of it that way."

"See? I'm a regular font of insight. Go on with your case."

I told him the rest of it.

He said, "Okay, so what do you want? Background checks on the mother? Both parents? The nurse?"

"I hadn't thought in those terms."

"No? What, then?"

"I really don't know, Milo. I guess I just wanted some counsel."

He placed his hands atop his belly, bowed his head, and raised it. "Honorable Buddha on duty. Honorable Buddha counsels as following: Shoot all bad guys. Let some other deity sort them out."

"Be good to know who the bad guys are."

"Exactly. That's why I suggested background checks. At least on your prime suspect."

"That would have to be the mother."

"Then she gets checked first. But as long as I'm punching buttons, I can throw in any others as a bonus. More fun than the payroll shit they're punishing me with."

"What would you check for?"

"Criminal history. It's a police data bank. Will your lady doctor friend be in on the fact that I'm checking?"

"Why?"

"I like to know my parameters when I snoop. What we're doing is technically a no-no."

"No. Let's keep her out of it—why put her in jeopardy?"

"Fine."

"In terms of a criminal history," I said, "Munchausens generally present as model citizens—just like your carpet cleaner. And we already know about the first child's death. It's been written off as SIDS."

He thought. "There'd be a coroner's report on that, but if no one had any suspicions of foul play, that's about it. I'll see what I can do about getting hold of the paperwork. You might even be able to do it yourself—check hospital records. If you can be discreet."

"Don't know if I can. The hospital's a different place now."

"In what way?"

"Lots more security—kind of heavy-handed."

"Well," he said, "you can't fault that. That part of town's gotten real nasty."

He got up, went to the fridge, found an orange and began peeling it over the sink. Frowning.

I said, "What is it?"

"I'm trying to frame some strategy on this. Seems to me the only way to solve something like this would be to catch the bad guy in the act. The kid gets sick at home?"

I nodded.

"So the only way to do it would be to surveil their house electronically. Hidden audio and video. Trying to record someone actually poisoning the baby."

"The Colonel's games," I said.

That made him frown.

"Yeah, exactly the kind of stuff that prick would delight in . . . He moved, you know."

"Where?"

"Washington, D.C. Where else? New enterprise for him. Corporation with one of those titles that tells you nothing about what it does. Ten to one he's living off the government. I got a note and a business card in the mail a while back. Congrats for entering the informational age and some free software to do my taxes."

"He knew what you were doing?"

"Evidently. Anyway, back to your baby-poisoner. Bugging her house. Unless you got a court order, anything you came up with would be inadmissible. But a court order means strong evidence, and all you've got are suspicions. Not to mention the fact that Grandpa's a pooh-bah, and you've got to tread extra carefully."

He finished peeling the orange, put it down, washed his hands, and began pulling apart the sections. "This one may be a heartbreaker—please don't tell me how cute the kid is."

"The kid's adorable."

"Thank you very much."

I said, "There were a couple of cases in England, reported in one of the pediatrics journals. They videotaped mothers smothering babies, and all *they* had were suspicions."

"They taped at home?"

"In the hospital."

"Big difference. And for all I know, the law's different in England. . . . Let me think on it, Alex. See if there's anything creative we *can* do. In the meantime I'll start playing with local records, NCIC, on the off chance that any of them has been naughty before, and we can build up *something* to get a warrant. Old Charlie's taught me well—you should see me ride those data bases."

"Don't put *yourself* in jeopardy," I said.

"Don't worry. The preliminary searches are no more than what an officer does every time he pulls someone over for a traffic stop. If and when I dig deeper, I'll be careful. Have the parents lived anyplace other than L.A.?"

"I don't know," I said. "I really don't know much about them, better start learning."

"Yeah, you dig your trench; I'll dig mine." He hunched over the counter, thinking out loud: "They're upper-crusties, which could mean private schools. Which is tough."

"The mother might be a public school girl. She doesn't come across as someone who was born to money."

"Social climber?"

"No, just simple. He's a college teacher. She might have been one of his students."

"Okay," he said, opening his note pad. "What else? Maybe military service for him, maybe officer's training—another tough nut to crack. Charlie *has* managed to hack into some of the military files, but nothing fancy, just V.A. benefits, cross-referencing, that kind of stuff."

"What do you guys do, play around with confidential data banks?"

"More like he plays, I watch. Where does the father teach?"

"West Valley Community College. Sociology."

"What about mom? Any job?"

"No, she's a full-time mom."

"Takes her job seriously, huh. Okay, give me a name to work with."

"Jones."

He looked at me.

I nodded.

His laughter was deep and loud, almost drunken.

8

The next morning, I arrived at the hospital at 9:45. The doctors' lot was nearly full and I had to drive up to the top level to find a space. A uniformed guard was leaning against a concrete abutment, half-concealed by shadows, smoking a cigarette. He kept his eyes on me as I got out of the Seville and didn't stop looking until I'd snapped my new badge to my lapel.

The private ward was as quiet as it had been yesterday. A single nurse sat at the desk and the unit clerk read *McCall's*.

I read Cassie's chart. Stephanie had been by for morning rounds, reported Cassie symptom-free but decided to keep her in for at least another day. I went to 505 W, knocked, and entered.

Cindy Jones and Vicki Bottomley were sitting on the sleeper couch. A deck of cards rested in Vicki's lap. The two of them looked up.

Cindy smiled. "Good morning."

"Good morning."

Vicki said, "Okay," and stood.

Cassie's bed had been cranked to an upright position. She sat playing with a Fisher-Price house. Other amusements, including a quorum of LuvBunnies, were scattered on the bedcover. A breakfast tray held a bowl of partially eaten oatmeal and a plastic cup of something red. Cartoon action flashed on the TV but the sound was off. Cassie was preoccupied with the house, arranging furniture and plastic figures. An I.V. pole was pushed into a corner.

I placed a new drawing on the bed. She glanced at it for a moment, then returned to her play.

Vicki was in rapid motion, handing the cards to Cindy, then clasping Cindy's hand briefly between both of hers. Avoiding eye contact with me, she walked over to the bed, tousled Cassie's head, and said, "See you, punkin."

Cassie looked up for an instant. Vicki tousled her hair again and left.

Cindy stood. A pink blouse replaced yesterday's plaid. Same jeans and sandals.

"Let's see, what did Dr. Delaware draw for you today?" She picked up the drawing. Cassie reached out and took it from her.

Cindy put an arm around her shoulder. "An elephant! Dr. Delaware drew you a cute blue elephant!"

Cassie brought the paper closer. "Eh-fa."

"Good, Cass, that's great! Did you hear that, Dr. Delaware? Elephant?"

I nodded. "Terrific."

"I don't know what you did, Dr. Delaware, but since yesterday she's been talking more. Cass, can you say elephant again?"

Cassie closed her mouth and crumpled the paper.

Cindy said, "Oh, my," cuddled her and stroked her cheek. Both of us watched Cassie labor to unfold the picture.

When she finally succeeded she said, "Eh-fa!" compressed the paper again, tighter, into a fist-sized ball, then looked at it, perplexed.

Cindy said, "Sorry, Dr. Delaware. Looks like your elephant isn't doing too well."

"Looks like Cassie is."

She forced a smile and nodded.

Cassie made another attempt to straighten the paper. This time, thimble-sized fingers weren't up to the task and Cindy helped her. "There you go, honey. . . . Yes, she's feeling great."

"Any problems with procedures?"

"There haven't been any procedures. Not since yesterday morning. We've just been sitting here—it's . . ."

"Something the matter?" I said.

She brought her braid forward and smoothed the fringe.

"People must think I'm crazy," she said.

"Why do you say that?"

"I don't know. It was a stupid thing to say—I'm sorry."

"What's the matter, Cindy?"

She turned away and played with her braid some more. Then she sat back down. Picking up the deck of cards, she passed it from hand to hand.

"It's just that . . ." she said, speaking so softly I had to move closer, "I . . . each time I bring her here she gets better. And then I take her home, thinking everything's going to be okay, and it is for a while, and then . . ."

"And then she gets sick again."

Keeping her head down, she nodded.

Cassie mumbled something to a plastic figure. Cindy said, "That's good, baby," but the little girl didn't seem to hear.

I said, "And then she gets sick all over again and you're let down."

Cassie threw the figure down, picked up another, and began shaking it.

Cindy said, "And then all of a sudden, she's okay—just like now. That's what I meant—about being crazy. Sometimes *I* think I'm crazy."

She shook her head and returned to Cassie's bedside. Taking a lock of the child's hair between her fingers, she let it slip away. Peering into the playhouse, she said, "Well, look at that—they're all eating what you made for dinner!" Her voice was so cheerful it made the roof of my mouth ache.

She stayed there, playing with Cassie's hair, pointing at the dolls, and prompting. Cassie made imitative sounds. Some of them sounded like words.

I said, "How about we go down for a cup of coffee? Vicki can stay with Cassie."

Cindy looked up. One hand rested on Cassie's shoulder. "No— no, I'm sorry, Dr. Delaware, I couldn't. I never leave her," she said.

"Never?"

She shook her head. "Not when she's in here. I know that sounds crazy, too, but I can't. You hear too many . . . things."

"What kinds of things?"

"Accidents—someone getting the wrong medicine. Not that I'm actually worried—this is a great hospital. But . . . I just need to be here. I'm sorry."

"It's okay. I understand."

"I'm sure it's more for me than for her, but . . ." She bent and hugged Cassie. Cassie squirmed and continued playing. Cindy gave me a helpless look.

"I know I'm being overprotective," she said.

"Not considering what you've been through."

"Well . . . thanks for saying that."

I pointed to the chair.

She gave a weak smile and sat down.

"It must be a real strain," I said. "Being here so often. It's one thing working in a hospital, but being dependent is something else."

She looked puzzled. "Working in a hospital?"

"You were a respiratory tech, right?" I said. "Didn't you do it at a hospital?"

"Oh, that. That was such a long time ago. No, I never got that far—didn't graduate."

"Lost interest?"

"Kind of." Picking up the box of cards, she tapped one knee. "Actually, going into R.T. in the first place was my aunt's idea. She was an R.N. Said a woman should have a skill even if she didn't use it, and that I should find something that would always be in demand, like health care. With the way we were ruining the air, people smoking, she felt there'd always be a call for R.T.'s."

"Your aunt sounds like someone with strong opinions."

She smiled. "Oh, she was. She's gone now." Rapid eyeblink.

"She was a fantastic person. My parents passed on when I was a kid and she basically raised me by herself."

"But she didn't encourage you to go into nursing? Even though she was an R.N.?"

"Actually she recommended *against* nursing. Said it was too much work for too little pay and not enough . ..."

She gave an embarrassed smile.

"Not enough respect from the doctors?"

"Like you said, Dr. Delaware, she had strong opinions on just about everything."

"Was she a hospital nurse?"

"No, she worked for the same G.P. for twenty-five years and they bickered the whole time like an old married couple. But he was a really nice man—old-fashioned family doctor, not too good about collecting his bills. Aunt Harriet was always on him for that. She was a real stickler for details, probably from her days in the army—she served in Korea, on the front. Made it to captain."

"Really," I said.

"Uh-huh. Because of her I tried out the service, too. Boy, this is really taking me back a few years."

"You were in the army?"

She gave a half-smile, as if expecting my surprise. "Strange for a girl, huh? It happened in my senior year in high school. The recruiter came out on careers day and made it sound pretty attractive—job training, scholarships. Aunt Harriet thought it would be a good idea, too, so that clinched it."

"How long were you in?"

"Just a few months." Her hands worked her braid. "A few months after I arrived I got sick and had to be discharged early."

"Sorry to hear that," I said. "Must have been serious."

She looked up. Blushing deeply. Yanking the braid.

"It was," she said. "Influenza—real bad flu—that developed into pneumonia. Acute viral pneumonia—there was a terrible epidemic in the barracks. Lots of girls got sick. After I recovered, they said my lungs might be weakened and they didn't want me in anymore." Shrug. "So that was it. My famous military career."

"Was it a big disappointment?"

"No, not really. Everything worked out for the best." She looked at Cassie.

"Where were you stationed?"

"Fort Jackson. Down in South Carolina. It was one of the few places they trained only women. It was the summer—you don't think of pneumonia in the summer, but a germ's a germ, right?"

"True."

"It was really humid. You could shower and feel dirty two seconds later. I wasn't used to it."

"Did you grow up in California?"

"California native," she said, waving an imaginary flag. "Ventura. My family came out from Oklahoma originally. Gold Rush days. One of my great-grandmothers was part Indian—according to my aunt, that's where the hair comes from."

She hefted the braid, then dropped it.

" 'Course, it's probably not true," she said, smiling. "Everyone wants to be Indian now. It's kind of fashionable." She looked at me: "Delaware. With that name you could be part Indian too."

"There's a family myth that says so—one third of one great-great-grandfather. I guess what I *am* is a mongrel—little bit of everything."

"Well, good for you. That makes you all-American, doesn't it?"

"Guess so," I said, smiling. "Was Chip ever in the service?"

"Chip?" The idea seemed to amuse her. "No."

"How'd the two of you meet?"

"At college. I did a year at WVCC, after R.T. school. Took Soc One-oh-one and he was my teacher."

Another look at Cassie. Still busy with the house. "Do you want to do your techniques now?"

"It's still a little soon," I said. "I want her to really trust me."

"Well . . . I think she does. She loves your drawings—we saved all the ones she didn't destroy."

I smiled. "It's still best to take it slow. And if she's not having any procedures, there's no need to rush."

"True," she said. "For all that's happening here, I guess we could go home right now."

"Do you want to?"

"I always want to. But what I *really* want is for her to get *better*."
Cassie glanced over and Cindy lowered her voice to a whisper again:
"Those seizures *really* scared me, Dr. Delaware. It was like . . ." She
shook her head.

"Like what?"

"Like something out of a movie. This is terrible to say, but it reminded me of *The Exorcist*." She shook her head. "I'm sure Dr. Eves will
get to the bottom of whatever's going on, eventually. Right? She said
we should stay at least one more night, maybe two, for observation. It's
probably for the best, anyway. Cassie's always so healthy *here*."

Her eyes moistened.

"Once you do go home," I said, "I'd like to come out and visit."

"Oh, sure . . ." Unasked questions flooded her face.

"In order to keep working on the rapport," I said. "If I can get
Cassie totally comfortable with me when she's not having procedures,
I'll be in a better position to help her when she does need me."

"Sure. That makes sense. Thank you, that's very kind. I . . .
didn't know doctors still made house calls."

"Once in a while. We call them home visits now."

"Oh. Well, sure, that would be great. I really appreciate your
taking the time."

"I'll call you after you're discharged and set up an appointment.
Why don't you give me your address and phone number?"

I tore a sheet out of my datebook and handed it to her along with
a pen.

She wrote and handed it back.

Fine, round hand, light touch.

Cassie B. Jones's house:
19547 Dunbar Court
Valley Hills, Ca.

A phone number with an 818 area code.

"That's out at the north end of Topanga Boulevard," she said.
"Near the Santa Susanna Pass."

"Pretty good ride to the hospital."

"Sure is." She wiped her eyes again. Bit her lip and tried to
smile.

"What is it?" I said.

"I was just thinking. When we come in, it's always the middle of the night and the freeway's clear. Sometimes I hate the night."

I squeezed her hand. Her fingers were slack.

I released them, looked at the paper again, folded it and put it in my pocket.

"Cassie B.," I said. "What does the B. stand for?"

"Brooks—that was my maiden name. It's sort of a tribute to Aunt Harriet. It's not exactly feminine, I guess. Brooke with an *e* would have been more of a girl's name. Like Brooke Shields. But I wanted to remember Aunt Harriet." She glanced sideways. "What're they doing now, Cass? Cleaning up the dishes?"

"Dih."

"Good! *Dishes!*"

She got up. I rose too. "Any questions before I go?"

"No . . . I don't think so."

"Then I'll stop by tomorrow."

"Sure. Great. Cass? Dr. Delaware's leaving. Say bye-bye?"

Cassie raised her eyes. Each hand clutched a plastic doll.

I said, "Bye-bye, Cassie."

"Bah-bah."

"Great!" said Cindy. "That was really great!"

"Bah . . . bah." The hands clapped, dolls clicking upon impact. "Bah! Bah!"

I walked over to the bed. Cassie looked up at me. Shiny eyes. Neutral expression. I touched her cheek. Warm and buttery.

"Bah!" A tiny finger probed my arm, just for a second. The puncture wound was healing nicely.

"Bye, cutie."

"Bah!"

Vicki was at the nursing station. I said hi, and when she didn't answer, I noted my visit in Cassie's chart, walked to Five East, and took the stairs down to the ground floor. Leaving the hospital, I drove to a gas station at Sunset and La Brea and used a pay phone to call Milo at Parker Center.

The line was busy. I tried twice more, same result, dialed Milo's home, and listened to Rick's sister do Peggy Lee.

One beep sounded. I talked quickly: "Hey, Mr. Blue, no emergency, but some data that might save you some time. Dad was never in the army but *mom* was—how's that for a switch? Maiden name: Brooks, as in babbling. She spent her time at Fort Jackson, South Carolina. Discharged early, due to a bout of viral pneumonia, she claims. But she blushed and got a little antsy when talking about it, so maybe it's not the whole truth. Maybe she misbehaved and got kicked out. She's twenty-six now, was a senior in high school when she joined up, so that gives you a time range to work with."

Returning to the car, I drove the rest of the way home thinking about pneumonia, respiratory therapy, and a baby boy lying still and gray in his crib. By the time I arrived, I was feeling short of breath.

I changed into shorts and a T-shirt, reviewed my chat with Cindy.

People must think I'm crazy. . . . Sometimes I *think I'm crazy.*

Guilt? A veiled confession? Or just tantalizing me?

Waltzing.

She'd been totally cooperative until I'd suggested we leave the room.

The "overly caring" Munchausen mother? Or simply the reasonable anxiety of a woman who's lost one child and suffered plenty with another?

I recalled the nervous surprise she'd shown when I told her of my plans for a home visit.

Something to hide? Or just surprise—a logical reaction—because doctors *didn't* do house calls anymore?

Another risk factor: Her mother-figure, the nurse. A woman who came across, even in Cindy's loving recollection, as something of a martinet.

A nurse who worked for a doctor but fought with him. Who disparaged physicians.

She'd guided Cindy into health care but away from nursing.

Ambivalence about doctors? About the health-care power structure? Preoccupation with sickness and treatment?

Had all that been communicated to Cindy at a young age?

Then there was the matter of her own illnesses—the flu and pneumonia that had disrupted her career plans.

Everything worked out for the best.

The blush, the yanking at her braid. The discharge was definitely a sensitive topic.

I got on the kitchen phone, obtained the 803 area code for South Carolina and dialed Information there. Fort Jackson turned out to be in Columbia. I wrote down the number and called it.

A drawling female voice answered. I asked for the base's chief medical officer.

"You want the commander of the hospital?"

"Yes, please."

"One moment."

A second later: "Colonel Hedgeworth's office."

"This is Dr. Delaware, from Los Angeles, California. I'd like to speak with the colonel, please."

"What was that name, sir?"

"Delaware." I added my professional title and medical school affiliation.

"Colonel Hedgeworth is out of the office, sir. Would you care to speak with Major Dunlap?"

"That would be fine."

"Please hold."

Half a dozen beats, then another drawling voice. Male baritone: "Major Dunlap."

"Major, this is Dr. Alex Delaware, from L.A." I repeated my credentials.

"Uh-huh. What can I do for you, Doctor?"

"We've been doing some pilot research—contagion patterns of viral epidemics, influenza and pneumonia, specifically—in relatively closed environments such as prisons, private schools, and military bases. Contrasting it with control groups in the general population."

"Epidemiological research?"

"We're working out of the Pediatrics department. Still in the process of assembling a preliminary data base, and Fort Jackson came up as a possible target site."

"Uh-huh," he said. Long pause. "Have you got a research grant on this?"

"Not yet, just some preliminary seed money. Whether or not we apply for full funding depends on how the data base shapes up. If we do write a proposal it would be as a collaborative effort—the target sites, plus us. We'd carry all the overhead, would just need access to facts and figures."

He chuckled. "We give you our stats and you put our names on any papers you write?"

"That would be part of it, but we'd always be open to scientific input."

"What med school was that?"

I told him.

"Uh-huh." Another laugh. "Well, I guess that would be pretty attractive, if I still cared about that kind of thing. But yeah, sure, I guess you can put our names down, for the time being—conditionally, no commitment. Got to check it with Colonel Hedgeworth, though, before I finalize anything."

"When will he be back?"

He laughed again. "*She'll* be back in a couple of days. Give me your number."

I gave him my home exchange, saying, "That's a private line, easier to reach."

"And what was your name?"

"Delaware."

"Like in the state?"

"Exactly."

"And you're with Pediatrics?"

"Yes," I said. Technically true, but I hoped he wouldn't delve too deeply and find out I had a clinical appointment but hadn't lectured in years.

"Fine," he said. "Get back to you soon as I can. If you don't hear from me in, say, a week—call back."

"Will do, Major. Thanks."

"No problem."

"In the meantime, though, if you could give me one bit of information, I'd appreciate it."

"What's that?"

"Do you recall any epidemics of either influenza or pneumonia at your base during the last ten years?"

"Ten years? Hmm. I haven't been here that long. We did have a meningitis outbreak a couple of years ago, but that was bacterial. Very nasty."

"We're limiting the inquiry to viral respiratory illnesses."

"Well," he said, "I guess the information's somewhere— hold on."

Two minutes passed.

"Captain Katz, how can I help you?"

I repeated my request.

"That far back wouldn't be on our computer," he said. "Can I get back to you on that?"

"Sure. Thanks."

Another exchange of numbers.

I put the receiver down, clogged with frustration, knowing the information was on someone's hard drive or floppy disc, accessible, instantly, at the push of the right button.

Milo didn't call back until four.

"Been trying to keep up with your Joneses," he said. "The coroner has a death form on file for the first kid. Charles Lyman Jones the Fourth. Nothing suspicious—sudden infant death syndrome, certified by your friend Stephanie and backed up by a Rita Kohler, M.D."

"She's the head of the General Pediatrics division. Stephanie's boss. She was originally their doctor, was out of town when Chad died."

"Uh-huh. Well, it all looks kosher. Now, in terms of the parents, here's what I've got so far. They live out in the West Valley and pay their property taxes on time—lots of taxes, 'cause they own lots of property. Fifty parcels."

"Fifty? Where?"

"Right where they live—the entire surrounding tract is theirs. Not bad for a college teacher, huh?"

"College teacher with a trust fund."

"No doubt. Other than that, they seem to live pretty simple and straight. Charles Lyman the Third drives a 1985 Volvo 240 four-door, received a speeding ticket last year and two parking citations, all paid. Cindy Brooks Jones drives a Plymouth Voyager van and is pure as the driven snow, infraction-wise. Ditto your surly nurse, if she's Victoria June Bottomley, DOB 4/24/36, with an address in Sun Valley."

"Sounds like her."

"So far, Beaver Cleaverland."

"You obviously didn't get my message."

"No. When and where?"

"Around eleven. I left it with Rick's sister."

"I didn't get any emergency call."

"That's 'cause I did a *one* beeper," I said. "Respecting your business procedures." I recounted the suspicions my talk with Cindy had aroused and my call to South Carolina.

"Joe Sleuth," he said. "Just can't control yourself."

"Hey, with your fees, I figured anything I could do myself would be a bargain."

He grunted. "*Knowing* me is a bargain. Pneumonia, huh? So what're you saying? Her lungs clog, it messes her plans up, so she fucks up her kids' lungs—whatchacallit, projecting?"

"Something like that. On top of that, she was trained in respiratory therapy."

"Then why would she move away from respiratory stuff? Why the stomach problems and the seizures?"

"I don't know, but the facts remain: Lung sickness disrupted her life. And/or gave her a lot of attention."

"So she passed it on to the kids in order to get more attention for herself? Or got *mad* at being sick and took it *out* on the kids?"

"Either. Neither. Both. I don't know. Maybe I'm just blowing air—no pun intended."

"That comment about being nuts. You think she suspects she's under watch?"

"It's possible. Or maybe she was just playing around with me. She's on edge, but who wouldn't be, with a child constantly sick? That's the problem with this whole case—anything I see can be explained several different ways. What does stick in my mind is the way she blushed and fiddled with her hair when she talked about the army. I'm wondering if the pneumonia story could be a cover for a psychiatric discharge or something else she doesn't want coming out. I'm hoping the army can confirm it, one way or the other."

"When's the army gonna call you back?"

"The guy I spoke to didn't commit himself. Said their health records that far back aren't computerized. Would health data be included in the military data banks Charlie's hacked into?"

"Don't know, but I'll ask him."

"Thanks."

"How's the baby doing?"

"Full recovery. No neurological problems that would have caused her to seize. Stephanie wants to watch her for a day or two. Mom says she wouldn't *mind* going home, but makes no effort to push it—Miss Compliant, doctor knows all. She's also claiming Cassie's talking more since I met her. She's certain it's something I did."

"The old kiss-up?"

"Munchausen moms are notorious for it—the staff generally loves them."

"Well," he said, "enjoy it while it lasts. You dig up some dirt on this lady, she's not gonna be kissing you anywhere."

9

After he hung up, I took the mail, the morning paper, and a month's worth of bills to a deli in West L.A. The place was nearly full—old people hunched over soup, young families with small children, two uniformed policemen at the rear joshing with the owner, mountainous sandwiches sharing table space with their walkie-talkies.

I sat at the corner table at the front, to the left of the counter, and had smoked turkey on onion roll, cole slaw, and Dr. Brown's CelRay soda.

Good stuff, but hospital thoughts intruded on my digestion.

At 9:00 P.M. I decided to go back to the hospital for an unscheduled visit. See how Mrs. Charles Lyman Jones the Third reacted to that.

Black night; the shadows on Sunset seemed to be moving in slow motion and the boulevard turned spooky nearer to the good side of town. After a few miles of hollow eyes, Thorazine shuffles, and scary motels, Western Peds's child-shaped logo and brightly lit Emergency Room arrow signaled a welcome outpost.

The parking lot was nearly deserted now. Small amber bulbs in grilled cases hung from the concrete ceiling, casting a hard-focus glow on every other parking slot. The remaining spaces were totally dark, creating a zebra-stripe effect. As I walked to the stairs I felt as if someone were watching me. When I looked back, I was alone.

The lobby was empty, too, the marble floors mirrors of nothing. One woman sat behind the Information window, methodically hand-stamping some papers. The page operator was getting paid for showing up. A clock ticked loudly. The smell of adhesive tape and a faint but definite sweat-spoor lingered, remembrances of stress gone by.

Something else I'd forgotten: Hospitals are different at night. The place was as spooky as the streets.

I took the elevator up to Five and walked through the ward, unnoticed. The doors to most of the rooms were closed; handwritten signs provided occasional distraction: *Protective Isolation*, *Infection Watch/No Visitors*. . . . The few doors that were open emitted TV sounds and the cricket-clicks of metered I.V.'s. I passed sleeping children and others entranced by the cathode ray. Parents sat, stiff as plaster. Waiting.

Chappy Ward's teak doors vacuum-sucked me into dead silence. No one was at the desk.

I walked over to 505 and rapped very softly. No answer. I opened the door and looked in.

Cassie's side rails were raised. She slept, guarded by stainless steel. Cindy slept, too, on the sofa bed, positioned so that her head was close to Cassie's feet. One of her hands extended through the bars, touching Cassie's sheet.

I closed the door softly.

A voice behind me said, "They're sleeping."

I turned.

Vicki Bottomley glared at me, hands on meaty hips.

"Another double shift?" I said.

She rolled her eyes and began walking off.

"Hold on," I said. The sharpness in my voice surprised both of us.

She stopped, turned slowly. "What?"

"What's the problem, Vicki?"

"There is no problem."

"I think there is."

"You're entitled." She started to leave again.

"Hold it." The empty corridor amplified my voice. Or maybe I really was that angry.

She said, "I've got work to do."

"So do I, Vicki. Same patient, as a matter of fact."

She stretched one arm toward the chart rack. "Be my guest."

I walked up to her. Close enough to crowd. She backed away. I moved forward.

"I don't know what your problem with me is, but I suggest we deal with it."

"I don't have any problem with anyone."

"Oh? Is what I've seen so far your usual level of charm?"

The pretty blue eyes blinked. Though they were dry, she wiped them quickly.

"Listen," I said, retreating a step, "I don't want to get into anything personal with you. But you've been hostile to me from the beginning and I'd like to know why."

She stared at me. Opened her mouth. Closed it.

"It's nothing," she said. "I'll be okay—no problem, I promise. Okay?"

She held out her hand.

I reached for it.

She gave me fingertips. A quick shake and she turned and started to walk away.

I said, "I'm going down to get some coffee. Care to join me?"

She stopped but didn't turn around.

"Can't. On duty."

"Want me to bring a cup up for you?"

Now she turned quickly. "What do you *want*?"

"Nothing," I said. "With your double-shifting, I figured you could use some coffee."

"I'm *fine*."

"I've heard you're terrific."

"What does that mean?"

"Dr. Eves thinks a lot of you. As a nurse. So does Cindy."

Her arms clamped across her chest, as if she were holding herself together. "I do my job."

"Do you see me getting in the way of that?"

Her shoulders climbed. She seemed to be phrasing an answer. But all she said was, "No. Everything will be okay. Okay?"

"Vicki—"

"I *promise,*" she said. "*Please?* Can I *go* now?"

"Sure," I said. "Sorry if I came on too strong."

She clamped her lips together, pivoted, and returned to her station.

I went to the Five East elevators. One lift was stuck on the sixth floor. The other two arrived simultaneously. Chip Jones stepped out of the central door, a cup of coffee in each hand. He had on faded jeans, a white turtleneck, and a denim jacket that matched the pants.

"Dr. Delaware."

"Professor."

He laughed and said, "Please," and stepped out into the hall. "How are my ladies doing?"

"They're both sleeping."

"Thank God. When I spoke to Cindy this afternoon, she sounded exhausted. I brought this from downstairs"—raising one cup—"to help fuel her. But sleep is what she really needs."

He began walking toward the teak doors. I tagged along. "Are we keeping you from hearth and home, Doctor?"

I shook my head. "Been and returned."

"Didn't know psychologists kept that kind of schedule."

"We don't when we can avoid it."

He smiled. "Well, the fact that Cindy's sleeping this early means Cassie must be getting healthy enough for her to relax. So that's good."

"She told me she never leaves Cassie."

"Never."

"Must be hard on her."

"Unbelievably hard. At first I tried to ease her away from it, but after being here a few times and seeing other mothers, I realized it was normal. Rational, actually. It's self-defense."

"Against what?"

"Screw-ups."

"Cindy talked about that, too," I said. "Have you seen a lot of medical error around here?"

"As a parent or as Chuck Jones's son?"

"Is there a difference?"

He gave a small, hard smile. "You bet there is. As Chuck Jones's son, I think this place is pediatric paradise, and I'll say so in the next banquet journal if they ask me. As a parent, I've seen things—the inevitable human errors. I'll give you an example—one that really shook me. A couple of months ago, the whole fifth floor was buzzing. Seems there was this little boy being treated for some kind of cancer—getting an experimental drug, so maybe there wasn't much hope anyway. But that's not the point. Someone misread a decimal point and he got a massive overdose. Brain damage, coma, the whole bit. All the parents on the floor heard the resuscitation page and saw the emergency team rush in. Heard his mother screaming for help. Including us—I was out in the hall, actually heard his mother scream for help."

He winced. "I saw her a couple of days later, Dr. Delaware. When he was still being respirated. She looked like a concentration camp victim. That look of being beaten down and betrayed? All because of one decimal point. Now that kind of thing probably happens all the time, on a smaller scale—things that can be smoothed over. Or don't even get picked up in the first place. So you can't blame parents for wanting to keep an eye out, can you?"

"No," I said. "Sounds like you don't have much confidence in this place."

"On the contrary, I do," he said impatiently. "Before we decided to have Cassie treated here, we did research—Dad notwithstanding. So I know this is *the* best place in the city for sick kids. But when it's your child, statistics don't matter much, do they? And human error is inevitable."

I held the doors to Chappy Ward open for him and he carried the coffee in.

Vicki's chunky form was visible through the glass door of the supply room behind the nursing station. She was placing something on a high shelf. We passed her and went to Cassie's room.

Chip stuck his head in, retracted it, and said, "Still out." Looking down at the cups, he held one out to me. "No sense wasting bad coffee."

"No, thanks," I said.

He laughed softly. "The voice of experience, huh? Has it always been this bad?"

"Always."

"Look at this—little *Exxon Valdez* we've got here." A faint, rainbowed slick floated on the black surface. Grimacing, he raised the other cup to his lips. "Yum—essence of grad school. But I need it to keep conscious."

"Long day?"

"On the contrary—too short. They seem to get shorter as you get older, don't they? Short and crammed with busywork. Then there's having to drive back and forth between work and home and here. Our glorious freeways—humanity at its nadir."

"Valley Hills means the Ventura Freeway," I said. "That's about as bad as it gets."

"Vile. When we were home-hunting, I purposely picked a place close to work to avoid commuting." He shrugged. "Best-laid plans. Sometimes I sit bumper to bumper and imagine it's what hell would be like."

He laughed again, sipped.

I said, "I'll be experiencing it firsthand in a couple of days—making a home visit."

"Yes, Cindy mentioned it. Ah, here comes Ms. Nightingale. . . . Hello, Vicki. Burning the midnight oil again?"

I turned and saw the nurse marching toward us, smiling, cap bobbing.

"Evening, Professor Jones." She sucked in air, as if preparing to power-lift, then nodded at me.

Chip handed her the untouched coffee. "Drink it or toss it."

"Thank you, Professor Jones."

He cocked his head at Cassie's door. "How long have the Sleeping Beauties been snoozing?"

"Cassie went down around eight. Mrs. Jones, around eight forty-five."

He looked at his watch. "Could you do me a favor, Vicki? I'm going to walk Dr. Delaware out, maybe get something to eat while I'm down there. Please have me paged if they wake up."

"If you like I can go down and get you something, Professor."

"No, thanks. I need to stretch—freewayitis."

Vicki clucked sympathetically. "Of course. I'll let you know soon as someone's up."

When we got to the other side of the teak doors, he stopped and said, "What do you think about the way we're being handled?"

"Handled in what way?"

He resumed walking. "Handled medically—this current hospitalization. No real evaluation's going on, as far as I can tell. No one's really checking Cassie out physically. Not that I mind—thank God she doesn't have to endure those godawful needles. But the message I'm starting to get is *placebo*. Hold our hands, send in a shrink—nothing personal—and let whatever's going on with Cassie just wind itself down."

"Do you find that insulting?"

"Not insulting—well, maybe a little. As if it's all in our heads. Believe me, it isn't. You people here haven't seen what we have—the blood, the seizures."

"You've seen all of it?"

"Not all of it. Cindy's the one who gets up at night. I tend to be a solid sleeper. But I've seen enough. You can't argue with blood. So why isn't more being done?"

"I can't answer for anyone else," I said. "But my best guess is, no one really knows what to do and they don't want to be unnecessarily intrusive."

"I suppose so," he said. "And, hey, for all I know it's exactly the right approach to take. Dr. Eves seems smart enough. Maybe Cassie's symptoms *are*—what's the term—self-restricting?"

"Self-limiting."

"Self-limiting." He smiled. "Doctors propagate more euphemisms than anyone. . . . I pray to God it *is* self-limiting. Be more than happy to remain an unsolved medical mystery if Cassie finally stays healthy. But hope comes hard by now."

"Chip," I said, "I haven't been called in because anyone thinks Cassie's problems are psychosomatic. My job is to help her deal with anxiety and pain. The reason I want to visit your home is to build up rapport with her in order to be useful for her when she needs me."

"Sure," he said. "I understand."

He looked at the ceiling and tapped one foot. A couple of nurses walked by. His eyes followed their trail, absently.

"I guess what I really have trouble handling is the irrationality," he said. "As if we're all floating around in some sea of random events. What the *hell* is making her *sick?*"

He punched the wall.

I sensed that anything I said would make matters worse, but I knew silence wouldn't help much either.

The elevator door opened and we stepped in.

"Pissed-off parents," he said, punching the DOWN button hard. "Pleasant way to end *your* day."

"My job."

"Some job."

"Beats honest labor."

He smiled.

I pointed to the cup in his hand. "That's got to be cold. How about we both get some fresh sludge?"

He thought for a moment. "Sure, why not?"

The cafeteria was closed, so we went down the hall, past the Residents' Lounge, where a row of vending machines stood next to the locker room. A thin young woman in surgical scrubs was walking away with two handfuls of candy bars. Chip and I each bought black coffee and he purchased a plastic-wrapped packet containing two chocolate chip cookies.

Farther down the corridor was a sitting area: orange plastic chairs arranged in an L, a low white table bearing food wrappers and out-of-date magazines. The Path Lab was a stone's throw away. I thought of his little boy and wondered if he'd make the association. But he ambled over and sat down, yawning.

Unwrapping the cookies, he dunked one in the coffee, said, "Health food," and ate the soggy part.

I sat perpendicular to him and sipped. The coffee was terrible but oddly comforting—like a favorite uncle's stale breath.

"So," he said, dunking again, "let me tell you about my daughter. Terrific disposition, good eater, good sleeper—she slept through at five weeks. For anyone else, good news, right? After what happened to Chad, it scared the *shit* out of us. We wanted her *awake*—used to take turns going in there, waking her up, poor thing. But what amazes me is how resilient she is—the way she just keeps bouncing back. You wouldn't think anything that small could be so tough.

"I feel kind of ridiculous, even discussing her with a psychologist. She's a *baby,* for God's sake—what kind of neuroses could she have? Though I guess with all this she could end up with plenty, couldn't she? All the stress. Are we talking major psychotherapy for the rest of her life?"

"No."

"Has anyone ever studied it?"

"There's been quite a bit of research," I said. "Chronically ill children tend to do better than experts predict—people do, in general."

"Tend to?"

"Most do."

He smiled. "I know. It's not physics. Okay, I'll allow myself some momentary optimism."

He tensed, then relaxed—deliberately, as if schooled in meditation. Letting his arms drop and dangle and stretching his legs. Dropping his head back and massaging his temples.

"Doesn't it get to you?" he said. "Listening to people all day? Having to nod and be sympathetic and tell them they're okay."

"Sometimes," I said. "But usually you get to know people, start to see their humanity."

"Well, this is sure the place to remind you of that—'A rarer spirit never did steer humanity; but you, gods, will give us some *faults* to make us men.' Words, Willy Shakespeare; italics, mine. I know it sounds pretentious, but I find the old bard reassures me—something for every situation. Wonder if *he* spent any time in hospitals."

"He may have. He lived during the height of the black plague, didn't he?"

"True . . . Well"—he sat up and unwrapped the second cookie—"all credit to you, I couldn't do it. Give me something neat and clean and theoretical, anytime."

"I never thought of sociology as hard science."

"Most of it isn't. But Formal Org has all sorts of nifty models and measurable hypotheses. The illusion of precision. I delude myself regularly."

"What kinds of things do you deal with? Industrial management? Systems analysis?"

He shook his head. "No, that's the applied side. I'm theoretical—setting up models of how groups and institutions function on a structural level, how components mesh, phenomenologically. Ivory tower stuff, but I find it great fun. I was schooled in the ivory tower."

"Where's that?"

"Yale, undergrad; University of Connecticut, grad. Never finished my dissertation after I found out teaching turns me on a lot more than research."

He stared down the empty basement corridor, watching the occasional passage of wraithlike white-coated figures in the distance.

"Scary," he said.

"What is?"

"This place." He yawned, glanced at his watch. "Think I'll go up and check on the ladies. Thanks for your time."

We both stood.

"If you ever need to talk to me," he said, "here's my office number."

He put his cup down, reached into a hip pocket, and pulled out an Indian silver money clasp inlaid with an irregular turquoise. Twenty-dollar bill on the outside, credit cards and assorted papers underneath. Removing the entire wad, he shuffled through it and found a white business card. Placing it on the table, he retrieved a blue Bic from another pocket and wrote something on the card, then handed it to me.

Snarling tiger logo, WVCC TYGERS circling it. Below that:

WEST VALLEY COMMUNITY COLLEGE
DEPARTMENT OF SOCIAL SCIENCES
(818) 509-3476

Two lines at the bottom. He'd filled them in using dark block letters:

CHIP JONES
EXT. 2359

"If I'm in class," he said, "this'll connect you to the message center. If you want me around when you come visiting at the house, try to give me a day's notice."

Before I could reply, heavy rapid footsteps from the far end of the hall made both of us turn. A figure came toward us. Athletic gait, dark jacket.

Black leather jacket. Blue slacks and hat. One of the rent-a-cops patrolling the halls of Pediatric Paradise for signs of evil?

He came closer. A mustachioed black man with a square face and brisk eyes. I got a look at his badge and realized he wasn't Security. LAPD. Three stripes. A sergeant.

"Excuse me, gentlemen," he said, speaking softly but giving us the once-over. His name tag read PERKINS.

Chip said, "What is it?"

The cop read my badge. It seemed to confuse him. "You're a doctor?"

I nodded.

"How long have you gentlemen been out here in the hall?"

Chip said, "Five or ten minutes. What's wrong?"

Perkins's gaze shifted to Chip's chest, taking in the beard, then the earring. "You a doctor too?"

"He's a parent," I said. "Visiting his child."

"Got a visiting badge, sir?"

Chip pulled one out and held it in front of Perkins's face.

Perkins chewed his cheek and swung back to me. He gave off a barbershop scent. "Have either of you seen anything unusual?"

"Such as?" said Chip.

"Anything out of the ordinary, sir. Someone who doesn't belong."

"Doesn't belong," said Chip. "Like somebody healthy?"

Perkins's eyes became slits.

I said, "We haven't seen anything, Sergeant. It's been quiet. Why?"

Perkins said, "Thank you," and left. I watched him slowing for a moment as he passed the pathology lab.

* * *

Chip and I took the stairs to the lobby. A crowd of night-shifters crowded the east end, pressing toward the glass doors that led outside. On the other side of the glass the darkness was cross-cut with the cherry-red pulse of police lights. White lights, too, refracting in starbursts.

Chip said, "What's going on?"

Without turning her head, a nurse nearby said, "Someone got attacked. In the parking lot."

"Attacked? By whom?"

The nurse looked at him, saw he was a civilian and moved away.

I looked around for a familiar face. None. Too many years.

A pale, thin orderly with short platinum hair and a white Fu Manchu said, "Enough, already," in a nasal voice. "All I want to do is go *home*."

Someone groaned a chorus.

Unintelligible whispers passed through the lobby. I saw a uniform on the other side of the glass, blocking the door. A burst of radio talk leaked through from the outside. Lots of movement. A vehicle swung its lights toward the glass, then turned away and sped off. I read a flash of letters: AMBULANCE. But no blinkers or siren.

"Whyn't they just bring her in here?" said someone.

"Who says it's a *her*?"

A woman said, "It's *always* a her."

"Dinja hear? No howler," someone answered. "Probably not an emergency."

"Or maybe," said the blond man, "it's too late."

The crowd rippled like gel in a petri dish.

Someone said, "I tried to get out the back way but they had it blocked. I'm like, this sucks."

"I think I heard one of them say it was a doctor."

"Who?"

"That's all I heard."

Buzz. Whisper.

Chip said, "Wonderful." Turning abruptly, he began pushing his way toward the rear of the crowd, back into the hospital. Before I could say anything, he was gone.

*   *   *

Five minutes later, the glass door opened and the crowd surged forward. Sergeant Perkins slipped through and held out a tan palm. He looked like a substitute teacher before an unruly high school class.

"Can I have your attention for a moment?" He waited for silence, finally settled for relative quiet. "An assault's occurred in your parking lot. We need you to file out one by one and answer some questions."

"What kind of assault?"

"Is he okay?"

"Who was it?"

"Was it a doctor?"

"Which lot did it happen in?"

Perkins did the slit-eye again. "Let's get this over with as quickly as possible, folks, and then you can all go home."

The man with the white Fu Manchu said, "How about telling us what happened so we can *protect* ourselves, Officer?"

Supportive rumblings.

Perkins said, "Let's just take it easy."

"No, *you* take it easy," said the blond man. "All you guys do is give *jay*walking tickets out on the boulevard. Then, when something real happens, you ask your questions and disappear and leave us to clean up the mess."

Perkins didn't move or speak.

"Come *on,* man," said another man, black and stooped, in a nursing uniform. "Some of us have *lives.* Tell us what happened."

"Yeah!"

Perkins's nostrils flared. He stared out at the crowd a while longer, then opened the door and backed out.

The people in the lobby twanged with anger.

A loud voice said, "*Deputy Dawg!*"

"*Damned jaywalking brigade.*"

"*Yeah, buncha stiffs—hospital sticks us across the street and then we get busted trying to get to work on time.*"

Another hum of consensus. No one was talking anymore about what had happened in the lot.

The door opened again. Another cop came through, young, white, female, grim.

"Okay, everyone," she said. "If you'll just file out one by one, the officer will check your ID and then you can go."

"Yo," said the black man. "Welcome to San Quentin. What's next? Body searches?"

More tunes in that key, but the crowd started to move, then quieted.

It took me twenty minutes to get out the door. A cop with a clipboard copied my name from my badge, asked for verifying identification, and recorded my driver's license number. Six squad cars were parked in random formation just outside the entrance, along with an unmarked sedan. Midway down the sloping walkway to the parking structure stood a huddle of men.

I asked the cop, "Where did it happen?"

He crooked a finger at the structure.

"I parked there."

He raised his eyebrows. "What time did you arrive?"

"Around nine-thirty."

"P.M.?"

"Yes."

"What level did you park on?"

"Two."

That opened his eyes. "Did you notice anything unusual at that time—anyone loitering or acting in a suspicious manner?"

Remembering the feeling of being watched as I left my car, I said, "No, but the lighting was uneven."

"What do you mean by uneven, sir?"

"Irregular. Half the spaces were lit; the others were dark. It would have been easy for someone to hide."

He looked at me. Clicked his teeth. Took another glance at my badge and said, "You can move on now, sir."

I walked down the pathway. As I passed the huddle I recognized one of the men. Presley Huenengarth. The head of hospital Security was smoking a cigarette and stargazing, though the sky was starless. One of the other suits wore a gold shield on his lapel and was talking. Huenengarth didn't seem to be paying attention.

Our eyes met but his gaze didn't linger. He blew smoke through his nostrils and looked around. For a man whose system had just failed miserably, he looked remarkably calm.

10

Wednesday's paper turned the assault into a homicide.

The victim, robbed and beaten to death, had indeed been a doctor. A name I didn't recognize: Laurence Ashmore. Forty-five years old, on the staff at Western Peds for just a year. He'd been struck from behind by the assailant and robbed of his wallet, keys, and the magnetized card key that admitted his car to the doctors' lot. An unnamed hospital spokesperson emphasized that all parking-gate entry codes had been changed but admitted that entry on foot would continue to be as easy as climbing a flight of stairs.

Assailant unknown, no leads.

I put the paper down and looked through my desk drawers until I found a hospital faculty photo roster. But it was five years old, predating Ashmore's arrival.

Shortly after eight I was back at the hospital, finding the doctors' lot sealed with a metal accordion gate and cars stack-parked in the circular drive fronting the main entrance. An ALL FULL sign was posted at the mouth of the driveway, and a security guard handed me a mimeographed sheet outlining the procedure for obtaining a new card key.

"Where do I park in the meantime?"

He pointed across the street, to the rutted outdoor lots used by nurses and orderlies. I backed up, circled the block, and ended up queuing for a quarter hour. It took another ten minutes to find a space. Jaywalking across the boulevard, I sprinted to the front door. Two guards instead of one in the lobby, but there was no other hint that a life had been snuffed out a couple of hundred feet away. I knew death was no stranger to this place but I'd have thought murder rated a stronger reaction. Then I looked at the faces of the people coming and going and waiting. Nothing like worry and grief to narrow one's perspective.

I headed for the rear stairway and noticed an up-to-date roster just past the Information desk. Laurence Ashmore's picture was on the top left. Specialty in Toxicology.

If the portrait was recent, he'd been a young-looking forty-five. Thin, serious face. Dark, unruly hair, hyphen mouth, horn-rimmed eyeglasses. Woody Allen with dyspepsia. Not the type to pose much of a challenge for a mugger. I wondered why it had been necessary to kill him for his wallet, then realized what an idiotic question that was.

As I prepared to ride up to Five, sounds from the far end of the hospital caught my attention. Lots of white coats. A squadron of people moving across my line of sight, rushing toward the patient-transport elevator.

Wheeling a child on a gurney, one orderly pushing, another holding an I.V. bottle and keeping pace.

A woman I recognized as Stephanie. Then two people in civvies. Chip and Cindy.

I went after them and caught up just as they entered the lift. Barely squeezing in, I edged my way next to Stephanie.

She acknowledged me with a twitch of her mouth. Cindy was holding one of Cassie's hands. She and Chip both looked defeated and neither of them glanced up.

We rode up in silence. As we got off the elevator Chip held out his hand and I grasped it for a second.

The orderlies wheeled Cassie through the ward and through the teak doors. Within moments her inert form had been lowered to the bed, the I.V. hooked up to a drip monitor, and the side rails raised.

Cassie's chart was on the gurney. Stephanie picked it up and said, "Thanks, guys." The orderlies left.

Cindy and Chip hovered near the bed. The room lights were off and slivers of gray morning peeked through the split of drawn drapes.

Cassie's face was swollen, yet it appeared drained—an inflated husk. Cindy took her hand once more. Chip shook his head and wrapped his arm around his wife's waist.

Stephanie said, "Dr. Bogner will be by again and so should that Swedish doctor."

Faint nods.

Stephanie cocked her head. The two of us stepped out into the hall.

"Another seizure?" I said.

"Four A.M. We've been in the E.R. since then, working her over."

"How's she doing?"

"Stabilized. Lethargic. Bogner's doing all of his diagnostic tricks but he's not coming up with much."

"Was she in any danger?"

"No mortal danger, but you know the kind of damage repetitive seizures can do. And if it's an escalating pattern, we can probably expect lots more." She rubbed her eyes.

I said, "Who's the Swedish doctor?"

"Neuroradiologist named Torgeson, published quite a bit on childhood epilepsy. He's giving a lecture over at the medical school. I thought, why not?"

We walked to the desk. A young dark-haired nurse was there now. Stephanie wrote in the chart and told her, "Call me immediately if there are any changes."

"Yes, Doctor."

Stephanie and I walked down the hall a bit.

"Where's Vicki?" I said.

"Home sleeping. I hope. She went off shift at seven, but was down in the E.R. until seven-thirty or so, holding Cindy's hand. She wanted to stay and do another shift, but I insisted she leave—she looked totally wiped out."

"Did she see the seizure?"

Stephanie nodded. "So did the unit clerk. Cindy pressed the call button, then ran out of the room, crying for help."

"When did Chip show up?"

"Soon as we had Cassie stabilized, Cindy called him at home and he came right over. I guess it must have been around four-thirty."

"Some night," I said.

"Well, at least we've got outside corroboration of the seizures. Kid's definitely grand mal."

"So now everyone knows Cindy's not nuts."

"What do you mean?"

"Yesterday she talked to me about people thinking she was crazy."

"She actually *said* that?"

"Sure did. The context was her being the only one who saw Cassie get sick, the way Cassie would recover as soon as she got to the hospital. As if her credibility was suspect. It could have been frustration, but maybe she knows she's under suspicion and was bringing it up to test my reaction. Or just to play games."

"How did you react?"

"Calm and reassuring, I hope."

"Hmm," she said, frowning. "One day she's worrying about her credibility; then all of a sudden we've got something organic to work with?"

"The timing *is* awfully cute," I said. "Who else besides Cindy was with Cassie last night?"

"No one. Not constantly. You think she slipped her something?"

"Or pinched her nose. Or squeezed her neck—carotid sinus pressure. Both came up when I was scanning the Munchausen literature and I'm sure there are a few more tricks that haven't been documented yet."

"Tricks a respiratory tech might know . . . Damn. So how in blazes do you detect something like that?"

She pulled her stethoscope from around her neck. Looped it around one hand and unwrapped it. Facing the wall, she pressed her forehead to it and closed her eyes.

"Are you going to put her on anything?" I said. "Dilantin or phenobarb?"

"I can't. Because if she doesn't have a bona fide disorder, meds can do more harm than good."

"Won't they suspect something if you don't medicate her?"

"Maybe . . . I'll just tell them the truth. The EEG tracings are inconclusive and I want to find the exact cause for the seizures before I dose her up. Bogner'll back me up on that—he's mad because *he* can't figure it out."

The teak doors swung open and George Plumb shot through, jaw leading, white coat flapping. He held the door for a man in his late sixties wearing a navy-blue pin-stripe suit. The man was much shorter than Plumb—five six or seven—stocky and bald, with a rapid, bowlegged walk and a malleable-looking face that appeared to have taken plenty of direct hits: broken nose, off-center chin, grizzled eyebrows, small eyes set in a sunburst pucker of wrinkles. He wore steel-rimmed eyeglasses, a white shirt with a spread collar, and a powder-blue silk tie fastened in a wide Windsor. His wingtips gleamed.

The two of them came straight to us. The short man looked busy even when standing still.

"Dr. Eves," said Plumb. "And Dr. . . . Delaware, was it?"

I nodded.

The short man seemed to be opting out of the introductions. He was looking around the ward—that same measuring appraisal Plumb had conducted two days ago.

Plumb said, "How's our little girl doing, Dr. Eves?"

"Resting," said Stephanie, focusing on the short man. "Good morning, Mr. Jones."

Quick turn of the bald head. The short man looked at her, then at me. Intense focus. As if he were a tailor and I were a bolt of cloth.

"What exactly happened?" he said in a gravelly voice.

Stephanie said, "Cassie experienced an epileptic seizure early this morning."

"Damn." The short man punched one hand with the other. "And still no idea what's causing it?"

"Not yet, I'm afraid. Last time she was admitted we ran every relevant test, but we're running them again and Dr. Bogner's coming over. There's also a visiting professor from Sweden who's arriving any minute. Childhood epilepsy's his specialty. Though when I spoke with him on the phone he felt we'd done everything right."

"Damn." The puckered eyes turned on me. A hand shot out. "Chuck Jones."

"Alex Delaware."

We shook hard and fast. His palm felt like a rasp blade. Everything about him seemed to run on fast-forward.

Plumb said, "Dr. Delaware is a psychologist, Chuck."

Jones blinked and stared at me.

"Dr. Delaware's been working with Cassie," said Stephanie, "to help her with her fear of needles."

Jones made a noncommittal sound, then said, "Well, let me know what goes on. Let's get to the bottom of this damned folderol."

He walked toward Cassie's room. Plumb followed like a puppy.

When they were inside I said, "Folderol?"

"How'd you like to have him for a grandpa?"

"He must love Chip's earring."

"One thing he doesn't love is shrinks. After Psychiatry was abolished a bunch of us went to him, trying to get some sort of mental health services restored. We might as well have asked him for an interest-free loan. Plumb was setting you up just now, when he told Jones what you do."

"The old corporate pissing game? Why?"

"Who knows? I'm just telling you so you'll keep your guard up. These people play a different game."

"Duly noted," I said.

She looked at her watch. "Time for clinic."

We left Chappy and headed for the elevator.

She said, "So what are we going to do, Alex?"

I considered telling her what I'd put Milo up to. Decided to keep her out of it. "From my reading, the only thing that seems to work is either catching someone in the act or having a direct confrontation that gets them to confess."

"Confrontation? As in coming out and accusing her?"

I nodded.

"I can't exactly do that at this point, can I?" she said. "Now that

she's got witnesses to a bona fide seizure and I'm bringing in specialists. Who knows, maybe I'm totally off-base and there really *is* some
kind of epilepsy, I don't know. . . . I received a letter from Rita this
morning. Express mail from New York—she's touring the art galleries. 'How are things progressing on the case?' Am I 'making any
headway' in my '*diagnosis?*' I got the feeling someone went around me
and called her."

"Plumb?"

"Uh-huh. Remember that meeting he wanted? We had it yesterday and it turned out to be all sweetness and light. Him telling me
how much he appreciates my commitment to the institution. Letting
me know the financial situation is lousy and going to get lousier but
implying that if I don't make waves, I can have a better job."

"Rita's."

"He didn't come out and say it but that was the message.
It would be just like him to then go and call *her*, set *her* against
me. . . . Anyway, none of that's important. What do I do about
Cassie?"

"Why don't you wait to see what this Torgeson says? If he feels
the seizures have been manufactured, you'd have more ammunition
for an eventual confrontation."

"Confrontation, huh? Can't wait."

As we neared the waiting room I commented on how little impact
Laurence Ashmore's murder seemed to have made.

"What do you mean?"

"No one's talking about it."

"Yes. You're right—it's terrible, isn't it. How hardened we get.
Caught up in our own stuff."

A few steps later she said, "I didn't really know him—
Ashmore. He kept to himself—kind of antisocial. Never attended a
staff meeting, never RSVP'd to party invitations."

"With those kinds of social skills, how'd he get any referrals?"

"He didn't *want* referrals—didn't do any clinical work. Pure
research."

"Lab rat?"

"Beady eyes and all. But I heard he was smart—knew his

toxicology. So when Cassie started coming in with those respiratory things, I asked him to go over Chad's chart."

"You tell him why?"

"You mean that I was suspicious? No. I wanted him to go in with an open mind. I just asked him to look for anything out of the ordinary. He was very reluctant. Almost resentful—as if I was imposing. A couple of days later I got a phone message saying he hadn't found anything. As in, don't bug me again!"

"How'd he pay his way? Grants?"

"I assume."

"I thought the hospital was discouraging them—didn't want to pay overhead."

"I don't know," she said. "Maybe he brought in his own overhead."

She frowned. "No matter what his social skills, what happened to him is horrible. There was a time, no matter how ugly things got out on the street, if you wore a white coat, or a steth around your neck, you were safe. Now that's all broken down. Sometimes it feels as if everything's breaking down."

We reached the clinic. The waiting room was overflowing and as noisy as a steam drill.

She said, "Enough whining. No one's forcing me. What I *wouldn't* mind is some time off."

"Why don't you take some?"

"Got a mortgage."

Several mothers waved at her and she returned the greetings. We passed through the door to the medical suite and headed for her office. A nurse said, "Morning, Dr. Eves. Your dance card is full."

Stephanie smiled gamely. Another nurse came up and handed her a stack of charts.

She said, "Merry Christmas to you, too, Joyce," and the nurse laughed and hurried off.

"See you," I said.

"Sure. Thanks. Oh, by the way, I learned something else about Vicki. A nurse I used to work with on Four told me she thought Vicki had a bad family situation. Alcoholic husband who roughed her up quite a bit. So maybe she's just a bit frayed—down on men. She still bugging you?"

"No. Actually we had a confrontation of our own and reached a truce of sorts."

"Good."

"She may be down on men," I said. "But not on Chip."

"Chip's no man. He's the boss's son."

"Touché," I said. "An abusive husband might explain why *I* put her teeth on edge. She could have turned to a therapist for help, gotten nowhere, developed a resentment. . . . Of course, major family stress could also lead her to act out in other ways—become a hero at work in order to raise her self-esteem. How'd she handle the seizure?"

"Competently. I wouldn't call it heroic. She calmed Cindy down, made sure Cassie was okay, then called me. Cool under fire, everything by the book."

"Textbook nurse, textbook case."

"But like you said before, how could she be involved, when all the other crises started at home?"

"But this one didn't. No, in all fairness, I can't say I really suspect her of anything. It just twangs my antennae that her home life's troubled and she comes over here and shines. . . . I'm probably just focusing on her because she's been such a pain."

"Fun referral, huh?"

"High intrigue, just like you said."

"I always keep my promises." Another glance at her watch. "Got to get through my morning exams, then drive out to Century City to pick up Torgeson. Got to make sure his car doesn't get caught up in the parking mess. Where'd they stick you?"

"Across the street, like everyone else."

"Sorry."

"Hey," I said, feigning insult, "some of us are international hotshots and some of us park across the street."

"Guy sounds like a cold fish over the phone," she said, "but he *is* hot stuff—served on the Nobel Committee."

"Hoo-hah."

"Hoo-hah in spades. Let's see if we can frustrate him too."

*   *   *

I called Milo from a pay phone and left him another one-beep message: "Vicki Bottomley has a husband who drinks and may beat her up. It probably doesn't mean anything, but could you please check if there are any domestic violence calls on record and if so, get me the dates?"

Textbook nurse . . .

Textbook Munchausen by proxy.

Textbook crib death.

Crib death evaluated by the late Dr. Ashmore.

The doctor who didn't see patients.

Just a grisly coincidence, no doubt. Stick around any hospital long enough and grisly becomes routine. But, not knowing what else to do, I decided to have a closer look at Chad Jones's chart myself.

Medical Records was still on the basement floor. I waited in line behind a couple of secretaries bearing requisition slips and a resident carrying a laptop computer, only to be informed that deceased patients' files were housed one floor down, in the sub-basement, in a place called SPI—status permanently inactive. It sounded like something the military had invented.

On the wall just outside the sub-basement stairwell was a map with one of those red YOU ARE HERE arrows in the lower left-hand corner. The rest was an aerial view of a grid of corridors. The actual hallways were walled with white tile and floored with gray linoleum patterned with black-and-pink triangles. Gray doors, red plaques. The hallway was fluorescent-lit and had the vinegary smell of a chem lab.

SPI was in the center of the webwork. Small box. Hard to extrapolate from two dimensions to the long stretch of corridor before me.

I began walking and reading door signs. BOILER ROOM. FURNITURE STORAGE. A series of several doors marked SUPPLIES. Lots of others that said nothing at all.

The hallway angled to the right.

CHEMICAL SPECTROGRAPHY. X-RAY ARCHIVES. SPECIMEN FILES. A double-width slab that said: MORGUE: NO UNAUTHORIZED ADMITTANCE.

I stopped. No smell of formalin, not a hint of what existed on the other side. Just silence and the acetic bite, and a chill that could have been due to a low thermostat setting.

I pictured the map in my head. If my memory was functioning properly, SPI was another right turn, a left, then a short jog. I started walking again, realized I hadn't seen another person since I'd been down here. The air got colder.

I picked up my pace, had managed to slip into a thought-free speed-walk when a door on the right wall swung open so suddenly I had to dodge to avoid getting hit.

No sign on this one. Two maintenance men in gray work clothes emerged from behind it carrying something. Computer. PC, but a big one—black and expensive-looking. As they huffed away, two more workers came out. Another computer. Then a single man, sleeves rolled up, biceps bunched, carrying a laser printer. A five-by-eight index card taped to the printer's console read L. ASHMORE, M.D.

I stepped past the door and saw Presley Huenengarth standing in the doorway, holding an armful of printout. Behind him were blank beige walls, charcoal-colored metal furniture, several more computers in various states of disconnection.

A white coat on a hook was the sole hint that anything more organic than differential equations had been contemplated here.

Huenengarth stared at me.

I said, "I'm Dr. Delaware. We met a couple of days ago. Over at General Pediatrics."

He gave a very small nod.

"Terrible thing about Dr. Ashmore," I said.

He nodded again, stepped back into the room, and closed the door.

I looked down the hall, watching the maintenance men carry off Ashmore's hardware and thinking of grave robbers. Suddenly a room full of post-mortem files seemed a warm and inviting prospect.

11

Status permanently inactive was a long narrow room lined with metal floor-to-ceiling shelves and human-width aisles. The shelves were filled with medical charts. Each chart bore a black tab. Hundreds of consecutive tabs created wavy, inch-thick black lines that seemed to cut the files in half.

Access was blocked by a waist-high counter. Behind it sat an Asian woman in her forties, reading a tabloid-sized Asian-language newspaper. Rounded characters—Thai or Laotian, I guessed. When she saw me she put it down and smiled as if I were delivering good news.

I asked to see the chart for Charles Lyman Jones IV. The name didn't appear to mean anything to her. She reached under the counter and produced a three-by-five card titled SPI REQUISITION. I filled it out, she took it, said "Jones," smiled again, and went into the files.

She looked for a while, walking up and down the aisles, pulling out charts, lifting tabs, consulting the slip. When she returned she was empty-handed.

"Not here, Doctor."

"Any idea where it might be?"

She shrugged. "Someone take."

"Someone's already checked it out?"

"Must be, Doctor."

"Hmm," I said, wondering who'd be interested in a two-year-old death file. "This is pretty important—for research. Is there any way I could talk to that someone?"

She thought for a moment, smiled, and pulled something else out from under the counter. El Producto cigar box. Inside were stacks of SPI requisition forms held together with spring clasps. Five stacks. She spread them on the counter. The top slips all bore the signature of pathologists. I read the patients' names, saw no evidence of alphabetization or any other system of classification.

She smiled again, said "Please," and returned to her newspaper.

I removed the clasp from the first pile and sifted through the forms. It soon became obvious that a system did exist. The slips had been classified by date of *request,* each stack representing a month, each piece of paper placed in daily chronological order. Five stacks because this was May.

No shortcuts—every slip had to be examined. And if Chad Jones's chart had been checked out before January 1, the form wouldn't be here at all.

I began reading the names of dead children. Pretending they were just random assemblages of letters.

A moment later I found what I was looking for, in the February stack. A slip dated February 14 and signed by someone with very poor penmanship. I studied the cramped scrawl, finally deciphered the last name as Herbert. D. Kent Herbert, or maybe it was *Dr.* Kent Herbert.

Other than the signature, the date, and a hospital phone extension, the slip was blank; POSITION/TITLE, DEPARTMENT, REASON FOR REQUEST hadn't been filled out. I copied the extension and thanked the woman behind the counter.

"Everything okay?" she said.

"Do you have any idea who this is?"

She came over and peered at the form.

"Habert . . . no. I just work here one month." Another smile. "Good hospital," she said cheerfully.

I began to wonder if she had any idea what she was filing.
"Do you have a hospital directory?"
She looked confused.
"A hospital phone book—the little orange ones?"
"Ah." She bent and produced one from under the counter.
No Herberts in the medical roster. In the following section, listing nonmedical staff, I found a Ronald Herbert, tagged as Assistant Food Services Manager. But the extension didn't match the one on the slip and I couldn't see a catering specialist having an interest in sudden infant death.

I thanked her and left. Just before the door closed, I heard her say, "Come again, Doctor."

I retraced my steps through the sub-basement, passing Laurence Ashmore's office again. The door was still closed and when I stopped to listen, I thought I heard movement on the other side.

I kept going, looking for a phone, finally spotted a pay unit just past the elevators. Before I got to it the elevator door opened and Presley Huenengarth stood there, looking at me. He hesitated, then walked out of the lift. Standing with his back to me, he removed a pack of Winstons from his suit pocket and took a long time cracking the seal.

The elevator door started to shut. I checked it with the heel of my hand and got on. The last thing I saw before it closed was the security man's placid stare behind a rising cloud of smoke.

After riding up to the first floor I used an in-house phone near Radiation Therapy to dial D. Kent Herbert's extension. The hospital's main switchboard answered.

"Western Pediatrics."
"I was dialing extension two-five-oh-six."
"One moment and I'll connect you, sir." A series of clicks and mechanical burps, then: "Sorry, sir, that extension's been disconnected."
"Since when?"
"I don't know, sir."
"Any idea whose extension it was?"
"No, sir. Who were you trying to reach?"

"D. Kent Herbert."

"Is that a doctor?"

"I don't know."

Pause. "One moment . . . The only Herbert I have listed is Ronald, in Food Services. Would you like me to connect you?"

"Why not?"

Five rings.

"Ron Herbert." Crisp voice.

"Mr. Herbert, this is Medical Records, calling about the chart you requisitioned?"

"Come again?"

"The medical chart you checked out in February? From SPI?"

"You must have the wrong guy, pal. This is the cafeteria."

"You never requested an SPI chart on February 14 of this year?"

Laughter. "Now why the heck would I do that?"

"Thank you, sir."

"No prob. Hope you find what you're after."

I hung up, took the stairs to the ground floor and entered the throng in the lobby. Easing my way through hard-packed bodies, I made it to the Information counter and, after spotting a hospital directory near the clerk's hand, slid it toward me.

The clerk, a dyed-blond black woman, was answering a Spanish-speaking man's question in English. Both of them looked tired and the acid of strife embittered the air. The clerk noticed the book in my hand and looked down her nose at me. The man's gaze followed. The queue behind him swayed and rumbled like a giant serpent.

"You can't have that," said the clerk.

I smiled, pointed at my badge, and said, "Just want to borrow it for a minute."

The clerk rolled her eyes and said, "Just for a minute, that's all."

I moved to the far end of the counter and flipped the book open to the first page, running my eyes and my index finger down the numbers column on the right side of each page, prepared to scan hundreds of extensions until I found 2506. But I hit the jackpot after only a couple of dozen.

ASHMORE, L. W.   (TOX.)   2506

I replaced the book and thanked the clerk. She glared again, snatched it, and placed it out of reach.

"Half a minute," I said. "Do I get a refund?"

Then I saw the faces of the people waiting in line and regretted being a wise-ass.

I went up to see Cassie, but there was a DO NOT DISTURB sign on her door and the nurse on duty told me both she and Cindy were sleeping.

On my way out of the hospital, my thoughts were intruded upon by someone calling my name. Looking up, I saw a tall, mustachioed man approaching from the main entrance. Late thirties, white coat, rimless glasses, Ivy League clothes. The mustache was an extravagant waxed black handlebar. The rest of him seemed arranged around it.

He waved.

I reached into the past and drew out a name.

Dan Kornblatt. Cardiologist. Former UC San Francisco chief resident. His first year at the hospital had been my last. Our relationship had been limited to case conferences and casual chats about the Bay Area—I'd done a fellowship at Langley Porter and Kornblatt delighted in pushing the proposition that no civilization existed south of Carmel. I remembered him as long on brains and short on tact with peers and parents, but tender with his young patients. Four other doctors were walking with him, two women, two men, all young. The five of them moved rapidly, accompanied by swinging arms—physical fitness or a strong sense of purpose. As they got closer I saw that Kornblatt's hair had grayed at the temples and his hawk face had taken on a few seams.

"Alex Delaware. My, my."

"Hi, Dan."

"To what do we owe the honor?"

"Here on a consult."

"Really? Gone private?"

"A few years ago."

"Where?"

"The West Side."

"But of course. Been back up to the *real* city lately?"

"Not lately."

"Me neither. Not since two Christmases ago. Miss that Tadich Grill, all that real-city culture."

He made introductions all around. Two of the other doctors were residents, one was a Cardiology fellow and one of the women—a short, dark, Mideastern woman—was an attending physician. Obligatory smiles and handshakes all around. Four names that passed right through me.

Kornblatt said, "Alex, here, was one of our star psychologists. Back when we had them." To me: "Speaking of which, I thought you guys were *verboten* around here. Has something changed in that regard?"

I shook my head. "It's just an isolated consult."

"Ah. So where you heading? Out?"

I nodded.

"If you're not crunched for time, why don't you come with us? Emergency staff meeting. Are you still on staff? Yeah, you must be if you're doing a consult." His brows creased. "How'd you manage to avoid the Psychiatry bloodbath?"

"Through a technicality. My affiliation was in Pediatrics, not Psychiatry."

"Pediatrics—that's interesting. Good loophole." To the others: "You see, there's always a loophole."

Four knowing looks. None of them was over thirty.

Kornblatt said, "So, you wanna hang with us? The meeting's an important one—that is, if you're still feeling sufficiently affiliated to care what goes on around here."

"Sure," I said, and fell in alongside him. "What's the topic?"

"The decline and fall of the Western Peds Empire. As evidenced by the murder of Larry Ashmore. Actually, it's a memorial for him." He frowned. "You heard about what happened, didn't you?"

I nodded. "Terrible."

"Symptomatic, Alex."

"Of what?"

"What's happened to this place. Look at the way the whole thing's been handled by the administration. A physician gets *mur-*

dered and no one even bothers to send around a memo. Not that they're paper-shy when it comes to disseminating *their* directives."

"I know," I said. "I happened to read one. On the door of the library."

He scowled and his mustache flared. "*What* library?"

"I saw that too."

"Sucks," he said. "Every time I have research to do I've got to drive over to the med school."

We walked across the lobby and came up against the queues. One of the doctors noticed a patient waiting in line, said "I'll join you in a moment," and left the group to greet the child.

"Don't miss the meeting," Kornblatt called after her, without breaking step. When we were clear of the crowd, he said, "No library, no Psych department, no overhead for grants, total hiring freeze. *Now,* there's talk about more cutbacks in all departments—straight across the board. *Entropy.* The bastards probably plan to tear the place down and sell the real estate."

"Not in this market."

"No, I'm serious, Alex. We don't make money and these are bottom-line people. Pave it over, put in lots of parking lots."

"Well," I said, "they might start by paving the ones across the street."

"Don't hold your breath. We are *peons* to these guys. Just another form of service staff."

"How'd they get control?"

"Jones—the new chairman—was managing the hospital's investments. Supposedly did a really good job, so when hard times got harder the board claimed they needed a financial pro and voted him in. He, in turn, fired all the old administration and brought in his own army."

Another crowd milled near the doors. Lots of tapping feet, weary head shakes, and needless punches of the buttons. Two of the lifts were stuck on upper floors. An OUT OF ORDER sign was taped across the door of the third.

"Onward, troops," said Kornblatt, pointing to the stairwell and increasing his pace to a near-run. All of them vaulted the first flight with the zest of triathlon junkies. When we got to the top, Kornblatt was bouncing like a boxer.

"Go, team!" he said, pushing the door open.

The auditorium was a few paces down. A couple of doctors were lounging near the entrance, which was topped by a handwritten banner that said ASHMORE MEMORIAL.

I said, "Whatever happened to Kent Herbert?"

Kornblatt said, "Who?"

"Herbert. The toxicologist. Didn't he work with Ashmore?"

"I didn't know *anyone* worked with Ashmore. The guy was a loner, a real—" He stopped himself. "Herbert? No, can't say I remember him."

We entered the big fan-shaped lecture hall; rows of gray cloth seats sloped sharply to a wooden lecture pit. A dusty green board on wheels stood at the rear of the pit. The upholstery on the seats was dingy and some of the cushions were tattered. The light, fluctuating hum of occasional conversation filled the room.

The auditorium held at least five hundred chairs but no more than seventy were occupied. The spotty attendance gave it the look of a pass-fail class. Kornblatt and his entourage headed down toward the front of the room, shaking hands and trading a few high-fives along the way. I hung back and sat by myself in the uppermost row.

Lots of white coats—full-time staffers. But where were the private practitioners? Unable to attend on short notice or choosing to stay away? Western Peds had always suffered from town-gown tension, but the full-timers and the physicians out in "the real world" had always managed to achieve a grudging symbiosis.

As I looked around some more, I was struck by another scarcity: gray heads. Where were all the senior people I'd known?

Before I could mull that, a man holding a cordless microphone stepped into the pit and called for quiet. Thirty-five; soft, pale baby face under a big blond Afro. His white coat was slightly yellowed and too big for him. Under it he wore a black shirt, and a brown knit tie.

He said, "Please," and the hum died. A few beepers went off, then silence.

"Thanks to all of you for coming. Could someone get the door?"

Faces turned. I realized I was closest to the exit, got up and shut the door.

"Okay," said Afro. "The first order of business is a moment of silence for our colleague Dr. Laurence Ashmore, so if you could all please rise. . . ."

Everyone stood. Heads drooped. A long minute passed.

Afro said, "Okay, please be seated." Walking to the board, he picked up a piece of chalk and wrote:

AGENDA

1. Ashmore memorial
2.
3.
4. . . . ?

Stepping away from the board, he said, "Is there someone who wants to say a few words about Dr. Ashmore?"

Silence.

"Let me say, then, that I know I speak for all of us in condemning the brutality of what happened to Larry. And in offering our deepest sympathy to his family. In lieu of flowers, I propose we get together a fund and donate it to an organization of the family's choice. Or our choice, if it would be too disruptive to ask the family at this point. We can decide now, or at a later date, depending on what people feel. Anyone care to comment?"

A short-haired woman in the third row said, "How about the Poison Control Center? He was a toxicologist."

"Poison Control Center sounds good," said Afro. "Anyone second that?"

A hand rose in the middle of the room.

"Thanks, Barb. So moved. Anyone know the family? To inform them of our plan?"

No response.

He looked at the woman who'd made the suggestion. "Barb, would you be in charge of collecting the funds?"

She nodded.

"All right, people, bring your donations to Barb Loman's office in Rheumatology and we'll see that the Poison Control Center gets the money, posthaste. Anything more along those lines?"

"Data," said someone. "As in, we don't have any."

"Could you stand and clarify, Greg?" said Afro.

A stocky, bearded man in a checked shirt and wide, floral, retro tie rose. I thought I remembered him, as a resident, without the beard. An Italian name . . .

". . . I'm saying, John, is that security stinks around here. What happened to him could have happened to any of us, and since it's *our* lives on the line we deserve to have full access to information. Exactly what happened, the progress of the police's investigation, as well as any measures we can take to assure our safety."

"There aren't any!" a bespectacled black man across the room called out. "Not unless the administration makes a real commitment to genuine security—twenty-four-hour guards at every entrance to the lot and at each and every stairwell."

"That means money, Hank," said the bearded man. "Good luck."

A ponytailed woman with dishwater hair got up.

"The money *would* be available, Greg," she said, "if they got their priorities straight. What we *don't* need are more paramilitary types obstructing our patients in the halls. What we *do* need is exactly what you and Hank just said: *genuine* security, including self-defense classes, karate, Mace, personal training, whatever. Especially for female staff. The nurses deal with this kind of threat every single day, coming from across the street. Especially the night shift—you know how a couple of them were beat up, and—"

"I know tha—"

". . . the open lots have no security at all. As all of us are learning, from direct experience. I drove in at five this morning on an emergency call, and let me tell you, it felt scary, people. I also have to say I think it was a *serious* mistake to limit this meeting to physicians. This is no time for elitism. There are nurses and ancillary staff out there suffering just like we are, working for the same goals. We should be getting together, empowering each other, not fractionating."

No one spoke.

The ponytailed woman looked around the auditorium and sat down.

Afro said, "Thank you, Elaine, your point is well taken. Though

I certainly don't think any deliberate attempt was made to be exclusionary."

"Well," said the ponytailed woman, standing again, "was anyone else other than physicians informed?"

Afro smiled. "This was an ad hoc *medical* staff meeting, Elaine, so it's only natural that physicians would——"

"Don't you think the rest of the staff *cares*, John?"

"Of course," said Afro. "I——"

"Western Peds women are *terrified*! Wake up, people! Everyone needs to be empowered. If you recall, the last two assault victims were women and——"

"Yes, I do recall, Elaine. We all do. And I assure you that in the event other meetings are scheduled—and it's certainly clear to me that they need to be—a definite effort will be made to reach out."

Elaine contemplated debate, then shook her head and sat.

Afro returned to the board, chalk poised. "I suppose we've moved on to another item, de facto, haven't we. Staff security?"

Scattered nods. The lack of group coherence was almost tangible. It reminded me of so many other meetings, years ago. Endless discussions, little or no resolution . . .

Afro placed a check next to ASHMORE MEMORIAL, wrote STF SECURITY on the next line, and faced the assembly.

"Okay. Any suggestions beyond guards and karate?"

"Yeah," said a balding, swarthy, thick-shouldered man. "Guns."

A few chuckles.

Afro gave a tight smile. "Thank you, Al. Was that the way things were handled in Houston?"

"You bet, John. S and W in every black bag. That's Smith and Wesson, for all you pacifist types."

Afro made a gun with his thumb and forefinger, pointed it at Bald, and winked. "Anything else, Al, short of turning the hospital into an armed camp?"

Dan Kornblatt stood. "I hate to say it but I think we're lapsing into tunnel vision here. What we need to do is address the larger issues."

"In what sense, Dan?"

"In the sense of our purpose—the institution's purpose."

Afro looked puzzled. "Are we through, then, with item two?"

Kornblatt said, "*I* certainly am. Security is just a symptom of the greater malaise."

Afro waited a moment, then checked off STF SECURITY.

"What malaise is that, Dan?"

"Chronic, end-stage apathy—institutionally *sanctioned* apathy. Just look around. How many private physicians are there on staff, John? Two hundred? Just take a look what percentage cared enough to brown-bag it today and make a statement with their presence."

"Dan—"

"Wait, let me finish. There's a *reason* so few private people are here. And it's the same reason they avoid sending their paying patients here if they can find semi-decent local facilities. Same reason so many of *our* top people have gone elsewhere. We've been tagged as a stepchild—an institutional *loser*. And the community's bought *into* that because the board itself *and* the administration hold this institution in low regard. And so do we. I'm sure we've all had enough psych to know what happens to the self-image of a kid who keeps being told he's a loser. He starts believing it. Same thing applies to—"

The door opened wide. Heads turned. George Plumb entered and straightened his tie, a blood-red paisley against a white shirt and light-gray raw silk suit. His shoes clicked as he descended to the pit. When he got to the bottom he stood next to Afro, as if assuming his rightful position.

"Afternoon, ladies and gentlemen," he said.

Kornblatt said, "We were just talking about institutional apathy, George."

Plumb gave a thoughtful look and placed one fist under his chin. "I was under the impression this was a memorial for Dr. Ashmore."

Afro said, "It was, but we've covered some additional ground."

Plumb turned and studied the writing on the board. "Quite a chunk of ground, it seems. Might I backtrack and talk a bit about Dr. Ashmore?"

Silence. Then nods. Looking disgusted, Kornblatt sat down.

"First of all," said Plumb, "I want to communicate the sympathy of the board of directors and the administration for the loss of Dr. Laurence Ashmore. Dr. Ashmore was a noted researcher and his absence will be profoundly felt. In lieu of flowers, Mrs. Ashmore has requested that funds be sent to UNICEF. My office will be pleased to handle all donations. Second, I want to assure you that progress *has* been made fabricating new parking cards. The cards are ready and can be picked up from Security between three and five, today and tomorrow. We regret any inconvenience. However, I'm sure all of you recognize the necessity of changing the keys. Any questions?"

The stocky bearded man named Greg said, "What about real security—guards at each stairwell?"

Plumb smiled. "I was just getting to that, Dr. Spironi. Yes, both the police and our own security staff inform us that the stairwells are a problem, and though the cost will be considerable, we are prepared to implement twenty-four-hour guards, one man per shift, for each level of the physicians' lot, as well as one guard per shift for each of the three open lots across the boulevard. That adds up to a total parking staff of fifteen guards, meaning a net hire of eleven guards added to the four already on staff. The cost, including benefits and insurance, should amount to slightly under four hundred thousand dollars."

"Four hundred!" said Kornblatt, springing to his feet. "Almost forty thousand a cop?"

"*Guards,* not cops, Dr. Kornblatt. Cops would cost much, much more. As I said, the figure includes benefits, insurance, workman's compensation, supplies and equipment, and site-specific ancillary costs such as orientation and in-house training. The company with which we've contracted has an excellent track record and their proposal includes self-defense and crime-prevention education for the entire staff. The administration didn't feel it was appropriate to bargain-hunt in this matter, Dr. Kornblatt. However, if you'd like to shop around for a more competitive price, be our guest. Bear in mind, however, that time is an issue—we want to restore a sense of security and well-being for everyone, with maximal haste."

Lacing his hands across his abdomen, he looked at Kornblatt.

The cardiologist said, "Last time I checked, *my* job was treating kids, George."

"Precisely," said Plumb. Turning his back on Kornblatt, he said, "Any additional questions?"

There was a moment of silence, as long as the one honoring Ashmore's memory.

Kornblatt stood and said, "I don't know about the rest of you but I'm feeling co-opted."

Plumb said, "Co-opted? In what sense, Dr. Kornblatt?"

"In the sense, George, that this was supposed to be a physicians' meeting and you've just walked in and taken over."

Plumb rubbed his jaw. Looked at the doctors. Smiled. Shook his head.

"Well," he said, "that certainly wasn't my intent."

"Maybe not, George, but it's sure coming out that way."

Plumb stepped forward, toward the front row. Lowering one leg to the cushion of an empty seat, he rested his elbow on the bent knee. Chin on hand again, and he was Rodin's "Thinker."

"Coopting," he said. "All I can say is that was not my intention."

Afro said, "George, what Dan—"

"No need to explain, Dr. Runge. The tragic incident with Dr. Ashmore has left all of us on edge."

Maintaining the thinker's pose, he turned back to Kornblatt: "I must say, Doctor, that I'm surprised to be hearing that kind of sectarian talk from you in particular. If I recall correctly, you drafted a memorandum last month calling for greater communication between the administration and the professional staff. I believe the term you used was cross-pollination?"

"I was talking about decision-making, George."

"And that's exactly what I'm attempting to do, Dr. Kornblatt. Cross-pollinate vis-à-vis security decisions. In that spirit I reiterate my offer to you—to any of you. Come up with your own security proposals. If you can develop one as comprehensive as ours, at equal or lower cost, the administration and the board will be more than happy to entertain it seriously. I mean that. I'm sure I don't need to remind you of the institution's financial situation. That four hundred thousand will have to come from somewhere."

"Patient care, no doubt," said Kornblatt.

Plumb gave a sad smile. "As I've stressed in the past, patient-care reduction is always the court of last resort," he said. "But each month strips us closer and closer to the bone. No one's fault—it's just present-day reality. In fact, perhaps it's good we've wandered afield of the issue of Dr. Ashmore's murder and are talking about it in open forum. To some extent, fiscal and security issues dovetail—both stem from demographic issues outside of anyone's control."

"There goes the neighborhood?" said Spironi.

"Unfortunately, Doctor, the neighborhood has *already* gone."

"So what do you suggest?" said Elaine, the ponytailed woman. "Closing down?"

Plumb shifted his gaze to her sharply. Lifting his foot from the chair, he straightened and sighed.

"What I suggest, Dr. Eubanks, is that we all remain painfully aware of the realities that, for all intents and purposes, imprison us. Institution-specific problems that augment the already difficult state of health care in this city, county, state, and to some extent, the entire country. I suggest that all of us work within a *realistic* framework in order to keep this institution going at some level."

"*Some* level?" said Kornblatt. "That sounds like more cuts a-comin', George. What's next, another pogrom, like Psychiatry? Or radical surgery on every division, like the rumors we've been hearing?"

"I really don't think," said Plumb, "that this is the right time to get into that kind of detail."

"Why not? It's an open forum."

"Because the facts simply aren't available at present."

"So you're not denying there will be cuts, soon?"

"No, Daniel," said Plumb, straightening and placing his hands behind his back. "I couldn't be honest and deny it. I'm neither denying nor confirming, because to do either would be to perform a disservice to you as well as to the institution. My reason for attending this meeting was to pay respect to Dr. Ashmore and to express solidarity—personal and institutional—with your well-intentioned memorial for him. The political nature of the meeting was never made clear to me and had I known I was intruding, I would have steered clear. So please excuse that intrusion, right now—though if I'm not mistaken, I do spot a few other Ph.D.'s out there." He looked at me briefly. "Good day."

He gave a small wave and headed up the stairs.

Afro said, "George—Dr. Plumb?"

Plumb stopped and turned. "Yes, Dr. Runge?"

"We do—I'm sure I speak for all of us in saying this—we do appreciate your presence."

"Thank you, John."

"Perhaps if this leads to greater communication between administration and the professional staff, Dr. Ashmore's death will have acquired a tiny bit of meaning."

"God willing, John," said Plumb. "God willing."

12

After Plumb left, the meeting lost its steam. Some of the doctors stayed behind, clustering in small discussion groups, but most disappeared. As I exited the auditorium I saw Stephanie coming down the hall.

"Is it over?" she said, walking faster. "I got hung up."

"Over and done. But you didn't miss much. No one seemed to have much to say about Ashmore. It started to evolve into a gripe session against the administration. Then Plumb showed up and took the wind out of the staff's sails by offering to do everything they were demanding."

"Like what?"

"Better security." I told her the details, then recounted Plumb's exchange with Dan Kornblatt.

"On a brighter note," she said, "we seem finally to have found something physical on Cassie. Look here."

She reached into her pocket and drew out a piece of paper. Cassie's name and hospital registration number were at the top. Below was a column of numbers.

"Fresh from this morning's labs."

She pointed to a number.

"Low sugar—hypoglycemia. Which could easily explain the grand mal, Alex. There were no focal sites on the EEG and very little if any wave abnormality—Bogner says it's one of those profiles that's open to interpretation. I'm sure you know that happens all the time in kids. So if we hadn't found low sugar, we would have really been stumped."

She pocketed the paper.

I said, "Hypoglycemia never showed up in her tests before, did it?"

"No, and I checked for it each time. When you see seizures in a kid you always look at sugar and calcium imbalance. The layman thinks of hypoglycemia as something minor but in babies it can really trash their nervous systems. Both times after her seizures, Cassie had normal sugar, but I asked Cindy if she'd given her anything to drink before she brought her into the E.R. and she said she had—juice or soda. Reasonable thing to do—kid looks dehydrated, get some fluids in her. But that, plus the time lag getting over here, could very well have messed up the other labs. So in some sense it's good she seized here in the hospital and we were able to check her out right away."

"Any idea why her sugar's low?"

She gave a grim look. "*That's* the question, Alex. Severe hypoglycemia with seizures is usually more common in infants than in toddlers. Preemies, babies of diabetic mothers, perinatal problems—anything that messes up the pancreas. In older kids, you tend to think more in terms of infection. Cassie's white count is normal, but maybe what we're seeing are residual effects. Gradual damage to the pancreas brought about by an old infection. I can't rule out metabolic disorders either, even though we checked for that back when she had breathing problems. She could have some sort of rare glycogen-storage problem that we don't have an assay for."

She looked up the hall and blew out air. "The other possibility's an insulin-secreting pancreatic tumor. Which is not good news."

"None of them sound like good news," I said.

"No, but at least we'll know what we're dealing with."

"Have you told Cindy and Chip?"

"I told them Cassie's sugar was low and she probably doesn't have classical epilepsy. I can't see any reason to go into any more detail while we're still groping for a diagnosis."

"How'd they react?"

"They were both kind of passive—wiped out. Like, 'Give me one more punch in the face.' Neither of them got much sleep last night. He just left to go to work and she's bunked out on the couch."

"What about Cassie?"

"Still drowsy. We're working on getting her sugar stabilized. She should be okay soon."

"What's in store for her, procedure-wise?"

"More blood tests, a tomographic scan of her gut. It may be necessary, eventually, to open her up surgically—get an actual look at her pancreas. But that's a ways off. Got to get back to Torgeson. He's reviewing the chart in my office. Turned out to be a nice guy, really casual."

"Is he reviewing Chad's chart too?"

"I called for it but they couldn't find it."

"I know," I said. "I was looking for it, too—for background. Someone named D. Kent Herbert pulled it—he worked for Ashmore."

"Herbert?" she said. "Never heard of him. Why would Ashmore be wanting the chart when he wasn't even interested the first time?"

"Good question."

"I'll put a tracer on it. Meantime, let's concentrate on Ms. Cassie's metabolic system."

We headed for the stairs.

I said, "Would hypoglycemia explain the other problems—breathing difficulties, bloody stools?"

"Not directly, but all the problems could have been symptoms of a generalized infectious process or a rare syndrome. New stuff is always coming at us—every time an enzyme is discovered, we find someone who doesn't have it. Or it could even be an *atypical* case of something we *did* test for that just didn't register in her blood for some God-knows-why reason."

She talked quickly, animatedly. Pleased to be dueling with familiar enemies.

"Do you still want me involved?" I said.

"Of course. Why do you ask?"

"Sounds like you've moved away from Munchausen and think it's genuine."

"Well," she said, "it would be nice for it to *be* genuine. And *treatable*. But even if that is the case, we're probably talking chronic disease. So they can use the support, if you don't mind."

"Not at all."

"Thanks much."

Down the stairs. At the next floor I said, "Could Cindy—or anyone else—have somehow caused the hypoglycemia?"

"Sure, if she gave Cassie a middle-of-the-night shot of insulin. I thought of that right away. But that would have required a lot of expertise with timing and dosage."

"Lots of practice injections?"

"Using Cassie as a pincushion. Which I can buy, theoretically. Cindy has plenty of time with Cassie. But given Cassie's reaction to needles, if her mom was sticking her, wouldn't she be freaking out every time she saw her? And I'm the only one she seems to despise. . . . Anyway, I never noticed any unusual injection marks when I did the physical."

"Would they be obvious, given all the other sticks she's had?"

"Not obvious, but I'm careful when I do my exams, Alex. The kids' bods get gone over pretty thoroughly."

"Could the insulin have been administered other than by injection?"

She shook her head as we continued to descend. "There *are* oral hypoglycemics, but their metabolites would show up on the tox panel."

Thinking of Cindy's health discharge from the army, I said, "Any diabetes in the family?"

"Someone sharing their insulin with Cassie?" She shook her head. "Back at the beginning, when we were looking at Cassie's metabolics, we had both Chip and Cindy tested. Normal."

"Okay," I said. "Good luck pinning it down."

She stopped and gave me a light kiss on the cheek. "I appreciate your comments, Alex. I'm so thrilled to be dealing with biochemistry, I run the risk of narrowing my perspective."

* * *

Back on the first floor I asked a guard where to find the Personnel office. He looked me over and told me right here, on the first floor.

It turned out to be exactly where I remembered it. Two women sat at typewriters; a third filed papers. The filer came up to me. She was straw-haired and hatchet-faced, in her late fifties. Under her ID was a circular badge that looked homemade, bearing a photo of a big hairy sheepdog. I told her I wanted to send a condolence card to Dr. Laurence Ashmore's widow and asked for his home address.

She said, "Oh, yes, isn't it terrible? What's this place coming to?" in a smoker's voice, and consulted a folder the size of a small-town phone book. "Here you go, Doctor—North Whittier Drive, over in Beverly Hills." She recited a street address in the 900's.

North Beverly Hills—prime real estate. The 900 block placed it just above Sunset. Prime of the prime; Ashmore had lived on more than research grants.

The clerk sighed. "Poor man. Just goes to show you, you can't buy your safety."

I said, "Isn't that the truth?"

"Isn't it, though?"

We traded wise smiles.

"Nice dog," I said, indicating the badge.

She beamed. "That's my honey—my champ. I breed true Old English, for temperament and working ability."

"Sounds like fun."

"It's more than that. Animals give without expecting anything in return. We could learn a few things from them."

I nodded. "One more thing. Dr. Ashmore had someone working with him—D. Kent Herbert? The medical staff would like him to be informed of the charity fund the hospital's establishing in Dr. Ashmore's honor but no one's been able to locate him. I was appointed to get hold of him but I'm not even sure he's still working here, so if you have some sort of an address, I'd be much obliged."

"Herbert," she said. "Hmm. So you think he terminated?"

"I don't know. I think he was still on the payroll in January or February, if that helps."

"It might. Herbert . . . let's see."

Walking to her desk, she pulled another thick folder from a wall shelf.

"Herbert, Herbert, Herbert . . . Well, I've got two here, but neither of them sound like yours. Herbert, Ronald, in Food Services, and Herbert, Dawn, in Toxicology."

"Maybe it's Dawn. Toxicology was Dr. Ashmore's specialty."

She screwed up her face. "Dawn's a girl's name. Thought you were trying to find a man."

I gave a helpless shrug. "Probably a mixup—the doctor who gave me the name didn't actually know this person, so both of us assumed it was a man. Sorry for the sexism."

"Oh, don't worry about *that*," she said. "I don't mess with all that stuff."

"Does this Dawn have a middle initial 'K'?"

She looked down. "Yes, she does."

"Then, there you go," I said. "The name I was given was D. *Kent*. What's her job description?"

"Um, five thirty-three A—let me see . . ." Thumbing through another book. "That looks like a research assistant, Level One."

"Did she transfer to another department in the hospital, by any chance?"

Consulting yet another volume, she said, "Nope. Looks like a termination."

"Hmm . . . Do you have an address for her?"

"Nope, nothing. We throw out personal stuff thirty days after they're gone—got a real space problem."

"When exactly did she terminate?"

"That I can tell you." She flipped a few pages and pointed to a code that I couldn't comprehend. "Here we go. You're right—about her being here in February. But that was her last month—she gave notice on the fifteenth, went officially off payroll on the twenty-eighth."

"The fifteenth," I said. The day after pulling Chad Jones's chart.

"That's right. See right here? Two slash fifteen?"

I stuck around for a few more minutes, listening to a story about her dogs. But I was thinking about two-legged creatures.

*   *   *

It was 3:45 when I drove out of the parking lot. A few feet from the exit a motorcycle cop was giving a jaywalking ticket to a nurse. The nurse looked furious; the cop's face was a blank tablet.

Traffic on Sunset was obstructed by a four-car fender-bender, and the accompanying turmoil wrought by rubberneckers and somnolent traffic officers. It took almost an hour to reach the inanimate green stretch that was Beverly Hills' piece of the boulevard. Tile-roofed ego monuments perched atop hillocks of Bermuda grass and dichondra, embellished by hostile gates, tennis court sheeting, and the requisite battalions of German cars.

I passed the stadium-sized weed-choked lot that had once housed the Arden mansion. The weeds had turned to hay, and all the trees on the property were dead. The Mediterranean palace had served briefly as a twenty-year-old Arab sheik's plaything before being torched by persons unknown—aesthetic sensibilities offended by puke-green paint and moronic statuary with blacked-in pubic hair, or just plain xenophobia. Whatever the reason for the arson, rumors had been circulating for years about subdivision and rebuilding. But the real estate slump had taken the luster off that kind of optimism.

A few blocks later the Beverly Hills Hotel came into view, ringed by a motorcade of white stretch limos. Someone getting married or promoting a new film.

As I approached Whittier Drive, I decided to keep going. But when the letters on the street sign achieved focus, I found myself making a sudden right turn and driving slowly up the jacaranda-lined street.

Laurence Ashmore's house was at the end of the block, a three-story, limestone Georgian affair on a double lot at least two hundred feet wide. The building was blocky, and impeccably maintained. A brick circular drive scythed through a perfect flat lawn. The landscaping was spare but good, with a preference for azaleas, camellias, and Hawaiian tree ferns—Georgian goes tropical. A weeping olive tree shaded half the lawn. The other half was sun-kissed.

To the left of the house was a porte-cochere long enough to shelter one of the stretches I'd just seen at the hotel. Beyond the wooden gates were treetops and the flaming red clouds of bougain-villea.

Prime of the prime. Even with the slump, at least four million.

A single car was parked in the circular drive. White Olds Cutlass, five or six years old. A hundred yards in either direction the curb was vacant. No black-garbed callers or bouquets on the door-stop. Shuttered windows; no sign of occupancy. The placard of a security company was staked in the perfect, clipped grass.

I drove on, made a U-turn, passed the house again and contin-ued home.

Routine calls from my service; nothing from Fort Jackson. I called the base anyway and asked for Captain Katz. He came on quickly.

I reminded him who I was and told him I hoped I hadn't interrupted his dinner.

He said, "No, that's fine, I was going to call you. Think I found what you're after."

"Great."

"One second—here it is. Influenza and pneumonia epidemics over the last ten years, right?"

"Exactly."

"Well, far as I can tell, we only had one major flu epidemic—one of the Thai strains—back in '73. Which is before your time."

"Nothing since?"

"Doesn't look like it. And no pneumonia, period. I mean, I'm sure we've had plenty of isolated flu cases, but nothing that would qualify as an epidemic. And we're real good about keeping those kinds of records. Only thing we usually have to worry about, in terms of contagion, is bacterial meningitis. You know how tough that can be in a closed environment."

"Sure," I said. "Have you had epidemics of meningitis?"

"A few. The most recent was two years ago. Before that, '83, then '78 and '75—almost looks cyclical, come to think of it. Might be worth checking *that* out, see if someone can come up with a pattern."

"How serious were the outbreaks?"

"Only one I observed personally was two years ago, and that was serious enough—soldiers died."

"What about sequellae—brain damage, seizure disorders?"

"Most probably. I don't have the data handy but I can get hold of them. Thinking of changing your research protocol?"

"Not quite yet," I said. "Just curious."

"Well," he said, "that can be a good thing, curiosity. At least out in the civilian world."

Stephanie had her hard data, and now I had mine.

Cindy had lied about her discharge.

Maybe Laurence Ashmore found some data too. Saw Cassie's name on the admission and discharge sheets and got curious.

What else could have caused him to take another look at Chad Jones's chart?

He'd never be able to tell me, but maybe his former assistant could.

I called 213, 310, and 818 Informations for a listing on Dawn Kent Herbert and got nowhere. Expanded my search to 805, 714, and 619 with the same result, then phoned Milo at Parker Center. He picked up and said, "Heard about your homicide last night."

"I was at the hospital when it happened." I told him about being questioned, the scene in the lobby. Feeling as if I'd been watched when I left the parking structure.

"Be careful, bucko. I got your message on Bottomley's hubby, but I've got no domestic violence calls to her address and there's no one on NCIC who could be her hubby. But she does have a trouble-maker living there. Reginald Douglas Bottomley, D.O.B. '70. Which would probably make him her son or maybe an errant nephew."

"What'd he do to get in trouble?"

"Lots—he's got a sheet long enough to cover Abdul-Jabbar's bed. Sealed juvenile file, then a bunch of DUIs, possession, shoplift-ing, petty theft, burglary, robbery, assault. Lots of busts, a few convictions, a teensy bit of jail time, mostly at County. Got a call in to a detective over at Foothill Division, see what he knows. What's the relevance of Bottomley's home situation to the little kid?"

"Don't know," I said. "Just looking for stress factors that might get her to act out. Probably because she was getting on my nerves. 'Course, if Reggie turned out bad because Vicki abused him, that would tell us something. Meanwhile, I've got something that definitely is relevant. Cindy Jones lied about her military discharge. I just talked to Fort Jackson and there was no pneumonia epidemic in '83."

"That so?"

"She might have had pneumonia, but it wasn't part of any outbreak. And she made a point about the epidemic."

"Seems a stupid thing to lie about."

"The Munchausen game," I said. "Or maybe she was covering up something. Remember I told you the discharge seemed a sensitive topic for her—how she blushed and yanked her braid? The public health officer at the army base said there *was* an epidemic in '83— just about the time Cindy would have been in. But it was bacterial *meningitis*. Which can lead to seizures. Giving us a link to another organ system Cassie's had problems with. In fact, she had a grand mal seizure last night. In the hospital."

"That's a first."

"Yup. First time anyone but Cindy saw it."

"Who else did?"

"Bottomley and the ward clerk. And what's interesting is, yesterday Cindy was talking to me about how Cassie always gets sick at home, then recovers right away in the hospital. So people start thinking her mother's crazy. And here we are, a few hours later, with eyewitnesses and chemical corroboration. The lab tests turned up hypoglycemia, and now Stephanie's convinced Cassie's really sick. But hypoglycemia can be faked, Milo, by anything that alters the blood sugar, like a shot of insulin. I mentioned that to Stephanie, but I'm not sure she's hearing it. She's really geared up, looking for rare metabolic diseases."

"Pretty sharp about-face," he said.

"I can't say that I blame her. After months of dealing with this, she's frustrated and wants to practice medicine, not play psychological guessing games."

"You, on the other hand . . ."

"I've got an evil mind—too much time hanging around you."

"Yeah," he said. "Well, I can see your point about the meningitis, if that's what the mom had. Seizures for all—like mother, like daughter. But you don't know that yet. And if she was covering up, why would she bring up the discharge in the first place? Why even tell you she was in the army?"

"Why'd your confessor make up his story? If she's a Munchausen, she'd get off on *teasing* me with half-truths. It would sure be nice to get hold of her discharge papers, Milo. Find out exactly what *did* happen to her in South Carolina."

"I can try, but it'll take time."

"Something else. I went looking for Chad Jones's post-mortem chart today but it was missing. Pulled by Ashmore's research assistant in February and never returned."

"Ashmore? The one who was killed?"

"The very same. He was a toxicologist. Stephanie had already asked him to review the chart half a year ago, when she started getting suspicious about Cassie. He did it reluctantly—pure researcher, didn't work with patients. And he told her he'd found nothing. So why would he pull the chart again, unless *he* discovered something new about Cassie?"

"If he didn't work with patients, how would he know about Cassie in the first place?"

"By seeing her name on the A and D's—the admission and discharge sheets. They come out daily and every doctor gets them. Seeing Cassie on them time after time might have finally gotten him curious enough to review her brother's death. The assistant's a woman by the name of Dawn Herbert. I tried to get hold of her but she quit the hospital the day after she pulled the chart—talk about more cute timing. And now Ashmore's dead. I don't want to sound like some kind of conspiracy nut, but it's weird, isn't it? Herbert might be able to clear things up, but there's no address or phone number listed for her from Santa Barbara down to San Diego."

"Dawn Herbert," he said. "As in the other Hoover."

"Middle name of Kent. As in Duke of."

"Fine. I'll try to squeeze in a trace before I go off shift."

"I appreciate it."

"Show it by feeding me. Got any decent grub in the house?"

"I suppose—"

"Better yet, *haute cuisine*. I'll pick. Gluttonous, overpriced, and on your credit card."

He showed up at eight, holding out a white box. On the cover was a cartoon of a grinning, grass-skirted islander finger-spinning a huge disc of dough.

"Pizza?" I said. "What happened to *haute* and overpriced?"

"Wait till you see the bill."

He carried the box into the kitchen, slit the tape with his fingernail, lifted the lid, removed a slice from the pie, and ate it standing at the counter. Then he pulled off a second wedge, handed it to me, got another one for himself, and sat at the table.

I looked at the slice in my hand. Molten desert of cheese, landscaped with mushrooms, onions, peppers, anchovies, sausage, and lots of things I couldn't identify. "What is this—pineapple?"

"And mango. And Canadian bacon and bratwurst and chorizo. What you've got there, pal, is authentic Spring Street Pogo-Pogo pizza. The ultimate democratic cuisine—little bit of every ethnicity, a lesson in gastronomic democracy."

He ate and spoke with his mouth full: "Little Indonesian guy sells it from a stand, near the Center. People line up."

"People line up to pay parking fines too."

"Suit yourself," he said, and dug in again, holding one hand under the slice to catch dripping cheese.

I went to the cupboard, found a couple of paper plates, and put them on the table, along with napkins.

"Whoa, the good china!" He wiped his chin. "Drink?"

I took two cans of Coke from the fridge. "This okay?"

"If it's cold."

Finishing his second slice, he popped his can and drank.

I sat and took a bite of pizza. "Not bad."

"Milo knows grub." He guzzled more Coke. "Regarding your Ms. Dawn K. Herbert, no wants or warrants. Another virgin."

He reached into his pocket, took out a piece of paper, and handed it to me. Typewritten on it was:

Dawn Kent Herbert, DOB 12/13/63, 5'5",
170 lb., brown and brown. Mazda Miata.

Under that was an address on Lindblade Street, in Culver City.

I thanked him and asked him if he'd heard anything new on the Ashmore murder.

He shook his head. "It's going down as your routine Hollywood mugging."

"Right guy to mug. He was rich." I described the house on North Whittier.

"Didn't know research paid that well," he said.

"It doesn't. Ashmore must have had some sort of independent income. That would explain why the hospital hired him at a time when they're getting rid of doctors and discouraging research grants. He probably brought some kind of endowment with him."

"Paid his way in?"

"It happens."

"Let me ask you this," he said. "In terms of your Ashmore-getting-curious theory. Cassie's been in and out of the hospital since she was born. Why would he wait until February to start snooping?"

"Good question," I said. "Hold on for a sec."

I went to the library and fetched the notes I'd taken on Cassie's medical history. Milo had sat down at the table and I joined him, turning pages.

"Here we are," I said. "February 10. Four days before Herbert pulled Chad's chart. It was Cassie's second hospitalization for stomach problems. The diagnosis was gastric distress of unknown origin, possible sepsis—the main symptom was bloody diarrhea. Which could have made Ashmore think of some specific kind of poisoning. Maybe his toxicology training overcame his apathy."

"Not enough for him to talk to Stephanie."

"True."

"So maybe he looked and didn't find anything."

"Then why not return the chart?" I said.

"Sloppy housekeeping. Herbert was supposed to but didn't. Knew she was leaving and didn't give a damn about her paperwork."

"When I see her I'll ask her."

"Yeah. Who knows, maybe she'll give you a ride in her Miata."

"Zoom zoom," I said. "Anything new on Reginald Bottomley?"

"Not yet. Fordebrand—the Foothill guy—is on vacation, so I've got a call in to the guy who's catching for him. Let's hope he cooperates."

He put the Coke down. Tension wounded his face and I thought I knew why. He was wondering if the other detective knew who *he* was. Would *bother* to return his call.

"Thanks," I said. "For everything."

"*De nada.*" He shook the can. Empty. Leaning on the counter with both elbows, he faced me.

"What's the matter?" I said.

"You sound low. Beaten down."

"Guess I am—all this theorizing and Cassie's no safer."

"Know what you mean," he said. "Best thing's to stay focused, not drift too far afield. It's a risk on cases with bad solve-prospects—God knows I've had plenty of them. You feel powerless, start throwing wild punches and end up no wiser and a helluva lot older."

He left shortly after that and I called Cassie's hospital room. It was after nine and direct access to patients had been cut off. I identified myself to the hospital operator and was put through. Vicki answered.

"Hi, it's Dr. Delaware."

"Oh . . . what can I do for you?"

"How's everything?"

"Fine."

"Are you in Cassie's room?"

"No—out here."

"At the desk?"

"Yes."

"How's Cassie doing?"

"Fine."

"Sleeping?"

"Uh-huh."

"What about Cindy?"

"Her too."

"Busy day for everyone, huh?"

"Uh-huh."

"Has Dr. Eves been by recently?"

"Around eight—you want the exact time?"

"No, thanks. Anything new, in terms of the hypoglycemia?"

"You'd have to ask Dr. Eves that."

"No new seizures?"

"Nope."

"All right," I said. "Tell Cindy I called. I'll be by tomorrow."

She hung up. Despite her hostility, I felt a strange—almost corrupt—sense of power. Because I knew about her unhappy past and she was unaware of it. Then I realized that what I knew put me no closer to the truth.

Far afield, Milo said.

I sat there, feeling the power diminish.

The next morning I woke up to clean spring light. I jogged a couple
of miles, ignoring the pain in my knees and fixing my thoughts on
the evening with Robin.

Afterward I showered, fed the fish, and read the paper while
eating breakfast. Nothing more on the Ashmore homicide.

I called Information, trying to match a phone number to the
address Milo had given me for Dawn Herbert. None was listed and
neither of the two other Herberts residing in Culver City knew any
Dawn.

I hung up, not sure it made much of a difference. Even if I
located her, what explanation would I use to ask her about Chad's
file?

I decided to concentrate on the job I'd been trained to do.
Dressing and clipping my hospital badge to my lapel, I left the
house, turned east on Sunset, and headed for Hollywood.

I reached Beverly Hills within minutes and passed Whittier
Drive without slowing. Something on the opposite side of the boulevard caught my eye:

White Cutlass, coming from the east. It turned onto Whittier and headed up the 900 block.

At the first break in the median, I hung a U. By the time I reached the big Georgian house, the Olds was parked in the same place I'd seen it yesterday and a black woman was stepping out on the driver's side.

She was young—late twenties or early thirties—short and slim. She had on a gray cotton turtleneck, black ankle-length skirt, and black flats. In one hand was a Bullock's bag; in the other, a brown leather purse.

Probably the housekeeper. Out doing a department store errand for Ashmore's grieving widow.

As she turned toward the house she saw me. I smiled. She gave me a quizzical look and began walking over slowly, with a short, light step. As she got closer I saw she was very pretty, her skin so dark it was almost blue. Her face was round, bottomed by a square chin; her features clean and broad like those of a Nubian mask. Large, searching eyes focused straight at me.

"Hello. Are you from the hospital?" British accent, public-school refined.

"Yes," I said, surprised, then realized she was looking at the badge on my lapel.

Her eyes blinked, then opened. Irises in two shades of brown—mahogany in the center, walnut rims.

Pink at the periphery. She'd been crying. Her mouth quivered a bit.

"It's very kind of you to come," she said.

"Alex Delaware," I said, extending my hand out the driver's window. She put the shopping bag on the grass and took it. Her hand was narrow and dry and very cold.

"Anna Ashmore. I didn't expect anyone so soon."

Feeling stupid about my assumptions, I said, "I didn't know Dr. Ashmore personally, but I did want to pay my respects."

She let her hand drop. Somewhere in the distance a lawn mower belched. "There's no formal service. My husband wasn't religious." She turned toward the big house. "Would you like to come in?"

*   *   *

The entry hall was two stories of cream plaster floored with black marble. A beautiful brass banister and marble stairs twisted upward to the second story. To the right, a large yellow dining room gleamed with dark, fluid Art Nouveau furniture that the real housekeeper was polishing. Art filled the wall behind the stairs, too—a mix of contemporary paintings and African batiks. Past the staircase, a short foyer led to glass doors that framed a California postcard: green lawn, blue pool sun-splashed silver, white cabanas behind a trellised colonnade, hedges and flower beds under the fluctuating shade of more specimen trees. Scrambling over the tiles of the cabana roof was a splash of scarlet—the bougainvillea I'd seen from the street.

The maid came out of the dining room and took Mrs. Ashmore's bag. Anna Ashmore thanked her, then pointed left, to a living room twice the size of the dining room, sunk two steps down.

"Please," she said, descending, and flipping a switch that ignited several floor lamps.

A black grand piano claimed one corner. The east wall was mostly tall, shuttered windows that let in knife-blades of light. The floors were blond planks under black-and-rust Persian rugs. A coffered white ceiling hovered over apricot plaster walls. More art: the same mix of oils and fabric. I thought I spotted a Hockney over the granite mantel.

The room was chilly and filled with furniture that looked straight out of the Design Center. White Italian suede sofas, a black Breuer chair, big, pockmarked post-Neanderthal stone tables, and a few smaller ones fashioned of convoluted brass rods and topped with blue-tinted glass. One of the stone tables fronted the largest of the sofas. Centered on it was a rosewood bowl filled with apples and oranges.

Mrs. Ashmore said, "Please," again, and I sat down directly behind the fruit.

"Can I offer you something to drink?"

"No, thank you."

She settled directly in front of me, straight and silent.

In the time it had taken to walk from the entry, her eyes had filled with tears.

"I'm sorry for your loss," I said.

She wiped her eyes with a finger and sat even straighter. "Thank you for coming."

Silence filled the room and made it seem even colder. She wiped her eyes again and laced her fingers.

I said, "You have a beautiful home."

She lifted her hands and made a helpless gesture. "I don't know what I'll do with it."

"Have you lived here long?"

"Just one year. Larry owned it long before that, but we never lived in it together. When we came to California, Larry said this should be our place."

She shrugged, raised her hands again, and let them drop back to her knees.

"Too big, it's really ridiculous. . . . We talked about selling it. . . ." Shaking her head. "Please—have something."

I took an apple from the bowl and nibbled. Watching me eat seemed to comfort her.

"Where did you move from?" I said.

"New York."

"Had Dr. Ashmore ever lived in Los Angeles before?"

"No, but he'd been here on buying trips—he had many houses. All over the country. That was his . . . thing."

"Buying real estate?"

"Buying and selling. Investing. He even had a house in France for a short while. Very old—a château. A duke bought it and told everyone it had been in his family for hundreds of years. Larry laughed at that—he hated pretentiousness. But he did love the buying and selling. The freedom it brought him."

I understood that, having achieved some financial independence myself by riding the land boom of the mid-seventies. But I'd operated on a far less exalted level.

"Upstairs," she said, "is all empty."

"Do you live here by yourself?"

"Yes. No children. Please—have an orange. They're from the tree in back, quite easy to peel."

I picked up an orange, removed its rind, and ate a segment. The sound of my jaws working seemed deafening.

"Larry and I don't know many people," she said, reverting to the present-tense denial of the brand-new mourner.

Remembering her remark about my arriving earlier than expected, I said, "Is someone from the hospital coming out?"

She nodded. "With the gift—the certificate of the donation to UNICEF. They're having it framed. A man called yesterday, checking to see if that was all right—giving to UNICEF."

"A man named Plumb?"

"No . . . I don't believe so. A long name—something German."

"Huenengarth?"

"Yes, that's it. He was very nice, said kind things about Larry."

Her gaze shifted, distractedly, to the ceiling. "Are you certain I can't get you something to drink?"

"Water would be fine."

She nodded and rose. "If we're lucky, the Sparkletts man has come. Beverly Hills water is disagreeable. The minerals. Larry and I don't drink it."

While she was gone, I got up and inspected the paintings. Hockney verified. Watercolor still life in a Plexiglas box frame. Next to that, a small abstract canvas that turned out to be a De Kooning. A Jasper Johns word salad, a Jim Dine bathrobe study, a Picasso satyr-and-nymph gambol in China ink. Lots of others I couldn't identify, interspersed with the earth-toned batiks. The wax pressings were tribal scenes and geometric designs that could have been talismans.

She returned with an empty glass, a bottle of Perrier, and a folded linen napkin on an oval lacquer tray. "I'm sorry, there's no spring water. I trust this will be acceptable."

"Of course. Thank you."

She poured the water for me and took her seat again.

"Lovely art," I said.

"Larry bought it in New York, when he worked at Sloan-Kettering."

"The cancer institute?"

"Yes. We were there for four years. Larry was very interested in cancer—the rise in frequency. Patterns. How the world was being poisoned. He worried about the world."

She closed her eyes again.

"Did the two of you meet there?"

"No. We met in my country—the Sudan. I'm from a village in the South. My father was the head of our community. I was schooled in Kenya and England because the big universities in Khartoum and Omdurman are Islamic and my family was Christian. The South is Christian and animist—do you know what that is?"

"Ancient tribal religions?"

"Yes. Primitive, but very enduring. The northerners resent that—the endurance. Everyone was supposed to embrace Islam. A hundred years ago they sold the southerners as slaves; now they try to enslave us with religion."

Her hands tightened. The rest of her remained unchanged.

"Was Dr. Ashmore doing research in the Sudan?"

She nodded. "With the U.N. Studying disease patterns—that's why Mr. Huenengarth felt the donation to UNICEF would be an appropriate tribute."

"Disease patterns," I said. "Epidemiology?"

She nodded. "His training was in toxicology and environmental medicine, but he did that only briefly. Mathematics was his true love, and with epidemiology he could combine mathematics with medicine. In the Sudan he studied the pace of bacterial contagion from village to village. My father admired his work and assigned me to help him take blood from the children—I'd just finished my nursing degree in Nairobi and had returned home." She smiled. "I became the needle lady—Larry didn't like hurting the children. We became friends. Then the Muslims came. My father was killed—my entire family. . . . Larry took me with him on the U.N. plane, to New York City."

She recounted the tragedy matter-of-factly, as if numbed by repeated insults. I wondered if exposure to suffering would help her deal with her husband's murder when the pain hit full force, or would make matters worse.

She said, "The children of my village . . . were slaughtered when the northerners came. The U.N. did nothing, and Larry became angry and disillusioned with them. When we got to New York he wrote letters and tried to talk to bureaucrats. When they wouldn't receive him, his anger grew and he turned inward. That's when the buying started."

"To deal with his anger?"

Hard nod. "Art became a kind of refuge for him, Dr. Delaware. He called it the highest place man could go. He would buy a new piece, hang it, stare at it for hours, and talk about the need to surround ourselves with *things* that couldn't hurt us."

She looked around the room and shook her head.

"Now I'm left with all of it, and most of it doesn't mean much to me." She shook her head again. "Pictures and the memory of his anger—he was an angry man. He even earned his money angrily."

She saw my puzzled look. "Please excuse me—I'm drifting. What I'm referring to is the way he started. Playing blackjack, craps—other games of chance. Though I guess *playing* isn't the right word. There was nothing playful about it—when he gambled he was in his own world, didn't stop to eat or sleep."

"Where did he gamble?"

"Everywhere. Las Vegas, Atlantic City, Reno, Lake Tahoe. The money he made there he invested in other schemes—the stock market, bonds." She waved an arm around the room.

"Did he win most of the time?"

"Nearly always."

"Did he have some kind of system?"

"He had many. Created them with his computers. He was a mathematical *genius,* Dr. Delaware. His systems required an extraordinary memory. He could add columns of numbers in his head, like a human computer. My father thought he was magical. When we took blood from the children, I had him do numbers tricks for them. They watched and were amazed, and didn't feel the sting."

She smiled and covered her mouth.

"He thought he could go on forever," she said, looking up, "making a profit at the casinos' expense. But they caught on and told him to leave. This was in Las Vegas. He flew to Reno but the casino there knew also. Larry was furious. A few months later he returned to the first casino in different clothing and an old man's beard. Played for higher stakes and won even more."

She stayed with that memory for a while, smiling. Talking seemed to be doing her good. That helped me rationalize my presence.

"Then," she said, "he just stopped. Gambling. Said he was

bored. Began buying and selling real estate . . . He was so good at it. . . . I don't know what to do with all this."

"Do you have any family here?"

She shook her head and clasped her hands. "Not here or anywhere. And Larry's parents are gone too. It's so . . . ironic. When the northerners came, shooting women and children, Larry looked at them in the face and screamed at them, calling them terrible names. He wasn't a big man. . . . Did you ever meet him?"

I shook my head.

"He was very small." Another smile. "Very small—behind his back my father called him a monkey. Affectionately. A monkey who thought he was a lion. It became a village joke and Larry didn't mind at all. Perhaps the Muslims believed he *was* a lion. They never hurt him. Allowed him to take me away on the plane. A month after we got to New *York,* I was robbed on the street by a drug addict. Terrified. But the city never frightened Larry. I used to joke that he frightened it. My fierce little monkey. And now . . ."

She shook her head. Covered her mouth again and looked away. Several moments passed before I said, "Why did you move to Los Angeles?"

"Larry was unhappy at Sloan-Kettering. Too many rules, too much politics. He said we should move to California and live in this house—it was the best piece of property he'd bought. He thought it was foolish that someone else should enjoy it while we lived in an apartment. So he evicted the tenant—some kind of film producer who hadn't paid his rent."

"Why did he choose Western Pediatrics?"

She hesitated. "Please don't be offended, Doctor, but his reasoning was that Western Peds was a hospital in . . . decline. Money problems. So his financial independence meant he'd be left alone to pursue his research."

"What kind of research was he doing?"

"Same as always, disease patterns. I don't know much about it—Larry didn't like to talk about his work." She shook her head. "He didn't talk much at all. After the Sudan, the cancer patients in New York, he wanted nothing to do with real people and their pain."

"I've heard he kept to himself."

She smiled tenderly. "He loved to be alone. Didn't even want a secretary. He said he could type faster and more accurately on his word processor, so what was the purpose?"

"He had research assistants, didn't he? Like Dawn Herbert."

"I don't know names, but yes, from time to time he'd hire graduate students from the university, but they never met his standards."

"The university over in Westwood?"

"Yes. His grant paid for lab assistance and there were tasks that he needn't have bothered himself with. But he was never happy with the work of others. The truth is, Doctor, Larry just didn't like depending on anyone else. Self-reliance became his religion. After my robbery in New York, he insisted we both learn self-defense. Said the police were lazy and didn't care. He found an old Korean man in lower Manhattan who taught us karate, kick-fighting—different techniques. I attended two or three lessons, then stopped. It seemed illogical—how could our hands protect us against a drug addict with a gun? But Larry kept going and practiced every night. Earned a belt."

"Black belt?"

"A brown one. Larry said brown was enough; anything more would have been ego."

Lowering her face, she cried softly into her hands. I took a napkin from the lacquer tray, stood by her chair, and had it ready when she looked up. Her hand gripped my fingers hard enough to sting, then let go. I sat back down.

She said, "Is there anything else I can get you?"

I shook my head. "Is there something I can do for you?"

"No, thank you. Just your coming to visit was gracious—we don't know many people."

She looked around the room once more.

I said, "Have you made funeral arrangements?"

"Through Larry's attorney . . . Apparently Larry planned it all out. The details—the plot. There's a plot for me too. I never knew. He took care of everything. . . . I'm not sure when the funeral will be. In these . . . cases, the coroner . . . Such a stupid way to . . ."

Her hand flew to her face. More tears.

"This is terrible. I'm being childish." She dabbed at her eyes with the napkin.

"It's a terrible loss, Mrs. Ashmore."

"Nothing I haven't seen before," she said quickly. Suddenly her voice was hard, plated with anger.

I kept quiet.

"Well," she said, "I suppose I'd better attend to business."

I got up. She walked me to the door. "Thank you for coming, Dr. Delaware."

"If there's anything I can do—"

"That's very kind, but I'm certain I'll be able to handle things as they come up."

She opened the door.

I said goodbye and the door closed behind me.

I began walking toward the Seville. The gardening noises had died and the street was beautiful and silent.

14

When I entered room 505 W, Cassie followed me with her eyes but the rest of her didn't move.

The drapes were drawn, and yellow light came from the half-open door of the bathroom. I saw wet clothes hanging over the shower rod. The bed rails were down and the room had the gluey smell of old bandages.

A metered I.V. line was still attached to Cassie's left arm. Clear fluid from a hanging bottle slow-dripped through the tubing. The whirr of the I.V. meter seemed louder. LuvBunnies surrounded Cassie. An untouched breakfast tray sat on the table.

I said, "Hi, sweetie."

She gave a small smile, closed her eyes, and moved her head back and forth the way a blind child might.

Cindy came out of the bathroom and said, "Hi, Dr. Delaware." Her braid was gathered atop her head and her blouse was untucked.

"Hi. How're you managing?"

"Okay."

I sat on the edge of Cassie's bed. Cindy came over and stood next to me. The pressure of my weight made Cassie's eyes open again. I smiled at her, touched her fingers. Her stomach rumbled and she shut her eyes once more. Her lips were dry and chapped. A small scrap of dead skin hung from the upper one. Each breath ruffled it.

I took her free hand. She didn't resist. Her skin was warm and silky, soft as a dolphin's belly.

I said, "Such a good girl," and saw her eyes move behind the lids.

"We had a rough night," said Cindy.

"I know. Sorry to hear it." I looked down at the hand in mine. No new wounds but plenty of old ones. The thumbnail was tiny, square-edged, in need of cleaning. I exerted gentle pressure and the digit rose, remained extended for a moment, then lowered, tapping the top of my hand. I repeated the pressure and the same thing happened. But her eyes remained shut and her face had grown loose. Within moments she was sleeping, breathing in time with the I.V. drip.

Cindy reached down and stroked her daughter's cheek. One of the bunnies fell to the floor. She picked it up and placed it next to the breakfast tray. The tray was farther away than she'd estimated and the movement threw her off balance. I caught her elbow and held it. Through the sleeve of her blouse, her arm was thin and pliable. I let go of it but she held on to my hand for a moment.

I noticed worry lines around her eyes and mouth, saw where aging would take her. Our eyes met. Hers were full of wonder and fear. She stepped away from me and went to sit on the sleeper couch.

I said, "What's been happening?" though I'd read the chart before coming in.

"Sticks and tests," she said. "All kinds of scans. She didn't get any dinner until late and couldn't hold it down."

"Poor thing."

She bit her lip. "Dr. Eves says the appetite loss is either anxiety or some sort of reaction to the isotopes they used in the scans."

"That sometimes happens," I said. "Especially when there are a lot of tests and the isotopes build up in the system."

She nodded. "She's pretty tired. I guess you can't draw with her today."

"Guess not."

"It's too bad—the way it worked out. You didn't have time to do your techniques."

"How'd she tolerate the procedures?"

"Actually, she was so tired—after the grand mal—that she was kind of passive."

She looked over at the bed, turned away quickly, and put the palms of her hands on the sofa, propping herself up.

Our eyes met again. She stifled a yawn and said, "Excuse me."

"Anything I can help with?"

"Thanks. Can't think of any."

She closed her eyes.

I said, "I'll let you rest," and walked to the door.

"Dr. Delaware?"

"Yes?"

"That home visit we spoke about," she said. "When we finally do get out of here, you're still planning on doing it, aren't you?"

"Sure."

"Good."

Something in her voice—a stridency I'd never heard before—made me stand there and wait.

But she just said "Good" again, and looked away, resigned. As if a critical moment had come and gone. When she started to play with her braid, I left.

No sign of Vicki Bottomley; the nurse on shift was a stranger. After completing my own notes, I reread Stephanie's, the neurologist's, and those of the consulting endocrinologist—someone named Alan Macauley, with strong, large handwriting.

The neurologist had found no abnormality on two successive EEGs and deferred to Macauley, who reported no evidence of any metabolic disorder, though his lab tests were still being analyzed. As far as medical science could tell, Cassie's pancreas was structurally and biochemically normal. Macauley suggested further genetic tests and scans to rule out some sort of brain tumor, and recommended further "intensive psychological consultation per Dr. Delaware."

I'd never met the man and was surprised to be referred to by name. Wanting to know what he meant by "intensive," I looked up his number in a hospital directory and called it.

"Macauley."

"Dr. Macauley, this is Alex Delaware—the psychologist who's seeing Cassie Jones."

"Lucky you. Been to see her recently?"

"About a minute ago."

"How's she doing?"

"Wiped out—post-seizural fatigue, I guess."

"Probably."

"Her mother said she didn't hold her dinner down."

"Her mother, huh? . . . So, what can I do for you?"

"I read your notes—about psychological support. Wondered if you had any suggestions."

Long pause.

"Where are you now?" he said.

"Chappy Ward nursing station."

"Okay, listen, I've got Diabetes Clinic in about twenty minutes. I can get there a little early—say in five. Why don't you catch me? Three East."

He waved when he saw me coming and I realized I'd seen him the day before at Ashmore's memorial. The husky, dark, bald man who'd talked about Texas and guns, a Smith & Wesson in every black bag.

Standing, he looked even bigger, with thick sloping shoulders and stevedore arms. He had on a white polo shirt over pressed jeans and western ostrich boots. His badge was pinned just above the jockey-and-horse logo. His stethoscope was in one hand. The other hand made aeronautic movements—nosedives and fast climbs—as he talked to a gangly boy of around seventeen.

Fifteen minutes before clinic was scheduled to start and the Endocrinology waiting room was filling up. Nutritional posters hung on the walls. Children's books and battered magazines were stacked on the table, along with brochures and packets of artificial sweetener.

Macauley slapped the boy's back and I heard him say, "You're doing great—keep it up. I know sticking yourself sucks the big hairy one, but depending on *Mommy* to stick you sucks even worse, doesn't it? So keep her the heck out of your life and go have some fun."

"Yeah, right," said the boy. He had a big chin and big nose. Big jug ears, each pierced with three gold wire loops. Well over six feet, but Macauley made him look small. His skin was oily-looking and sallow, spotted with pimples on cheeks and brow. His hair had been mowed in a new-wave do with more levels and angles than an architect's wet dream. "Party on," he said glumly.

"Hey, party *hearty,* man," said Macauley, "just as long as it's sugar-free."

"Fuck," said the boy.

"Now, *that's* okay, Kev. *That* you can do to your horny little heart's content, long as you use a condom."

The boy grinned despite himself.

Macauley slapped him again and said, "Okay, scram, get, vamoose, clear out of here. I've got *sick* people to deal with."

"Yeah, right." The boy pulled out a pack of cigarettes, stuck a smoke in his mouth, but didn't light it.

Macauley said, "Hey, turkey, your lungs are someone else's problem."

The boy laughed and shambled off.

Macauley came over to me. "Noncompliant adolescents with brittle diabetes. When I die I *know* I'm going to heaven, 'cause I've already been to hell."

He shot a thick arm forward. The hand at the end of it was big but his grip was restrained. His face was basset with a touch of bull terrier: thick nose, full lips, small, drooping dark eyes. The baldness and perpetual five o'clock shadow gave him a middle-aged look, but I guessed he was thirty-five or so.

"Al Macauley."

"Alex Delaware."

"Meeting of the Als," he said. "C'mon out of here before the natives grow restless."

He took me behind swinging doors just like those in Stephanie's clinic, past a similar mix of clerks, nurses, residents, ringing phones, and scratching pens, to an examining room decorated with a sugar-content chart issued by one of the big fast-food chains. The five food groups with an emphasis on burgers and fries.

"What can I do for you?" he said, sitting on a stool and spinning back and forth in small semicircles.

"Any insights on Cassie?" I said.

"Insights? Isn't that your department?"

"In a perfect world it would be, Al. Unfortunately, reality's refusing to cooperate."

He snorted and ran his hand over his head, smoothing nonexistent hair. Someone had left a rubber reflex hammer on the examining table. He picked it up and touched the tip to his knee.

"You recommended intensive psych support," I said, "and I just wondered—"

"If I was being an especially sensitive guy or if I thought the case was suspicious, right? The answer is b. I read your notes in the chart, asked around about you, and found out you were good. So I figured I'd put in my two cents."

"Suspicious," I said. "As in Munchausen by proxy?"

"Call it what you want—I'm a gland-hand, not a shrink. But there's nothing wrong with the kid's metabolism, I can tell you that."

"You're sure of that?"

"Look, this isn't the first time I've been involved in the case—I worked her up months ago, when she supposedly presented with bloody stools. No one ever actually *saw* the stools except the mom, and red spots on a diaper don't make it in my book. We could be talking diaper rash. And my first go-round was *rigorous*. Every endocrine test in the book, some that weren't."

"Someone saw this latest seizure."

"I know that," he said impatiently. "The nurse and the U.C. And low sugar does explain it, physiologically. But what it *doesn't* explain is *why*. She's got no genetic or metabolic abnormality of any kind, no glycogen storage disorder, and her pancreas is functioning perfectly. At this point, all I'm doing is plowing old ground and throwing in some experimental assays I borrowed from the med school—basic science stuff they're still getting baselines on. We might just have the most tested two-year-old kid in the Western Hemisphere. Wanna call Guinness?"

"What about something idiopathic—a rare variant of a known disease?"

He looked at me, passed the hammer from hand to hand. "Anything's possible."

"But you don't think so."

"What I *don't* think is that there's anything wrong with her glands. This is a healthy kid, presenting with hypoglycemia because of something else."

"Something someone gave her?"

He tossed the hammer up in the air and snagged it with two fingers. Repeated the exercise a couple more times, then said, "What do *you* think?" He smiled. "Always wanted to do that with one of you guys. Seriously, though, yeah, that's what I think. It's logical, isn't it, considering the history? And that sib who died."

"Did you consult on his case?"

"No, why would I? That was respiratory. And I'm not saying that was necessarily ominous—babies do die of SIDS. But in this case it makes you think, doesn't it?"

I nodded. "When I heard about the hypoglycemia, one of the first things I thought about was insulin poisoning. But Stephanie said there were no fresh injection marks on Cassie's body."

He shrugged. "Could be. I didn't do a complete physical. But there are ways to stick someone and be subtle: Use a really small needle—a newborn spike. Pick a site that's easy to miss—the folds of the buttocks, knee folds, between the toes, right under the scalp. My doper patients get creative all the time, and insulin goes right into the skin. Little pinprick like that can heal really quickly."

"Have you mentioned your suspicions to Stephanie?"

He nodded. "Sure I did, but she's still hopped up on something esoteric. Between you and me, I didn't get the feeling she wanted to hear it. Not that it matters to me personally. I'm off the case—quits, vamoose. Out of *here,* as a matter of fact."

"Leaving the hospital?"

"You bet. One more month, then off for quieter pastures. I need the time I have left to wrap up my own cases. It's gonna be a mess— lots of angry families. So the last thing I want to do is muck around in Chuck Jones's family affairs when there's nothing I can do about it anyway."

"*Because* it's his family?"

He shook his head. "It would be nice to say yup, that's it, the whole thing's politics. But actually, it's the case itself. She could be *anyone's* granddaughter and we'd still be spitting into the wind because we have no facts. Just look at you and me, right here. *You* know what's going on; *I* know what's going on; Stephanie *used* to know what was going on until she got all horny about the hypoglycemia. But knowing doesn't mean a thing, legally, does it? 'Cause we can't do anything. That's what I hate about abuse cases—someone accuses parents; they deny it, walk away or just ask for another doc. And even if you *could* prove something was going on, you'd get into a circus of lawyers, paperwork, years in court, dragging *our* reputations through the mud. Meantime the kid's a basket case and you couldn't even get a restraining order."

"Sounds like you've had experience."

"My wife's a county social worker. The system's so overloaded, even kids with broken bones aren't considered a priority anymore. But it's the same all over—I had a case back in Texas, diabetic kid. The mother was *witholding* insulin and we still had a hell of a time keeping the kid safe. And she was a nurse. Top O.R. gal."

"Speaking of nurses," I said, "what do you think of Cassie's primary R.N.?"

"Who's that? Oh, yeah, Vicki. I think Vicki's a cranky bitch but generally real good at what she does—" The droopy eyes perked. "Her? Shit, I never thought about that, but that doesn't make sense, does it? Till this last seizure, the problems started at home?"

"Vicki visited the home, but only a couple of times. Not enough to do all the damage."

"Besides," he said, "it's always the mother, isn't it, these Munchausens? And this one's strange—at least in my uneducated opinion."

"How so?"

"I don't know. She's just too damned nice. Especially considering how inept we've been diagnosing her kid. That were me, I'd be pissed, demanding action. But she keeps smiling. Smiles *too* much for my taste. 'Hi, Doctor, how are you, Doctor?' Never trust a smiler, Al. I was married to one the first time. Those white teeth were always hiding something—you can probably give me all the psychodynamics behind it, right?"

I shrugged and said, "Perfect world."

He laughed. "Lot of good you are."

I said, "Any impressions of the father?"

"Never met him. Why? Is he strange too?"

"I wouldn't say strange. He's just not what you'd expect of Chuck Jones's son. Beard, earring. Doesn't seem to have much affection for the hospital."

"Well, at least he and Chuck have something in common. . . . Far as I'm concerned the case is a loser and I'm tired of losing. That's why I punted to you. And now you're telling me you've got squat. Too bad."

He retrieved the hammer, tossed it, caught it, used it to drum the top of the table.

I said, "Would hypoglycemia explain any of Cassie's earlier symptoms?"

"Maybe the diarrhea. But she also had fevers, so there was probably some kind of infectious process going on. In terms of the breathing problems, it's also possible. Mess with the metabolism, *anything's* possible."

He picked up his stethoscope and looked at his watch. "Got work to do. Some of the kids out there, this'll be the last time I see them."

I got up and thanked him.

"For what? I've accomplished squat on this one."

I laughed. "Same way I feel, Al."

"Consultancy blues. You know the story of the oversexed rooster who was bothering the hens in the henhouse? Sneaking up behind 'em and jumping their bones, just generally making a nuisance of himself? So the farmer had him castrated and turned him into a *consultant.* Now he just sits on the fence, watching and giving advice to the other roosters. Trying to remember what it felt like."

I laughed again. We left the exam room and returned to the waiting room. A nurse came up to Macauley and handed him a pile of charts without comment. She looked angry as she walked away.

"Good morning to you, too, darling," he said. To me: "I'm a rotten deserter. Next few weeks are gonna be my punishment."

He looked out at the turmoil and his hound face sagged.

"Does quieter pastures mean private practice?" I said.

"Group practice. Small town in Colorado, not far from Vail. Ski in the winter, fish in the summer, find new modes of mischief for the rest of the year."

"Doesn't sound too bad."

"Shouldn't be. No one else in the group does endocrinology, so maybe I'll even have a chance to use my training once in a while."

"How long have you been at Western Peds?"

"Two years. One and a half too long."

"The financial situation?"

"That's a big part of it but not all of it. I was no Pollyanna when I came here, knew an inner-city hospital would always be struggling to balance the books. It's the attitude that bugs me."

"Grandpa Chuck?"

"And his boys. They're trying to run this place like just another company. We could be manufacturing widgets for all they're concerned. *That's* what grinds—their not understanding. Even the gypsies know things are bad—you know about our Hollywood gypsies?"

"Sure," I said. "Big white Cadillacs, twelve to a car, camp-outs in the hallways, the barter system."

He grinned. "I've been paid with food, spare parts for my MG, an old mandolin. Actually, it's a better reimbursement rate than I get from the government. Anyway, one of my diabetics is one of them. Nine years old, in line to be king of the tribe. His mother's this good-looking woman, educated, about a hundred years of living behind her. Usually when she comes in she's full of laughs, buttering me up, telling me I'm God's answer to medical science. This time she was really quiet, as if she was upset about something. And it was just a routine exam—the boy's doing well, medically. So I asked her what the matter was and she said, 'This place, Dr. Al. Bad vibrations.' She was narrowing her eyes at me like some storefront fortuneteller. I said, what do you mean? But she wouldn't explain, just touched my hand and said, 'I like you, Dr. Al, and Anton likes you. But we won't be coming back here. Bad vibrations.'"

He hefted the charts and transferred them to one hand. "Pretty dicey, huh?"

I said, "Maybe we should consult her on Cassie."

He smiled. Patients continued to stream in, even though there was no room for them. Some of them greeted him and he responded with winks.

I thanked him again for his time.

He said, "Sorry we won't have a chance to work together."

"Good luck in Colorado."

"Yup," he said. "You ski?"

"No."

"Me neither . . ." He looked back at the waiting room, shook his head. "What a place . . . Originally, I was gonna be a surgeon, slice and dice. Then, when I was a second-year med student, I came down with diabetes. No dramatic symptoms, just some weight loss that I didn't think much about because I wasn't eating properly. I went into shock in the middle of gross anatomy lab, collapsed on top of my cadaver. It was just before Christmas. I got home and my family handled it by passing the honey-baked ham right by me, no one saying anything. *I* handled *that* by rolling my pants up, hoisting my leg up on the table and jabbing it, in front of everyone. Eventually, I figured it was time to forget about scalpels and think about people. That's what appealed to me about *this* place—working with kids and families. But when I got here I found out that was all gone. Bad vibes is right. That gypsy lady could tell the *moment* she walked in the door. It might sound nuts to you, but she crystallized what had been going on in my head for a while. Sure, Colorado's gonna be boring—sniffles and sneezes and diaper rash. And I haven't been here long enough to collect any pension, so financially the two years have been a wash. But at least I won't be sitting on the fence. Cock-a-doodle-doo."

15

Robin called at seven to say she was on her way over. She was at my door a half hour later, hair drawn back and French-braided, accentuating the sweet, clean lines of her neck. She wore black teardrop earrings and a cool-pink denim dress that hugged her hips. In her arms were bags of Chinese takeout.

When we'd lived together, Chinese had been the cue for dinner in bed. Back in the good old days I'd have led her into the bedroom, Joe Suave. But two years apart and a reconciliation that was still confusing had shaken my instincts. I took the bags, placed them on the dining room table, and kissed her lightly on the lips.

She put an arm around me, pressed the back of my head, and enlarged the kiss.

When we broke for breath she said, "I hope this is okay—not going out?"

"I've been out plenty today."

"Me too. Delivering the Stealths to the *boys'* hotel. They wanted me to stay and party."

"They've got better taste in women than in music."

She laughed, kissed me again, pulled back, and did some exaggerated heavy breathing.

"Enough with the hormones," she said. "First things first. Let me heat this up and we'll have ourselves an indoor picnic."

She took the food into the kitchen. I hung back and watched her move. All these years I'd never tired of watching her move.

The dress was nouveau-rodeo sweetheart—lots of leather fringe and old lace on the yoke. She wore ankle-high boots that echoed sharply on the kitchen floor. Her braid swung as she walked. So did the rest of her but I found myself looking at the braid. Shorter than Cindy Jones's and auburn instead of dark-brown, but it got me thinking about the hospital again.

She deposited the bags on the counter, started to say something, then realized I hadn't followed her in. Looking over her shoulder, she said, "Something the matter, Alex?"

"No," I lied, "just admiring."

One of her hands darted to her hair and I realized she was nervous. That made me want to kiss her again.

I said, "You look gorgeous."

She flashed a smile that tightened my chest and held out her arms. I went into the kitchen.

"Tricky," she said later, trying to knit my chest hair with chopsticks.

"The idea," I said, "is to show your devotion by knitting me a sweater. Not turning me into one."

She laughed. "Cold moo goo. What a gourmet treat."

"At this moment, wet sand on toast would be okay." I stroked her face.

Placing the chopsticks on the nightstand, she moved closer. Our sweaty flanks stuck together and made wet-plastic noises. She turned her hand into a glider and flew it over my chest, barely touching skin. Propping herself up, she bumped her nose against mine, kissed my chin. Her hair was still braided. As we'd made love, I'd held it, passing the smooth rope between my fingers, finally letting go when I began to lose control, for fear of hurting her. Some of the curly strands had come loose and they tickled my face. I smoothed them back and nuzzled her under her chin.

Her head lifted. She massaged my chest some more, stopped, inspected, looped a finger under a single hair, and said, "Hmm."

"What?"

"A *gray* one—isn't that *cute*."

"Adorable."

"It is, Alex. You're *maturing*."

"What's that, the euphemism of the day?"

"The *truth,* Doctor. Time's a sexist pig—women decay; men acquire a vintage. Even guys who weren't all that cute when they were young have a second shot at studliness if they don't let themselves go completely to seed. The ones like you, who were adorable to begin with, can really clean up."

I started panting.

"I'm serious, Alex. You'll probably get all craggy and wise—look like you really understand the mysteries of life."

"Talk about false advertising."

She inspected each of my temples, turning my head gently with strong fingers and burrowing through the hair.

"This is the ideal place to start silvering," she said in a teacher's voice. "Maximum class-and-wisdom quotient. Hmm, nope, I don't see anything yet, just this one little guy, down here." Touching a nail to the chest hair, she brushed my nipple again. "Too bad you're still a callow youth."

"Hey, babe, let's party."

She put her head back down and reached lower, under the blanket.

"Well," she said, "there's something to be said for callow too."

We moved to the living room and listened to some tapes she'd brought. The new Warren Zevon casting cold light upon the dark side of life—a novel in miniature. A Texas genius named Eric Johnson who produced musical textures from the guitar that made me want to burn my instruments. A young woman named Lucinda Williams with a beautiful, bruised voice and lyrics straight from the heart.

Robin sat on my lap, curled small, her head on my chest, breathing shallowly.

When the music was over she said, "Is everything okay?"

"Sure. Why?"

"You seem a little distracted."

"Don't mean to be," I said, wondering how she could tell.

She sat up and undid her braid. Her curls had matted and she began separating the strands. When she'd fluffed them and restored the natural perm, she said, "Anything you want to talk about?"

"It really isn't anything," I said. "Just work—a tough case. I'm probably letting it get to me too much."

I expected her to let that go, but she said, "Confidential, right?" with just a trace of regret.

"Limited confidentiality," I said. "I'm a consultant and this one may spill over into the criminal justice system."

"Oh. *That* kind of case."

She touched my face. Waited.

I told her the story of Cassie Jones, leaving out names and identifying marks.

When I finished, she said, "Isn't there anything that can be done?"

"I'm open to suggestions," I said. "I've got Milo running background checks on the parents and the nurse, and I'm doing my best to get a feel for all of them. Problem is, there isn't a shred of real evidence, just logic, and logic isn't worth much, legally. The only fishy thing so far is the mother lying to me about being the victim of an influenza epidemic when she was in the army. I called the base and managed to find out there'd been no epidemic."

"Why would she lie about something like that?"

"The real reason she was discharged could be something she wants to hide. Or, if she's a Munchausen personality, she just likes lying."

"Disgusting," she said. "A person doing that to their own flesh and blood. To any kid . . . How does it feel to be back at the hospital?"

"Kind of depressing, actually. Like meeting an old friend who's gone downhill. The place seems gloomy, Rob. Morale's low, cash flow's worse than ever, lots of staff have left—remember Raoul Melendez-Lynch?"

"The cancer specialist?"

"Uh-huh. He was *married* to the hospital. I watched him weather crisis after crisis and keep on ticking. Even he's gone—took a job in Florida. *All* the senior physicians seem to be gone. The faces I pass in the halls are new. And young. Or maybe I'm just getting old."

"Mature," she said. "Repeat after me: ma-ture."

"I thought I was callow."

"Mature *and* callow. Secret of your charm."

"Top of all that, the crime problems out on the street are leaking in more and more. Nurses beaten and robbed . . . A couple of nights ago there was a murder in one of the parking lots. A doctor."

"I know. I heard it on the radio. Didn't know you were back working there or I would have freaked."

"I was there the night it happened."

Her fingers dug into my hand, then loosened. "Well, that's reassuring. . . . Just be careful, okay? As if my saying it makes a difference."

"It does. I promise."

She sighed and put her head on my shoulder. We sat there without talking.

"I'll be careful," I said. "I mean it. Old guys can't afford to be reckless."

"Okay," she said. A moment later: "So that's why you're down. I thought it might be me."

"You? Why?"

She shrugged. "The changes—everything that's happened."

"No way," I said. "You're the bright spot in my life."

She moved closer and rested a hand on my chest. "What you said before—the hospital being gloomy? I've *always* thought of hospitals that way."

"Western Peds was different, Rob. It used to be . . . vital. Everything meshing together like this wonderful organic *machine.*"

"I'm sure it was, Alex," she said softly. "But when you get down to it, no matter how vital or caring a hospital is, it's always going to be a place of death, isn't it? Mention the word *hospital* to me and what comes to my mind is my dad. Lying there, all tubed and punctured and helpless. Mom screaming for the nurse every time he moaned, no one really caring . . . The fact that *your* place treats kids only makes it worse, as far as I'm concerned. 'Cause what's worse than suffering kids? I never understood how you stayed there as long as you did."

"You build up a shell," I said. "Do your job, let in just enough emotion so you can be useful to your patients. It's like that old toothpaste commercial. The invisible shield."

"Maybe that's what's really bothering you, coming back after all these years, and your shield's gone."

"You're probably right." I sounded glum.

"Some shrink I am," she said.

"No, no. It's good talking about it."

She snuggled up against me. "You're sweet to say so, whether it's true or not. And I'm glad you told me what's on your mind. You never used to talk much about your work. The few times I tried, you changed the subject, so I could tell you weren't comfortable with it and I never pushed. I know part of it was confidentiality, but I really wasn't after gory details, Alex. I just wanted to know what you were going through so I could support you. I guess you were protecting me."

"Maybe I was," I said. "But to tell the truth, I never really knew you wanted to hear any of it."

"Why's that?"

"You always seemed more interested in—how can I say this—angles and planes."

She gave a small laugh. "Yeah, you're right. I never was much for touchy-feely. In fact, when we first met, the one thing that I wasn't sure I liked about you was that you were a psychologist. Not that it stopped me from chasing you shamelessly, but it did surprise me—being attracted to a shrink. I didn't know a thing about psychology, never even took a course in college. Probably because of Dad. He was always making comments about crazy psychiatrists, crooked doctors. Going on about how anyone who didn't work with his hands couldn't be trusted. But as I got to know you and saw how serious you were about what you did, I loosened up. Tried to learn—I even read some of your psych books. Did you know that?"

I shook my head.

She smiled. "At night, in the library. I used to sneak in when you were sleeping and I couldn't. *Schedules of Reinforcement. Cognitive Theory.* Pretty strange stuff for a woodchopper like me."

"I never knew," I said, amazed.

She shrugged. "I was . . . embarrassed. I don't really know why. Not that I was trying to be an expert or anything. Just wanted to be closer to you. I'm sure I didn't send out a clear message . . . not sympathetic enough. I guess what I'm saying is, I hope we can continue this way. Letting each other in a little more."

"Sure we can," I said. "I never found you unsympathetic, just—"

"Preoccupied? Self-obsessed?"

She looked up at me with another chest-tightening smile. Big white upper incisors. The ones I liked to lick.

"Strongly focused," I said. "You're one a them artsy-fartsy creative types. Need intense concentration."

"Strongly focused, huh?"

"Definitely."

She laughed. "We've definitely got a thing for each other, Dr. Delaware. Probably chemical—pheromones or whatever."

"That we do, that we do."

She put her head on my chest. I stroked her hair and thought of her going into the library, reading my books.

"Can we try again?" I said. "Will you come back?"

She tensed hard as bone.

"Yes," she said. "God, yes."

She sat up, took my face in her hands and kissed it. Scrambled on me, straddling me, her arms down over my shoulders, gripping.

I ran my hands over her back, held her hips, raised myself to her. We fused once more, rocked and rolled together, silent and intent.

Afterward she lay back, panting. I was breathing hard, too, and it took a long time to wind down.

I rolled on my side and wrapped my arms around her. She pressed her belly up against mine, glued herself to me.

We stayed together for a long while. When she started to get restless, the way she always did, and began to pull away, I didn't let her go.

16

She stayed the night and, as usual, was up early.

What wasn't usual was her sticking around for another hour to drink coffee and read the paper. She sat next to me at the table, one hand on my knee, finishing the arts section as I skimmed the sports scores. Afterward, we went down to the pond and threw pellets to the fish. The heat had come on early for spring, overpowering the ocean currents, and the air smelled like summer vacation.

Saturday, but I felt like working.

She remained at my side. We touched a lot but the signs of her restlessness were beginning: flexing muscles, random glances, minuscule lags in the conversation that only a lover or a paranoiac would have noticed.

I said, "Got a busy one planned?"

"Just a few things to catch up on. How about you?"

"The same. I'm planning to hit the hospital sometime today."

She nodded, put both arms around my waist, and we walked back up to the house, entwined. After she got her purse we descended to the carport.

A new truck was parked next to the Seville. Royal-blue Chevy pickup with a white racing stripe along the side. New car registration sticker on the windshield.

"Nice," I said. "When'd you get it?"

"Yesterday. The Toyota developed serious engine problems and the estimates I got ranged from one to two thousand, so I thought I'd treat myself."

I walked her to the truck.

She said, "Dad would've liked it. He was always a Chevy man— didn't have much use for anything else. When I drove the other one I sometimes felt he was looking over my shoulder, scowling and telling me Iwo Jima stories."

She got in, put her bag on the passenger seat, and stuck her face out the window for a kiss.

"Yum," she said. "Let's do it again soon, cutie. What was your name again? Felix? Ajax?"

"Mr. Clean."

"How true," she said, laughing as she sped away.

I paged Stephanie, and the operator came back on the line saying Dr. Eves would call back. I hung up, pulled out my Thomas Guide, and pinpointed Dawn Herbert's address on Lindblade Street. I'd just located it when the phone rang.

"Steph?"

"No, *Mile*. Am I interrupting something?"

"Just waiting for a callback from the hospital."

"And of course you don't have call-waiting."

"Of course."

Milo gave a long, equine snort that the phone amplified into something thunderous. "Have you had your gas lamps converted to Dr. Edison's miracle wires yet?"

"If God had wanted man to be electric, he would have given him batteries."

He snort-laughed. "I'm at the Center. Phone me as soon as you're finished with *Steph*."

He hung up. I waited another ten minutes before Stephanie's call came in.

"Morning, Alex," she said. "What's up?"

"That's what I wanted to ask you."

"Nothing much. I saw her about an hour ago," she said. "She's feeling better—awake, alert, and screaming at the sight of me."

"What's the latest on the hypoglycemia?"

"The metabolic people say there are no metabolic problems, her pancreas has been examined from every possible angle—clean as a whistle—and my Swedish friend and everyone else is back on Munchausen. So I guess *I'm* back to square one, too."

"How long are you planning to keep her in?"

"Two or three days, then back home if nothing else comes up. I know it's dangerous letting her out, but what can I do, turn the hospital into her foster home? Unless you've got some suggestions."

"None yet."

"You know," she said, "I really let myself go with that sugar thing. Thinking it was real."

"Don't bludgeon yourself. It's a crazy case. How did Cindy and Chip react to the continuing uncertainty?"

"I only saw Cindy. The usual quiet resignation."

Remembering Al Macauley's comment, I said, "Any smiles?"

"Smiles? No. Oh, you mean those spacey ones she sometimes gives? No. Not this morning. Alex, I'm worried sick over this. By discharging Cassie, what am I sentencing her to?"

Having no balm, I offered a Band-Aid. "At least discharging her will give me the chance to make a home visit."

"While you're there, why don't you sneak around and look for hot clues?"

"Such as?"

"Needles in bureau drawers, insulin spansules in the fridge. I'm kidding—no, actually I'm only half-kidding. I'm *this* close to confronting Cindy, let the chips fall. The next time that little girl gets sick, I just may do it, and if they get mad and go elsewhere, at least I'll know I did everything I could— Oops, that's me on page— Neonatology, one of my preemies. Gotta go, Alex. Call me if you learn anything, okay?"

*   *   *

I phoned Milo back. "Working weekends?"

"Did a trade with Charlie. Saturdays on in exchange for some flexibility in my moonlighting. How's old *Steph*?"

"Off organic disease, back on Munchausen. No one can find an organic reason for the hypoglycemia."

"Too bad," he said. "Meantime, I've got the lowdown on Reggie Bottomley, the nurse's bad seed. Guy's been dead for a couple of years. For some reason his name never got off the files. Suicide."

"How?"

"He went into the bathroom, got naked, sat on the toilet, smoked crack, jacked off, then turned his head into bad fruit with a shotgun. Very messy. The Tujunga detective—a gal, actually, named Dunn—said Vicki was home when it happened, watching TV in the next room."

"Jesus."

"Yeah. The two of them had just had some kind of spat over Reggie's dissolute life-style and Reggie stomped off, got his works out of his dresser drawer and the gun, locked himself in the can, and kaboom. Mom heard the shot, couldn't get the door open, tried to use a hatchet and still couldn't do it. The paramedics found her sitting on the floor, crying and screaming for him to please come out, talk it over. They broke the door down and when they saw what he looked like, tried to hold her back. But she got a look at some of it. So that could explain her sour disposition."

"Oh, man," I said. "What a thing to go through. Anything on the family history that led up to the suicide?"

"Dunn said there was no history of child abuse—she saw it as basically a nice mom with a rotten kid. And she busted Reggie lots of times, knew him well."

"What about dad?"

"Died when Reggie was little. Heavy drinker, like you said. Reggie was in trouble right out of the chute, smoking dope and moving on up the pharmaceutical ladder. Dunn describes him as a little skinny jerk, learning disabilities, not too bright, couldn't hold a job. Incompetent criminal, too—got caught all the time, but he was so pitiful-looking, judges usually went easy on him. He didn't get violent until near the end—the assault rap. And even that was relatively dinky—bar fight, he used a pool cue on some other scrote's head. Dunn said he was getting feistier because of the crack, it was just a matter of time before he ended up prematurely *muerto*. According to her, mom was the long-suffering type, tried her best. End of story. It tell you anything about mom as a suspect?"

"Not really. Thanks anyway."

"What's your next step?"

"Lacking anything else, I guess a visit with Dawn Herbert. I spoke to Ashmore's wife yesterday, and she said he hired grad students from the university. So maybe Herbert has enough technical knowledge to know what Ashmore was looking for in Chad's chart."

"Ashmore's wife? What'd you do, pay a grief call?"

"Yes. Nice lady. Ashmore was quite an interesting fellow." I told him about the couple's time in the Sudan, Ashmore's gambling systems and investments.

"Blackjack, huh? Must have been good."

"She said he was a math genius—computer wizard. Brown belt in several martial arts, too. Not exactly easy prey for a mugger."

"No? I know you used to do all that good stuff, and I never wanted to disillusion you, but I've seen plenty of martial *artists* with tags on their toes. It's one thing in a *dojo*, bowing and jumping around and screaming like there's a hatpin in your colon. Whole different story out on the streets. Incidentally, I checked with Hollywood Division on Ashmore's murder and they're giving a low solve probability. Hope the widow isn't pinning her hopes on law enforcement."

"The widow is still too dazed to hope."

"Yeah . . ."

"What?"

"Well," he said, "I've been thinking a lot about your case—the psychology of this whole Munchausen thing—and it seems to me we've missed a potential suspect."

"Who?"

"Your buddy Steph."

"Stephanie? Why?"

"Female, medical background, likes to test authority, wants to be in the center of things."

"I never thought of her as attention-seeking."

"Didn't you tell me she was some big radical in the old days, Chairman of the interns' union?"

"Sure, but she seemed sincere. Idealistic."

"Maybe. But look at it this way: Treating Cassie puts her smack at the center of things, and the sicker the kid is, the more Stephanie gets the spotlight. Playing rescuer, big hero, rushing over to the Emergency Room and taking charge. The fact that Cassie's a big shot's kid makes it even tastier, from that standpoint. And these sudden shifts she's making—Munchausen one day, pancreatic disease the next, then back to Munchausen. Doesn't that have a *hysterical* feeling to it? Your goddam waltz?"

I digested all that.

"Maybe there's a *reason* the kid goes nuts when she sees her, Alex."

"But the same logic that applies to Vicki applies to her," I said. "Until this last seizure, all of Cassie's problems began at home. How could Stephanie have been involved?"

"Has *she* ever been out to the home?"

"Just early on—once or twice, setting up the sleep monitor."

"Okay, what about this? The first problems the kid had were real—the croup, or whatever. Steph treated them and found out being doctor to the chairman of the board's grandchild was a kick. Power trip—you yourself said she plans on being head of the department."

"If that was her goal, *curing* Cassie would have made her look a lot better."

"The parents haven't dropped her yet, have they?"

"No. They think she's great."

"There you go. She gets them to depend on her, and tinkers with Cassie—best of both worlds. And you yourself told me Cassie gets sick soon after appointments. What if that's because Stephanie's doing something to her—dosing her up during a checkup and sending her home like a medical time bomb?"

"What could she have done with Cindy right there in the exam room?"

"How do you know she was there?"

"Because she never leaves Cassie's side. And some of those

medical visits were with other doctors—specialists, not Stephanie."

"Do you know for a fact that Stephanie didn't also see the kid the same day the specialists did?"

"No. I guess I could look at the outpatient chart and find out."

"If she even charted it. It could have been something subtle— checking the kid's throat and the tongue depressor's coated with something. Whatever, it's something to consider, right?"

"Doctor sends baby home with more than a lollipop? That's pretty obscene."

"Any worse than a mother poisoning her own child? The other thing you might want to think of, in terms of her motivation, is revenge: She hates Grandpa because of what he's doing to the hospital, so she gets to him through Cassie."

"Sounds like you've been doing a lot of thinking."

"Evil mind, Alex. They used to pay me for it. Actually, what got me going was talking to Rick. He'd heard of Munchausen—the adult type. Said he'd seen nurses *and* doctors with those tendencies. Mistakes in dosage that aren't accidental, heroes rushing in and saving the day—like pyromaniac firemen."

"Chip talked about that," I said. "Medical errors, dosage miscalculations. Maybe he senses something about Stephanie without realizing it. . . . So why's she calling me in? To play with me? We never worked that closely together. I can't mean that much to her, psychologically."

"Calling you in proves she's doing a thorough job. And you've got a rep as a smart guy—real challenge for her if she's a Munchie. Plus, all the other shrinks are gone."

"True, but I don't know . . . Stephanie?"

"There's no reason to get an ulcer over it—it's all theory. I can peel 'em off, right and left."

"It makes my stomach turn, but I'll start looking at her more closely. Guess I'd better watch what I say to her, stop thinking in terms of teamwork."

"Ain't it always that way? One guy, walking the road alone."

"Yeah . . . Meantime, as long as we're peeling off theories, how about this one? We're not making headway because we're concentrating on one bad guy. What if there's some kind of collusion going on?"

"Who?"

"Cindy and Chip are the obvious choice. The typical Munchausen husband is described as passive and weak-willed. Which doesn't fit Chip at all. He's a savvy guy, smart, opinionated. So if his wife's abusing Cassie, why isn't he aware of it? But it could also be Cindy and Vicki—"

"What? Some romantic thing?"

"Or just some twisted mother-*daughter* thing. Cindy rediscovering her dead aunt in Vicki—another tough R.N. And Vicki, with her own child rearing a failure, ripe for a surrogate daughter. It's possible their pathology's meshed in some bizarre way. Hell, maybe Cindy and *Stephanie* have a thing going. And maybe it *is* romantic. I don't know anything about Stephanie's private life. Back in the old days she hardly seemed to have one."

"Long as you're piling it on, what about dad and Stephanie?"

"Sure," I said. "Dad and doc, dad and nurse—Vicki sure kisses up plenty to Chip. Nurse and doc, et cetera. *Ad nauseum. E pluribus unum.* Maybe it's *all* of them, Milo. Munchausen team—the Orient Express gone pediatric. Maybe half the damn world's psychopathic."

"Too conservative an estimate," he said.

"Probably."

"You need a vacation, Doc."

"Impossible," I said. "So much psychopathology, so little time. Thanks for reminding me."

He laughed. "Glad to brighten your day. You want me to run Steph through the files?"

"Sure. And as long as you're punching keys, why not Ashmore? Dead men can't sue."

"Done. Anyone else? Take advantage of my good mood and the LAPD's hardware."

"How about me?"

"Already did that," he said. "Years ago, when I thought we might become friends."

I took a ride to Culver City, hoping Dawn Herbert stayed home on Saturday morning. The drive took me past the site of the cheesy apartment structure on Overland where I'd spent my student/intern days. The body shop next door was still standing, but my building had been torn down and replaced with a used-car lot.

At Washington Boulevard, I headed west to Sepulveda, then continued south until a block past Culver. I turned left at a tropical fish store with a coral-reef mural painted on the windows and drove down the block, searching for the address Milo had pulled out of the DMV files.

Lindblade was packed with small, boxy, one-story bungalows with composition roofs and lawns just big enough for hopscotch. Liberal use of texture-coat; the color of the month was butter. Big Chinese elms shaded the street. Most of the houses were neatly maintained, though the landscaping—old birds of paradise, arbor-vitaes, spindly tree roses—seemed haphazard.

Dawn Herbert's residence was a pale-blue box one lot from the corner. An old brown VW bus was parked in the driveway. Travel decals crowded the lower edge of the rear window. The brown paint was dull as cocoa powder.

A man and a woman were gardening out in front, accompanied by a large golden retriever and a small black mutt with spaniel pretensions.

The people were in their late thirties or early forties. Both had pasty, desk-job complexions lobstered with patches of fresh sunburn on upper arm and shoulder, light-brown hair that hung past their shoulders, and rimless glasses. They wore tank tops, shorts, and rubber sandals.

The man stood at a hydrangea bush, clippers in hand. Shorn flowers clumped around his feet like pink fleece. He was thin and sinewy, with mutton-chop sideburns that trailed down his jaw, and his shorts were held up by leather suspenders. A beaded band circled his head.

The woman wore no bra and as she knelt, bending to weed, her breasts hung nearly to the lawn, brown nipples visible. She looked to be the man's height—five nine or ten—but probably outweighed him by thirty pounds, most of it in the chest and thighs. A possible match for the physical dimensions on Dawn Herbert's driver's license but at least a decade too old for the '63 birthdate.

As I pulled up I realized that the two of them looked vaguely familiar. But I couldn't figure out why.

I parked and turned off the engine. Neither of them looked up. The little dog started to bark, the man said, "Down, Homer," and continued clipping.

That was a cue for the bark to go nuclear. As the mutt scrunched his eyes and tested the limits of his vocal cords, the retriever looked on, bemused. The woman stopped weeding and searched for the source of irritation.

She found it and stared. I got out of the car. The mutt stood his ground but went into the face-down submissive posture.

I said, "Hey, boy," bent and petted him. The man lowered his clippers. All four of them were staring at me now.

"Morning," I said.

The woman stood. Too *tall* for Dawn Herbert, too. Her thick, flushed face would have looked right at a barn raising.

"What can I do for you?" she said. Her voice was melodious and I was certain I'd heard it before. But where?

"I'm looking for Dawn Herbert."

The look that passed between them made me feel like a cop.

"That so?" said the man. "She doesn't live here anymore."

"Do you know where she does live?"

Another exchange of glances. More fear than wariness.

"Nothing ominous," I said. "I'm a doctor, over at Western Pediatric Hospital—in Hollywood. Dawn used to work there and she may have some information on a patient that's important. This is the only address I have for her."

The woman walked over to the man. It seemed like a self-defense move but I wasn't clear who was protecting who.

The man used his free hand to brush petals off his shorts. His bony jaw was set hard. The sunburn had gotten his nose, too, and the tip was raw.

"You come all the way here just to get information?" he said.

"It's complicated," I said, fudging for enough time to build a credible story. "An important case—a small child at risk. Dawn checked his medical chart out of the hospital and never returned it. Normally I'd have gone to Dawn's boss. A doctor named Ashmore. But he's dead. Mugged a couple of days ago in the hospital parking lot—you may have heard about it."

New look on their faces. Fear and bafflement. The news had

obviously caught them off guard and they didn't know how to respond. Finally they chose suspicion, locking hands and glaring at me.

The retriever didn't like the tension. He looked back at his masters and started to whine.

"Jethro," said the woman, and the dog quieted. The black mutt perked up his ears and growled.

She said, "Mellow out, Homer," in a singsong voice, almost crooning it.

"Homer and Jethro," I said. "Do they play their own instruments or use backup?"

Not a trace of a smile. Then I finally remembered where I'd seen them. Robin's shop, last year. Repair customers. A guitar and a mandolin, the former in pretty bad shape. Two folkies with a lot of integrity, some talent, not much money. Robin had done five hundred bucks' worth of work for some self-produced record albums, a plate of home-baked muffins, and seventy-five in cash. I'd watched the transaction, unnoticed, from up in the bedroom loft. Later, Robin and I had listened to a couple of the albums. Public domain songs, mostly—ballads and reels, done traditionally and pretty well.

"You're Bobby and Ben, aren't you?"

Being recognized cracked their suspicion and brought back the confusion.

"Robin Castagna's a friend of mine," I said.

"That so?" said the man.

"She patched up your gear last winter. Gibson A-four with a headstock crack? D-eighteen with loose braces, bowed neck, bad frets, and a popped bridge? Whoever baked those muffins was good."

"Who *are* you?" said the woman.

"Exactly who I said I was. Call Robin—she's at her shop, right now. Ask her about Alex Delaware. Or if you don't want to bother, could you please tell me where I can find Dawn Herbert? I'm not out to hassle her, just want to get the chart back."

They didn't answer. The man placed a thumb behind one of his suspender straps.

"Go call," the woman told him.

He went into the house. She stayed behind, watching me, breathing deeply, bosoms flopping. The dogs watched me too. No one spoke. My eyes caught motion from the west end of the block and I turned and saw a camper back out of a driveway and lumber toward Sepulveda. Someone on the opposite side of the street was flying an American flag. Just beyond that, an old man sat slumped in a lawn chair. Hard to be sure but I thought he was watching me too.

Belle of the ball in Culver City.

The suspendered man came back a few minutes later, smiling as if he'd run into the Messiah. Carrying a pale-blue plate. Cookies and muffins.

He nodded. That and his smile relaxed the woman. The dogs began wagging their tails.

I waited for someone to ask me to dance.

"Get this, Bob," he said to the woman. "This boy's her main squeeze."

"Small world," said the woman, finally smiling. I remembered her singing voice from the album, high and clear, with a subtle vibrato. Her speaking voice was nice too. She could have made money delivering phone sex.

"That's a terrific woman you've got there," she said, still checking me out. "Do you appreciate her?"

"Every day."

She nodded, stuck out her hand, and said, "Bobby Murtaugh. This is Ben. You've already been introduced to *these* characters."

Greetings all around. I petted the dogs and Ben passed the plate. The three of us took muffins and ate. It felt like a tribal ritual. But even as they chewed, they looked worried.

Bobby finished her muffin first, ate a cookie, then another, chewing nonstop. Crumbs settled atop her breasts. She brushed them off and said, "Let's go inside."

The dogs followed us in and kept going, into the kitchen. A moment later I heard them slurping. The front room was flat-ceilinged and darkened by drawn shades. It smelled of Crisco and sugar and wet canine. Tan walls, pine floor in need of finishing, odd-sized home-made bookshelves, several instrument cases where a coffee table would have been. A music stand in the corner was stacked with sheet music. The furniture was heavy Depression-era stuff—thrift-shop treasures. On the walls were a Vienna Regulator that had stopped at two o'clock, a framed and glassed Martin guitar poster, and several handbills commemorating the Topanga Fiddle and Banjo Contest.

Ben said, "Have a seat."

Before I could comply, he said, "Sorry to tell you this, friend, but Dawn's dead. Someone killed her. That's why we got freaked out when you mentioned her name, and the other murder. I'm sorry."

He looked down at the muffin plate and shook his head.

"We still haven't gotten it out of our heads," said Bobby. "You can still sit down. If you want to."

She sank into a tired green sofa. Ben sat next to her, balancing the plate on one bony knee.

I lowered myself to a needlepoint chair and said, "When did it happen?"

"A couple of months ago," said Bobby. "March. It was on a weekend—middle of the month, the tenth, I think. No, the ninth." Looking at Ben.

"Something like that," he said.

"I'm pretty sure it was the ninth, babe. It was the weekend of Sonoma, remember? We played on the ninth and came back to L.A. on the tenth—'member how late it was because of the problems with the van in San Simeon? Least that's when he said it happened—the cop. The ninth. It *was* the ninth."

He said, "Yeah, you're right."

She looked at me: "We were out of town—playing a festival up north. Had car trouble, got stuck for a while, and didn't get back till late on the tenth—early morning of the eleventh, actually. There was a cop's business card in the mailbox with a number to call. Homicide detective. We didn't know what to do and didn't call him, but he called us. Told us what happened and asked us lots of questions. We didn't have anything to tell him. The next day he and a couple of other guys came by and went through the house. They had a warrant and everything, but they were okay."

A glance at Ben. He said, "Not too bad."

"They just wanted to go through her stuff, see if they could find anything that might relate. 'Course they didn't—that was no surprise. It didn't happen here and they told us from the beginning they didn't suspect anyone she knew."

"Why's that?"

"He—this detective—said it was . . ." She closed her eyes and reached for a cookie. Managed to find it and ate half.

"According to the cop, it was a sick psycho thing," said Ben. "He said she was really . . ."

Shaking his head.

"A mess," said Bobby.

"They didn't find anything here," said Ben. The two of them looked shaken.

"What a thing to come home to," I said.

"Oh, yeah," said Bobby. "It really scared us—to have it be someone we knew." She reached for another cookie, even though half of the first one was still in her hand.

"Was she your roommate?"

"Tenant," said Bobby. "We own the house." Saying it with wonderment. "We have a spare bedroom, used to use it as a practice room, do some home recording. Then I lost my job over at the day-care center, so we decided to rent it out for the money. Put a card up on the bulletin board at the university 'cause we figured a student might want just a room. Dawn was the first to call."

"How long ago was this?"

"July."

She ate both cookies. Ben patted her thigh and squeezed it gently. The soft flesh cottage-cheesed. She sighed.

"What you said before," he said, "about this medical chart. Was her taking it uncool?"

"She was supposed to return it."

They looked at each other.

"Did she have a 'taking' problem?" I said.

"Well," he said, uncomfortably.

"Not at first," said Bobby. "At first she was a great tenant—cleaned up after herself, minded her own business. Actually, we didn't see her much because we had our day jobs, and then sometimes we'd go out to sing at night. When we didn't, we went to sleep early. She was out all the time—real night owl. It was a pretty good arrangement."

"Only problem," said Ben, "was her coming in at all hours, because Homer's a good watchdog and when she came in he used to bark and wake us up. But we couldn't very well tell her when to come in and out, could we? Mostly, she was okay."

"When did she start taking things?"

"That was later," he said.

"A couple of months after she arrived," said Bobby. "At first we didn't put it together. It was just small stuff—pens, guitar picks. We don't own anything valuable, except the instruments, and stuff gets lost, right? Look at all those one-of-a-kind socks, right? Then it got more obvious. Some cassette tapes, a six-pack of beer—which she could have had if she'd asked. We're pretty free with our food, even though the deal was she was supposed to buy her own. Then some jewelry—a couple pairs of my earrings. And one of Ben's bandannas, plus an antique pair of suspenders he got up in Seattle. Real nice, heavy leather braces, the kind they don't make anymore. The last thing she took was the one that bothered me the most. An old English brooch I got handed down from my grandmother—silver and garnet. The stone was chipped but it had sentimental value. I left it out on the dresser and the next day it was gone."

"Did you ask her about it?" I said.

"I didn't come out and accuse her, but I did ask her if she'd seen it. Or the earrings. She said no, real casual. But we knew it had to be her. Who else could it have been? She's the only other person ever stepped in here, and things never disappeared until she came."

"It must have been an emotional problem," said Ben. "Kleptomania, or something like that. She couldn't have gotten any serious money for any of it. Not that she needed dough. She had plenty of clothes and a brand-new car."

"What kind of car?"

"One of those little convertibles—a Mazda, I think. She got it after Christmas, didn't have it when she first started living with us or we might have asked for a little more rent, actually. All we charged her was a hundred a month. We thought she was a starving student."

Bobby said, "She definitely had a head problem. I found all the junk she stole out in the garage, buried under the floorboards, in a box, along with a picture of her—like she was trying to stake claim to it, put away a little squirrel's nest or something. To tell the truth, she was greedy, too—I know that's not charitable but it's the truth. It wasn't until later that I put two and two together."

"Greedy in what way?"

"Grabbing the best for herself. Like if there'd be a half-gallon of fudge ripple in the freezer, you'd come back and find all the fudge dug out and just the vanilla left. Or with a bowl of cherries, all the dark ones would be picked out."

"Did she pay her rent on time?"

"More or less. Sometimes she was a week or two late. We never said anything, and she always paid, eventually."

Ben said, "But it was turning into a tense scene."

"We were getting to the point where we would have asked her to leave," said Bobby. "Talked about how to do it for a couple of weeks. Then we got the gig in Sonoma and got all tied up, practicing. Then we came home and . . ."

"Where was she murdered?"

"Somewhere downtown. A club."

"A nightclub?"

Both of them nodded. Bobby said, "From what I gather it was one of those New Wave places. What was the name of it, Ben? Something Indian, right?"

"Mayan," he said. "The Moody Mayan. Or something like that." Thin smile. "The cop asked us if we'd been there. Right."

"Was Dawn a New Waver?"

"Not at first," said Bobby. "I mean, when we met her she was pretty straight-looking. Almost too straight—kind of prim, actually. We thought she might think *we* were too loose. Then gradually she punked up. One thing she was, was smart, I'll tell you that. Always reading textbooks. Studying for a Ph.D. Biomathematics or something like that. But at night she used to change—she'd dress up to go out. That's what Ben meant by her having the clothes—punk stuff, lots of black. She used to smear on that temporary hair dye that washes right out. And all this Addams Family makeup—sometimes she'd mousse up her hair and spike it. Like a costume. The next morning she'd be straight again, going to work. You wouldn't have recognized her."

"Did she actually get killed at this club?"

"I don't know," she said. "We really weren't listening to the details, just wanted the cops to get her stuff out of here, get the whole thing out of our systems."

"Do you remember the detective's name?"

"Gomez," they said in unison.

"Ray Gomez," said Bobby. "He was a Los Lobos fan and he liked doo-wop. Not a bad guy."

Ben nodded. Their knees were pressed up against each other, white from pressure.

"What a thing to happen," she said. "Is this child going to suffer because Dawn stole the chart?"

"We can work around it," I said. "It just would have been nice to have."

"Shame," said Ben. "Sorry we can't help you. The police took all her stuff and I didn't see any medical chart in there. Not that I was looking that close."

"What about the things she stole?"

"No," said Bobby, "no charts there, either. Not too thorough of the cops not to find it, huh? But let me just check, to make sure—maybe inside the flaps or something."

She went into the kitchen and came back shortly with a shoebox and a strip of paper. "Empty—this here's the picture she laid on top. Like she was staking her claim."

I took the photo. One of those black-and-white, four-for-a-quarter self-portraits you get out of a bus terminal machine. Four versions of a face that had once been pretty, now padded with suet and marred by distrust. Straight dark hair, big dark eyes. Bruised eyes. I started to hand it back. Bobby said, "You keep it. I don't want it."

I took another look at the photo before pocketing it. Four identical poses, grim and watchful.

"Sad," I said.

"Yeah," said Bobby, "she never smiled much."

"Maybe," said Ben, "she left it at her office at the U—the chart, I mean."

"Do you know what department she was in?"

"No, but she had an extension there that she gave us. Two-two-three-eight, right?"

"Think so," said Bobby.

I took paper and pen out of my briefcase and copied that down. "She was a doctoral student?"

"That's what she told us when she applied. Biomathematics, or something."

"Did she ever mention her professor's name?"

"She gave a name for a reference," said Bobby, "but to tell the truth we never called it."

Sheepish smile.

"Things were tight," said Ben. "We wanted to get a tenant quickly, and she looked okay."

"The only boss she ever talked about was the guy at the hospital—the one who got killed. But she never mentioned him by name."

Ben nodded. "She didn't like him much."

"Why's that?"

"I dunno. She never went into details—just said he was an asshole, really picky, and she was gonna quit. Then she did, back in February."

"Did she get another job?"

"Not that she told us about," said Bobby.

"Any idea how she paid her bills?"

"Nope, but she always had money to spend."

Ben gave a sick smile.

Bobby said, "What?"

"Her and her boss. She hated him but now they're both in the same boat. L.A. got 'em."

Bobby shuddered and ate a muffin.

17

Learning about Dawn Herbert's murder and her penchant for stealing got me thinking.

I'd assumed she'd pulled Chad's chart for Laurence Ashmore. But what if she'd done it for herself because she'd learned something damaging to the Jones family and planned to profit from it?

And now she was dead.

I drove to the fish store, bought a forty-pound bag of koi food, and asked if I could use the phone to make a local call. The kid behind the counter thought for a while, looked at the total on the register, and said, "Over there," pointing to an old black dial unit on the wall. Next to it was a big saltwater aquarium housing a small leopard shark. A couple of goldfish thrashed at the water's surface. The shark glided peacefully. Its eyes were steady and blue, almost as pretty as Vicki Bottomley's.

I called Parker Center. The man who answered said Milo wasn't there and he didn't know when he'd be back.

"Is this Charlie?" I said.

"No."

Click.

I dialed Milo's home number. The kid behind the counter was watching me. I smiled and gave him the one-minute index finger while listening to the rings.

Peggy Lee delivered the Blue Investigations pitch. I said, "Dawn Herbert was murdered in March. Probably March 9, somewhere downtown, near a punk music club. The investigating detective was named Ray Gomez. I should be at the hospital within an hour—you can have me paged if you want to talk about it."

I hung up and started walking out. A froth of movement caught the corner of my eye and I turned toward the aquarium. Both the goldfish were gone.

The Hollywood part of Sunset was weekend-quiet. The banks and entertainment firms preceding Hospital Row were closed, and a scatter of poor families and drifters massaged the sidewalk. Auto traffic was thin—mostly weekend workers and tourists who'd gone too far past Vine. I made it to the gate of the doctors' parking structure in less than half an hour. The lot was functioning again. Plenty of spaces.

Before heading up to the wards, I stopped at the cafeteria for coffee.

It was the tail end of lunch hour but the room was nearly empty. Dan Kornblatt was getting change from the cashier just as I stepped up to pay. The cardiologist was carrying a lidded plastic cup. Coffee had leaked out and was running down the cup's sides in mud-colored rivulets. Kornblatt's handlebars drooped and he looked preoccupied. He dropped the change in his pocket and saw me, gave a choppy nod.

"Hey, Dan. What's up?"

My smile seemed to bother him. "Read the paper this morning?" he said.

"Actually," I said, "I just skimmed."

He squinted at me. Definitely peeved. I felt as if I'd gotten the wrong answer on an oral exam.

"What can I say," he snapped, and walked away.

I paid for my coffee and wondered what in the paper was eating him. Looking around the cafeteria for a discarded paper, I failed to spot one. I took a couple of swallows of coffee, tossed the cup, and went to the library's reading room. This time it was locked.

Chappy Ward was deserted and the door to every room but Cassie's was open. Lights off, stripped beds, the tainted meadow smell of fresh deodorization. A man in yellow maintenance scrubs vacuumed the hallway. The piped-in music was something Viennese, slow and syrupy.

Vicki Bottomley sat at the nursing station reading a chart. Her cap sat slightly off-kilter.

I said, "Hi, anything new?"

She shook her head and held out the chart without looking up.

"Go ahead and finish it," I said.

"Finished." She waved the chart.

I took it but didn't open it. Leaning against the counter, I said, "How's Cassie feeling today?"

"Bit better." Still no eye contact.

"When did she wake up?"

"Around nine."

"Dad here yet?"

"It's all in there," she said, keeping her head down and pointing at the chart.

I flipped it open, turned to this morning's pages, and read Al Macauley's summary notes and those of the neurologist.

She picked up some kind of form and began to write.

"Cassie's latest seizure," I said, "sounds like it was a strong one."

"Nothing I haven't seen before."

I put the chart down and just stood there. Finally she looked up. The blue eyes blinked rapidly.

"Have you seen lots of childhood epilepsy?" I said.

"Seen everything. Worked Onco. Took care of babies with brain tumors." Shrug.

"I did oncology, too. Years ago. Psychosocial support."

"Uh-huh." Back to the form.

"Well," I said, "at least Cassie doesn't seem to have a tumor."

No answer.

"Dr. Eves told me she's planning to discharge her soon."

"Uh-huh."

"I thought I'd go out and make a home visit."

Her pen raced.

"You've been out there yourself, haven't you?"

No answer.

I repeated the question. She stopped writing and looked up. "If I have, is there something wrong with that?"

"No, I was just—"

"You were just making talky-talk is what you were doing. Right?" She put the pen down and wheeled backward. A smug smile was on her lips. "Or are you checking me out? Wanting to know if I went out and *did* something to her?"

She wheeled back farther, keeping her eyes on me, still smiling.

"Why would I think that?" I said.

" 'Cause I know the way you people think."

"It was a simple question, Vicki."

"Yeah, right. That's what this has all been about, from the beginning. All this phony talky-talk. You're checking me out to see if I'm like that nurse in New Jersey."

"What nurse is that?"

"The one killed the babies. They wrote a book about it and it was on TV."

"You think you're under suspicion?"

"Aren't I? Isn't it always the nurse who gets blamed?"

"Was the nurse in New Jersey blamed falsely?"

Her smile managed to turn into a grimace without a movement.

"I'm sick of this game," she said, standing and shoving the chair away. "With you people it's always games."

" 'You people' meaning psychologists?"

She folded her hands across her chest and muttered something. Then she turned her back on me.

"Vicki?"

No answer.

"What this is all *about*," I said, fighting to keep my voice even, "is finding out what the hell's going on with Cassie."

She pretended to read the bulletin board behind the desk.

"So much for our little truce," I said.

"Don't worry," she said, turning quickly and facing me. Her voice had risen, a sour reed solo superimposed on the Sacher-torte music.

"Don't worry," she repeated, "I won't get in your way. You want something, just ask. 'Cause you're the *doctor*. And I'll do anything that'll help that poor little baby—contrary to what you think, I *care* about her, okay? Fact is, I'll even go down and get you *coffee* if that impresses you and keeps your attention on her, where it should be. I'm not one of those *feminists* think it's a sin to do something other than push meds. But don't pretend to be my *friend*, okay? Let's both of us just do our jobs without talky-talk, and go about our merry ways, okay? And in answer to your question, I was out at the house exactly two times—months ago. Okay?"

She walked to the opposite end of the station, found another form, picked it up and began reading. Squinting, she held it at arm's length. She needed reading glasses. The smug smile returned.

I said, "*Are* you doing something to her, Vicki?"

Her hands jerked and the paper dropped. She bent to pick it up and her cap fell off. Bowing a second time, she retrieved it and stood up rigidly. She was wearing a lot of mascara and a couple of specks had come loose below one eye.

I didn't budge.

"No!" A whisper with lots of force behind it.

Footsteps turned both of our heads. The maintenance man came out into the hall, pulling his vacuum. He was middle-aged and Hispanic, with old eyes and a Cantinflas mustache.

"Sumtin' else?" he said.

"No," said Vicki. "*Go.*"

He looked at her, raised an eyebrow, then yanked on the machine and towed it toward the teak doors. Vicki watched him, hands clenched.

When he was gone, she said, "That was a *horrible* question! Why do you have to think such *ugly* thoughts—why does *any*one have to be *doing* anything to her? She's sick!"

"All her symptoms are some sort of mystery illness?"

"Why *not*?" she said. "Why not? This is a hospital. That's what we get here—sick *kids*. That's what *real* doctors do. Treat sick *kids*."

I maintained my silence.

Her arms began to rise and she fought to keep them down, like a subject resisting a hypnotist. Where the cap had been, her stiff hair had bunched in a hat-sized dome.

I said, "The real doctors aren't having much luck, are they?"

She exhaled through her nose.

"Games," she said, whispering again. "Always games with you people."

"You seem to know a lot about us people."

She looked startled and swiped at her eyes. Her mascara had started to run and the knuckles came away gray but she didn't notice them; her glare was fixed on me.

I met it, absorbed it.

The smug smile came back on her face. "Is there anything else you want, *sir*?" She pulled bobby pins out of her hair and used them to fasten the wedge of white starch.

"Have you told the Joneses your feelings about therapists?" I said.

"I keep my feelings to myself. I'm a professional."

"Have you told them someone suspects foul play?"

"Of course not. Like I said, I'm a professional!"

"A professional," I said. "You just don't like therapists. Bunch of quacks who promise to help but don't come through."

Her head jerked back. The hat bobbled and one hand shot up t o keep it in place.

"You don't know me," she said. "You don't know anythir g about me."

"That's true," I lied. "And that's become a problem for Cassi e."

"That's ridic—"

"Your behavior's getting in the way of her care, Vicki. Let's not discuss it out here anymore." I pointed to the nurse's room behind the station.

She slammed her hands on her hips. "For what?"

"A discussion."

"You have no right."

"Actually, I do. And the only reason you're still on the case is through my good graces. Dr. Eves admires your technical sk ills but your attitude's getting on her nerves, as well."

"Right."

I picked up the phone. "Call her."

She sucked in her breath. Touched her cap. Licked her lips. "What do you *want* from me?" Trace of whine.

"Not out here," I said. "In there, Vicki. Please."

She started to protest. No words came out. A tremor surged across her lips. She put a hand up to cover it.

"Let's just drop it," she said. "I'm sorry, okay?"

Her eyes were full of fear. Remembering her final view of her son and feeling like a louse, I shook my head.

"No more hassles," she said. "I promise—I really mean it this time. You're right, I *shouldn't* have mouthed off. It's because I'm worried about her, same as you. I'll be fine. Sorry. It won't happen again—"

"Please, Vicki." I pointed to the nurse's room.

"—I swear. Come on, cut me a little slack."

I held my ground.

She moved toward me, hands fisted, as if ready to strike. Then she dropped them. Turned suddenly, and walked to the room. Moving slowly, shoulders down, barely lifting her shoes from the carpet.

The room was furnished with an orange Naugahyde couch and matching chair, and a coffee table. A phone sat on the table next to an unplugged coffee maker that hadn't been used or cleaned in a long time. Cat and puppy posters were taped to the wall above a bumper sticker that read NURSES DO IT WITH TENDER LOVING CARE.

I closed the door and sat on the couch.

"This stinks," she said, without conviction. "You have no right— I *am* calling Dr. Eves."

I picked up the phone, called the page operator and asked for Stephanie.

"Wait," she said. "Hang up."

I canceled the page and replaced the receiver. She did a little toe-heel dance, finally sank into the chair, fiddling with her cap, both feet flat on the ground. I noticed something I hadn't seen before: a tiny daisy drawn in nail polish marker, on her new badge, just above her photo. The polish was starting to flake and the flower looked shredded.

She put her hands in her spreading lap. A condemned-prisoner look filled her face.

"I have work to do," she said. "Still have to change the sheets, check to make sure Dietary gets the dinner order right."

"The nurse in New Jersey," I said. "What made you bring that up?"

"Still on that?"

I waited.

"No big deal," she said. "I told you, there was a book and I read it, that's all. I don't like to read those kinds of things usually, but someone gave it to me, so I read it. Okay?"

She was smiling, but suddenly her eyes had filled with tears. She flailed at her face, trying to dry it with her fingers. I looked around the room. No tissues. My handkerchief was clean and I gave it to her.

She looked at it, ignored it. Her face stayed wet, mascara tracing black cat-scratches through the impasto of her makeup.

"Who gave you the book?" I said.

Her face clogged with pain. I felt as if I'd stabbed her.

"It had nothing to do with Cassie. Believe me."

"Okay. What exactly did this nurse do?"

"Poisoned babies—with lidocaine. But she was no nurse. Nurses love kids. Real nurses." Her eyes shifted to the bumper sticker on the wall and she cried harder.

When she stopped, I held out the handkerchief again. She pretended it wasn't there. "What do you *want* from me?"

"Some honesty—"

"About what?"

"All the hostility I've been getting from you—"

"I said I was sorry about that."

"I don't need an apology, Vicki. My honor isn't the issue and we don't have to be buddies—make talky-talk. But we do have to communicate well enough to take care of Cassie. And your behavior's getting in the way."

"I disag—"

"It *is*, Vicki. And I know it can't be anything I've said or done because you were hostile before I opened my mouth. So it's obvious you have something against psychologists, and I suspect it's because they've failed you—or mistreated you."

"What are you doing? Analyzing me?"

"If I need to."

"That's not fair."

"If you want to keep working the case, let's get it out in the open. Lord knows it's difficult enough as is. Cassie's getting sicker each time she comes in; no one knows what the hell's going on. A few more seizures like the one you saw and she could be at risk for some serious brain damage. We can't afford to get distracted by interpersonal crap."

Her lip shook and scooted forward.

"There's no need," she said, "to swear."

"Sorry. Besides my foul mouth, what do you have against me?"

"Nothing."

"Baloney, Vicki."

"There's really no—"

"You don't like shrinks," I said, "and my intuition is you've got a good reason."

She sat back. "That so?"

I nodded. "There are plenty of bad ones out there, happy to take your money without doing anything for you. I happen not to *be* one of them but I don't expect you to believe that just because I say so."

She screwed up her mouth. Relaxed it. Puckers remained above her upper lip. Her face was streaked and smudged and weary and I felt like the Grand Inquisitor.

"On the other hand," I said, "maybe it's just me you resent— some sort of turf thing over Cassie, your wanting to be the boss."

"That's not it at *all*!"

"Then what *is* it, Vicki?"

She didn't answer. Looked down at her hands. Used a nail to push back a cuticle. Her expression was blank but the tears hadn't stopped.

"Why not get it out into the open and be done with it?" I said. "If it's not related to Cassie, it won't leave this room."

She sniffed and pinched the tip of her nose.

I moved forward and softened my tone: "Look, this needn't be a marathon. I'm not out to expose you in any way. All I want to do is clear the air—work out a real truce."

"Won't leave this room, huh?" Return of the smug smile. "I've heard that before."

Our eyes met. Hers blinked. Mine didn't waver.

Suddenly her arms flew upward, hands scissoring. Ripping her cap from her hair, she hurled it across the room. It landed on the floor. She started to get up, but didn't.

"Damn you!" she said. The top of her head was a bird's nest.

I'd folded the handkerchief and rested it on one of my knees. Such a neat boy, the Inquisitor.

She put her hands to her temples.

I got up and placed a hand on her shoulder, certain she'd fling it off. But she didn't.

"I'm sorry," I said.

She sobbed and started to talk, and I had nothing to do but listen.

She told only part of it. Ripping open old wounds while struggling to hold on to some dignity.

The felonious Reggie transformed into an "active boy with school problems."

"He was smart enough, but he just couldn't find anything that interested him and his mind used to wander all over the place."

The boy growing into a "restless" young man who "just couldn't seem to settle down."

Years of petty crime reduced to "some problems."

She sobbed some more. This time she took my handkerchief.

Weeping and whispering the punch line: her only child's death at nineteen, due to "an accident."

Relieved of his secret, the Inquisitor held his tongue.

She was silent for a long time, dried her eyes, wiped her face, then began talking again:

Alcoholic husband upgraded to blue-collar hero. Dead at thirty-eight, the victim of "high cholesterol."

"Thank God we owned the house," she said. "Besides that, the only other thing Jimmy left us worth anything was an old Harley-Davidson motorcycle—one of those choppers. He was always tinkering with that thing, making a mess. Putting Reggie on the back and racing through the neighborhood. He used to call it his hog. Till Reggie was four he actually thought that's what a hog was."

Smiling.

"It was the first thing I sold," she said. "I didn't want Reggie getting ideas that it was his birthright to just go out and crack himself up on the freeway. He always liked speed. Just like his dad. So I sold it to one of the doctors where I worked—over at Foothill General. I'd worked there before Reggie was born. After Jimmy died, I had to go back there again."

I said, "Pediatrics?"

She shook her head. "General ward—they didn't do peds there. I would have preferred peds, but I needed a place that was close to home, so I could be close to Reggie—he was ten but he still wasn't good by himself. I wanted to be home when he was. So I worked nights. Used to put him in at nine, wait till he was asleep, grab a nap for an hour, then go off at ten forty-five so I could be on shift by eleven."

She waited for judgment.

The Inquisitor didn't oblige.

"He was all alone," she said. "Every night. But I figured with him sleeping it would be okay. What they call latchkey now, but they didn't have a name for it back then. There was no choice—I had no one to help me. No family, no such thing as day care back then. You could only get all-night babysitters from an agency and they charged as much as I was making."

She dabbed at her face. Looked at the poster again, and forced back tears.

"I never stopped worrying about that boy. But after he grew up he accused me of not caring about him, saying I left him because I didn't care. He even got on me for selling his dad's bike—making it into a mean thing instead of because I cared."

I said, "Raising a kid alone," and shook my head in what I hoped was sympathy.

"I used to *race* home at seven in the morning, hoping he'd still be asleep and I could wake him up and pretend I'd been there with him all night. In the beginning it worked, but pretty soon he caught on and he'd start to hide from me. Like a game—locking himself in the bathroom . . ." She mashed the handkerchief and a terrible look came onto her face.

"It's okay," I said. "You don't have to—"

"You don't have kids. You don't understand what it's like. When he was older—a teenager—he'd stay out all night, never calling in, sometimes for a couple days at a time. When I grounded him, he'd sneak out anyway. Any punishment I tried, he just laughed. When I tried to talk to him about it, he threw it back in my face. My working and leaving him. Tit for tat: *you* went out—now *I* go out. He never . . ."

She shook her head.

"Never got a lick of help," she said. "Not one single lick . . . from any of them. *Your* crowd, the experts. Counselors, special-ed experts, you name it. Everyone was an expert except me. 'Cause I was the *problem,* right? They were all good at blaming. Real experts at that. Not that any of them could help him—he couldn't learn a thing in school. It got worse and worse each year and all I got was the runaround. Finally, I took him to . . . one of you. Private clown. All the way over in Encino. Not that I could afford it."

She spat out a name I didn't recognize.

I said, "Never heard of him."

"Big office," she said. "View of the mountains and all these little dolls in the bookshelf instead of books. Sixty dollars an hour, which was a lot back then. Still is . . . specially for a total waste of time. Two years of fakery is what I got."

"Where'd you find him?"

"He came recommended—*highly* recommended—from one of the doctors at Foothill. And I thought he was pretty smart myself, at first. He spent a couple of weeks with Reggie, not telling me anything, then called me in for a conference and told me how Reggie had serious problems because of the way he'd grown up. Said it was gonna take a long time to fix it but he would fix it. *If.* Whole list of *if*s. *If* I didn't put any pressure on Reggie to perform. *If* I respected Reggie as a person. Respected his *confidentiality.* I said what's my part in all this? He said paying the bills and minding my own business. Reggie had to develop his own responsibility—long as I did it for him he'd never straighten out. Not that he kept what *I* said to *him* about Reggie confidential. Two years I paid that faker and at the end of it I got a boy who hated me because of what that man put in his head. It wasn't till later that I found out he'd repeated everything I'd told him. Blown it way up and made it worse."

"Did you complain?"

"Why? *I* was the stupid one. For believing. You wanna know how stupid? After . . . after Reggie . . . after he had his . . . after he was . . . gone—a *year* after, I went to another one. Of your crowd. Because my supervisor thought I should—not that she'd pay for it. And not that I wasn't doing my job properly, 'cause I was. But I wasn't sleeping well or eating or enjoying anything. It wasn't like being alive at all. So she gave me a referral. I figured maybe a woman would be a better judge of character. . . . *This* joker was in Beverly *Hills.* Hundred and *twenty* an hour. Inflation, right? Not that the value went up. Though in the beginning this one seemed even more on the ball than the first one. Quiet. Polite. A real gentleman. And he seemed to understand. I felt . . . talking to him made me feel better. In the beginning. I started to be able to work again. Then . . ."

She stopped, clamping her mouth shut. Shifting her attention from me to the walls to the floor to the handkerchief in her hand. Staring at the sodden cloth with surprise and revulsion.

She dropped it as if it were lice-ridden.

"Forget it," she said. "Water under the dam."

I nodded.

She tossed the handkerchief at me and I caught it.

She said, "Baseball Bob," with reflexive quickness. Laughed. Shut it off.

I put the handkerchief on the table. "Baseball Bob?"

"We used to say that," she said defensively. "Jimmy and me and Reggie. When Reggie was little. When someone would make a good catch, he was Baseball Bob—it was stupid."

"In my family it was 'You can be on my team.' "

"Yeah, I've heard that one."

We sat in silence, resigned to each other, like boxers in the thirteenth round.

She said, "That's it. My secrets. Happy?"

The phone rang. I picked it up. The operator said, "Dr. Delaware, please?"

"Speaking."

"There's a call for you from a Dr. Sturgis. He's been paging you for the last ten minutes."

Vicki stood.

I motioned her to wait. "Tell him I'll call him back."

I hung up. She remained on her feet.

"That second therapist," I said. "He abused you, didn't he?"

"Abuse?" The word seemed to amuse her. "What? Like some kind of abused child?"

"It's pretty much the same thing, isn't it?" I said. "Breaking a trust?"

"Breaking a trust, huh? How about blowing it *up*? But that's okay. I learned from it—it made me stronger. Now I watch myself."

"You never complained about him either?"

"Nope. Told you I'm stupid."

"I—"

"Sure," she said. "That's all I needed, his word against mine—who're they gonna believe? He'd get lawyers to go into my life and dig it all up—Reggie. Probably get *experts* to say I was a liar and a rotten mother . . ." Tears. "I wanted my boy to rest in peace, okay? Even though . . ."

She threw up her hands, put her palms together.

"Even though what, Vicki?"

"Even though he never gave *me* peace." Her voice soared in pitch, teetering on hysteria.

"He blamed me till the *end*. Never got rid of those feelings that first faker planted in his head. *I* was the bad one. *I'd* never cared about him. *I'd* made him not learn, not do his homework. *I* didn't force him to go to school because I didn't care a hoot. It was 'cause of me he dropped out and started . . . running around with bad influences and . . . I was one hundred percent of it, hundred and five. . . ."

She let out a laugh that raised the hair on the back of my neck.

"Wanna hear something *confidential*—kind of stuff *you* people like to hear? *He* was the one gave me that book about that bitch from New Jersey. *That* was his Mother's Day gift to me, okay? All wrapped up in a little box with ribbons and the word *Mom* on it. In printing, 'cause he couldn't do cursive, never mastered it—even his printing was all crooked, like a first-grader's. He hadn't given me a present for years, not since he stopped bringing home his shop projects. But there it was, little gift-wrapped package, and inside this little used paperback book on dead babies. I nearly threw up, but I read it anyway. Trying to see if there was something I'd missed. That he was trying to tell me something I wasn't getting. But there wasn't. It was just plain ugly. She was a monster. No real nurse. And one thing I know—one thing I've worked into my own head, without experts—is that she has nothing to do with me, okay? She and me didn't even live on the same planet. I make kids feel *better.* I'm *good* at that. And I never hurt them, okay? *Never.* And I'm gonna keep helping them the rest of my natural life."

18

"Can I go now?" she said. "I'd like to wash my face."

Unable to think of a reason to keep her there, I said, "Sure."

She righted her cap. "Listen, I don't need any more grief, okay? The main thing is for Cassie to get better. Not that . . ." She colored and began walking to the door.

"Not that I can do any good in that department?" I said.

"I *meant,* not that it's gonna be *easy.* If you're the one ends up diagnosing her, hats off to you."

"What do you think about the fact that the doctors can't find anything?"

Her hand rested on the doorknob. "Doctors can't find lots of things. If patients knew how much guessing goes on, they'd . . ." She stopped. "I keep on, I'm gonna get myself in trouble again."

"Why are you so certain it's organic?"

"Because what else could it be? These aren't *abusers.* Cindy's one of the best mothers I've ever seen, and Dr. Jones is a real gentleman. And despite *who* they are, you'd never know it, because they don't lord it over anyone, okay? That's *real* class, far as I'm concerned. Go out and see for yourself—they love that little girl. It's just a matter of time."

"Before what?"

"Before someone figures out what's *wrong*. I've seen it lots of times. Doctors can't figure things out so they call it psychosomatic. Then poof, all of a sudden someone finds something that hasn't been looked for before and you've got yourself a new disease. They call that medical progress."

"What do you call it?"

She stared at me. "I call it progress too."

She walked away and I stayed behind, thinking. I'd gotten her to talk but had I learned anything?

My thoughts shifted to the cruel gift her son had given her. Pure spite? Or had he been telling her something?

Had she told *me* about it as part of a game? Told me just what she wanted me to know?

I stayed with it a while and came up with nothing. Cleared my head and walked to 505 W.

Cassie sat propped up in bed, wearing red floral pajamas with white collar and cuffs. Her cheeks were raspberry-pink and her hair was gathered in a topknot tied with a white bow. The I.V. had been disconnected and it stood in the corner, like a metal scarecrow. Depleted glucose bags hung from the arms. The only evidence her veins had been punctured was a small round Band-Aid atop one hand and the yellow Betadine stain below it. Her eyes glistened as they followed me.

Cindy sat near her on the bed, spoon-feeding her cereal. She wore a SAVE THE OCEANS T-shirt over a denim skirt and sandals. Dolphins cavorted across her bustline. She and Cassie looked more similar than ever.

As I approached, Cassie opened a mouth full of cereal-mush. A stray speck dotted her upper lip.

Cindy picked it off. "Swallow, honey. Hi, Dr. Delaware. We didn't expect to see you today."

I put my briefcase down and sat on the foot of the bed. Cassie looked confused but not fearful.

"Why's that?" I said.

"It's the weekend."

"You're here, so I'm here."

"That's very nice of you. Look, sweetie, Dr. Delaware came all the way to see you on a Saturday."

Cassie looked at Cindy, then back at me, still muddled.

Wondering about the mental effects of the seizure, I said, "How's everything?"

"Oh, fine."

I touched Cassie's hand. She didn't move for a second, then drew away, slowly. When I chucked her chin, she looked down at my hand.

"Hi, Cassie," I said.

She continued to stare. Some milk dribbled out of her mouth. Cindy wiped it and closed her mouth gently. Cassie started to chew. Then she parted her lips and said, "Hah," through the mush.

"Right!" said Cindy. "*Hi!* That's great, Cass!"

"Hah."

"We did very well with our food today, Dr. Delaware. Juice and fruit and crackers for breakfast. Then we had our breakfast Krispies for lunch."

"Great."

"Real great." Her voice was tight.

Remembering the short-lived moment of tension last time I'd talked to her—the feeling that she was about to tell me something important—I said, "Is there anything you want to discuss with me?"

She touched Cassie's hair. Cassie started to play with another drawing. "No, I don't think so."

"Dr. Eves tells me you'll be going home soon."

"That's what she says." She adjusted Cassie's topknot. "I'm sure looking forward to it."

"Bet you are," I said. "No more doctors for a while."

She looked at me. "The doctors have been great. I know they're doing their best."

"You've seen some of the best," I agreed. "Bogner, Torgeson, Macauley, Dawn Herbert."

No reaction.

"Got anything planned when you get back home?"

"Just getting back to normal."

Wondering what that meant, I said, "I'd like to come out pretty soon."

"Oh—of course. You can draw with Cassie at her play table. I'm sure we can find a chair to fit you—can't we, Cass?"

"Fip."

"Right! Fi*t*."

"*Fip.*"

"Excellent, Cass. Do you want Dr. Delaware to draw with you at your little bear table?" When Cassie didn't answer she said, "Draw? Draw pictures?" and made scrawling motions with one hand.

"Daw."

"Yes, draw. With Dr. Delaware."

Cassie looked at her, then me. Then she nodded. Then she smiled.

I stayed awhile, providing entertainment and looking for signs of post-seizural damage. Cassie seemed okay but I knew brain effects could be subtle. For the thousandth time I wondered what was going on in her little body.

Cindy was friendly enough, but I couldn't shake the feeling that her enthusiasm for my services had waned. She sat on the sleeper, brushing out her hair while scanning *TV Guide*. The hospital air was cool and dry and the hair crackled with each stroke. Northern light came in through the room's single window, a straw-colored beam that burned through the smog and burst against the fairy-tale wallpaper. The lower edge of the beam touched upon the long dark strands, tracing a metallic streak through them.

It created an odd cosmetic effect and made her look beautiful. I'd never thought of her as desirable—too busy wondering if she was a monster. But seeing her gilded that way made me realize how little she exploited her looks.

Before I could mull that any longer, the door swung open and Chip came in, carrying coffee. He had on navy sweats and running shoes and his hair looked freshly washed. A diamond sparkled in his ear.

His greeting was tavern-buddy friendly but a ribbon of steel ran through the amiability—resistance not unlike Cindy's. It made me wonder if the two of them had discussed me. When he sat down between Cassie and me I got up and said, "See you later."

No one argued, though Cassie kept looking at me. I smiled at her. She stared a while longer before shifting her attention to a drawing. I collected my stuff and headed for the door.

"Bye, Dr. Delaware," said Cindy.

"Bye," said Chip. "Thanks for everything."

I looked over his shoulder at Cassie. Waved at her. She raised a hand and curled her fingers. The topknot was in disarray again. I wanted to swoop her up and take her home with me.

"Bye, sweetie."

"Bah."

I had to get away from the hospital.

Feeling like a teething puppy with nothing to chomp, I turned out of the lot and drove up Hillhurst, heading for a restaurant at the top of the street that I'd learned about from Milo but never went to alone. Continental food of the old school, autographed photos of near-celebrities, dark panel walls saturated with nicotine bitters, waiters without SAG cards.

A sign in the lobby said the restaurant wouldn't be serving for another half hour but the cocktail lounge was accepting sandwich orders.

A middle-aged, tuxedoed woman with improbable red hair worked behind the bar. A few serious drinkers sat at the padded horseshoe chewing ice cubes, snuffling salted freebies, and devoting what little attention they had left to an auto-chase scene on the tube. The TV was mounted on a ceiling bracket. It reminded me of the one I'd just seen in Cassie's room.

The hospital . . . dominating my thoughts the way it had years ago. I loosened my tie, sat down, and ordered a club sandwich and beer. When the bartender turned to prepare it, I went to the pay phone at the back of the lounge and called Parker Center.

"Records," said Milo.

"*Doctor* Sturgis?"

"Well, if it isn't *Doctor* Hard-to-Get. Yeah, I figured easiest way to get some action in that place was use the title."

"If only it were so," I said. "Sorry for the delay getting back to you but I was tied up with Vicki Bottomley, then Cassie and her parents."

"Anything new?"

"Not much, except the Joneses seemed a little cool."

"Maybe you're threatening them. Getting too close."

"Can't see why. As for Vicki, she and I had a little psycho-drama—I was trying to clear the air, leaned on her a bit. She accused me of suspecting her of harming Cassie. So I asked her if she was, and she went nuclear. Ended up giving me a sanitized version of her son's story and adding something I hadn't known: Reggie gave her a book as a Mother's Day gift. True-crime thing about some nurse in New Jersey who murdered babies."

"Some gift. Think she was trying to tell you something?"

"I don't know. Maybe I should tell Stephanie to pull her off the case and see what happens. If *Stephanie* can be trusted. Meanwhile, this Dawn Herbert thing. On top of being murdered, she was a bit of a kleptomaniac."

I gave him my blackmail theory. "What do you think?"

"Uh-huh . . . well," he said, clearing his throat, "that's certainly a good question, sir, but that information's not currently available on our present data base."

"Bad time to talk?"

"Yes, sir. Right away, sir." A moment later, he lowered his voice: "Brass coming through on tour, some kind of police-biggie convention this weekend. I'm off in five minutes. How about late lunch, early dinner—let's say half an hour?"

"Started without you," I said.

"What a pal. Where are you?"

I told him.

Still talking quietly, he said, "Good. Order me a pea soup with a ham bone and the breast of chicken with the cornbread stuffing, extra stuffing."

"They're only making sandwiches right now."

"By the time I get there, they'll be serving real food. Tell 'em it's for me. Remember the order?"

"Soup, bone, chicken, extra stuffing."

"They ever remake *The Thirty-nine Steps,* you can play Mr. Memory. Have 'em time the order so nothing's cold. Also a dark draft. The Irish stuff—they'll know what I mean."

I returned to the bar, relayed Milo's order to the bartender, and told her to delay my sandwich until he arrived. She nodded, called the kitchen, then served my beer with a dish of almonds. I asked her if she had a newspaper.

"Sorry," she said, glancing toward the barflies. "No one around here reads. Try the machines out front."

I went back to Hillhurst and caught a faceful of sunglare. Four coin-op newspaper dispensers lined the sidewalk. Three were empty; one of them was vandalized and graffitied. The last one was fully stocked with a tabloid promising SAFE SEX, RAUNCHY GIRLS, AND DIRTY FUN.

I went back into the lounge. The channel had been switched to an old western. Square jaws, moping dogies, and long shots of scrubland. The barflies stared up at the screen, entranced. As if it hadn't been filmed just over the hill, in Burbank.

Thirty-six minutes later Milo appeared, waving me over as he strode past the bar, toward the restaurant section. I took my beer and caught up with him. His jacket was over his shoulder and his tie was tucked into his waistband. The band was crushed by the weight of his belly. A couple of the lushes looked up and watched him, dulled, but still wary. He never noticed. But I knew he would've been pleased to see how much cop-scent he still gave off.

The main dining room was empty except for a busboy running a manual carpet-sweeper over a corner. A stringy old waiter appeared—American Gothic on a crash diet—bearing soft rolls, Milo's ale, and a plate of cherry peppers and stuffed olives.

"Him, too, Irv," said Milo.

"Certainly, Mr. Sturgis."

When the waiter left, Milo touched my beer glass and said, "You're replacing that with dark draft, lad. From the weariness in your eyes, I'd say you've earned it."

"Gee, thanks, Dad. Can I have a two-wheeler without training wheels too?"

He grinned, tugged his tie lower, then loosened the knot completely and pulled it off. Running his hand over his face, he sat back in the booth and snorted.

"How'd you find out about Herbert's murder?" he said.

"From her former landlords." I summarized my talk with Bobby and Ben Murtaugh.

"They seem on the level?"

I nodded. "They're still pretty shaken."

"Well," he said, "there's nothing new on the case. She's on file as a Central Division open. The overall picture is a sadistic-psycho thing. Very little physical evidence."

"Another low-probability one?"

"Uh-huh. Best bet on these wacko ones is the bad guy does it again and gets caught. Nasty one, too. She was hit over the head, had her throat cut and something wooden shoved up her vagina—coroner found splinters. That's about all they've got physically. It happened near a punk club operating out of a garment contractor's place in the Union District. Not far from the Convention Center."

"The Moody Mayan," I said.

"Where'd you hear that?"

"The Murtaughs."

"They got it half right," he said. "It was the Mayan *Mortgage*. Place went out of business a couple of weeks later."

"Because of the murder?"

"Hell, no. If anything, that would have helped business. We're talking the night-crawler scene, Alex. Spoiled kids from Brentwood and Beverly Hills putting on *Rocky Horror Show* duds and playing 'Look, Mom, no common sense.' Blood and entrails—someone *else's*—would be just what they're looking for."

"That fits with what the Murtaughs said about Herbert. Grad student by day, but she used to punk herself up at night. Used the kind of hair dye that washes out the next morning."

"L.A. shuffle," he said. "Nothing's what it seems. . . . Anyway, the place probably closed down because that crowd gets bored easily—the whole kick is to move from place to place. Kind of a metaphor for life itself, huh?"

I did a finger-down-the-throat pantomime.

He laughed.

I said, "Do you know this particular club?"

"No, but they're all the same—fly-by-night setups, no occupancy permits, no liquor licenses. Sometimes they take over an abandoned building and don't bother to pay rent. By the time the landlord catches on or the fire department gets around to shutting them down, they're gone. What'll change it is a couple hundred clowns getting roasted."

He raised his glass and buried his upper lip in foam. He wiped it and said, "According to Central, one of the bartenders saw Herbert leave the club shortly before two A.M. with a guy. He recognized her because she'd been dancing at the club and was one of the few heavyset girls they let in. But he couldn't give any specifics on the guy other than that he was straight-looking and older than her. The time frame fits with the coroner's ETD of between two and four. The coroner also found cocaine and booze in her system."

"A lot?"

"Enough to dull her judgment. If she had any in the first place—which is doubtful, seeing as she was traipsing around the Union District in the wee hours, all alone."

"The landlords said she was smart—Ph.D. student in biomath."

"Yeah. Well, there's smart and there's smart. The actual killing took place on a side street a couple of blocks away from the club. In that little Mazda of hers. The keys were still in the ignition."

"She was killed in the car?"

"Right in the driver's seat, judging from the spatter pattern. Afterward, she slumped across both seats. The body was found just after sunrise by a couple of garment workers arriving for the early shift. Blood had seeped through the door and into the street. The slant of the street made it run down into the curb and pool. It was the pool they noticed."

The waiter brought my ale, a bowl of soup oysters, and Milo's pea soup. He waited while Milo tasted. Milo said, "Perfect, Irv," and the old man nodded and disappeared.

Milo took a couple more spoonfuls, licked his lips, and spoke through the steam. "The Mazda's convertible top was up but there was no blood on the headliner, so the coroner's certain the top was down when it happened. The spatter pattern also indicates that whoever did it was outside the car, standing on the driver's side. Standing over her, maybe a foot or two behind her. He hit her on the head. From the skull damage it must've knocked her out, may even have killed her. Then he used some kind of blade to sever her jugular and her windpipe. Once that was done, he did the mechanical rape, so maybe we've got ourselves a necrophile."

"Sounds like overkill," I said. "Some kind of frenzy."

"Or thoroughness," he said, sipping soup. "He was cool enough to raise the top."

"Was she seen dancing with anyone in the club?"

"Nothing on record. Only reason the bartender remembered her leaving was he was on a smoke break, just outside."

"He wasn't considered a suspect?"

"Nope. Tell you one thing, the asshole who did it came prepared—think about all those weapons. We're talking a predator, Alex. Maybe someone watching the club, prowling the area 'cause he knows there's lots of women around. He waits until he sees exactly what he's been looking for. Lone target, maybe a certain physical type, maybe he's just decided tonight's the night. With the added bonus of a *convertible* on a quiet, dark street. With the *top* down. Which is like 'You are cordially invited to assault me.' "

"Makes sense," I said, feeling my gorge rise.

"A grad student, huh? Too bad she flunked Logic One-A. I'm not trying to blame the victim, Alex, but add the dope and booze to her behavioral pattern and it doesn't sound like a lady with strong instincts for self-preservation. What'd she steal?"

As I told him, he ate more soup, used his spoon to wedge marrow out of the bone, and ate that too.

I said, "The Murtaughs said she seemed to have plenty of money even after she quit her job. And you've just added cocaine to her budget. So blackmail makes some sense, doesn't it? She latches on to the fact that one Jones kid died and the other keeps coming back into the hospital with unexplained illnesses. She steals the evidence and tries to exploit it. And now she's dead. Just like Ashmore."

He put his glass down slowly. "Big leap, from petty pilfering to putting the squeeze on biggies, Alex. And there's no reason, from the facts of the case, to think a psycho didn't cut her up. In terms of where she got her money, we still don't know her family didn't give it to her. For that matter, the coke could have been asset, not a debit— maybe she *dealt* dope, too."

"If she had family money, why would she rent a cheap single room from the Murtaughs?"

"Slumming. We already know she played roles—the whole punk bit. And the thefts she pulled on her landlords were illogical, not for profit. Exactly the kind of thing that's likely to get discovered. She comes across *disorganized* to me, Alex. Not the type to plan and execute a high-level blackmail scheme."

"No one said she was good at it. Look at the way she ended up."

He looked around the empty room as if suddenly concerned about being overheard. He drained his ale glass, then lifted his spoon and pushed the soup bone around his bowl like a kid playing toy boat in a tiny green harbor.

"The way she ended up," he finally said. "So who killed her? Daddy? Mommy? Grandpa?"

"Wouldn't you say hired help? Those types don't do their own dirty work."

"Hired to slice her and do a mechanical rape?"

"Hired to make it look like a 'psycho thing' that'll never get solved unless the psycho does it again. Hell, maybe Ashmore was involved, too, and the same guy was paid to set up a phony mugging."

"Imaginative," he said. "You just sat there with those people, playing with their kid, making chitchat, and thinking all this?"

"You think I'm totally off-base?"

He ate more soup before answering. "Listen, Alex, I've known you long enough to appreciate the way your mind works. I just don't think you have much more than fantasy at this point."

"Maybe so," I said. "But it sure beats thinking about Cassie and everything we're not doing for her."

The rest of the food came. I watched him carve up his chicken. He took a long time to section the meat, showing more surgical skill and deliberation than I'd ever seen before.

"Phony psycho job on Herbert," he said. "Phony mugging for Ashmore."

"He was Herbert's boss. Owned the computers and had done a toxicology check on Chad Jones. It was logical to think he knew whatever Herbert did. Even if he didn't, whoever killed her might have taken care of him, too, just to be careful."

"Why would he be involved in blackmail? He *was* independently wealthy."

"He invested in real estate," I said, "and the market's sliding. What if he was leveraged to the hilt? Or maybe he hadn't quit gambling, as his wife believed. Lost big at the tables and needed some cash. Rich folk can get poor, right? The L.A. shuffle."

"If Ashmore was in on it—and I'm just playing along at this point—why would he want Herbert for a partner?"

"Who says he did? She could have found out on her own—gotten hold of his computer data and decided to free-lance."

He said nothing. Wiped his lips with his napkin, even though he hadn't eaten any chicken.

I said, "One problem, though. Ashmore was killed two months after Herbert. If their murders are related, why take so long to eliminate him?"

He tapped his fingers on the table. "Well . . . another way to look at it is, Ashmore had no knowledge of what Herbert was up to at first, but found out later. From data *she'd* stashed in the computer. And he either tried to capitalize on it, or told the wrong person."

"You know, that dovetails with something I saw the other day. Huenengarth—the head of Security—removing Ashmore's computers the morning after Ashmore's murder. My first impression was he was getting hold of Ashmore's equipment. But maybe what Huenengarth was really after was *in* the machines. The data. He works for Plumb—meaning he really works for Chuck Jones. Guy's a real corporate henchman type, Milo. Plus, his name came up yesterday when I was speaking to Mrs. Ashmore. He was the one who called to offer the hospital's sympathies. Was coming by with the UNICEF certificate and the plaque. Strange job for head of Security, wouldn't you say? Unless his real intention was to learn if Ashmore kept a computer at home and, if he did, to get it out of there."

Milo looked down at his plate. Finally ate. Quickly, mechanically, without much apparent pleasure. I knew how much food meant to him and felt bad for ruining his dinner.

"Intriguing," he said, "but it's still one big *if.*"

"You're right," I said. "Let's give it a rest."

He put his fork down. "There's a basic flaw with all of it, Alex. If Grandpa knew about Junior and/or Mrs. Junior killing Chad, and cared enough about hushing it up to pay blackmail money *and* hire a killer, why would he allow Cassie to be brought back to the same hospital?"

"Maybe he didn't know, until Herbert and/or Ashmore put the arm on him."

"Even so. Why not send Cassie somewhere else for treatment? Why run the risk of dealing with the exact same doctors who'd treated Chad and having them make the same connection the black-mailers had made? It's not like the family wouldn't have been justified. Cassie isn't getting any better—you yourself said Jones Junior's talking about medical errors. No one would blame them for getting a second opinion. Also, it's one thing to say the parents are abusers and Grandpa's protecting them, even to the point of eliminating a black-mailer. But if Grandpa *knew* Cassie was being poisoned, wouldn't he want to step in and stop it?"

"Maybe he's no better than they are," I said.

"Family of psychos?"

"Where do you think it starts?"

"I don't know—"

"Maybe Chuck Jones was an abusive father and that's where Chip learned it. The way he's tearing down the hospital sure doesn't make him Mr. Compassionate."

"Corporate greed is one thing, Alex. Watching your grand-daughter get messed with to the point of epileptic seizures is another."

"Yeah," I said, "it's probably all fantasy—getting far afield. Would you please eat? Your pickiness is making me nervous."

He smiled for my benefit and took fork in hand. Both of us faked fascination with our food.

"Huenengarth," he said. "Don't imagine there'd be too many of that name on file. What's the first name?"

"Presley."

He smiled. "Even better. Speaking of which, I ran Ashmore and Steph. He's clean except for a couple of traffic tickets that he didn't get around to paying before he died. She's been clean for a long time, but a few years ago she had a DUI."

"Drunk driving?"

"Uh-huh. Caused a collision, no injuries. First offense, she got probation. Probably got sent to AA or a treatment center."

"So maybe *that's* why she's changed."

"Changed how?"

"Got thin, started putting on makeup, got into fashion. Image of the young professional. She has a designer coffee maker in her office. Real espresso."

"Could be," he said. "Strong coffee's part of the reformed alkie thing—to replace the booze."

Thinking of his off-and-on flirtation with the bottle, I said, "You think it means anything?"

"What, the DUI? You see any evidence she's still boozing?"

"No, but I haven't been looking for any."

"Any clear relationship between alcoholism and Munchausen?"

"No. But whatever problem you've got, booze makes it worse. And if she had the typical Munchausen background—abuse, incest, illness—I could understand her hitting the bottle."

He shrugged. "So you answer your own question. At the very least it means she's got something she'd like to forget. Which makes her like most of us."

20

As we left the restaurant Milo said, "I'll try to find out what I can about Dawn Herbert, for what it's worth. What's your next step?"

"Home visit. Maybe seeing them in their natural habitat will give me *some* kind of insight."

"Makes sense. Hell, while you're out there you can do a little snooping—you've got the perfect cover."

"That's exactly what Stephanie said. She suggested I nose around in their medicine cabinet. Half-joking."

"Why not? You shrinks get paid to poke and probe. Don't even need a search warrant."

On the way home I stopped off at the Ashmore house—still curious about Huenengarth and wanting to see how the widow was doing. A black wreath hung on the front door and no one answered my ring.

I got back in the car, cranked up the stereo, and made it all the way home without thinking about death and disease. I checked in with my service. Robin had left word she'd be back around six. The morning paper was still on the dining room table, neatly folded, the way she always left it.

Recalling Dan Kornblatt's peevish comment in the cafeteria, I paged through the paper, trying to find what had upset him. Nothing in the front pages or Metro, but it jumped out at me from the second page of the Business section.

I never read the financial pages, but even if I did, I could have missed it. Small piece, lower bottom corner, next to the foreign exchange rates.

The headline read HEALTH CARE IN THE PRIVATE SECTOR: THE OPTIMISM FADES. The gist of the article was that the for-profit hospital business, once seen by Wall Street as a rich financial lode, had turned out to be anything but. That premise was backed up by examples of hospitals and HMOs gone bust, and interviews with financial honchos, one of them George Plumb, formerly CEO of MGS Healthcare Consultants, Pittsburgh, and currently CEO of Western Pediatric Medical Center, Los Angeles.

Pittsburgh . . . The outfit revamping the library with an outmoded computer system—BIO-DAT—was from Pittsburgh too.

One hand feeding the other? I read on.

The honchos' main complaints centered on government meddling and "market-restricting" fee schedules but also touched upon difficulties dealing with insurance companies, the skyrocketing cost of new technologies, the salary demands of doctors and nurses, and the failure of sick people to behave like statistics.

"One AIDS patient, alone, can cost us millions," lamented one East Coast administrator. "And we still haven't seen the light at the end of that tunnel. This is a disease no one knew about when any of the plans were put together. The rules have been changed in the middle of the game."

The HIV epidemic was cited repeatedly by executives, as if the plague were a bit of naughtiness devised to throw the actuaries off track.

Plumb's special contribution to the gripe-fest had to do with the difficulties of running inner-city hospitals due to "unfavorable demographics and social problems that seep into the institution from the surrounding neighborhoods. Add to that, rapidly deteriorating physical plants and shrinking revenues, and the paying consumer and his or her provider is unwilling to contract for care."

When asked for solutions, Plumb suggested that the wave of the future might be "decentralization—replacing the large urban hospital with smaller, easily managed health-care units strategically located in positive-growth suburban areas.

"However," he cautioned, "careful economic analyses need to be done before planning anything of that magnitude. And nonpecuniary issues must also be considered. Many established institutions inspire a high degree of loyalty in those whose memories are grounded in the good old days."

It sounded awfully like a trial balloon—testing public opinion before proposing radical surgery: putting the "physical plant" up for sale and heading for suburban pastures. And if cornered, Plumb could always brush off his comments as detached expert analysis.

Kornblatt's remark about selling off the hospital's real estate began to sound less like paranoia and more like an educated guess.

Of course, Plumb was only a mouthpiece. Speaking for the man I'd just proposed as a possible murder contractor and accessory to child abuse.

I remembered what Stephanie had told me about Chuck Jones's background. Before becoming Western Peds's chairman of the board, he'd managed the hospital's investment portfolio. Who'd know more about the precise value of Western Peds's assets—including the land—than the man who kept the books?

I visualized him and Plumb and the gray-twin numbers crunchers, Roberts and Novak, hunched over a moldy ledger, like predators out of a Thomas Nast cartoon.

Could the hospital's dismal financial situation be due to more than unfortunate demographics and shrinking revenues? Had Jones mismanaged Western Peds's money to the point of crisis, and was he now planning to cover his losses with a flashy real estate sale?

Adding insult to injury by taking a nice fat commission on the deal?

Strategically located in positive-growth suburban areas.

Like the fifty lots Chip Jones owned out in the West Valley?

One hand feeding the other . . .

But to pull off that kind of thing, appearances would have to be kept up, Jones and company exhibiting unwavering loyalty to the urban dinosaur until it drew its last breath.

Pulling the chairman's granddaughter out of treatment wouldn't be part of that.

In the meantime, though, steps could be taken to hasten the dinosaur's death.

Shut down clinical programs. Discourage research. Freeze salaries and keep the wards understaffed.

Encourage senior doctors to leave and replace them with inexperienced help, so that private physicians lost confidence and stopped referring their paying patients.

Then, when redemption was out of the question, give an impassioned speech about insoluble social issues and the need to move fearlessly into the future.

Destroying the hospital to save it.

If Jones and his minions pulled it off, they'd be viewed as visionaries with the courage and foresight to put a tottering almshouse out of its misery and replace it with healing grounds for the upper middle class.

There was a certain vicious beauty to it.

Thin-lipped men planning a war of attrition with flow-charts, balance sheets, computer printouts.

Printouts . . .

Huenengarth confiscating Ashmore's computers.

Was he after data that had nothing to do with sudden infant death syndrome or poisoned babies?

Ashmore had no interest in patient care, but a *strong* attraction to finance. Had he stumbled upon Jones's and Plumb's machinations—overheard something down in the sub-basement, or hacked into the wrong data base?

Had he tried to profit from the knowledge and paid for it?

Big leap, Milo would say.

I remembered the glimpse I'd caught of Ashmore's office before Huenengarth shut the door.

What kind of toxicology research could be carried out without test tubes or microscopes?

Ashmore, crunching numbers and dying because of it . . . Then what of Dawn Herbert? Why had she pulled a dead infant's chart? Why had she been murdered two months before Ashmore?

Separate schemes?

Some sort of collusion?

Big leap . . . And even if any of it was true, what the hell did it have to do with Cassie Jones's ordeal?

I phoned the hospital and requested room 505 W. No one answered. Dialing again, I asked to be put through to the Chappy Ward nursing desk. The nurse who picked up had a Spanish accent. She informed me the Jones family was off the floor, taking a walk.

"Anything new?" I said. "In terms of her status?"

"I'm not sure—you'll have to ask the primary. I believe that's Dr. . . ."

"Eves."

"Yeah, that's right. I'm just a float, not really familiar with the case."

I hung up, looked out the kitchen window at treetops graying under a descending lemon-colored sun. Mulled the financial angle some more.

I thought of someone who might be able to educate me financially. Lou Cestare, once a stocks-and-bonds golden boy, now a chastened veteran of Black Monday.

The crash had caught him off guard and he was still scouring the tarnish from his reputation. But he remained on *my* A list.

Years ago I'd saved up some cash, working eighty hours a week and not spending much. Lou had given me financial security by investing the money in pre-boom beachfront real estate, selling for healthy profits and putting the gain into blue-chip securities and tax-free bonds. Avoiding the speculative stuff, because he knew I'd never be rich from practicing psychology and couldn't afford to lose big.

The income from those investments was still coming in, slow and steady, augmenting what I brought in doing forensic consults. I'd never be able to buy French Impressionist paintings, but if I kept my life-style reasonable, I probably wouldn't have to work when I didn't want to.

Lou, on the other hand, was a very wealthy man, even after losing most of his assets and nearly all of his clients. He split his time now between a boat in the South Pacific and an estate in the Willamette Valley.

I called Oregon and spoke to his wife. She sounded serene, as always, and I wondered if it was strength of character or a good facade. We made small talk for a while and then she told me Lou was up in Washington State, hiking near Mount Rainier with their son, and wasn't expected until tomorrow night or Monday morning. I gave her my want-list. It didn't mean much to her, but I knew she and Lou never talked money.

Wishing her well and thanking her, I hung up.

Then I drank another cup of coffee and waited for Robin to come home and help me forget the day.

21

She was carrying two suitcases and looking cheerful. A third valise
was down in her new truck. I brought it up and watched her unpack
and hang her clothes. Filling the space in the closet that I'd left
empty for more than two years.

Sitting down on the bed, she smiled. "There."

We necked for a while, watched the fish, went out and had rack
of lamb at a sedate place in Brentwood where we were the youngest
patrons. After returning home, we spent the rest of the evening
listening to music, reading, and playing gin. It felt romantic, a little
geriatric, and very satisfying. The next morning, we went walking in
the glen, pretending we were birdwatchers and making up names for
the winged things we saw.

Sunday lunch was hamburgers and iced tea up on the terrace.
After we did the dishes she got involved in the Sunday crossword
puzzle, biting her pencil and frowning a lot. I stretched out on a
lounge chair, feigning relaxation. Shortly after 2:00 P.M. she put the
puzzle down, saying, "Forget it. Too many French words."

She lay down beside me. We absorbed sun, until I noticed her starting to fidget.

I leaned over and kissed her forehead.

"Ummm . . . anything I can do for you?" she said.

"No, thanks."

"Sure?"

"Uh-huh."

She tried to sleep, grew more restless.

I said, "I'd like to get over to the hospital some time today."

"Oh, sure . . . As long as you're going out, I might as well get over to the shop, take care of a few odds and ends."

Cassie's room was empty, the bed stripped, the drapes drawn. Vacuum tracks striped the carpet. The bathroom was bare and disinfected; a paper runner was wrapped around the toilet.

As I stepped out of the room a voice said, "Hold it."

I came face to face with a security guard. Wet-sanded triangular face, grim lips, and black-framed glasses. Same hero I'd met the first day, enforcing the badge law.

He blocked the doorway. Looked ready to charge San Juan Hill.

I said, "Excuse me."

He didn't move. There was barely enough space between us for me to glance down and read his badge. *Sylvester, A.D.*

He looked at mine and took a single step backwards. Partial retreat but not enough to allow me through.

"See, got a new one," I said. "All bright and shiny, full color. Now could you please get out of the way so I can go about my business?"

He looked up and down a couple of times, matching my face to the photo. Stepping aside, he said, "This ward's closed."

"So I see. For how long?"

"Till they open it."

I walked past him and headed for the teak doors.

He said, "Looking for anything in particular?"

I stopped and faced him again. One hand rested on his holster; the other gripped his baton.

Resisting the urge to bark, "Draw, pardner," I said, "I came to see a *patient*. They used to treat them here."

I used a phone on the public ward to call Admissions and Discharge and confirmed that Cassie had been released an hour ago. I took the stairs down to the first floor and bought a watery cola from a vending machine. I was carrying it across the entrance lobby when I crossed paths with George Plumb and Charles Jones, Jr. They were laughing, keeping up a brisk pace that caused Jones's short bowlegs to pump. So much for concerned grandpa.

They got to the door just as I emerged. Jones saw me and his mouth stood still. A few seconds later his feet did the same. Plumb stopped, too, remaining just behind his boss. The pink in his complexion was more vivid than ever.

"Dr. Delaware," said Jones. His gravel voice made it sound like a warning growl.

"Mr. Jones."

"Do you have a moment, Doctor?"

Caught off guard, I said, "Sure."

Casting an eye at Plumb, he said, "I'll catch up with you later, George."

Plumb nodded and marched off, arms swinging.

When we were alone Jones said, "How's my granddaughter?"

"Last time I saw her she was looking better."

"Good, good. I'm on my way to see her."

"She's been discharged."

His grizzled eyebrows crinkled unevenly, each thatch of steely hair pointing randomly. Beneath the brows were lumps of scar tissue. His eyes got tiny. For the first time I noticed they were a watery brown.

"That so? When?"

"An hour ago."

"Damn." He squeezed his broken nose and jiggled the tip back and forth. "I came by expressly to see her because I didn't get a chance to see her yesterday—blasted meetings all day. She's my only grand-child, you know. Beautiful little thing, isn't she?"

"Yes, she is. Be nice if she were healthy."

He stared up at me. Put his hands in his pocket and tapped a wingtip on the marble floor. The lobby was nearly empty and the sound echoed. He repeated it. His posture had lost some of its stiffness, but he straightened quickly. The watery eyes sagged.

"Let's find a place to talk," he said, and barreled forward through the lobby, confident once more. A solid little fireplug of a man who carried himself as if self-doubt wasn't in his DNA. Jingling as he walked.

"I don't keep an office here," he said. "With all the money problems, the space shortage, last thing I want is to be seen as playing fast and loose."

As we passed the elevators one of them arrived. Tycoon's luck. He strode right in, as if he'd reserved the lift, and jabbed the basement button.

"How about the dining room?" he said as we rode down.

"It's closed."

"I know it is," he said. "I'm the one who curtailed the hours."

The door opened. He strode out and headed for the cafeteria's locked doors. Pulling a ring of keys out of his trouser pocket—the jingle—he thumbed and selected a key. "Early on we did a resource-utilization survey. It showed no one was using the room much during this time of day."

He unlocked the door and held it open.

"Executive privilege," he said. "Not too democratic, but democracy doesn't work in a place like this."

I stepped in. The room was pitch-dark. I groped the wall for a light switch but he walked right to it and flipped it. A section of fluorescent panels stuttered and brightened.

He pointed to a booth in the center of the room. I sat down and he went behind the counter, filled a cup with tap water, and dropped a lemon wedge in it. Then he got something from under the counter—a Danish—and put it on a plate. Moving briskly, familiarly, as if he were puttering in his own kitchen.

He came back, took a bite and a sip, and exhaled with satisfaction.

"She *should* be healthy, dammit," he said. "I really don't understand why the hell she isn't, and no one's been able to give me a straight story."

"Have you talked to Dr. Eves?"

"Eves, the others, all of them. No one seems to know a damn thing. You have anything to offer yet?"

"Afraid not."

He leaned forward. "What I don't understand is why they called you in. Nothing personal—I just don't see the point of a psychologist here."

"I really can't discuss that, Mr. Jones."

"Chuck. Mr. Jones is a song by that curly character, whatsisname—Bob Dylan?" Tiny smile. "Surprised I know that, right? Your era, not mine. But it's a family joke. From way back when. Chip's high school days. He used to ride me, fight everything. Everything was like this."

He made hooks of his hands, linked them, then strained to pull them apart, as if they'd become glued.

"Those were the days," he said, smiling suddenly. "He was my only one, but he was like half a dozen, in terms of rebellion. Anytime I'd try to get him to do something he didn't want to do, he'd rear up and buck, tell me I was acting just like the song by that Dylan Thomas character, that guy who doesn't know what's going on—Mr. Jones. He'd play it loud. I never actually listened to the lyrics, but I got the point. Nowadays he and I are best of friends. We laugh about those days."

Thinking of friendship cemented by real estate deals, I smiled.

"He's a solid boy," he said. "The earring and the hair are just part of the image—you know he's a college professor, don't you?"

I nodded.

"The kids he teaches *eat* that kind of thing up. He's a great teacher, won awards for it."

"That so?"

"Lots of them. You'll never hear him toot his own horn. He was always like that. Modest. I've got to do his bragging for him. He was winning them back when he was a student. Went to Yale. Always had a flair for it, teaching. Used to tutor the slow boys in his fraternity and get them up to grade. Tutored high school kids, too—got a commendation for it. It's a gift, like anything else."

His hands were still linked together, two stubby, fleshy grapples. He separated them, fanned them on the table. Closed the fingers. Scratched the Formica.

"Sounds like you're pretty proud of him," I said.

"I most certainly am. Cindy too. Lovely girl, no pretensions. They've created something solid—proof of the pudding is Cassie. I know I'm not objective but that little girl is adorable and beautiful and smart. Great disposition to boot."

"No mean feat," I said. "Considering."

His eyes wandered. Closed and opened.

"You know we lost one before her, don't you? Beautiful little boy—crib death. They still don't know why that happens, do they?"

I shook my head.

"That was *hell* on earth, Doctor. Clear out of the blue—one day he's here; the next . . . I just can't understand why no one can tell me what's wrong with this one."

"No one really knows, Chuck."

He waved that off. "I still don't understand why you're involved. Don't take that personally. I know you've heard all sorts of horror stories about why we abolished the Psychiatry division. But the truth is, that had nothing to do with approving or disapproving of mental health treatment. I certainly do approve—what's not to approve? Some people need help. But the fact is that the weak sisters running Psychiatry had no idea how to construct a budget and stick to it, let alone do their own jobs competently. The clear picture I got from the other doctors was that they were inept. Of course, to hear it now, they were all geniuses—we destroyed a center of psychiatric brilliance."

He rolled his eyes. "No matter. Hopefully, one day we'll be able to establish a good, solid department. Bring in some top people. You used to work here, didn't you?"

"Years ago."

"Would you ever consider returning?"

I shook my head.

"Why'd you leave?"

"Various reasons."

"The freedom of the private sector? Be your own boss?"

"That was part of it."

"So maybe if you step back you can be objective and understand what I mean. About the need for efficiency. Being realistic. In general, I'm finding doctors out in the private sector do understand. Because running a practice is running a business. It's only the ones who live off the— But no matter. Getting back to what I was saying, about your involvement with my granddaughter. No one's got the gall to say her problems are in her *head,* do they?"

"I really can't talk about details, Chuck."

"Why the hell not?"

"Confidentiality."

"Chip and Cindy don't keep secrets from me."

"I need to hear that from them. It's the law."

"You're a tough one, aren't you?"

"Not particularly." I smiled.

He smiled back. Linked his hands again. Drank hot water.

"All right. This is *your* business and you have to stick to your own rules. Guess I've got to get some kind of permission note from them."

"Guess so."

He smiled wide. His teeth were severely misaligned and brown.

"In the meantime," he said, "am *I* allowed to talk to *you?*"

"Sure."

He locked in on my face, studying it, with a mixture of interest and skepticism, as if it were a quarterly report. "I'll just assume no one seriously thinks Cassie's problems are mental, because that's just too ridiculous."

Pause. Assess. Hoping for a nonverbal clue?

I made sure not to move.

He said, "So, the only other thing I can come up with to explain your getting involved is that someone thinks something's wrong with Cindy or Chip. Which is ridiculous."

He sat back. Kept studying. A triumphant look came on his face. I was sure I hadn't even blinked. Wondered if he'd seen something or was just finessing.

I said, "Psychologists aren't called in only to analyze, Chuck. We also give support to people under stress."

"Being a hired friend, huh?" He jiggled his nose again, stood, smiled. "Well, then, be a *good* friend. They're good kids. All three of them."

22

I drove away trying to figure out what he'd been after and whether I'd given it to him.

Wanting me to see him as a concerned grandfather?

Chip and Cindy don't keep secrets from me.

Yet Chip and Cindy hadn't taken the trouble to inform him Cassie was being discharged. I realized that during all the contacts I'd had with both of them, his name hadn't come up once.

A tightly wound little man who was *all* business—even during our few minutes together, he'd mixed family matters with hospital affairs.

He hadn't wasted a moment on debate, had never tried to change my opinion.

Choosing, instead, to *shape* the conversation.

Even the choice of meeting place had been calculated. The dining room he closed and now treated as his personal galley. Getting refreshments for himself, but not me.

Brandishing a ring of keys to let me know he could open any

door in the hospital. Bragging about it, but letting me know he had too much integrity to grab office space.

Bringing my presumed hostility toward the despoiler of the Psychiatry department out in the open, then trying to neutralize me by appending a bribe just subtle enough to be taken as casual conversation:

Hopefully, one day we'll be able to establish a good, solid department. Bring in some top people . . . Would you ever consider returning?

When I'd demurred, he'd backed off immediately. Empathized with my good sense, then used it to support his point of view.

If he'd been a hog farmer, he'd have found a way to use the squeal.

So I had to believe that though ours had been a chance encounter, if we hadn't bumped into each other soon, he would have arranged a meeting.

I was too small a fry for him to care what I thought about him.

Except as it related to Cassie and Chip and Cindy.

Wanting to know what I'd learned about his family.

Meaning there was probably something to hide and he didn't know if I'd discovered it.

I thought of Cindy's worry: *People must think I'm crazy.*

Was there a breakdown in her past?

The entire family fearful of a psychological probe?

If so, what better place to avoid scrutiny than a hospital without a Psychiatry department?

Another reason not to transfer Cassie.

Then Stephanie had gone and ruined things by bringing in a free-lance.

I remembered Plumb's surprise when she told him what I was.

Now his boss had checked me out personally.

Shaping, molding. Painting a rosy picture of Chip and Cindy.

Mostly Chip—I realized he'd spent very little time on Cindy.

Paternal pride? Or directing me *away* from his daughter-in-law because the less said about her the better?

I stopped for a red light at Sunset and La Brea.

My hands were tight on the steering wheel. I'd cruised a couple of miles without knowing it.

When I got home I was in a bad mood and thankful that Robin wasn't there to share it.

The operator at my service said, "Nothing, Dr. Delaware. Isn't that nice?"

"You bet." We told each other to have a nice day.

Unable to get Ashmore and Dawn Herbert out of my head, I drove over to the university, hooking into the campus at the north end and continuing southward until I came to the Medical Center.

A new exhibit on the history of leeching lined the hallway leading to the Biomed library—medieval etchings and wax simulations of patients being feasted upon by rubbery parasites. The main reading room was open for another two hours. One librarian, a good-looking blond woman, sat at the reference desk.

I searched through a decade of the *Index Medicus* for articles by Ashmore and Herbert and came up with four by him, all published during the last ten years.

The earliest appeared in the World Health Organization's public-health bulletin—Ashmore's summary of his work on infectious diseases in the southern Sudan, emphasizing the difficulty of conducting research in a war-torn environment. His writing style was cool, but the anger leaked through.

The other three pieces had been published in biomathematics journals. The first, funded by a grant from the National Institutes of Health, was Ashmore's take on the Love Canal disaster. The second was a federally funded review of mathematical applications to the life sciences. Ashmore's final sentence: "There are lies, damn lies, and statistics."

The last report was the work Mrs. Ashmore had described: analyzing the relationship between soil-concentration of pesticides and rates of leukemia, brain tumors, and lymphatic and liver cancers in children. The results were less than dramatic—a small numerical link between chemicals and disease, but one that wasn't statistically significant. But Ashmore said if even one life was saved, the study had justified itself.

A little strident and self-serving for scientific writing. I checked the funding on the study: The Ferris Dixon Institute for Chemical Research, Norfolk, Virginia. Grant #37958.

It sounded like an industry front, though Ashmore's point of view wouldn't have made him a likely candidate for the chemical industry's largesse. I wondered if the absence of any more publications meant the institute had cut off his grant money.

If so, who paid his bills at Western Peds?

I went over to the librarian and asked her if there was a compilation of scientific grants issued by private agencies.

"Sure," she said. "Life science or physical?"

Not sure how Ashmore's work would be categorized, I said, "Both."

She got up and walked briskly back to the reference shelves. Heading straight for a case in the center of the section, she pulled down two thick soft-cover books.

"Here you go—these are the most recent. Anything prior to this year is bound, over there. If you want federally funded research, that's over there to the right."

I thanked her, took the books to a table, and read their covers. CATALOGUE OF PRIVATELY FUNDED RESEARCH: VOLUME I: THE BIOMEDICAL AND LIFE SCIENCES.

Ditto, VOLUME II: ENGINEERING, MATHEMATICS, AND THE PHYSICAL SCIENCES.

I opened the first one and turned to the "Grantee" section at the back. Laurence Ashmore's name popped out at me midway through the As, cross-referenced to a page number in the "Grantor" section. I flipped to it:

THE FERRIS DIXON INSTITUTE FOR CHEMICAL RESEARCH
NORFOLK, VIRGINIA

The institute had funded only two projects for the current academic year:

#37959: Ashmore, Laurence Allan. Western Pediatric Medical Center, Los Angeles, CA. *Soil toxicity as a factor in the etiology of pediatric neoplasms: a follow-up study.* $973,652.75, three years.

#37960: Zimberg, Walter William. University of Maryland, Baltimore, MD. *Non-parametric statistics versus Pearson correlations in scientific prediction: the investigative, heuristic, and predictive value of* a priori *determination of sample distribution.* $124,731.00, three years.

The second study was quite a mouthful, but Ferris Dixon obviously wasn't paying by the word. Ashmore had received nearly 90 percent of its total funding.

Nearly a million dollars for three years.

Very big bucks for a one-man project that was basically a rehash. I was curious about what it took to impress the folks at Ferris Dixon. But it was Sunday and even those with deep pockets rested.

I returned home, changed into soft clothes, and puttered, pretending the fact that it was the weekend meant something to me. At six o'clock, no longer able to fake it, I called the Jones house. As the phone rang, the front door opened and Robin stepped in. She waved, stopped in the kitchen to kiss my cheek, then kept going toward the bedroom. Just as she disappeared from view Cindy's voice came on the line.

"Hello."

"Hi. It's Alex Delaware."

"Oh, hi. How are you, Dr. Delaware?"

"Fine. And you?"

"Oh . . . pretty good." She sounded edgy.

"Something the matter, Cindy?"

"No . . . Um, could you hold for just one second?"

She covered the receiver and the next time I heard her voice it was muffled and her words were unintelligible. But I made out another voice answering—from the low tones, Chip.

"Sorry," she said. "We're just getting settled. I thought I heard Cassie—she's taking a nap."

Definitely edgy.

"Tired from the ride?" I said.

"Um . . . that and just getting readjusted. She had a great big dinner, plus dessert, then just dropped off. I'm across the hall from her right now. Keeping my ears open . . . you know."

"Sure," I said.

"I keep her door open to our bathroom—it connects to our room—and a night light on inside. So I can look in on her regularly."

"How do you get any sleep that way?"

"Oh, I manage. If I'm tired, I nap when she does. Being together so much, we've kind of gotten on to the same schedule."

"Do you and Chip ever take shifts?"

"No, I couldn't do that—his course load's really heavy this semester. Are you coming out to visit us, soon?"

"How about tomorrow?"

"Tomorrow? Sure. Um . . . how about in the afternoon—around four?"

Thinking of the 101 freeway snarl, I said, "Would earlier be possible?"

"Um, okay—three-thirty?"

"I was thinking even earlier, Cindy, like two?"

"Oh, sure . . . I've got some things to do—would two-thirty be okay?"

"Fine."

"Great, Dr. Delaware. We're looking forward to seeing you."

I walked to the bedroom, thinking how much more nervous she sounded at home than in the hospital. Something about home setting her off—raising her anxiety and leading to Munchausen manipulation?

Though, even if she was virgin-innocent, I supposed it made sense for her house to spook her. For her, home was where the harm was.

Robin was slipping into a little black dress I'd never seen before. I zipped her up, pressed my cheek to the warmth between her shoulder blades, and finally managed to complete the process. We drove to the top of the Glen, to an Italian place in the shopping center just below Mulholland. No reservation, and we had to wait at a cold onyx bar. Frantic singles scene tonight, lots of tanned flesh and triple entendres. We enjoyed not being part of it, reveled in silence. I started to have real faith in our reunion—something pleasant to think about.

A half hour later we were seated at a corner table and ordering before the waiter could escape. We ate veal and drank wine for a peaceful hour, drove back home, got out of our clothes and straight into bed. Despite the wine, our union was quick, limber, almost jovial. Afterward, Robin ran a bath, got in, and called for me to join her. Just as I was about to, the phone rang.

"Dr. Delaware, this is Janie at your service. I've got a call from a Chip Jones."

"Thanks. Put him on, please."

"Dr. Delaware?"

"Hi, Chip, what's up?"

"Nothing—nothing medical, that is, thank God. I hope I'm not calling too late?"

"Not at all."

"Cindy just phoned me to say you're coming by, tomorrow afternoon. I'm checking to see if you need me to be there."

"Your input's always welcome, Chip."

"Hmm."

"Is there a problem?"

"I'm afraid there is. I've got an afternoon class at one-thirty, then a meeting with some of my students right afterward. Nothing earth-shattering—just routine office hours—but with finals approaching, the undergraduate panic level's been rising at a precipitous rate."

"No problem," I said, "I'll catch you the next time."

"Great—and if something comes up that you want to ask me about, just call. I gave you my number here, didn't I?"

"Yes, you did."

"Great. Then it's all set."

I hung up, bothered by his call but not sure why. Robin called from the bathroom and I went in. The light was dim and she was up to her neck in suds, head tilted back against the rim of the tub. A few clusters of bubbles dotted her pinned-up hair, shiny as gems. Her eyes were closed and she kept them that way as I got in.

Covering her breasts, she said, "Shudder, shudder—hope that's not Norman Bates."

"Norman preferred showers."

"Oh. Right. Norman's meditative brother, then."

"Norman's wet brother—Merman."

She laughed. I stretched out, closed my eyes too. She put her legs atop mine. I sank, feeling myself warm, massaging her toes, trying to loosen up. But I kept thinking of the conversation I'd just had with Chip and remained tight.

Cindy just phoned me to say you're coming by, tomorrow afternoon.

Meaning he hadn't been home when I'd called.

Hadn't been the man I'd heard Cindy speaking to.

The edginess . . .

Robin said, "What's the matter? Your shoulders are all bunched."

I told her.

"Maybe you're reading too much into it, Alex. It could have been a relative visiting—her father or her brother."

"She doesn't have either."

"So it was a cousin or an uncle. Or a service call—the plumber, the electrician, whatever."

"Try getting one of those guys on a Sunday evening," I said.

"They're rich. The rich get what they want when they want it."

"Yeah, maybe that's all it was. . . . Still, I thought she sounded nervous. As if I'd caught her off guard."

"Okay, let's say she's having a fling. You already suspect her of poisoning her kid. Adultery's a misdemeanor in comparison."

"Having a fling the first day back from the hospital?"

"Hubby didn't see anything wrong with flying off to his office the first day, did he? If that's his usual pattern, she's probably a lonely lady, Alex. He isn't giving her what she needs, so she's getting it elsewhere. Anyway, does adultery relate to this Munchausen business?"

"Anything that makes someone with those tendencies feel helpless could have an effect. But it's more than that, Robin. If Cindy's having an affair, that could provide a motive. Ditch hubby and kids, get free to be with her lover."

"There are easier ways to get free of your family."

"We're talking about someone sick."

"Really sick."

"I don't get paid to deal with healthy heads."

She leaned forward and touched my face. "This is really getting to you."

"Sure is. Cassie's so damned dependent and everyone's failing her."

"You're doing everything *you* can."

"I suppose."

We stayed in the water. I worked at relaxing again, settled finally for loose muscles and a tight mind. Soap-sud clouds gathered around Robin's shoulders like an ermine stole. She looked beautiful and I told her so.

She said, "What a flatterer, Mer." But her grin was deep and heartfelt. At least I'd made someone feel good.

We got back into bed and tackled the Sunday paper. I read carefully this time, searching for anything on Western Peds or Laurence Ashmore but finding nothing. The phone rang at ten forty-five. Robin answered. "Hi, Milo."

He said something that made her laugh. She said, "Absolutely," handed me the receiver, and returned to her crossword puzzle.

"Nice to hear her voice again," he said. "Finally, you show some good judgment." The connection was clear, but it sounded distant.

"Where are you?"

"Alley behind a leather-goods store, little pilfering surveillance, nothing so far. Am I interrupting something?"

"Domestic bliss," I said, stroking Robin's arm. She was concentrating hard on the puzzle, pencil in mouth, but her hand rose to meet mine and we laced fingers.

"Let's hear it for any kind of bliss," said Milo. "Got a couple of things for you. First, your Mr. Huenengarth has an interesting pattern. Valid driver's license and social security number, but the address on the license traces to a mail drop in Tarzana, and he's got no phone number, credit history, or IRS file. No county records either. No record of him in the military or on the voter roster. Similar pattern to a long-term con just out of the joint—someone who hasn't voted or paid taxes. Though he doesn't show up on NCIC or the parole rolls either, so maybe it's a computer glitch or I screwed up technically. I'll have Charlie try tomorrow."

"Phantom of the hospital," I said. "I feel so much better knowing he's head of Security."

Robin looked up briefly, then down again.

"Yeah," said Milo. "You'd be surprised how many strange types get into security—nutcases who try out for police departments, don't pass the psych evaluation. Meantime, keep your distance from him until I can find out more. Second thing is, I've been nosing around the Herbert file and plan to do a little late-night downtown prowl—talk to that bartender witness."

"Does he have something new to offer?"

"No, but Gomez and his partner didn't follow through enough for my taste. The guy has a serious dope record and they figured him for an unreliable witness. So they let him off easy, not enough questions. I got hold of his number, spoke to his girlfriend, and found out he got a job at another club nearby, over in Newton Division. Thought I'd go over and talk to him. Thought you might be interested in a tag-along. But you've obviously got better things to do."

Robin looked up. I realized my fingers had tightened around hers and eased my grip.

"When are you going?" I said.

"Hour or so. Figured I'd make it over there after midnight, when the scene just starts. I want to catch him in his element, but before it gets too intense. Anyway, enjoy your bliss."

"Wait. I've got a few things for *you*. Got time?"

"Sure. Nothing here in this alley but us cats. What's up?"

"I got buttonholed by Grandpa Chuck today, just as I left the hospital. He gave me a one-big-happy-family speech—defending the clan's honor, just like we discussed. Topped it off by offering me a job. The implication I got was I should behave myself, not dig too deeply."

"Not very subtle."

"Actually, he managed to do it quite subtly. Even if it had been taped, he could never have been pinned down. Not that the offer was worth much, because a job at Western Peds isn't likely to have much security."

I recounted Plumb's newspaper interview, and the financial-scheme hypotheses that had led me to look further into Laurence Ashmore's research. By the time I got to the Ferris Dixon Institute, Robin had put her puzzle down and was listening intently.

"Virginia," said Milo. "Been there a couple of times for fed training seminars. Pretty state, but anything down there always spells government to me."

"The institute's listed in a roster of private agencies. I figured it for some kind of corporate front."

"What kind of grant was it?"

"Pesticides in the soil, Ashmore analyzing his old data. Way too much money for that kind of thing, Milo. I thought I'd call the institute tomorrow morning, see what else I can learn. I'm also going to try to contact Mrs. Ashmore again. Find out if Huenengarth the Mystery Man's dropped by."

"Like I said, Alex, keep your distance."

"Don't worry, I won't get any closer than the phone. Afternoon I'll be doing what I went to school for over at Chip and Cindy's. Who may *not* be in a state of domestic bliss."

I reviewed my suspicions, including the caveats Robin had raised. "What do you think?"

"I think, who the hell knows? Maybe she did have a leaky faucet, or maybe she's the Hester Prynne of the San Fernando Valley. Tell you one thing, if she is stepping out on the Chipper, she's being pretty sloppy about it, wouldn't you say? Letting you hear Lover Boy's voice."

"Maybe she didn't mean to—I caught her off guard. She sounded antsy—covered the phone almost immediately. All I actually made out were a few low tones. And if she's a Munchausen type, flirting with another kind of danger would be right up her alley."

"Low tones, huh? Sure it wasn't the TV?"

"No, this was a real-life conversation. Cindy talked and the guy answered. I assumed it was Chip. If he hadn't called me later, I'd never have known it wasn't."

"Hmm," he said. "So what does it mean? In terms of Cassie?"

I repeated my motive theory.

He said, "Don't forget Chip's dough—that's one hell of an incentive."

"One hell of a family embarrassment, too, if it blows wide open and there's a nasty divorce. Maybe *that's* what Chuck's trying to keep me away from. He talked about Chip and Cindy creating something solid—called Cindy a lovely girl. Even though she doesn't seem like the girl a guy in his position would have wanted for his only daughter-in-law. On the other hand, from the look of his teeth, he came up the hard way himself. So maybe he's not a snob."

"His teeth?"

"They're crooked and discolored. No one ever shelled out on orthodontia on his account. Fact is, his entire manner's pretty rough."

"Self-made man," he said. "Maybe he respects Cindy for doing the same thing."

"Who knows? Anything on why she left the army?"

"Not yet. Gotta press Charlie on that . . . Okay, I'll check with you tomorrow."

"If you find out anything from the bartender, call me first thing."

There was a strain in my voice. My shoulders had bunched again.

Robin touched them and said, "What is it?"

I covered the phone and turned to her. "He's found a lead to something that may or may not be related to the case."

"And he called to invite you along."

"Yes, but—"

"And you want to go."

"No, I—"

"Is it anything dangerous?"

"No, just interviewing a witness."

She gave me a gentle shove. "Go."

"It's not necessary, Robin."

She laughed. "Go anyway."

"I don't need to. This is nice."

"Domestic bliss?"

"Mega-bliss." I put my arm around her.

She kissed it, then removed it.

"Go, Alex. I don't want to lie here listening to you toss."

"I won't."

"You know you will."

"Being alone is preferable?"

"I won't be. Not in my head. Not with what we've got going for us now."

23

I tucked her in bed and went out to the living room to wait. Milo knocked softly just before midnight. He was carrying a hard-shell case the size of an attaché and had on a polo shirt, twill pants, and windbreaker. All in black. Regular-guy parody of the L.A. hipster ensemble.

I said, "Trying to fade into the night, Zorro?"

"We're taking your car. I'm not bringing the Porsche down there."

I pulled out the Seville; he put the case in the trunk, got in the passenger seat. "Let's roll."

I followed his directions, taking Sunset west to the 405 south, merging with hurtling trucks and the red-eye crowd heading out to the airport. At the junction with the Santa Monica Freeway, I hooked over toward L.A. and traveled east in the fast lane. The highway was emptier than I'd ever seen it, softened to something impressionistic by a warm, moist haze.

Milo lowered the window, lit up a panatela, and blew smoke out at the city. He seemed tired, as if he'd talked himself out over the phone. I felt weary, too, and neither of us said a word. Near La Brea a loud, low sports car rode our tail, belched and flashed its brights before passing us at close to a hundred. Milo sat up suddenly—cop's reflex—and watched it disappear before settling back down and staring out the windshield.

I followed his gaze upward to an ivory moon, cloud-streaked and fat, though not quite full. It dangled before us like a giant yo-yo, ivory mottled with green-cheese verdigris.

"Three-quarter moon," I said.

"More like seven-eighths. That means *almost* all the nuts're out. Stay on the Ten past the interchange and get off at Santa Fe."

He kept grumbling directions in a low voice, taking us into a broad, silent district of storehouses, foundries, and wholesale jobbers. No streetlights, no movement; the only vehicles I spotted were penned behind prison-grade security fences. As we'd traveled away from the ocean, the haze had lifted and the downtown skyline had turned chiseled and crisp. But here I could barely make out the shapes, miragelike against the matte-black stasis of the city's outer limits. The silence seemed glum—a failure of spirit. As if L.A.'s geographical boundaries had exceeded its energy.

He directed me through a series of quick, sharp turns down asphalt strips that could have been streets or alleys—a maze that I'd never be able to reverse from memory. He'd allowed his cigar to go cold but the smell of tobacco stuck to the car. Though the breeze streaming in was warm and pleasant, he began raising the window. I realized why before he finished: A new smell overpowered the burnt-cloth stink of cheap leaf. Sweet and bitter at the same time, metallic, yet rotten. It leaked through the glass. So did noise—cold and resonant, like giant steel hands clapping—scraping the night-lull from somewhere far away.

"Packing houses," he said. "East L.A. all the way down to Vernon, but the sound carries. When I first came on the force I drove a cruiser down here, on the night watch. Sometimes they slaughtered the hogs at night. You could hear them howling, smashing into things, and rattling their chains. Nowadays I think they tranquilize them— Here, turn right, then immediately left. Go a block and park anywhere you can."

The maze ended on a skinny block-long straightaway bounded

on both sides by cyclone fencing. No sidewalks. Weeds erupted through the tar like hairs on a wen. Cars lined both sides of the street, pushed up close to the fence.

I pulled into the first space I saw, behind an old BMW with a K-ROQ window sticker and a rear deck piled high with trash. We got out of the Seville. The air had cooled but the slaughterhouse smell remained—dribs and drabs of stench, rather than a constant assault. Changing wind, probably, though I couldn't sense it. The machine scrape was gone, replaced by music—electric organ elf-squeaks and a murky bass, middle-range tones that might have come from guitars. If there was a beat, I couldn't sense that either.

"Party time," I said. "What's the dance of the week?"

"Felony lambada," said Milo. "Sidle up against your partner and rifle through his/her pockets." He shoved his hands in *his* pockets and slouched forward.

We began walking up the street. It dead-ended at a tall, windowless building. Pale-painted brick walls that a couple of red lights turned pink. Three stories—a trio of successively smaller cubes stacked atop one another. Flat roof, steel doors asymmetrically placed under a random assortment of shuttered windows. A tangle of fire-escape ladders hugged the facade like cast-iron ivy. As we got closer I saw huge, faded letters painted above the dock: BAKER FERTILIZER AND POTASH CO.

The music got louder. Heavy, slow, keyboard solo. Voices became audible in between notes. As we got closer, I saw a line of people S-curved in front of one of the doors—a fifty-foot ant-trail that dipped into the street and clogged it.

We began passing the line. Faces turned toward us sequentially, like animated dominoes. Black duds were the uniform, sullen pouts the mask. Boot chains, cigarettes—legal and otherwise—mumbles and shuffles and sneers, an amphetamine jerk here and there. Flashes of bare flesh, whiter than the moonlight. A rude comment harmonized with the organ and somebody laughed.

The age range was eighteen to twenty-five, skewed toward the lower end. I heard a cat snarl at my back, then more laughter. Prom from Hell.

The door that had drawn the crowd was a rust-colored sheet-metal rectangle blocked by a slide bolt. A big man wearing a sleeveless black turtleneck, green-flowered surfing shorts, and high-laced boots stood in front of it. He was in his early twenties, had clotted features, dreamy eyes, and skin that would have been florid even without the red bulb above his head. His black hair was trimmed to a buzz on top and engraved with lightning bolts of scalp on both sides. I noticed a couple of thin spots that hadn't been barbered—downy patches, as if he was recovering from chemo-therapy. But his body was huge and inflated. The hair at the back of his head was long and knotted in a tight, oiled queue that hung over one shoulder. The shoulder and its mate were graveled with acne. Steroid rash—that explained the hair loss.

The kids at the head of the line were talking to him. He wasn't answering, didn't notice our approach or chose to ignore it.

Milo walked up to him and said, "Evening, champ."

The bouncer kept looking the other way.

Milo repeated himself. The bouncer jerked his head around and growled. If not for his size, it would have been comical. The people at the head of the line were impressed.

Someone said, "Yo, kung-fu." The bouncer smiled, looked away again, cracked his knuckles and yawned.

Milo moved quickly, stepping up nose to nose with him while shoving his badge in the meaty face. I hadn't seen him remove it from his pocket.

The bouncer growled again but the rest of him was acquiescent. I looked over my shoulder. A girl with hair the color of deoxygenated blood stuck her tongue out at me and wiggled it. The boy fondling her chest spit and flipped me the bird.

Milo moved his badge back and forth in front of the bouncer's eyes. The bouncer followed it, as if hypnotized.

Milo held it still. The bouncer read laboriously.

Someone cursed. Someone else howled like a wolf. That caught on and soon the street sounded like something out of Jack London.

Milo said, "Open up, Spike, or we start checking IDs and health codes."

The lupine chorus grew louder, almost blotting out the music. The bouncer crunched his brows, digesting. It looked painful. Finally he laughed and reached behind himself.

Milo grabbed his wrist, big fingers barely making it around the joint. "Easy."

"Op'ning it, man," said the bouncer. "Key." His voice was unnaturally deep, like a tape played at slo-mo, but whiny nonetheless.

Milo backed away, gave him some space, and watched his hands. The bouncer pulled a key out of his surf-shorts, popped a lock on the bolt, and lifted the bar.

The door opened an inch. Heat and light and noise poured out through it. The wolf-pack charged.

The bouncer leaped forward, hands shaped into what he thought were karate blades, baring his teeth. The pack stopped, retreated, but a few protests sounded. The bouncer raised his hands high in the air and made pawing movements. The light from above turned his irises red. His armpits were shaven. Pimples there, too.

"*The fuck back!*" he bellowed.

The wolfies went still.

Milo said, "Impressive, Spike."

The bouncer kept his eyes fixed on the line. His mouth hung open. He was panting and sweating. Sound kept pouring out of the door crack.

Milo put his hand on the bolt. It creaked and stole the bouncer's attention. He faced Milo.

"Fuck him," said a voice from behind us.

"We're going in now, Spike," said Milo. "Keep those assholes calm."

The bouncer closed his mouth and breathed loudly through his nose. A bubble of snot filled one nostril.

"It's not Spike," he said. "It's James."

Milo smiled. "Okay. You do good work, James. Ever work at the Mayan Mortgage?"

The bouncer wiped his nose with his arm and said, "Huh?"

Working hard at processing.

"Forget it."

The bouncer looked injured. "Whaddya say, man? Seriously."

"I said you've got a bright future, James. This gig ever gets old, you can always run for Vice President."

* * *

The room was big, harshly lit in a few spots, but mostly dark. The floors were cement; the walls that I could see, painted brick. A network of conduits, wheels, gears, and pipes adhered to the ceiling, ragged in places, as if ripped apart in a frenzy.

Off to the left was the bar—wooden doors on sawhorses fronting a metal rack full of bottles. Next to the rack were half a dozen white bowls filled with ice.

Shiny porcelain bowls. Raised lids.

Toilets.

Two men worked nonstop to service a thirsty throng of minors, filling and squirting and scooping cubes from the commodes. No faucets; the soda and water came from bottles.

The rest of the space was a dance floor. No boundary separated the bar crowd from pressure-packed bodies writhing and jerking like beached grunion. Up close, the music was even more formless. But loud enough to keep the Richter scale over at Cal Tech busy.

The geniuses creating it stood at the back, on a makeshift stage. Five hollow-cheeked, leotarded things who could have been junkies had they been healthier-looking. Marshall Stacks big as vacation cabins formed a black felt wall behind them. The bass drum bore the legend OFFAL.

High on the wall behind the amps was another BAKER FERTIL-IZER sign, partially blocked by a hand-lettered banner tacked diagonally.

WELCOME TO THE SHIT HOUSE.

The accompanying artwork was even more charming.

"Creative," I said, loud enough to feel my palate vibrate, but inaudible.

Milo must have read my lips because he grinned and shook his head. Then he lowered it and charged through the dancers, toward the bar.

I dived in after him.

We arrived, battered but intact, at the front of the drinkers. Dishes of unshelled peanuts sat beside toilet paper squares improvising as napkins. The bartop needed wiping. The floor was carpeted with husks where it wasn't wet and slick.

Milo managed to bull his way behind the bar. Both of the barkeeps were thin, dark, and bearded, wearing sleeveless gray undershirts and baggy white pajama bottoms. The one closer to Milo was bald. The other was Rapunzel in drag.

Milo went over to Baldy. The bartender jabbed one hand defensively while pouring Jolt Cola into a glass quarter-filled with rum. Milo's hand fit all the way around this wrist. He gave it a short, sharp twist—not enough to cause injury, but the bartender's eyes and mouth opened and he put the cola can down and tried to jerk away.

Milo held fast, doing the badge thing again, but discreetly. Keeping the ID at an angle that hid it from the drinkers. A hand from the crowd reached out and snared the rum and cola. Several others began slapping the bartop. A few mouths opened in soundless shouts.

Baldy gave Milo a panicked look.

Milo talked in his ear.

Baldy said something back.

Milo kept talking.

Baldy pointed at the other mix-master. Milo released his grip. Baldy went over to Rapunzel and the two of them conferred. Rapunzel nodded and Baldy returned to Milo, looking resigned.

I followed the two of them on a sweaty, buffeted trek through and around the dance floor. Slow going—part ballet, part jungle clearance. Finally we ended up at the back of the room, behind the band's amps and a snarl of electric wires, and walked through a wooden door marked TOILETS.

On the other side was a long, cold, cement-floored hall littered with paper scraps and nasty-looking puddles. Several couples groped in the shadows. A few loners sat on the floor, heads lowered to laps. Marijuana and vomit fought for olfactory dominance. The sound level had sunk to jet-takeoff roar.

We passed doors stenciled STANDERS and SQUATTERS, stepped over legs, tried to skirt the garbage. Baldy was good at it, moving with a light, nimble gait, his pajama pants billowing. At the end of the hallway was yet another door, rusted metal, identical to the one the bouncer had guarded.

Baldy said, "Outside okay?" in a squeaky voice.

"What's out there, Robert?"

The bartender shrugged and scratched his chin. "The back." He was anywhere from thirty-five to forty-five. The beard was little more than fuzz and didn't conceal much of his face. It was a face worth concealing, skimpy and rattish and brooding and mean.

Milo pushed the door open, looked outside, and took hold of the bartender's arm.

The three of us went outside to a small fenced parking lot. A U-Haul two-ton truck was parked there, along with three cars. Lots more trash was spread across the ground in clumps, a foot high in places, fluttering in the breeze. Beyond the fence was the fat moon.

Milo led the bald man to a relatively clean spot near the center of the lot, away from the cars.

"This is Robert Gabray," he said to me. "Mixologist extraordinaire." To the bartender: "You've got fast hands, Robert."

The barkeep wiggled his fingers. "Gotta work."

"The old Protestant ethic?"

Blank look.

"You like working, Robert?"

"Gotta. They keep a record a everything."

"Who's they?"

"The owners."

"They in there watching you?"

"No. But they got eyes."

"Sounds like the CIA, Robert."

The bartender didn't answer.

"Who pays your salary, Robert?"

"Some guys."

"Which guys?"

"They own the building."

"What's the name on your payroll check?"

"Ain't no checks."

"Cash deal, Robert?"

Nod.

"You holding out on the Internal Revenue?"

Gabray crossed his arms and rubbed his shoulders. "C'mon, what'd I do?"

"You'd know that better than me, wouldn't you, Robert?"

"Bunch a A-rabs, the owners."

"Names."

"Fahrizad, Nahrizhad, Nahrishit, whatever."

"Sounds Iranian, not Arab."

"Whatever."

"How long you been working here?"

"Couple of months."

Milo shook his head. "No, I don't think so, Robert. Wanna give it another try?"

"What?" Gabray looked puzzled.

"Think back where you *really* were a couple of months ago, Robert."

Gabray rubbed his shoulders some more.

"Cold, Robert?"

"I'm okay . . . Okay, yeah, it's been a couple of *weeks*."

"Ah," said Milo, "that's better."

"Whatever."

"Weeks, months, it's all the same to you?"

Gabray didn't answer.

"It just *seemed* like months?"

"Whatever."

"Time goes quickly when you're having fun?"

"Whatever."

"Two weeks," said Milo. "That makes a lot more sense, Robert. Probably what you meant to say. You wouldn't think of giving me a hard time—you were just making an honest error, right?"

"Yeah."

"You forgot that two months ago you weren't working anywhere because you were at County lockup on a pissanty mary-joo-anna rap."

The bartender shrugged.

"Really bright, Robert, running those red lights with that brick in the trunk of your car."

"It wasn't my stuff."

"Ah."

"It's true, man."

"You took the heat for someone else?"

"Yeah."

"You're just a nice guy, huh? Real hero."

Shrug. Another rub of the shoulders. One of Gabray's arms rose higher and he scratched the bare skin atop his head.

"Got an itch, Robert?"

"I'm fine, man."

"Sure you're not dope-chilled?"

"I'm okay, man."

Milo looked at me. "Robert mixes powders as well as fluids. Quite an amateur chemist—isn't that right, Robert?"

Another shrug.

"Got a day job, Robert?"

Shake of the head.

"Your P.O. know you're working here?"

"Why shouldn't I?"

Milo leaned in closer and smiled patiently. "Because you, as a habitual although petty felon, are supposed to stay away from bad influences, and those folks in there don't look any too wholesome."

Gabray sucked his teeth and looked at the ground. "Who told you I was here?"

Milo said, "Spare me the questions, Robert."

"It was that bitch, wasn't it?"

"What bitch is that?"

"You know."

"Do I?"

"You musta—you knew I was here."

"Angry at her, Robert?"

"Nah."

"Not at all?"

"I don't get mad."

"What do you get?"

"Nothing."

"You get even?"

Gabray said, "Can I smoke?"

"She paid your bail, Robert. In my book that makes *her* the hero."

"I'll marry her. Can I smoke?"

"Sure, Robert, you're a free man. Least till your trial. 'Cause *the bitch* made your bail."

Gabray pulled a pack of Kools out of his p.j. pants. Milo was ready with a match.

"Let's talk about where you were *three* months ago, Robert."

Gabray smoked and gave another foggy look.

"A month before you got busted, Robert. March."

"What about it?"

"The Mayan Mortgage."

Gabray smoked and looked at the sky.

"Remember it, Robert?"

"What about it?"

"This."

Milo slid something out of his shirt pocket. Penlight and a color photo. He held the picture in front of Gabray's eyes and shined the light on it. I stepped behind Gabray and peered over his shoulder.

Same face as in the snapshot the Murtaughs had given me. Below the hairline. Above it, the skull was flattened to something that was incapable of holding a brain. What was left of the hair was a matted red-black cloud. Eggshell-colored skin. A black-red necklace encircled the throat. The eyes were two purple eggplants.

Gabray looked at it, smoked, said, "So?"

"Remember her, Robert?"

"Should I?"

"Her name's Dawn Herbert. She was offed near the Mayan and you told some detectives you saw her with some guy."

Gabray flicked ashes and smiled. "*That's* what this is about? Yeah, I told them. I guess."

"You guess?"

"It was a long time ago, man."

"Three months."

"That's a long time, man."

Milo moved closer to Gabray and stared down at the smaller man. "You gonna help me on this? Yes or no?" Waving the homicide photo.

"What happened to the other cops? One a them was a beaner, I think."

"They took early retirement."

Gabray laughed. "Where? In Tia Wanna?"

"Talk to me, Robert."

"I don't know nothing."

"You saw her with a guy."

Shrug.

"Did you lie to those poor hardworking detectives, Robert?"

"Me? Never." Smile. "Perish my thoughts."

"Tell me what you told them."

"Didn't they write it down?"

"Tell me anyway."

"It was a long time ago."

"Three months."

"That's long, man."

"Sure is, Robert. Ninety whole days, and think about this: Your record, even a little weed could put you away for two, three times that long. Think of three hundred cold days—that was a lot of grass in your trunk."

Gabray looked at the photo, turned his head, and smoked.

"It wasn't mine. The weed."

Milo's turn to laugh. "That gonna be your defense?"

Gabray frowned, pinched his cigarette, sucked smoke through it. "You're saying you can help me?"

"Depends on what you come up with."

"I seen her."

"With a guy?"

Nod.

"Tell me the whole thing, Robert."

"That's it."

"Tell it like a story. Once upon a time."

Gabray snickered. "Yeah, sure. Once upon a time . . . I seen her with a guy. The end."

"In the club?"

"Outside."

"Where outside?"

"Like . . . a block away."

"That the only time you saw her?"

Gabray contemplated. "Maybe I seen her another time, inside."

"Was she a regular?"

"Whatever."

Milo sighed and patted the barkeep's shoulder. "Robert, Robert, Robert."

Gabray flinched with each mention of his name. "What?"

"That's not much of a story."

Gabray ground out his cigarette and produced another. He waited for Milo to light it and when that didn't happen, pulled out a book of matches and did it himself.

"I seen her maybe one more time," he said. "That's it. I only worked there a couple of weeks."

"Trouble holding down a job, Robert?"

"I like to move around, man."

"A ramblin' guy."

"Whatever."

"Twice in a couple of weeks," said Milo. "Sounds like she enjoyed the place."

"Fuckheads," said Gabray with sudden passion. "All a them, rich dumb fucks, coming down to play street-life, then running back to Rodeo Drive."

"Dawn Herbert come across as a rich bitch?"

"They're all the same, man."

"Ever talk to her?"

Alarm in the barkeep's eyes. "Nah. Like I said, I only seen her once, maybe twice. That's it. I didn't know her from shit—I had nothing to do with her and nothing to do with *that*." Pointing at the photo.

"You're sure about that."

"Real sure. *Really* real sure, man. That is *not* my thing."

"Tell me about seeing her with this guy."

"Like I said, once upon a time I was working there and once upon a time I went to take a smoke and seen her. Only reason I remembered was 'cause a the guy. He wasn't one a them."

"One of who?"

"The fuckheads. *She* was, but not *him*. He, like, stood out."

"Stood out how?"

"Straight."

"Businessman?"

"Nah."

"What then?"

Gabray shrugged.

"Was he wearing a suit, Robert?"

Gabray smoked hard and thought. "Nah. Kinda like you—

Sears Roebuck, that kind of jacket." Drawing his hands across his waist.

"A windbreaker?"

"Yeah."

"What color?"

"I dunno—dark. It was a long—"

"Time ago," said Milo. "What else was he wearing?"

"Pants, shoes, whatever. He looked like you." Smile. Smoke.

"In what way?"

"I dunno."

"Heavyset?"

"Yeah."

"My age?"

"Yeah."

"My height?"

"Yeah."

"Same hair as me?"

"Yeah."

"You have two dicks?"

"Ye— Huh?"

"Cut the crap, Robert. What was his hair like?"

"Short."

"Bald or a full head?"

Gabray frowned and touched his own bare dome. "He had hair," he said grudgingly.

"Beard or mustache?"

"I dunno. It was far."

"But you don't remember any facial hair?"

"No."

"How old was he?"

"I dunno—fifty, forty, whatever."

"You're twenty-nine and he was much older than you?"

"Eight. Next *month* I'm twenty-nine."

"Happy birthday. He was older than you?"

"A lot older."

"Old enough to be your father?"

"Maybe."

"Maybe?"

"Nah—not old enough. Forty, forty-five."

"Hair color?"

"I dunno—brown."

"Maybe or definitely?"

"Probably."

"Light or dark brown?"

"I dunno. It was nighttime."

"What color was *her* hair?"

"You got the picture there."

Milo shoved the photo in the barkeep's face. "Is this what she looked like when you saw her?"

Gabray pulled back and licked his lips. "Uh-uh—it was . . . her hair was different."

"Sure it was," said Milo. "It was sitting on an intact skull."

"Yeah—no—I mean the color. You know, yellow. Real yellow— like scrambled eggs. You could see it in the light."

"She was under a light?"

"I guess . . . yeah. The two a them were— a streetlight. Just for a sec, till they heard me and split."

"You didn't tell the other detectives about any light."

"They didn't ask."

Milo lowered the picture. Gabray smoked and looked away.

Milo said, "What were Ms. Herbert and this straight-looking guy doing under the light?"

"Talking."

"His hair wasn't blond?"

"I told you, *hers* was. You could *see* it, man—it was like a . . . banana." Gabray chuckled.

"And his was brown."

"Yeah. Hey, if this is so important, how come you're not writing it down?"

"What else do you remember about him, Robert?"

"That's it."

"Middle-aged, dark windbreaker, dark hair. That's not much to trade with, Robert."

"I'm telling you what I saw, man."

Milo turned his back on Gabray and looked at me. "Well, we tried to help him."

"You got someone, like tight?" said the bartender.

Milo kept his back turned. "What do you mean, Robert?"

"Tight *case,* man. I don't want to be telling you something and have some dude walk on some *Miranda* or something and come looking for me, you know?"

"You haven't told me much, Robert."

"You got someone tight?"

Milo pivoted slowly and faced him. "What I got is you, Robert, trying to jerk me around, withholding evidence on top of that brick in your trunk. I figure six months minimum—get the wrong judge, you might even be talking a year or so."

Gabray held out his hands. "Hey, I just don't want someone walking and coming after me. This guy was . . ."

"What?"

Gabray was silent.

"This guy was what, Robert?"

"A con—okay? He looked like serious business. A hard-case."

"You could tell that from far away?"

"Some things you can tell, okay? The way he stood, I dunno. He had these shoes—big and ugly, like you get in the joint."

"You could see his shoes?"

"Not up close—the light. But they were big—I seen shoes like that before. Whaddya want from me—I'm trying to help."

"Well, Robert, don't you worry. There's no one in custody."

"What *if*?" said Gabray.

"What if what?"

"I tell you and 'cause a that you *bust* him? How do I know he's not gonna get out and come looking for me?"

Milo held up the photo again. "Look what he did, Robert. What do you think? We're gonna let him walk?"

"That don't mean *nothing* to me, man. I don't have confidence in the system."

"That so?"

"Yeah. I see guys all the time, do bad stuff and walk on technos."

"Tsk, tsk," said Milo. "What's this world coming to? Listen, genius, we find him, he won't walk. And you tell me something that'll help me find him, you'll walk too. With brownie points. Hell,

Robert, all the points you'll have, you'll be able to screw up a couple *more* times and coast."

Gabray smoked and tapped his foot and frowned.

"What is it, Robert?"

"I'm *thinking*."

"Ah." To me: "Let's be real quiet."

"His face," said the bartender. "I seen it. But just for a second."

"That so? Was he angry or anything?"

"Nah, just talking to her."

"And what was she doing?"

"Listening. I thought when I saw it: this punk cunt's listening to Mr. Straight. Don't make sense."

"Mr. Con."

"Yeah. But he still didn't fit the scene—all you see down there at that hour is freaks and beaners and niggers. And cops—I thought first that he was a cop. Then I thought that he looked like a con. Same difference."

"What was he talking to her about?"

"I couldn't *hear* it, man! It was—"

"Was he holding anything?"

"Like what?"

"Like anything."

"You mean like to hurt her with? Nothing I saw. You really think he's the one did her?"

"What did his face look like?"

"Regular . . . uh, kinda . . . square." Gabray put the cigarette in his mouth and used his hands to frame a wobbly quadrangle. "A regular face."

"Complexion?"

"He was white."

"Pale, swarthy—on the dark side?"

"I dunno, just a white guy."

"Same color as her?"

"She had on makeup—that real white shit they like? He was darker than that. Regular white. Normal."

"Eye color?"

"I was too far away for that, man."

"How far?"

"I dunno, half a block."

"But you could see his shoes?"

"Maybe it was closer . . . I seen 'em. But I didn't see no eye color."

"How tall was he?"

"Taller than her."

"Taller than you?"

"Uh . . . maybe. Not much."

"What're you?"

"Five ten."

"So he was what, five eleven or six feet?"

"Guess so."

"Heavy build?"

"Yeah, but not fat, you know."

"If I knew I wouldn't be asking you."

"Heavy—big—you know—like from working out. On the yard."

"Muscular."

"Yeah."

"Would you remember this guy if you saw him again?"

"Why?" Another alarm flash. "You *do* got someone?"

"No. Would you remember him if you saw his picture?"

"Yeah, sure." Flippantly. "I got a good memory. Put him in a lineup and I'll give you a beaucoup ID, you treat me good."

"You trying to hustle me, Robert?"

Gabray smiled and shrugged. "Taking care of biz."

"Well," said Milo, "let's take care of some now."

We took Gabray across the rear lot, walked through a rubble-filled ditch on the east side of the building, and got back on the street. The line at the front door hadn't shrunk much. This time the bouncer noticed as we walked by.

Gabray said, "Yo, fuckin' King Kong," under his breath.

Milo said, "The guy with Ms. Herbert as big as James?"

Gabray laughed. "No—no way. That's not human. That they got outa the fuckin' zoo."

Milo pushed him forward, questioning him all the way to the car without extracting anything further.

"Nice wheels," said Gabray when we stopped at the Seville. "Get it from impound or something?"

"Hard work, Robert. That old Protestant ethic."

"I'm Catholic, man. Used to be, anyway. All of that religion shit's bullshit."

Milo said, "Shut up, Robert," and opened the trunk.

He removed the hard-shell case, put Gabray in the rear seat of the car, and got in next to him, leaving the door open for light. I stood outside and watched him open the case. Inside was a book that said IDENTIKIT. Milo showed Gabray transparencies with facial features drawn on them. Gabray selected some and put them together. When he was finished, a bland-looking Caucasian face gazed up. A face out of a *Dick and Jane* primer. Someone's dad.

Milo stared at it, fixed it in place, wrote something down; then he had Gabray designate spots on a street map with a yellow marker. After a few more questions, he got out of the car. Gabray followed. Despite the warm breeze, the barkeep's bare shoulders were fuzzed with goose bumps.

"Okay?" he said.

"For the time being, Robert. I'm sure I don't have to tell you this, but I'm gonna anyway: Don't change addresses. Stay where I can reach you."

"No prob." Gabray started to walk away.

Milo blocked him with a straight-arm. "Meanwhile, *I'm* gonna be writing letters. One to your P.O. saying you worked here without telling him, another to Mr. Fahrizad and his buddies informing them you finked on them and that's why the fire department's closing them down, and a third to the IRS telling them you've been taking cash for God knows how long and not declaring it."

Gabray bent at the waist as if seized by a cramp. "Oh, man—"

"Plus a report to the prosecutor on your weed thing, letting him know you were uncooperative and obstructive and a poor risk for plea bargain. I don't like writing letters, Robert. Writing letters makes me grumpy. If I have to waste my time looking for you, I'm gonna get even grumpier and all of those letters get hand-delivered. You behave yourself, I tear them up. *Comprende?*"

"Aw, man, that's *rude.* I been strai—"

"No problems if you behave yourself, Robert."

"Yeah, yeah, sure."

"Will you?"

"Yeah, yeah. Can I go now? I gotta work."

"Are you *hearing* me, Robert?"

"I'm hearing. Stay in one place, be a fucking boy scout. No jamming, no scamming. Okay? Can I go?"

"One more thing, Robert. Your lady."

"Yeah?" said Gabray, in a hard voice that turned him into something more than a sniveling loser. "What about her?"

"She's gone. Flew the coop. Don't even think about going after her. And *especially* don't think about hurting her for talking to me. Because I woulda found you anyway. You've got no gripe with her."

Gabray's eyes widened. "Gone? What the—whaddya mean?"

"Gone. She wanted out, Robert."

"Aw, shit—"

"She was packing her bags when I spoke to her. Pretty shaken up by your approach to domestic life."

Gabray said nothing.

Milo said, "She had enough of being pounded on, Robert."

Gabray dropped the cigarette and stomped it out hard.

"She *lies,*" he said. "Fucking *bitch.*"

"She made your bail."

"She *owed* me. She *still* owes me."

"Let it go, Robert. Think of those letters."

"Yeah," said Gabray, tapping his foot. "Whatever. I'm cool with it. I got a good attitude about life."

24

When we were out of the maze and back on San Pedro, Milo turned on his penlight and studied the Identikit face.

"Think he's reliable?" I said.

"Not very. But in the unlikely event a real suspect ever shows up, this might help."

I stopped for a red light and glanced at the composite. "Not very distinctive."

"Nope."

I leaned over and gave a closer look. "It could be Huenengarth, minus the mustache."

"That so?"

"Huenengarth's younger than the guy Gabray described—mid-thirties—and his face is a bit fuller. But he's thickly built and his hair's styled like that. His mustache could have been grown since March, and even if not, it's very faint—might have been hard to spot from a distance. And you said he might be an ex-con."

"Hmm."

The light turned green, and I headed back toward the freeway.

He chuckled.

"What?"

"Just thinking. If I ever actually make sense out of the Herbert thing, my troubles will just be beginning. Sneaking her file out. Moving in on Central's territory, offering Gabray protection I had no permission to authorize. Far as the department's concerned, I'm a goddam clerk."

"Solving a homicide wouldn't impress the department?"

"Not nearly as much as rank conformity—but hell, I suppose I can work something out if it comes to that. Give a gift to Gomez and Wicker—let them take the glory and hope for half a gold star. Gabray may get sold out in the process . . . Hell, he's no innocent—screw him. If his info turns out to be real, he'll do okay."

He closed the kit and placed it on the floor.

"Listen to me," he said, "talking like a goddam politician."

I drove up the ramp. All lanes were empty and the freeway looked like a giant drag strip.

He said, "Putting some bad guys out of commission should be enough satisfaction, right? What you guys call intrinsic motivation."

"Sure," I said. "Be good for goodness' sake and Santa will remember you."

We arrived back at my house just after three. He drove away in the Porsche and I slipped into bed, trying to be silent. Robin awoke anyway and reached for my hand. We locked fingers and fell asleep.

She was up and gone before my eyes cleared. A toasted English muffin and juice were at my place on the kitchen table. I finished them off while planning my day.

Afternoon at the Joneses'.

Morning on the phone.

But the phone rang before I could get to it.

"Alex," said Lou Cestare, "all those interesting questions. Branching out into investment banking?"

"Not yet. How was the hike?"

"Long. I kept thinking my little guy would tire but he wanted to play Edmund Hillary. Why do you want to know about Chuck Jones?"

"He's chairman of the board of the hospital where I used to work. He also manages the hospital's portfolio. I'm still on staff there, feel some affection for the place. Things aren't going well there financially, and there's been talk of Jones running the place down so he can dissolve it and sell the land."

"Doesn't sound like his style."

"You know him?"

"Met him a couple of times at parties. Quick hello-goodbye— he wouldn't remember. But I do know his style."

"Which is?"

"Building up, not tearing down. He's one of the best money managers around, Alex. Pays no attention to what other people are doing and goes after solid companies at cut-rate prices. True bargains—the stock-buys everyone dreams about. But *he* finds them better than anyone else."

"How?"

"He knows how to really figure out how a company's doing. Which means going way beyond quarterly reports. Once he ferrets out an undervalued stock about to pop, he buys in, waits, sells, repeats the process. His timing's impeccable."

"Does he ferret using inside information?"

Pause. "This hour of the morning and you're already talking dirty?"

"So he does."

"Alex, the whole inside trading thing has been blown way out of proportion. As far as I'm concerned, no one's even come up with a good definition."

"Come on, Lou."

"Do *you* have one?"

"Sure," I said. "Using data unavailable to the average person in order to make buy-and-sell decisions."

"Okay, then, what about an investor who wines and dines a key employee in order to find out if the company's doing its job properly? Someone who takes the time to really get into the nuts and bolts of company operations? Is that corrupt or just being thorough?"

"If bribery's involved, it's corrupt."

"What, the wining and dining? Why's that different from a reporter buttering up a source? Or a cop encouraging a witness with a doughnut and a cup of coffee? I don't know of any law that makes dinner between business people illegal. Theoretically, anyone could do it, if they were willing to put out the effort. *But no one ever bothers, Alex.* That's the thing. Even professional researchers usually rely on graphs and charts and the numbers the company gives them. Lots of them never even bother to visit the company they're analyzing."

"I guess it depends on what the investor learns from the wining and dining."

"Exactly. If the employee tells him someone's going to make a serious takeover bid on such and such a date, that's illegal. But if that same employee tells him the company's in a financial position that makes it ripe for takeover, that's valid data. It's a thin line—see what I mean? Chuck Jones does his homework, that's all. He's a bulldog."

"What's his background?"

"I don't think he even went to college. We're talking rags to riches. I think he shod horses or something when he was a kid. Doesn't that appeal to your sensibilities? The guy came out of Black Monday a hero because he dumped his stocks months before the crash and shifted to T-bills and metals. Even though his stocks were shooting *up.* If anyone had known, they would have thought he was going senile. But when the market crashed, he was able to bottom-fish, bought in again and made another fortune."

"Why didn't anyone know?"

"He's got a thing for privacy—his kind of strategy depends upon it. He buys and sells constantly, avoids big block trades, stays away from computerized trading. It wasn't until months later that I found out, myself."

"How'd you find out?"

"The scuttlebutt—twenty-twenty hindsight, while the rest of us licked our wounds."

"How was he able to predict the crash?"

"Prescience. The best players have it. It's a combination of a great data base and a kind of ESP you get from being in the game a long time. I used to think I had it, but I got chastened—no big deal. Life was getting boring, and rebuilding's more fun than just treading water. But Chuck Jones *does* have it. I'm not saying he never loses. Everyone does. But he wins a lot more than he loses."

"What's he into now?"

"I don't know—like I said, close-to-the-cuff's his style. Invests only for himself, so he's got no shareholders to deal with. I doubt, though, that he's high on real estate."

"Why's that?"

"Because real estate's a turkey. I don't mean for someone like you who bought in years ago and is just looking for some stable income. But for traders out for a quick profit, the party's over, at least for now. I divested myself a while ago, moved back into stocks. Jones is smarter than me, so odds to evens he got there before I did."

"His son owns a big block of land out in the Valley."

"Who said wisdom is genetic?"

"His son's a college professor. I don't think he was able to buy fifty parcels for himself."

"Probably his trust fund—I don't know. You'll still have to convince me Chuck's getting into r.e. in a big way. The land the hospital's on is Hollywood, right?"

"Several acres," I said. "Purchased a long time ago—the hospital's seventy years old—so it's probably all paid for. Even in a slump, a sale would be pure profit."

"Sure it would, Alex. But to the hospital itself. What's *Jones's* incentive?"

"Commission on the deal."

"How many acres are we talking about and where exactly are they?"

"Five or so." I told him Western Peds's address.

"Okay, so that's ten, fifteen million—let's even say twenty because of contiguous lots. Which is liberal, because that big of a chunk would be hard to unload, so you might have to subdivide into smaller parcels. That could take time—there'd be zoning hassles, hearings, permits, environmental shenanigans. The biggest cut Chuck could take for himself without attracting a commotion would be twenty-five percent—ten's more likely. Meaning two to five mil in his pocket . . . No, I can't see Chuck messing around for that kind of money."

"What if there's more to it?" I said. "What if he not only plans to close down one hospital but is also figuring to open up a new one on his son's land?"

"All of a sudden he's in the hospital business? I doubt it, Alex.

No offense, but health care's a turkey too. Hospitals have been going belly-up almost as fast as savings and loans."

"I know, but maybe Jones figures he can do a good job anyway, bucking the trend. You just said he doesn't pay attention to what everyone else is doing."

"Anything's possible, Alex, but once again you'd have to prove it to me. Where'd you come up with all this theorizing, anyway?"

I told him about Plumb's comments in the paper.

"Ah, the other name on your list. Him, I'd never heard of him, so I looked him up in every directory I've got. What emerges is your basic corporate drone: M.B.A., doctorate, a series of management jobs, climbing the ladder. His first job was at a national accounting firm named Smothers and Crimp. Then he moved into the head office at another place."

"Where?"

"Hold on—I wrote it down somewhere . . . Here we go. Plumb, George Haversford. Born, '34; married Mary Ann Champlin, '58; two kids, blah blah blah . . . out of grad school in '60 with a D.B.A.; Smothers and Crimp, 1960 through '63, left as a partner. Controller, Hardfast Steel in Pittsburgh, '63 till '65; Controller and chief operating officer, Readilite Manufacturing, Reading, Pennsylvania, '65 through '68; a step up to CEO at an outfit called Baxter Consulting, stayed there till '71; '71 through '74 at Advent Management Specialists; went out on his own with the Plumb Group, '74 till '77; then back into the corporate world in '78 at a place called Vantage Health Planning, CEO till '81—"

"The guy hops around a lot."

"Not really, Alex. Moving around every couple of years in order to up your ante is your basic corporate drone pattern. It's one of the main reasons I dropped out of it early. Hell on the family—lots of booze-hound wives who smile a lot and kids who turn delinquency into an art form. . . . Where was I? Vantage Health till '81; then it looks as if he began specializing in medical stuff. Arthur-McClennan Diagnostics for three years, NeoDyne Biologicals for another three, then MGS Healthcare Consultants—the Pittsburgh place you asked me to look up."

"What'd you find out about it?"

"Small-to-medium hospital outfit specializing in acute-care facilities in small-to-medium cities in the northern states. Established in '82 by a group of doctors, went public in '85, OTC issue, poor stock performance, got reprivatized the next year—bought out by a syndicate and shut down."

"Why would a syndicate buy it, then shut it down?"

"Could be any number of reasons. Maybe they discovered buying it was a mistake and tried to cut their losses fast. Or they wanted the company's resources, rather than the company itself."

"What kinds of resources?"

"Hardware, investments, the pension fund. The other group you asked about—BIO-DAT—was originally a subsidiary of MGS. The data analysis arm. Before the buy-out it got sold to another concern—Northern Holdings, in Missoula, Montana—and was maintained."

"Is it a public company?"

"Private."

"What about the other companies Plumb worked for? Are you familiar with any of them?"

"Not a one."

"Are any of *them* public?"

"One second and I'll tell you. . . . Got the old PC cooking. Let me make a scan list. You want to go all the way back to the accountants—Smothers and whatever?"

"If you've got the time."

"Got more time than I'm used to. Hold on just one second."

I waited, listening to keyboard clicks.

"All right," he said, "now let's scroll up the exchanges and run a search . . . here we go."

Beep. "Nothing on the New York."

Beep. "No Amex listings on any of them, either. Let's see about the Nasdaq . . ."

Beep. Beep. Beep. Beep.

"No listings, Alex. Let me check the list of private holdings."
Beep.

"Doesn't look like it, Alex." A slight edge in his voice.

"Meaning none of them are in business?"

"Looks like it."

"Do you find that unusual?"

"Well," he said, "businesses do fail or close down at a pretty high rate, but this Plumb guy does seem to be the kiss of death."

"Chuck Jones hired him to run the hospital, Lou. Care to revise your thinking about his intentions?"

"Think he's a spoiler, huh?"

"What happened to the other companies Plumb was associated with?"

"That would be hard to find out—they were all small, and if they were privately held, there'd be no stock ramifications, little or no coverage in the business press."

"What about the local press?"

"If it was a company town with lots of people being thrown out of work, maybe. But good luck tracking that down."

"Okay, thanks."

"Is this really important, Alex?"

"I don't know."

"It would be a hell of a lot easier for *me* to track," he said, "knowing the ropes. Let me play Tarzan and climb a few."

After he hung up, I called Virginia Information and got the number of the Ferris Dixon Institute for Chemical Research. A pleasant female voice answered, "Ferris Dixon, good afternoon, how may I help you?"

"This is Dr. Schweitzer from Western Pediatric Medical Center in Los Angeles. I'm an associate of Dr. Laurence Ashmore."

"Just one second, please."

Long pause. Music. The Hollywood Strings doing The Police's *Every Breath You Take.*

The voice returned: "Yes, Dr. Schweitzer, how may I help you?"

"Your institute funds Dr. Ashmore's research."

"Yes?"

"I was just wondering if you knew he was deceased."

"Oh, how horrible," she said, but she didn't sound surprised. "But I'm afraid the person who can help you with that isn't in."

I hadn't asked for help, but I let that pass. "Who might that be?"

"I'm not exactly sure, Doctor. I'd have to check that."

"Could you, please?"

"Certainly, but it may take a while, Doctor. Why don't you give me your number and I'll get back to you."

"I'll be moving around. How about if I get back to you?"

"Certainly, Doctor. Have a nice—"

"Excuse me," I said. "As long as we're talking, could you give me some information on the institute? For purposes of my own research?"

"What would you like to know, Dr. Schweitzer?"

"What kinds of projects do you prefer to fund?"

"That would be a technical question, sir," she said. "I'm afraid I can't help you with that, either."

"Is there some kind of brochure you could send me? A list of previous studies you've funded?"

"I'm afraid not—we're a fairly young agency."

"Really? How young?"

"One moment, please."

Another long break. More Muzak, then she was back.

"Sorry for taking so long, Doctor, and I'm afraid I can't stay with you—I've got several other incoming calls. Why don't you get back to us with *all* your questions. I'm sure the right person will be able to help you."

"The right person," I said.

"Exactly," she said with sudden cheer. "Have a nice day, Doctor."

Click.

I called back. The line was busy. I asked the operator to put through an emergency interruption, and waited until she came back on the line.

"I'm sorry, sir, that number's out of order."

I sat there, still hearing the pleasant voice.

Smooth . . . well rehearsed.

One word she'd used jumped out at me.

"We're a fairly young *agency*."

Odd way to describe a private foundation.

Virginia . . . anything down there always spells government to me.

I tried the number again. Still off the hook. Checked my notes for the other study the institute had funded.

Zimberg, Walter William. University of Maryland, Baltimore. Something to do with statistics in scientific research.

The med school? Mathematics? Public health?

I got the university's number and called it. No Zimbergs on the medical school faculty. Same at the math department.

At Public Health a male voice answered.

"Professor Zimberg, please."

"Zimberg? No such person here."

"Sorry," I said. "I must have gotten the wrong information. Do you have a faculty roster handy?"

"One moment . . . I've got a Professor *Walter* Zimberg but he's in the Department of Economics."

"Could you please connect me to his office?"

Click. Female voice: "Economics."

"Professor Zimberg, please."

"Hold, please."

Click. Another female voice: "Professor Zimberg's office."

"Professor Zimberg, please."

"I'm afraid he's out of town, sir."

I threw out a guess: "Is he over in Washington?"

"Um . . . Who is this, please?"

"Professor Schweitzer, an old colleague. Is Wal—Professor Zimberg at the convention?"

"What convention is that, sir?"

"National Association of Biostatisticians—over at the Capital Hilton? I heard he was going to present some new data on nonparametrics. The study the Ferris Dixon Institute's funding."

"I'm— The professor should be calling in soon, sir. Why don't you give me your number and I'll have him get back to you."

"Appreciate the offer," I said, "but I'm about to hop on a plane myself. That's why I didn't make the convention. Did the professor write up an abstract on his paper before he left? Something I could read when I get back?"

"You'd have to talk to the professor about that."

"When do you expect him back?"

"Actually," she said, "the professor's on sabbatical."

"No kidding? I didn't hear that. . . . Well, he's due, isn't he? Where's he off to?"

"Various places, Professor . . ."

"Schweitzer."

"Various places, Professor Schweitzer. However, as I said, he does call in frequently. Why don't you give me your number and I'll have him get back to you."

Repeating, almost word for word, what she'd just said a minute ago.

Word for word what another friendly female voice had said, *five* minutes ago, speaking from the hallowed offices of the Ferris Dixon Institute for Chemical Research.

25

To hell with Alexander Graham Bell.

I drove back to some hallowed halls I could see and touch.

There was one parking meter free near the university administration building. I went to the registrar's office and asked an Indian
clerk in a peach-colored sari to look up Dawn Kent Herbert.

"Sorry, sir, we don't give out personal information."

I flashed my clinical faculty card from the med school across
town. "I don't want anything personal—just need to know in which
department she's enrolled. It has to do with a job. Verification of
education."

The clerk read the card, had me repeat Herbert's name, and
walked away.

A moment later she returned. "I show her as a graduate student
in the School of Public Health, sir. But her enrollment's been terminated."

I knew Public Health was in the Health Sciences building, but
I'd never actually been there. Shoving more money in the meter, I
headed toward south campus, passing the Psych building, where I'd

learned to train rats and listen with the third ear, crossing the Science quad, and entering the Center at the west end, near the Dental School.

The long hall that led to Public Health was a quick jog from the library, where I'd just studied Ashmore's academic history. Walls on both sides were lined with group photos of every class the medical school had graduated. Brand-new doctors looking like kids. The white-coats milling in the halls seemed just as young. By the time I reached the School of Public Health, the corridor had quieted. A woman was leaving the main office. I caught the door for her and stepped in.

Another counter, another clerk working in cramped space. This one was very young, black, with straightened hennaed hair and a smile that seemed real. She wore a fuzzy lime-green sweater with a yellow-and-pink parrot embroidered on it. The bird was smiling too.

"I'm Dr. Delaware from Western Pediatric Hospital. One of your graduate students worked at our hospital and I'd like to know who her faculty adviser is."

"Oh, sure. Her name, please."

"Dawn Herbert."

No reaction. "What department is she in?"

"Public Health."

The smile broadened. "This is the *School* of Public Health, Doctor. We have several departments, each with its own faculty." She lifted a brochure from a stack near my elbow, opened it and pointed to the table of contents.

DEPARTMENTS OF THE SCHOOL

BIOSTATISTICS

COMMUNITY HEALTH SCIENCES

ENVIRONMENTAL HEALTH SCIENCES

ENVIRONMENTAL SCIENCE AND ENGINEERING

EPIDEMIOLOGY

HEALTH SERVICES

Thinking of the kind of work Ashmore had done, I said, "Either Biostatistics or Epidemiology."

She went to the files and pulled down a blue fabric loose-leaf folder. The spine was lettered BIOSTAT.

"Yes, here we go. She's in the Ph.D. program in Biostat and her adviser's Dr. Yanosh."

"Where can I find Dr. Yanosh?"

"One floor down—office B-three-forty-five. Would you like me to call and see if she's in?"

"Please."

She picked up a phone and punched an extension. "Dr. Yanosh? Hi. Merilee here. There's a doctor from some hospital wanting to talk to you about one of your students . . . Dawn Herbert . . . Oh . . . Sure." Frowning. "What was your name again, sir?"

"Delaware. From Western Pediatric Medical Center."

She repeated that into the receiver. "Yes, of course, Dr. Yanosh . . . Could I see some identification, please, Dr. Delaware?"

Out came the faculty card again.

"Yes, he does, Dr. Yanosh." Spelling my name. "Okay, Doctor, I'll tell him."

Hanging up, she said, "She doesn't have much time but she can see you right now." Sounding angry.

As I opened the door, she said, "She was *murdered*?"

"I'm afraid so."

"That's really *ugly*."

There was an elevator just past the office, next to a darkened lecture hall. I rode it down one flight. B-345 was a few doors to the left.

Closed and locked. A slide-in sign said ALICE JANOS, M.P.H., PH.D.

I knocked. Between the first and second raps a voice said, "One minute."

Heel-clicks. The door opened. A woman in her fifties said, "Dr. Delaware."

I held out my hand. She took it, gave an abrupt shake, and let go. She was short, plump, blond, bubble-coiffed, and expertly made up and wore a red-and-white dress that had been tailored for her. Red shoes, matching nails, gold jewelry. Her face was small and attractive in a chipmunkish way; when she was young she'd probably been the cutest girl in school.

"Come in, please." European accent. The intellectual Gabor sister.

I stepped into the office. She left the door open and came in after me. The room was pin-neat, minimally furnished, scented with perfume, and hung with art posters in chromium frames. Miró and Albers and Stella and one that commemorated a Gwathmey-Siegel exhibit at the Boston Museum.

An open box of chocolate truffles sat on a round glass table. Next to it was a sprig of mint. On a stand perpendicular to the desk were a computer and a printer, each sheathed with a zippered cover. Atop the printer was a red leather designer purse. The desk was university-issue metal, prettified with a diagonally set lace coverlet, a floral-patterned Limoges blotter, and family photos. Big family. Albert Einstein look-alike husband and five good-looking, college-age kids.

She sat close to the chocolate and crossed her legs at the ankles. I faced her. Her calves were ballet-thick.

"You are a physician?"

"Psychologist."

"And what connection do you have to Ms. Herbert?"

"I'm consulting on a case at the hospital. Dawn obtained a medical chart belonging to the patient's sibling and never returned it. I thought she might have left it here."

"This patient's name?"

When I hesitated, she said, "I can't very well answer your question without knowing what I'm looking for."

"Jones."

"Charles Lyman Jones the Fourth?"

Surprised, I said, "You have it?"

"No. But you are the second person who's come asking for it. Is there a genetic issue at stake that makes this so urgent? Sibling tissue typing or something like that?"

"It's a complex case," I said.

She recrossed her legs. "The first person didn't give me an adequate explanation either."

"Who was that?"

She gave me an analytic look and sat back in her chair. "Forgive me, Doctor, but I'd appreciate seeing the identification you just showed Merilee upstairs."

For the third time in half an hour I presented my faculty card, augmenting it with my brand-new full-color hospital badge.

Putting on gold-framed half-glasses, she examined both, taking her time. The hospital ID held her interest longer.

"The other man had one of these too," she said, holding it up. "He said he was in charge of hospital security."

"A man named Huenengarth?"

She nodded. "The two of you seem to be duplicating each other's efforts."

"When was he here?"

"Last Thursday. Does Western Pediatrics generally give this type of personal service to all its patients?"

"As I said, it's a complex case."

She smiled. "Medically or socio-culturally?"

"I'm sorry," I said. "I can't get into details."

"Psychotherapeutic confidentiality?"

I nodded.

"Well, I certainly respect that, Dr. Delaware. Mr. Huenengarth used another phrase to protect *his* secrecy. 'Privileged information.' I thought that sounded rather cloak-and-dagger and told him so. He wasn't amused. A rather grim fellow, actually."

"Did you give him the chart?"

"No, because I don't *have* it, Doctor. Dawn left no medical charts of any kind behind. Sorry to have misled you, but all the attention she's generated lately has led me to be cautious. That and her murder, of course. When the police came by to ask questions, I cleaned out her graduate locker personally. All that I found were some textbooks and the computer disks from her dissertation research."

"Have you booted up the disks?"

"Is that question related to your complex case?"

"Possibly."

"Possibly," she said. "Well, at least you're not getting pushy the way Mr. Huenengarth did. Trying to pressure me to turn them over."

Removing her glasses, she got up, returned my ID, closed the door. Back in her chair, she said, "Was Dawn involved in something unsavory?"

"She may have been."

"Mr. Huenengarth was a bit more forthcoming than you, Doctor. He came right out and said Dawn had *stolen* the chart. Informed me it was my *duty* to see that it was returned—quite imperious. I had to ask him to leave."

"He's not Mr. Charm."

"An understatement—his approach is pure KGB. More like a policeman than the real policemen who investigated Dawn's murder, as far as I'm concerned. *They* weren't pushy *enough*. A few cursory questions and goodbye—I grade them C-minus. Weeks later I called to see what kind of progress was being made, and no one would take my call. I left messages and none were returned."

"What kind of questions did they ask about her?"

"Who her friends were, had she ever associated with criminal types, did she use drugs. Unfortunately, I wasn't able to answer any of them. Even after having her as my student for four years, I knew virtually nothing about her. Have you served on any doctoral committees?"

"A few."

"Then you know. Some students one really gets close to; others pass through without making a mark. I'm afraid Dawn was one of the latter. Not because she wasn't bright. She was *extremely* sharp, mathematically. It's why I accepted her in the first place, even though I had reservations about her motivation. I'm always looking for women who aren't intimidated by numbers and she had a true gift for math. But we never . . . jelled."

"What was the matter with her motivation?"

"She didn't *have* any. I always got the feeling she'd drifted into grad school because it was the path of least resistance. She'd applied to medical school and gotten rejected. Kept applying even after she enrolled here—a lost cause, really, because her non-math grades weren't very good and her M-CAT scores were significantly below average. Her math scores were so high I decided to accept her, though. I went so far as to get her funding—a Graduate Advanced Placement fellowship. This past fall, I had to cut that off. That's when she found the job at your hospital."

"Poor performance?"

"Poor progress on her dissertation. She finished her course work with adequate grades, submitted a research proposal that looked promising, dropped it, submitted another, dropped that, et cetera. Finally she came up with one that she seemed to like. Then she just froze. Went absolutely nowhere with it. You know how it is— students either zip through or languish for years. I've been able to help plenty of the languishers and I tried to help Dawn. But she rejected counseling. Didn't show up for appointments, made excuses, kept saying she could handle it, just needed more time. I never felt I was getting through to her. I was at the point of considering dropping her from the program. Then she was . . ."

She rubbed a fingertip over one blood-colored nail. "I suppose none of that seems very important now. Would you like a chocolate?"

"No, thanks."

She looked down at the truffles. Closed the box.

"Consider that little speech," she said, "as an elongated answer to your question about her disks. But yes, I did boot them up, and there was nothing meaningful on them. She'd accomplished *nothing* on the dissertation. As a matter of fact, I hadn't even bothered to look at them when your Mr. Huenengarth showed up—had put them away and forgotten about them, I was so upset by her death. Going through that locker felt ghoulish enough. But *he* made such a point of trying to get them that I booted them up the moment he was gone. It was worse than I'd imagined. All she'd produced, after all my encouragement, were statements and restatements of her hypotheses and a random numbers table."

"A random numbers table?"

"For random sampling. You know how it's done, I'm sure."

I nodded. "Generate a collection of random numbers with a computer or some other technique, then use it to select subjects from a general pool. If the table says five, twenty-three, seven, choose the fifth, twenty-third, and seventh people on the list."

"Exactly. Dawn's table was huge—thousands of numbers. Pages and pages generated on the department's mainframe. What a foolish waste of computer time. She was nowhere near ready to select her sample. Hadn't even gotten her basic methodology straight."

"What was her research topic?"

"Predicting cancer incidence by geographical location. That's as specific as she'd gotten. It was really pathetic, reading those disks. Even the little bit she had written was totally unacceptable. Disorganized, out of sequence. I had to wonder if indeed she *had* been using drugs."

"Did she show any other signs of that?"

"I suppose the unreliability could be considered a symptom. And sometimes she did seem agitated—almost manic. Trying to convince me—or herself—that she was making progress. But I know she wasn't taking amphetamines. She gained lots of weight over the last four years—at least forty pounds. She was actually quite pretty when she enrolled."

"Could be cocaine," I said.

"Yes, I suppose so, but I've seen the same things happen to students who *weren't* on drugs. The stress of grad school can drive anyone temporarily mad."

"How true," I said.

She rubbed her nails, glanced over at the photos of her family. "When I found out she'd been murdered, it changed my perception of her. Up till then I'd been absolutely *furious* with her. But hearing about her death—the way she'd been found . . . well, I just felt sorry for her. The police told me she was dressed like some kind of punk-rocker. It made me realize she'd had an outside life she'd kept hidden from me. She was simply one of those people to whom the world of ideas would never be important."

"Could her lack of motivation have been due to an independent income?"

"Oh, no," she said. "She was poor. When I accepted her she begged me to get her funding, told me she couldn't enroll without it."

I thought of the carefree attitude about money she'd shown the Murtaughs. The brand-new car she'd died in.

"What about her family?" I said.

"I seem to remember there was a mother—an alcoholic. But the policemen said they hadn't been able to locate anyone to claim the body. We actually took up a collection here at the school in order to bury her."

"Sad."

"Extremely."

"What part of the country was she from?" I said.

"Somewhere back east. No, she wasn't a rich girl, Dr. Delaware. Her lack of drive was due to something else."

"How did she react to losing her fellowship?"

"She didn't react at *all*. I'd expected some anger, tears, anything—hoped it would help clear the air and we'd reach an understanding. But she never even tried to contact me. Finally, I called *her* in, asked her how she was planning to support herself. She told me about the job at your hospital. Made it sound like something prestigious—was quite snotty, actually. Though your Mr. Huenengarth said she'd been little more than a bottle washer."

No bottles in Ashmore's lab. I was silent.

She looked at her watch, then over at her purse. For a moment I thought she was going to get up. But instead, she moved her chair closer and stared at me. Her eyes were hazel, hot, unmoving. An inquisitive heat. Chipmunk searching for the acorn hoard.

"Why all the questions, Doctor? What are you really after?"

"I really can't give any details because of the confidentiality issue," I said. "I know it doesn't seem fair."

She said nothing for a moment. Then: "She *was* a thief. Those textbooks in her locker had been stolen from another student. I found other things too. Another student's sweater. A gold pen that had belonged to me. So I won't be surprised if she *was* involved in something unsavory."

"She may have been."

"Something that led to her being murdered?"

"It's possible."

"And what's *your* involvement with all of this, Doctor?"

"My patient's welfare may be at stake."

"Charles Jones's sister?"

I nodded, surprised that Huenengarth had revealed that much.

"Is some type of child abuse suspected?" she said. "Something Dawn found out about and tried to profit from?"

Swallowing my amazement, I managed to shrug and run a finger across my lips.

She smiled. "I'm no Sherlock Holmes, Dr. Delaware. But Mr.

Huenengarth's visit made me very curious—all that pressure. I've studied health-care systems too long to believe anyone would go to that kind of effort for an average patient. So I asked my husband to make inquiries about the Jones boy. He's a vascular surgeon, has privileges at Western Peds, though he hasn't operated there in years. So I know who the Joneses are and the role the grandfather's playing in the turmoil the hospital's going through. I also know that the boy died of SIDS and another child keeps getting sick. Rumors are floating. Put that together with the fact that Dawn stole the first child's chart and went from abject student poverty to being quite cavalier about money, add two separate visits from professionals personally looking for that chart, and one doesn't need to be a detective."

"I'm still impressed."

"Are you and Mr. Huenengarth working at cross-purposes?"

"We're not working together."

"Whose side are you on?"

"The little girl's."

"Who's paying your fee?"

"Officially, the parents."

"Don't you consider that a conflict of interest?"

"If it turns out to be, I won't submit a bill."

She studied me for several moments. "I do believe you might mean that. Now tell me this: Does possession of the disks put *me* in any danger?"

"I doubt it, but it can't be ruled out."

"Not a very comforting answer."

"I don't want to mislead you."

"I appreciate that. I survived the Russian tanks in Budapest in '56, and my survival instincts have been well developed ever since. What do you suspect might be the importance of the disks?"

"They may contain some kind of coded data," I said, "imbedded in the random number table."

"I must say I thought of the same thing—there really was no logical reason for her to have generated that table at such an early stage of her research. So I scanned it, ran a few basic programs, and no obvious algorithms jumped out. Do you have any cryptographic skills?"

"None whatsoever."

"Neither do I, though good decoding programs do exist, so one no longer needs to be an expert. However, why don't we take a look right now, and see if our combined wisdom produces anything. After that, I'll hand the disks over to you and be rid of them. I'll also be sending a letter to Huenengarth and the police, carbon-copied to my dean, stating that I passed the disks along to you and have no interest in them."

"How about just to the police? I can give you a detective's name."

"No." She walked back to the desk, picked up the designer purse and unclasped it. Removing a small key, she fit it into the lock of the top desk drawer.

"I usually don't lock up like this," she said. "That man made me feel as if I were back in Hungary."

Sliding open a left-hand file drawer, she looked down into it. Frowned. Stuck her arm in, moved it around, pulled it out empty.

"Gone," she said, looking up. "How interesting."

26

The two of us went up to the department office and Janos asked Merilee to get Dawn Herbert's student file. Five-by-eight index card.

"This is all of it?" she said, frowning.

"We recycle all the old paper now, Dr. Janos, remember?"

"Ah, yes. How politically correct . . ." Janos and I read the card: DE-ENROLLED stamped at the top in red. Four typed lines under that:

> Herbert, D.K. Prog: Ph.D., Bio-St.
> D.O.B.: 12/13/63
> POB: Poughkeepsie, N.Y.
> A.B., Math, Poughkeepsie Coll.

"Not much," I said.

Janos gave a cold smile and handed the card back to Merilee. "I've got a seminar, Dr. Delaware, if you'll please excuse me."

She left the office.

Merilee stood there holding the card, looking as if she'd been an unwilling witness to a marital spat.

"Have a nice day," she said, then turned her back on me.

*   *   *

I sat in the car and tried to untangle the knots the Jones family had tied in my head.

Grandpa Chuck, doing something to the hospital.

Chip and/or Cindy doing something to their kids.

Ashmore and/or Herbert learning about some or all of it. Ashmore's data confiscated by Huenengarth. Herbert's data stolen by Huenengarth. Herbert probably murdered by a man who looked like Huenengarth.

The blackmail scenario obvious even to a casual observer like Janos.

But if Ashmore and Herbert had both been up to something, why had she been the first to die?

And why had Huenengarth waited so long after her death to search for her disks, when he'd moved in on Ashmore's computers the day after the toxicologist's murder?

Unless he'd only *learned* about Herbert's data after reading Ashmore's files.

I stayed with that for a while and came up with a possible chronology:

Herbert the first to suspect a tie-in between Chad Jones's death and Cassie's illnesses—student leading the teacher, because the teacher couldn't care less about patients.

She pulled Chad's chart, confirmed her suspicions, recorded her findings—encoded as random numbers—on the university computer, printed out a floppy disk, stashed it in her graduate locker, and put the squeeze on the Jones family.

But not before making a duplicate record and filing it in one of Ashmore's computers, *without* Ashmore's knowledge.

Two months after her murder, Ashmore found the file and tried to use it too.

Greedy, despite his million-dollar grant.

I thought of the Ferris Dixon money. Way too much for what Ashmore claimed to be doing with it. Why had the largesse of a chemical foundation extended to a man who criticized chemical companies? A foundation no one seemed to know much about, supposedly dedicated to life-science research, but its only other grantee was an *economist*.

The elusive Professor Zimberg . . . the sound-alike secretaries at his office and Ferris Dixon.

Some kind of game . . .

The waltz.

Maybe Ashmore and Herbert had worked *different* angles.

He, leaning on Chuck Jones because he'd latched on to a financial scam. She, trying to milk Chip and Cindy on the child-abuse secret.

Two blackmailers operating out of one lab?

I worked with it a while longer.

Money and death, dollars and science.

I couldn't get it to mesh.

The parking meter's red VIOLATION flag popped up like toast. I looked at my watch. Just after noon. Over two hours until my appointment with Cassie and mommy.

In the meantime, why not a visit with daddy?

I used a pay phone in the administration building to call West Valley Community College and get directions.

Forty-five-minute drive, if traffic was thin. Leaving the campus and heading north, I turned west on Sunset and got onto the 405. At the interchange I transferred to the Ventura Freeway, drove toward the western end of the Valley, and got off at Topanga Canyon Boulevard.

The northward cruise took me through a commercial cross-section: upscale shopping plazas still pretending trickle-down economics was working, shabby storefront businesses that had never believed it in the first place, insta-bilt strip malls without any ideological underpinnings.

Up above Nordhoff, the street turned residential and I was treated to a lean stretch of budget-box apartments and motor courts, condo complexes plastered with happy-talk banners. A few citrus groves and U-pick farms had resisted progress. Essences of manure, petroleum, and lemon leaves mingled, not quite masking the burnt-supper smell of simmering dust.

I drove to the Santa Susanna Pass, but the road was closed for no apparent reason and blockaded by CalTrans barriers. I kept going to the end of Topanga, where a jumble of freeway overpasses butted up against the mountains. Off to the right a group of sleek women cantered on beautiful horses. Some of the riders wore fox-hunting garb; all looked content.

I found the 118 on-ramp within the concrete pretzel, traveled west for a few miles, and got off on a brand-new exit marked COLLEGE ROAD. West Valley C.C. was a half-mile up—the only thing in sight.

Nothing at all like the campus I'd just left. This one was announced by a huge, near-empty parking lot. Beyond that, a series of one-story prefab bungalows and trailers were distributed gracelessly over a ten-acre patchwork of concrete and dirt. The landscaping was tentative, unsuccessful in places. A sprinkling of students walked on plain-wrap concrete pathways.

I got out and made my way to the nearest trailer. The midday sun cast a tinfoil glare over the Valley and I had to squint. Most of the students were walking alone. Very little conversation filtered through the heat.

After a series of false starts, I managed to locate someone who could tell me where Sociology was. Bungalows 3A through 3F.

The departmental office was in 3A. The departmental secretary was blond and thin and looked just out of high school. She seemed put-upon when I asked her where Professor Jones's office was, but said, "Two buildings up, in Three-C."

Dirt separated the bungalows, cracked and trenched. So hard and dry that not a single footprint showed. A far cry from the Ivy League. Chip Jones's office was one of six in the small pink stucco building. His door was locked and the card listing his office hours was marked:

ALWAYS
FIRST COME, FIRST SERVED.

All the other offices were locked too. I went back to the secretary and asked her if Professor Jones was on campus. She consulted a schedule and said, "Oh, yeah. He's teaching Soc One-oh-two over in Five-J."

"When's the class over?"

"In an hour—it's a two-hour seminar, twelve to two."

"Do they take a break in the middle?"

"I don't know."

She turned her back on me. I said, "Excuse me," managed to get her to tell me where 5J was, and walked there.

The building was a trailer, one of three on the western edge of the campus, overlooking a shallow ravine.

Despite the heat, Chip Jones was conducting class outside, sitting on one of the few patches of grass in sight, in the partial shade of a young oak, facing ten or so students, all but two of them women. The men sat at the back; the women circled close to his knees.

I stopped a hundred feet away.

His face was half-turned away from me and his arms were moving. He had on a white polo shirt and jeans. Despite his position, he was able to inject a lot of body English into his delivery. As he moved from side to side the students' heads followed and a lot of long female hair swayed.

I realized I had nothing to say to him—had no reason to be there—and turned to leave.

Then I heard a shout, looked over my shoulder and saw him waving.

He said something to the class, sprang to his feet, and loped toward me. I waited for him and when he got to me, he looked scared.

"I thought it was you. Is everything okay?"

"Everything's fine," I said. "Didn't want to alarm you. Just thought I'd drop by before heading over to your house."

"Oh—sure." He blew out breath. "Well, that's a relief. I just wish you'd told me you were coming, so I could've scheduled some time for us to talk. As it stands, I've got a two-hour seminar until two—you're welcome to sit in, but I don't imagine you want to hear about the structure of organizations. And after that there's a faculty meeting till three and another class."

"Sounds like a busy day."

He smiled. "My kind of day." The smile vanished. "Actually, Cindy's the one with the tough job. *I* can escape."

He smoothed his beard. Today's earring was a tiny sapphire, inflamed by the sun. His bare arms were tan and hairless and sinewy.

"Is there anything specific you wanted to talk to me about?" he said. "I can have them break for a few minutes."

"No, not really." I looked around at all the empty space.

"Not exactly Yale," he said, as if reading me. "I keep telling them a few trees would help. But I like being on the cutting edge—building something from scratch. This whole area's *the* high-growth region of the L.A. basin. Come back in a few years and it'll be teeming."

"Despite the slump?"

He frowned, tugged on his beard, and said, "Yes, I think so. The population can only go one way." Smile. "Or at least that's what my demographer friends tell me."

He turned toward the students, who were staring at us, and held up a hand. "Do you know how to get to the house from here?"

"Approximately."

"Let me tell you exactly. Just get back on the freeway—on the One-eighteen—and get off at the seventh exit. After that you can't miss it."

"Great. I won't keep you," I said.

He looked at me but seemed to be somewhere else.

"Thanks," he said. Another backward glance. "This is what keeps me sane—gives me the illusion of freedom. I'm sure you know what I mean."

"Absolutely."

"Well," he said, "I'd better be getting back. Love to my ladies."

27

The ride to the house wouldn't take more than fifteen minutes, leaving forty-five to go before my two-thirty with Cassie.

Remembering Cindy's odd resistance to my coming out any earlier, I decided to head over there right now. Do things on my terms, for a change.

Each exit on the 118 took me farther into the isolation of brown mountains, deforested by five years of drought. The seventh was marked Westview, and it deposited me on a gently curving road of red clay darkened by the mountain's hulk. A few minutes later the clay turned to twin lanes of new asphalt, and red pennants on high metal poles began appearing at fifty-foot intervals. A yellow backhoe was parked on a turnoff. No other vehicles were in sight. Baked hillside and blue sky filled my eyes. The pennant poles flashed by like jail bars.

The asphalt tabled at a hundred square feet of brick, shaded by olive trees. High metal gates were rolled wide open. A big wooden sign to the left of the aperture read WESTVIEW ESTATES in red block letters. Below the legend was an artist's rendition of a spreading pastel-hued housing development set into too-green alps.

I rolled close enough to the sign to read it. A timetable beneath the painting listed six construction phases, each with "twenty to a hundred custom estate homesites, 1/2 to 5 acres." According to the dates, three phases should have been completed. When I looked through the gates I saw a sprinkle of rooftops, lots of brown. Chip's comments about population growth, a few minutes ago, seemed a bit of wishful thinking.

I drove past an untended guardhouse whose windows still bore masking-tape Xs, into a completely empty parking lot fringed with yellow gazania. The exit from the lot fed to a wide, empty street named Sequoia Lane. The sidewalks were so new they looked white-washed.

The left side of the street was an ivy-covered embankment. A half-block in, to the right, sat the first houses, a quartet of big, bright, creatively windowed structures, but unmistakably a tract.

Mock Tudor, mock hacienda, mock Regency, mock Ponderosa Ranch, all fronted by sod lawns crosscut with beds of succulents and more gazania. Tennis court tarp backed the Tudor house; peacock-blue pool water glimmered behind the open lots of the others. Signs on the doors of all four read MODEL. Business hours were posted on a small billboard on the lawn of the Regency, along with the phone number of a real estate company in Agoura. More red pennants. All four doors were closed and the windows were dark.

I kept going, looking for Dunbar Court. The side streets were all "Courts"—wide, squat strips ending in cul-de-sacs, and ribbing east-ward from Sequoia. Very few cars were parked along curbs and in driveways. I saw a bicycle on its side in the center of a half-dead lawn, a garden hose that lay unfurled like a somnolent snake—but no people. A momentary breeze produced sound but no relief from the heat.

Dunbar was the sixth Court. The Jones house was at the mouth of the dead end, a wide, one-story ranch, white stucco trimmed with used-brick. In the center of the front yard a wagon wheel leaned against a young birch tree too thin to support it. Flower beds edged the facade. The windows sparkled. The loom of mountains behind the house made it look like something constructed from a child's kit. The air smelled of grass pollen.

A gray-blue Plymouth Voyager van was parked in the driveway. A brown pickup truck with a bed full of hoses, nets, and plastic bottles

was idling in the driveway of the house next door. The sign on the
door said VALLEYBRITE POOL SERVICE. Just as I pulled up to the curb
the truck shot out. The driver saw me and stopped short. I waved him
on. A young, shirtless, ponytailed man stuck his head out and stared.
Then he grinned suddenly and gave me the thumb-up, instant buddy
sign. Dropping a bronze arm over the driver's door, he finished
backing up and was off.

I walked to the front door. Cindy opened it before I had a chance
to knock, brushing hair out of her face and glancing at her Swatch.

"Hi," she said. Her voice sounded choked, as if she'd just caught
her breath.

"Hi." I smiled. "Traffic was better than I thought."

"Oh . . . sure. C'mon in." The hair was unbraided but still
waved by constriction. She wore a black T-shirt and very short white
shorts. Her legs were smooth and pale, a little skinny but well-shaped
above narrow bare feet. The sleeves of the T-shirt were cut high and
on the bias, revealing lots of slender arm and a bit of shoulder. The
bottom hem of her shirt barely reached her waist. As she held the door
open she hugged herself and looked uncomfortable. Showing more
skin than she'd intended for me, I supposed.

I walked in and she closed the door after me, taking care not to
slam it. A modest entry hall ended at ten feet of wall papered in a
teal-blue miniprint and hung with at least a dozen framed photographs. Cindy and Chip and Cassie, posed and candid, and a couple of
a pretty, dark-haired baby in blue.

Smiling baby boy. I looked away from him and let my eyes settle
on an enlarged snapshot of Cindy and an older woman. Cindy appeared
around eighteen. She wore a white bare-midriff blouse and tight jeans
tucked into white boots, and her hair was a wide, windblown fan. The
older woman was leathery-looking, thin but wide-hipped, and had on
a red-and-white striped sleeveless knit top over white stretch pants
and white shoes. Her hair was dark-gray and cut very short, her lips so
skinny they were nearly invisible. Both she and Cindy wore sunglasses; both were smiling. The older woman's smile said No Nonsense. Boat masts and gray-green water backgrounded the shot.

"That's my Aunt Harriet," said Cindy.

Remembering she'd grown up in Ventura, I said, "Where is
this, Oxnard Harbor?"

"Uh-huh. Channel Islands. We used to go there for lunch, on her days off. . . ." Another look at her watch. "Cassie's still sleeping. She takes her nap around now."

"Back to routine pretty quickly." I smiled. "That's good."

"She's a good girl. . . . I guess she'll be up soon."

She sounded edgy again.

"Can I get you something to drink?" she said, moving away from the picture wall. "There's iced tea in the fridge."

"Sure, thanks."

I followed her through a generously dimensioned living room lined on three sides with floor-to-ceiling mahogany bookshelves and furnished with oxblood leather couches and club chairs that looked new. The shelves were full of hardcovers. A brown afghan was draped over one of the chairs. The fourth wall had two curtained windows and was papered in a black-and-green plaid that darkened the room further and gave it a clubby look, unmistakably masculine.

Chip's dominance? Or indifference to interior decorating on her part? I trailed slightly behind her, watching her bare feet sink into brown plush carpet. A grass stain spotted one buttock of her shorts. She had a stiff stride and held her arms pressed to her sides.

A dining room papered in a brown mini-print led to a white-tile and oak kitchen large enough to accommodate a distressed pine table and four chairs. The appliances were chrome-fronted and spotless. Glassed cabinets revealed neatly stacked crockery and size-ordered glassware. The dish drainer was empty; the counters, bare.

The window above the sink was a greenhouse affair filled with painted clay pots stuffed with summer flowers and herbs. A larger window to the left afforded a view of the backyard. Flagstone patio, rectangular pool covered with blue plastic and fenced with wrought iron. Then a long, perfect strip of grass, interrupted only by a wooden play-set, that ended at a hedge of orange trees espaliered against a six-foot cinder-block wall. Beyond the wall the ubiquitous mountains hung like drapery. Maybe miles away, maybe yards. I tried to get some perspective, couldn't. The grass began looking like a runway to eternity.

She said, "Please, have a seat."

Setting a place mat before me, she put a tall glass of iced tea upon it. "Just a mix—hope that's all right." Before I could answer, she returned to the refrigerator and touched the door.

I drank and said, "It's fine."

She picked up a washcloth and ran it over clean counter tiles, avoiding my eyes.

I sipped a bit, waited till we finally made contact, and tried another smile.

Her return smile was quick and tight and I thought I saw some color in her cheeks. She tugged her shirt down, kept her legs pressed together as she wiped the counter some more, washed the cloth, rung it out, folded it. Held it in both hands as if unsure what to do with it.

"So," she said.

I looked out at the mountains. "Beautiful day."

She nodded, snapped her face to the side, cast a downward glance, and placed the washcloth over the faucet spout. She ripped a square of paper towel from a wooden roller and began wiping the spigot. Her hands were wet. A Lady Macbeth thing or just her way of dealing with the tension?

I watched her clean some more. Then she gave another downward look and I followed it. To her chest. Nipples poking sharply through the thin black cotton of her shirt, small but erect.

When she looked up, my eyes were elsewhere.

"She should be up soon," she said. "She usually sleeps from about one to two."

"Sorry for coming so early."

"Oh, no, that's okay. I wasn't doing anything anyway."

She dried the spigot and stowed the paper towel in a wastebasket beneath the sink.

"While we wait," I said, "do you have any questions about Cassie's development? Or anything else?"

"Um . . . not really." She bit her lip, polished the faucet. "I just wish I . . . someone could tell me what's going on—not that I expect you to."

I gave a nod, but she was looking out the greenhouse window and didn't notice it.

Suddenly she leaned over the sink on tiptoe and adjusted one of the potted plants. Her back was to me and I saw her shirt ride up, revealing a couple of inches of tight waist and spine-knob. As she puttered, her long hair swayed like a horsetail. The stretch made her calves ride up and her thighs tighten. She straightened the pot, then another, stretched farther, and fumbled. One of the planters fell, hitting the rim of the sink, shattering, and showering planter's mix onto the floor.

She was down on all fours in an instant, scooping and collecting. Dirt crusted her hands and streaked her shorts. I got up but before I could help her, she bounded to her feet, hurried to a utility closet and retrieved a broom. Her sweeping was hard and angry. I tore a paper square off the roller and handed it to her after she put the broom away.

She was flushed now, and her eyes were wet. She took the towel without looking at me. Wiping her hands, she said, "I'm sorry—I have to go change."

She left the kitchen through a side door. I used the time to walk around the room, opening drawers and doors and feeling like an imbecile. Nothing more ominous in the cupboards than housekeeping aids and convenience foods. I looked out the door through which she'd left, found a small bathroom and service porch, and checked them out too. Washer and dryer, cabinets choked with detergents and cleansers, softeners and brighteners—a treasury of things promising to make life shiny and sweet-smelling. Most of them toxic, but what did that prove?

I heard footsteps and hurried back to the table. She came in wearing a loose yellow blouse, baggy jeans, sandals—her hospital uniform. Her hair was loosely braided and her face looked scrubbed.

"Sorry. What a klutz," she said.

She walked to the refrigerator. No independent movement from her chest region, no nipples.

"More iced tea?"

"No, thanks."

She took a can of Pepsi, popped it open, and sat down facing me.

"Did you have a nice ride over?"

"Very nice."

"It's good when there's no traffic."

"Yes, it is."

"I forgot to tell you, they closed off the pass to widen the road. . . ."

She continued to talk. About the weather and gardening, creasing her forehead.

Working hard at being casual.

But she seemed a stranger in her home. Talking stiffly, as if she'd rehearsed her lines but had no confidence in her memory.

Out the big window, the view was static as death.

Why were they living here? Why would Chuck Jones's only son choose exurban quarantine in his own faltering housing development when he could have afforded to live anywhere?

Proximity to the junior college didn't explain it. Gorgeous ranchland and plenty of country-club communities dotted the west end of the Valley. And funk-chic was still alive in Topanga Canyon.

Some kind of rebellion? A bit of ideology on Chip's part— wanting to be part of the community he planned to build? Just the kind of thing a rebel might use to dampen any guilt over making big profits. Though, from the looks of it, profits were a long way off.

Another scenario fit, too: abusive parents often secreted their families from the prying eyes of potential rescuers.

I became aware of Cindy's voice. Talking about her dishwasher, letting out words in a nervous stream. Saying she rarely used it, preferred gloving up and using steaming water so that the dishes dried almost instantly. Getting animated, as if she hadn't talked to anyone in a long time.

She probably hadn't. I couldn't imagine Chip sitting around for chitchat about housework.

I wondered how many of the books in the living room were hers. Wondered what the two of them had in common.

When she paused for breath, I said, "It really is a nice house."

Out of context, but it perked her up.

She gave a big smile, sloe-eyed, lips moist. I realized how good-looking she could be when she was happy.

"Would you like to see the rest of it?" she said.

"Sure."

We retraced our steps to the dining room and she pulled pieces of wedding silver out of a hutch and showed them to me, one by one. Next came the book-lined living room, where she talked about how hard it had been to find skilled carpenters to build solid shelving, no plywood. "Plywood gasses out—we want the house to be as clean as possible."

I pretended to listen while inspecting the books' spines.

Academic texts: sociology, psychology, political science. A bit of fiction, but none of it dated after Hemingway.

Interspersed among the volumes were certificates and trophies. The brass plate on one was inscribed: SINCERE THANKS TO MR. C. L. JONES III, FROM LOURDES HIGH SCHOOL ADVANCED PLACEMENT CLUB. YOU SHOWED US THAT TEACHING AND LEARNING WERE JUST PART OF FRIENDSHIP. Dated ten years ago.

Right below it was a scroll presented by the Yale Tutorial Project to CHARLES "CHIP" JONES FOR DEDICATED SERVICES TO THE CHILDREN OF THE NEW HAVEN FREE CLINIC.

On a higher shelf was yet another tutoring award, issued by a fraternity at Yale. Two more plasticized plaques, granted by the College of Arts and Sciences at the University of Connecticut at Storrs, attested to Chip's excellence in graduate teaching. Papa Chuck hadn't lied.

Several more recent testimonials from West Valley Junior College: the Department of Sociology's Undergraduate Teaching Citation, a gavel on a plaque from the WVJC Student Council thanking PROF. C. L. JONES FOR SERVING AS FACULTY ADVISOR, a group photo of Chip and fifty or so smiling, shiny-cheeked sorority girls on an athletic field, both he and the girls in red T-shirts emblazoned with Greek letters. The picture was autographed: "Best, Wendy." "Thanks, Prof. Jones—Debra." "Love, Kristie." Chip was squatting on a baseline, arms around two of the girls, beaming, looking like a team mascot.

Cindy's got the tough job. I can escape.

I wondered what Cindy did for attention, realized she'd stopped talking, and turned to see her looking at me.

"He's a great teacher," she said. "Would you like to see the den?"

More soft furniture, crammed shelves, Chip's triumphs preserved in brass and wood and plastic, plus a wide-screen TV, stereo components, an alphabetized rack of classical and jazz compact discs.

That same clubby feel. The sole strip of wall not covered with shelves was papered in another plaid—blue and red—and hung with

Chip's two diplomas. Below the foolscaps, placed so low I had to kneel to get a good look, were a couple of watercolors.

Snow and bare trees and rough-wood barns. The frame of the first was labeled NEW ENGLAND WINTER. The one just above the floor molding was SYRUP TAPPING TIME. No signature. Tourist-trap quality, done by someone who admired the Wyeth family but lacked the talent.

Cindy said, "Mrs. Jones—Chip's mom—painted those."

"Did she live back east?"

She nodded. "Years ago, back when he was a boy. Uh-oh, I think I hear Cassie."

She held up an index finger, as if testing the wind.

A whimper, distant and mechanical, came from one of the bookcases. I turned toward it, located the sound at a small brown box resting on a high shelf. Portable intercom.

"I put it on when she sleeps," she said.

The box cried again.

We left the room and walked down a blue-carpeted hall, passing a front bedroom that had been converted into an office for Chip. The door was open. A wooden sign nailed to it said SKOLLAR AT WIRK. Yet another book-filled leathery space.

Next came a deep-blue master bedroom and a closed door that I assumed led to the connecting bathroom Cindy had told me about. Cassie's room was at the end of the hall, a generous corner space done up in rainbow paper and white cotton curtains with pink trim. Cassie was sitting up in a canopied crib, wearing a pink nightshirt, hands fisted, crying halfheartedly. The room smelled baby-sweet.

Cindy picked her up and held her close. Cassie's head was propped on her shoulder. Cassie looked at me, closed her eyes, flopped her face down.

Cindy cooed something. Cassie's face relaxed and her mouth opened. Her breathing became rhythmic. Cindy rocked her.

I looked around the room. Two doors on the southern wall. Two windows. Bunny and duck decals appliquéd to furniture. A wicker-back rocker next to the crib. Boxed games, toys, and enough books for a year's worth of bedtime reading.

In the center three tiny chairs surrounded a circular play table. On the table were a stack of paper, a new box of crayons, three sharpened pencils, a gum eraser, and a piece of shirt cardboard hand-lettered WELCOME DR. DELAWARE. LuvBunnies—more than a dozen of them—sat on the floor, propped against the wall, spaced as precisely as cadets at inspection.

Cindy settled in the rocker with Cassie in her arms. Cassie molded to her like butter on bread. Not a trace of tension in the little body.

Cindy closed her eyes and rocked, stroking Cassie's back, smoothing sleep-moistened strands of hair. Cassie took a deep breath, let it out, nestled her head under Cindy's chin, and made high-pitched contented sounds.

I lowered myself to the floor and sat cross-legged—shrink's analytical lotus—watching, thinking, suspecting, imagining worst-cases and beyond.

After a few minutes my joints began to ache and I got up and stretched. Cindy's eyes followed me. We traded smiles. She pressed her cheek to Cassie's head and shrugged.

I whispered, "Take your time," and began walking around the room. Running my hands along the dustless surfaces of furniture, inspecting the contents of the toy case while trying not to look too inquisitive.

Good stuff. The right stuff. Each game and plaything safe, and age-appropriate, and educational.

Something white caught the corner of my eye. The buckteeth of one of the LuvBunnies. In the dim light of the nursery the critter's grin and those of its mates seemed malevolent—mocking.

I remembered those grins from Cassie's hospital room and a crazy thought hit me.

Toxic toys. *Accidental* poisoning.

I'd read about a case in a child health journal—stuffed animals from Korea that turned out to be filled with waste fibers from a chemical plant.

Delaware solves the mystery and everyone goes home happy.

Picking up the nearest bunny—a yellow one—I squeezed its belly, felt the give-and-rebound of firm foam. Raising the toy to my nose, I smelled nothing. The label said MADE IN TAIWAN OF LUV-PURE AND FIREPROOF MATERIALS. Below that was an approval seal from one of the family magazines.

Something along the seam—two snaps. A trapdoor flap that could be undone. I pulled it open. The sound made Cindy turn. Her eyebrows were up.

I poked around, found nothing, fastened the snap, and put the toy back.

"Allergies, right?" she said, talking just above a whisper. "To the stuffing—I thought of that too. But Dr. Eves had her tested and she's not allergic to anything. For a while, though, I washed the bunnies every day. Washed all her cloth toys and her bedding with Ivory Liquid. It's the gentlest."

I nodded.

"We pulled up the carpeting, too, to see if there was mold in the padding or something in the glue. Chip had heard of people getting sick in office buildings—'sick buildings,' they call them. We had a company come out and clean the air-conditioning ducts, and Chip had the paint checked, to see if there was lead or chemicals."

Her voice had risen and taken on an edge again. Cassie squirmed. Cindy rocked her quiet.

"I'm always looking," she whispered. "All the time—ever since . . . the beginning."

She covered her mouth with her hand. Removed the hand and slapped it down to her knee, pinkening the white skin.

Cassie's eyes shot open.

Cindy rocked harder, faster. Fighting for composure.

"First one, now the other," she whispered—loud, almost hissing. "Maybe I'm just not supposed to be a mother!"

I went over and placed my hand on her shoulder. She slid out from under it, shot up out of the rocker, and thrust Cassie at me. Tears streamed from her eyes, and her hands shook.

"Here! Here! I don't know what I'm doing. I'm not meant to be a mother!"

Cassie began whimpering, then gulping air.

Cindy thrust her at me again and, when I took her, ran across the room. My hands were around Cassie's waist. She was arching her back. Wailing, fighting me.

I tried to comfort her. She wouldn't let me.

Cindy threw open a door, exposing blue tile. Running into the bathroom, she slammed the door. I heard the sound of retching, followed by a toilet flush.

Cassie squirmed and kicked and screamed louder. I got a firm grasp around her middle and patted her back. "It's okay, honey. Mommy's coming right back. It's okay."

She coiled more violently, punching at my face, continuing to caterwaul. I tried to contain her while providing comfort. She jerked and turned scarlet, threw her little head back and howled, nearly slipping out of my grasp.

"Mommy's coming right back, Cass—"

The bathroom door opened and Cindy rushed out, wiping her eyes. I expected her to grab Cassie away but she just held out her hands and said, "Please," mouthing the word over Cassie's shrieks and looking as if she expected me to withhold her child.

I handed Cassie back to her.

She hugged the little girl and started to circle the room very fast. Taking large, hard steps that made her thin thighs quiver, and muttering things to Cassie that I couldn't hear.

Two dozen circuits and Cassie's cries got softer. Another dozen and she was quiet.

Cindy kept moving, but as she passed me she said, "I'm sorry— I really am. I'm sorry."

Her eyes and cheeks were wet. I told her it was okay. The sound of my voice made Cassie crank up again.

Cindy began walking faster, saying, "Baby, baby, baby."

I went over to the play table and sat as best I could on one of the tiny chairs. The welcome cardboard stared up at me like some kind of sick joke.

A few moments later, gasps and sucking sobs took the place of Cassie's cries. Then she silenced and I saw that her eyes were closed.

Cindy returned to the rocking chair and began to whisper harshly: "I'm really, really, really sorry. I'm so— That was— God, I'm a *horrible* mother!"

Barely audible, but the anguish in her voice opened Cassie's eyes. The little girl stared up at her mother and mewled.

"No, no, baby, it's okay. I'm sorry—it's okay."

Mouthing to me: "I'm horrible."

Cassie started to cry again.

"No, no, it's okay, honey. I'm good. If you want me to be good, I'm good. I'm a *good* mommy, yes, I am, yes—yes, honey, everything's okay. Okay?"

Forcing herself to smile down at Cassie. Cassie reached up and touched one of Cindy's cheeks.

"Oh, you are *so* good, little girl," said Cindy, in a crumbling voice. "You are *so* good to your mommy. You are *so, so good*!"

"Ma ma."

"Mama *loves* you."

"Ma ma."

"You're so good to your mama. Cassie Brooks Jones is the best girl, the sweetest girl."

"Ma ma. Mamama."

"Mama loves you *so* much. Mama loves you *so* much." Cindy looked at me. Looked at the play table.

"Mama loves you," she said into Cassie's ear. "And Dr. Delaware's a very good friend, honey. Here, see?"

She turned Cassie's head toward me. I tried another smile, hoping it looked better than it felt.

Cassie shook her head violently and said, "Nuh!"

"Remember, he's our friend, honey? All those pretty drawings he did for you at the hospita—"

"Nuh!"

"The animals—"

"Nuh *nuh*!"

"C'mon, honey, there's nothing to be scared of—"

"*Nuuuh!*"

"Okay, okay. It's okay, Cass."

I got up.

"Are you going?" said Cindy. Alarm in her voice.

I pointed to the bathroom. "May I?"

"Oh. Sure. There's one just off the entry hall too."

"This is fine."

"Sure . . . Meantime, I'll try to calm her down. . . . I'm really, really sorry."

* * *

I locked the door and the one leading to the master bedroom, flushed the toilet, and let out my breath. The water was as blue as the tiles. I found myself staring down at a tiny azure whirlpool. Turning on the water, I washed my face and dried it, catching a glimpse of myself in the mirror.

Dire and old with suspicion. I tried on a few smiles, finally settled on one that didn't approximate the leer of a used-car salesman. The mirror was the face of a medicine cabinet.

Child-proof latch. I undid it.

Four shelves. I turned the water up full blast, rifled quickly, starting at the top and working down.

Aspirin, Tylenol, razor blades, shaving cream. Men's cologne, deodorant, an emery board, a bottle of liquid antacid. A small yellow box of spermicidal jelly capsules. Hydrogen peroxide, a tube of earwax-dissolving ointment, suntan lotion . . .

I closed the cabinet. When I turned off the water I heard Cindy's voice through the door, saying something comforting and maternal.

Until she'd thrust Cassie at me, the little girl had accepted me. *Maybe I'm not supposed to be a mother. . . . I'm a horrible mother.*

Stretched past the breaking point? Or trying to sabotage my visit?

I rubbed my eyes. Another cabinet beneath the sink. Another child-proof latch. Such careful parents, pulling up the carpets, washing the toys . . .

Cindy was cooing to Cassie.

Silently, I got down on my knees, freed the latch, and opened the door.

Beneath the snake of the drainpipe were boxes of tissues and rolls of plastic-wrapped toilet paper. Behind those sat two bottles of green mint mouthwash and an aerosol can. I examined the can. Pine-scented disinfectant. As I replaced it, it fell and my arm shot forward to catch it and mask the noise. I succeeded but the back of my hand knocked against something, off to the right, with sharp corners.

I pushed the paper goods aside and drew it out.

White cardboard box, about five inches square, imprinted on top with a red-arrow logo above stylized red script that read HOLLO-WAY MEDICAL CORP. Above that was an arrow-shaped gold foil sticker: SAMPLE, PRESENTED TO: *Ralph Benedict, M.D.*

A string-and-disc tie held the box shut. I unwound it, pushed back the flaps, and exposed a sheet of corrugated brown paper. Under that was a row of white plastic cylinders the size of ballpoint pens, nestled in a bed of Styrofoam peanuts. A folded slip of printed paper was rubber-banded to each one.

I fished out a cylinder. Feather-light, almost flimsy. A numbered ring girdled the bottom of the shaft. At the tip was a hole surrounded by screw thread; on the other end, a cap that twisted but didn't come off.

Black letters on the barrel said INSUJECT. I removed the printed paper. Manufacturer's brochure, copyrighted five years ago. Holloway Medical's home office was in San Francisco.

The first paragraph read:

INSUJECT (TM) is a dose-adjustable ultra-lightweight delivery system for the subcutaneous administration of human or purified pork insulin in 1 to 3 unit doses. INSUJECT should be used in conjunction with other components of the Holloway INSU-EASE (TM) system, namely, INSUJECT disposable needles and INSUFILL (TM) cartridges.

The second paragraph highlighted the selling points of the system: portability, an ultra-thin needle that reduced pain and the risk of subdermal abscesses, increased "ease of administration and precise calibration of dosage." A series of boxed line drawings illustrated needle attachment, loading of the cartridge into the cylinder, and the proper way to inject insulin beneath the skin.

Ease of administration.

An ultra-thin needle would leave a minuscule puncture wound, just as Al Macauley had described. If the injection site was concealed, the mark just might escape detection.

I groped around inside the box, looking for needles.

None, just the cylinders. Shoving my hands into the recesses of the cabinet yielded nothing more.

Probably cool enough to store insulin, but maybe someone was picky. Could Insufill cartridges be sitting on one of the shelves of the chrome-faced refrigerator in the kitchen?

Standing, I placed the box on the counter and the brochure in my pocket. The water in the toilet bowl had just stopped spinning. I cleared my throat, coughed, flushed again, looking around the room for another hiding place.

The only possibility I could see was the toilet tank. I lifted the cap and peered in. Just plumbing and the gizmo that dyed the water.

Ultra-thin needle . . . The bathroom was an ideal hiding place—perfect conduit from the master suite to the nursery.

Perfect for fixing up a middle-of-the-night injection:

Lock the door to the master suite, fetch the gear from beneath the sink, assemble it, and tiptoe into Cassie's room.

The bite of the needle would startle the little girl awake, probably make her cry, but she wouldn't know what had happened.

Neither would anyone else. Waking up in tears was normal for a child her age. Especially one who'd been sick so often.

Would darkness conceal the needle-wielder's face?

On the other side of the nursery door Cindy was talking, sounding sweet.

Then again, maybe there was an alternative explanation. The cylinders were meant for her. Or Chip.

No—Stephanie had said she'd tested both of them for metabolic disease and found them healthy.

I looked at the door to the master bedroom, then down at my watch. I'd spent three minutes in this blue-tile dungeon, but it felt like a weekend. Unlocking the door, I padded across the threshold into the bedroom, grateful for thick, tight-weave carpeting that swallowed my footsteps.

The room was darkened by drawn shutters and furnished with a king-size bed and clumsy Victorian furniture. Books were stacked high on one of the nightstands. A phone sat atop the stack. Next to the table was a brass-and-wood valet over which hung a pair of jeans. The other stand bore a Tiffany revival lamp and a coffee mug. The bedcovers were turned down but folded neatly. The room smelled of the pine disinfectant I'd found in the bathroom.

Lots of disinfectant. Why?

A double chest ran along the wall facing the bed. I opened a top drawer. Bras and panties and hose and floral sachet in a packet. I felt around, closed the drawer, got to work on the one below, wondering what thrill Dawn Herbert had gotten from petty theft.

Nine drawers. Clothing, a couple of cameras, canisters of film, and a pair of binoculars. Across the room was a closet. More clothes, tennis rackets and canisters of balls, a fold-up rowing machine, garment bags and suitcases, more books—all on sociology. A telephone directory, light bulbs, travel maps, a knee brace. Another box of contraceptive jelly. Empty.

I searched garment pockets, found nothing but lint. Maybe the dark corners of the closet concealed something but I'd been there too long. Shutting the closet door, I snuck back to the bathroom. The toilet had stopped gurgling and Cindy was no longer talking.

Had she grown suspicious about my prolonged absence? I cleared my throat again, turned on the water, heard Cassie's voice—some kind of protest—then the resumption of mommy-talk.

Detaching the toilet paper holder, I slid off the old roll and tossed it into the cabinet. Unwrapping a refill, I slipped it onto the dispenser. The ad copy on the wrapper promised to be gentle.

Picking up the white box, I pushed open the door to Cassie's room, wearing a smile that hurt my teeth.

They were at the play table, holding crayons. Some of the papers were covered with colored scrawl.

When Cassie saw me she gripped her mother's arm and began whining.

"It's okay, hon. Dr. Delaware's our friend." Cindy noticed the box in my hands and squinted.

I came closer and showed it to her. She stared at it, then up at me. I stared back, searching for any sign of self-indictment.

Just confusion.

"I was looking for toilet paper," I said, "and came across this."

She leaned forward and read the gold sticker.

Cassie watched her, then picked up a crayon and threw it. When that didn't capture her mother's attention, she whined some more.

"Shh, baby." Cindy's squint tightened. She continued to look baffled. "How strange."

Cassie threw her arms up and said, "Uh uh uh!"

Cindy pulled her closer and said, "Haven't seen those in a long time."

"Didn't mean to snoop," I said, "but I knew Holloway made equipment for diabetics and when I saw the label I got curious— thinking about Cassie's blood sugar. Are you or Chip diabetic?"

"Oh, no," she said. "Those were Aunt Harriet's. *Where* did you find them?"

"Beneath the sink."

"How odd. No, Cass, these are for drawing, not throwing." She picked up a red crayon and drew a jagged line.

Cassie followed the movement, then buried her head in Cindy's blouse.

"Boy, I haven't seen those in a really long time. I cleaned out her house, but I thought I threw all her medicines out."

"Was Dr. Benedict her doctor?"

"And her boss."

She bounced Cassie gently. Cassie peeked out from under her arm, then began poking her under the chin.

Cindy laughed and said, "You're tickling me. . . . Isn't that odd, under the sink all this time?" She gave an uneasy smile. "Guess that doesn't make me much of a housekeeper. Sorry you had to go looking for paper—I usually notice when the roller's low."

"No problem," I said, realizing there'd been no dust on the box. Pulling out a cylinder, I rolled it between my fingers.

Cassie said, "Peh-il."

"No, it's not a pencil, honey." No anxiety. "It's just a . . . thing."

Cassie reached for it. I gave it to her and Cindy's eyes got wide. Cassie put it to her mouth, grimaced, lowered it to the paper and tried to draw.

"See, I told you, Cass. Here, if you want to draw, use this."

Cassie ignored the proffered crayon and kept looking at the cylinder. Finally she threw it down on the table and began to fuss.

"C'mon, sweetie, let's draw with Dr. Delaware."

My name evoked a whimper.

"Cassie *Brooks,* Dr. Delaware came all the way to play with you, to draw animals—hippos, kangaroos. Remember the kangaroos?"

Cassie whimpered louder.

"Hush, honey," said Cindy, but without conviction. "No, don't break your crayons, honey. You can't— C'mon, Cass."

"Uh uh uh." Cassie tried to get off Cindy's lap.

Cindy looked at me.

I offered no advice.

"Should I let her?"

"Sure," I said. "I don't want to be associated with confining her."

Cindy released her and Cassie made her way to the floor and crawled under the table.

"We did a little drawing while we were waiting for you," said Cindy. "I guess she's had enough."

She bent and looked under the table. "Are you tired of drawing, Cass? Do you want to do something else?"

Cassie ignored her and picked at the carpet fibers.

Cindy sighed. "I'm really sorry—for before. I . . . it just . . . I really blew it, didn't I? I really, really screwed things up—don't know what came over me."

"Sometimes things just pile up," I said, shifting the Insuject box from one hand to another. Keeping it in her view, looking for any sign of nervousness.

"Yes, but I still blew it for you and Cassie."

"Maybe it's more important for you and me to talk, anyway."

"Sure," she said, touching her braid and casting a glance under the table. "I could sure use some help, couldn't I? How about coming out now, Miss Cassie?"

No answer.

"Could I trouble you for another iced tea?" I said.

"Oh, sure, no trouble at all. Cass, Dr. Delaware and I are going into the kitchen."

Cindy and I walked to the door of the nursery. Just as we reached the threshold, Cassie crawled out, tottered upright, and came running toward Cindy, arms outstretched. Cindy picked her up and carried her on one hip. I followed, carrying the white box.

In the kitchen Cindy opened the refrigerator door with one hand and reached in for the pitcher. But before she could pull it out, Cassie slipped lower and Cindy needed both hands to hold her.

"Why don't you concentrate on her," I said, placing the box on the kitchen table and taking hold of the pitcher.

"Let me at least get you a glass." She went to the open cupboards across the room.

The moment her back was turned, I conducted a manic visual scan of the fridge. The most medicinal thing on the shelves was a tub of no-cholesterol margarine. Butter was in the butter compartment, the one marked CHEESE held a packet of sliced American.

Taking hold of the pitcher, I closed the door. Cindy was setting a glass on a place mat. I poured it half-full and drank. My throat felt raw. The tea tasted sweeter than before—almost sickly. Or maybe it was just my mind, lingering on thoughts of sugar.

Cassie watched me with a child's piercing suspicion. My smile caused her to frown. Wondering if trust could ever be regained, I put the glass down.

"Can I get you something else?" said Cindy.

"No, thanks. Better be going. Here." Offering her the box.

"Oh, I don't need it," she said. "Maybe someone at the hospital can use it. They're very expensive—that's why Dr. Ralph used to give us samples."

Us.

"That's very nice of you." I picked up the box.

"Well," she said, "we sure can't use them." She shook her head. "How strange, your finding them—kind of brings back memories."

Her mouth turned down. Cassie saw it, said, "Uh," and squirmed.

Cindy replaced the pout with a wide, abrupt smile. "Hello, sweetie."

Cassie poked at her mouth. Cindy kissed her fingers. "Yes, Mama loves you. Now let's walk Dr. Delaware bye-bye."

When we got to the entrance I stopped to look at the photos, realizing there were none of Chip's parents. My eyes settled back on the shot of Cindy and her aunt.

"We were walking that day," she said softly. "Along the dock. She used to take lots of walks. Long ones, for her diabetes—the exercise helped her control it."

"Did she have it pretty much under control?"

"Oh, yes—that wasn't what . . . what took her. That was an S-T-R-O-K-E. She had really great control—careful about every-thing that went into her mouth. When I lived with her, I wasn't allowed any sweets or junk. So I never developed a taste for it, and we don't keep much around the house."

She kissed Cassie's cheek. "I figure if she doesn't get a taste of it now, maybe she won't want it later."

I turned away from the photo.

"We do everything," she said, "to keep her healthy. Without health, there's . . . nothing. Right? That's the kind of thing you hear when you're young but it's only later that you start to believe it."

Anguish filled her eyes.

Cassie wiggled and made wordless sounds.

"True," I said. "How about you and me getting together tomorrow, right here."

"Sure."

"When would be a good time?"

"With or without . . . H-E-R?"

"Without, if possible."

"Then it would have to be when she's asleep. She generally naps from one to two or two-thirty, then goes down for the night at seven or eight. How about eight, in order to play it safe? If that's not too late for you."

"Eight's fine."

"Chip will probably be able to be here, too—that should be good, don't you think?"

"Absolutely," I said. "See you then."

She touched my arm. "Thanks for everything, and I'm really sorry. I know you'll help us get through this."

Back on Topanga, I pulled into the first gas station I saw and used the pay phone to call Milo at work.

"Perfect timing," he said. "Just got off the phone with Fort Jackson. Seems little Cindy was sick all right. *And* back in '83. But not pneumonia or meningitis. *Gonorrhea.* They drummed her out because of it, on an ELS—entry-level status. That means she served less than a hundred and eighty days and they wanted to get rid of her before they had to pay benefits."

"Just because of a dose?"

"A dose plus what led up to it. Seems during the four months she was there, she set some kind of record for sexual promiscuity. So if she's fooling around on hubby, that just means she's being consistent."

"Promiscuity," I said. "I just finished my home visit and this was the first time I got a sense of her sexuality. I arrived early, on purpose—curious about why she didn't want me out there until two-thirty. She'd let her hair down. Literally. Was wearing short shorts and a T-shirt with no bra."

"Coming on to you?"

"No. In fact she seemed really uncomfortable. A few minutes later she spilled some dirt on her clothes, hurried off to change and came back dowdied up."

"Maybe you just missed her boyfriend."

"Could be. She told me one-to-two was Cassie's nap time and Chip teaches a class that day from twelve to two, so what better time for an affair? And the bedroom smelled of disinfectant."

"Masking the smell of love," he said. "You didn't see anyone? Pass any cars speeding away?"

"Just the pool man pulling out of the driveway next door— Oh, shit, you don't think?"

"Sure I do." He laughed. "I see the worst in everyone." More laughter. "The pool man. Now there's your basic SoCal *thang*."

"He was next door, not at her house."

"So what? It's not unusual for those guys to service several pools on one block—that far out of town, he might do the whole damned neighborhood. More ways than one. Do the Joneses have a pool?"

"Yes, but it was covered."

"Get a look at Mr. Chlorine?"

"Young, tan, ponytail. The sign on his truck said ValleyBrite Pool Service, with an I-T-E."

"He see you pull up?"

"Yup. He stopped short, stuck his head out the window and stared, then gave this big grin with the thumb-up sign."

"Friendly, huh? Even if he'd just screwed her, he may not be the only one. Back in the army she was no nun."

"How'd you find out about it?"

"Wasn't easy. The army buries stuff just on principle. Charlie spent a lot of time trying to get into her file and couldn't. Finally, I swallowed my pride and called the colonel—only for you, bucko."

"Much appreciated."

"Yeah . . . To his credit, the asshole didn't gloat. Hooked me right up with an unlisted military number in D.C. Some kind of archive. They had no details—just name, rank, serial number, and her ELS designation, but I was lucky to get a records officer who'd done rice-paddy duty same time as me, and I convinced him to call South Carolina and find me someone to talk to. He came up with a female captain who'd been a corporal back when Cindy was a grunt. She remembered Cindy very well. Seems our gal was the talk of the barracks."

"It's an all-female base," I said. "Are we talking lesbian promiscuity?"

"Nope. She messed around in town—used to go on leave and party in the local bars. It ended, according to this captain, when Cindy hooked up with a bunch of teenagers and one of them happened to be the son of a local big shot. She gave him the clap. Mayor paid a visit to the base commander, and bye-bye. Sordid little tale, huh? Any relevance to the Munchausen thing?"

"Promiscuity's not part of the profile, but if you consider it another form of attention seeking, I guess it would be consistent. Also, Munchausens often report incest in childhood, and promiscuity could be another reaction to that. What *definitely* fits the profile is early experience with serious illness, and V.D. wasn't *her* first. The aunt who raised her was diabetic."

"Sugar screw-up. Interesting."

"Wait, there's more." I told him about finding the Insujects and showing them to Cindy.

"I thought it might be the confrontation we've been waiting for. But she didn't show any guilt or anxiety. Just puzzlement about what they were doing beneath the sink. She said they were leftovers from the aunt—something she thought she'd gotten rid of when she cleaned out the aunt's house after she died. But there was no dust on the box, so that's probably another lie."

"How long ago did the aunt die?"

"Four years. The doctor the samples were sent to was the aunt's physician and boss."

"Name?"

"Ralph Benedict. Hell, for all I know, *he's* the mystery lover.

Who'd be better at faking illnesses than a doctor? And we know she goes for older men—she married one."

"Younger ones too."

"Yeah. But it makes sense, doesn't it—a doctor boyfriend? Benedict could be supplying her with drugs and apparatus. Coaching her in faking illness."

"What's his motive?"

"True love. He sees the kids as encumbrances, wants to get rid of them and have Cindy all to himself. Maybe with some of Chip's money thrown in. As an M.D., he'd know how to set it up. Know how to be careful. Because two kids from one family dying, one right after another, is suspicious, but if the deaths were different and each looked medically valid, it could be pulled off."

"Ralph Benedict," he said. "I'll check with the medical board."

"Cindy grew up in Ventura. He might still be there."

"What's the name of the company who shipped him these cylinders?"

"Holloway Medical. San Francisco."

"Let's see what else they sent him and when. Cylinders—like empty tubes?"

"They're part of a kit." I described the Insuject system.

"No needles or drugs under the sink?"

"Nope, the needles and the insulin spansules come separately." I recounted my search of the bedroom and the refrigerator. "But they could be anywhere in that house. Any possibility of getting a search warrant now?"

"Just on the basis of tubes? Doubtful. With needles attached and the insulin all loaded up, maybe. That would be evidence of premeditation, though she could still claim the stuff was left over from the aunt."

"Not if the insulin was still fresh. I'm not sure of insulin's exact shelf life, but it's not four years."

"Yeah. So find me some fresh insulin and I'll visit a judge. Right now, there's no evidentiary chain."

"Even with Cassie's low sugar?"

"Even with. Sorry. Wonder why she left it under the sink like that."

"She probably never imagined anyone would look there. It was stuck in a corner—you'd have to be groping around to find it."

"And she wasn't pissed at all that you were snooping in her john?"

"If she was, she didn't show it. I made up a story about running out of toilet paper and going under the sink for a fresh roll. She apologized for not being a better housekeeper."

"Eager to please, huh? The boys back in South Carolina sure took advantage of it."

"Or she gets people to do what she wants by playing dumb and passive. I didn't walk out of that house feeling in control."

"Ye olde bathroom detective. Sounds like you're ready for the Vice Squad."

"I'll pass. The whole thing was surreal. Not that I was doing much good as a therapist."

I told him how Cindy had thrust Cassie at me, and Cassie's subsequent panic.

"Up till then my rapport with Cassie had been progressing pretty well. Now, it's shot to hell, Milo. So I have to wonder if Cindy was deliberately trying to sabotage me."

"Waltzing and leading, huh?"

"Something she told me suggests that control is a big issue for her. When she was a kid, the aunt wouldn't let her eat any sweets at all, even though there was nothing wrong with *her* pancreas. That's a far cry from Munchausen, but there is a hint of pathology there—not allowing a healthy child to have an occasional ice cream."

"Aunt projecting the diabetes onto her?"

"Exactly. And who knows if there were other aspects of the disease the aunt projected—like injections. Not insulin, but maybe some kind of vitamin shots. I'm just guessing. Cindy also told me that she restricts Cassie's sweets. At face value, that sounds like good mothering. Reasonable health-consciousness from someone who's already lost one child. But maybe there's a whole weird thing going on with regard to sugar."

"Sins of the mothers," he said.

"The aunt was *Cindy's* functional mother. And look at the role model she provided: a health professional who had a chronic disease and *controlled* it—Cindy spoke of that with pride. She may have grown up associating being female—being *maternal*—with being sick and emotionally rigid: controlled and control*ling*. It's no surprise she chose the military right after high school—from one structured environment to another. When that didn't work out, her next step was respiratory tech school. Because Aunt Harriet told her it was a good profession. Control and illness—it keeps repeating itself."

"She ever mention why she didn't finish respiratory tech school?"

"No. What are you thinking—more promiscuity?"

"I'm a big believer in patterns. What'd she do after that?"

"Junior college. Where she met Chip. She dropped out, got married. Got pregnant right away—more big changes that might have made her feel out of control. The marriage was a step up for her socially, but she ended up living in a very lonely place."

I described Dunbar Court and the surrounding tract.

"Slow death for someone who craves attention, Milo. And when Chip gets home, I'll bet the situation doesn't change much. He's really into the academic life—big fish in a small pond. I dropped by the J.C. before I went to the house and caught a glimpse of him teaching. Guru on the grass, disciples at his feet. A whole world she's not part of. The house reflects it—room after room of *his* books, *his* trophies, masculine furniture. Even in her own home she hasn't made an imprint."

"So she makes an imprint on the kid."

"Using familiar tools, things she remembers from her childhood. Insulin, needles. Other poisons—manipulating what goes into Cassie's mouth the same way her aunt controlled her."

"What about Chad?"

"Maybe he actually did die of SIDS—yet another traumatic illness in Cindy's life—and *that* was the stress that drove her over the edge. Or maybe she smothered him."

"You think your finding the cylinders will scare her off?"

"That would be logical, but with Munchausen, the whole power game, I suppose it could do just the opposite—raise the ante, challenge her to get the better of me. So maybe I just made things more dangerous for Cassie—hell if I know."

"Don't flog yourself. Where are the cylinders now?"

"Right here. In the car. Can you have them dusted for prints?"

"Sure, but Cindy's or Chip's prints on it wouldn't mean much—one of them stashed it years ago and forgot about it."

"What about the lack of dust?"

"It's a clean cabinet. Or you knocked off whatever dust was on it when you took it out. I'm talking like a defense attorney now, though we're not even close to making anyone need one. And if this Benedict guy touched it, that's cool too. They were sent to him in the first place."

"With the aunt dead, there'd be no reason for him to give them to Cindy."

"True. If we can pin down this shipment to him *after* the aunt died, that would be great. Any serial numbers on the things? Or an invoice?"

"Let me check . . . no invoice. But there are serial numbers. And the copyright on the manufacturer's brochure is five years old."

"Good. Give me those numbers and I'll get on it. In the meantime, I still think your best bet is to continue playing with Cindy's head. Give her a taste of her own medicine."

"How?"

"Pull her in for a meeting, without the kid—"

"That's already set up for tomorrow evening. Chip'll be there too."

"Even better. Confront her, straight on. Tell her you think someone is making Cassie sick and you know *how*. Hold up a cylinder and say you're not buying any of this leftover crap. You want to take chances, go for a big bluff: say you've talked to the D.A. and he's ready to file charges for attempted murder. Then pray she cracks."

"And if she doesn't?"

"You get thrown off the case, but at least she'll know someone's wise to her. I don't see what you can gain by waiting any longer, Alex."

"What about Stephanie? Do I clue her in? Are we eliminating her as a suspect?"

"Like we said before, she could be Cindy's secret lover, but there's no sign of that. And if she *was* involved, why would Cindy mess with Benedict? Stephanie's a doctor—she could get the same stuff he could. Anything's possible, but far as I can tell, the mom started out looking good and she keeps getting better."

"If Stephanie's off the hook," I said, "I should let her in on it—she's the primary doc. Pulling something this strong without her knowledge is probably unethical."

"Why don't you just sound her out and see how she reacts? Tell her about the cylinders and see where she goes with it. If you're satisfied she's clean, take her along with you when you play with Cindy's head. Strength in numbers."

"Play with her head? Sounds fun."

"It rarely is," he said. "If I could do it for you, I would."

"Thanks. For everything."

"Anything else?"

Finding the Insujects had pushed the visit to Dr. Janos's office out of my head.

"Plenty," I said, and told him how Huenengarth had beat me to Dawn Herbert's computer disks. Then I threw in my calls to Ferris Dixon and Professor W. W. Zimberg's office, and my updated blackmail theories on Herbert and Ashmore.

"High intrigue, Alex—maybe some of it's even true. But don't let yourself get distracted from Cassie. I'm still checking on Huenengarth. Nothing yet, but I'll stay on it. Where will you be in case something does come up?"

"I'll call Stephanie soon as we hang up. If she's in her office I'll run over to the hospital. If not, I'll be home."

"All right. How about we get together later tonight, trade miseries. Eight okay?"

"Eight's fine. Thanks again."

"Don't thank me. We're a long way from feeling good about this one."

29.

The General Peds receptionist said, "Dr. Eves stepped out. Let me page her."

I waited, looking out through the clouded walls of the phone booth at traffic and dust. The equestrians came into view again, cantering up a side street, heading back from what must have been a circuit. Slim jodhpured legs clamped around glistening torsos. Lots of smiles.

Probably heading back to the club for cold drinks and conversation. I thought of all the ways Cindy Jones could have chosen to fill her time.

Just as the horses vanished, the receptionist came back on the line. "She's not answering, Doctor. Would you like to leave a message?"

"Any idea when she'll be back?"

"I know she's coming back for a five o'clock meeting—you might try her just before then."

Five P.M. was almost two hours away. I drove down Topanga

thinking of all the damage that could be done to a child in that time. Kept heading south to the on-ramp.

Traffic was backed up to the street. I nosed into the snail-trail and oozed eastward. Nasty drive to Hollywood. At night, though, the ambulance would fairly zip.

I pulled into the doctors' lot just before four, clipped my badge to my lapel, and walked to the lobby, where I paged Stephanie. The anxiety that had hit me only a week ago was gone. In its place, a driving sense of anger.

What a difference seven days make . . .

No answer. I phoned her office again, got the same receptionist, the same answer, delivered in a slightly annoyed tone.

I went up to the General Peds clinic and walked into the examination suite, passing patients, nurses, and doctors without notice.

Stephanie's door was closed. I wrote a note for her to call me and was bending to slip it under the door when a husky female voice said, "Can I help you?"

I straightened. A woman in her late sixties was looking at me. She had on the whitest white coat I'd ever seen, worn buttoned over a black dress. Her face was deeply tanned, wrinkled, and pinch-featured under a helmet of straight white hair. Her posture would have made a marine correct his own.

She saw my badge and said, "Oh, excuse me, Doctor." Her accent was Marlene Dietrich infused with London. Her eyes were small, green-blue, electrically alert. A gold pen was clipped to her breast pocket. She wore a thin gold chain from which a single pearl dangled, set in a golden nest like a nacreous egg.

"Dr. Kohler," I said. "Alex Delaware."

We shook hands and she read my badge. Confusion didn't suit her.

"I used to be on the staff," I said. "We worked together on some cases. Crohn's disease. Adaptation to the ostomy?"

"Ah, of course." Her smile was warm and it made the lie inoffensive. She'd always had that smile, wore it even while cutting down a resident's faulty diagnosis. Charm planted by an upper-class Prague childhood cut short by Hitler, then fertilized by marriage to The Famous Conductor. I remembered how she'd offered to use her connections to bring funds to the hospital. How the board had turned her down, calling that kind of fund-raising "crass."

"Looking for Stephanie?" she said.

"I need to talk to her about a patient."

The smile hung there but her eyes iced over. "I happen to be looking for her myself. She's scheduled to be here. But I suppose our future division head must be busy."

I feigned surprise.

"Oh, yes," she said. "Those in the know say her promotion is imminent."

The smile got wider and took on a hungry cast. "Well, all the best to her . . . though I hope she learns to anticipate events a bit better. One of her teenage patients just showed up without an appointment and is creating a scene out in the waiting room. And Stephanie left without checking out."

"Doesn't sound like her," I said.

"Really? Lately, it's *become* like her. Perhaps she sees herself as having already ascended."

A nurse passed by. Kohler said, "Juanita?"

"Yes, Dr. Kohler?"

"Have you seen Stephanie?"

"I think she went out."

"Out of the hospital?"

"I think so, Doctor. She had her purse."

"Thank you, Juanita."

When the nurse had gone, Kohler pulled a set of keys out of a pocket.

"Here," she said, jamming one of the keys into Stephanie's lock and turning. Just as I caught the door, she yanked the key out sharply and walked away.

The espresso machine was off but a half-full demitasse sat on the desk, next to Stephanie's stethoscope. The smell of fresh roast overpowered the alcohol bite seeping in from the examining rooms. Also on the desk were a pile of charts and a memo pad stuffed with drug company stationery. As I slipped my note under it I noticed writing on the top sheet.

Dosages, journal references, hospital extensions. Below that, a solitary notation, scrawled hastily, barely legible.

B, Brwsrs, 4

Browsers—the place where she'd gotten the leather-bound Byron. I saw the book, up in the shelf.

B for Byron? Getting another one?

Or meeting someone at the bookstore? If it meant today, she was there now.

It seemed an odd assignation in the middle of a hectic afternoon. Not like her.

Until recently, if Kohler was to be believed.

Something romantic that she wanted segregated from the hospital rumor mill? Or just seeking out some privacy—a quiet moment among the mildew and the verse.

Lord knew she was entitled to her privacy.

Too bad I was going to violate it.

Only a half-mile from the hospital to Los Feliz and Hollywood, but traffic was lobotomized and it took ten minutes to get there.

The bookstore was on the west side of the street, its facade the same as it had been a decade ago: cream-colored sign with black gothic letters spelling out ANTIQUARIAN BOOK MERCHANT above dusty windows. I cruised past, looking for a parking space. On my second go-round I spotted an old Pontiac with its back-up lights on, and waited as a very small, very old woman eased away from the curb. Just as I finished pulling in, someone came out of the bookstore.

Presley Huenengarth.

Even at this distance his mustache was nearly invisible.

I slumped low in the car. He fiddled with his tie, took a pair of sunglasses out, slipped them on, and shot quick looks up and down the street. I ducked lower, pretty sure he hadn't seen me. He touched his tie again, then began walking south until he came to the corner. Turning right, he was gone.

I sat up.

Coincidence? There'd been no book in his hand.

But it was hard to believe he was the one Stephanie was meeting. Why would she call him "B"?

She didn't like him, had called him spooky.

Gotten *me* thinking of him as spooky.

Yet *his* bosses were promoting her.

Had she been talking the rebel line while fraternizing with the enemy?

All for the sake of career advancement?

Do you see me as a division head, Alex?

Every other doctor I'd spoken to was talking about leaving, but *her* eye was on a promotion.

Rita Kohler's hostility implied it wouldn't be a bloodless transition. Was Stephanie being rewarded for good behavior—treating the chairman's grandchild without making waves?

I remembered her absence at the Ashmore memorial. Her showing up late, claiming she'd been tied up.

Maybe true, but in the old days she'd have found a way to be there. Would have been up on the dais.

I kept thinking about it as I sat there, wanting to see it another way. Then Stephanie came out of the store and I knew I couldn't.

Satisfied smile on her face.

No books in her hand either.

She looked up and down the block the same way he had.

Big plans for Dr. Eves.

Rat jumping *onto* a sinking ship?

I'd driven over intending to show her the Insuject cartridges. Ready to study her reaction, declare her innocent and make her a part of tomorrow night's confrontation of Cindy Jones.

Now, I didn't know where she stood. Milo's first suspicions of her began to solidify.

Something wrong—something off.

I lowered my head again.

She began walking. In the same direction *he* had.

Came to the corner, looked to the right. Where *he'd* gone.

She lingered there for a while. Still smiling. Finally crossed the street and kept going.

I waited until she was out of sight, then drove away. The moment I cleared the space, someone zipped in.

First time all day I'd felt useful.

When I got home, just before five, I found a note from Robin saying she'd be working late unless I had something else on my mind. I had plenty, but none of it included fun. I called her, got a machine and told her I loved her and that I'd be working too. Though as I said it, I realized I didn't know at what.

I phoned Parker Center. A nasal, high-pitched male voice answered.

"Records."

"Detective Sturgis, please."

"He's not *he-ere.*"

"When will he be back?"

"Who is this?"

"Alex Delaware. A friend."

He pronounced my name as if it were a disease, then said, "I have absolutely no *ide-a,* Mr. Delaware."

"Do you know if he's gone for the day?"

"I wouldn't know that *either.*"

"Is this Charlie?"

Pause. Throat clear. "This is *Charles* Flannery. Do I *know* you?"

"No, but Milo's talked about how much you've taught him."

Longer pause, more throat clears. "How *grand* of him. If you're interested in your *friend's* schedule, I suggest you call the deputy chief's office."

"Why would they know?"

"Because he's *there,* Mr. Delaware. As of half an hour ago. And please don't ask me why, because I don't *kno-ow.* No one tells me *anything.*"

*   *   *

The deputy chief's. Milo in trouble again. I hoped it wasn't because of something he'd done for me. As I thought about it, Robin called back.

"Hi, how's the little girl?"

"I may have pinned down what's happening to her, but I'm worried it may have made things worse for her."

"How could that be?"

I told her.

She said, "Have you told Milo yet?"

"I just tried to reach him and he's been called into the deputy chief's office. He's been free-lancing for me on the department computer. I hope it didn't mess him up."

"Oh," she said. "Well, he can handle himself—he's shown that."

"What a mess," I said. "This case is bringing back too many memories, Robin. All those years at the hospital—eighty-hour weeks and all the suffering you can eat. So much garbage I couldn't do anything *about*. The doctors weren't always effective either, but at least they had their pills and their scalpels. All I had were words and nods and meaningful pauses and some fancy behavioral technology that I rarely got a chance to use. Half the time I walked around the wards feeling like a carpenter with bad tools."

She said nothing.

"Yeah, I know," I said. "Self-pity's a bore."

"You can't suckle the world, Alex."

"Now there's an image for you."

"I mean it. You're as masculine as they come but sometimes I think you're a frustrated mother—wanting to *feed* everyone. Take *care* of everything. That can be good—look at all the people you've helped. *Including* Milo, but—"

"Milo?"

"Sure. Look at what he's got to deal with. A gay *cop* in a department that denies there's any such thing. Officially, he doesn't exist. Think of the alienation, day in and day out. Sure he's got Rick, but that's his other world. Your friendship's a connection for him—an extension to the rest of the world."

"I'm not his friend out of charity, Robin. It's no big political thing. I just like him as a human being."

"Exactly. He knows the kind of friend you are—he once told me it took him six months to get used to having a straight friend. Someone who would just take him at face value. Told me he hadn't had a friend like that since junior high. He also appreciates the fact that you don't play therapist with him. That's why he extends himself for you. And if he's gotten in trouble because of it, he can deal with it. Lord knows he's dealt with worse— Oops, gotta turn off the saw. That's all the profundity you get out of me today."

"When did you get so wise?"

"It's always been there, Curly. You just have to have your eyes open."

Alone again, I felt like jumping out of my skin. I called my service. Four messages: a lawyer asking me to consult on a child custody case, someone with an M.B.A. promising to help me build my practice, the county psychological association wanting to know if I was going to attend the next monthly meeting and, if so, did I want chicken or fish. The last, from Lou Cestare, letting me know he'd found nothing new on George Plumb's former employers but would keep trying.

I tried Milo again, on the off chance he'd returned from the deputy chief's office. Charles Flannery's voice came on and I hung up.

What *was* Stephanie up to, meeting with Huenengarth?

Just malignant careerism or had someone leaned on her, too— the old drunk-driving arrest.

Or maybe her drinking wasn't ancient history. What if the drinking was still out of control and they were exploiting *that*?

Exploiting while grooming her for division head?

It didn't make sense—but maybe it did.

If I was right about Chuck Jones wanting to dissolve the hospital, hiring an impaired division head would fit beautifully.

Rat climbing aboard a sinking ship . . .

I thought of someone who'd jumped off.

What *had* made Melendez-Lynch finally leave?

I didn't know if he'd talk to me. Our last contact, years ago, had been tainted by his humiliation—a case gone very bad, a lapse of ethics on his part that I'd learned about without wanting to.

But what was there to lose?

Miami Information had one listing for him. Our Lady of Mercy Hospital. It was eight-thirty in Florida. His secretary would be gone, but unless Raoul had undergone a personality transplant, he'd still be working.

I dialed. A recorded voice, female and cultured, informed me I'd reached the chief physician's office, which was now closed, and enunciated a series of touch-tone codes for reaching Dr. Melendez-Lynch's voice mail.

I pressed the Instant Page code and waited for a callback, wondering when machines were going to start calling one another and eliminating the messiness of the human factor.

A still-familiar voice said, "Dr. Melendez-Lynch."

"Raoul? It's Alex Delaware."

"*Ahleex?* No keeding. How *are* you?"

"Fine, Raoul. And you?"

"Much too fat and much too busy, but otherwise superb . . . What a surprise. Are you here in Miami?"

"No, still in L.A."

"Ahh . . . So tell me, how have you been spending the last few years?"

"Same as before."

"Back in practice?"

"Short-term consults."

"Short term . . . still retired, eh?"

"Not exactly. How about you?"

"Also more of the same, Alex. We are doing some very exciting things—advanced cell-wall permeability studies in the carcinogenesis lab, several pilot grants on experimental drugs. So tell me, to what do I owe the honor of this call?"

"I've got a question for you," I said, "but it's personal, not professional, so if you don't want to answer it, just say so."

"Personal?"

"About your leaving."

"What do you want to know about it?"

"Why you did it."

"And why, may I ask, are you suddenly so curious about my motivation?"

"Because I'm back at Western Peds, consulting on a case. And the place looks really *sad,* Raoul. Low morale, people quitting—people I never thought would leave. You're the one I know best, so I'm calling you."

"Yes, that is personal," he said. "But I don't mind answering." He laughed. "The answer is very simple, Alex. I left because I was unwanted."

"By the new administration?"

"Yes. The Visigoths. The choice they gave me was simple. Leave, or die professionally. It was a matter of survival. Despite what anyone will tell you, money had nothing to do with it. No one ever worked at Western Peds for the money—you know that. Though the money got worse, too, when the Visigoths took control. Wage freezes, hiring freezes, eating away at our secretarial staff, a totally arrogant attitude toward the physicians—as if we were their servants. They even stuck us out on the street in trailers. Like derelicts. I could tolerate all of that because of the *work.* The research. But when that ended, there was simply no reason to stay on."

"They cut off your research?"

"Not explicitly. However, at the beginning of the last academic year the board announced a new policy: Because of financial difficulties, the hospital would no longer chip in for overhead on research grants. You know how the government works—on so many grants, any money they give you depends upon the host institution contributing expenses. Some of the private foundations are also insisting upon it now. All of my funding came from NCI. A no-overhead rule essentially *nullified* all of my projects. I tried to argue, yelled, screamed, showed them figures and facts—what we were trying to *do* with our research; this was pediatric *cancer,* for God's sake. No use. So I flew to Washington and talked with *government* Visigoths, trying to get them to suspend the rules. That, too, was futile. Our kinder and gentler bunch, eh? None of them functions at a human level. So what were my options, Alex? Stay on as an overeducated technician and give up fifteen years of work?"

"Fifteen years," I said. "Must have been hard."

"It wasn't easy, but it turned out to be a *fantastic* decision. Here, at Mercy, I sit on the board as a voting member. There are plenty of idiots here, too, but I can ignore them. As a bonus, my second child—Amelia—is enrolled at the medical school in Miami and lives with me. My condominium overlooks the ocean and on the rare occasion I visit Little Havana, it makes me feel like a little boy. It was like surgery, Alex. The process was painful but the results were worth it."

"They were stupid to lose you."

"Of course they were. Fifteen years and not even a gold watch." He laughed. "These are not people who hold physicians in awe. All that matters to them is money."

"Jones and Plumb?"

"And that pair of dogs trailing after them—Novak and whatever. They may be accountants but they remind me of Fidel's thugs. Take my advice, Alex: Don't get too involved there. Why don't you come out to Miami and put your skills to use where they'll be appreciated? We'll write a grant together. The AIDS thing is paramount now—so much sadness. Two thirds of our hemophiliacs have received infected blood. You could be useful here, Alex."

"Thanks for the invitation, Raoul."

"It's a sincere one. I remember the good we did together."

"So do I."

"Think about it, Alex."

"Okay."

"But of course you won't."

Both of us laughed.

I said, "Could I ask you one more thing?"

"Also personal?"

"No. What do you know about the Ferris Dixon Institute for Chemical Research?"

"Never heard of it. Why?"

"It funded a doctor at Western Peds. *With* overhead."

"Really. And which guy is this?"

"A toxicologist named Laurence Ashmore. He's done some epidemiologic work on childhood cancer."

"Ashmore . . . never heard of him either. What kind of epidemiology does he do?"

"Pesticides and malignancy rates. Mostly theoretical stuff, playing with numbers."

He snorted. "How much did this institute give him?"

"Nearly a million dollars."

Silence.

"What?"

"It's true," I said.

"With *overhead*?"

"High, huh?"

"Absurd. What's the name of this institute?"

"Ferris Dixon. They only funded one other study, much smaller. An economist named Zimberg."

"With overhead . . . Hmm, I'll have to check into that. Thank you for the tip, Alex. And think about my offer. The sun shines here too."

30

I didn't hear from Milo and had doubts if he'd make our eight o'clock
meeting. When he hadn't shown up by twenty after, I figured
whatever had held him up at Parker Center had gotten in the way. But
at 8:37 the bell rang, and when I opened the door it was him.
Someone was standing behind him.

Presley Huenengarth. His face floated over Milo's shoulder like a
malignant moon. His mouth was as small as a baby's.

Milo saw the look in my eyes, gave an it's-okay wink, put his
hand on my shoulder, and walked in. Huenengarth hesitated for a
moment before following. His hands were at his sides. No gun. No
bulge in his jacket; no sign of coercion.

The two of them could have been a cop team.

Milo said, "Be right with you," and went into the kitchen.

Huenengarth stood there. His hands were thick and mottled
and his eyes were everywhere. The door was still open. When I closed
it, he didn't move.

I walked into the living room. Though I couldn't hear him, I
knew he was following me.

He waited for me to sit on the leather sofa, unbuttoned his jacket, then sank into an armchair. His belly bulged over his belt, straining the white broadcloth of his button-down shirt. The rest of him was broad and hard. His neck flesh was cherry-blossom pink and swelled over his collar. A carotid pulse plinked through, steady and rapid.

I heard Milo messing in the kitchen.

Huenengarth said, "Nice place. Any view?"

It was the first time I'd heard his voice. Midwest inflections, medium-pitched, on the reedy side. On the phone it would conjure a much smaller man.

I didn't answer.

He put a hand on each knee and looked around the room some more.

More kitchen noise.

He turned toward it and said, "Far as I'm concerned, people's personal lives are their own business. As long as what he is doesn't get in the way of the job, I could care less. Matter of fact, I can help him."

"Great. You want to tell me who you are?"

"Sturgis claims you know how to keep a secret. Few people do."

"Especially in Washington?"

Blank stare.

"Or is it Norfolk, Virginia?"

He pursed his lips and turned his mouth into a peeved little blossom. The mustache above it was little more than a mouse-colored stain. His ears were close-set, lobeless, and pulled down into his bull neck. Despite the season, the gray suit was a heavy worsted. Cuffed pants, black oxfords that had been resoled, blue pen in his breast pocket. He was sweating just below the hairline.

"You've been trying to follow me," he said. "But you really have no idea what's going on."

"Funny, I felt followed."

He shook his head. Gave a stern look. As if he were the teacher and I'd guessed wrong.

"So educate me," I said.

"I need a pledge of total discretion."

"About what?"

"Anything I tell you."

"That's pretty broad."

"That's what I need."

"Does it have to do with Cassie Jones?"

The fingers on his knees began drumming. "Not directly."

"But indirectly."

He didn't answer.

I said, "You want a pledge from me, but you won't give an inch. You've *got* to work for the government."

Silence. He examined the pattern of my Persian rug.

"If it compromises Cassie," I said, "I can't pledge anything."

"You're wrong," he said, and gave another headshake. "If you really cared about her, you wouldn't obstruct me."

"Why's that?"

"I can help her too."

"You're a pretty helpful guy, aren't you?"

He shrugged.

"If you're able to stop the abuse, why haven't you?"

He ceased drumming and touched one index finger to the other. "I didn't say I was *omniscient*. But I can be useful. *You* haven't made much progress so far, have you?"

Before I could answer, he was up and headed for the kitchen. He returned with Milo, who was carrying three cups of coffee.

Taking one for himself, Milo put the remaining two on the coffee table and settled on the other end of the sofa. Our eyes met. He gave a small nod. Trace of apology.

Huenengarth sat back down, in a different chair from the one he'd just gotten out of. Neither he nor I touched our coffee.

Milo said, "Skoal," and drank.

"Now what?" I said.

"Yeah," said Milo. "He's low on charm, but maybe he can do what he says he can."

Huenengarth turned toward him and glared.

Milo sipped, crossed his legs.

I said, "You're here of your own free will, huh?"

Milo said, "Well, everything's relative." To Huenengarth: "Stop playing Junior G-man and give the man some data."

Huenengarth glared some more. Turned to me. Looked at his coffee cup. Touched his mustache.

"This theory you have," he told me, "about Charles Jones and George Plumb destroying the hospital—who've you discussed it with so far?"

"It's not *my* theory. The entire staff thinks the administration's screwing the place over."

"The entire staff hasn't taken it as far as you have. Who've you talked to besides Louis B. Cestare?"

I hid my surprise and my fear. "Lou's not involved in this."

Huenengarth half-smiled. "Unfortunately, he is, Doctor. A man in his position, all those links to the financial world—he could have turned out to be a knotty problem for me. Fortunately, he's being cooperative. At this very moment. Conferring with one of my colleagues up in Oregon. My colleague says Mr. Cestare's estate is quite lovely."

Full smile. "Don't worry, Doctor, we only bring out the thumbscrews as a last resort."

Milo put down his coffee. "Why don't you just cut to the chase, bucko?"

Huenengarth's smile vanished. He sat up straighter and looked at Milo.

Silent stare.

Milo gave a disgusted look and drank coffee.

Huenengarth waited a while before turning back to me. "Is there anyone else you've spoken to in addition to Mr. Cestare? Not counting your girlfriend, Ms.—uh—Castagna. Don't worry, Doctor. From what I know about her, she isn't likely to leak a story to *The Wall Street Journal*."

"What the hell do you want?" I said.

"The names of anyone you've included in your fantasy. Specifically, people with business connections or a reason to harbor a grudge against Jones or Plumb."

I glanced at Milo. He nodded, though he didn't look happy.

"Just one other person," I said. "A doctor who used to work at Western Peds. Now he lives in Florida. But I didn't tell him anything he didn't already know and we didn't go into any details—"

"Dr. Lynch," said Huenengarth.

I swore. "What'd you do, tap my phone?"

"No, that wasn't necessary. Dr. Lynch and I talk once in a while. Have been talking for a while."

"*He* tipped you off?"

"Let's not get sidetracked, Dr. Delaware. The main thing is *you* told me about speaking to *him*. That's good. Admirably frank. I also like the way you wrestled with it. Moral dilemmas mean something to you—I don't get to see that too often. So now I trust you more than when I walked into this room, and that's good for both of us."

"Gee, I'm touched," I said. "What's my reward? Learning your real name?"

"Cooperation. Maybe we can be mutually helpful. To Cassie Jones."

"How can you help her?"

He folded his arms across his barrel chest. "Your theory—the *entire staff's* theory—is appealing. For a one-hour TV episode. Greedy capitalists sucking the lifeblood out of a beloved institution; the good guys come in and clean it up; cut to commercial."

"Who're the good guys here?"

He put a hand to his chest. "I'm hurt, Doctor."

"What are you, FBI?"

"A different collection of letters—it wouldn't mean anything to you. Let's get back to your theory: appealing, but wrong. Do you remember Cestare's first reaction when you floated it by him?"

"He said it was unlikely."

"Why?"

"Because Chuck Jones was a builder, not a destroyer."

"Ah."

"But then he looked up *Plumb's* job history and found out companies *he's* been associated with tend not to live long. So maybe Jones has changed his style and is going for slash and burn."

"Plumb *is* a slash-and-burn man," he said. "Got a long history of setting up companies for raiders, then taking fat commissions on the buy-out. But those were companies backed up by *assets* that made them worth plundering. Where's the incentive to destroy a nonprofit money-loser like Western Pediatrics? Where are the *assets*, Doctor?"

"The real estate the hospital sits on, for a start."

"The real estate." Another headshake, accompanied by a finger wag. The guy had a definite tutorial bent. "As a matter of fact, the land is owned by the city and leased to the hospital under a ninety-nine-year contract, the contract's renewable for another ninety-nine at the hospital's request, and the rent's a dollar a year. Public record—look it up at the assessor's office, just as I did."

"You're not here because Jones and his gang are innocents," I said. "What are they after?"

He moved forward on his chair. "Think *convertible* assets, Doctor. A massive supply of high-quality stocks and bonds at Chuck Jones's disposal."

"The hospital's investment portfolio—Jones manages it. What's he doing, skimming?"

Yet another headshake. "Proximate but no panatela, Doctor. Though that's also a reasonable assumption. As it turns out, the hospital's portfolio is a joke. Thirty years of dipping into it to balance the operating budget has stripped it down to bare bones. In fact, Chuck Jones has built it up some—he's a very savvy investor. But rising costs keep eating away at it. There'll never be enough in there to make it worth fooling with—not at Jones's level."

"What's his level?"

"Eight figures. Major-league financial manipulation. Fisk and Gould would have counted their fingers after shaking hands with Chuck Jones. His public image is that of a financial wizard and he's even saved a few companies along the way. But it's his *plundering* that fuels it all. The man's destroyed more businesses than the Bolsheviks."

"So he's a slash-and-burn man, too, as long as the price is high enough."

Huenengarth looked up at the ceiling.

"Why doesn't anyone know about it?" I said.

He scooted forward a bit more. Very little of him was touching the chair.

"They will soon," he said quietly. "I've been on his trail for four and a half years and the end's finally in sight. No one's going to fuck it up—that's why I need total discretion. I *won't* get derailed. Understand?"

The pink of his neck had deepened to tomato-aspic. He fingered his collar, loosened his tie and opened it.

"*He's* discreet," he said. "Covers himself beautifully. But I'm going to beat him at his own game."

"Covers himself how?"

"Layers of shadow corporations and holding companies, phony syndicates, foreign bank accounts. Literally *hundreds* of trading accounts, operating simultaneously. Plus battalions of lackeys like Plumb and Roberts and Novak, most of whom only know a small part of each picture. It's a screen so effective that even people like Mr. Cestare don't see through it. But when he falls, he's going to fall hard, Doctor, I promise you. He's made mistakes and I've got him in my sights."

"So what's he plundering at Western Peds?"

"You really don't need to know the details."

He picked up his coffee cup and drank.

I thought back to my conversation with Lou.

Why would a syndicate buy it, then shut it down?

Could be any number of reasons . . . They wanted the company's resources, rather than the company itself.

What kinds of resources?

Hardware, investments, the pension fund . . .

"The doctors' pension fund," I said. "Jones manages that, too, doesn't he?"

He put down the cup. "The hospital charter says it's his responsibility."

"What's he done with it? Turned it into his personal cashbox?"

He said nothing.

Milo said, "Shit."

"Something like that," said Huenengarth, frowning.

"The pension fund is eight figures?" I said.

"A healthy eight."

"Come on, how's that possible?"

"Some luck, some skill, but mostly just the passage of time, Doctor. Ever calculate what a thousand dollars left in a five percent savings account for seventy years would be worth? Try it some time. The doctors' pension fund is seventy years' worth of blue chip stocks and corporate bonds that have increased ten, twenty, fifty, hundreds of times over, split and resplit dozens of times, and paid out dividends that are reinvested in the fund. Since World War Two the stock market's been on a steady upward swing. The fund's full of gems like IBM purchased at two dollars a share, Xerox at one. And, unlike a commercial investment fund, almost nothing goes out. The rules of the fund say it can't be used for hospital expenses, so the only outflow is payments to doctors who retire. And that's only a trickle, because the rules also minimize payments to anyone who leaves before twenty-five years."

"The actuarial structure," I said, remembering what Al Macauley had said about not collecting any pension. "Anyone who leaves before a certain period gets paid nothing."

He gave an enthusiastic nod. The student was finally getting things right.

"It's called the fractional rule, Doctor. Most pension funds are set up that way—supposedly to reward loyalty. When the medical school agreed to contribute to the fund seventy years ago, it stipulated that a doctor who left before five years wouldn't get a penny. Same goes for one who leaves after *any* time period and continues to work as a physician at a comparable salary. Doctors are very employable, so those two groups account for over eighty-nine percent of cases. Of the remaining eleven percent, very few doctors serve out the full twenty-five and qualify for full pension. But the money paid into the fund for every doctor who's ever worked at the hospital stays right there, earning interest."

"Who contributes besides the med school?"

"You were on staff there. Didn't you read your benefits package?"

"Psychologists weren't included in the fund."

"Yes, you're right. It does stipulate M.D. . . . Well, count yourself lucky to be a Ph.D."

"Who contributes?" I repeated.

"The hospital kicks in the rest."

"The doctors don't pay anything?"

"Not a penny. That's why they accepted such strict regulations. But it was very shortsighted. For most of them, the pension's worthless."

"Stacked deck," I said. "Giving Jones an eight-figure cashbox—that's why he's making the staff's lives miserable. He doesn't want to destroy the hospital—he wants to keep it limping along with no doctor staying very long. Keep turnover high—staff leaving before five years or when they're young enough to get comparable jobs. The pension keeps accruing dividends, he doesn't have to pay out, and he's able to rape the surplus."

He nodded with passion. "Gang rape, Doctor. It's happening all over the country. There are over nine hundred thousand corporate pension funds in the U.S. Two *trillion* dollars held in trust for eighty million workers. When this last bull market created billions of dollars of surplus, corporations got Congress to ease up on how surpluses can be used. The money's now considered a *company* asset, rather than the property of the workers. Last year alone, the sixty largest corporations in the U.S. had sixty billion dollars to play around with. Some companies have started buying insurance policies so they can use the *principal*. It's part of what fueled the whole takeover mania—pension status is one of the first things raiders look at when they choose their targets. They dissolve the company, use the surplus to buy the next company, and dissolve *it*. And so on and so on. People get thrown out of jobs—too bad."

"Getting rich with other people's money."

"Without having to create any goods or services. Plus, once you start thinking you own something, it gets easier to bend the rules. Illegal pension manipulations have skyrocketed—embezzlement, taking personal loans out of the fund, awarding management contracts to cronies and taking kickbacks while the cronies charge outrageous management fees—that's organized crime's contribution. Up in Alaska we had a situation where the mob cleaned out a union fund and workers lost every cent. Companies have also changed the rules in the middle of the game by switching over to defined-contribution plans. Instead of monthly payments the retiree gets one lump sum based on his life expectancy, and the company buys itself predictability. It's legal, for the time being, but it defeats the whole purpose of pensions—old-age security for working people. Your average blue-collar guy doesn't have any idea how to invest. Only five percent ever do. Most defined-benefit payouts get frittered away on miscellaneous expenses, and the worker's left high and dry."

"Surpluses," I said. "Bull markets. What happens when the economy slows, like right now?"

"If the company goes belly-up and the plan's been looted, the workers have to collect from any private insurance companies that hold paper. There's also a federal fund—PBGC. Pension Benefits Guarantee Corporation. But just like FDIC and FSLIC, it's grossly underfunded. If enough companies with looted plans start folding, you'll have a crisis that'll make the S and L thing look like a picnic. But even with PBGC functioning, it can take years for a worker to collect on a claim. The employees with the most to lose are the oldest and sickest—the loyal ones who gave their lives to the company. People go on welfare, waiting. Die."

His whole face had gone red and his hands were big mottled fists.

"Is the doctors' fund in jeopardy?" I said.

"Not yet. As Mr. Cestare told you, Jones saw Black Monday coming and turned mega-profits. The hospital board of directors loves him."

"Building up his cashbox, for future plundering?"

"No, he's plundering right now. As he's putting dollars in, he's slipping them out."

"How can he get away with it?"

"He's the only one who's got a handle on each and every transaction—the total picture. He's also using the fund as leverage for personal purchases. Parking stock in it, merging fund accounts with his own—moving money around hourly. *Playing* with it. He buys and sells under scores of aliases that change daily. *Hundreds* of transactions daily."

"Lots of commission for him?"

"Lots. Plus, it makes it incredibly difficult to keep track of him."

"But you have."

He nodded, still flushed—the hunter's glow. "It's taken me four and a half years but I've finally gained access to his data banks, and so far, he doesn't know it. There's no reason for him to suspect he's being watched, because normally the government doesn't pay any attention to nonprofit pension funds. If he hadn't made some mistakes with some of the corporations he killed, he'd be home free, in fiduciary heaven."

"What kinds of mistakes?"

"Not important," Huenengarth barked.

I stared at him.

He forced himself to smile and held out one hand. "The point is, his shell's finally cracked and I'm prying it open—getting *exquisitely* close to shattering it. It's a crucial moment, Doctor. That's why I get cranky when people start following me. Understand? Now, are you satisfied?"

"Not really."

He stiffened. "What's your problem?"

"A couple of murders, for starts. Why did Laurence Ashmore and Dawn Herbert die?"

"Ashmore," he said, shaking his head. "Ashmore was a weird bird. A doctor who actually understood economics and had the technical skills to put his knowledge to use. He got rich, and like most rich people he started to believe he was smarter than anyone else. So smart he didn't have to pay his share of taxes. He got away with it for a while, but the IRS finally caught on. He could've gone to jail for a long time. So I helped him."

"Go west, young swindler," I said. "He was your hacker into Jones's data, wasn't he? The perfect wedge—an M.D. who doesn't see patients. Was his degree real?"

"Hundred percent."

"You bought him a job with a million-dollar grant, plus over-head. Basically, the hospital got *paid* to hire him."

He gave a satisfied smile. "Greed. Works every time."

"You're IRS?" I said.

Still smiling, he shook his head. "Very occasionally, one tentacle strokes the other."

"What'd you do? Just put your order in to the IRS? Give me a physician in tax trouble who also has computer skills—and they filled it?"

"It wasn't that simple. Finding someone like Ashmore took a long time. And finding him was one of the factors that helped convince . . . my superiors to fund my project."

"Your superiors," I said. "The Ferris Dixon Institute for Chemi-cal Research—FDIC. What does the R stand for?"

"Rip-off. It was Ashmore's idea of a joke—everything was a game with him. What he really wanted was something that conformed to PBGC—the Paul Bowles Garden Club was his favorite. He prided himself on being literary. But I convinced him to be subtle."

"Who's Professor Walter William Zimberg? Your boss? Another hacker?"

"No one," he said. "Literally."

"He doesn't exist?"

"Not in any real sense."

"Munchausen man," Milo muttered.

Huenengarth shot him a sharp look.

I said, "He's got an office at the University of Maryland. I spoke to his secretary."

He lifted his cup, took a long time drinking.

I said, "Why was it so important for Ashmore to work out of the hospital?"

"Because that's where Jones's main terminal is. I wanted him to have direct access to Jones's hardware and software."

"Jones is using the hospital as a business center? He told me he doesn't have an office there."

"Technically that's true. You won't see his name on any door. But his apparatus is buried within some of the space he's taken away from the doctors."

"Down in the sub-basement?"

"Let's just say buried deeply. Somewhere hard to find. As head of Security, I made sure of that."

"Getting *yourself* in must have been quite a challenge."

No answer.

"You still haven't answered me," I said. "Why'd Ashmore die?"

"I don't know. Yet."

"What'd he do?" I said. "Make an end-run around you? Use what he'd learned working for you to extort money from Chuck Jones?"

He licked his lips. "It's possible. The data he collected are still being analyzed."

"By whom?"

"People."

"What about Dawn Herbert? Was she in on it?"

"I don't know what her game was," he said. "Don't know if she had one."

His frustration seemed real.

I said, "Then why'd you chase down her computer disks?"

"Because *Ashmore* was interested in them. After we started to decode *his* files, her name came up."

"In what context?"

"He'd made a coded notation to take her seriously. Called her a 'negative integer'—his term for someone suspicious. But she was already dead."

"What else did he say about her?"

"That's all we've gotten so far. He put everything in code—complex codes. It's taking time to unravel them."

"He was your boy," I said. "Didn't he leave you the keys?"

"Only some of them." Anger narrowed the round eyes.

"So you stole her disks."

"Not stole, appropriated. They were mine. She compiled them while working for Ashmore, and Ashmore worked for me, so legally they're my property."

He blurted the last two words. The possessiveness of a kid with a new toy.

I said, "This isn't just a job with you, is it?"

His gaze flicked across the room and back to me. "That's exactly what it is. I just happen to love my work."

"So you have no idea why Herbert was murdered."

He shrugged. "The police say it was a sex killing."

"Do *you* think it was?"

"I'm not a policeman."

"No?" I said, and the look in his eyes made me go on. "I'll bet you were some kind of cop before you went back to school. Before you learned to talk like a business school professor."

He gave another eye-flick, quick and sharp as a switchblade. "What's this, free psychoanalysis?"

"Business administration," I said. "Or maybe economics."

"I'm a humble civil servant, Doctor. Your taxes pay my salary."

"Humble civil servant with a false identity and over a million dollars of phony grant money," I said. "You're Zimberg, aren't you? But that's probably not your real name, either. What does the 'B' on Stephanie's note pad stand for?"

He stared at me, stood, walked around the room. Touched a picture frame. The hair on his crown was thinning.

"Four and a half years," I said. "You've given up a lot to catch him."

He didn't answer but his neck tightened.

"What's Stephanie's involvement in all this?" I said. "Besides true love."

He turned and faced me, flushed again. Not anger this time— embarrassment. A teenager caught necking.

"Why don't you ask her?" he said softly.

She was in a car parked at the mouth of my driveway, dark Buick Regal, just behind the hedges, out of sight from the terrace. A dot of light darted around the interior like a trapped firefly.

Penlight. Stephanie sat in the front passenger seat, using it to read. Her window was open. She wore a gold choker that caught starlight, and had put on perfume.

"Evening," I said.

She looked up, closed the book, and pushed the door open. As the penlight clicked off, the dome-light switched on, highlighting her as if she were a soloist onstage. Her dress was shorter than usual. I thought: heavy date. Her beeper sat on the dashboard.

She scooted over into the driver's seat. I sat where she'd just been. The vinyl was warm.

When the car was dark again, she said, "Sorry for not telling you, but he needs secrecy."

"What do you call him, Pres or Wally?"

She bit her lip. "Bill."

"As in Walter William."

She frowned. "It's his nickname—his friends call him that."

"He didn't tell *me*. Guess I'm not his friend."

She looked out the windshield and took hold of the wheel. "Look, I know I misled you a bit, but it's personal. What I do with my private life is really none of your concern, okay?"

"Misled me a bit? Mr. Spooky's your main squeeze. What else haven't you told me about?"

"Nothing—nothing to do with the case."

"That so? He says he can help Cassie. So why didn't you get him to pitch in sooner?"

She put her hands on the steering wheel. "Shit."

A moment later: "It's complicated."

"I'll bet it is."

"Look," she said, nearly shouting, "I told you he was spooky because that's the image he wants to project, okay? It's important that he be seen as a bad guy to get the job done. What he's doing is *important,* Alex. As important as medicine. He's been working on it for a long time."

"Four and a half years," I said. "I've heard all about the noble quest. Is getting you in as division head part of the master plan?"

She turned and faced me. "I don't have to answer that. I *deserve* that promotion. Rita's a dinosaur, for God's sake. She's been coasting on her reputation for years. Let me tell you a story: A couple of months ago we were doing rounds up on Five East. Someone had eaten a McDonald's hamburger at the nursing station and left the box up on the counter—one of those Styrofoam boxes for takeout? With the arches embossed right on it? Rita picks it up and asks what it is. Everyone thought she was kidding. Then we realized she wasn't. *McDonald's,* Alex. That's how out of touch she is. How can she relate to our patient mix?"

"What does that have to do with Cassie?"

Stephanie held her book next to her, like body armor. My night-accustomed eyes made out the title. *Pediatric Emergencies.*

"Light reading?" I said. "Or career advancement?"

"Damn you!" She grabbed the door handle. Let go. Sank back. "Sure it'd be good for him if I was head—the more friends he can get close to *them,* the better chance he has of picking up more information to nail them with. So what's wrong with that? If he doesn't get them, there'll be no hospital at all, soon."

"Friends?" I said. "You sure he knows what that means? Laurence Ashmore worked for him, too, and he doesn't speak very fondly of him."

"Ashmore was a jerk—an obnoxious little schmuck."

"Thought you didn't know him very well."

"I didn't—didn't have to. I told you how he treated me—how blasé he was when I needed help."

"Whose idea was it to have him review Chad's chart in the first place? Yours? Or *Bill's*? Trying to dish up some additional dirt on the Joneses?"

"What's the difference?"

"Be nice to know if we're doing medicine or politics here."

"What's the difference, Alex? What's the damned *difference*! The important thing is results. Yes, he's my friend. Yes, he's helped me a lot, so if I want to help him back, that's okay! What's *wrong* with that! Our goals are *consistent*!"

"Then why not help *Cassie*?" Shouting myself. "I'm sure the two of you have discussed her! Why put her through one more second of misery if Mr. *Helpful* can put an end to it?"

She cowered. Her back was up against the driver's door. "What the hell do you *want* from me? Perfection? Well, sorry, I can't fill that bill. I tried that—it's a short road to misery. So just lay off, okay? *Okay?*"

She began to cry.

I said, "Forget it. Let's just concentrate on Cassie."

"I *am*," she said in a small voice. "Believe me, Alex, I *am* concentrating on her—always have been. We couldn't do anything, because we didn't *know*—had to be sure. That's why I called you in. Bill didn't want me to, but I insisted on that. I put my foot down—I really did."

I kept silent.

"I needed your help to find out," she said. "To know for sure that Cindy was really doing it to her. *Then* Bill could help. At that point, we could confront them."

"*Then?*" I said. "Or were you just waiting until Bill gave the signal? Until his plan was in place and he was ready to take down the whole family?"

"No! He . . . We just wanted to do it in a way that would . . . be effective. Just jumping in and accusing them wouldn't be . . ."

"Strategic?"

"*Effective!* Or ethical—it wouldn't be the right thing. What if she wasn't guilty?"

"Something organic? Something metabolic?"

"Why not! I'm a doctor, dammit, not God. How the hell could I know? Just because Chuck's a piece of slime didn't mean Cindy was! I wasn't *sure*, dammit! Getting to the bottom of it is *your* job—that's why I called you in."

"Thanks for the referral."

"Alex," she said plaintively, "why are you making this so *painful* for me? You know the kind of doctor I am."

She sniffed and rubbed her eyes.

I said, "Since you called me in, I feel I've been running a maze."

"Me too. You think it's easy having meetings with those sleaze-balls and pretending to be their little stooge? Plumb thinks his hand was created in order to rest on my knee."

She grimaced and pulled her dress lower. "You think it's easy being with a bunch of docs, passing Bill in the hall and hearing what they say about him? Look, I know he's not your idea of a nice guy, but you don't really know him. He's *good*. He *helped* me."

She looked out the driver's window. "I had a problem. . . . You don't need to know the details. Oh, hell, why not? I had a *drinking* problem, okay?"

"Okay."

She turned around quickly. "You're not surprised? Did I show it—did I act pathologic?"

"No, but it happens to nice people too."

"I never showed it at all?"

"You're not exactly a drooling drunk."

"No." She laughed. "More like a *comatose* drunk, just like my mom—good old genetics."

She laughed again. Squeezed the steering wheel.

"Now my dad," she said, "there was your *angry* drunk. And my brother, Tom, he was a *genteel* drunk. Witty, charming—very Noel Cowardish. Everyone loved it when *he'd* had a few too many. He was an industrial designer, much smarter than me. Artistic, creative. He died two years ago of cirrhosis. He was thirty-eight."

She shrugged. "I postponed becoming an alcoholic for a while—always the contrary kid. Then, during my internship, I finally decided to join the family tradition. Binges on the day off. I was really good at it, Alex. I knew how to clean up just in time to look clever-and-together on rounds. But then I started to slip. Got my timing mixed up. Timing's always a tricky thing when you're a closet lush. . . . A few years ago I got busted for drunk driving. Caused an accident. Isn't that a pretty picture? Imagine if I'd killed someone, Alex. Killed a kid. Pediatrician turns toddler into road pizza—what a headline."

She cried again. Dried her eyes so hard it looked as if she were hitting herself.

"Shit, enough with the self-pity—my AA buddies always used to get on me for that. I did AA for a year. Then I broke away from it—no spare time and I was doing fine, right? Then last year, with all the stress—some personal things that didn't work out—I started again. Those teeny little bottles you get on airplanes? I picked some up on a flight, coming home from an AMA convention. Just a nip before bed. Then a few more . . . then I started taking the little buggers to the office. For that *mellow* moment at the end of the day. But I was cool, always careful to put the empties back in my purse, leave no evidence. See, I'm good at subterfuge. You didn't know that about me till now, did you? But I got you, too, didn't I? Oh, shit!"

She hit the wheel, then rested her head on it.

"It's okay," I said. "Forget it."

"Sure, it is. It's okay, it's great, it's terrific, it's wonderful. . . . One night—a really shitty one, sick kids up the wazoo—I polished off a *bunch* of little bottles and passed out at my desk. Bill was making a security check and found me at three in the morning. I'd vomited all over my charts. When I saw him standing over me I thought I was going to die. But he held me and cleaned me up and took me home— took *care* of me, Alex. *No* one ever did that for me. I was always taking care of my mother because she was always . . ."

She rolled her brow on the steering wheel.

"It's because of him that I'm pulling it together. Did you notice all the weight I've lost? My hair?"

"You look great."

"I learned how to dress, Alex. Because it finally mattered. Bill bought me my coffee machine. He *understood,* because *his* family was also . . . His dad was a *real* nasty drunk. Weekend lush, but he held down a job in the same factory for twenty-five years. Then the company got taken over and dissolved, and his dad lost his job, and they found out the pension fund had been looted. Completely stripped. His dad couldn't find another job and drank himself to death. Bled out, right in his bed. Bill was in high school. He came home from football practice and found him. Do you see why he understands? Why he needs to do what he's doing?"

"Sure," I said, wondering how much of the story was true. Thinking of the Identikit face of the man seen walking into the darkness with Dawn Herbert.

"He raised *his* mom, too," she said. "He's a natural problem solver. That's why he became a cop, why he took the time to go back to school and learn about finance. He has a Ph.D., Alex. It took him ten years because he was working." She lifted her head and her profile was transformed by a smile. "But don't try calling him Doctor."

"Who's Presley Huenengarth?"

She hesitated.

"Another state secret?" I said.

"It . . . Okay, I'll tell you because I want you to trust me. And it's no big deal. Presley was a friend of his when he was a kid. A little boy who died of a brain tumor when he was eight years old. Bill used his identity because it was safe—there was nothing on file but a birth certificate, and the two of them were the same age, so it was perfect."

She sounded breathless—excited—and I knew "Bill" and his world had offered her more than just succor.

"Please, Alex," she said, "can we just forget all this and work together? I know about the insulin injectors—your friend told Bill. You see, *he* trusts him. Let's put our heads together and get her. Bill will help us."

"How?"

"I don't know, but he will. You'll see."

She hooked her beeper over her belt and the two of us went back up to the house. Milo was still on the couch. Huenengarth/Zimberg/Bill was standing across the room, in a corner, leafing through a magazine.

Stephanie said, "Hi, guys," in a too-chirpy voice.

Huenengarth closed the magazine, took her by the elbow, and seated her in a chair. Pulling another one close to her, he sat down.

She didn't take her eyes off him. He moved his arm as if to touch her, but unbuttoned his jacket instead.

"Where are Dawn Herbert's disks?" I said. "And don't tell me it's not relevant, because I'll bet you it is. Herbert may or may not have latched on to what Ashmore was doing for you, but I'm pretty sure she had suspicions about the Jones kids. Speaking of which, have you found Chad's chart?"

"Not yet."

"What about the disks?"

"I just sent them over to be analyzed."

"Do the people analyzing even know what they're looking at? The random number table?"

He nodded. "It's probably a substitution code—shouldn't be too much of a problem."

"You haven't unscrambled all of Ashmore's numbers yet. What makes you think you'll do better with Herbert's?"

He looked at Stephanie and gave another half-smile. "I like this guy."

Her return smile was nervous.

"Man raises a good point," said Milo.

"Ashmore was a special case," said Huenengarth. "Real puzzle-freak, high IQ."

"Herbert wasn't?"

"Not from what I've learned about her."

"Which is?"

"Just what you know," he said. "Some smarts in math, but basically she was a klepto and a lowlife—doper and a loser."

As he spat out each noun, Stephanie flinched. He noticed it, turned and touched her hand briefly, let go.

"If something comes up on the disk that concerns you," he said, "rest assured I'll let you know."

"We need to know now. Herbert's information could give us some direction." I turned to Milo. "Did you tell him about our friend the bartender?"

Milo nodded.

"Everything?"

"Don't bother being subtle," said Huenengarth. "I saw the

masterpiece your junkie bartender produced and no, it's not me. I don't hack up women."

"What are you talking about?" said Stephanie.

"Stupidity," he told her. "They've got a description of a murder suspect—someone who may or may not have murdered this Herbert character—and they thought it bore a resemblance to yours truly."

She put her hand to her mouth.

He laughed. "Not even close, Steph. Last time I was that thin was back in high school." To me: "Can we get to work now?"

"I've never stopped," I said. "Do you have any information on Vicki Bottomley?"

Huenengarth waved a hand at Milo. "Tell him."

"We've done phone traces from her home to the Jones house and Chip's office."

"We?" said Huenengarth.

"Him," said Milo. "Federal warrant. Next week he sprouts a fucking pair of wings."

"Find anything?" I said.

Milo shook his head. "No calls. And none of Bottomley's neighbors have seen Cindy or Chip around, so if there is a link, it's pretty damn hidden. My intuition is she's got nothing to do with it. She's certainly not the main poisoner. Once the chips fall, we'll see if she fits in, anywhere."

"So where do we go now?"

Milo looked at Huenengarth. Huenengarth looked at me and held his hand out toward the couch.

"Been sitting all day," I said.

He frowned and touched his tie. Stared at everyone else.

Milo said, "Any more federal doublespeak and I'm outa here."

"All right," said Huenengarth. "First, I want to reiterate my demand of total discretion—total cooperation from both of you. *No* improvisation. I mean it."

"In return for what?" I said.

"Probably enough technical support to bust Cindy. Because I've got federal warrants on Chuck Jones, and with a two-minute phone call I can include Junior and everything *he* owns in the deal. We're talking audio, video, home, place of business—they go bowling, I can have someone peeking from behind the pins. Give me two hours alone in their house and I can rig it with peep-toys you wouldn't believe. Got a camera that goes right in their TV so when they're watching it, it's watching them. I can toss the house for insulin or whatever crap you're looking for and they'll never know it. All you have to do is keep your mouths shut."

"Cassie's room is the one that needs to be rigged," I said. "And the bathroom connecting it to the master bedroom."

"Tile walls in the bathroom?"

"Tile walls and one window."

"No problem—whatever toys I don't have at hand, I can have delivered in twenty-four hours."

Milo said, "Your tax dollars busy at work."

Huenengarth frowned. "Sometimes they are."

I wondered if he knew what a joke was. Stephanie didn't care if he did; her expression said he danced on water.

"I've got a meeting scheduled at the house tomorrow night," I said. "I'll try to change it to the hospital. Can you have your equipment ready by then?"

"Probably. If not, it will be soon after—day or two. But can you assure me the house will be totally empty? I'm ready to pounce on Daddy, I can't afford *any* screwups."

I said to Stephanie, "Why don't you call Chip and Cindy in for a meeting? Tell them something came up on the lab tests, you need to examine Cassie and then speak with them. Once they get there, make sure they stay for a long time."

"Fine," she said. "I'll keep them waiting, tell them the labs got lost or something."

"Action, camera," said Huenengarth.

"How come you can get Chip included in the warrant?" I asked him. "Is he involved in his father's financial dealings?"

No answer.

I said, "I thought we were being frank."

"He's a sleaze, too," Huenengarth said, irritated.

"The fifty parcels he owns? Is that really one of Chuck's deals?"

He shook his head. "The land deal's for shit—Chuck's too smart for that. Junior's a loser, can't hold on to a dollar. Gone through plenty of Daddy's already."

"What's he spending it on besides land?" I said. "His life-style's pretty ordinary."

"Sure, on the surface it is. But that's just part of the image: Mr. Self-made. It's a crock. That dinky junior college he teaches at pays him twenty-four thousand a year—think you can buy a house in *Watts* on that, let alone that entire tract? Not that he owns it, anymore."

"Who does?"

"The bank that financed the deal."

"Foreclosure?"

"Any minute." Big smile. "Daddy bought the land at a bargain price, years ago. Gave it to Junior, the idea being that Junior would sell at the right time and get rich on his own. He even told Junior when the right time was, but Junior didn't listen."

The smile became a lottery-winner's grin. "Not the first time, either. Back when Junior was at Yale, he started his own business: competition with Cliff Notes because he could do it better. Daddy bankrolled him, hundred thousand or so. Down the drain, because apart from its being a harebrained scheme, Junior lost interest. That's his pattern. He has a problem with finishing things. A few years later, when he was in graduate school, he decided he was going to be a publisher—start a sociology magazine for the lay public. Another quarter of a million of Daddy's dough. There've been others, all along the same lines. By my calculation, around a million or so urinated away, not including the land. Not much by Daddy's standards, but you'd figure someone with half a brain could do something constructive with that kind of grubstake, right? Not Junior. He's too *creative*."

"What went wrong with the land?" I said.

"Nothing, but we're in a recession and property values dropped. Instead of cashing in and cutting his losses, Junior decided to go into the construction business. Daddy knew it was stupid and refused to bankroll it, so Junior went out and got a loan from a bank using Daddy's name as collateral. Junior lost interest as usual, the sub-contractors saw they had a real chicken on their hands and started plucking. Those houses are built like garbage."

"Six phases," I said, remembering the architectural rendering. "Not much completed."

"Maybe half of one phase. The plan was for an entire city. Junior's own personal Levittown." He laughed. "You should see the proposal he wrote up when he sent it to Daddy. Like a term paper—delusions of grandeur. No doubt the bank'll go to Daddy first, before taking over the deed. And Daddy may just divvy up. Because he *loves* Junior, tells everyone who'll listen what a scholar his baby boy is—another joke. Junior changed his major a bunch of times in college. Didn't finish his Ph.D.—the old boredom thing."

"One thing he has stuck with is teaching," I said. "And he seems to be good at it—he's won awards."

Huenengarth let his tongue protrude through his small lips as he shook his head. "Yeah. Formal Organizations, New Age Management Techniques. We're talking Marxist theory and rock 'n' roll. He's an *entertainer.* I've got tapes of his lectures, and basically what he does is pander to the students. Lots of anti-capitalist rhetoric, the evils of corporate corruption. You don't have to be Freud to figure *that* one out, right? He likes rubbing the old man's face in it—even the wife's part of that program, wouldn't you say?"

"In what way?"

"C'mon, Doctor. Milo, here, told me you found out about her military *career.* The woman's a *slut.* A lowlife *loser.* On *top* of what she's doing to the kid. Can't exactly be what the old man had in mind for Junior."

He grinned. Scarlet again, and sweating heavily. Nearly levitating off his chair in rage and delight. His hatred was tangible, poisonous. Stephanie felt it; her eyes were thrilled.

"What about Chip's mother?" I said. "How did she die?"

He shrugged. "Suicide. Sleeping pills. Entire family's fucked up. Though I can't say I blame her. Don't imagine living with Chuck was any barrel of primates. He's been known to play around—likes 'em in groups of three or four, young, chesty, blond, borderline intelligence."

I said, "You'd like to get all of them, wouldn't you?"

"I've got no use for them," he said quickly. Then he got up, took a few steps, turned his back on us, and stretched.

"So," he said. "Let's aim for tomorrow. You get 'em out, we move in and play Captain Video."

"Great, Bill," said Stephanie. Her beeper went off. She removed it from her belt and examined the digital readout. "Where's your phone, Alex?"

I walked her into the kitchen and hung around as she punched numbers.

"This is Dr. Eves. I just got . . . What? . . . When? . . . All right, give me the resident on call. . . . Jim? This is Stephanie. What's up? . . . Yes, yes, there's a history of that. It's all in the chart. . . . Absolutely, keep that drip going. Sounds like you're doing everything right, but get me a full tox panel, stat. Make sure to check for hypoglycemic metabolites. Check all over for puncture wounds, too, but don't let on, okay? It's important, Jim. Please. . . . Thanks. And keep her totally isolated. *No* one goes in. . . . Especially not them . . . What? . . . Out in the hall. Leave the drapes open so they can see her, but *no one goes inside.* . . . I don't care. . . . I know. Let it be on my head, Jim. . . . What? . . . *No.* Keep her in ICU. Even *if* things lighten up . . . I don't *care,* Jim. Find a bed somewhere. This one's crucial. . . . What? . . . Soon. Soon as I can— maybe an hour. Just— What? . . . Yes, I will. . . . Okay. Thanks. I owe you."

She hung up. Her face was white and her chest heaved.

"Again," I said.

She looked past me. Held her head.

"Again," she said. "This time she's unconscious."

31

Quiet night on Chappy Ward. No shortage of empty rooms.

This one was two doors down from 505 W. Cassie's room.

That cold, clean hospital smell.

The images on the TV I was watching were black-and-white and fuzzy and small, a miniaturized, capsulated reality.

Cold and clean and a medicinal staleness—though no one had been in this room for a long time.

I'd been in it most of the day and all of the evening.

Into the night . . .

The door was bolted shut. The room was dark, except for a focused yellow parabola from a corner floor lamp. Double drapes blotted out Hollywood. I sat on an orange chair, as confined as a patient. The piped music barely leaked through from the hallway.

The man who called himself Huenengarth sat across the room, near the lamp, cradled by a chair identical to mine that he'd pushed up to the empty bed. A small black hand radio rested in his lap.

The bed was stripped down to the mattress. Resting on the ticking was a sloping paper ramp. Government documents.

The one he was reading had kept his interest for more than an hour. Down at the bottom was a line of numbers and asterisks and a word that I thought was UPDATE. But I couldn't be sure because I was too far away and neither of us wanted to change that.

I had things to read, too: the latest lab reports on Cassie and a brand-new article Huenengarth had shoved at me. Five typed pages on the subject of pension fraud by Professor W. W. Zimberg, written in starchy legalese with lots of words blacked out by a broad-tipped marker.

My eyes went back to the TV. No movement on the screen other than the slow drip of sugar-water through plastic tubing. I inspected the small, colorless world from edge to edge. For the thousandth time . . .

Bedclothes and railings, a blur of dark hair and puffy cheek. The I.V. gauge, with its inlets and outlets and locks . . .

I sensed movement across the room without seeing it. Huenengarth took out a pen and crossed something out.

According to documents he showed Milo in the deputy chief's office, he'd been in Washington, D.C., the night Dawn Herbert was butchered in her little car. Milo told me he'd corroborated it, as the two of us drove to the hospital just before sunrise.

"Who exactly is he working for?" I said.

"Don't know the details but it's some sort of covert task force, probably in cahoots with the Treasury Department."

"Secret agent man? Think he knows our friend the colonel?"

"Wondered about that myself. He found out pretty damn fast that I was playing computer games. After we got out of the D.C.'s office, I shot the colonel's name at him and got a blank stare, but it wouldn't surprise me if the two of them attended some of the same parties. Tell you one thing, Alex—asshole's more than just a field agent, got some real juice behind him."

"Juice and motivation," I said. "Four and a half years to avenge his father. How do you think he managed the million-dollar budget?"

"Who knows? Probably kissed the right ass, stabbed the right back. Or maybe it was just a matter of the right person's ox getting gored. Whatever, he's a smart cookie."

"Good actor, too—getting that close to Jones and Plumb."

"So one day he'll run for President. Did you know you were going twenty over the limit?"

"If I get a ticket, you can fix it for me, right? Now that you're a real policeman again."

"Yeah."

"How'd you pull it off?"

"I didn't pull off anything. When I got to the D.C.'s, Huenengarth was already there. He gets right in my face, demands to know why I've been tracing him. I think about it and tell him the truth, because what's my choice? Play hard to get and have the department cite me for improper use of departmental time and facilities? He then proceeds to ask me lots of questions about the Jones family. All this time, the D.C. is just sitting behind his desk, hasn't said a word, and I figure this is it, start thinking private enterprise. But soon as I finish, Huenengarth thanks me for my cooperation, says it's a shame, the crime rate being what it is, that a guy with my experience is sitting in front of a screen instead of working cases. The D.C. looks as if he just sucked pigshit through a straw, but he keeps quiet. Huenengarth asks if I can be assigned to his investigation—LAPD liaison to the Feds. D.C. squirms and says sure, getting me back on active duty was the department's plan all along. Huenengarth and I leave the office together and the minute we're alone he tells me he doesn't give a fuck about me personally, but his case on Jones is just about to break and I'd better not get in his way while he moves in with the killing thrust."

"Killing thrust, huh?"

"Gentle soul, probably doesn't wear fur . . . Then he said, 'Maybe we can cut a deal. Don't fuck me up and I'll help you.' Then he told me how he knew about Cassie from Stephanie, but hadn't done anything because there wasn't enough evidence, but maybe now there was."

"Why all of a sudden?"

"Probably because he's close enough to getting Grandpa and wouldn't mind doing a total destruct on the family. I also wouldn't be surprised if on some level he enjoys seeing Cassie suffer—the curse of the Jones family. He really hates them, Alex. . . . On the other hand, where would we be without him? So let's use the hell out of him, see what happens. How does this look on me?"

"High fashion, Ben Casey."

"Yeah. Take a picture. When it's over."

Movement on the screen.

Then nothing.

My neck was stiff. I shifted position while keeping my eyes on the TV.

Huenengarth continued to do his homework. It had been hours since anything I did caught his attention.

Time passed, slothfully cruel.

More movement.

Shadowing one corner. Upper right-hand.

Then nothing, for a long time.

Then . . .

"Hey!" I said.

Huenengarth peered over his pamphlet. Bored.

The shadow grew. Lightened.

Took shape. White and fuzzy.

Starfish . . . human hand.

Something grasped between thumb and forefinger.

Huenengarth sat up.

"Go!" I said. "This is it!"

He smiled.

The hand on the screen advanced. Grew larger. Big, white . . .

"C'mon!" I said.

Huenengarth put down his article.

The hand jabbed . . . poking at something.

Huenengarth seemed to be savoring the picture.

He looked at me as if I'd interrupted a terrific dream.

The thing between the fingers probed.

Huenengarth's smile stretched under his little mustache.

"Damn you," I said.

He picked up the little black radio and held it to his mouth.

"On your mark," he said.

The hand was at the I.V. gauge now, using the thing between its fingers to nuzzle a rubber-tipped inlet.

Sharp-tipped thing.

White cylinder, much like a pen. Ultra-thin needle.

It darted, a bird pecking a wormhole.

Plunged.

Huenengarth said, "Go," to the radio.

It was only later that I realized he'd skipped "Get set."

He moved toward the door, but I threw the bolt and was out first. All those years of jogging and treadmilling finally paid off.

The door to 505W was already wide open.

Cassie was on her back in the bed, breathing through her mouth.

Post-seizure slumber.

She was covered to the neck. I.V. tubing curled from under the blankets.

Cindy was sleeping, too, flat on her stomach, one arm dangling.

Milo stood next to the I.V. pole, baggy in green surgical scrubs. A hospital ID badge was pinned to his shirt. M. B. STURGIS, M.D., his photographed face cross and bearish.

The real face was policeman-stoic. One of his big hands was clamped over Chip Jones's wrist. The other bent Chip's arm behind his back. Chip cried out in pain.

Milo ignored him and told him his rights.

Chip had on a camel-colored jogging suit and brown suede running shoes with diagonal leather stripes. His back was arched in Milo's grip and his eyes were splayed and bright, sick with terror.

It was his fear that made me want to kill him.

I ran to the bed and checked the I.V. gauge. Locked—sealed with Krazy Glue. Stephanie's idea. None of what was in the cylinder was entering Cassie's bloodstream. Creative, but a risk: seconds later, Chip would have felt the pressure build behind the needle. And known.

Milo had him cuffed now. Chip started crying, then stopped.

Huenengarth licked his lips and said, "You're fucked, Junior." I hadn't seen him come in.

Chip stared at him. His mouth was still open. His beard trembled. He dropped something on the floor. White cylinder with a tiny, sharp tip. It rolled on the carpet before coming to a stop. Chip raised a foot and tried to step on it.

Milo yanked him away. Huenengarth put on a surgical glove and picked up the cylinder.

He waved it in front of Chip's face.

Chip made a whimpering noise and Huenengarth responded with a masturbatory movement of one arm.

I went over to Cindy and nudged her. She rolled and didn't waken. A shake of her shoulders failed to rouse her. I shook harder, said her name. Nothing.

A cup was on the floor, near her dangling hand. Half-filled with coffee.

"What did you drug her with?" I asked Chip.

He didn't answer. I repeated the question and he looked at the floor. His earring tonight was an emerald.

"What'd you give her?" I said, dialing the phone.

He pouted.

The page operator came on and I called for an emergency resuscitation.

Chip watched, wide-eyed.

Huenengarth advanced toward him again. Milo stilled him with a look and said, "If she's in danger and you don't tell us, you're only making matters worse for yourself."

Chip cleared his throat, as if preparing for an important announcement. But he said nothing.

I went to Cassie's bed.

"Okay," said Milo, "let's go to jail." He pushed Chip forward. "We'll let the lab figure it out."

Chip said, "Probably diazepam—Valium. But I didn't give it to her."

"How much?" I said.

"Forty milligrams is what she usually takes."

Milo looked at me.

"Probably not lethal," I said. "But it's a heavy dose for someone her size."

"Not really," said Chip. "She's habituated."

"Bet she is," I said, lacing my fingers to keep my hands still.

"Don't be stupid," said Chip. "Search me—see if you find drugs of any kind."

"You're not holding because you gave it all to her," said Huenengarth.

Chip managed to laugh, though his eyes were frightened. "Go ahead, search."

Huenengarth patted him down, turned his pockets inside out, and found only a wallet and keys.

Chip looked at him, shook hair out of eyes, and smiled.

"Something funny, Junior?"

"You are making a big mistake," said Chip. "If I wasn't the victim, I'd really feel sorry for you."

Huenengarth smiled. "That so?"

"Very much so."

"Junior, here, thinks this is funny, gents." He wheeled on Chip: "What the fuck do you think is going on here? You think one of Daddy's *attorneys* is going to get you out of this? We've got you on videotape trying to kill your kid—everything from loading the needle to sticking it in. Want to guess where the camera is?"

Chip kept smiling but panic fueled his eyes. They blinked, popped, raced around the room. Suddenly he shut them and dropped his head to his chest, muttering.

"What's that?" said Huenengarth. "What'd you say?"

"Discussion closed."

Huenengarth came closer. "Atttempted murder's not some dinky-shit Chapter Eleven. What kind of scum would do this to his own flesh and blood?"

Chip kept his head down.

"Well," said Huenengarth, "you can always start a new project—Cliff Notes for jailhouse lawyers. Those big bucks in maximum lockup are gonna love your educated anus."

Chip didn't move. His body had gone loose—meditative—and Milo had to work at holding him upright.

A sound came from the bed. Cassie shifting position. Chip looked at her.

She moved again, but remained asleep.

A terrible look came onto his face—disappointment at an unfinished job.

Enough hatred to fuel a war.

All three of us saw it. The room got very small.

Huenengarth reddened and puffed like a bullfrog.

"Happy rest of your life, fuckhead," he whispered. Then he stomped out.

When the door closed, Chip snickered, but it sounded forced.

Milo pushed him toward the door. They got out just before Stephanie arrived with the emergency team.

33

I watched Cassie sleep. Stephanie left with the team, but came back about a half hour later.

"How's Cindy doing?" I said.

"She'll probably have a monster headache but she'll survive."

"She may need to be detoxed," I said, lowering my voice to a whisper. "He said she was habituated, though he denied dosing her—made a real big point of saying he didn't have any drugs on him. But I'm sure he slipped it in her coffee, did it plenty of times before tonight. Every time I saw him here, he had a cup with him."

She shook her head, sat on the bed, and pulled her stethoscope from around her neck. Warming the disk with her breath, she placed it on Cassie's chest and listened.

When she was through, I said, "Any dope in Cassie's system?"

"No, just low sugar." Her whisper was weak. She lifted Cassie's free arm and took a pulse. "Nice and regular." She put the arm down.

She sat there for a moment, then tucked the covers up around Cassie's neck and touched a soft cheek. The drapes were open. I saw her look out at the night with tired eyes.

"It makes no sense," she said. "Why did he use insulin, right after you found the injectors? Unless Cindy didn't tell him you found them. Was their communication that bad?"

"I'm sure she did tell him, and that's *exactly* why he used them. He planted them there for me to find. Made a special call to verify that I was coming out and making sure he wouldn't be there. Playing concerned daddy, but he was really pinpointing the time. Because he knew we had to suspect Munchausen by now, and he was hoping I'd snoop, discover the cylinders, and suspect Cindy, just as I did. What could be more logical: They were *her* aunt's samples. *She* was in charge of the house, so she'd be the most likely one to hide them there. And she was the *mother*—that stacked the deck against her from the beginning. The first time I met him he made a point of telling me they had a traditional marriage—child rearing was her bailiwick."

"Pointing a finger at her right from the beginning." She shook her head in disbelief. "So . . . orchestrated."

"Meticulously. And if I hadn't found the cylinders during yesterday's visit, there would have been plenty of other opportunities for him to set her up."

"What a monster," she said.

"The devil wears jogging clothes."

She hugged herself.

I said, "How big of a dosage was loaded into the Insuject?"

She looked at Cassie and lowered her voice to a whisper. "More than enough."

"So tonight was to be the final chapter," I said. "Cassie seizing fatally, Cindy right there snoozing, with all of us suspecting her. If we hadn't caught him he probably would have stashed the needle in her purse or somewhere else incriminating. And the Valium in her system would have added to the picture of guilt: suicide attempt. Remorse for killing her baby, or just an unbalanced mind."

Stephanie rubbed her eyes. Rested her head on one hand. "What an incredible prick . . . How'd he get in without going through Security?"

"Your friend Bill said he didn't enter the hospital through the front door, so he probably used one of his father's keys and came in through the back. Maybe one of the loading docks. At this hour there'd be no one there. We know from the hallway camera that he took the stairs up and waited until the Five East nurse went into the back room before entering Chappy. Probably did the same thing when Cassie had that first seizure here in the hospital. Dress rehearsal. Sneaking up in the wee hours, injecting her with just enough insulin to provide a delayed reaction, then driving home to the Valley and waiting for Cindy's call before coming back to comfort her in the E.R. The fact that Chappy's nearly always empty made it easier for him to come and go unnoticed."

"And all this time I was obsessing on Cindy. Brilliant, Eves."

"I zeroed in on her too. We all did. She was a perfect Munchausen suspect. Low self-esteem, easygoing manner, early experiences with serious illness, health-care training. He probably came across the syndrome in his readings, saw the fit, and realized he had an opportunity to get her. *That's* why he didn't have Cassie transferred to another hospital. He wanted to give us time to develop our suspicions. Worked us like an audience—the way he works his students. *He's* the exhibitionist, Steph. But we never saw it because the books say it's always a woman."

Silence.

"He killed Chad, didn't he?" she said.

"It's a strong possibility."

"Why, Alex? Why use his own kids to get at Cindy?"

"I don't know, but I'll tell you one thing. He hates Cassie. Before they took him away he gave her a look that was really disturbing. Pure contempt. If the tape caught it and it's ruled admissible in court, it's all the prosecutor will need."

Shaking her head, she returned to the bed and stroked Cassie's hair.

"Poor little baby. Poor little innocent baby."

I sat there, not wanting to think or do or talk or feel.

A trio of LuvBunnies sat on the floor near my feet.

I picked one up. Passed it from hand to hand. Something hard in the belly.

Undoing the flap, I poked around the foam stuffing, just as I had in Cassie's bedroom. This time, I found something tucked into a fold near the groin.

I drew it out. A packet. About an inch in diameter. Tissue paper fastened with cellophane tape.

I unwrapped it. Four pills. Pale-blue, each with a heart-shaped cutout.

Stephanie said, "Valium."

"Here's our secret stash." I rewrapped the packet and set it aside for Milo. "He made such a big deal about not having any dope with him. Everything's a game with him."

"Vicki bought those bunnies," Stephanie said. "Vicki's the one who got Cassie started on them."

"Vicki will be talked to after this," I said.

"Too weird," she said. "The stuff they don't teach you in sch—"

A squeak came from the bed. Cassie's eyes blinked spasmodically, then opened. Her little mouth turned down. She blinked some more.

"It's okay, baby," said Stephanie.

Cassie's mouth worked, finally producing a sound:

"Eh eh eh."

"It's okay, honey. Everything's gonna be fine. You're gonna be fine now."

"Eh eh eh eh."

More blinks. A shudder. Cassie tried to move, failed, cried out in frustration. Scrunched her eyes. Crinkled her chin.

Stephanie held her and rocked her. Cassie tried to twist away from Stephanie's caress.

I remembered the way she'd fought me in her bedroom.

Reacting to her mother's anxiety? Or memories of another man who came in the night, shrouded by darkness, and hurt her?

But then, why hadn't she panicked whenever she saw Chip? Why had she jumped up into his arms, so willingly, the first time I'd seen them together?

"Eh eh eh . . ."

"Shh, baby."

"Eh . . . eh eh . . . eh."

"Go back to sleep, honey. Go back to sleep."

Very faintly: "Eh . . ."

"Shh."

"Eh . . ."

Closed eyes.

Soft snores.

Stephanie held her for several moments, then slipped her hands free.

"Must be the magic touch," she said sadly. Looping her stethoscope over her neck, she walked out of the room.

34

A nurse and a policewoman arrived soon after.

I gave the cop the packet of pills and sleepwalked my way to the teak doors.

Out in Five East, people were moving and talking, but I didn't focus on them. I rode the elevator down to the basement. The cafeteria was closed. Wondering if Chip had a key to that, too, I bought coffee from a machine, found a pay phone, and sipped as I asked information for a number on a Jennifer Leavitt. Nothing.

Before the operator could break the connection, I had him check for any Leavitts in the Fairfax district. Two. One of them matched my vague memory of Jennifer's parents' home number.

My watch said 9:30. I knew Mr. Leavitt went to sleep early in order to make it to the bakery by 5:00 A.M. Hoping it wasn't too late, I punched numbers.

"Hello."

"Mrs. Leavitt? It's Dr. Delaware."

"Doctor. How *are* you?"

"Fine, and you?"

"Very good."

"Am I calling too late?"

"Oh, no. We're just watching television. But Jenny's not here. She has her own apartment now—my daughter the doctor, very independent."

"You must be proud of her."

"What's not to be proud of? She's always made me proud. Do you want her new number?"

"Please."

"Hold on . . . She's in Westwood Village, right near the U. With another girl, a nice girl . . . Here it is. If she's not there, she's probably in her office—she's got an office, too." Chuckle.

"That's great." I copied down the numbers.

"An office," she said. "You know, raising a child like that, it's a privilege. . . . I miss her. For my taste, the house is too quiet."

"I'll bet."

"You were very helpful to her, Dr. Delaware. College at her age wasn't so easy—you should be proud of *yourself*."

No one answered at Jennifer's apartment. But she picked up her office phone after one ring: "Leavitt."

"Jennifer, it's Alex Delaware."

"Hi, Alex. Did you solve your Munchausen by proxy?"

"The *who*dunit," I said. "But the whydunit's not clear yet. It turned out to be the father."

"Well, *that's* a twist," she said. "So it isn't *always* the mother."

"He was counting on our assuming it was. He set her up."

"How Machiavellian."

"He fancies himself an intellectual. He's a professor."

"Here?"

"No, at a junior college. But he does his serious research at the U, which is why I'm calling you. My bet is he read up exhaustively on the syndrome in order to create a textbook case. His first child died of SIDS. Another textbook case, so I'm wondering if he set that up too."

"Oh, no—this sounds *grotesque*."

"I was thinking about the SAP system," I said. "If he's got a faculty account, would there be some way to find out?"

"The library keeps a record of all users, for billing."

"Do the bills list which articles were pulled?"

"Absolutely. What time is it? Nine forty-seven. The library's open till ten. I could call down there and see if anyone I know is working. Give me the bastard's name."

"Jones, Charles L. Sociology, West Valley Community College."

"Got it. I'm going to put you on hold and call them on the other line. Just in case we get cut off, give me your number."

Five minutes later she clicked in.

"*Voilà,* Alex. The idiot left a beautiful paper trail. Pulled everything the system's got on three topics—Munchausen, sudden infant death, and the sociological structure of hospitals. Plus a few isolated articles on two other topics: diazepam toxicity and—are you ready for this?—women's fantasies about penis size. It's all there: names, dates, exact hour. I'll get a printout for you tomorrow."

"Fantastic. I really appreciate it, Jennifer."

"One more thing," she said. "He's not the only one who used the account. There's another signature on some of the searches—a Kristie Kirkash. Know anyone by that name?"

"No," I said, "but I wouldn't be surprised if she's young, cute, and one of his students. Maybe even plays sorority softball."

"Sleazy affair for the prof? How do you figure?"

"He's a creature of habit."

35

Hot morning and the Valley was frying. A big rig had overturned on the freeway, showering all lanes with eggs. Even the shoulder was blocked and Milo cursed until the highway patrolman waved us through.

We arrived at the junior college ten minutes behind schedule. Made it to class just as the last students were entering.

"Damn," said Milo. "Improv time." We climbed the stairs to the trailer. I remained in the doorway and he went up to the blackboard.

It was a small room—half the trailer, partitioned by an accordion wall and set up with a conference table and a dozen folding chairs.

Ten of the chairs were occupied. Eight women, two men. One of the women was in her sixties; the rest were girls. Both men were fortyish. One was white, with a full head of light-brown hair; the other, Hispanic and bearded. The white man looked up briefly, then buried himself in a book.

Milo picked up a pointer and tapped the board. "Mr. Jones won't be making it today. I'm Mr. Sturgis, your substitute."

All eyes on him, except those of the reader.

One of the girls said, "Is he okay?" in a strained voice. She had very long, dark, frizzy hair, a thin, pretty face, and wore dangling earrings constructed of lavender-and-white plastic balls on nylon fishing line. Her black tube top showed off a big chest and smooth, tan shoulders. Too-blue eye shadow, too-pale lipstick, too much of both.

Despite that, better-looking than the photo in her student file.

Milo said, "Not really, Kristie."

She opened her mouth. The other students looked at her.

She said, "Hey, what's going on?" and grabbed her purse.

Milo reached into his pocket and pulled out his police badge. "You tell me, Kristie."

She froze. The other students gawked. The reader's eyes floated above the pages of his book. Moving slowly.

I saw Milo look at him. Look down at the floor.

Shoes.

Clunky black oxfords with bubble toes. They didn't go with his silk shirt and his designer jeans.

Milo's eyes narrowed. The reader's fixed on mine, then sank out of view as he raised the book higher.

Theories of Organizations.

Kristie started to cry.

The other students were statues.

Milo said, "Yo Joe! Cavity check!"

The reader looked up reflexively. Just for a second, but it was enough.

Bland face. Dick and Jane's dad from a half-block distance. Up close, details destroyed the paternal image: five o'clock shadow, pockmarks on the cheeks, a scar across the forehead. Tattoo on one hand.

And the sweat—a coat of it, shiny as fresh lacquer.

He stood up. His eyes were hard and narrow; his hands huge, the forearms thick. More tattoos, blue-green, crude. Reptilian.

He picked up his books and stepped away from the table while keeping his head down.

Milo said, "Hey, c'mon, stay. I'm an easy grader."

The man stopped, began to lower himself, then he threw the books at Milo and made a rush for the door.

I stepped in front of him, locking my hands in a double-arm block.

He shouldered me full-force. The impact slammed me against the door and pushed it open.

I fell backward onto the cement, landing hard and feeling my tailbone hum. Reaching out, I grabbed two handfuls of silk. He was on top of me, clawing and punching and spraying sweat.

Milo pulled him off, hit him very fast in the face and the belly and shoved him hard against the bungalow. The man struggled. Milo kidney-punched him, hard, and cuffed him as he sank, groaning.

Milo forced him down on the ground and put one foot on the small of his back.

A pat-down produced a wad of cash, a flick-knife with a black handle, a vial of pills, and a cheap plastic billfold stamped RENO: NEVADA'S PLAYGROUND. Milo pulled three different driver's licenses out of the fold.

"Well, well, well, what have we here? Sobran comma Karl with a K, Sebring comma Carl with a C, and . . . Ramsey comma Clark Edward. Which one's real, turkey, or are you suffering from multiple personality syndrome?"

The man said nothing.

Milo nudged one of the black shoes with a toe.

"Good old prison clumpers. County or state?"

No answer.

"You need new heels, genius."

The man's back muscles moved under his shirt.

Milo turned to me. "Find a phone and call the Devonshire substation. Tell them we've got a suspect on a Central Division homicide and give them Dawn Herbert's full name."

The man on the ground said, "Bullshit." His voice was deep and muddy.

One of the young students came out onto the stairs. Twenty or twenty-one, short blond pageboy, sleeveless white dress, Mary Pickford face.

She said, "Kristie's pretty upset," in a very timid voice.

"Tell her I'll be with her in a minute," said Milo.

"Um . . . sure. What did Karl do?"

"Sloppy homework," said Milo.

The man on the ground growled and the girl looked startled.

Milo kept his knee on the man's back and said, "Shut up."

The blond girl gripped the doorjamb.

Softening his voice, Milo said, "It's okay—nothing to worry about. Just go inside and wait."

"This isn't some kind of experiment or anything, is it?"

"Experiment?"

"A role-play. You know? Professor Jones likes to use them to raise our awareness."

"Bet he does. No, miss, this is real. Sociology in action. Take a good look—it'll be on the final."

36

The envelope arrived by messenger at 7:00 P.M., just before Robin got home. I put it aside and tried to have a normal evening with her. After she went to sleep, I took it to the library. Turned on all the lights and read.

TRANSCRIPT OF INTERROGATION

DR# 102—789 793
DR# 64—458 990
DR# 135—935 827

PLACE:	L.A.C. JAIL, BLOCK: HIGH-POWER
T/DATE:	6/1/89, 7:30 P.M.
SUSPECT:	JONES, CHARLES LYMAN III, MW, 6'3", BRO, BLU AGE: 38
DEF ATTORNEY:	TOKARIK, ANTHONY M., ESQ.
LAPD:	MILO B. STURGIS #15994, WLA (SPEC. ASSIGNMENT) STEPHEN MARTINEZ, #26782, DEVSHR.

DET. STURGIS: This is video-audiotape session number two with Suspect Charles Lyman Jones the Third. Suspect was informed of his rights at the time of arrest for attempted murder. Miranda warning was repeated and taped at a previous session, eleven A.M. June 1, 1989, and transcribed on that day at two P.M. Said session was terminated on advice of suspect's counsel, Mr. Anthony Tokarik, Esquire. This session represents resumption of interview at request of Mr. Tokarik. Do I need to re-Mirandize him, Counselor, or does that second warning hold for this session?

MR. TOKARIK: It will hold, unless Professor Jones requests re-Mirandization. Do you want to be warned again, Chip?

MR. JONES: No. Let's get on with this.

MR. TOKARIK: Go ahead.

DET. STURGIS: Evening, Chip.

MR. TOKARIK: I'd prefer that you address my client respectfully, Detective.

DET. STURGIS: Professor be okay?

MR. TOKARIK: Yes. However, if that's too difficult for you, "Mr. Jones" would suffice.

DET. STURGIS: You just called him Chip.

MR. TOKARIK: I'm his lawyer.

DET. STURGIS: Uh-huh . . . okay . . . sure. Hey, I'd even call him "Doctor," but he never finished his Ph.D., did you, Chip—Mr. Jones? What's that? Can't hear you.

MR. JONES: (unintelligible)

DET. STURGIS: Got to speak up, Mr. Jones. Grunts don't make it.

MR. TOKARIK: Hold on, Detective. Unless the tone of this interview changes, I'm going to call a halt to it immediately.

DET. STURGIS: Suit yourself—your loss. I just thought you guys might want to hear some of the evidence we've compiled against old Chip, here. 'Scuse me—Mister Jones.

MR. TOKARIK: I can get anything you have from the district attorney under the rules of recovery, Detective.

DET. STURGIS: Fine. Then wait till the trial. Let's go, Steve.

DET. MARTINEZ: Sure.

MR. JONES: Hold on. (unintelligible)

MR. TOKARIK: Wait, Chip. (unintelligible) I'd like to confer with my client privately, if you don't mind.

DET. STURGIS: If it doesn't take too long.

Tape off: 7:39 P.M.
Tape on: 7:51 P.M.

MR. TOKARIK: Go ahead, show us what you've got.

DET. STURGIS: Yeah, sure, but is Mr. Jones going to be answering questions or is it gonna be a one-way show-and-tell?

MR. TOKARIK: I reserve my client's right to refuse to answer any questions. Proceed if you wish, Detective.

DET. STURGIS: What do you think, Steve?

DET. MARTINEZ: I don't know.

MR. TOKARIK: Decision, gentlemen?

DET. STURGIS: Yeah, okay . . . Well, Chip—Mr. Jones— I'm glad you've got yourself a high-priced lawyer like Mr. Tokarik here, 'cause you're sure gonna—

MR. TOKARIK: This is definitely getting off on the wrong foot. My fees have nothing to—

DET. STURGIS: What are we doing here, Counselor, interrogating a suspect or critiquing my style?

MR. TOKARIK: I strenuously object to your—

DET. STURGIS: Object all you want. This isn't court.

MR. TOKARIK: I request another conference with my client.

DET. STURGIS: No way. Let's split, Steve.

DET. MARTINEZ: You bet.

MR. JONES: Hold on. Sit down.

DET. STURGIS: You ordering me around, Junior?

MR. TOKARIK: I object to—

DET. STURGIS: Come on, Steve, we're outa here.

MR. JONES: Hold on!

MR. TOKARIK: Chip, it's—

MR. JONES: Shut up!

MR. TOKARIK: Chip—

MR. JONES: Shut up!

DET. STURGIS: Uh-uh, no way do I proceed with this kind of friction going on between the two of you. Then he complains he wasn't represented by counsel of choice? No way.

MR. TOKARIK: Don't play lawyer with me, Detective.

MR. JONES: Just shut the hell up, Tony! This whole thing is preposterous!

DET. STURGIS: What is, Professor Jones?

MR. JONES: Your supposed case.

DET. STURGIS: You didn't attempt to inject your daughter, Cassandra Brooks, with insulin?

MR. JONES: Of course not. I found the needle in Cindy's purse, got upset because it confirmed my suspicions about her, and was trying to see if she'd already—

MR. TOKARIK: Chip—

MR. JONES: . . . jected it into Cassie's I.V. Stop giving me looks, Tony—it's my future at stake here. I want to hear what kind of folderol they think they've got, so I can clear it up once and for all.

DET. STURGIS: Folderol?

MR. TOKARIK: Chip—

DET. STURGIS: I don't want to continue if—

MR. JONES: He's my attorney of choice, okay? Go on.

DET. STURGIS: You're sure?

MR. JONES: (unintelligible)

DET. STURGIS: Speak right into that mike over there.

MR. JONES: Get on with it. I want out of here, posthaste.

DET. STURGIS: Yes, sir, massah sir.

MR. TOKARIK: Detecti—

MR. JONES: Shut up, Tony.

DET. STURGIS: Everyone ready? Okay. First of all, we've got you on videotape, trying to shoot insulin into—

MR. JONES: Wrong. I told you what that was about. I was just trying to see what Cindy was up to.

DET. STURGIS: Like I said, we've got you on videotape, trying to shoot insulin into your daughter's intravenous line. Plus video logs of the cameras at the entrance to Western Pediatric Medical Center confirming that you didn't enter the hospital through the front door. One of the keys on your ring has been identified as a hospital master. You probably used it to sneak in through the—

MR. TOKARIK: I obj—

MR. JONES: Tony.

MR. TOKARIK: I request a brief conference with my—

MR. JONES: Cut it out, Tony. I'm not one of your idiot sociopaths. Go on with your fairy tale, Detective. And you're right, I did use one of Dad's keys. So what? Whenever I go to that place I avoid the front door. I try to be inconspicuous. Is discretion an egregious felony?

DET. STURGIS: Let's go on. You bought two cups of coffee from a hospital machine, then took the stairs up to the fifth floor. We've got you on video up there too. Out in the hall where Five East meets Chappell Ward, carrying the coffee and looking through a crack in the door. What it looks like to me is you're waiting until the nurse on duty goes into a back room. Then you go into room 505 West where you stay for fifty-five minutes until I come in and find you jabbing that needle into your daughter's I.V. line. We're going to show you all those videotapes now, okay?

MR. JONES: Seems eminently superfluous, but suit yourself.

DET. STURGIS: Action, camera.

Tape off: 8:22 P.M.
Tape on: 9:10 P.M.

DET. STURGIS: Okay. Any comments?

MR. JONES: Godard it's not.

DET. STURGIS: No? I thought it had a lot of *vérité*.

MR. JONES: Are you a fan of *cinéma vérité*, Detective?

DET. STURGIS: Not really, Mr. Jones. Too much like work.

MR. JONES: Hah, I like that.

MR. TOKARIK: Is that it? That's your evidence, in toto?

DET. STURGIS: In toto? Hardly. Okay, so now we've got you jabbing that needle—

MR. JONES: I told you what that was about—I was testing it. Checking the I.V. inlet to see if Cindy'd already injected Cassie.

DET. STURGIS: Why?

MR. JONES: Why? To protect my child!

DET. STURGIS: Why did you suspect your wife of harming Cassie?

MR. JONES: Circumstances. The data at hand.

DET. STURGIS: The data.

MR. JONES: Exactly.

DET. STURGIS: Want to tell me more about the data?

MR. JONES: Her personality—things I noticed. She'd been acting strange—elusive. And Cassie always seemed to fall ill after she'd spent time with her mother.

DET. STURGIS: Okay . . . We've also got a puncture wound in the fleshy part of Cassie's armpit.

MR. JONES: No doubt you do, but I didn't put it there.

DET. STURGIS: Aha . . . what about the Valium you put in your wife's coffee?

MR. JONES: I explained it in the room, Detective. I didn't

give it to her. It was for her nerves, remember. She's been really on edge—been taking it for a while. If she denies that, she's lying.

DET. STURGIS: She does indeed deny it. She says she was never aware you were dosing her up.

MR. JONES: She lies habitually—that's the point. Accusing me based purely on what she says is like constructing a syllogism based on totally false premises. Do you understand what I mean by that?

DET. STURGIS: Sure, Prof. Valium tablets were found in one of Cassie's toys—a stuffed bunny.

MR. JONES: There you go. How would I know anything about that?

DET. STURGIS: Your wife says you bought several of them for Cassie.

MR. JONES: I bought Cassie all sorts of toys. Other people bought LuvBunnies too. A nurse named Bottomley—very iffy personality. Why don't you check her out, see if she's involved.

DET. STURGIS: Why should she be?

MR. JONES: She and Cindy seem awfully close—too close, I always thought. I wanted her transferred off the case, but Cindy refused. Check her out—she's strange, believe me.

DET. STURGIS: We did. She's passed a polygraph and every other test we threw at her.

MR. JONES: Polygraphs are inadmissible in court.

DET. STURGIS: Would you take one?

MR. TOKARIK: Chip, don't—

MR. JONES: I don't see any reason to. This whole thing is preposterous.

DET. STURGIS: Onward. Did you have a prescription for the Valium we found at your campus office?

MR. JONES: (laughs) No. Is that a crime?

DET. STURGIS: As a matter of fact, it is. Where'd you get it?

MR. JONES: Somewhere—I don't remember.

DET. STURGIS: One of your students?

MR. JONES: Of course not.

DET. STURGIS: A student named Kristie Marie Kirkash?

MR. JONES: Uh—absolutely not. I may have had it around from before.

DET. STURGIS: For yourself?

MR. JONES: Sure. From years ago—I was under some stress.

Now that I think about it, I'm sure that's what it was. Someone lent it to me—a faculty colleague.

DET. STURGIS: What's this colleague's name?

MR. JONES: I don't remember. It wasn't that significant. Valium's like candy nowadays. I plead guilty to having it without a prescription, okay?

DET. STURGIS: Okay.

MR. TOKARIK: What did you just take out of your briefcase, Detective?

DET. STURGIS: Something for the record. I'm going to read it out loud—

MR. TOKARIK: I want a copy first. Two copies—for myself and for Professor Jones.

DET. STURGIS: Duly noted. We'll get the Xerox going soon as we're finished here.

MR. TOKARIK: No, I want it simultaneous with your—

MR. JONES: Stop obstructing, Tony. Let him read whatever it is. I want out of here today.

MR. TOKARIK: Chip, nothing's of greater importance to me than your imminent release, but I—

MR. JONES: Quiet, Tony. Read, Detective.

MR. TOKARIK: Not at all. I'm unhappy with thi—

MR. JONES: Fine. Read, Detective.

DET. STURGIS: That settled? Sure? Okay. This is a transcript of an encoded computer floppy disk, 3M Brand, DS, DD, RH, double-sided, double-density, Q Mark. Further designated with Federal Bureau of Investigation Evidence Tag Number 133355678345 dash 452948. The disk was decoded by the cryptography division of the FBI National Crime Laboratory in Washington, D.C., and was received at Los Angeles Police Department Headquarters, this morning, 6:45 A.M., via government pouch. Once I start, I'm going to read it in its entirety, even if you choose to leave the room with your client, Counselor. In order to make it clear that this evidence was offered to you and you declined to hear it. Understood?

MR. TOKARIK: We exercise all of our rights without prejudice.

MR. JONES: Read on, Detective. I'm intrigued.

DET. STURGIS: Here goes:

> I'm putting this in code to protect myself, but it's not a complicated code, just a basic substitution—numbers for

letters with a couple of reversals, so you should be able to handle that, Ashmore. And if something's happened to me, have fun with it.

Charles Lyman Jones the Third, known as Chip, is a monster.

He came to my high school as a volunteer tutor and seduced me sexually and emotionally. This was ten years ago. I was seventeen and a senior and in the honors program in math, but I needed help with English and Social Sciences because I found it boring. He was twenty-eight and a graduate student. He seduced me and we had sex repeatedly over a six-month period at his apartment and at the school, including activities that I found personally repulsive. He was frequently impotent and did sick things to me in order to arouse himself. Eventually, I got pregnant and he said he'd marry me. We never got married, just lived together in a dive near the University of Connecticut, at Storrs. Then it got worse.

1. He didn't tell his family about me. He kept another apartment in town and went there whenever his father came to visit.

2. He started to act really crazy. Doing things to my body—putting drugs in my drinks and sticking me with needles when I was sleeping. At first I wasn't sure what was happening, used to wake up with marks all over, feeling sore. He said I was anemic and it was petechiae—broken capillaries due to pregnancy. Since he told me he'd been pre-med at Yale, I believed him. Then one time I woke up and caught him trying to inject me with something brown and disgusting-looking—I'm sure now it was feces. Apparently he hadn't given me enough dope to put me out, or maybe I'd become hooked and needed more to pass out. He explained the needle by saying it was all for my good—some kind of organic vitamin tonic.

I was young and I believed all his lies. Then it got too weird and I left and tried to live with my mother but she was drunk all the time and wouldn't take me in. Also, I think he paid her off, because right around then she got lots of new clothes. So I went back to him and the more pregnant I got, the meaner and more vicious he got. One time he pulled a really hysterical fit and told me the baby would ruin everything between us and that it had to go. Then he claimed it wasn't even his, which was ridiculous because I was a virgin when I met him and never fooled around with anyone else. Eventually, the stress he put me through made me miscarry. But that didn't make him happy either, and he kept sneaking up on me when I was sleeping, shouting in my ear and sometimes sticking me. I was getting fevers and bad headaches and hearing voices and becoming dizzy. For a while I thought I was going crazy.

I finally left Storrs and went back to Poughkeepsie. He followed me and we had a real screaming fit in Victor Waryas Park. Then he gave me a check for ten thousand dollars and told me to get out of his life and stay there. That was a lot of money to me at the time and I agreed. I was feeling too down and screwed up to work, so I got out on the street and got ripped off and ended up marrying Willie Kent, a black guy who pimped once in a while. That lasted about six months. Then I got into detox and got my equivalency and got into college.

I majored in math and computer science and did really well and then I got seduced by another teacher named Ross M. Herbert and was married to him for two years. He wasn't a monster like Chip Jones but he was boring and unhygienic and I divorced him and left college after three years.

I got a job in computers but that was pretty noncreative so I decided to be a doctor and went back to school to study pre-med. I had to work nights and squeeze in my studying. That's why my grades and my M-CAT scores weren't as high as they should have been, but I did get straight As in math.

I finally finished and applied to a bunch of medical schools but didn't get in. I worked as a lab assistant for a year and took the M-CATs again and did better. So I applied again and made some waiting lists. I also applied to some Public Health programs in order to get a related degree, and the best one that accepted me was in Los Angeles, so I came out here.

I scraped by for four years, kept applying to med school. Then I was reading the paper and saw an article on Charles Lyman Jones, Jr., and realized it was his father. That's when I realized how rich they were and how I'd been ripped off. So I decided to get some of what was coming to me. I tried to call his father but couldn't get through to him, even wrote letters he never answered. So I looked up Chip in city records and found he was living out in the Valley and went out to see what his house looked like. I did it at night, so no one could see me. I did it a bunch of times and got a look at his wife. What freaked me out was how much like me she looked, before I gained weight. His little daughter was real cute, and boy, did I feel sorry for the two of them.

I really didn't want to hurt them—the wife and the little girl—but I also felt I should warn them what they were up against. And he owed me.

I went back there several times, thinking about what to do, and then one night I saw an ambulance pull up in front of the house. He came out right afterward, in his Volvo, and I followed him at a distance, to Western Pediatric Medical Center. I stayed behind him all the way to the Emergency Room and heard him ask about his daughter, Cassie.

The next morning I went back, to Medical Records, wearing my white lab coat and saying I was Dr. Herbert. It was really easy, no security. Later, they beefed things up. Anyway, the daughter: her chart was gone but a card was there listing all these other admissions for her, so I knew he was up to his tricks. The poor little thing.

That's what really got me going—it wasn't just the money. Believe it or don't, Ashmore, but it's the truth. When I saw that card on the little girl, I knew I had to get him. So I went to Personnel and applied for a job. Three weeks later they called and offered me a half-time. With you, Ashmore. Shitty job, but I could watch Chip without him knowing. I finally got hold of Cassie's chart and found out everything he was doing to her. I also read in there that they'd had a boy who died. So I looked up his chart and found out he'd had crib death. So Chip had finally murdered someone. Next time I saw Cassie's name on the A and D sheets, I watched for him and finally saw him and followed him out to the parking lot and said, "Surprise."

He was really freaked out, tried to pretend he didn't know me. Then he tried to put me on the defensive by saying how much weight I'd gained. I just told him I knew what he was up to and that he'd better stop. Also, if he didn't give me a million dollars, I'd go to the police. He actually started crying, said he never meant to hurt anyone—just like he used to do when we were together. But this time it didn't work. I said no dice.

Then he said he'd give me a good-will payment of ten thousand dollars and try to come up with some more, but I had to give him time and it wouldn't be anything near a million—he didn't have that kind of money. I said fifty up front and we finally agreed on twenty-seven five. The next day he met me up at Barnsdale Park in Hollywood and gave me the money in cash. I told him he'd better come up with at least two hundred thousand more by the end of the month. He started crying again and said he'd do his best. Then he asked me to forgive him. I left and used the money to buy a new car because my old one was broken down, and in L.A. you're nothing without a good car. I put Chad Jones's chart in a locker at the airport—LAX, United Airlines, Number 5632—and the next day I quit the hospital.

So now I'm waiting till the end of the month and writing this down as collateral. I want to be rich and I want to be a doctor. I deserve all that. But just in case he tries to renege, I'm leaving this floppy in a locked drawer each night, then collecting it in the morning. There's also a copy in my locker at school. If you're reading it, I'm probably in Dutch, but so what. I've got no other alternatives.

March 7, 1989
Dawn Rose Rockwell Kent Herbert

DET. STURGIS: That's it.

MR. TOKARIK: Are we supposed to be impressed? Decoded hocus-pocus? You know this is totally inadmissible.

DET. STURGIS: If you say so.

MR. TOKARIK: Come on, Chip, let's get out of here—Chip?

MR. JONES: Uh-huh.

DET. STURGIS: Sure you wanna go? There's more.

MR. TOKARIK: We've heard quite enough.

DET. STURGIS: Suit yourself, Counselor. But don't waste your time asking for bail. D.A.'s filing Murder One as we speak.

MR. TOKARIK: Murder One! That's outrageous. Who's the victim?

DET. STURGIS: Dawn Herbert.

MR. TOKARIK: Murder One? On the basis of that fantasy?

DET. STURGIS: On the basis of eyewitness testimony, Counselor. Collaborator testimony. Upstanding citizen named Karl Sobran. You do have a thing for your students, don't you, Prof.

MR. TOKARIK: Who?

DET. STURGIS: Ask the prof.

MR. TOKARIK: I'm asking you, Detective.

DET. STURGIS: Karl Edward Sobran. We've got a windbreaker with blood on it and a confession implicating your client. And Sobran's credentials are impeccable. Bachelor's degree in interpersonal violence from Soledad, postgraduate training from numerous other institutions. Your client hired him to kill Ms. Herbert and make it look like a sex thing. Not much of a challenge, because Sobran likes to get violent with women—did time for rape and assault. His last paid vacation was for larceny and he spent it up in the Ventura County Jail. That's where old Professor Chip, here, met him. Volunteer tutoring—a class project his sociology students were doing. Sobran got an A. Old Chip sent a letter recommending parole, calling Sobran graduate-school material and promising to keep him under his wing. Sobran got out and enrolled at West Valley Community College as a sociology major. What he did to Dawn— What was that, Prof? Fieldwork?

MR. TOKARIK: This is the most ridiculous thing I've ever heard of.

DET. STURGIS: D.A. doesn't think so.

MR. TOKARIK: The D.A. is totally politically motivated. If my client was any other Jones, we wouldn't even be sitting here.

DET. STURGIS: Okay . . . have a nice day. Steve?

DET. MARTINEZ: See y'all.

MR. TOKARIK: Coded disks, the alleged testimony of a convicted felon—absurd.

DET. STURGIS: Ask your client if it's absurd.

MR. TOKARIK: I'll do no such thing. Let's go, Chip. Come on.

MR. JONES: Can you get me bail, Tony?

MR. TOKARIK: This isn't the place to—

MR. JONES: I want out of this place, Tony. Things are piling up. I've got papers to grade.

MR. TOKARIK: Of course, Chip. But it may take—

DET. STURGIS: He's not going anywhere and you know it, Counselor. Level with him.

MR. JONES: I want out. This place is depressing. I can't concentrate.

MR. TOKARIK: I understand, Chip, but—

MR. JONES: No buts, Tony. I want out. A l'extérieur. O.U.T.

MR. TOKARIK: Of course, Chip. You know I'll do everything I—

MR. JONES: I want out, Tony. I'm a good person. This is totally Kafkaesque.

DET. STURGIS: Good person, huh? Liar, torturer, murderer . . . Yeah, I guess if you don't count those minor technicalities, you're up for sainthood, Junior.

MR. JONES: I am a good person.

DET. STURGIS: Tell that to your daughter.

MR. JONES: She's not my daughter.

MR. TOKARIK: Chip—

DET. STURGIS: Cassie's not your daughter?

MR. JONES: Not strictly speaking, Detective. Not that it's relevant—I wouldn't hurt anyone's child.

DET. STURGIS: She's not yours?

MR. JONES: No. Even though I've raised her as if she were. All the responsibility but none of the ownership.

DET. MARTINEZ: Whose is she, then?

MR. JONES: Who knows? Her mother's such a compulsive roundheels, jumps anything with a— In pants. God only knows who the father is. I sure don't.

DET. STURGIS: By "her mother" you're referring to your wife? Cindy Brooks Jones.

MR. JONES: Wife in name only.

MR. TOKARIK: Chip—

MR. JONES: She's a barracuda, Detective. Don't believe that innocent exterior. Pure predator. Once she snagged me, she reverted to type.

DET. STURGIS: What type is that?

MR. TOKARIK: I'm calling this session to a halt right now. Any further questions are at your legal risk, Detective.

DET. STURGIS: Sorry, Chip. Your legal beagle, here, says zip the lip.

MR. JONES: I'll talk to whom I want, when I want, Tony.

MR. TOKARIK: For God's sake, Chip—

MR. JONES: Shut up, Tony. You're growing tedious.

DET. STURGIS: Better listen to him, Prof. He's the expert.

MR. TOKARIK: Exactly. Session ended.

DET. STURGIS: Whatever you say.

MR. JONES: Stop infantilizing me—all of you. I'm the one stuck in this hellhole. My rights are the ones being abridged. What do I have to do to get out of here, Detective?

MR. TOKARIK: Chip, at this point there's nothing you can do—

MR. JONES: Then what do I need you for? You're fired.

MR. TOKARIK: Chip—

MR. JONES: Just shut up and let me get a thought out, okay?

MR. TOKARIK: Chip, I can't in good conscience—

MR. JONES: You don't have a conscience, Tony. You're a lawyer. Quoth the Bard: "Let's kill all the lawyers." Okay? So just hold on . . . okay . . . Listen, you guys are cops—you understand street people, how they lie. That's the way Cindy is. She lies atavistically—it's an ingrained habit. She fooled me for a long time because I loved her—"When my love swears that she is made of truth, I do believe her, though I know she lies." Shakespeare—everything's in Shakespeare. Where was I . . . ?

MR. TOKARIK: Chip, for your own sake—

MR. JONES: She's amazing, Detective. Could charm the bark off a tree. Serve me dinner and smile and ask me how my day had been—and an hour before, she was in our marital bed, screwing the pool man. The pool man, for God's sake. We're talking urban legend here. But she lived it.

DET. STURGIS: By "the pool man" you're referring to Greg Worley of ValleyBrite Pool Service?

MR. JONES: Him, others—what's the difference? Carpenters, plumbers, anything in jeans and a tool belt. No trouble getting tradesmen out to our place—oh, no. Our place was Disneyland for every blue-collar cocksman in town. It's a disease, Detective. She can't help herself. Okay, rationally, I can understand that. Ungovernable impulses. But she destroyed me in the process. I was the victim.

MR. TOKARIK: (unintelligible)

DET. STURGIS: What's that, Counselor?

MR. TOKARIK: I register my objection to this entire session.

MR. JONES: Suppress your ego, Tony. I'm the victim—don't exploit me for your ego. That's my problem in general—people tend to take advantage of me because they know I'm fairly naïve.

DET. STURGIS: Dawn Herbert do that?

MR. JONES: Absolutely. That folderol you read was absolute fantasy. She was a dope addict when I found her. I tried to help her and she paid me back with paranoia.

DET. STURGIS: What about Kristie Kirkash?

MR. JONES: (unintelligible)

DET. STURGIS: What's that, Prof?

MR. JONES: Kristie's my student. Why? Does she say it's more than that?

DET. STURGIS: Actually she does.

MR. JONES: Then she's lying—another one.

DET. STURGIS: Another what?

MR. JONES: Predator. Believe me, she's old beyond her years. I must attract them. What happened with Kristie is that I caught her cheating on a test and was working with her on her ethics. Take my advice and don't accept anything she says at face value.

DET. STURGIS: She says she rented a post office box for you out in Agoura Hills. You have the number handy, Steve?

DET. MARTINEZ: Mailboxes Plus, Agoura, box number 1498.

MR. JONES: That was for research.

DET. STURGIS: What kind of research?

MR. JONES: I've been thinking of a possible project: pornography research—recurrent images in an overly organized society—as a form of ritual. Obviously, I didn't want material sent to my home or my campus office—you get on pervert lists, and I didn't want a flood of garbage coming in. So Kristie rented the POB for me.

DET. STURGIS: Any reason you didn't rent it yourself?

MR. JONES: I was busy, Kristie lived out there, and it just seemed convenient.

DET. STURGIS: Any reason you rented it under the name of Ralph Benedict, M.D.? A physician who's been dead for two and a half years and just happened to have treated your wife's aunt for diabetes?

MR. TOKARIK: Don't answer that.

DET. STURGIS: Any reason you had medical apparatus shipped out to that post office box using Ralph Benedict, M.D.'s name and medical license number?

MR. TOKARIK: Don't answer that.

DET. STURGIS: Any reason you had insulin and Insuject insulin-delivery systems, such as the one we found in your hand in your daughter's hospital room, shipped to that post office box in Ralph Benedict, M.D.'s name?

MR. TOKARIK: Don't answer that.

MR. JONES: Ridiculous. Cindy knew about the POB, too. I gave her my spare key. She must have used it for that.

DET. STURGIS: She says she didn't.

MR. JONES: She's lying.

DET. STURGIS: Okay, but even so, why'd *you* use Benedict's name to *get* the box? It's your name on the application form.

MR. TOKARIK: Don't answer that.

MR. JONES: I want to—I want to clear my name, Tony. In all honesty, Detective, I can't really answer that one. It must have been subconscious. Cindy must have mentioned Benedict's name—yes, I'm sure she did. As you said, he was her aunt's doctor, she talked about him a lot, and it stuck in my mind—so when I needed a name for the box, it just popped into my head.

DET. STURGIS: Why'd you need an alias in the first place?

MR. JONES: I already explained that. For the pornography— some of the stuff I received was really disgusting.

DET. STURGIS: Your wife says she knew nothing about the box.

MR. JONES: Of·course she does. She's lying. Really, Detective, it's all a matter of context—seeing things in a different light, using a new lens.

DET. STURGIS: Uh-huh.

MR. TOKARIK: Now what are you pulling out?

DET. STURGIS: I think it's obvious. This is a mask.

MR. TOKARIK: I fail to see—

MR. JONES: No big deal. It's from the carnival—Delta Psi's carnival. They dressed me up as a witch. I kept the mask for a souvenir.

DET. STURGIS: Kristie Kirkash kept it. You gave it to her last week and told her to keep it.

MR. JONES: So?

DET. STURGIS: So I think you put this on when you injected Cassie. So you'd look like a woman—the wicked witch.

MR. TOKARIK: Ridiculous.

MR. JONES: I agree with you there, Tony.

DET. STURGIS: A souvenir, huh? Why'd you give it to Kristie?

MR. JONES: She's a Delta Psi. I thought the sorority would like to have it.

DET. STURGIS: Considerate.

MR. JONES: I'm their faculty adviser. What's the big—

DET. STURGIS: You have a thing for your students, don't you? That's how you met your wife, isn't it? She was your student.

MR. JONES: It's not unusual—the teacher-student relationship . . .

DET. STURGIS: What about it?

MR. JONES: Often . . . sometimes it leads to intimacy.

DET. STURGIS: You tutor her, too? Your wife?

MR. JONES: As a matter of fact, I did. But she was hopeless—not very bright at all.

DET. STURGIS: But you married her anyway. How come? A smart guy like you.

MR. JONES: I was smitten—"this spring of love."

DET. STURGIS: You met in the spring?

MR. JONES: It's a quotation—

DET. STURGIS: Shakespeare?

MR. JONES: As a matter of fact, yes. I fell deeply in love and was taken advantage of. A romantic nature. My bête noire.

DET. STURGIS: What about Karl Sobran? He take advantage of you too?

MR. JONES: With Karl it was different—with him, ironically, I wasn't naïve. I knew what he was, right away, but I felt I could help him channel his impulses.

DET. STURGIS: What did you know he was?

MR. JONES: Classic antisocial sociopath. But contrary to popular belief, those types don't lack consciences. They merely suspend them at their convenience—read Samenow. As a police officer, you really should. Where was I? Karl. Karl is very bright. I was hoping to direct his intelligence in a constructive manner.

DET. STURGIS: Like murder for hire?

MR. TOKARIK: Don't answer that.

MR. JONES: Stop sighing, Tony. That's ridiculous. Of course not. Did Karl actually say that?

DET. STURGIS: How else would I know about him, Prof?

MR. JONES: Ludicrous. But he is a sociopath—don't forget that. Genetic liar. At worst I'm guilty of underestimating him—not realizing how truly dangerous he was. As much as I didn't respect Dawn as a human being, I was horrified to find out she was murdered. If I'd known, I'd never have written that letter to Karl's parole board. Never have . . . Oh, my God.

DET. STURGIS: Never have what?

MR. JONES: Talked idly to Karl.

DET. STURGIS: About Dawn?

MR. TOKARIK: Don't answer that.

MR. JONES: You're sighing again—it's very wearisome, Tony. Yes, about her, as well as other things. I'm afraid I must have thrown out idle comments about Dawn that Karl must have misinterpreted horribly.

DET. STURGIS: What kinds of comments?

MR. JONES: Oh, no, I can't believe he actually— How she was harassing me. He misunderstood. God, what a horrible misunderstanding!

DET. STURGIS: You're saying he misunderstood your comments and killed her on his own?

MR. JONES: Believe me, Detective, the thought makes me sick. But it's an inescapable conclusion.

DET. STURGIS: What exactly did you tell Sobran about Dawn?

MR. JONES: That she was someone from my past who was bothering me.

DET. STURGIS: That's it?

MR. JONES: That's it.

DET. STURGIS: There was no solicitation? To kill or hurt her?

MR. JONES: Absolutely not.

DET. STURGIS: But there was payment, Prof. Two thousand dollars that Sobran deposited in his account the day after her murder. He had some of it in his pocket when I arrested him. He says he got it from you.

MR. JONES: No problem. I've been helping Karl for a long time—so he could get on his feet, wouldn't have to revert.

DET. STURGIS: Two thousand dollars?

MR. JONES: Sometimes I get a little loose with the purse strings. It's an occupational hazard.

DET. STURGIS: Of being a sociology professor?

MR. JONES: Of growing up wealthy—it can be a real curse, you know. That's why I always tried to live my life as if the money didn't exist. Keeping my life-style unpretentious— keeping away from all the things that have the potential to corrupt.

DET. STURGIS: Like real estate deals?

MR. JONES: My investments were for them—Cindy and the kids. I wanted them to have some kind of financial stability, because teaching school sure won't give you that. That was before I realized what she was doing.

DET. STURGIS: By "doing," you mean sexual behavior?

MR. JONES: Exactly. With everything that walked in through the door. The children weren't even mine, but I took care of them anyway. I'm a soft touch—it's something I need to work on.

DET. STURGIS: Uh-huh . . . Was Chad yours?

MR. JONES: Not a chance.

DET. STURGIS: How do you know?

MR. JONES: One look at him. He was the spitting image of a roofer we had working out on the tract. Spitting image— total clone.

DET. STURGIS: Is that why you killed him?

MR. JONES: Don't be tedious, Detective. Chad died of sudden infant death syndrome.

DET. STURGIS: How can you be sure?

MR. JONES: Textbook case. I read up on it—SIDS—after the little guy died. Trying to understand—to work it through. It was a horrible time for me. He wasn't my flesh and blood, but I still loved him.

DET. STURGIS: Okay, let's move on. Your mother. Why'd you kill her?

MR. TOKARIK: I object!

MR. JONES: You fuck—

DET. STURGIS: See, I did some studying, too—

MR. JONES: You fat fu—

MR. TOKARIK: I object! I most strenuously object to thi—

DET. STURGIS: —trying to understand you, Prof. Talked to people all about your mom. You'd be amazed at how willing people are to talk once someone's down—

MR. JONES: You are stupid. You are psychotic and . . . and . . . egregiously stupid and ignorant. I should have known better than to bare my soul to someone like—

MR. TOKARIK: Chip—

DET. STURGIS: One thing they all agree on was that old Mom was a hypochondriac. Healthy as a horse but convinced she was terminally ill. One person I spoke to said her bedroom was like a hospital room—that she actually had a hospital bed. With the little table? All these pills and syrups lying around. Needles too. Lots of needles. She stick herself, or get you to do it?

MR. JONES: Oh, God . . .

MR. TOKARIK: Take my handkerchief, Chip. Detective, I demand that you cease this line of questioning.

DET. STURGIS: Sure. Bye.

MR. JONES: She was the one who did the sticking! Herself and me—she hurt me! Vitamin B-12 shots twice a day. Protein shots. Antihistamine shots, even though I wasn't allergic to anything! My bottom was her fucking pincushion! Antibiotics the minute I coughed. Tetanus shots if I got a scrape. I was the Azazel goat—cod liver oil and castor oil, and if I threw it up, I had to clean it up and to take a double dosage. She could always get hold of medicine because she used to be a nurse—that's how she met him. Army hospital, he was wounded at Anzio—big hero. She took care of him, but to me she was a sadistic maniac—you have no idea what it was like!

DET. STURGIS: Sounds like no one protected you.

MR. JONES: No one! It was a living hell. Every day brought a new surprise. That's why I hate surprises. Hate them. Detest them.

DET. STURGIS: You prefer everything planned out, huh?

MR. JONES: Organization. I like organization.

DET. STURGIS: Sounds like your dad let you down.

MR. JONES: (laughs) That's his hobby.

DET. STURGIS: So you go your own way.

MR. JONES: Mother's the— Necessity's the mother of invention. (laughs) Thank you, Herr Freud.

DET. STURGIS: Getting back to mom for a minute—

MR. JONES: Let's not.

DET. STURGIS: The way she died—Valium O.D., plastic bag over the head—guess we'll never prove it wasn't suicide.

MR. JONES: That's because it was. And that's all I have to say about that.

DET. STURGIS: Want to say anything about why you hung two pictures she painted in your house but really low to the ground? What was that, a symbolic demeaning or something?

MR. JONES: I have nothing to say about that.

DET. STURGIS: Uh-huh . . . yeah . . . So what you're trying to tell me is, you're the victim and this is all a big misunderstanding.

MR. JONES: (unintelligible)

DET. STURGIS: What?

MR. JONES: Context, Detective. Context.

DET. STURGIS: New lens.

MR. JONES: Exactly.

DET. STURGIS: Your reading up on sudden infant death was because you were trying to understand your . . . Chad's death?

MR. JONES: Exactly.

DET. STURGIS: Did you read up on Munchausen syndrome by proxy because you were trying to understand Cassie's illnesses?

MR. JONES: As a matter of fact, I did. Research is what I'm trained to do, Detective. All the experts seemed to be baffled by Cassie's symptoms. I figured I'd learn what I could.

DET. STURGIS: Dawn Herbert said you were once pre-med.

MR. JONES: Very briefly. I lost interest.

DET. STURGIS: Why?

MR. JONES: Too concrete, no imagination involved. Doctors are really nothing more than glorified plumbers.

DET. STURGIS: So . . . you read up on Munchausen syndrome—doing the old professor thing.

MR. JONES: (laughs) What can I tell you? In the end we all revert. . . . It was a revelation, believe me. Learning about the syndrome. Not that I ever imagined, in the beginning, that Cindy might be doing something to her— Perhaps I was too slow to suspect, but my own childhood . . . too painful. I suppose I repressed. But then . . . when I read . . .

DET. STURGIS: What? Why are you shaking your head?

MR. JONES: It's hard to talk about . . . so cruel . . . You think you know someone and then . . . But the fit— everything started to fit. Cindy's history. Her obsession with health. The techniques she must have used . . . disgusting.

DET. STURGIS: Such as?

MR. JONES: Smothering to simulate asphyxia. Cindy was always the one who got up when Cassie cried—she only called me when things got bad. Then those terrible GI— gastrointestinal—problems and fevers. Once I saw something brown in Cassie's baby bottle. Cindy said it was organic apple juice and I believed her. Now I realize it must have been some sort of fecal matter. Poisoning Cassie with her own filth so that she'd get an infection but it would be an autologous one—self-infection, so that no foreign organism would show up on the blood tests. Disgusting, isn't it?

DET. STURGIS: That it is, Prof. What's your theory on the seizures?

MR. JONES: Low blood sugar, obviously. Overdose of insulin. Cindy knew all about insulin, because of her aunt. I guess I should have figured it out—she talked about her aunt's diabetes all the time, wouldn't let Cassie have any junk food—but it really didn't sink in. I guess I really didn't want to believe it, but . . . the evidence. I mean, at some point one simply has to stop denying, doesn't one? But still . . . Cindy had—*has*—her frailties, and sure, I was furious with her for her sexual acting-out. But her own child . . .

DET. STURGIS: Hers, only.

MR. JONES: Yes, but that's beside the point. Who wants to see any child suffer?

DET. STURGIS: So you went over to the university and pulled medical articles out of the SAP data bank.

MR. JONES: (unintelligible)

DET. STURGIS: What's that?

MR. JONES: No more questions, okay? I'm getting a little tired.

DET. STURGIS: Did I say something that offended you?

MR. JONES: Tony, make him stop.

MR. TOKARIK: Session ended.

DET. STURGIS: Sure. Absolutely. But I just don't get it. We're having a good talk, all convivial, and then all of a sudden I say something about the SAP data bank—that great computerized system they've got, where you can pull articles right off the computer and Xerox them? Something just click about that, Professor? Like the fact that professors can open an account and get an itemized monthly bill?

MR. TOKARIK: My client and I have no idea what you're talking abou—

DET. STURGIS: Steve?

DET. MARTINEZ: Here you go.

MR. TOKARIK: Ah, more tricks from the police bag.

DET. STURGIS: Here. You look at it, Counselor. The articles with the red stars are on sudden infant death. Check the dates your client and Ms. Kirkash pulled 'em out of the computer. Six months before Chad died. The blue ones are on

Munchausen syndrome. Check those dates and you'll see he pulled those two months after Cassie was born—long before her symptoms started. To me that spells premeditation, don't you think, Counselor? Though I have enjoyed the little comedy routine he's just done for us—maybe the fellas on cell block will enjoy it, too. Hell, maybe you can get him off High-Power and into the main population, Counselor. So he can teach those sociopaths some sociology—what do you say? What's that?

MR. JONES: (unintelligible)

MR. TOKARIK: Chip—

DET. STURGIS: Are those tears I see, Chipper? Poor baby. Speak up—I can't hear you.

MR. JONES: Let's deal.

DET. STURGIS: Deal? For what?

MR. JONES: Reduced charges: assault—assault with a deadly weapon. That's all you've got evidence of, anyway.

DET. STURGIS: Your client wants to negotiate, Counselor. I suggest you advise him.

MR. TOKARIK: Don't say anything, Chip. Let me handle this.

MR. JONES: I want to deal, goddamit! I want out!

DET. STURGIS: What do you have to deal with, Chipper?

MR. JONES: Information—hard facts. Things my dad's been doing. Real murder. There was a doctor at the hospital named Ashmore—he must have been bothering my dad about something. Because I overheard my dad and one of his lackeys—a worm named Novak—I heard them talking about it when I went to visit my dad at his house. They were in the library and didn't know I was standing right outside the door—they never paid much attention to me. They were saying this guy, this doctor, would have to be handled. That with all the security problems at the hospital it shouldn't be a problem. I didn't really think much of it, but then a month later, Ashmore was murdered in the hospital parking lot. So there had to be a connection, right? I'm sure my dad had him killed. Take a close look at it—believe me, it'll make all this nonsense look trivial.

DET. STURGIS: All this folderol, huh?

MR. JONES: Believe me, just investigate.

DET. STURGIS: Selling the old man down the river, huh?

MR. JONES: He never did a thing for me. Never protected me—not once, not a single time!

DET. STURGIS: Hear that, Counselor? There's your defense: a bad childhood. Bye, Chip. C'mon, Steve.
DET. MARTINEZ: See y'all in court.
MR. JONES: Wait—
MR. TOKARIK: Chip, there's no nee—

END OF TAPE

37

The indictment made the third page of a news-thin Saturday paper. The headline was PROFESSOR CHARGED WITH MURDER AND CHILD ABUSE, and an old college photo of Chip was included. In it, he looked like a happy hippie; the article described him as a "sociological researcher and recipient of several teaching awards." The mandatory sample of disbelieving colleagues was quoted.

Next week's story swallowed that one up: Chuck Jones and George Plumb's arrests for conspiracy to commit the murder of Laurence Ashmore.

A co-conspirator named Warren Novak—one of the gray accountants—had cut a deal and was telling all, including the fact that Plumb had instructed him to draw cash out of a hospital account to pay a hired killer. The man who'd actually cracked Ashmore's skull was described as a former bodyguard for Charles Jones named Henry Lee Kudey. A photo showed him being escorted to jail by an unnamed federal agent. Kudey was big and heavy and sloppy-looking and appeared to have just woken up. The marshal was blond and wore black-framed spectacles. His face was a nearly equilateral triangle. As a Western Peds Security guard he'd called himself A. D. Sylvester.

I wondered why a government agent would be doing the arresting on a homicide until I came to the final paragraph: Federal charges against Chuck Jones and his gang for "alleged financial wrongdoings based upon a lengthy government probe" were imminent. Anonymous "federal officials" were quoted. The names Huenengarth and Zimberg never appeared.

At four o'clock on a Tuesday, I made my fourth attempt to reach Anna Ashmore. The first three times, no one had answered at the house on Whittier Drive. This time, a man did.

"Who's calling?" he said.

"Alex Delaware. I'm on the staff at Western Pediatric Hospital. Paid a condolence call last week and just wanted to see how she's doing."

"Oh. Well, this is her attorney, Nathan Best. She's doing as well as can be expected. Left for New York last night to visit with some old friends."

"Any idea when she'll be back?"

"I'm not sure she will."

"Okay," I said. "If you speak to her, give her my best."

"All right. What did you say your name was?"

"Delaware."

"Are you a doctor?"

"Psychologist."

"You wouldn't be in the market for some bargain real estate, would you, Doctor? The estate will be divesting itself of several properties."

"No, thanks."

"Well, if you know someone who is, tell them. Bye."

At five o'clock, I stuck to a recently acquired routine and drove to a small white house on a shady dead-end street in West L.A., just east of Santa Monica.

This time Robin came along with me. I parked and got out. "Shouldn't be long."

"Take your time." She pushed the seat back, put her feet up on the dash, and began sketching pearl-inlay designs on a piece of Bristol board.

As usual, the house was curtained. I walked up the path of railroad ties that split the lawn. Vermilion-and-white petunias struggled in the borders. A Plymouth Voyager van was parked in the driveway. Behind it was a dented copper-colored Honda. The heat was really settling in and the air felt thick and greasy. I couldn't detect any breeze. But something was causing the bamboo chimes over the doorway to clank.

I knocked. The peephole slid open and a pretty blue eye filled it. The door swung back and Vicki Bottomley stood aside and let me pass. She wore a lime-green nurse's smock over white stretch pants. Her hair was sprayed tight. A pumpkin-colored mug was in her hand.

"Coffee?" she said. "There's a little left."

"No, thanks. How's it going today?"

"Seems to be better, actually."

"Both of them?"

"Mostly the little one—she's really come out of her shell. Running around like a real little bandit."

"Good."

"Talking to herself, too—is that okay?"

"I'm sure it is."

"Yeah. That's what I thought."

"What's she talking about, Vicki?"

"Can't make it out—mostly babbling. She looks happy enough, though."

"Tough little kid," I said, walking in.

"Most kids are. . . . She's looking forward to seeing you."

"That so?"

"Yup. I mentioned your name and she smiled. 'Bout time, huh?"

"Sure is. Must have earned my stripes."

"Got to, with the little ones."

"How's she sleeping?"

"Good. Cindy's not sleeping so good, though. I keep hearing her get up and turn on the TV a bunch of times every night. Maybe the Valium withdrawal, huh? Though I don't notice any other symptoms."

"Maybe that, or just plain anxiety."

"Yeah. Last night she fell asleep in front of the TV, and I woke her and sent her back to her room. But she'll be okay. Doesn't have much choice, does she?"

"Why's that?"

"Being a mother."

The two of us began walking through the living room. White walls, beige carpet, brand-new furniture barely out of the rental warehouse. The kitchen was to the left. Straight ahead were sliding glass doors that had been left wide open. The backyard was a strip of Astroturfed patio followed by real grass, pale in comparison. An orange tree heavy with ripening fruit served as a centerpiece. At the rear was a scallop-topped redwood fence backed by phone wires and the roofline of the neighboring garage.

Cassie sat on the grass, sucking her fingers while inspecting a pink plastic doll. Doll clothes were strewn on the grass. Cindy sat nearby, cross-legged.

Vicki said, "Guess so."

"What's that?"

"Guess you've earned your stripes."

"Guess we both have."

"Yeah . . . You know I wasn't too happy having to take that lie detector."

"I can imagine."

"Answering all those questions—being *thought* of like that." She shook her head. "That was really hurtful."

"The whole thing was hurtful," I said. "He set it up that way."

"Yeah . . . I guess he knocked us all around—using my bunnies. They should have capital punishment for people like that. I'm gonna *enjoy* getting up on the stand and telling the world about *him*. When do you think that'll happen—the trial?"

"Probably within a few months."

"Probably . . . Okay, have fun. Talk to you later."

"Any time, Vicki."

"Any time what?"

"Any time you want to talk."

"I'll bet." She grinned. "I'll just bet. You and me talky-talking—wouldn't that be a hoot?"

She slapped me lightly on the back and turned around. I stepped out onto the patio.

Cassie looked at me, then returned to the naked doll. She was barefoot and had on red shorts and a pink T-shirt patterned with silver hearts. Her hair was topknotted and her face was grimy. She appeared to have gained a little weight.

Cindy uncrossed her legs and stood without effort. She wore shorts, too. The skimpy white ones I'd seen at her house, below a white T-shirt. Her hair was loose and brushed straight back from her forehead. She'd broken out a bit on her cheeks and chin, and tried to patch it with makeup.

"Hi," she said.

"Hi." I smiled and got down on the ground with Cassie. Cindy stood there for a moment, then walked into the house. Cassie turned to watch her, lifted her chin and opened her mouth.

"Mommy'll be right back," I said, and lifted her onto my lap.

She resisted for a moment. I let go. When she made no attempt to get off, I put one hand around her soft little waist and held her. She didn't move for a while; then she said, "Ho-ee."

"Horsey ride?"

"Ho-ee."

"Big horsey or little horsey?"

"Ho-ee."

"Okay, here we go, little horsey." I bounced her gently. "Gid-dyap."

"Gi-ap."

She bounced harder and I moved my knee a little faster. She giggled and threw her arms up into the air. Her topknot tickled my nose on each assent.

"Giii-ahp! Giii-*ahhp*!"

When we stopped, she laughed, scrambled off my lap, and toddled toward the house. I followed her into the kitchen. The room was half the size of the one on Dunbar Drive and furnished with tired-looking appliances. Vicki stood by the sink, one arm elbow-deep in a chromium coffeepot.

She said, "Well, look what the wind blew in." The arm in the pot kept rotating.

Cassie ran to the refrigerator and tried to pull it open. She wasn't successful and began to fuss.

Vicki put the pot down, along with a piece of scouring cloth, and placed her hands on her hips. "And what do *you* want, young lady?"

Cassie looked up at her and pointed to the fridge.

"We have to *talk* to get things around here, Miss Jonesy."

Cassie pointed again.

"Sorry, I don't understand pointy-language."

"Eh!"

"What kind of *eh*? Potato or tomato?"

Cassie shook her head.

"Lamb or jam?" said Vicki. "Toast or roast, juice or moose?"

Giggle.

"Well, what is it? An ice cream or a sunbeam?"

"Eye-ee."

"What's that? Speak up."

"Eye-ee!"

"I *thought* so."

Vicki opened the freezer compartment and took out a quart container.

"Mint chip," she said to me, frowning. "Frozen toothpaste, if you ask me, but she loves it—all the kids do. You want some?"

"No, thanks."

Cassie danced a quick little two-step of anticipation.

"Let's sit down at the table, young lady, and eat like a human being."

Cassie toddled to the table. Vicki put her on a chair, then pulled a tablespoon out of a drawer and began to scoop ice cream.

"Sure you don't want some?" she asked me.

"I'm sure, thanks."

Cindy came in, drying her hands on a paper towel.

"Snack time, Mom," said Vicki. "Probably ruin her dinner, but she did pretty good on lunch. Okay with you?"

"Sure," said Cindy. She smiled at Cassie, kissed the top of her head.

"I cleaned out the coffeepot," said Vicki. "Down to the dregs. Want some more?"

"No, I'm fine."

"Probably go out later to Von's. Need anything?"

"No, I'm fine, Vicki. Thanks."

Vicki set a bowl of ice cream in front of Cassie and pressed the round part of the spoon into the green, speckled mass.

"Let me soften this up—then you can go at it."

Cassie licked her lips again and bounced in her chair. "Eye-ee!"

Cindy said, "Enjoy, sweetie-pie. I'll be outside if you need me."

Cassie waved bye-bye and turned to Vicki.

Vicki said, "Eat up. Enjoy yourself."

I went back outside. Cindy was standing against the fence. Dirt was clumped up around the redwood slats and she imbedded her toes in it.

"God, it's hot," she said, brushing hair out of her eyes.

"Sure is. Any questions today?"

"No . . . not really. She seems to be fine. . . . I guess it'll be . . . I guess when he's on trial is when it's going to be hard, right? All the attention."

"Harder for you than her," I said. "We'll be able to keep her out of the limelight."

"Yeah . . . I guess so."

"Not that the press won't try to get pictures of both of you. It may mean moving around a bit—more rented houses—but she can be shielded."

"That's okay—that's all I care about. How's Dr. Eves?"

"I spoke to her last night. She said she'd be coming by this evening."

"When's she leaving for Washington?"

"Couple of weeks."

"Was moving something she planned or just . . ."

"You'd have to ask her that," I said. "But I know it didn't have anything directly to do with you."

"Directly," she said. "What does that mean?"

"Her moving was personal, Cindy. Nothing to do with you or Cassie."

"She's a nice lady—kind of . . . intense. But I liked her. I guess she'll be coming back for the trial."

"Yes, she will."

A citrus smell drifted over from the orange tree. White blossoms dusted the grass at the tree's base, fruit that would never be. She opened her mouth to speak, but shielded her lips with her hand instead.

I said, "You suspected him, didn't you?"

"Me? I— Why do you say that?"

"The last couple of times we talked, before the arrest, I felt you wanted to tell me something but were holding back. You just had that same look now."

"I— It really wasn't *suspicion*. You just wonder—I started to wonder, that's all."

She stared at the dirt. Kicked it again.

"When did you start wondering?" I said.

"I don't know—it's hard to remember. You think you know someone and then things happen. . . . I don't know."

"You're going to have to talk about all of it, eventually," I said. "For lawyers and policemen."

"I know, I know, and it scares me, believe me."

I patted her shoulder. She moved away and hit the fence with her back. The boards vibrated.

"I'm sorry," she said. "I just don't want to think about that now. It's just too . . ."

She looked down at the dirt again. It wasn't until I saw the tears drip from her face and dot the soil that I realized she was crying.

I reached out and held her. She resisted, then relented, leaning her full weight against me.

"You think you know someone," she said, between sobs. "You think you— You think someone loves you and they're . . . and then . . . your whole world falls apart. Everything you thought was real is just . . . *fake*. Nothing— Everything's wiped out. I . . . I . . ."

I could feel her shaking.

Pausing for breath, she said "I" again.

"What is it, Cindy?"

"I— It's . . ." Shaking her head. Her hair brushing against my face.

"It's okay, Cindy. Tell me."

"I should have— It didn't make sense!"

"What didn't?"

"The time— He was . . . *he* was the one who found Chad. *I* was always the one who got up when Chad cried or was sick. *I* was the mother—that was *my* job. He *never* got up. But that night he *did*. I didn't hear a thing. I couldn't *understand* that. Why didn't I hear a *thing? Why?* I *always* heard when my babies cried. I was always getting up all the *time* and letting him *sleep*, but this time I *didn't*. I should have *known!*"

She punched my chest, growled, rubbed her head against my shirt as if trying to grind her pain away.

"I should've known it was wrong when he came to get me and told me Chad didn't look good. Didn't *look* good! He was *blue!* He was . . . I went in and found him *lying* there—just lying there, not moving. His color . . . it was . . . all . . . It was wrong! He *never* was the one to get up when they cried! It was *wrong*. It was *wrong*— I should have . . . I should have known from the beginning! I could have . . . I . . ."

"You couldn't have," I said. "No one could have known."

"I'm the *mother!* I *should* have!"

Tearing away from me, she kicked the fence, hard.

Kicked it again, even harder. Began slapping the boards with the flats of her hands.

She said, "Ohhh! Oh, God, oh!" and kept striking out.

Redwood dust rained down on her.

She gave out a wail that pierced the heat. Pushed herself up against the fence, as if trying to force herself through it.

I stood there, smelling oranges. Planning my words and my pauses and my silences.

When I got back to the car, Robin had filled the board with designs and was studying them. I got behind the wheel and she put them back in her folio.

"You're *drenched*," she said, wiping sweat from my face. "Are you okay?"

"Hanging in. The heat." I started the car.

"No progress?"

"Some. It's going to be a marathon."

"You'll make it to the finish."

"Thanks," I said. Hanging a three-point turn, I drove away.

Halfway down the block I pulled over to the curb, jammed the transmission into PARK, leaned across the seat, and kissed her hard. She flung both arms around me and we held each other for a long time.

A loud "ahem" broke us apart.

We looked up and saw an old man watering his lawn with a dribbling hose. Watering and scowling and mumbling. He wore a wide-brimmed straw hat with a ragged crown, shorts, rubber sandals. Bare-chested—his teats sagged like those of a woman wasted by famine. His upper arms were stringy and sunburnt. The hat shadowed a pouchy, sour face but couldn't conceal his disgust.

Robin smiled at him.

He shook his head and the water from his hose arced and sprayed the sidewalk.

One of his hands gave a dismissive wave.

Robin stuck her head out the window and said, "Whatsamatter, don't you approve of true love?"

"Goddam *kids*," he said, turning his back on us.

We drove away without thanking him.

To my daughter, Rachel.
Brains, beauty, grace, wit, style.
And a heart of gold.

———————

Special thanks to
Sheriff's Deputy Kurt Ebert

1

It came in a plain brown wrapper.

Padded envelope, book rate, book sized. I assumed it was an academic text I'd forgotten ordering.

It went on to the mail table, along with Monday's bills and announcements of scholarly seminars in Hawaii and St. Croix. I returned to the library and tried to figure out what I was going to do in ten minutes when Tiffani and Chondra Wallace showed up for their second session.

A year ago their mother had been murdered by their father up on a ridge in the Angeles Crest Forest.

He told it as a crime of passion and maybe he was right, in the very worst sense. I'd learned from court documents that absence of passion had never been a problem for Ruthanne and Donald Dell Wallace. She'd never been a strong-willed woman, and despite the ugliness of their divorce, she had held on to "love feelings" for Donald Dell. So no one had been surprised when he cajoled her into taking a night ride with sweet words, the promise of a lobster dinner, and good marijuana.

Shortly after parking on a shaded crest overlooking the forest, the two of them got high, made love, talked, argued, fought, raged, and finally clawed at one another. Then Donald Dell took his buck knife to the woman who still bore his name, slashed and stabbed her thirty-three times, and kicked her corpse out of his pickup, leaving behind an Indian-silver clip stuffed with cash and his membership card in the Iron Priests motorcycle club.

A docket-clearing plea bargain landed him in Folsom Prison on a five to ten for second-degree murder. There he was free to hang out in the yard with his meth-cooking Aryan Brotherhood bunkmates, take an auto mechanics course he could have taught, accrue good behavior brownie points in the chapel, and bench press until his pectorals threatened to explode.

Four months into his sentence, he was ready to see his daughters.

The law said his paternal rights had to be considered.

An L.A. family court judge named Stephen Huff—one of the better ones—asked me to evaluate. We met in his chambers on a September morning and he told me the details while drinking ginger ale and stroking his bald head. The room had beautiful old oak paneling and cheap country furniture. Pictures of his own children were all over the place.

"Just when does he plan on seeing them, Steve?"

"Up at the prison, twice a month."

"That's a plane ride."

"Friends will chip in for the fare."

"What kind of friends?"

"Some idiocy called The Donald Dell Wallace Defense Fund."

"Biker buddies?"

"Vroom vroom."

"Meaning it's probably amphetamine money."

His smile was weary and grudging. "Not the issue before us, Alex."

"What's next, Steve? Disability payments because he's stressed out being a single parent?"

"So it smells. So what else is new? Talk to the poor kids a few times, write up a report saying visitation's injurious to their psyches, and we'll bury the issue."

"For how long?"

He put down the ginger ale and watched the glass raise wet circles on his blotter. "I can kibosh it for at least a year."

"Then what?"

"If he puts in another claim, the kids can be reevaluated and we'll kibosh it again. Time's on their side, right? They'll be getting older and hopefully tougher."

"In a year they'll be ten and eleven, Steve."

He picked at his tie. "What can I tell you, Alex? I don't want to see these kids screwed up, either. I'm asking you to evaluate because you're tough-minded—for a shrink."

"Meaning someone else might recommend visitation?"

"It's possible. You should see some of the opinions your colleagues render. I had one the other day, said the fact that a mother was severely depressed was good for the kid—teach her the value of true emotions."

"Okay," I said. "But I want to do a real evaluation, not some rubber stamp. Something that may have some use for them in the future."

"Therapy? Why not? Sure, do whatever you want. You are now shrink of record. Send your bill straight to me and I'll see you get paid within fifteen working days."

"Who's paying, our leather-clad friends?"

"Don't worry, I'll make sure they pay up."

"Just as long as they don't try to deliver the check in person."

"I wouldn't worry about it, Alex. Those types shy away from insight."

The girls arrived right on time, just as they had last week, linked, like suitcases, to the arms of their grandmother.

"Well, here they are," Evelyn Rodriguez announced. She remained in the entry and pushed them forward.

"Morning," I said. "Hi, girls."

Tiffani smiled uneasily. Her older sister looked away.

"Have an easy ride?"

Evelyn shrugged, twisted her lips and untwisted them. Maintaining her grip on the girls, she backed away. The girls allowed themselves to be tugged, but unwillingly, like nonviolent protesters. Feeling the burden, Evelyn let go. Crossing her arms over her chest, she coughed and looked away from me.

Rodriguez was her fourth husband. She was Anglo, stout, bottom-heavy, an old fifty-eight, with dimpled elbows and knuckles, nicotine skin, and lips as thin and straight as a surgical incision. Talk came hard for her and I was pretty sure it was a character trait that preceded her daughter's murder.

This morning she wore a sleeveless, formless blouse—a faded

mauve and powder blue floral print that reminded me of a decorative tissue box. It billowed, untucked, over black stretch jeans piped with red. Her blue tennis shoes were speckled with bleach spots. Her hair was short and wavy, corn colored above dark roots. Earring slits creased her lobes but she wore no jewelry. Behind bifocals, her eyes continued to reject mine.

She patted Chondra's head, and the girl pressed her face against a thick, soft arm. Tiffani had walked into the living room and was staring at a picture on the wall, tapping one foot fast.

Evelyn Rodriguez said, "Okay, then, I'll just wait down in the car."

"If it gets too hot, feel free to come up."

"The heat don't bother me." She raised a forearm and glanced at a too-small wristwatch. "How long we talking about this time?"

"Let's aim for an hour, give or take."

"Last time was twenty minutes."

"I'd like to try for a little longer today."

She frowned. "Okay . . . can I smoke down there?"

"Outside the house? Sure."

She muttered something.

"Anything you'd like to tell me?" I said.

"Me?" She freed one finger, poked a breast, and smiled. "Nah. Be good, girlies."

Stepping out on the terrace, she closed the door. Tiffani kept examining the picture. Chondra touched the doorknob and licked her lips. She had on a white Snoopy T-shirt, red shorts, and sandals with no socks. A paper-wrapped Fruit Roll-Up extended from one pocket of the shorts. Her arms and legs were pasty and chubby, her face broad and puggish, topped by white-blond hair drawn into very long, very tight pigtails. The hair gleamed, almost metallic, incongruous above the plain face. Puberty might turn her pretty. I wondered what else it might bring.

She nibbled her lower lip. My smile went unnoticed or unbelieved.

"How are you, Chondra?"

She shrugged again, kept her shoulders up, and looked at the floor. Ten months her sister's senior, she was an inch shorter and seemed less mature. During the first session, she hadn't said a word, content to sit with her hands in her lap as Tiffani talked on.

"Do anything fun this week?"

She shook her head. I placed a hand on her shoulder and she

went rigid until I removed it. The reaction made me wonder about some kind of abuse. How many layers of this family would I be able to peel back?

The file on my nightstand was my preliminary research. Before-bed reading for the strong stomached.

Legal jargon, police prose, unspeakable snapshots. Perfectly typed transcripts with impeccable margins.

Ruthanne Wallace reduced to a coroner's afternoon.

Wound depths, bone rills . . .

Donald Dell's mug shot, wild-eyed, black-bearded, sweaty.

"And then she got mean on me—she knew I didn't handle mean but that didn't stop her, no way. And then I just—you know—lost it. It shouldn'ta happened. What can I say?"

I said, "Do you like to draw, Chondra?"

"Sometimes."

"Well, maybe we'll find something you like in the playroom."

She shrugged and looked down at the carpet.

Tiffani was fingering the frame of the picture. A George Bellows boxing print. I'd bought it, impulsively, in the company of a woman I no longer saw.

"Like the drawing?" I said.

She turned around and nodded, all cheekbones and nose and chin. Her mouth was very narrow and crowded with big, misaligned teeth that forced it open and made her look perpetually confused. Her hair was dishwater, cut institutionally short, the bangs hacked crookedly. Some kind of food stain specked her upper lip. Her nails were dirty, her eyes an unremarkable brown. Then she smiled and the look of confusion vanished. At that moment she could have modeled, sold anything.

"Yeah, it's cool."

"What do you especially like about it?"

"The fighting."

"The fighting?"

"Yeah," she said, punching air. "Action. Like WWA."

"WWA," I said. "World Wrestling?"

She pantomimed an uppercut. "Pow poom." Then she looked at her sister and scowled, as if expecting support.

Chondra didn't move.

"Pow poom," said Tiffani, advancing toward her. "Welcome to WWA fighting, I'm Crusher Creeper and this is the Red Viper in a grudge match of the century. *Ding!*" Bell-pull pantomime.

She laughed, nervously. Chondra chewed her lip and tried to smile.

"Aar," said Tiffani, coming closer. She pulled the imaginary cord again. "Ding. Pow poom." Hooking her hands, she lurched forward with Frankenstein-monster unsteadiness. "Die, Viper! *Aaar!*"

She grabbed Chondra and began tickling her arms. The older girl giggled and tickled back, clumsily. Tiffani broke free and began circling, punching air. Chondra started chewing her lip, again.

I said, "C'mon, guys," and took them to the library. Chondra sat immediately at the play table. Tiffani paced and shadowboxed, hugging the periphery of the room like a toy on a track, muttering and jabbing.

Chondra watched her, then plucked a sheet of paper off the top of a stack and picked up a crayon. I waited for her to draw, but she put the crayon down and watched her sister.

"Do you guys watch wrestling at home?" I said.

"Roddy does," said Tiffani, without breaking step.

"Roddy's your grandmother's husband?"

Nod. Jab. "He's not our grampa. He's Mexican."

"He likes wrestling?"

"Uh-huh. Pow poom."

I turned to Chondra. She hadn't moved. "Do you watch wrestling on TV, too?"

Shake of the head.

"She likes *Surfriders*," said Tiffani. "I do, too, sometimes. And *Millionaire's Row*."

Chondra bit her lip.

"*Millionaire's Row*," I said. "Is that the one where rich people have all sorts of problems?"

"They *die*," said Tiffani. "Sometimes. It's really for real." She put her arms down and stopped circling. Coming over to us, she said, "They die because money and materials are the roots of sins and when you lay down with Satan, your rest is never peaceful."

"Do the rich people on *Millionaire's Row* lay down with Satan?"

"Sometimes." She resumed her circuit, striking out at unseen enemies.

"How's school?" I asked Chondra.

She shook her head and looked away.

"We didn't start yet," said Tiffani.

"How come?"

"Gramma said we didn't have to."

"Do you miss seeing your friends?"

Hesitation. "Maybe."

"Can I talk to Gramma about that?"

She looked at Chondra. The older girl was peeling the paper wrapper off a crayon.

Tiffani nodded. Then: "Don't do that. They're his."

"It's okay," I said.

"You shouldn't destroy other people's stuff."

"True," I said. "But some things are meant to be used up. Like crayons. And these crayons are here for you."

"Who bought them?" said Tiffani.

"I did."

"Destroying's Satan's work," said Tiffani, spreading her arms and rotating them in wide circles.

I said, "Did you hear that in church?"

She didn't seem to hear. Punched the air. "*He* laid down with Satan."

"Who?"

"*Wallace.*"

Chondra's mouth dropped open. "Stop," she said, very softly.

Tiffani came over and dropped her arm over her sister's shoulder. "It's okay. He's not our dad anymore, remember? Satan turned him into a bad spirit and he got all his sins wrapped up like one. Like a big burrito."

Chondra turned away from her.

"Come on," said Tiffani, rubbing her sister's back. "Don't worry."

"Wrapped up?" I said.

"Like one," she explained to me. "The Lord counts up all your good deeds and your sins and wraps them up. So when you die, He can look right away and know if you go up or down. *He's* going down. When he gets there, the angels'll look at the package and know all he done. And then he'll burn."

She shrugged. "That's the truth."

Chondra's eyes pooled with tears. She tried to remove Tiffani's arm from her shoulder, but the younger girl held fast.

"It's okay," said Tiffani. "You got to talk about the truth."

"Stop," said Chondra.

"It's okay," Tiffani insisted. "You got to talk to him." She looked at me. "So he'll write a good book for the judge and *he'll* never get out."

Chondra looked at me.

I said, "Actually, what I write won't change how much time he spends in jail."

"Maybe," insisted Tiffani. "If your book tells the judge how evil he is, then *maybe* he could put him in longer."

"Was he ever evil to you?"

No answer.

Chondra shook her head.

Tiffani said, "He *hit* us."

"A lot?"

"Sometimes."

"With his hand or something else?"

"His hand."

"Never a stick or a belt or something else?"

Another headshake from Chondra. Tiffani's was slower, reluctant.

"Not a lot, but sometimes," I said.

"When we were bad."

"Bad?"

"Making a mess—going near his bike—he hit Mom more. Right?" Prodding Chondra. "He *did*."

Chondra gave a tiny nod, grabbed the crayon, and started peeling again. Tiffani watched but didn't stop her.

"That's why we left him," she said. "He hit her all the time. And then he came after her with lust and sin in his heart and killed her—tell the judge that, you're rich, he'll listen to you!"

Chondra began crying. Tiffani patted her and said, "It's okay, we got to."

I got a tissue box. Tiffani took it from me and wiped her sister's eyes. Chondra pressed the crayon to her lips.

"Don't eat it," said Tiffani. "It's poison."

Chondra let go and the crayon flew out of her hand and landed on the floor. Tiffani retrieved it and placed it neatly alongside the box.

Chondra was licking her lips. Her eyes were closed and one soft hand was fisted.

"Actually," I said, "it's not poisonous, just wax with color in it. But it probably doesn't taste too good."

Chondra opened her eyes. I smiled and she tried to smile, producing only a small rise in one corner of her mouth.

Tiffani said, "Well, it's not food."

"No, it isn't."

She paced some more. Boxed and muttered.

I said, "Let me go over what I told you last week. You're here because your father wants you to visit him in jail. My job is to find out how you feel about that, so I can tell the judge."

"Why doesn't the judge ask *us*?"

"He will," I said. "He'll be talking to you, but first he wants me to—"

"Why?"

"Because that's my job—talking to kids about their feelings. Finding out how they really—"

"We don't *want* to see him," said Tiffani. "He's an insument of Satan."

"An—"

"An *insument*! He laid all down with Satan and became a sinful spirit. When he dies, he's going to burn in hell, that's for sure."

Chondra's hands flew to her face.

"Stop!" said Tiffani. She rushed over to her sister, but before she got there, Chondra stood and let out a single, deep sob. Then she ran for the door, swinging it open so hard it almost threw her off balance.

She caught it, then she was out.

Tiffani watched her go, looking tiny and helpless.

"You got to tell the truth," she said.

I said, "Absolutely. But sometimes it's hard."

She nodded. Now her eyes were wet.

She paced some more.

I said, "Your sister's older but it looks like you take care of her."

She stopped, faced me, gave a defiant stare, but seemed comforted.

"You take good care of her," I said.

Shrug.

"That must get hard sometimes."

Her eyes flickered. She put her hands on her hips and jutted her chin.

"It's okay," she said.

I smiled.

"She's my sister." She stood there, knocking her hands against her legs.

I patted her shoulder.

She sniffed, then walked away.

"You got to tell the truth," she said.

"Yes, you do."

Punch, jab. "Pow poom . . . I wanna go home."

Chondra was already with Evelyn, sharing the front seat of the thirty-year-old, plum-colored Chevy. The car had nearly bald blackwalls and a broken antenna. The paint job was homemade, the color nothing GM had ever conceived. One edge of the car's rear bumper had been broken and it nearly scraped the ground.

I got to the driver's window as Tiffani made her way down the steps from the landing. Evelyn Rodriguez didn't look up. A cigarette drooped from her lips. A hardpack of Winstons sat on the dashboard. The driver's half of the windshield was coated with greasy fog. Her fingers were busy tying a lanyard keychain. The rest of her was inert.

Chondra was pressed up against the passenger door, legs curled beneath her, staring at her lap.

Tiffani arrived, making her way to the passenger side while keeping her eyes on me. Opening the rear door, she dove inside.

Evelyn finally took her eyes off her work, but her fingers kept moving. The lanyard was brown and white, a diamond stitch that reminded me of rattlesnake skin.

"Well, that was quick," she said. "Close that door now, don't kill the battery."

Tiffani scooted over and slammed the door.

I said, "The girls haven't started school yet."

Evelyn Rodriguez looked at Tiffani for a second, then turned to me. "That's right."

"Do you need any help with that?"

"Help?"

"Getting them started. Is there some kind of problem?"

"Nah, we been busy—I make 'em read at home. They're okay."

"Planning to send them soon?"

"Sure, when things calm down—so what's next? They have to come again?"

"Let's try again tomorrow. Same time okay?"

"Nope," she said. "Matter of fact, it isn't. Got things to do."

"What's a good time for you, then?"

She sucked the cigarette, adjusted her glasses, and placed the lanyard on the seat. Her slash lips twitched, searching for an expression.

"There are no good times. All the good times already been rolled."

She started the car. Her lips were trembling and the cigarette bobbed. She removed it and turned the wheel sharply without shifting out of park. The car was low on steering fluid and shrieked in protest. The front tires swung outward and scraped the asphalt.

"I'd like to see them again fairly soon," I said.

"What for?"

Before I could answer, Tiffani stretched herself out along the back seat, belly down, and began kicking the door panel with both feet.

"Cut that *out!*" said Mrs. Rodriguez, without looking back. "What for?" she repeated. "So we can be told what to do and how to do it, as usual?"

"No, I—"

"The problem is, things are upside *down. Nonsensical.* Those that *should* be dead *aren't,* and those that *are,* shouldn't *be.* No amount of talking's gonna change that, so what's the difference? Upside down, completely, and now I got to be a mama all over again."

"He can write a book," said Tiffani. "So that—"

Evelyn cut her off with a look. "You don't worry yourself about things. We got to be heading back—if there's time, I'll get you an ice cream."

She yanked the gear lever down. The Chevy grumbled and bucked, then drove off, rear bumper flirting with the road.

I stood there a while, sucking up exhaust fumes, then went back up to the house, returned to the library, and charted:

"*Strong resistance to eval. on part of m.g.m. T overtly angry, hos-*

tile to father, talks in terms of sin, retribution. C still not communic. Will follow."

Profound.

I went to the bedroom and retrieved Ruthanne Wallace's police file.

Big as a phone book.

"Trial transcripts," Milo had said, hefting it as he handed it over. "Sure isn't because of any hotshot detection. Your basic moron murder."

He'd pulled it from Foothill Division's CLOSED files, filling my request without question. Now I flipped pages, not knowing why I'd asked for it. Closing the folder, I took it into the library and crammed it down into a desk drawer.

Ten in the morning and I was already tired.

I went to the kitchen, loaded some coffee into the machine, and started going through the mail, discarding junk mail, signing checks, filing paper, then coming to the brown-wrapped package that I'd assumed was a book.

Slitting the padded envelope, I stuck my hand in, expecting the bulk of a hardcover. But my fingers touched nothing and I reached deeper, finally coming upon something hard and smooth. Plastic. Wedged tightly in a corner.

I shook the envelope. An audiocassette fell out and clattered onto the table.

Black, no label or markings on either side.

I examined the padded envelope. My name and address had been typed on a white sticker. No zip code. No return address either. The postmark was four days old, recorded at the Terminal Annex.

Curious, I took the tape into the living room, slipped it into the deck, and sank back onto the old leather couch.

Click. A stretch of static-fuzzed nothing started me wondering if this was some sort of practical joke.

Then a shock of noise killed that theory and made my chest tighten.

A human voice. Screaming.

Howling.

Male. Hoarse. Loud. Wet—as if gargling in pain.

Unbearable pain. A terrible incoherence that went on and on as I sat there, too surprised to move.

A throat-ripping howling interspersed with trapped-animal panting.

Heavy breathing.

Then more screams—louder. Ear-clapping expulsions that had no shape or meaning . . . like the soundtrack from the rancid core of a nightmare.

I pictured a torture chamber, shrieking black mouths, convulsing bodies.

The howling bore through my head. I strained to make out words amid the torrent but heard only the pain.

Louder.

I leaped up to turn down the volume on the machine. Found it already set low.

I started to turn it off, but before I could, the screaming died.

More static-quiet.

Then a new voice.

Soft. High-pitched. Nasal.

A child's voice:

> Bad love. Bad love.
> Don't give me the bad love.

Child's timbre—but with no childish lilt.

Unnaturally flat—*robot*like.

> Bad love. Bad love.
> Don't give me the bad love . . .

Repeating it. Three times. Four.

A chant, Druidish and mournful—so oddly metallic.

Almost like a prayer.

> Bad love. Bad love . . .

No. Too hollow for prayer—too faithless.

Idolatrous.

A prayer for the dead.

By the dead.

2

I turned the recorder off. My fingers were stiff from clenching, my heart thumped, and my mouth was dry.

Coffee smells drew me to the kitchen. I filled a cup, returned to the living room, and rewound the tape. When the spool filled, I turned the volume to near inaudible and pressed PLAY. My gut knotted in anticipation. Then the screams came on.

Even that soft, it was hideous.

Someone being *hurt*.

Then the child's chant again, even worse in replay. The robotic drone conjured a gray face, sunken eyes, a small mouth barely moving.

Bad love. Bad love . . .

What had been done to strip the voice so completely of emotion?

I'd heard that kind of voice before—on the terminal wards, in holding cells and shelters.

Bad love . . .

The phrase was vaguely familiar, but why?

I sat there for a long time, trying to remember, letting my coffee go cold and untouched. Finally I got up, ejected the tape, and took it into the library.

Down into the desk drawer, next to Ruthanne's file.

Dr. Delaware's Black Museum.

My heart was still chopping away. The screams and chants replayed themselves in my mind.

The house felt too empty. Robin was not due back from Oakland till Thursday.

At least she hadn't been home to hear it.

Old protective instincts.

During our years together I'd worked hard at shielding her from the uglier aspects of my work. Eventually, I realized I'd erected the barrier higher than it needed to be and had been trying to let her in more.

But not this. No need for her to hear this.

I sank lower into my desk chair, wondering what the damned thing meant.

Bad love . . . what should I do about it?

A sick joke?

The child's voice . . .

Bad love . . . I knew I'd heard the phrase before. I repeated it out loud, trying to trigger a memory. But the words just hovered, chattering like bats.

A psychological phrase? Something out of a textbook?

It did have a psychoanalytic ring.

Why had the tape been sent to *me*?

Stupid question. I'd never been able to answer it for anyone else.

Bad love . . . most likely something orthodox Freudian. Melanie Klein had theorized about good breasts and bad breasts—perhaps there was someone out there with a sick sense of humor and a side interest in neo-Freudian theory.

I went to my bookshelves, pulled out a dictionary of psychological terms. Nothing. Tried lots of other books, scanning indexes.

Not a clue.

I returned to the desk.

A former patient taunting me for services poorly rendered?

Or something more recent—Donald Dell Wallace, festering up in Folsom, seeing me as his enemy and trying to play with my head?

His attorney, a dimwit named Sherman Bucklear, had called me several times before I'd seen the girls, trying to convince me his client was a devoted father.

"It was Ruthanne neglected them, Doctor. Whatever else Donald Dell did, he cared about them."

"How was he on child support?"

"Times are rough. He did the best he could—does that prejudice you, Doctor?"

"I haven't formed an opinion yet, Mr. Bucklear."

"No, of course not. No one's saying you should. The question is, are you willing to form one at all or do you have your mind made up just because of what Donald Dell did?"

"I'll spend time with the girls. Then I'll form my opinion."

" 'Cause there's a lot of potential for prejudice against my client."

"Because he murdered his wife?"

"That's exactly what I mean, Doctor—you know, I can always bring in my own experts."

"Feel free."

"I feel very free, Doctor. This is a free country. You'd do well to remember that."

Other experts. Was this bit of craziness an attempt to intimidate me so that I'd drop out of the case and clear the way for Bucklear's hired guns? Donald Dell's gang, the Iron Priests, had a history of bullying rivals in the meth trade, but I still didn't see it. How could anyone assume I'd make a connection between screams and chants and two little girls?

Unless this was only the first step in a campaign of intimidation. Even so, it was almost clownishly heavyhanded.

Then again, Donald Dell's leaving his ID at the murder scene didn't indicate finesse.

I'd consult an expert of my own. Dialing the West L.A. police station, I was connected to Robbery-Homicide, where I asked for Detective Sturgis.

Milo was out of the office—no big surprise. He'd endured a demotion and six months' unpaid suspension for breaking the jaw of a homophobic lieutenant who'd put his life in danger, then a butt-numbing year as a computer clerk at Parker Center. The department had hoped inertia would finally drive him into disability retirement; the LAPD still denied the existence of gay cops, and Milo's very presence was an assault upon that ostrich logic. But he'd stuck it out and finally gotten back into active service as a Detective II. Back on the streets now, he was making the most of it.

"Any word when he'll be back?" I asked the detective who answered.

"Nope," he said, sounding put upon.

I left my name. He said, "Uh-huh," and hung up.

I decided nothing further could be gained by worrying, changed into a T-shirt, shorts, and sneakers, and trotted out the front door, ready for a half-hour run, knees be damned.

Bounding down the steps, I jogged across the motor court, passing the spot where Evelyn Rodriguez's car had leaked oil. Just as I rounded the eugenia hedge that blocked my house from the old bridle path winding above the Glen, something stepped in front of me and stopped.

And stared.

A dog, but I'd never seen one like it.

Small dog—about a foot high, maybe twice that in length. Short, black coat brindled with yellow hairs. A lot of muscle crammed into the compact package; its body bulged and gleamed in the sunlight. It had thick legs, a bull neck, a barrel chest, and a tight, tucked-in belly. Its head was disproportionately wide and square, its face flat, deeply wrinkled, and pendulously jowled.

Somewhere between frog, monkey, and extraterrestrial.

A strand of drool dangled from its flews.

It continued to look me straight in the eye, arching forward, as if ready to spring. Its tail was an inch of stub. Male. Neutered.

I stared back. He snorted and yawned, showing big, sharp, white teeth. A banana-sized tongue curled upward and licked meaty lips.

A diamond of white hair in the center of his chest throbbed with cardiac excitement. Around his beefy neck was a nailhead-studded collar, but no tag.

"Hi, fella."

His eyes were light brown and unmoving. I thought I detected a softness that contradicted the fighter's stance.

Another yawn. Purple maw. He panted faster and remained rooted in place.

Some kind of bulldog or mini-mastiff. From the crust around his eyes and the heaving of his chest, the early autumn heat wasn't doing him any good. Not a pug—considerably bigger than a pug, and the ears stood upright, like those of a Boston terrier—in fact, he looked a bit like a Boston. But shorter and a lot heavier—a Boston on steroids.

An exotic dwarf fighter bred to go for the kneecaps, or a pup that would turn massive?

He yawned again and snorted harshly.

We continued to face off.

A bird chirped.

The dog cocked his head toward the sound for half a second, then peered back at me. His eyes were preternaturally alert, almost human.

He licked his lips. The drool strand stretched, broke, and fell to the pavement.

Pant, pant, pant.

"Thirsty?"

No movement.

"Friend or foe?"

Another display of teeth that seemed more smile than snarl, but who knew?

Another moment of standoff, then I decided letting something this pint-sized obstruct me was ridiculous. Even with the bulk, he couldn't weigh more than twenty or twenty-five pounds. If he did attack, I could probably punt-kick him onto the Glen.

I took a step forward, then another.

The dog came toward me deliberately, head lowered, muscles meshing, in a rolling, pantherish gait. Wheezing.

I stopped. He kept going.

I lifted my hands out of mouth range, suddenly aware of my exposed legs.

He came up to me. Up to my legs. Rubbed his head against my shin.

His face felt like hot suede. Too hot and dry for canine health.

I reached down and touched his head. He snorted and panted faster, letting his tongue loll. I lowered my hand slowly and dangled it, receiving a long lick on the palm. But my skin remained bone dry.

The pants had turned into unhealthy-sounding clicks.

He tremored for a second, then worked his tongue over his arid face.

I kneeled and patted his head again, feeling a flat plate of thick, ridged bone beneath the glossy coat. He looked up at me with a bulldog's sad-clown dignity. The crust around his eyes looked calcified. The folds of his face were encrusted, too.

The nearest water source was the garden-hose outlet near the pond. I stood and gestured toward it.

"Come on, buster—hydration."

The dog strained but stayed in place, head cocked, letting out raspy breaths that grew faster and faster and began to sound labored. I thought I saw his front legs quaver.

I began walking to the garden. Heard soft pads and looked behind me to see him following a few paces behind. Keeping to the left—a trained heeler?

But as I opened the gate to the pond, he hung back, remaining well outside the fence.

I went in. The pond water was greening due to the heat, but still clear. The koi were circling lazily. A couple of them saw me and approached the rim for feeding—babies who'd survived the surprise spawn of two summers ago. Most were over a foot long now. A few were colored brilliantly.

The dog just stood there, nose pointed at the water, suffering.

"Come on, pal." I picked up the hose.

Nothing.

Uncoiling a couple of feet, I opened the valve. The rubber hummed between my fingers.

"C'mere. H₂O."

The dog stared through the gateway, panting, gasping, legs bowed with fatigue. But he didn't budge.

"C'mon, what's the problem, sport? Some kind of phobia, or don't you like seafood?"

Blink. He stayed in place. Swayed a bit.

The hose began to dribble. I dragged it out the gate, sprinkling plants as I walked.

The dog stood his ground until the water was an inch from his fleshy mouth. Then he craned his neck and began lapping. Then gulping. Then bathing in it, shaking his head and showering me before opening his maw and heading in for more.

Long time since the last tipple.

He shook and sprayed me again, turned his head away from the water, and sat.

When I returned from replacing the hose, he was still there, settled on his ample haunches.

"What now?" I said.

He ambled up to me, jauntily, a bit of roll in his stride. Putting his head against my leg, he kept it there.

I rubbed him behind the ears and his body went loose. He

stayed relaxed as I used my handkerchief to wipe the crust from his face. When I was through, he let out a grumble of contentment.

"You're welcome."

He put his head against my leg once more, blowing out breath as I petted.

What a morning. I sighed.

He snorted. A reply?

I tried it again, sighing audibly. The dog produced an adenoidal grunt.

"A conversationalist," I said. "Someone talks to you, don't they? Someone cares about you."

Grunt.

"How'd you get here?"

Grumble.

My voice was loud against the quiet of the Glen, harsh counterpoint to the flow of the waterfall.

Nut mail and talking to a dog. This is what it's come to, Delaware.

The dog gazed up at me with a look I was willing to classify as friendship.

You take what you can get.

He watched as I pulled the Seville out of the carport, and when I opened the passenger door, he jumped in as if he owned the vehicle. For the next hour and a half, he looked out the window as I drove around the canyon, watching for LOST DOG posters on trees and talking to neighbors I'd never met. No one belonged to him and no one recognized him, though the checkout girl at the Beverly Glen Market opined that he was "a little stud," and several other shoppers concurred.

While I was there, I bought a few groceries and a small bag of kibble. When I got home, the dog bounced up the stairs after me and watched as I unloaded the staples. I poured the kibble into a bowl and set it on the kitchen floor, along with another bowl of water. The dog ignored it, choosing instead to station himself in front of the refrigerator door.

I moistened the kibble but that had no effect. This time the stubby tail was wagging.

I pointed to the bowl.

The dog began nudging the fridge door and looking up at me. I opened the door and he tried to stick his head in. Restraining him by the collar, I scrounged and found some leftover meatloaf.

The dog jumped away from my grasp, leaping nearly to my waist.

"A gourmet, huh?"

I crumbled some meatloaf into the kibble and mixed it with my fingers. The dog was snarfing before my hand was free, coating my fingers with a slick layer of drool.

I watched him feast. When he finished, he cocked his head, stared at me for a moment, then walked toward the back of the kitchen, circling and sniffing the floor.

"What now? Sorbet to clean your palate?"

He circled some more, walked to the service porch door, and began butting and scratching at the lower panel.

"Ah," I said, bounding up. I unlatched the door and he zipped out. I watched him race down the stairs and find a soft, shaded spot near a juniper bush before lifting his leg.

He climbed back up, looking content and dignified.

"Thank you," I said.

He stared at me until I petted him, then trailed me into the dining room, settling next to my leg, frog face lifted expectantly. I scratched him under his chin and he promptly flipped onto his back, paws upright.

I scratched his belly and he let out a long, low, phlegmy moan. When I tried to stop, one paw pressed down on my hand and bade me continue.

Finally he turned back on his belly and fell asleep, snoring, jowls shaking like mudflaps.

"Someone's got to be looking for you."

I slid the morning paper across the table. Plenty of lost-dog ads in the classifieds, but none of the animals remotely matched the creature stretched out on the floor.

I got animal control's number from information and told the woman who answered it what I'd found.

"He sounds cute," she said.

"Any idea what he is?"

"Not offhand—could be some kind of bulldog, I guess. Maybe a mix."

"What should I do with him?"

"Well," she said, "the law says you have to try to return him. You could bring him in and leave him with us, but we're pretty crowded and I can't honestly tell you he'll get anything more than basic care."

"What if you have him and no one claims him?"

"Well . . . you know."

"What're my alternatives?"

"You could put an ad in the paper—'founds' are sometimes free. You might also want to take him to a vet—make sure he's not carrying anything that could cause you problems."

I thanked her, called the newspaper, and placed the ad. Then I pulled out the Yellow Pages and looked under veterinarians. There was an animal hospital on Sepulveda near Olympic that advertised "walk-ins and emergencies."

I let the the dog sleep for an hour, then took him for another ride.

The clinic was a milky blue, cement-block building set between a wrought iron foundry and a discount clothing barn. The traffic on Sepulveda looked angry, so I carried my guest to the front door, upping the weight estimate to thirty pounds.

The waiting room was empty except for an old man wearing a golf cap, comforting a giant white German shepherd. The dog was prone on the black linoleum floor, weeping and trembling from fright. The man kept saying, "It's okay, Rexie."

I tapped on a frosted glass window and registered, using my name because I didn't know the dog's. Rex was summoned five minutes later, then a college-age girl opened the door and called out, "Alex?"

The bulldog was stretched on the floor, sleeping and snoring. I picked him up and carried him in. He opened one eye but stayed limp.

"What's the matter with Alex, today?" said the girl.

"Long story," I said and followed her to a small exam room outfitted with lots of surgical steel. The disinfectant smell reminded *me* of traumas gone by, but the dog stayed calm.

The vet arrived soon after—a young, crewcut, Asian man in a blue smock, smiling and drying his hands with a paper towel.

"Hi, I'm Dr. Uno—ah, a Frenchie, don't see too many of those."

"A what?"

He one-handed the towel into a waste bin. "A French bull-dog."

"Oh."

He looked at me. "You don't know what he is?"

"I found him."

"Oh," he said. "Well, that's a pretty rare dog you've got there—*someone'll* claim him." He petted the dog. "These little guys are pretty expensive, and this one looks like a good specimen." He lifted his flews. "Well cared for, too—these teeth have been scaled pretty recently and his ears are clean—these upright ears can be receptacles for all kinds of stuff . . . anyway, what seems to be your problem with him?"

"Apart from a fear of water, nothing," I said. "I just wanted him checked out."

"Fear of water? How so?"

I recounted the dog's avoidance of the pond.

"Interesting," said the vet. "Probably means he's been perimeter trained for his own safety. Bulldog pups can drown pretty easily—real heavy boned, so they sink like rocks. On top of that, they have no nose to speak of, so they have trouble getting their head clear. Another patient of mine lost a couple of English bull babies that way. So this guy's actually being smart by shying away."

"He's housebroken and he heels, too," I said.

The vet smiled and I realized something very close to owner's pride had crept into my voice.

"Why don't you put him up here on the table and let's see what else he can do."

The dog was probed, vaccinated, and given a clean bill of health.

"Someone definitely took good care of him," said Uno. "The basic thing to watch out for is heatstroke, specially now, when the temperature is rising. These brachycephalic dogs are really prone to it, so keep him out of the heat."

He handed me some brochures on basic dog care, reiterated the heat danger, and said, "That's about it. Good luck finding the owner."

"Any suggestions along those lines?"

"Put an ad in the paper, or if there's a local Frenchie club, you could try getting in touch with them."

"Do you have a list of club addresses?"

"Nope, sorry, we do mostly ER work. Maybe the AKC—American Kennel Club—could help. They register most of the purebreds."

"Where are they?"

"New York."

He walked me to the door.

"These dogs generally have good temperament?" I said.

He looked down at the dog, who was staring up at us and wagging his stub.

"From the little I've heard and read, what you're seeing right now is pretty much it."

"They ever attack?"

"Attack?" He laughed. "I guess if he got attached to you he might try to protect you, but I wouldn't count on it. They're really not good for much but being a friend."

"Well, that's something," I said.

"Sure it is," he said. "That's where it's at, bottom line, right?"

3

I drove away from the clinic stroking the dog and thinking of the child's voice on the tape. I wasn't hungry but figured I'd need some lunch eventually. Spotting a hamburger stand farther up on Sepulveda, I bought a takeout half-pounder. The aroma kept the dog awake and drooling all the way home, and a couple of times he tried to stick his nose in the bag. Back in the kitchen, he convinced me to part with a third of the patty. Then he carried his booty to a corner, sat, masticated noisily, and promptly went to sleep, chin to the floor.

I phoned my service and found out Milo had called back. This time he answered at Robbery-Homicide. "Sturgis."

"How's it going, Joe Friday?"

"The usual buckets of blood. How's by you?"

I told him about receiving the tape. "Probably just a prank, but imagine getting a kid to do that."

I expected him to slough it off, but he said, " 'Bad love'? That's weird."

"What is?"

"Those exact same words popped up in a case a couple of months ago. Remember that social worker who got murdered at the mental health center? Rebecca Basille?"

"It was all over the news," I said, remembering headlines and sound bites, the smiling picture of a pretty, dark-haired young woman butchered in a soundproof therapy room. "You never said it was your case."

"It wasn't really anyone's case because there was no investigation to speak of. The psycho who stabbed her died trying to take another caseworker hostage."

"I remember."

"I got stuck filling out the paperwork."

"How did 'bad love' pop up?"

"The psycho screamed it when he ran out after cutting Becky. Clinic director was standing in the hall, heard him before she ducked into her office and hid. I figured it was schizo talk."

"It may be something psychological—jargon that he picked up somewhere in the mental health system. 'Cause I think I've heard it, too, but I can't remember where."

"That's probably it," he said. "A kid, huh?"

"A kid chanting in this strange, flat voice. It may be related to a case I'm working on, Milo. Remember that file you got me—the woman murdered by her husband?"

"The biker?"

"He's been locked up for six months. Two months ago he started asking for visitation with his daughters—around the same time as the Basille murder, come to think of it. If Becky's murderer screaming 'bad love' *was* in the news, I guess he could have taken notice and filed it away for future use."

"Intimidate the shrink—maybe remind you of what can happen to therapists who don't behave themselves?"

"Exactly. There'd be nothing criminal in that, would there? Just sending a tape."

"Wouldn't even buy him snack bar demerits, but how could he figure you'd make the connection?"

"I don't know. Unless this is just an appetizer and there's more coming."

"What's this fool's name, again?"

"Donald Dell Wallace."

He repeated it and said, "I never read the file. Refresh me on him."

"He used to hang out with a biker gang called the Iron Priests—small-time Tujunga bunch. In between prison sentences, he worked as a motorcycle mechanic. Dealt speed on the side. I think he's a member of the Aryan Brotherhood."

"Well, there's a character reference for you. Let me see what I find out."

"You think this is something I should worry about?"

"Not really—you might think of locking your doors."

"I already do."

"Congratulations. You going to be home tonight?"

"Yup."

"How's Robin?"

"Fine. She's up in Oakland, giving a seminar—medieval lutes."

"Smart kid, working with inanimate objects. All right, I'll come by, rescue you from your hermitude. If you want me to I can fingerprint the tape, check it against Wallace's. If it's him, we'll report him to his keepers, at least let him know you're not going to roll over."

"Okay—thanks."

"Yeah . . . don't handle it anymore, hard plastic's a real good surface for preservation. . . . *Bad love.* Sounds like something out of a movie. Sci-fi, splatter flick, whatever."

"I couldn't find it in any of my psych books, so maybe that's it. Maybe that's where Becky's murderer got it, too—all of us are children of the silver screen. The tape was mailed from the Terminal Annex, not Folsom. Meaning if Wallace *is* behind it, someone's helping him."

"I can check the rest of his gang, too. At least the ones with records. Don't lose any sleep over it. I'll try to get by around eight. Meanwhile, back to the slaughter."

"Buckets of blood, huh?"

"Big *sloshing* buckets. Every morning I wake up, praise the Lord, and thank Him for all the iniquity—how's that for perverse?"

"Hey," I said, "you love your work."

"Yeah," he said. "Yeah, I do. Demotion never felt so goddamn glorious."

"Department treating you well?"

"Let's not lapse into fantasy. The department's *tolerating* me, because they think they've wounded me *deeply* with their pissanty pay cut and I'll eventually cave in and take disability like every other goldbricking pension junkie. The fact that one night of moonlighting more than makes up for the difference in take-home has eluded the brass. As has the fact that I'm a contrary bastard."

"They're not very observant, are they?"

"That's why they're administrators."

After he hung up, I called Evelyn Rodriguez's house in Sunland. As the phone rang, I pictured the man who'd carved up her daughter playing with a tape recorder in his cell.

No one answered. I put the phone down.

I thought of Rebecca Basille, hacked to death in a soundproof room. Her murder had really gotten to me—gotten to lots of therapists. But I'd put it out of my head until Milo reminded me.

I drummed my fists on the counter. The dog looked up from his empty bowl and stared. I'd forgotten he was there.

What happens to therapists who don't behave themselves . . .

What if Wallace had nothing to do with the tape? Someone else, from my past.

I went into the library and the dog followed. The closet was stacked with boxes of inactive patient files, loosely alphabetized with no strict chronological order, because some patients had been treated at several different time periods.

I put the radio on for background and started with the A's, looking for children whom I'd tagged with psychopathic or antisocial tendencies and cases that hadn't turned out well. Even long-term deadbeats I'd sent to collections.

I made it halfway through. A sour history lesson with no tangible results: nothing popped out at me. By the end of the afternoon, my eyes hurt and I was exhausted.

I stopped reading, realized grumbly snores had overpowered the music. Reaching down, I kneaded the bulldog's muscular neck. He shuddered but remained asleep. A few charts were fanned on the desk. Even if I came up with something suggestive, patient confidentiality meant I couldn't discuss it with Milo.

I returned to the kitchen, fixed kibble and meatloaf and fresh water, watched my companion sup, burp, then circle and sniff. I left the service door open and he bounced down the stairs.

While he was out, I called Robin's hotel in Oakland again, but she was still out.

The dog came back. He and I went into the living room and

watched the evening news. Current events were none too cheerful, but he didn't seem to mind.

The doorbell rang at eight-fifteen. The dog didn't bark, but his ears stiffened and tilted forward and he trailed me to the door, remaining at my heels as I squinted through the peephole.

Milo's face was a wide-angle blur, big and pocked, its paleness turned sallow by the bug light over the doorway.

"Police. Open up or I'll shoot."

He bared his teeth in a Halloween grimace. I unlocked the door and he came in, carrying a black briefcase. He was dressed for work: blue hopsack blazer, gray slacks, white shirt stretched tight over his belly, blue and gray plaid tie tugged loose, suede desert boots in need of new soles.

His haircut was recent, the usual: clipped short at sides and back, long and shaggy on top, sideburns down to the earlobes. Country yokels had looked that way back in the fifties. Melrose Avenue hipsters were doing it nowadays. I doubted Milo was aware of either fact. The black forelock that shadowed his forehead showed a few more gray streaks. His green eyes were clear. Some of the weight he'd lost had come back; he looked to be carrying at least two hundred and forty pounds on his seventy-five inches.

He stared at the dog and said, "*What?*"

"Gee, Dad, he followed me home. Can I keep him?"

The dog gazed up at him and yawned.

"Yeah, I'm bored, too," Milo told him. "What the hell *is* it, Alex?"

"French bulldog," I said. "Rare and pricey, according to a vet. And this one's a damned good specimen."

"Specimen." He shook his head. "Is it civilized?"

"Compared to what you're used to, very."

He frowned, patted the dog gingerly, and got slurped.

"Charming," he said, wiping his hand on his slacks. Then he looked at me. "*Why*, Marlin Perkins?"

"I'm serious—he just showed up this morning. I'm trying to locate the owner, have an ad running in the paper. The vet said he's been well cared for. It's just a matter of time before somebody claims him."

"For a moment I thought this tape stuff had gotten to you and you'd gone out and bought yourself some protection."

"This?" I laughed, remembering Dr. Uno's amusement. "I don't think so."

"Hey," he said, "sometimes bad things come in small packages—for all I know it's trained to go for the gonads."

The dog stood on his hind legs and touched Milo's trousers with his forepaws.

"Down, Rover," he said.

"What's the matter, you don't like animals?"

"Cooked, I do. Didja name it yet?"

I shook my head.

"Then 'Rover' will have to do." He took his jacket off and tossed it onto a chair. "Here's what I've got so far on Wallace. He keeps a low profile in slam and has some associations with the Aryan Brotherhood, but he's not a full member. As for what kind of hardware he's got in his cell, I don't know yet. Now where's the alleged tape?"

"In the alleged tapedeck."

He went over and turned on the stereo. The dog stayed with me.

I said, "You know where the meatloaf comes from, don't you?"

He cocked his head and licked my hand.

Then the screams came on and the hairs rose on the back of his neck.

Hearing it the third time was worse.

Milo's face registered revulsion, but after the sound died, he said nothing. Taking his briefcase over to the deck, he switched it off, ejected the tape, and removed it by inserting a pencil in one of the reel holes.

"Black surface," he muttered. "Ye olde white powder."

Placing the cassette atop the plastic cover of my turntable, he removed a small brush and a vial from the case. Dipping the brush into the vial, he dusted the cassette with a pale, ashlike powder, squinting as he worked.

"Well, looks like we've got some nice ridges and swirls," he said. "But they could all be yours. Your prints are on file with the medical board, right, so I can check?"

"They printed me when I got my license."

"Meaning a week or two going through channels in order to pry it loose from Sacramento—noncriminal stuff's not on PRIN-TRAK yet. You haven't been arrested for anything recently, have you?"

"Nothing I can remember."

"Too bad. Okay, let's get a quick fix on your digits right now."

He took an inkpad and fingerprint form from the case. The dog watched as he inked my fingers and rolled them on the form. The audiocassette was near my hand and I looked at the concentric white patches on its surface.

"Keep that pinkie loose," said Milo. "Feel like a scumbag felon yet?"

"I don't say squat without my lawyer, pig."

He chuckled and handed me a cloth. As I wiped my fingers, he took a small camera out of the case and photographed the prints on the tape. Flipping the cartridge over with the pencil, he dusted, raised more prints on the other side, and took pictures of them, muttering, "Might as well do it right." Then he lowered the cassette into a small box lined with cotton, sealed the container, and put it into the case.

"What do you think?" I said.

He looked at my print form, then at the tape, and shook his head. "They always look the same to me. Let the lab deal with it."

"I meant about the tape. Sound like any movie you know?"

He ran his hand over his face, as if washing without water. "Not really."

"Me neither. Didn't the kid's voice have a brainwashed quality to it?"

"More like brain *dead*," he said. "Yeah, it was ugly. But that doesn't make it real. Far as I'm concerned, it's still filed under B for 'bad joke.' "

"Someone getting a child to chant as a joke?"

He nodded. "We're living in weird times, Doc."

"But what if it *is* real? What if we're dealing with a sadist who's abducted and tortured a child and is telling me about it in order to heighten the kick?"

"The *screamer* was the one who sounded tortured, Alex. And that was an adult. Someone's messing with your head."

"If it's not Wallace," I said, "maybe it's some psychopath picking me as his audience because I treat kids and sometimes my name gets in the papers. Someone who read about Becky's murderer screaming 'bad love' and got an idea. And for all I know, I'm not the only therapist he's contacted."

"Could be. When was the last time you *were* in the papers?"

"This summer—when the Jones case went to trial."

"Anything's possible," he said.

"Or maybe it's more direct, Milo. A former patient, telling me I failed him. I started going through my files, got halfway and couldn't find anything. But who knows? My patients were all children. In most cases I have no idea what kind of adults they turned into."

"If you found anything funny, would you give me the names?"

"Couldn't," I said. "Without some kind of clear danger, I couldn't justify breaking confidentiality."

He scowled. The dog watched him unwaveringly.

"What're *you* staring at?" he demanded.

Wag, wag.

Milo began to smile, fought it, picked up his case, and put a heavy hand on my shoulder.

"Listen, Alex, I still wouldn't lose any sleep over it. Let me take these to the lab right now instead of tomorrow, see if I can get some night-shifter to put some speed on. I'll also make a copy and start a case file—private one, just for my eyes. When in doubt, be a goddamn clerk."

After he left, I tried to read a psychology journal but couldn't concentrate. I watched the news, did fifty pushups, and had another go at my charts. I made it through all of them. Kids' names, vaguely remembered pathologies. No allusions to "bad love." No one I could see wanting to frighten me.

At ten, Robin called. "Hi, honey."

"Hi," I said. "You sound good."

"I am good, but I miss you. Maybe I'll come home early."

"That would be great. Just say when and I'll be at the airport."

"Everything okay?"

"Peachy. We've got a visitor."

I described the bulldog's arrival.

"Oh," she said, "he sounds adorable. Now I definitely want to come home early."

"He snorts and drools."

"How cute. You know, we should get a dog of our own. We're nurturant, right? And you had one when you were a kid. Don't you miss it?"

"My father had one," I said. "A hunting cur that didn't like children. It died when I was five and we never got another, but sure, I like dogs—how about something big and protective?"

"Long as it's also warm and furry."

"What breeds do you like?"

"I don't know—something solid and dependable. Let me think about it and when I get back we can go shopping."

"Sounds good, bowwow."

"We can do other stuff, too," she said.

"Sounds even better."

Just before midnight, I fashioned a bed for the dog out of a couple of towels, placed it on the floor of the service porch, and turned out the light. The dog stared at it, then trotted over to the fridge.

"No way," I said. "Time to sleep."

He turned his back on me and sat. I left for the bedroom. He heeled along. Feeling like Simon Legree, I closed the door on his supplicating eyes.

As soon as I got under the covers I heard scratching, then heavy breathing. Then something that sounded like an old man choking.

I jumped out of bed and opened the door. The dog raced through my feet and hurled himself up on the bed.

"Forget it," I said and put him on the carpet.

He made the choking sound again, stared, and tried to climb up.

I returned him to the floor.

A couple more tries and he gave up, turning his back on me and staying hunkered against the dust ruffle.

It seemed a reasonable compromise.

But when I awoke in the middle of the night, thinking about pain screams and robot chants, he was right next to me, soft eyes full of pity. I left him there. A moment later, he was snoring and it helped put me back to sleep.

4

The next morning I woke up tasting the metal and bite of bad dreams. I fed the dog and called the Rodriguez house again. Still no answer, but this time a machine fed me Evelyn's tired voice over a background of Conway Twitty singing "Slow Hand."

I asked her to call me. She hadn't by the time I finished showering and shaving. Neither had anyone else.

Determined to get outdoors, I left the dog with a big biscuit and walked the couple of miles to the university campus. The computers at the biomed library yielded no references to "bad love" in any medical or psychological journals, and I returned home at noon. The dog licked my hand and jumped up and down. I petted him, gave him some cheese, and received a drool-covered hand by way of thanks.

After boxing my charts, I carried them back to the closet. A single carton had remained on the shelf. Wondering if it contained files I'd missed, I pulled it down.

No patient records: it was crammed with charts and reprints of technical articles I'd set aside as references. A thick roll of papers bound with a rubber band was wedged between the folders. The word "PROFUNDITIES" was scrawled across it, in my handwriting. I remembered myself younger, angrier, sarcastic.

Removing the band from the roll, I flattened the sheaf and inhaled a snootful of dust.

More nostalgia: a collection of articles *I'd* authored, and programs from scientific meetings at which I'd presented papers.

I leafed through it absently until a brochure near the bottom caught my eye. Strong black letters on stiff blue paper, a coffee stain on one corner.

GOOD LOVE/BAD LOVE

*Psychoanalytic Perspectives and
Strategies in a Changing World*

November 28–29, 1979
Western Pediatric Medical Center
Los Angeles, California

A Conference Examining the Relevance
and Application of de Boschian Theory
to Social and Psychobiological Issues

and Commemorating Fifty Years of
Teaching, Research, and Clinical Work by

ANDRES B. DE BOSCH, Ph.D.

Co-sponsored by WPMC
and
The de Bosch Institute and Corrective School,
Santa Barbara, California

Conference Co-Chairs

Katarina V. de Bosch, Ph.D.
Practicing Psychoanalyst and Acting Director,
The de Bosch Institute and Corrective School

Alexander Delaware, Ph.D.
Assistant Professor of Pediatrics
and Psychology, WPMC

Harvey M. Rosenblatt, M.D.
Practicing Psychoanalyst and Clinical Professor of
Psychiatry
New York University School of Medicine

Headshot photos of all three of us. Katarina de Bosch, thin and brooding; Rosenblatt and I, bearded and professorial.

The rest was a list of scheduled speakers—more photos—and details of registration.

"Good Love/Bad Love." I remembered it clearly now. Wondered how I could have forgotten.

Nineteen seventy-nine had been my fourth year on staff at Western Peds, a period marked by long days and longer nights on the cancer ward and the genetic disorders unit, holding the hands of dying children and listening to families with unanswerable questions.

In March of that year, the head of psychiatry and the chief psychologist both chose to go on sabbatical. Though they weren't on speaking terms and the chief never returned, their last official cooperative venture was designating me interim chief.

Slapping my back and grinding their teeth around their pipe bits, they worked hard at making it sound like a stepping-stone to something wonderful. What it had amounted to was more administrative chores and just enough of a temporary pay raise to kick me into the next tax bracket, but I'd been too young to know any better.

Back then, Western Peds had been a prestigious place, and I learned quickly that one aspect of my new job was fielding requests from other agencies and institutions wanting to associate with the hospital. Most common were proposals for jointly sponsored conferences, to which the hospital would contribute its good name and its physical premises in return for continuing-education credits for the medical staff and a percentage of the box office. Of the scores of requests received yearly, a good many were psychiatric or psychological in nature. Of those, only two or three were accepted.

Katarina de Bosch's letter had been one of several I received, just weeks after assuming my new post. I scanned it and rejected it.

Not a tough decision—the subject matter didn't interest me or my staff: the front-line battles we were waging on the wards placed the theorizations of classical psychoanalysis low on our want list. And from my readings of his work, Andres de Bosch was a middleweight analyst—a prolific but superficial writer who'd produced little in the way of original thought and had

parlayed a year in Vienna as one of Freud's students and membership in the French resistance into an international reputation. I
wasn't even sure he was still alive; the letter from his daughter
didn't make it clear, and the conference she proposed had a memorial flavor to it.

I wrote her a polite letter.

Two weeks later I was called in to see the medical director, a
pediatric surgeon named Henry Bork who favored Hickey-Free-
man suits, Jamaican cigars, and sawtooth abstract art, and who
hadn't operated in years.

"Alex." He smiled and motioned to a Breuer chair. A slender
woman was sitting in a matching nest of leather and chrome on
the other side of the room.

She looked to be slightly older than me—early thirties, I
guessed—but her face was one of those long, sallow constructions
that would always seem aged. The beginnings of worry lines suggested themselves at crucial junctures, like a portrait artist's initial
tracings. Her lips were chapped—all of her looked dry—and her
only makeup was a couple of grudging lines of mascara.

Her eyes were large enough without the shadowing, dark,
heavy lidded, slightly bloodshot, close set. Her nose was promi-
nent, down tilted, and sharp, with a small bulb at the tip. Full
wide lips were set sternly. Her legs were pressed together at the
knees, feet set squarely on the floor.

She wore a coarse, black, scallop-necked wool sweater over a
pleated black skirt, stockings tinted to mimic a Caribbean tan, and
black loafers. No jewelry. Her hair was straight, brown, and long,
drawn back very tightly from a low, flat brow, and fastened above
each ear with wide, black, wooden barrettes. A houndstooth jacket
was draped over her lap. Near one shoe was a black leatherette
attaché case.

As I sat down, she watched me, hands resting upon one another, spindly and white. The top one was sprinkled with some
sort of eczematous rash. Her nails were cut short. One cuticle
looked raw.

Bork stepped between us and spread his arms as if preparing
to conduct a symphony.

"Dr. Delaware, Dr. Katarina de Bosch. Dr. de Bosch, Alex Delaware, our acting chief psychologist."

I turned to her and smiled. She gave a nod so tiny I might
have imagined it.

Bork backed away, rested a buttock on his desk, and cupped both his hands over one knee. The desk surface was twenty square feet of lacquered walnut shaped like a surfboard, topped with an antique padded leather blotter and a green marble inkwell. Centered on the blotter was a single rectangle of stiff blue paper. He picked it up and used it to rap his knuckles.

"Do you recall Dr. de Bosch's writing to you suggesting a collaborative venture with your division, Alex?"

I nodded.

"And the disposition of that request?"

"I turned it down."

"Might I ask why?"

"The staff's been asking for things directly related to inpatient management, Henry."

Looking pained, Bork shook his head, then handed the blue paper to me.

A program for the conference, still smelling of printer's ink. Full schedule, speakers, and registration. My name was listed below Katarina de Bosch's as co-chair. My picture below, lifted off the professional staff roster.

My face broiled. I took a deep breath. "Looks like a fait accompli, Henry." I tried to hand him the brochure, but he put his hands back on his knees.

"Keep it for your records, Alex." Standing, he sidled in front of the desk, taking tiny steps, like a man on a ledge. Finally, he managed to get behind the surfboard and sat down.

Katarina de Bosch was inspecting her knuckles.

I considered maintaining my dignity but decided against it. "Nice to know what I'm doing in November, Henry. Care to give me my schedule for the rest of the decade?"

A small, sniffing sound came from Katarina's chair. Bork smiled at her, then turned to me, shifting his lips into neutral.

"An unfortunate misunderstanding, Alex—a snafu. 'Something naturally always fouls up,' right?"

He looked at Katarina again, got nothing in return, and lowered his eyes to the blotter.

I fanned the blue brochure.

"Snafu," Bork repeated. "One of those interim decisions that had to be made during the transition between Dr. Greiloff's and Dr. Franks' sabbaticals and your stepping in. The board offers its regrets."

"Then why bother with a letter of application?"

Katarina said, "Because I'm polite."

"I didn't know the board got involved in scheduling conferences, Henry."

Bork smiled. "Everything, Alex, is the province of the board. But you're right. It's not typical for us to get directly involved in that type of thing. However . . ."

He paused, looked again at Katarina, who gave another tiny nod. Clearing his throat, he began fingering a cellophaned cigar— one of a trio of Davidoffs sharing pocket space with a white silk handkerchief.

"The fact that we *have* gotten involved should tell you something, Alex," he said. His smile was gone.

"What's that, Henry?"

"Dr. de Bosch—*both* Dr. de Bosches are held in extremely high esteem by . . . Western's medical community."

Are. So the old man was still alive.

"I see," I said.

"Yes, indeed." The color had risen in his cheeks, and his usual glibness had given way to something tentative, shaky.

He removed the cigar from his pocket and held it between his index fingers.

From the corner of my eye I saw Katarina. Watching me.

Neither of them spoke; I felt as if the next line was mine and I'd flubbed it.

"High esteem," said Bork finally, sounding more tense.

I wondered what was bugging him, then remembered a rumor of a few years ago. Doctors' dining room gossip, the kind I tried to avoid.

A Bork problem child, the youngest of four daughters. A teenaged chronic truant with learning disorders and a tendency toward sexual experimentation, sent away, two or three summers ago, hush-hush, for some kind of live-in remediation. The family tight-lipped with humiliation.

One of Bork's many detractors had told the story with relish. *The de Bosch Institute and Corrective School . . .*

Bork was watching me. The look on his face told me I shouldn't push it any further.

"Of course," I said.

It sounded hollow. Katarina de Bosch frowned.

But it made Bork smile again. "Yes," he said. "So obviously, we're eager for this conference to take place. Expeditiously. I hope you and Dr. de Bosch will enjoy working together."

"Will I be working with both Drs. de Bosch?"

"My father isn't well," said Katarina, as if I should have known it. "He had a stroke last winter."

"Sorry to hear that."

She stood, smoothed her skirt with brief flogging movements, and picked up her attaché. In the chair she'd seemed tall—willowy—but upright she was only five two or three, maybe ninety-five bony pounds. Her legs were short and her feet pointed out. The skirt hung an inch below her knees.

"In fact, I need to get back to take care of him," she said. "Walk me back to my car, Dr. Delaware, and I'll give you details on the conference."

Bork winced at her imperiousness, then looked at me with some of that same desperation.

Thinking of what he was going through with his daughter, I stood and said, "Sure."

He put the cigar in his mouth. "Splendid," he said. "Thank you, Alex."

She said, "Henry," without looking at him and stomped toward the door.

He rushed from behind his desk and managed to get to it soon enough to hold it open for her.

He was a politician and a hack—a skilled physician who'd lost interest in healing and had lost sight of the human factor. In the coming years he never acknowledged my empathy of that afternoon, never displayed any gratitude or particular graciousness to me. If anything, he became increasingly hostile and obstructive and I came to dislike him intensely. But I never regretted what I'd done.

The moment we were out the door, she said, "You're a behaviorist, aren't you?"

"Eclectic," I said. "Whatever works. Including behavior therapy."

She smirked and began walking very fast, swinging the attaché in a wide, dangerous arc through the crowded hospital corridor. Neither of us talked on the way to the glass doors that fronted the building. She moved her short legs furiously, intent upon maintaining a half-step advantage. When we reached the entrance, she stopped, gripped the attaché with both hands, and waited until I held one of the doors open, just as she'd done with Bork. I pictured her growing up with servants.

Her car was parked right in front, in the NO STOPPING ambulance zone—a brand-new Buick, big and heavy, black with a silver vinyl top, buffed shiny as a general's boot. A hospital security guard was standing watch over it. When he saw her approaching he touched his hat.

Another door held open. I half expected to hear a bugle burst as she slid into the driver's seat.

She started the car with a sharp twist, and I stood there, looking at her through a closed window.

She ignored me, gunned the engine, finally looked at me and raised an eyebrow, as if surprised I was still there.

The window lowered electrically. "Yes?"

"We were supposed to discuss details," I said.

"The *details*," she said, "are, I'll do everything. Don't worry about it, don't complicate things, and it will all fall into place. All right?"

My throat got very tight.

She put the car into drive.

"Yes, *ma'am*," I said, but before the second word was out she'd roared off.

I went back into the hospital, got coffee from a machine near the admittance desk, and took it up to my office, trying to forget about what had happened and determined to focus myself on the day's challenges. Later, seated at my desk, charting the morning's rounds, my hand slipped and some of the coffee spilled on the blue brochure.

I didn't hear from her again until a week before the conference, when she sent a starchily phrased letter inquiring if I cared to deliver a paper. I called and declined and she sounded relieved.

"But it would be nice if you at least welcomed the attendees," she said.

"Would it?"

"Yes." She hung up.

I did show up on the first day to offer brief words of welcome and, unable to escape graciously, remained on stage for the entire morning, with the other co-chair—Harvey Rosenblatt, the psychiatrist from New York. Trying to feign interest as Katarina strode to the podium, wondering if I'd see another side of her, softened for public consumption.

Not that there was much of a public. Attendance was thin— maybe seventy or eighty therapists and graduate students in an auditorium that seated four hundred.

She introduced herself by name and title, then read a prepared speech in a strident monotone. She favored complex, meandering sentences that lost meaning by the second or third twist, and soon the audience was looking glazed. But she didn't seem to care—didn't seem to be talking to anyone but herself.

Reminiscing about her father's glory days.

Such as they were.

Anticipating the symposium, I'd taken the time to review Andres de Bosch's collected writings, and I hadn't raised my opinion of him.

His prose style was clear, but his theories about child rearing —the good love/bad love spectrum of maternal involvement that his daughter had used to title the conference—seemed nothing more than extensions and recombinations of other people's work. A little Anna Freud here, a little Melanie Klein there, tossed with croutons of Winnicott, Jung, Harry Stack Sullivan, Bruno Bettelheim.

He leavened the obvious with clinical anecdotes about the children he'd treated at his school, managed to work both his Vienna pilgrimage and his war experiences into his summaries, name dropping and adopting the overly casual manner of one truly self-impressed.

Emperor's new clothes, and the audience at the conference didn't show any great excitement. But from the rapt look on Faithful Daughter's face, she thought it was cashmere.

By the second day, attendance was down by half and even the speakers on the dais—three L.A.-based analysts—looked unhappy to be there. I might have felt sorry for Katarina, but she seemed unaware of it all, continuing to flash slides of her father—dark-haired and goateed in healthier days—working at a big, carved desk surrounded by talismans and books, drawing in crayon with a young patient, writing in the brandied light of a Tiffany lamp.

Then another batch: posing with his arm around *her*—even as a teenager, she'd looked old, and they could have been lovers— followed by shots of a blanket-swaddled old man sunk low in an electric wheelchair, positioned atop a high, brown bluff. Behind him the ocean was beautiful and blue, mocking his senescence.

A sad variation upon the home-movie trap. The few remaining attendees looked away in embarrassment.

Harvey Rosenblatt seemed especially pained; I saw him shade his eyes and study some scribbled notes that he'd already read from.

A tall, shambling, gray-bearded fellow in his forties, he struck up a conversation with me as we waited for the afternoon session to begin. His warmth seemed more than just therapeutic veneer. Unusually forthcoming for an analyst, he talked easily about his practice in mid-Manhattan, his twenty-year marriage to a psychologist, and the joys and challenges of raising three children. The youngest was a fifteen-year-old boy whom he'd brought with him.

"He's back at the hotel," he said, "watching movies on pay-TV—probably the dirty ones, right? I promised to get back in an hour and take him out to Disneyland—do you have any idea how late they're open?"

"During the winter, I think only till six or so."

"Oh." He frowned. "Guess we'll have to do that tomorrow; hopefully, Josh can deal with it."

"Does he like arcade games?" I said.

"Does a duck quack?"

"Why don't you try the Santa Monica pier. It's open late."

"Okay—that sounds good, thanks. Do they have good hot dogs by any chance?"

"I know they have hot dogs, but I can't vouch for them being gourmet."

He smiled. "Josh is a hot dog connoisseur, Alex." He puffed his cheeks and smoothed his beard. "Too bad about Disneyland. I hate to disappoint him."

"Challenges of parenthood, huh?" I said.

He smiled. "He's a sweet kid. I brought him with me hoping to turn it into a semi-vacation for both of us. I try to do that with each of them when they're old enough. It's hard to reconcile working with other people's kids when you can't find time for your own—you have any?"

I shook my head.

"It's an education, believe me. Worth more than ten years of school."

"Do you treat only children?" I said.

"Half and half. Actually, I find myself doing less and less child work as time goes on."

"Why's that?"

"To be honest, kid work's just too nonverbal for me. Three hours in a row of play therapy makes my eyes cross—narcissistic, I know, but I figure I'm not doing them much good if I'm fading away. My wife, on the other hand, doesn't mind. She's a real artist with it. Great mom, too."

We walked to the cafeteria, had coffee and donuts, and chatted for a while about other places he could take his son. As we headed back to the auditorium, I asked him about his connection to the de Bosches.

"Andres was my teacher," he said, "in England. I did a fellowship eleven years ago at Southwick Hospital—near Manchester. Child psychiatry and pediatric neurology. I'd toyed with the idea of working for the government and I wanted to see how the Brits ran their system."

"Neurology?" I said. "Didn't know de Bosch was interested in the organic side of things."

"He wasn't. Southwick was heavily biological—still is—but Andres was their token analyst. Kind of a . . ." He smiled. "I was about to say 'throwback,' but that wouldn't be kind. It's not as if he was some sort of relic. Quite vital, actually—a gadfly to the hard-wire boys, and don't we all need gadflies."

We entered the conference room. Ten minutes until the next speech and the place was nearly empty.

"Was it a good year?" I said after we were seated.

"The fellowship? Sure. I got to do lots of long-term depth work with kids from poor and working-class families, and Andres was a wonderful teacher—great at communicating his knowledge."

I thought: it's not genetic. I said, "He is a clear writer."

Rosenblatt nodded, crossed his legs, and looked around the deserted auditorium.

"How's child analysis accepted here?" he said.

"It's not used much," I said. "We deal mostly with kids with serious physical illnesses, so the emphasis is on short-term treatment. Pain control, family counseling, compliance with treatment."

"Not much tolerance for delayed gratification?"

"Not much."

"Do you find that satisfying—as an analyst?"

"I'm not an analyst."

"Oh." He blushed around his beard. "I guess I assumed you were—then how'd you get involved in the conference?"

"Katarina de Bosch's powers of persuasion."

He smiled. "She can be a real ball-breaker, can't she? When I knew her back in England she was just a kid—fourteen or fifteen —but even then she had a forceful personality. She used to attend our graduate seminars. Spoke up as if she was a peer."

"Daddy's girl."

"Very much so."

"Fourteen or fifteen," I said. "So she's only twenty-five or -six?"

He thought for a moment. "That's about right."

"She seems older."

"Yes, she does," he said, as if coming up with an insight. "She has an old soul, as the Chinese say."

"Is she married?"

He shook his head. "There was a time I thought she might be gay, but I don't think so. More likely asexual."

I said, "The temptation to think Oedipally is darn near irresistible, Harvey."

"For girls it's Elektra," he said, wagging a finger with amusement. "Get your complexes straight."

"She drives one, too."

"What?"

"Her car's an Electra—a big Buick."

He laughed. "There you go—now if that doesn't convert you to fervid belief in Freud, I don't know what will."

"Anna Freud never married, either, did she?" I said. "Neither did Melanie Klein."

"What, a neurotic pattern?" he said, still chuckling.

"Just presenting the data, Harvey. Draw your own conclusions."

"Well, *my* daughter's damned *boy* crazy, so I wouldn't get ready to publish just yet." He turned serious. "Though I'm sure the impact of such a powerful paternal—"

He stopped talking. I followed his gaze and saw Katarina heading toward us from the left side of the auditorium. Carrying a clipboard and marching forward while looking at her watch.

When she reached us, Rosenblatt stood.

"Katarina. How's everything going?" There was guilt in his voice—he'd make a very bad liar.

"Fine, Harvey," she said, looking down at her board. "You're up in two minutes. Might as well take your place on stage."

I never saw either of them again, and the events of that autumn soon faded from memory, sparked briefly, the following January, by a newspaper obituary of Andres de Bosch. Cause of death was suicide by overdose—prescription tranquilizers. The eighty-year-old analyst was described as despondent due to ill health. His professional achievements were listed in loving, inflated detail, and I knew who'd provided them.

Now, years later, another spark.

Good love/*bad love*. De Bosch's term for mothering gone bad. The psychic damage inflicted when a trusted figure betrays the innocent.

So Donald Dell Wallace probably wasn't behind it. Someone else had picked me—because of the *conference*?

Someone with a long, festering memory? Of what? Some transgression committed by de Bosch? In the name of de Boschian therapy?

My co-chairmanship made me seem like a disciple, but that was my only link.

Some kind of grievance? Was it even real, or just a delusion?

A psychotic sitting at the conference, listening, boiling . . .

I thought back to the seventy strangers in the auditorium. A collective blur.

And why had Becky Basille's murderer howled "bad love"?

Another madman?

Katarina might have the answer. But she hadn't had much use for me back in seventy-nine, and there was no reason to believe she'd talk to me now.

Unless she'd gotten a tape, too, and was frightened.

I punched 805 information. There was no Santa Barbara list-ing for either the de Bosch Institute or the Corrective School. Nei-ther was there an office number for Katarina de Bosch, Ph.D. Before the operator could get away, I asked her to check for a home number. Zilch.

I hung up and pulled out the latest American Psychological Association directory. Nothing there, either. Retrieving some older volumes, I finally found Katarina's most recent entry. Five years ago. But the address and number were those of the Santa Barbara school. On the off chance the phone company had messed up, I called.

A woman answered, "Taco Bonanza." Metallic clatter and shouts nearly drowned her out.

I cut the connection and sat at my desk, stroking the top of the bulldog's head and gazing at the coffee stain on the brochure. Wondering how and when enlightenment had given way to enchi-ladas.

Harvey Rosenblatt.

Half past one made it four-thirty in New York. I got the num-ber for NYU's med school and asked for the department of psychi-atry. After a couple of minutes on hold, I was informed that there was no Dr. Harvey Rosenblatt on either the permanent or the part-time clinical staff.

"We do have a *Leonard* Rosenblatt," said the secretary. "His office is out in New Rochelle—and a Shirley Rosenblatt in Man-hattan, on East Sixty-fifth Street."

"Is Shirley an M.D. or a Ph.D.?"

"Um—one second—a Ph.D. She's a clinical psychologist."

"But no Harvey?"

"No, sir."

"Do you have any old rosters on hand? Lists of staff members who've retired?"

"There may be something like that somewhere, sir, but I really don't have the time to search. Now if you'll—"

"Could I have Dr. Shirley Rosenblatt's number please?"

"One moment."

I copied it down, called Manhattan information for a listing on Harvey Rosenblatt, M.D., learned there was none, and dialed Shirley, Ph.D.'s exchange.

A soft, female voice with Brooklyn overtones said, "This is

Dr. Shirley Rosenblatt. I'm in session or out of the office, and can't come to the phone. If your call is a true emergency, please press one. If not, please press two, wait for the beep, and leave your message. Thank you and have a lovely day."

Mozart in the background . . . *beep.*

"Dr. Rosenblatt, this is Dr. Alex Delaware, from Los Angeles. I'm not sure if you're married to Dr. Harvey Rosenblatt or even know him, but I met him several years ago at a conference out here and wanted to touch base with him on something—for research purposes. If you can help me reach him, I'd appreciate your passing along my number."

I recited the ten digits and put the phone back in its cradle. The mail came a half hour later. Nothing out of the ordinary, but when I heard it drop into the bin, my hands had clenched.

5

I went down to feed the fish, and when I got back the phone was ringing.

The operator at my service said, "This is Joan, Dr. Delaware, are you free? There's someone on the line about a dog, sounds like a kid."

"Sure."

A second later a thin, young voice said, "Hello?"

"Hi, this is Dr. Delaware."

"Um . . . this is Karen Alnord. My dog got lost and you said in the paper that you found a bulldog?"

"Yes, I did. He's a little French bulldog."

"Oh . . . mine's a boxer." Dejected.

"Sorry. This one's not a boxer, Karen."

"Oh . . . I just thought—you know, sometimes people think they're bulldogs."

"I can see the resemblance," I said. "The flat face—"

"Yeah."

"But the one I've found's much smaller than a boxer."

"Mine's a puppy," she said. "He's not too big yet."

I put her age at between nine and eleven.

"This one's definitely full-grown, Karen. I know because I took him to the veterinarian."

"Oh . . . um . . . okay. Thank you, sir."

"Where'd you lose your dog, Karen?"

"Near my house. We have a gate, but somebody left it open and he got out."

"I'm really sorry. Hope you find him."

"I will," she said, in a breaking voice. "I've got an ad, too, and I'm calling all the other ads, even though my mom says none of them are probably the right one. I'm paying a reward, too— twenty dollars, so if you do find him you can get it. His name's Bo and there's a bone-shaped tag on his collar that says Bo and my phone number."

"I'll keep an eye out, Karen. Whereabouts do you live?"

"Reseda. On Cohasset between Sherman Way and Saticoy. His ears haven't been cropped. If you find him, here's my phone number."

I wrote it down, even though Reseda was over the hill to the north, fifteen or twenty miles away.

"Good luck, Karen."

"Thank you, sir. I hope your bulldog finds his owner."

That reminded me that I hadn't yet called the Kennel Club. Information gave me the number in New York and another one in North Carolina. Both answered with recorded messages and told me business hours were over.

"Tomorrow," I told the bulldog.

He'd been observing me, maintaining that curious, cocked head stance. The fact that someone was probably grieving for him bothered me, but I didn't know what else to do other than take good care of him.

That meant food, water, shelter. A walk, when it got cool enough.

A walk meant a leash.

He and I took a drive to a pet store in south Westwood and I bought a lead, more dog food, biscuits in various flavors, and a couple of nylon bones the salesman assured me were excellent for chewing. When we returned, it seemed temperate enough for a stroll if we stayed in the shade. The dog stood still, tail wagging rapidly, while I put the leash on. The two of us explored the Glen for half an hour, hugging the brush, walking against traffic. Like regular guys.

When I got back, I called my service. Joan said, "There's just one, from a Mrs. Rodriguez—hold on, that's your board . . . there's someone ringing in right now."

I waited a moment, and then she said, "I've got a Mr. Silk on the line, says he wants to make an appointment."

"Thanks, put him on."

Click.

"Dr. Delaware."

Silence.

"Hello?"

Nothing.

"Mr. Silk?"

No answer. Just as I was about to hang up and redial the service, a low sound came through the receiver. Mumbles—no. Laughter.

A deep, throaty giggle.

"Huh huh huh."

"Who is this?" I said.

"Huh huh huh." Gloating.

I said nothing.

"Huh huh huh."

The line went dead.

I got the operator back on the line.

"Joan, that guy who just called. Did he leave anything other than his name?"

"No, he just asked if you treated adults as well as children and I said he'd have to speak to you about that."

"And his name was Silk? As in the fabric?"

"That's what I heard. Why, doctor, is something wrong?"

"He didn't say anything, just laughed."

"Well that's kind of crazy, but that's your business, isn't it, doctor?"

Evelyn Rodriguez answered on the first ring. When she heard my voice, hers went dead.

"How's everything?" I said.

"Fine."

"I know it's a hassle for you, but I would like to see the girls."

"Yeah, it's a hassle," she said. "Driving all the way out there."

"How about if I come out to you?"

No answer.

"Mrs. Rodriguez?"

"You'd do that?"

"I would."

"What's the catch?"

"No catch, I'd just like to make this whole thing as easy as possible for you."

"Why?"

To show Donald Dell Wallace I can't be intimidated. "To help the girls."

"Uh-huh . . . *they're* paying for your time, right? His . . . bunch a heathens."

"The judge made Donald Dell responsible for the costs of the evaluation, Mrs. Rodriguez, but as we talked about the first time, that doesn't obligate me to him in any way."

"Uh-huh."

"Has that been a problem for you?" I said. "The fact that he's paying?"

She said nothing for a moment, then: "Bet you're charging plenty."

"I'm charging my usual fee," I said, realizing I sounded like a Watergate witness.

"Bet it includes your driving time and all. Door to door, just like the lawyers."

"Yes, it does."

"*Good*," she said, stretching the word. "Then *you* can drive instead of me—drive *slow*. Keep your meter running and make them devils *pay*."

Angry laughter.

I said, "When can I come out?"

"How 'bout right now? They're running around like wild Injuns, maybe you can settle 'em down. How about you drive out here right this *minute* and see 'em? You ready for that?"

"I can probably be there in forty-five minutes."

"Whenever. We'll be right here. We're not taking any vacations to Hono-*lulu*."

She hung up before I could ask for directions. I looked up her address in my case file—the ten thousand block of McVine Terrace in Sunland—and matched it to my Thomas map. Setting the dog up with water, food, and a bone, I left, not at all unhappy about running up the Iron Priests' tab.

*   *   *

The 405 freeway deposited me in a scramble of northbound traffic just beginning to clot, facing hills so smogged they were no more than shrouded, gray lumps on the horizon. I did the L.A. stop-and-go boogie for a while, listening to music and trying to be patient, finally made it to the 118 east, then the 210, and cruised into the high desert northeast of the city, picking up speed as both the road and the air got clearer.

Exiting at Sunland, I hooked north again and got onto a commercial stretch of Foothill Boulevard that ran parallel to the mountains: auto parts barns, body shops, unfinished furniture outlets, and more roofers than I'd ever seen in one area.

I spotted McVine a few minutes later and turned left. The street was narrow, with grass growing down to the curb instead of sidewalks, and planted haphazardly with eucalyptus and willow. The curb grass was dry and yellow. The houses behind it were small and low, some of them no more than trailers on raised foundations.

The Rodriguez residence was on a northwest corner, a boxcar of mocha stucco with a gutterless, black composition roof and a flat, porchless face broken by three metal-sashed windows. One of the windows was blocked by a tilting sheet of lattice. The squares were broken in spots, warped in others, and a few dead branches wormed around them. A high, pink block wall enveloped the rear of the property.

I got out and walked up a hardpack lawn stippled with blemishlike patches of some sort of low-growing succulent and split by a foot-worn rut. Evelyn's plum-colored Chevy was parked to the left of the pathway, next to a red half-ton pickup with two stickers on the bumper. One sang the praises of the Raiders, the other dared me to keep kids off drugs. A stick-on sign on the door said R AND R MASONRY.

I pressed the bell and a wasp-buzz sounded. A woman opened the door and looked at me through the smoke vining upward from a freshly lit Virginia Slim.

In her late twenties, five seven and lanky, she had dirty blond hair gathered in a high, streaked ponytail and pale skin. Slanted, dark eyes and broad cheekbones gave her a Slavic look. The rest of her features were sharp, beginning to pinch. Her shape was perfect for the hardbody era: sinewy arms, high breasts, straightedge tummy, long legs leading up to flaring hips just a little wider than a boy's. She wore skintight, low-riding jeans and a baby-blue, sleeveless midriff top that showcased an apostrophe of a navel some obstetrician should have been mighty proud of. Her feet were bare. One of them tapped arrhythmically.

"You the doctor?" she said, in a husky voice, talking around the cigarette, just the way I'd seen Evelyn Rodriguez do.

"Dr. Delaware," I said, and extended my hand.

She took it and smiled—amusement rather than friendliness —gave a hard squeeze, then dropped it.

"I'm Bonnie. They're waiting for you. C'mon in."

The living room was half the width of the boxcar and smelled like a drowned cigar. Carpeted in olive shag and paneled with knotty pine, it was darkened by drawn drapes. A long, brown corduroy sofa ran along the back wall. Above it hung a born-again fish symbol. To the left was a console TV topped with some sort of cable decoder and a VCR, and a beige velveteen recliner. On a hexagonal table, an ashtray brimmed over with butts.

The other half of the front space was a kitchen–dining area combo. Between the two rooms was an ochre-colored door. Bonnie pushed it open, letting in a lot of bright, western light, and took me down a short, shagged hall. At the end was a den, walled in grayish mock birch and backed by sliding glass doors that looked out to the backyard. More recliners, another TV, porcelain figurines on the mantel, below three mounted rifles.

Bonnie slid open a glass door. The yard was a small, flat square of scorched grass surrounded by the high pink walls. An avocado tree grew at the rear, huge and twisted. Barely out of its shade was an inflatable swimming pool, oval and bluer than anyone's heaven. Chondra sat in it, splashing herself without enthusiasm. Tiffani was in a corner of the property, back to us, jumping rope.

Evelyn Rodriguez sat between them in a folding chair, working on her lanyard and smoking. She had on white shorts, a dark blue T-shirt, and rubber beach sandals. On the grass next to her was her purse.

Bonnie said, "Hey," and all three of them looked up.

I waved. The girls stared.

Evelyn said, "Go get him a chair."

Bonnie raised her eyebrows and went back into the house, putting some wiggle in her walk.

Evelyn shaded her face, looked at her watch, and smiled. "Forty-two minutes. Couldn't ya have stopped for coffee or something?"

I forced a chuckle.

"Course," she said, "don't really matter what you actually do, you can always *say* you done it, right? Just like a lawyer. You can say anything you *please*."

She stubbed her cigarette out on the grass.

I went over to the pool. Chondra returned my "Hi" with a small, silent smile. Some teeth this time: progress.

Tiffani said, "You write your book yet?"

"Not yet. I need more information from you."

She nodded gravely. "I got lots of truth—we don't want to ever see him."

She grabbed hold of a branch and started swinging. Humming something.

I said, "Have fun," but she didn't answer.

Bonnie came out with a folded chair. I went and took it from her. She winked and went back into the house, rear twitching violently. Evelyn wrinkled her nose and said, "Well, does it?"

I unfolded the chair. "Does it what?"

"Does it matter? What actually happens? You're just gonna do what you want to, write what you want to anyway, right?"

I sat down next to her, positioning myself so I could see the girls. Chondra was motionless in the pool, gazing at the trunk of the avocado.

Evelyn humphed. "You ready to come out?"

Chondra shook her head and began splashing herself again, doing it slowly, as if it were a chore. Her white pigtails were soaked the color of old brass. Above the pink walls the sky was static and blue, bottomed by a soot-colored cloud bank that hid the horizon. Someone in the neighborhood was barbecuing, and a mixture of scorching fat and lighter fluid spread its cheerful toxin through the autumn heat.

"You don't think I'll be honest, huh?" I said. "Been burned by other doctors, or is it something about me?"

She turned toward me slowly and put her lanyard in her lap.

"I think you do your job and go home," she said. "Just like everyone else. I think you do what's best for *you*, just like everyone else."

"Fair enough," I said. "I'm not going to sit here and tell you

I'm some saint who'd work for free or that I really know what you've been going through, 'cause I don't—thank God. But I think I understand your rage. If someone had done it to my child, I'd be ready to kill him, no question about it."

She took her Winstons out of her pocket and knocked a cigarette loose. Sliding it out and taking it between two fingers, she said, "Oh you would, would you? Well that would be revenge, and the Bible says revenge is a negational action."

She lit up with a pink disposable lighter, inhaled very deeply, and held it. When she let the smoke out, her nostrils twitched.

Tiffani began jumping very fast. I wondered if we were within her earshot.

Evelyn shook her head. "Gonna break her head one of these days."

"Lots of energy," I said.

"Apple don't fall far."

"Ruthanne was like that?"

She smoked, nodded, and started to cry, letting her tears drip down her face and wiping them with short, furious movements. Her torso pushed forward and for a moment I thought she was going to leave.

"Ruthanne was *just* like that when she was little. Always moving. I never felt I could . . . she had spirit, she was—she had . . . wonderful spirit."

She tugged her shorts down and sniffed.

"Want some coffee?"

"Sure."

"Wait right here." She went into the house.

"Hey, girls," I called out.

Tiffani kept jumping. Chondra looked up. Her mouth hung slightly open and water droplets bubbled her forehead, like oversized sweat.

I went over to her. "Swim a lot?"

She gave a very small nod and splashed one arm, turning away and facing the avocado tree. Young fruit hung from the branches, veiled by a cloud of whiteflies. Some of it was blackened with disease.

Tiffani waved at me. Then she began to chant in a loud voice:

"I went to the Chinese restaurant,
to get a loaf of bread bread bread,

a man was there with a big mustache,
and this is what he said said said.
El eye el eye chicholo beauty, pom-pom cutie . . ."

Evelyn came back holding a couple of mugs. Bonnie marched behind her carrying a small plate of sugar wafers. The look on her face said she'd been created for better things.

I walked back to the lawn chairs.

Bonnie said, "Here you go," handed me the plate, and sashayed off.

Evelyn gave me a mug. "Black or cream?"

"Black."

We sat and sipped. I balanced the cookie plate on my lap.

"Have one," she said, "or are you one of those health-food types?"

I took a wafer and chewed on it. Lemon-flavored and slightly stale.

"I dunno," she said, "maybe *I* shoulda been a health fooder, too. I always gave my kids sugar and stuff, whatever they wanted —maybe I shouldn'ta. Got a boy went AWOL over in Germany two years ago, don't even *know* where he is, the baby don't know *zero* about what she wants to do with her life, and Ruthie . . ."

She shook her head and looked over at Tiffani. "Watch your head on that *branch*, you!"

"Bonnie's the baby?" I said.

Nod. "She got all the brains and the looks. Just like her daddy —he coulda been a movie star. Only time I ever went gaga for the looks, and boy, what a mistake *that* was."

She gave a full smile. "He cleaned me out thirteen months after we were married. Left me with the baby in diapers and went down to Louisiana to work the deep-sea rigs. Got killed soon after in a fall that they *said* was an accident. Never took out the right insurance for himself, so I got nothing."

She smiled wider. "He had a temper on him. All my men do. Roddy's got a fuse on him, too, though it takes a while to get it lit. He's a Mexican, but he's the best of the lot."

She patted the T-shirt pocket that held the cigarette pack. "Sugar and bad tempers and cancer sticks. I really go for all the good things in life, huh?"

Her eyes watered again. She lit up.

"All the good things," she said. "All the blessed good things."

She kept the cigarette in her mouth, busied her hands by squeezing them together, letting go, repeating the motion. The lanyard lay on the grass, neglected.

"There's no room for your guilt," I said.

She yanked the cigarette out of her mouth and stared at me. *"What'd* you say?"

"There's no room for your guilt. All the guilt belongs to Donald Dell. One hundred percent of it."

She started to say something, but stopped.

I said, "No one else should carry that burden, Evelyn. Not Ruthanne for going with him that night, and certainly not you for the way you raised her. Junk food had nothing to do with what happened. Neither did anything but Donald Dell's impulses. It's *his* cross to bear now."

Her eyes were on me, but wavering.

I said, "He's a bad guy, he does bad things, no one knows why. And now you're having to be a mom, all over again, when you weren't planning on it. And you're going to do it without complaining too much and you're going to do your best. No one's going to pay you or give you any credit, so at least give *yourself* some."

"You talk sweet," she said. "Telling me what I want to hear." Wary, but not angry. "Sounds like you got a temper on you, too."

"I talk straight. For my own sake—you're right about that. All of us do what we think's best for us. And I do like to make money —I went to school a long time to learn what I do. I'm worth a high fee, so I charge it. But I also like to sleep well at night."

"Me, too. So what?" She smoked, coughed, ground out the cigarette with disgust. "Been a long time since I slept peacefully."

"Takes time."

"Yeah . . . how long?"

"I don't know, Evelyn."

"Least you're honest." Smile. "Maybe."

"What about the girls?" I said. "How do they sleep?"

"Not good," she said. "How could they? The little one wakes complaining she's hungry—which is a laugh, 'cause she eats all day, though you wouldn't know it to look at her, would you? I used to be like that, believe it or not." Squeezing her thigh. "She gets up two, three times a night, wanting Hersheys and licorice and *ice* cream."

"Does she ever get those things?"

"Hel—heck no. There's a *limit*. I give her a piece of orange or something—maybe a half a cookie—and send her right back. Not that it stops her the next time."

"What about Chondra?"

"*She* don't get up, but I hear her crying in her bed—under the blanket." She looked over at the older girl, who was sitting motionless in the center of the pool. "She's the soft one. Soft as jelly."

She sighed and looked down at her coffee with disdain. "Instant. Shoulda made real stuff."

"It's fine," I said, and drank to prove it.

"It's okay, but it's not great—don't see great around here too often. My second husband—Brian's dad—owned a big place up near Fresno—table grapes and alfalfa, some quarter horses. We lived up there for a few years—that was *close* to great, all that space. Then he went back to his drinking—Brian, Senior—and it all went to—straight down the tubes. Ruthie used to love that place—especially the horses. There's riding stables around here, too, out in Shadow Hills, but it's expensive. We always said we'd get over there but we never did."

The sun dropped behind the cloud bank, and the yard dimmed.

"What're you gonna do to us?" she said.

"*To* you?"

"What's your plan?"

"I'd like to help you."

"If you wanna *help* them, keep them away from *him*, that's all. He's a devil."

"Tiffani called him an instrument of Satan."

"I told her that," she said defiantly. "You see something wrong with that?"

"Not at all."

"It's my faith—it props me up. And he *is* one."

"How'd Ruthanne meet him?"

Her shoulders dropped. "She was waitressin' at a place out in Tujunga—okay, it was a bar. He and his *bunch* hung out there. She went out with him for months before tellin' me. Then she brought him home and the first look I got I said no, no, no—my experiences, I can spot a bad apple like that." Snap of fingers. "I warned her, but that didn't do no good. Maybe I gave up too easy, I don't know. I was havin' problems of my own, and Ruthie didn't think I had a single intelligent thing to say to her."

She lit another cigarette and took several hard, fast drags. "She was stubborn. That was her only real sin."

I drank more coffee.

"Nothing to say anymore, doc? Or am I boring you?" She flicked ashes onto the dirt.

"I'd rather listen."

"And they pay you all that money for that? Good racket you got there."

"Beats honest labor," I said.

She smiled. First friendly one I'd seen.

"Stubborn," she said. She smoked and sighed and called out, "Five more minutes, then into the house for homework, both a you!"

The girls ignored her. She kept looking at them. Drifted off, as if she'd forgotten I was there. But then she turned and looked at me.

"So, Mr. Easy Listener, what *do* you want from me and my little girls?"

Same question she'd asked me the first time she met me. I said, "Enough time to find out exactly how they've been affected by their mom's death."

"How do you *think* they've been affected? They loved their mama. They're crushed to dirt."

"I need to get specific for the court."

"What do you mean?"

"I need to list symptoms that prove they're suffering psychologically."

"You gonna say they're crazy?"

"No, nothing like that. I'll talk about symptoms of anxiety— like the sleep problems, changes in appetite, things that make them vulnerable to seeing him. Otherwise they're going to get swept up in the system. Some of it you can tell me, but I'll also need to hear things directly from them."

"Won't that mess them up more, talking about it?"

"No," I said. "Just the opposite—keeping things inside is more likely to create problems."

She gave a skeptical look. "I don't see them talkin' to you much, so far."

"I need time with them—need to build up their trust."

She thought about that. "So what do we do, just sit here jawing?"

"We could start with a history—you telling me as much as you remember about what they were like as babies. Anything else you think might be important."

"A history, huh?" She took a deep drag, as if trying to suck maximum poison out of the cigarette. "So now we've got a history . . . yeah, I've got *plenty* to tell you. Why don't you get out a pencil and start writing?"

6

She talked as the sky darkened further, letting the girls play on as she recounted nightmares and weeping spells, the terrors of orphanhood. At five-thirty Bonnie came out and switched on floodlights that turned the yard sallow. It stilled her mother's voice, and Evelyn stood and told the girls, "Go in the house, you."

Right after they did, a man came out, rubbing his hands together and sniffing the air. Five three or so, in his late fifties or early sixties, low waisted, dark skinned and weak chinned, with long, tattooed arms. Bowlegs gave him a tottering walk. His eyes were shadowed by thick, gray thatches, and a drooping, iron-colored Zapata mustache obscured his mouth. His bushy gray hair was slicked straight back. He wore a khaki workshirt and blue jeans with hand-rolled cuffs. His hands were caked with plaster and he rubbed them more vigorously as he approached.

Evelyn saluted him.

He returned the gesture and looked at me, stretching to stand taller.

"This here's that doctor," she said. "We been having a nice talk."

He nodded. The shirt was embroidered with a white oval tag that said "Roddy" in red script. Up close I saw that his face was severely pockmarked. A couple of crescent-shaped scars ran down his chin.

I held out a hand.

He looked at his palm, gave an embarrassed smile, and said, "Dirty." His voice was soft and hoarse. I put my hand down. He smiled again and saluted me.

"Dr. Delaware."

"Roddy. Pleased to meetchu." Boyle Heights accent. As he lowered his fingers, I noticed tattooed letters across the knuckles. L-O-V-E. Homemade job. On the other hand was the inevitable H-A-T-E. In the fold between his thumb and forefinger was a crude blue crucifix. Next to that, a tiny red-eyed spider climbed a tiny web above the legend NR.

He put his hands in his pockets.

"How's your day?" Evelyn asked him. She looked as if she wanted to touch him.

"Okay." He sniffed.

"Hungry?"

"Yeah, I could eat." The tattooed hands emerged and rubbed together. "Gotta wash up."

"Sure, *patron*."

He went into the house.

"Well," she told me, "I'd better get into the kitchen. Guess it's too late for you to talk to them, but you can come back tomorrow."

"Great."

We walked inside. Chondra and Tiffani were on the sofa in the rear den, watching cartoons on TV. A cat was being cheerfully decapitated. Tiffani held the remote control.

"Bye, girls."

Glazed eyes.

"Say bye to the doctor."

The girls looked up. Small waves and smiles.

"I'm leaving now," I said. "I'll be coming out here tomorrow —maybe we can get a chance to talk."

"See you," said Tiffani. She nudged her sister. Chondra said, "Bye."

Evelyn was gone. I found her out in the kitchen, pulling something out of the freezer. Rodriguez was stretched back in the velveteen recliner, eyes closed, a beer in his hand.

"See you tomorrow," I said.

"One sec." Evelyn came over. The package in her hand was a

diet frozen entree. Enchilada Fiesta. "Better be the day after—I forgot there's some things I got to do."

"Okay. Same time?"

"Sure." She looked at the frozen package and shook her head. "How 'bout New York steak?" she called out to her husband.

"Yeah," he said, without opening his eyes.

"He likes his steak," she said quietly. "For a fella his size, he's a real meat eater."

She followed me all the way out to the front lawn. Looked at the TV dinner in her hand. "No one likes this one. Maybe I'll have it."

I hit bad traffic on the western end of the 210, and by the time I pulled into the carport, it was after seven. When I got in the house, the dog greeted me, but he had his head down and looked subdued. I smelled the reason first, then saw it, on the service porch floor near the door.

"Oh," I said.

He drooped lower.

"My mistake for locking you in." I rubbed his neck, and he gave me a grateful lick, then trotted over to the fridge.

"Let's not push things, bucko."

I cleaned up the mess, reflecting on the responsibilities of pet foster-parenthood, and phoned in for messages, wondering if anyone had responded to my ad. No one had. Nothing from Shirley Rosenblatt, Ph.D., either. Or Mr. Silk. The operator gave me a few business calls. I decided to put the tape out of my mind, but the child's chant stayed there and I couldn't sit still.

I fed the dog and was contemplating what to do about my own dinner when Milo called at eight-ten.

"No prints on the tape except yours. Any mail problems today?" He sounded tired.

"No, but I did get a call." I told him about the giggling man.

"Silk, huh? Well, that's a pisser."

"What is?"

"Sounds like you've got a nutcase on your hands."

"You don't think it's serious?"

Pause. "Most of these guys are cowards, like to stay in the background. But to be honest, Alex, who knows?"

I said, "I think I may have found what 'bad love' means," and filled him in about the symposium.

"Seventy-nine," he said. "Nut with a real long memory."

"Think that's a bad sign?"

"I—let's put our heads together and hash it out. You eat yet?"

"Nope."

"I'm over in Palms, got to finish up a few things. I could meet you at that place on Ocean in about half an hour."

"Don't think I'd better," I said. "Left my guest alone too long already."

"What guest? Oh, him. Why can't you leave him? Is he lonely and depressed?"

"It's more of a gastrointestinal issue," I said, rubbing the dog behind the ears. "He just ate and will be needing easy ingress and egress."

"Ingr—oh . . . *fun*. Well, get a dog door, Alex. Then, get a *life*."

"A dog door means sawing a hole. He's only a short-term lodger."

"Suit yourself."

"Fine," I said. "I'll put a door in—Robin wants a dog anyway. How about you bring one over, I'll install it, and then we can go out."

"Where the hell am I gonna find a dog door at this hour?"

"You're the detective."

Slam.

He arrived at nine-fifteen, pulling an unmarked Ford into the carport. His tie was loose, he looked wilted, and he carried two bags—one from a pet store, the other from a Chinese restaurant.

The dog came up and nuzzled his cuffs and he gave the animal a grudging pat and said, "Ingress and egress."

Removing a metal and plastic contraption from the pet store bag, he handed it to me. "Seeing as I don't feel like manual labor before dinner and the *handy* resident of this household is out of town, I figured we'd better do takeout."

He went over to the fridge, dog following.

Watching his slow trudge, I said, "You look wiped. New blood buckets?"

He got a Grolsch, opened it, and nodded. "Armed robbery, what I was working on in Palms. Little mom-and-pop grocery. Pop died a few months ago, mom's eighty, barely hanging on. Two little shits came in this afternoon, flashed knives, and threatened to rape her and cut off her breasts if she didn't hand over the cashbox. Old lady puts them at around thirteen or fourteen. She's too shook to say much else, chest pains, shortness of breath. They admitted her to St. John's for observation."

"Poor thing. Thirteen or fourteen?"

"Yeah. The timing of the robbery might mean the little assholes waited till after school to do it—how's that for your extracurricular activities? Or maybe they're just your basic truant psychopaths out for a fun day."

"Urban Huck and Tom," I said.

"Sure. Smoke a corncob of crack, gangbang Becky Thatcher."

He sat down at the table and sniffed the top of the beer bottle. The dog had remained at the refrigerator and was looking at him, as if contemplating approach, but Milo's tone and expression stilled him and he came over and settled at my feet.

I said, "So no one else's prints were on the tape."

"Not a one."

"What does that mean? Someone took the trouble to wipe it clean?"

"Or handled it with gloves. Or there *were* prints and they got smeared when you touched the tape." He stretched his legs. "So show me this brochure you found."

I went to the library, got the conference program, and gave it to him. He scanned it, "No one named Silk here."

"Maybe he was in the audience."

"You look intense," he said, pointing to my photo. "That beard—kind of rabbinic."

"Actually, I was bored." I told him how I'd become a co-chair.

He put down his bottle. "Nineteen seventy-nine. Someone carrying around a grudge all this time?"

"Or something happened recently that triggered a recollection from seventy-nine. I tried calling Katarina and Rosenblatt, to see if maybe they'd gotten anything in the mail, but she's closed up shop in Santa Barbara and he's no longer practicing in Manhattan. I found a psychologist in New York who may be his wife and left her a message."

He examined the brochure again. "So what could the grudge be about?"

"I have no idea, Milo. Maybe it's not even the conference,

maybe it's someone who sees himself as victimized by the therapist—or the therapy. Maybe the grievance isn't even real—
something paranoid—a delusion that would never occur to you or
me."

"Meaning we're normal?"

"Everything's relative."

He smiled. "So you can't remember anything weird happening at the conference."

"Nothing at all."

"This de Bosch—was he controversial in any way? The kind
to make enemies?"

"Not that I know, but my only contact with him was through
his writings. They're not controversial."

"What about the daughter?"

I thought about that. "Yeah, she could have made enemies—a
real sourpuss. But if she's the target of someone's resentment, why
would I be? My only link to her was the conference."

He waved the brochure. "Reading this, someone could believe you were esteemed colleagues. She hemmed you in, huh?"

"Expertly. She had clout with the medical director of the hospital. My guess was that it was because she'd treated one of his
daughters—a kid with problems—and called in a marker. But it
could have been something else completely."

He put his beer bottle down on the coffee table. The dog
looked up, then lowered his chin to the floor.

"The kid's voice on the tape," I said. "How does that figure
in? And the guy who killed Becky Basille—"

"Hewitt. Dorsey Hewitt. Yeah, I know—what does he have to
do with it?"

"Maybe he was treated by the de Bosches, too. Maybe 'bad
love' was a phrase they used in therapy. But what does that
mean? A whole slew of therapy graduates freaking out—getting
back at their doctors?"

"Wait a second," said Milo. "I'm sorry about your tape and
your nut-call, but that's a far cry from murder." He handed the
brochure back to me. "Wonder if Donald Wallace was ever treated
by the de Bosches—still waiting for more info from the prison.
How're those girls doing?"

"The kinds of problems you'd expect. Documenting a good
case against visitation shouldn't be a problem. The grandmother's

opening up a bit, too. I went out to the house this afternoon. Her latest husband looks like a retired cholo—lots of homemade tattoos." I described Rodriguez's skin art.

"Dealing with the elite," he said. "You and me both." He crossed his legs and glanced down at the dog: "C'mere, Rove."

The dog ignored him.

"Good dog," he said, and drank his beer.

He left at ten-thirty. I decided to put off installing the dog door till the next day. Robin called at ten-fifty and told me she'd decided, definitely, to come home early—tomorrow evening at nine. I wrote down her flight number and said I'd be at LAX to pick her up, told her I loved her, and went to sleep.

I was dreaming about something pleasantly sexual when the dog woke me just after three in the morning, growling and pawing the dust ruffle.

I groaned. My eyes felt glued shut.

He pawed some more.

"What?"

Silence.

Scratch scratch.

I sat up. "What is it?"

He did the old-man-choking bit.

Ingress and egress . . .

Cursing myself for not installing the door, I forced myself out of bed and made my way, blindly, through the dark house to the kitchen. When I opened the service porch door, the dog raced down the stairs. I waited, yawning and groggy, muttering, "Make it fast."

Instead of stopping to squat near the bushes, he kept going and was soon out of sight.

"Ah, exploring new ground." I forced one eye to stay open. Cool air blew in through the door. I looked outside, couldn't see him in the darkness.

When he didn't return after a minute or so, I went down to get him. It took a while to find him, but I finally did—sitting near the carport, as if guarding the Seville. Huffing, and moving his head from side to side.

"What is it, guy?"

Pant, pant. He moved his head faster but didn't budge his body.

I looked around some more, still unable to see much. The mixed smells of night-blooming plants hit my nose, and the first spray of dew moistened my skin. The night sky was hazy, just a hint of moonlight peeking through. Just enough to turn the dog's eyes yellow.

"Hound of the Basketballs," I said, remembering an old *Mad* magazine sketch.

The dog scratched the ground and sniffed, started turning his head from side to side.

"*What?*"

He began walking toward the pond, stopping several feet from the fence, just as he had during our first encounter. Then he came to a dead halt.

The gate was closed. It had been hours since the timed lights had shut off. I could hear the waterfall. Peering over the fence, I caught a glimpse of moonstreaked wetness as my eyes started to accommodate.

I looked back at the dog.

Still as a rock.

"Did you hear something?"

Head cock.

"Probably a cat or a possum, pal. Or maybe a coyote, which might be a little too much for you, no offense."

Head cock. Pant. He pawed the ground.

"Listen, I appreciate your watchfulness, but can we go back up now?"

He stared at me. Yawned. Gave a low growl.

"I'm bushed, too," I said, and headed for the stairs. He did nothing until I'd gotten all the way up, then raced up with a swiftness that belied his bulk.

"No more interruptions, okay?"

He wagged his stub cheerfully, jumped on the bed, and sprawled across Robin's side.

Too exhausted to argue, I left him there.

He was snoring long before I was.

Wednesday morning I assessed my life: crank letters and calls, but I could handle that if it didn't accelerate. And my true love returning from the wilds of Oakland. A balance I could live with. The dog licking my face belonged in the plus column, too, I supposed. When I let him out, he disappeared again and stayed out.

This time he'd gotten closer to the gate, stopping only a couple of feet from the latch. I pushed it open and he took another step.

Then he stopped, stout body angling forward.

His little frog face was tilted upward at me. Something had caused it to screw up, the eyes narrowing to slits.

I anthropomorphized it as conflict—struggling to get over his water phobia. Canine self-help hampered by the life-saving training some devoted owner had given him.

He growled and jutted his head toward the gate.

Looking *angry*.

Wrong guess? Something near the pond bothering him?

The growls grew louder. I looked over the fence and saw it.

One of my koi—a red and white *kohaku*, the largest and prettiest of the surviving babies—was lying on the moss near the water's edge.

A jumper. Damn.

Sometimes it happened. Or maybe a cat or coyote *had* gotten in. And that's what he'd heard . . .

But the body didn't look torn up.

I opened the gate and went in. The bulldog stepped up to the gatepost and waited as I kneeled to inspect the fish.

It *had* been torn. But no four-legged predator had done it.

Something was sticking out of its mouth—a twig, thin, stiff, a single shriveled red leaf still attached.

A branch from the dwarf maple I'd planted last winter.

I glanced over at the tree, saw where the bough had been cut off, the wound oxidized almost black.

Clean cut. Hours old. A knife.

I forced my eyes back to the carp.

The branch had been jammed down its gullet and forced down through its body, like a spit. It exited near the anus, through a ragged hole, ripping through beautiful skin and letting loose a rush of entrails and blood that stained the moss cream-gray and rusty brown.

I filled with anger and disgust. Other details began to leap out at me, painful as spattering grease.

A spray of scales littering the moss.

Indentations that might have been footprints.

I took a closer look at them. To my untrained eye, they remained characterless gouges.

Leaves beneath the maple, where the branch had been sheared.

The fish's dead eyes stared up at me.

The dog was growling.

I joined in and we did a duet.

7

I dug a grave for the fish. The sky was Alpine clear, and the beauty of the morning was a mockery of my task.

I thought of another beautiful sky—Katarina de Bosch's slide show. Azure heavens draping her father's wheelchaired form.

Good love/bad love.

Definitely more than just a sick joke now.

Flies were divebombing the koi's torn corpse. I nudged the body into the hole and shoveled dirt over it as the bulldog watched.

"Should have taken you more seriously last night."

He cocked his head and blinked, brown eyes gentle.

The dirt over the grave was a small umber disc that I tamped with my foot. After taking one last look, I dragged myself up to the house. Feeling like a dependent child, I called Milo. He wasn't in and I sat at my desk, baffled and angry.

Someone had trespassed on my property. Someone had watched me.

The blue brochure was on my desk, my name and photo—the perfect logic of trumped-up evidence.

Reading this, someone could believe you were esteemed colleagues.

I phoned my service. Still no callback from Shirley Rosenblatt, Ph.D. Maybe she wasn't Harvey's wife. . . . I tried her number again, got the same recorded message, and slammed down the phone in disgust.

My hand started to close around the brochure, crumpling it, then my eyes dropped to the bottom of the page and I stopped and smoothed the stiff paper.

Other names.

The three other speakers.

Wilbert Harrison, M.D., FACP
Practicing Psychoanalyst
Beverly Hills, California

Grant P. Stoumen, M.D., FACP
Practicing Psychoanalyst
Beverly Hills, California

Mitchell A. Lerner, M.S.W., ACSW
Psychoanalytic Therapist
North Hollywood, California

Harrison, chubby, around fifty, fair, and jolly looking, with dark-rimmed glasses. Stoumen older, bald and prune faced, with a waxed, white mustache. Lerner, the youngest of the three, Afroed and turtlenecked, full bearded, like Rosenblatt and myself.

I had no memory beyond that. The topics of their papers meant nothing to me. I'd sat up on the dais, mind wandering, angry about being there.

Three locals.

I opened the phone book. Neither Harrison nor Lerner was in there, but Grant P. Stoumen, M.D., still had an office on North Bedford Drive—Beverly Hills couch row. A service operator answered, "Beverly Hills Psychiatric, this is Joan."

Same service I used. Same voice I'd just spoken to.

"It's Dr. Delaware, Joan."

"Hi, Dr. Delaware! Fancy talking to you so soon."

"Small world," I said.

"Yeah—no, actually, it happens all the time, we handle lots of psych docs. Who in the group are you trying to reach?"

"Dr. Stoumen."

"Dr. Stoumen?" Her voice lowered. "But he's gone."

"From the group?"

"From—uh . . . from life, Dr. Delaware. He died six months ago. Didn't you hear?"

"No," I said. "I didn't know him."

"Oh . . . well, it was really pretty sad. So unexpected, even though he was pretty old."

"What did he die of?"

"A car accident. Last May, I think it was. Out of town, I forget exactly where. He was at some kind of convention and got run over by a car. Isn't that terrible?"

"A convention?"

"You know, one of those medical meetings. He was a *nice* man, too—never lost patience the way some of the—" Nervous laugh. "Scratch *that* comment, Dr. D. Anyway, if you're calling about a patient, Dr. Stoumen's were divided up among the rest of the doctors in the group, and I can't be sure which one took the one you're calling about."

"How many doctors are in the group?"

"Carney, Langenbaum, and Wolf. Langenbaum's on vacation, but the other two are in town—take your pick."

"Any recommendations?"

"Well . . ." Another nervous laugh. "They're both—all right. Wolf tends to be a little better about returning calls."

"Wolf'll be fine. Is that a him or a her?"

"A him. Stanley Wolf, M.D. He's in session right now. I'll put a message on his board to call you."

"Thanks a lot, Joan."

"Sure bet, Dr. D. Have a nice day."

I installed the dog door, making slow progress because I kept pausing between saw swings and hammer blows, convinced I'd heard footsteps in the house or unwarranted noise out on the terrace.

A couple of times I actually went down to the garden and looked around, hands clenched.

The grave was a dark ellipse of dirt. Dried fish scales and a slick gray-brown stain marked the pond bank.

I went back up, did some touch-up painting around the door frame, cleaned up, and had a beer. The dog tried his new passageway, ingressing and egressing several times and enjoying himself.

Finally, tired and panting, he fell asleep at my feet. I thought about who'd want to scare me or hurt me. The dead fish stayed in my head, a cognitive stench, and I remained wide-awake. At eleven, he awoke and raced for the front door. A moment later, the mail chute filled.

Standard-sized envelopes that I sorted through. One had a Folsom POB return address and an eleven-digit serial number hand-printed above it in red ink. Inside was a single sheet of ruled notebook paper, printed in the same red.

Doctor A. Delaware, Ph.D.

Dear Dr. Delaware, Ph.D.:

I am writing to you to express my feelings about seeing my daughters, namely Chondra Wallace and Tiffani Wallace, as their natural father and legal guardian.

Whatever was done to our family including done by my-self and no matter how bad is in my opinion, water under the bridge. And such as it is, I should not be denied permission and my paternity rights to see my lawful, legal daughters, Chondra Wallace and Tiffani Wallace.

I have never done anything to hurt them and have always worked hard to support them even when this was hard. I don't have any other children and need to see them for us to have a family.

Children need their fathers as I'm sure I don't have to tell a trained doctor like yourself. One day I will be out of incarceration. I am their father and will be taking care of them. Chondra Wallace and Tiffani Wallace need me. Please pay attention to these facts.

Yours sincerely,
Donald Dell Wallace

I filed the letter in the thick folder, next to the coroner's report on Ruthanne. Milo called at noon and I told him about the fish. "Makes it more than a prank, doesn't it?"

Pause. "More than I expected."

"Donald Dell knows my address. I just got a letter from him."

"Saying what?"

"One day he'll be out and wanting to be a full-time dad, so I shouldn't deny him his rights now."

"Subtle threat?"

"Could you prove it?"

"No, he could have gotten your address through his lawyer—you're reviewing his claim, so he'd be entitled to it legally. Incidentally, according to my sources he doesn't have an audio recorder in his cell. TV and VCR, yes."

"Cruel and unusual. So what do I do?"

"Let me come over and check out your pond. Notice any footprints or obvious evidence?"

"There were some prints," I said, "though they didn't look like much to my amateur eyes. Maybe there's some other evidence that I wasn't sophisticated enough to spot. I was careful not to disturb anything—oh, hell, I buried the fish. Was that a screwup?"

"Don't worry about it, it's not like we're gonna do an autopsy." He sounded uneasy.

"What's the matter?" I said.

"Nothing. I'll come by and have a look as soon as I can. Probably the afternoon."

He spoke the last words tentatively, almost turning the statement into a question.

I said, "What is it, Milo?"

"What it *is*, is that I can't do any full-court press for you on this. Killing a fish just isn't a major felony—at the most, we've got trespassing and malicious mischief."

"I understand."

"I can probably take some footprint molds myself," he said. "For what it's worth."

"Look," I said, "I still don't consider it a federal case. This is cowardly bullshit. Whoever's behind it probably doesn't want a confrontation."

"Probably not," he said. But he still sounded troubled, and that started to rattle me.

"Something else," I said. "Though it's also probably no big deal. I was looking at the conference brochure again and tried to contact the three local therapists who gave speeches. Two weren't listed, but the one who was had been killed this past spring. Hit by a car while attending a psychiatric symposium. I found out because his answering service just happens to be the same one I use and the operator told me."

"Killed here in L.A.?"

"Out of town, she didn't remember where. I've got a call in to one of his associates."

"Symposium," he said. "Curse of the conference?"

"Like I said, it's probably nothing—the only thing that is starting to bug me is I can't reach anyone associated with the de Bosch meeting. Then again, it's been a long time, people move."

"Yeah."

"Milo, *you're* bugged about something. What is it?"

Pause. "I think, given everything that's been happening—putting it all together—you'd be justified getting a little . . . watchful. No paranoia, just be extra careful."

"Fine," I said. "Robin's coming home early—tonight. I'm picking her up at the airport. What do I tell her?"

"Tell her the truth—she's a tough kid."

"Some welcome home."

"What time are you picking her up?"

"Nine."

"I'll get over well before then and we'll put our heads together. You want, I can stay at the house while you're gone. Just feed me and water me and tell Rover not to make demands."

"Rover's a hero as far as I'm concerned—he's the one who heard the intruder."

"Yeah, but there was no *follow-through*, Alex. Instead of *eating* the sucker, he just stood around and watched. What you've *got* is a four-legged bureaucrat."

"That's cold," I said. "Didn't you ever watch *Lassie*?"

"Screw that, my thing was *Godzilla*. There's a useful pet."

By three, no one had returned my calls and I felt like a cartoon man on a desert island. I did paperwork and looked out the window a lot. At three-thirty, the dog and I hazarded a walk around the Glen, and when I arrived back home, there were no signs of intrusion.

Shortly after four, Milo arrived, looking hurried and bothered. When the dog came up to him, he paid no mind.

He held an audiocassette in one hand, his vinyl attaché case in the other. Instead of making his usual beeline to the kitchen, he went into the living room and loosened his tie. Putting the case on the coffee table, he handed me the tape.

"The original's in my file. This is your copy."

Seeing it brought back the screams and the chants. That child. . . . I put it in my desk and we went down to the pond, where I showed him the footprints.

He kneeled and inspected for a long time. Stood, frowning. "You're right, these are useless. Looks to me like someone took the time to mess them up."

He checked around the pond area some more, taking his time, getting his pants dirty. "Nope, nothing here worth a damn. Sorry."

That same troubled tone in his voice that I'd heard over the phone. He was holding back something, but I knew it was useless to probe.

Back in the living room, I said, "Something to drink?"

"Later." He opened the vinyl case and took out a brown plastic box. Removing a videocassette from it, he bounced it against one thigh.

The tape was unmarked, but the box was printed with the call letters of a local TV station. Rubber-stamped diagonally across the label was the legend PROPERTY LAPD: EVIDENCE RM. and a serial number.

"Dorsey Hewitt's last stand," he said. "Definitely not for prime time, but there's something I want you to check out—if your stomach can take it."

"I'll cope."

We went into the library. Before inserting the cartridge into the VCR, he peered into the machine's load slot.

"When's the last time you lubricated this?"

"Never," I said. "I hardly use it except to record sessions when the court wants visuals."

He sighed, slid the cartridge in, picked up the remote control, pressed PLAY, and stood back, watching the monitor with his hands folded across his waist. The dog jumped up on a big leather chair, settled, and regarded him. The screen went from black to bright blue and a hiss filtered through the speakers.

A half minute more of blue, then the TV station logo flashed over a digital date, two months old.

Another few moments of video stutter were followed by a long shot of an attractive, one-story brick building, with a central arch leading to a courtyard and wood-grilled windows. Tile roof, brown door to the right of the arch.

Close up on a sign: LOS ANGELES COUNTY MENTAL HEALTH CENTER, WESTSIDE.

Swing back to a long shot: two small, dark-garbed figures crouched on opposite sides of the arch—toylike: G.I. Joe figurines holding rifles.

A side shot revealed police barriers fencing the street.

No sound other than static, but the dog's ears had perked and pitched forward.

Milo raised the volume, and a soup of incomprehensible background speech could be heard above the white noise.

Nothing for a few seconds, then one of the dark figures moved, still squatting, and repositioned itself to the left of the door. Another figure came from around a corner and lowered itself to a deep crouch, both hands on its weapon.

A close-up inflated the new arrival, turning dark cloth into navy blue, revealing the bulk of protective vesting, white letters spelling out LAPD across a broad back. Combat boots. Blue ski mask revealing only eyes; I thought of Munich terrorists and knew something bad was going to happen.

But nothing did for the next few moments. The dog's ears were still stiff and his breathing had quickened.

Milo rubbed one shoe with another and ran his hand over his face. Then the brown door on the screen swung open on two people.

A man, bearded, long-haired, scrawny. The beard, a matted frenzy of blond and gray corkscrews. Above a blemished, knotted forehead, his hair haloed in spiky clumps, recalling a child's clumsily drawn sun.

The camera moved in on him, highlighting dirty flesh, sunken cheeks, bloodshot eyes so wide and bulging they threatened to shoot off the shaggy launchpad of his face.

He was naked from the waist up and sweating furiously. The wild eyes began rotating madly, never blinking, never settling. His mouth was agape, like a dental patient's, but no sound issued forth. He appeared to be toothless.

His left arm was clamped around a heavy black woman, im-

bedded so tightly in her soft, skirted waist that the fingers disappeared.

The skirt was green. Over it the woman wore a white blouse
that had come partially untucked. She was around thirty-five and
her face was wet, too—perspiration and tears. *Her* teeth were visible, lips stretched back in a rictus of horror.

The man's right arm was a bony yoke around her neck. Something silvery flashed in his hand as he pressed it up against her
throat.

She closed her eyes and kept them clenched.

The man was leaning her back, pressing her to him, convex-
ing her neck and revealing the full breadth of a big, shiny carving
knife. Red-stained hands. Red-stained blade. Only her heels
touched the pavement. She was off balance, an unwilling dancer.

The man blinked, darted his eyes, and looked at one of the
SWAT cops. Several rifles were aimed at him. No one moved.

The woman trembled and the collaring hand moved involuntarily and brought forth a small red mark from her neck. The
blotch stood out like a ruby.

She opened her eyes and stared straight ahead. The man
screamed something to her, shook her, and they closed again.

The camera stayed on the two of them, then shifted smoothly
to another of the SWAT men.

No one moved.

The dog was standing on the chair, breathing hard.

The bearded man's knife elbow quivered.

The man closed his mouth, opened it. Looked to be screaming
at the top of his lungs, but the sound wasn't carrying.

The woman's mouth was still open. Her wound had already
coagulated—just a nick.

The man propelled her onto the sidewalk, very slowly. One of
her shoes came off. He didn't notice it, was looking from side to
side, cop to cop, screaming nonstop.

All at once the sound came on. Very loud. New microphone.

The dog began barking.

The man with the knife screamed, a howling, hoarse and wet.
Panting. Wordless.

Pain scream.

My hands dug into my thighs. Milo faced the screen, immo-
bile.

The bearded man shifted his head from side to side some more, faster, harder, as if being slapped. Screaming louder. Pressing the knife up under the woman's chin.

Her eyes shot open.

The dog's barks turned to growls, guttural and bearish, loud enough to be scary and a lot more threatening than the warning sounds he'd uttered last night.

The man with the knife was directing his screams at a SWAT man to his left, haranguing wordlessly, as if the two of them were friends turned hateful.

The cop might have said something because the madman upped his volume.

Roaring. Shrieking.

The man backed away, hugging the woman more tightly, concealing his face behind hers as he dragged her into the doorway.

Then a smile and a short, sharp twist of his wrist.

Another spot of blood—larger than the first—formed on the woman's throat.

She raised her hands reflexively, trying to bend out from under the knife, losing her balance and stumbling.

Her weight and the movement surprised the man, and for one brief moment, as he tried to keep her upright and haul her backward, he lowered his right arm.

A quick, sharp sound—like a single handclap—and a red dot appeared on the man's right cheek.

He spread his arms. Another dot materialized, just left of the first one.

The woman fell to the pavement as a rain of gunfire sounded —corn popping in an echo chamber. The man's hair blew back. His chest burst, and the front of his face turned into something amoebic and rosy—a pink and white kaleidoscope that seemed to unfold as it imploded.

The hostage was facedown, fetal. Bloodspray showered down on her.

The man, now faceless, slumped and sagged, but he remained on his feet for one hellish second, a gore-topped scarecrow, still gripping the knife as red juice poured out of his head. He had to be dead but he continued to stand, bending at the knees, his ruined head shadowing the hostage's shoulder.

Then all at once he let go of the knife and collapsed, falling on the woman, limp as a blanket. She twisted and struck out at him, finally freed herself and managed to rise to her knees, sobbing and covering her head with her hands.

Policemen ran to her.

One of the dead man's bare feet was touching her leg. She didn't notice it, but a cop did and kicked it away. Another officer, still ski-masked, stood over the faceless corpse, legs spread, gun pointed.

The screen went black. Then bright blue.

The dog was barking again, loud and insistent.

I made a shushing sound. He looked at me, cocked his head. Stared at me, confused. I went over to him and patted his back. His back muscles were jumping and drool trickled from his flews.

"It's okay, fella." My voice sounded false and my hands were cold. The dog licked one of them and looked up at me.

"It's okay," I repeated.

Milo rewound the tape. His jaw was bunched.

How long had the scene lasted—a few minutes? I felt as if I'd aged watching it.

I stroked the dog some more. Milo stared at the numbers on the VCR's counter.

"It's him, isn't it?" I said. "Hewitt. Screaming on my tape."

"Him or a good imitation."

"Who's the poor woman?"

"Another social worker at the center. Adeline Potthurst. She just happened to be sitting at the wrong desk when he ran out after killing Becky."

"How is she?"

"Physically, she's okay—minor lacerations. Emotionally?" He shrugged. "She took disability leave. Refused to talk to me or anyone else."

He ran a hand along the edge of a bookshelf, grazing book spines and toys.

"How'd you figure it out?" I said. "Hewitt on the 'bad love' tape?"

"I'm not sure what I figured, actually."

He shrugged. His forelock cast a hat-brim shadow over his brow, and in the weak light of the library, his green eyes were drab.

The tape ejected. Milo put it on an end table and sat down.

The dog waddled over to him, and this time Milo looked pleased to see him.

Rubbing the animal's thick neck, he said, "When I first heard *your* tape, something about it bugged me—*reminded* me of something. But I didn't know what it was, so I didn't say anything to you. I figured it was probably 'bad love'—Hewitt's using the phrase, my reading about it in the clinic director's witness report."

"Had you watched the video before?"

He nodded. "But at the station, with half an ear—a bunch of other detectives sitting around, cheering when Hewitt bit it. Splatter's never been my thing. I was filling out forms, doing paperwork. . . . When you told me about the tape, it still didn't trigger, but I wasn't that bugged. I figured what you did—a bad joke."

"The phone call and the fish make it more than a joke, don't they?"

"The phone call, by itself, is stupidity—like you said, cowardly shit. Someone coming on your property in the middle of the night and *killing* something *is* more. All of it put *together* is more. How *much* more I don't know, but I'd rather be a little paranoid than get taken by surprise. After we spoke on the phone this afternoon I really wracked my brains about what was bothering me. Went back into the Basille files, found the video, and watched it. And realized it wasn't the phrase that I remembered, it was the *screams*. Someone had stuck Hewitt's screams on your little gift."

He pulled his wet hand away from the dog's maw, looked at it, wiped it on his jacket.

"Where'd the video come from?" I said. "TV station's raw footage?"

He nodded.

"How much of it was actually broadcast?"

"Not much at all. This TV station has a twenty-four-hour crime-watch van with a scanner—anything for the ratings, right? They got to the scene first and were the only ones to actually record the whole thing. Their total footage is ten minutes or so, mostly no-action standoff before Hewitt comes out with Adeline. What you just saw is thirty-five seconds."

"That's all? It seemed a lot longer."

"Seemed like a goddamn eternity, but that's what it was. The part that actually made it to the six o'clock news was *nine* seconds.

Five of Hewitt with Adeline, three of Rambo close-ups on the SWAT guys, and one second of Hewitt down. No blood, no screaming, no standing dead man."

"Wouldn't sell deodorant," I said, pushing the image of the teetering corpse out of my head. "Why was the sound off for most of it? Technical difficulties?"

"Yup. Loose cable on their parabolic mike. The sound man caught it midway through."

"What did the other stations broadcast?"

"Postmortem analysis by the department mouthpiece."

"So if the screams on my tape were lifted, the source had to be this particular piece of footage."

"Looks that way."

"Meaning what? Mr. Silk's an employee of the TV station?"

"Or a spouse, kid, lover, pal, significant other, whatever. If you give me your patient list, I can try to get hold of the station's personnel records and cross-check."

"Be better if you give me the personnel list," I said. "Let me check it against my patients, so I can preserve confidentiality."

"Fine. Another list you might try to get is the one for your 'bad love' conference. Anyone who attended. It was a long time ago, but maybe the hospital keeps records."

"I'll call tomorrow."

He got up and touched his throat. "*Now* I'm thirsty."

We went into the kitchen, opened beers, and sat at the table, drinking and brooding.

The dog positioned himself between us, licking his lips.

Milo said, "He doesn't get to go for the gusto?"

"Teetotaler." I got up and slid the water bowl over. The dog ignored it.

"Bullshit. He wants hops and malt," said Milo. "Looks like he's closed a few taverns in his day."

"*There's* a marketing opportunity for you," I said. "Brew a hearty lager for quadrupeds. Though I'm not sure you could set your criteria too high for a species that imbibes out of the toilet."

He laughed. I managed a smile. Both of us trying to forget the videotape. And everything else.

"There's another possibility," I said. "Maybe Hewitt's voice wasn't lifted from the video footage. Maybe he was taped simultaneously by someone at the mental health center. Someone who happened to have a recorder handy the day of the murder and switched it on during the standoff. There'd probably be machines lying around the center, for therapy."

"You're saying there's a therapist behind this?"

"I was thinking more of a patient. Some paranoids make a fetish of keeping records. I've seen some lug tape recorders around with them. Someone who'd been bearing a grudge since seventy-nine could very well be highly paranoid."

He thought about that. "Nutcase with a pocket Sony, huh? Someone you once treated who ended up at the mental health center?"

"Or just someone who remembered me from the conference and ended up at the center. Someone tying me in with bad love— whatever it means to him. Probably anger at bad therapy. Or therapy he perceived as bad. De Bosch's theory has to do with bad mothers letting their kids down. Betrayal. If you think of therapists as surrogate parents, the stretch isn't hard to make."

He put down his bottle and looked at the ceiling. "So we've got a nut, one of your old patients, gone downhill, can't afford private treatment so he's getting county help. Happens to be at the center the day Hewitt freaks out and butchers Becky. Recorder in his pocket—keeping tabs on all the people talking behind his back. He hears the screams, presses RECORD . . . I guess it's possible— anything's *possible* in this city."

"If we're dealing with someone who's been stewing for a long time, witnessing Becky Basille's murder and the SWAT scene could have set him off. Hearing Hewitt screaming about bad love could have done it, too, if he'd had experiences with de Bosch or a de Boschian therapist."

He rolled the bottle between his palms. "Maybe. But two nuts with a 'bad love' fixation just *happening* to show up at the same place on the same day is too damned cute for my taste."

"Mine, too," I said.

He drank some more.

"What if it wasn't a coincidence at all, Milo? What if Hewitt and the taper *knew* each other—even shared a common rage about bad love, de Bosch, therapists in general? If the mental health center's typical, it's a crowded place, patients waiting for hours. It wouldn't be that strange for two disturbed people to get together and discover a mutual resentment, would it? If they were paranoid to begin with, they could have played upon each other's fears and delusions. *Confirming* for each other that the way they saw the world was valid. The taper might even be someone who wouldn't have been violent under different circumstances. But seeing Hewitt murder *his* therapist and then seeing Hewitt's face blown off could have pushed him over."

"So now he's ready to do his own therapist? So what's the tape and the call and the fish?"

"Preparing the scene. Or maybe he won't go any further—I don't know. And something else: I might not even be his only target. He might have a current therapist who's in danger."

"Any idea who it could be? From your patient list?"

"No, that's the thing. There's no one who fits. But my patients were all kids. Lots can happen over time."

He sat back in his chair and looked up at the ceiling.

"Speaking of kids," he said. "Where does the kid's voice fit in with your two-nut scenario?"

"I don't know, dammit. Maybe the taper's got a kid. Or he's abducted one—God, I hope not, but that voice stank of coercion, didn't it? So flat—did *Hewitt* have any children?"

"Nope. The report has him as unmarried, unemployed, un-everything."

"Be good to know who he hung out with at the center. We could also try to verify that my tape was taken from the video footage. Because if it wasn't, we wouldn't have to bother cross-referencing the station personnel list."

He smiled. "And you wouldn't have to expose your patient list, right?"

"Right. That would be a major betrayal. I still can't justify it."

"You're sure it's not any of them?"

"No, I'm not sure, but what am I going to do? Call hundreds of people and ask them if they've grown up to be hate-crazed nuts?"

"No Mr. Silk in your past, huh?"

"Only silk I know is in my ties."

"One thing I can tell you, your tape's not an *exact* lift off the video. The footage has Hewitt screaming for just over twenty-seven seconds out of the thirty-five, and your segment only lasts sixteen. I had a brief go at it before I came over here—tried running both tapes simultaneously on two machines to see if I could pick out any segments that coincided exactly. I couldn't—it was tricky, going from machine to machine, on-off, on-off, trying to synchronize. And it's not like we're dealing with words, here—doesn't take long before all the screaming starts to sound the same."

"What about doing some kind of voiceprint analysis? Trying to get an electronic match."

"From what I know, you need actual words for a match. And the department doesn't do voiceprints anymore."

"Why not?"

"Probably not enough call. What they're useful for, mostly, is kidnapping ransom calls, and that's usually the FBI's game. Also phone scams, bunco stuff, which is low priority with all the buckets of blood. I think one guy at the sheriff's is still doing them. I'll find out."

The dog finally put his head in the bowl and began slurping water. Milo lifted his bottle, said, "Cheers," and emptied it.

"Why don't you and I try a little bit of low-tech teamwork right now?" I said. "You take audio, I'll take video—"

"And I'll be in Screamland afore ye."

He took the portable tapedeck into the library and loaded the video. We sat across from one another, listening to screams, trying to shut out the context. Even with two people it was difficult—hard to divide the howls into discrete segments.

We played and rewound, doing it over and over, trying to locate the sixteen seconds of the bad love tape amid the pain and noise of the longer video segment. The dog tolerated only a minute or so before scooting out of the room.

Milo and I stayed and sweated.

After half an hour, a triumph of sorts.

A discrepancy.

A second or two of sing-song, wordless jabber at the tail end of my tape that didn't materialize anywhere on the soundtrack of the video.

Ya ya ya . . . the screamer lowering his volume just a bit—a barely discernible shift not much longer than an eyeblink. But once I pointed it out, it mushroomed, as obvious as a billboard.

"Two separate taping sessions," I said, as stunned as Milo

looked. "Has to be, otherwise why would the shorter tape have something on it that's missing from the longer segment?"

"Yeah," he said quietly, and I knew he was angry at himself for not catching it first.

He sprang to his feet and paced. Looked at his Timex. "When'd you say you were going to the airport?"

"Nine."

"If you're comfortable leaving the place unguarded, I could go get something done."

"Sure," I said, rising. "What?"

"Talk to the clinic director about Hewitt's social life."

He collected his things and we walked to the door.

"Okay, I'm off," he said. "Got the Porsche and the cellular, so you can always reach me if you need to."

"Thanks for everything, Milo."

"What're friends for?"

Ugly answers flashed in my head, but I kept them to myself.

8

Just as I was preparing to head out for LAX, Dr. Stanley Wolf returned my call. He sounded middle-aged and spoke softly and hesitantly, as if doubting his own credibility.

I thanked him and said I'd called about Dr. Grant Stoumen.

"Yes, I got the message." He asked several tortuous questions about my credentials. Then: "Were you a student of Grant's?"

"No, we never met."

"Oh . . . what do you need to know?"

"I'm being harassed by someone, Dr. Wolf, and I thought Dr. Stoumen might be able to shed some light on it."

"Harassed?"

"Annoying mail. Phone calls. It may be linked to a conference I co-chaired several years ago. Dr. Stoumen delivered a paper there."

"A conference? I don't understand."

"A symposium on the work of Andres de Bosch entitled 'Good Love/Bad Love.' The term 'bad love' was used in the harassment."

"How long ago was this?"

"Seventy-nine."

"De Bosch—the child analyst?"

"Did you know him?"

"No, child analysis is outside of my . . . purview."

"Did Dr. Stoumen ever talk about de Bosch—or this particular conference?"

"Not to my recollection. Nor did he mention any . . . annoying mail?"

"Maybe 'annoying' is too mild," I said. "It's fairly nasty stuff."

"Uh-hm." He didn't sound convinced.

I said, "Last night it went a little further. Someone trespassed on my property. I have a fish pond. They took a fish out, killed it, and left it for me to see."

"Hmm. How . . . bizarre. And you think this symposium's the link?"

"I don't know, but it's all I've got so far. I'm trying to contact anyone who appeared on the dais, to see if they've been harassed. So far everyone I've tried to reach has moved out of town. Do you happen to know a psychiatrist named Wilbert Harrison or a social worker named Mitchell Lerner?"

"No."

"They also delivered papers. The co-chairs were de Bosch's daughter, Katarina, and a New York analyst named Harvey Rosenblatt."

"I see. . . . Well, as I mentioned I'm not a child analyst. And unfortunately, Grant's no longer with us, so I'm afraid—"

"Where did his accident take place?"

"Seattle," he said, with sudden strength in his voice. "At a conference, as a matter of fact. And it wasn't a simple accident. It was a hit-and-run. Grant was heading out for a late-night walk; he stepped off the curb in front of his hotel and was struck down."

"I'm sorry."

"Yes, it was terrible."

"What was the topic of the conference?"

"Something to do with child welfare—the Northwest Symposium on Child Welfare, I believe. Grant was always an advocate for children."

"Terrible," I said. "And this was in May?"

"Early June. Grant was on in years—his eyesight and hearing weren't too good. We prefer to think he never saw it or heard it coming."

"How old was he?"

"Eighty-nine."

"Was he still in practice?"

"A few old patients stopped by from time to time, and he kept an office in the suite and insisted on paying his share of the rent. But mostly he traveled. Art exhibitions, concerts. And conferences."

"His age made him a contemporary of Andres de Bosch," I said. "Did he ever mention him?"

"If he did, I don't recall it. Grant knew lots of people. He was in practice for almost sixty years."

"Did he treat especially disturbed or violent patients?"

"You know I can't discuss his cases, Dr. Delaware."

"I'm not asking about specific cases, just the general tenor of his practice."

"The little that I saw was pretty conventional—children with adjustment problems."

"Okay, thanks. Is there anyone else who could talk to me about him?"

"Just Dr. Langenbaum, and he knows about as much as I do."

"Did Dr. Stoumen leave a widow?"

"His wife died several years ago and they had no children. Now I really do have to get going."

"Thanks for your time, Dr. Wolf."

"Yes . . . hmm. Good luck on . . . working this through."

I got my car keys, left a lot of lights on in the house, and turned on the stereo to loud jazz. The dog was sleeping noisily on his towel bed, but he roused himself and followed me to the door.

"Stay and guard the home front," I said, and he harrumphed, stared for a moment, finally sat down.

I walked out, closed the door, listened for a protest, and when I didn't hear any, went down to the carport. The night had cooled, massaged by sea current. The waterfall seemed deafening and I drove away listening to it diminish.

As I coasted down toward the Glen, a sense of dread dropped over me, dark and smothering, like a condemned man's hood.

I paused at the bottom of the road, looking at black treetops and slate sky. A faint bit of light from a distant house blinked through the foliage like an earthbound star.

No way to gauge its distance. I had no real neighbors because an acre-wide strip of county land, unbuildable due to a quirky water table, cut through this section of the Glen. Mine was the only buildable site on the plot plan.

Years ago the isolation had been just what I wanted. Now a nosy streetmate didn't seem half bad.

A car sped down the Glen from the north, appearing suddenly around a blind curve, going too fast, its engine flatulent with power.

I tensed as it passed, took another look backward, and hooked right, toward the Sunset on-ramp of the 405 south. By the time I got on the freeway, I was thinking of Robin's smile and pretending nothing else mattered.

Slow night at the airport. Cabbies circled the terminals and skycaps looked at their watches. I found a space in the passenger loading zone and managed to stay there until Robin came out, toting her carry-on.

I kissed her and hugged her, took the suitcase, and put it in the trunk of the Seville. A man in a Hawaiian shirt was looking at her over cigarette smoke. So were a couple of kids with backpacks and surfer hair.

She had on a black silk T-shirt and black jeans, and over that a purple and red kimono-type shirt tied around her waist. The jeans were tucked into black boots with tooled silver toes. Her hair was loose and longer than ever—well past her shoulder blades, the auburn curls bronzed by the light from the baggage claim area. Her skin gleamed and her dark eyes were clear and peaceful. It had been five days since I'd seen her, but it seemed like a long separation.

She touched my cheek and smiled. I leaned in for a longer kiss.

"Whoa," she said, when we stopped, "I'll go away more often."

"Not necessary," I said. "Sometimes there is gain without pain."

She laughed and hugged me and put her arm around my waist. I held the door open as she got in the car. The man in the Hawaiian shirt had turned his back on us.

As I drove away she put her hand on my knee and looked over at the back seat. "Where's the dog?"

"Guarding hearth and home. How was your talk?"

"Fine. Plus I may have sold that archtop guitar I did last summer—the one Joey Shah defaulted on. I met a jazz musician from Dublin who wants it."

"Great," I said. "You put a lot of time into that one."

"Five hundred hours, but who's counting."

She stifled a yawn and put her head on my shoulder. I drove all the way to Sunset before she woke up, shaking her curls. "Boy . . . must have hit me all of a sudden." Sitting up, she blinked at the streets of Bel Air.

"Home sweet home," she said softly.

I waited until she'd roused herself before telling her the bad news.

She took it well.

"Okay," she said, "I guess it goes with the territory. Maybe we should move out for a while and stay at the shop."

"Move out?"

"At least till you know what's going on."

I thought of her studio, separated from the mean streets of Venice by a thin veneer of white windows and locks. Saws and drills and wood shavings on the ground floor. The sleeping loft in which we'd made love so many times . . .

"Thanks," I said, "but I can't stay away indefinitely—the house needs maintenance. Not to mention the fish that're left."

That sounded trivial, but she said, "That poor fish. And you worked so hard to keep them alive."

She touched my cheek.

"Welcome home," I said glumly.

"Don't worry about *that*, Alex. Let's just figure out how to deal with this stupidity until it's resolved."

"I don't want to put you in any danger. Maybe *you* should move to the shop—"

"And leave you alone in the middle of this?"

"I just want to make sure you're okay."

"How okay do you think I'm going to be, worrying every minute about you? I mean, the fish are wonderful, Alex, but you can hire someone to feed them. Hire someone to look after the whole house, for that matter."

"Pack up the wagons and head out?"

"What's wrong with being a little cautious, honey?"

"I don't know . . . it just seems awfully drastic—all that's really happened is malicious mischief."

"So why were you so upset when you told me about it?"

"Sorry. I didn't want to upset you."

"Of *course* it upsets me," she said. "Someone sending you weird tapes, sneaking in and . . ." She put her arm around my shoulder. The light changed to green and I turned left.

"Goes with the territory," she repeated. "All those troubled people you've worked with over the years. All that misdirected passion. The surprising thing isn't that it happened. It's how long it took."

"You never said it worried you."

"It wasn't a matter of worry—I didn't obsess on it. Just thought about it from time to time."

"You never said anything."

"What would have been the point? I didn't want to upset *you*."

I lifted her hand from my shoulder and kissed it.

"Okay," she said, "so we protect each other, Curly. Ain't that what true love's all about?"

I pulled up in front of the house. No obvious signs of intrusion.

I said, "Just let me check around for a sec before you get out."

"Oh, really," she said. But she stayed in the car.

I gave the pond a quick inspection. The fish moved with nighttime languor, and none was missing.

I jogged up the stairs to the landing, checked the front door, peered in through the living room window. Something moved as the drapes parted. The dog's face pressed against the glass, wetting it. I raised my hand in greeting. He pawed the window. I could hear the jazz through the redwood walls.

By the time I got back down, Robin was lifting her valise from the trunk. When I tried to take it from her, she said, "I've got it," and headed for the steps.

As I unlocked the front door, she said, "We could at least get an alarm. Everyone else has one."

"Never been a slave to fashion," I said, but when she didn't smile, I added, "Okay. I'll call a company tomorrow."

We walked in and almost tripped over the bulldog, who'd

positioned himself on the welcome mat. He stared from Robin to me, then back to her, where he lingered with Churchillian dignity.

Robin said, "My God."

"What?" I said.

"He *invented* cute, Alex. Come here, sweetie." She bent down to his level with one hand extended, palm down.

He trotted forward without hesitation, jumped up, put his paws on her shoulders, and embarked on a lick-fest.

"Ooh!" She laughed. "What a *handsome* boy you are—what a *cutie*—look at those *muscles!*"

She stood, wiping her face, still laughing. The dog continued to nuzzle and paw her legs. His tongue was out and he was panting.

She placed a hand on my shoulder and gave me a grave look. "Sorry, Alex. There is now another man in my life." Bending, she rubbed him behind the ears.

"Crushed," I said, placing a hand over my heart. "And you might reconsider—he doesn't have gonads."

"Them's the breaks," she said, smiling. "Look at that *face!*"

"Also, he snores."

"So do you, once in a while."

"You never told me."

She shrugged. "I kick you and usually you stop—well, just look at *you*, you little hunk. Apathy's not *your* problem, *is* it?"

She knelt back down and got her face rebathed. "What a doll!"

"Think of the ramifications on your social life," I said. "Meatloaf and kibble by candlelight."

She laughed again and roughed the dog's fur.

As the two of them played, I picked up the suitcase and carried it into the bedroom, checking rooms as I passed, trying not to be obvious. Everything looked fine. I took Robin's clothes out and arranged them on the bed.

When I got back, she was on the leather couch, the dog's head in her lap. "I know this is heartless, Alex, but I hope his owner never calls. How long, legally, do you have to run the ad?"

"I'm not sure."

"There's got to be a limit, right? Some sort of statute of limitations?"

"Probably."

Her smile disappeared. "With my luck someone'll show up tomorrow and cart him off."

She covered another yawn. The dog looked at her, fascinated.

"Tired?" I said.

"A little. Everything okay around here? I'm sure you looked."

"Perfect."

"I'll get unpacked."

"Did it," I said. "Why don't you run a bath? I'll put your stuff away, then join you."

"That's sweet of you, thanks." She looked at the dog. "See, he really is a nice guy, our Dr. D. How 'bout you—you like baths, too?"

"As a matter of fact, he hates the water. Won't even get near it. So it's just you and me, kid."

"How Machiavellian of you—where does he sleep?"

"Last night he slept in the bed. Tonight he moves back into the kitchen."

She pouted.

I shook my head. "Uh-uh, no way."

"Oh, c'mon, Alex. It's just temporary."

"Do you want those eyes watching us?"

"Watching us do what?"

"The crossword puzzle."

"He'll be lonely out there, Alex."

"All of a sudden we're into voyeurism?"

"I'm sure he's a gentleman. And as you so unkindly pointed out, he has no . . ."

"Balls or no balls, he's a *nudist*, Robin. And he's got the hots for you. The kitchen."

She tried a bigger pout.

I said, "Put it out of your mind."

"Cruel," she said. "Heartless and cruel."

"Sounds like a law firm. Heartless, Cruel, and Horny—think I'll put 'em on retainer."

The dog posted himself at the bathroom door as Robin stepped into the suds. She soaped up, and I picked him up and carried him, grumbling, to his towel bed. The moment I put him down, he tried to escape. I closed the kitchen doors and gave him a Milk-Bone and as he began chewing, I snuck out.

He fussed for a while, attempting a sonorous rendition of the old-man-choking bit, but I applied sound behavior theory principles and ignored him, while trying to suppress my guilt. After a minute or so he calmed down and soon I heard him snoring in two-four time.

When I got back, Robin looked at me reproachfully. Her hair was up and the water's soapy surface reached just below her nipples.

"He's fine." I got out of my clothes. "Enjoying the slumber of the truly virtuous."

"Well," she said, putting her arms behind her head and watching, "I suppose it's best."

"Forgiven?" I said, sinking into the heat of the bath.

She contemplated. Breathed in. Smiled.

"I don't know . . ."

I kissed her. She kissed back. I touched one breast, kissed a soapy nipple.

"Umm," she said, breaking away. "Well . . ."

"Well, what?"

"You can forget Mr. Cruel and Mr. Heartless, but I think it's time to take a meeting with their partner—what's his name?"

9

Thursday morning she was up and out of the shower by six-fif-
teen. When I got to the kitchen I expected to see her dressed for
work, that restless look in her eyes.

But she was still in her robe, drinking coffee and reading
ArtForum. She'd set out food for the dog and only a few bits remained. He was at her feet and looked up at me only briefly before returning his head to the side of her leg.

She put the magazine down and smiled up at me.

I kissed her and said, "You can get going, I'll be fine."

"What if I just want to be with you?"

"That would be great."

"Of course, if *you* have other plans . . ."

"Nothing till the afternoon."

"What's then?"

"Patient appointment out in Sun Valley at three-thirty."

"Making a house call?"

I nodded. "Custody case. Some resistance and I want to see
the kids in their natural environment."

"Three-thirty? That's good. We can hang out together till
then."

"Terrific." I poured myself a cup, sat down, and pointed to
the magazine. "What's new in the art world?"

"The usual foolishness." She closed it and pushed it aside.

"Actually I have no idea what's going on in the art world or anywhere else. I can't concentrate, Alex. Woke up in the middle of the night, thinking about everything that's been happening to you and that poor psychiatrist up in Seattle. Do you really think there is a connection?"

"I don't know. It was a hit-and-run, but he was eighty-nine and couldn't see or hear well. Like Freud said, sometimes a cigar is just a cigar—did you get any sleep?"

"A bit."

"Was I snoring?"

"No."

"Would you tell me if I was?"

"Yes!" She gave my hand a gentle cuff.

"Why didn't you wake me to talk?" I said.

"You were deep asleep. I didn't have the heart."

"Next time wake me."

"We can talk right now, if you want. This whole thing's giving me very definite creeps the more I think about it. I'm worried about you—what will the next call or mail delivery bring?"

"Milo's looking into it," I said. "We'll get to the bottom of it."

I took her hand and squeezed it. She squeezed back hard. "You can't think of anyone who'd want to get back at you? Out of all the patients you've known?"

"Not really. When I worked at the hospital, I saw physically ill kids. In practice, it was basically normal children with adjustment problems." The same kinds of patients Grant Stoumen had treated.

"What about your legal cases? All that custody garbage?"

"Anything's possible, theoretically," I said. "But I've gone through my files and found nothing. The conference has to be the link—bad love."

"What about that madman—Hewitt? Why was he shouting it?"

"I don't know," I said.

She let go of my hand. "He killed his therapist, Alex."

"Guess I could switch careers. But I'm really not good for anything else."

"Be serious."

"Okay—what happened to Becky Basille is the extreme. It's a long way from tapes and a crank call and a mangled carp to murder."

The look on her face made me add: "I'll be careful—scout's honor. I'll call an alarm company—get a referral from Milo."

"You won't consider moving out—just for a while?"

"Let's just see what happens over the next few days."

"What are you waiting for, Alex? Things to get worse? Oh, never mind, let's not bicker."

She got up, shaking her head, and went to the coffeepot for a refill. Stayed there drinking and looking out the window.

"Honey, I'm not trying to tough it out," I said. "I just want to see what Milo comes up with before I shake up our lives completely. Let's at least give him a day or two to look into it, okay? If he doesn't, we'll move to the studio temporarily."

"A day or two? You've got a deal." The dog padded over to her. She smiled at him, then at me. "Maybe I'm overdoing it. Was the tape that bad?"

"Bizarre," I said. "Like some kind of sick gag."

"It's the *sick* part that bothers me."

The dog snorted and jangled his collar. She took some cheese out of the fridge, told him to sit, and rewarded his obedience with small bites. He gobbled noisily and licked his flews.

"What do you call this?" she said. "Operant conditioning?"

"A-plus," I said. "Next week's topic is stress management."

She grinned. The last bit of cheese disappeared amid the soft folds of the dog's mouth. Robin washed her hands. The dog continued to sit and stare at her. "Shouldn't we give him a name, Alex?"

"Milo calls him Rover."

"Figures."

"I've stuck with 'hey, you' because I keep expecting someone to call and claim him."

"True . . . why get attached . . . are you hungry? I can dish something up."

"Why don't we go out?"

"Go out?"

"Like normal people."

"Sure, I'll go change."

The sparkle in her eyes made me say, "How about changing into something semi-fancy and we can hit the Bel Air?"

"The Bel Air? What are we celebrating?"

"The new world order."

"If only there was one. What about him?"

"Milk-Bone *en le kitchen*," I said. "I don't have a suit that fits him."

She put on a silver crepe de chine blouse and a black skirt and I found a lightweight sportcoat, brown turtleneck, and khaki slacks that looked decent. I told my service where I'd be and we took Sunset to Stone Canyon Road and drove up the half mile to the Bel Air Hotel. Pink-shirted valets opened our doors and we walked across the covered bridge to the main entrance.

Swans glided below in the still, green pond, cutting through the water with blissful ignorance. A white lattice marriage canopy was being set up on the banks. Huge pine and eucalyptus umbrellaed the grounds, air-conditioning the morning.

We passed through the pink stucco arcade hung with black-and-white photos of monarchs gone by. The stone pathways had been freshly watered, the ferns dripped dew, and the azaleas were in bloom. Room service waiters rolled carts to sequestered suites. An emaciated, androgynous, long-haired thing in brown velvet sweats walked past us unsteadily, carrying *The Wall Street Journal* under one atrophied arm. Death was in its eyes, and Robin bit her lip.

I held her arm tighter and we entered the dining room, exchanged smiles with the hostess, and were seated near the French doors. Several years ago—soon after we'd met—we'd lingered right here over dinner and seen Bette Davis through those same doors, gliding across the patio in a long, black gown and coronation-quality diamonds, looking as serene as the swans.

This morning, the room was nearly empty and none of the faces had a measurable Q-rating, though all looked well tended. An Arab in an ice cream suit drank tea, alone, at a corner table. An elderly, dewlapped couple who could have been pretenders to a minor throne whispered to each other and nibbled on toast. In a big booth at the far end, half a dozen dark suits sat listening to a crewcut, white-haired man in a red T-shirt and khakis. He was telling a joke, gesturing expansively with an unlit cigar. The other men's body language was half humble servant, half Iago.

We had coffee and took a long time deciding what to eat. Neither of us felt like talking. After a few moments, the silence began to feel like a luxury and I relaxed.

We finished a couple of fresh grapefruit juices and put in our breakfast order, holding hands until the food came. I'd just taken the first bite of my omelet when I spotted the hostess approaching. Two steps ahead of someone else.

A tall, broad someone, easily visible over her coiffure. Milo's jacket was light blue—a tint that clashed with his aqua shirt. Pigeon-gray pants and brown-and-blue-striped tie rounded off the ensemble. He had his hands in his pockets and looked dangerous.

The hostess kept her distance from him, clearly wanting to be somewhere else. Just before she reached our table, he stepped ahead of her. After kissing Robin, he took a chair from another table and pulled it up perpendicular to us.

"Will you be ordering, sir?" said the hostess.

"Coffee."

"Yes, sir." She walked away hastily.

Milo turned to Robin. "Welcome home. You look gorgeous, as ever."

"Thank you, Milo—"

"Flight okay?"

"Just fine."

"Every time I'm up in one of those things I wonder what gives us the right to break the law of gravity."

Robin smiled. "To what do we owe the honor?"

He ran his hand over his face. "Has he told you about what's going on?"

She nodded. "We're thinking of moving into the shop until things clear up."

Milo grunted and looked at the tablecloth.

The waiter brought the coffee and a place setting. Milo unfolded the napkin over his lap and drummed a spoon on the table. As the coffee was being poured, he glanced around the room, lingering on the suits in the far booth.

"Meals and deals," he said, after the waiter left. "Either showbiz or crime."

"There's a difference?" I said.

His smile was immediate but very weak—it seemed to torment his face.

"There's a new complication," he said. "This morning I decided to have a go at the computer, tracking down any references to 'bad love' in the case files. I really didn't expect to find anything, just trying to be thorough. But I did. Two unsolved homicides, one three years old, the other five. One beating, one stabbing."

"Oh God," said Robin.

He covered her hand with his. "Hate to spoil your breakfast, kids, but I wasn't sure when I'd be able to catch both of you. Service said you were here."

"No, no, I'm glad you came." She pushed her plate away and gripped Milo's hand.

"Who got killed?" I said.

"Does the name Rodney Shipler mean anything to you?"

"No. Is he a victim or a suspect?"

"Victim. What about Myra Paprock?"

He spelled it. I shook my head.

"You're sure?" he said. "Neither of them could have been old patients?"

I repeated both names to myself. "No—never heard of them. How does 'bad love' figure into their murders?"

"With Shipler—he was the beating—it was scrawled on a wall at the crime scene. With Paprock, I'm not sure what the connection is yet. The computer just threw out 'bad love' under 'miscellaneous factors'—no explanation."

"Did the same detectives work both cases?"

He shook his head. "Shipler was in Southwest Division, Paprock over in the valley. Far as I can tell, the cases were never cross-referenced—two years apart, different parts of the city. I'm going to try to get the actual case files this afternoon."

"For what it's worth," I said, "I spoke to Dr. Stoumen's associate last night. The accident was a hit-and-run. It happened in Seattle, in June of last year."

Milo's eyebrows rose.

"It may have just been a hit-and-run," I said. "Stoumen was almost ninety, couldn't see or hear well. Someone ran into him as he stepped off a curb."

"At a psych conference."

"Yes, but unless Shipler or Paprock were therapists, what link could there be?"

"Don't know what they were yet. The computer doesn't give out that level of detail."

Robin's head had dropped, curls spilling onto the table. She looked up, clear eyed. "So what do we do?"

"Well," said Milo, "you know I'm not Mr. Impulsive, but with everything we've got here—nut mail, nut call, dead fish, two cold-case homicides, hazardous conferences—" He looked at me. "Moving's not a bad idea. At least till we find out what the hell's going on. But I wouldn't go to the shop. Just in case whoever's bothering Alex has done enough research on him to know the location."

She looked out the window and shook her head. He patted her shoulder.

She said, "I'm fine. Let's just figure out where we're going to live." She looked around. "This place ain't shabby—too bad we're not oil sheiks."

"As a matter of fact," said Milo, "I think I've got an option for you. Private client of mine—investment banker I moonlighted for last year. He's in England for a year, put his house up for rent, and hired me to keep an eye on the premises. It's a nice size place and not that far from you. Beverly Hills PO, off Benedict Canyon. It's still empty—you know the real estate market—and he's coming back in three months, so he unlisted it. I'm sure I can get his permission for you to use it."

"Benedict Canyon." Robin smiled. "Close to the Sharon Tate house?"

"Not far, but the place is as safe as you're gonna get. The owner's security conscious—has a big art collection. Electric gates, closed-circuit TV, screaming siren alarm."

It sounded like prison. I didn't say a thing.

"The alarm's hooked up to Beverly Hills PD," he went on. "And their response time's averaging two minutes—maybe a little longer up in the hills, but still damn good. I'm not going to tell you it's home, chillun, but for temporary lodgings you could do worse."

"And this client of yours won't mind?"

"Nah, it's a piece of cake."

"Thanks, Milo," said Robin. "You're a doll."

"No big deal."

"What do I do about my work? Can I go to the shop?"

"Wouldn't hurt to avoid it for a few days. At least until I find out more about these unsolveds."

She said, "I had orders piled up before I went to Oakland, Milo. The time I spent up there already set me back." She grabbed her napkin and crushed it. "I'm sorry, here you are getting threatened, baby, and I'm griping . . ."

I took her hand and kissed it.

Milo said, "In terms of work, you could set up shop in the garage. It's a triple and there's only one car in it."

"That's big enough," said Robin, "but I can't just pack up the table saw and the band saw and cart them over."

"I may be able to help you with that, too," said Milo.

"An alternative," I said, "would be moving to the studio and hiring a guard."

"Why take a chance?" said Milo. "My philosophy is when trouble calls, don't be there to answer the doorbell. You can even take Rover with. Owner keeps cats—a friend's taking care of them now, but we're not talking pristine environment."

"Sounds good," I said, but my throat had gone dry and a refugee numbness was rising up from my feet. "As long as we're talking critters, there're the rest of the koi. The pond maintenance people can probably board them for a while—time to get organized."

Robin began folding her napkin, over and over, ending up with a small, thick wad that she pressed between her hands. Her knuckles were ivory knobs and her lips were clamped together. She gazed over my shoulder, as if peering into an uncertain future.

The waiter came over with the coffeepot, and Milo waved him away.

From the big booth came the sound of male laughter. The levity had probably been going on for a while, but I heard it now because the three of us had stopped talking.

The Arab got up from his table, smoothed his suit, put cash on the table, and left the dining room.

Robin said, "Guess it's time to hitch up the wagons," but she didn't move.

"This whole thing seems so unreal," I said.

"Maybe it'll turn out we've hassled for nothing," Milo said, "but you two are among the few humans I hold any positive regard for, so I do feel an obligation to protect and serve."

He looked at our barely touched food and frowned. "This'll set you back some."

"Have some." I pushed my plate toward him.

He shook his head.

"The stress diet," I said. "Let's write a book and hit the talk-show circuit."

He followed us home in an unmarked Ford. When the three of us stepped into the house, the dog thought it was a party and began jumping around.

"Take a Valium, Rover," said Milo.

"Be nice to him," said Robin, kneeling and holding her arms out. The dog charged her and she tussled with him for a second, then stood. "I'd better figure out what I'm going to need to take."

She left for the bedroom, dog at heel.

"True love," said Milo.

I said, "Is there anything more you want to tell me?"

"You mean, am I shielding her from gory details? No. Didn't figure I should."

"No, of course not," I said. "I just—I guess *I* still want to protect her."

"Then you're doing the right thing by moving."

I didn't answer.

"Nothing to be ashamed of," he said. "The protective instinct. I keep my work out of Rick's face, he does the same for me."

"If anything happened to her . . ." From the back of the house came Robin's footsteps, rapid and intermittent.

Pause and decision.

Dull sounds as clothing hit the bed. Soft, sweet words as she talked to the dog.

I paced some more, circling, trying to focus . . . what to take, what to leave . . . looking at things I wouldn't be seeing for a while.

"Ring around the rosy," he said. "Now you're looking like me when I'm uptight."

I ran my hand over my face. He laughed, unbuttoned his jacket, and pulled a notepad and pen out of an inner pocket. He was wearing his revolver in a brown cowhide hip holster.

"Do *you* have any more details for me?" he said. "Like about the psychiatrist—Stoumen?"

"Just the approximate date—early June—and the fact that the conference was the Northwest Symposium on Child Welfare. I'm pretty sure it's sponsored by the Child Welfare League, and they have an office here in town. Maybe you can pry an attendance roster out of them."

"You have a go at the Western Pediatric roster yet?"

"No. I'll try right now."

I called the hospital and asked for the Office of Continuing Education. The secretary told me records of past symposia were only kept for one year. I asked her to check anyway and she did.

"Nothing, doctor."

"There're no archives or anything?"

"Archives? With our budget problems we're lucky to get bed-pans, doctor."

Milo was listening in. When I hung up, he said, "Okay, scratch that. Onward. I'm going to hook up with the FBI's violent crime data bank and see if 'bad love' shows up on any out-of-town homicides."

"What about Dorsey Hewitt?" I said. "Could he have killed Shipler and Paprock?"

"Let me try to find out if he was living in L.A. during their murders. I'm still trying to get hold of Jean Jeffers, the clinic direc-tor—see if Hewitt had clinic buddies."

"The taper," I said. "You know, that second session could have taken place the day of the murder—someone taping Hewitt right after he killed Becky. Before he ran out and the TV mikes picked him up. That's pretty damn cold—almost premeditated. Same kind of mind who could turn a child's voice robotic. What if the taper knew exactly what Hewitt was going to do and was ready to tape him?"

"An accomplice?"

"Or at least a knowing confederate. Someone who knew Becky was going to die, but didn't stop it."

He stared at me. Grimaced. Wrote something down. Said, "Ready to start packing now?"

It took an hour or so for Robin and me to throw together suitcases, plastic shopping bags, and cardboard cartons. A smaller collection than I would have expected.

Milo and I carried all of it into the living room, then I called my pond maintenance people and arranged for them to collect the fish.

When I returned to the pile, Milo and Robin were staring at it. She said, "I'm going to go over to the shop and get the small tools and the breakable things together—if that's okay."

"Sure, just be careful," said Milo. "Anyone weird hanging around, just turn around and come back."

"Weird? This is Venice we're talking about."

"Relatively speaking."

"Gotcha." She took the dog with her. I walked her down to her truck and watched as they drove away. Milo and I had a couple of Cokes, then the doorbell rang and he went to get it. After looking through the peephole, he opened the door and let in three men—boys, really, around nineteen or twenty.

They were thick faced and had power lifters' rhino physiques. Two white, one black. One of the white ones was tall. They wore perforated tank tops, knee-length baggies in nauseating color combinations, and black lace-up boots that barely closed around their tree-stump calves. The white boys had their hair cut very short, except at the back, where it fringed around their excessive shoulders. The black's head was shaved clean. Despite their bulk, all three seemed awkward—intimidated.

Milo said, "Morning, campers, this is Dr. Delaware. He's a psychologist, so he knows how to read your minds. Doctor, this is Keenan, Chuck, and DeLongpre. They haven't figured out what to do with their lives yet, so they abuse themselves over at Silver's Gym and spend Keenan's money. Right, boys?"

The three of them smiled and cuffed one another. Through the open door I saw a black van parked near the carport. Jacked-up suspension, black-matte reversed hubcaps, darkened windows, diamond-shaped bulb of black plastic set into the side panel, a skull-and-crossbones decal just below that.

"Tasteful, huh?" said Milo. "Tell Dr. Delaware who recovered your wheels for you, after a miscreant scumbag junkie made off with it because you left it on Santa Monica Boulevard with the key in the ignition."

"You did, Mr. Sturgis," said the shorter white boy. He had a crushed nose, puffy lips, a very deep voice, and a slight lisp. The confession seemed to relieve him and he gave a big grin. One of his canines was missing.

"And who didn't charge you his usual private fee because you'd run out of trust fund that month, Keenan?"

"You didn't, sir."

"Was that a gift?"

"No, sir."

"Am I a chump?"

Shake of the thick head.

"What did I demand in return, boys?"

"Slave labor!" they shouted in unison.

He nodded and rapped the back of one hand against the palm of the other. "Payoff time. All this stuff goes into the Deathmobile. The really heavy gear's over in Venice—Pacific Avenue. Know where that is?"

"Sure," said Keenan. "Near Muscle Beach, right?"

"Very good. Follow me there and we'll see what you're made of. Once you're finished, you'll keep your mouths shut about it. Period. Understood?"

"Yes, sir."

"And be careful with it—pretend it's bottles of liver shake or something."

10

We met up with Robin and loaded her pickup. Watching her shop empty made her blink, but she wiped her eyes quickly and said, "Let's go."

We set up a caravan—Milo in the lead, Robin and the dog in the truck, me in the Seville, the van trailing—and headed back to Sunset, passing Beverly Glen as if it were someone else's neighborhood, entering Beverly Hills, and driving north onto Benedict Canyon.

Milo turned off on a narrow road, poorly paved and sided with eucalyptus. A cheerless, white iron gate appeared fifty feet up. He slipped a card key into a slot and it opened. The caravan continued up a steep pebbled drive hedged with very high columns of Italian cypress that looked slightly moth-eaten. Then the road kinked and we descended another two or three hundred feet, toward a shallow bowl of an unshaded lot, maybe half an acre wide.

A low, off-white one-story house sat in the bowl. A long, straight, concrete drive led to the front door. As I got closer I saw that the entire property was hilltop, the depression an artificial crater scalped from the tip.

Canyon and mountain views surrounded the property. Lots of brown slopes and a few green spots, flecked with the lint of occasional houses. I wondered if mine could be seen from up here, looked around but couldn't get my bearings.

The house was wide and free of detail, roofed too heavily with deep brown aluminum tile supposed to simulate shake, and windowed with aluminum-cased rectangles.

A flat-topped detached garage was separated from the main building by an unfenced paddle tennis court. A ten-foot satellite dish perched atop it, aimed at the cosmos.

A few cactus and yuccas grew near the house, but that was it in terms of landscaping. What could have been front lawn had been converted to concrete pad. An empty terra cotta planter sat next to the coffee-colored double doors. As I got out of the car, I noticed the TV camera above the lintel. The air was hot and smelled sterile.

I got out and went over to Robin's truck.

She smiled. "Looks like a motel, doesn't it?"

"Long as the owner's not named Norman."

The black van dieseled as its ignition shut down. The three beef-boys exited and threw open the rear doors. Tarped machines filled the cabin. The boys did some squats and grunts and began unloading.

Milo said something to them, then waved to us. His jacket was off but he still wore his gun. The heat had returned.

"Crazy weather," I said.

Robin got out and lifted the dog out of the pickup. We walked to the front door, and Milo let us into the house.

The floor was white marble streaked with pink, the furniture teakwood and ebony and bright blue velour. The far wall was taken up by single, light French doors. All the others were covered with paintings—hung frame to frame, so that only scraps of white plaster were visible.

The doors looked out onto a yard encircled by a nearly invisible fence—glass panes in thin iron frames. A strip of sod-grass separated a cement patio from a long, narrow lap pool. The pool had been dug at the edge of the lot—someone aiming for a merge-with-the-sky effect. But the water was blue and the sky was gray and the whole thing ended up looking like an off-balance cubist sculpture.

The dog ran to the French doors and tapped the glass with his paws. Milo let him out and he squatted in the grass before returning.

"Make yourself right at home, why don't you." To us: "Called London, everything's set up. There'll be a token rent, but you don't have to worry about it until he gets back."

We thanked him. He dusted off one of the couches and I studied the art. Impressionist pictures that looked French and important nudged up against pre-Raphaelite mythology. Syrupy, Orientalist harem scenes neighbored with English hunt paintings. Modern pieces, too: a Mondrian, a Frank Stella chevron, a Red Grooms subway cartoon, something amorphous fashioned out of neon.

The dining area was all Maxfield Parrish: cobalt skies, heavenly forests, and beautiful blond boys.

Lots of nude male statuary, too. A lamp whose black granite base was a limbless, muscular torso—Venus de Milo in drag. A framed cover from *The Advocate* commemorating the Christopher Street riot side by side with a Paul Cadmus drawing of a reclining Adonis. A framed Arrow Man shirt ad from an old issue of *Collier's* kept company with a black-and-white gelatin print of a Paul Newman lookalike in nothing but a G-string. I felt less comfortable than I would have expected. Or maybe it was just the suddenness of the move.

Milo brought us back to the door and demonstrated the closed-circuit surveillance system. Two cameras—one in front, the other panning the rear of the house, two black-and-white monitors mounted over the door. One of them captured the three behemoths, shlepping and swearing.

Milo opened the door and shouted, "Careful!" Closing it, he said, "What do you think?"

"Great," I said. "Plenty of space—thanks a lot."

"Beautiful view," said Robin. "Really gorgeous."

We followed him into the kitchen and he opened the door of a Sub-Zero cooler. Empty except for a bottle of cooking sherry. "I'll get you some provisions."

Robin said, "Don't worry, I can take care of that."

"Whatever. . . . Let's get you a bedroom—you've got your choice of three."

He took us down a wide, windowless hallway lined with prints. A wall clock in a mother-of-pearl case read two thirty-five. In less than an hour, I was expected in Sunland.

Robin read my mind: "Your afternoon appointment?"

"What time?" said Milo.

"Three-thirty," I said.

"Where?"

"Wallace's mother-in-law. I'm supposed to see the girls out there. No reason not to go, is there?"

He thought for a moment. "None that I can see."

Robin caught the hesitation. "Why should there be a reason?"

"This particular case," I said, "is potentially ugly. Two little girls, their father killed their mother and now wants visitation—"

"That's absurd."

"Among other things. The court asked me to evaluate and make a recommendation. In the very beginning Milo and I talked about the father possibly being behind the tape. Trying to intimidate me. He's got a criminal record and hangs with an outlaw motorcycle gang that's been known to use strongarm tactics."

"This creep's walking free?"

"No, he's locked up in prison. Maximum security at Folsom, I just got a letter from him, telling me he's a good father."

"Wonderful," she said.

"He's not behind this. It was just a working guess, until I learned about the 'bad love' symposium. My problems have something to do with de Bosch."

She looked at Milo. He nodded.

"All right," she said, taking hold of my jacket lapel and kissing my chin. "I'm going to stop being Mama Bear and go about my business."

I held her around the waist. Milo looked away.

"I'll be careful," I said.

She put her head on my chest.

The dog began pawing the floor.

"Oedipus Rover," said Milo.

Robin pushed me away gently. "Go help those poor little girls."

I took Benedict into the valley and picked up the Ventura Freeway at Van Nuys Boulevard. Traffic was hideous all the way to the 210 and beyond, and I didn't make it to McVine until 3:40. When I got to the Rodriguez house, no cars were parked in front and no one answered my ring.

Evelyn showing her displeasure at my tardiness?

I tried again, knocked once, then harder, and when that brought no response, went around to the back. Managing to hoist myself up high enough to peer over the pink block wall, I scanned the yard.

Empty. Not a toy or a piece of furniture in sight. The inflatable pool had been put away, the garage was shut, and drawn drapes blocked the rear windows.

Returning to the front, I checked the mailbox and found yesterday's and today's deliveries. Bulk stuff, coupon giveaways, and something from the gas company.

I put it back and looked up and down the street. A boy of around ten zoomed by on rollerblade skates. A few seconds later, a red truck came speeding down from Foothill and for an instant I thought it was Roddy Rodriguez's. But as it passed, I saw that it was lighter in shade than his and a decade newer. A blond woman sat in the driver's seat. A big yellow dog rode in the bed, tongue out, watchful.

I returned to the Seville and waited for another twenty-five minutes, but no one showed up. I tried to recall the name of Rodriguez's masonry company and finally did—R and R.

Driving back to Foothill Boulevard, I headed east until I spotted a phone booth at an Arco station. The directory had been yanked off the chain, so I called information and asked for R and R's address and phone number. The operator ignored me and switched over to the automated message, leaving me only the number. I called it. No one answered. I tried information a second time and got a street address—right on Foothill, about ten blocks east.

The place was a gray-topped lot, forty or fifty feet behind a shabby brown building. Surrounded by barbed link, it had a green clapboard beer bar on one side, a pawnshop on the other.

The property was empty except for a few brick fragments and some paper litter. The brown building looked to have once been a double garage. Two sets of old-fashioned hinge doors took up most of the front. Above them, ornate yellow letters shouted R AND R MASONRY: CEMENT, CINDER, AND CUSTOM BRICK. Below that: RETAINING WALLS OUR SPECIALTY, followed by an overlapping R's logo meant to evoke Rolls-Royce fantasies.

I parked and got out. No signs of life. The padlock on the gate was the size of a baseball.

I went over to the pawnshop. The door was locked and a sign above a red button said, PRESS AND WAIT. I obeyed and the door buzzed but didn't open. I leaned in close to the window. A man stood behind a nipple-high counter, shielded by a Plexiglas window.

He ignored me.

I buzzed again.

He made a stabbing motion and the door gave.

I walked past cases filled with cameras, cheap guitars, cassette decks and boomboxes, pocket knives and fishing rods.

The man was managing to examine a watch and check me over at the same time.

He was sixty or so, with slicked, dyed-black hair and a pumpkin-colored bottle tan. His face was long and baggy.

I cleared my throat.

He said, "Yeah?" through the plastic and kept looking at the watch, turning it over with nicotined fingers and working his lips as if preparing to spit. The window was scratched and cloudy and outfitted with a ticket-taker remote speaker that he hadn't switched on. The store had soft, wooden floors and stank of WD-40, sulfur matches, and body odor. A sign over the gun display said NO LOONIES.

"I'm looking for Roddy Rodriguez next door," I said. "Have some work for him to do on a retaining wall."

He put the watch down and picked up another.

"Excuse me," I said.

"Got something to buy or sell?"

"No, I was just wondering if you knew when Rodriguez was—"

He turned his back on me and walked away. Through the Plexiglas I saw an old desk full of papers and other timepieces. A semiautomatic pistol served as a paperweight. He scratched his butt and held the watch up to a fluorescent bulb.

I left and walked over to the bar two doors down. The green board was rubbed to raw timber in spots and the front door was unmarked. A sun-shaped neon sign said, SUNNY'S SUN VALLEY. A single window below it was filled with a Budweiser sign.

I walked in, expecting darkness, billiard clicks, and a cowboy jukebox. Instead, I got bright lights, ZZ Top going on about a Mexican whore, and a nearly empty room not much larger than my kitchen.

No pool table—no tables of any kind. Just a long, pressed-wood bar with a black vinyl bumper and matching stools, some of them patched with duct tape. Up against the facing wall were a cigarette machine and a pocket comb dispenser. The floor was grubby concrete.

The man working the bar was thirtyish, fair, balding, stubbled. He wore tinted eyeglasses and one of his ears was double pierced, hosting a tiny gold stud and a white metal hoop. He had on a soiled white apron over a black T-shirt, and his chest was flabby. His arms were soft looking, too, white and tattooed. He wasn't doing much when I came in, and he continued along those lines. Two men sat at the bar, far from each other. More tattoos. They didn't move either. It looked like a poster for National Brain Death Week.

I took a stool between the men and ordered a beer.

"Draft or bottle?"

"Draft."

The bartender took a long time to fill a mug, and as I waited I snuck glances at my companions. Both wore billed caps, T-shirts, jeans, and work shoes. One was skinny, the other muscular. Their hands were dirty. They smoked and drank and had tired faces.

My beer came and I took a swallow. Not much head and not great, but not as bad as I'd expected.

"Any idea when Roddy'll be back?" I said.

"Who?" said the bartender.

"Rodriguez—the masonry guy next door. He's supposed to be doing a retaining wall for me and he didn't show up."

He shrugged.

"Place is closed," I said.

No answer.

"Great," I said. "Guy's got my goddamned deposit."

The bartender began soaking glasses in a gray plastic tub.

I drank some more.

ZZ gave way to a disc jockey's voice, hawking car insurance for people with bad driving records. Then a series of commercials for ambulance-chasing lawyers polluted the air some more.

"When's the last time you've seen him around?" I said.

The bartender turned around. "Who?"

"Rodriguez."

Shrug.

"Has his place been closed for a while?"

Another shrug. He returned to soaking.

"Great," I said.

He looked over his shoulder. "He never comes in here, I got nothing to do with him, okay?"

"Not much of a drinker?"

Shrug.

"Fucking asshole," said the man on my right.

The skinny one. Sallow and pimpled, barely above drinking age. His cigarette was dead in the ashtray. One of his index fingers played with the ashes.

I said, "Who? Rodriguez?"

He gave a depressed nod. "Fucking greaser don't pay."

"You worked for him?"

"Fucking A, digging his fucking ditches. Then the roach coach comes by for lunch and I wanna advance so's to get a burrito. He says sorry, amigo, not till payday. So I'm adios, amigo, man."

He shook his head, still pained by the rejection.

"Asshole," he said, and returned to his beer.

"So he shafted you, too," I said.

"Fucking A, man."

"Any idea where I can find him?"

"Maybe Mexico, man."

"Mexico?"

"Yeah, all a them beaners got second homes there, got they extra wives and they little taco-tico kids, send all they money there."

I heard a metallic click to the left, looked over, and saw the muscular man light up a cigarette. Late twenties or early thirties, two-day growth of heavy beard, thick, black Fu Manchu mustache. His cap was black and said CAT. He blew smoke toward the bar.

I said, "You know Rodriguez, too?"

He gave a long, slow headshake and held out his mug.

The bartender filled it, then extended his own hand. The mustachioed man jostled the pack until a cigarette slid forward. The bartender took it, nodded, and lit up.

Guns 'n Roses came on the radio.

The bartender looked at my half-empty mug. "Anything else?"

I shook my head, put money down on the bar, and left.

"Asshole," said the skinny man, raising his voice to be heard over the music.

I drove back to the Rodriguez house. Still dark and empty. A woman across the street was holding a broom, and she began looking at me suspiciously.

I called over: "Any idea when they'll be back?"

She went inside her house. I drove away and got back on the freeway, exiting on Sunset and heading north on Beverly Glen. I realized my error just as I completed the turn, but continued on to my house anyway, pulling up in front of the carport. Looking over my shoulder with paranoid fervor, I decided it was safe to get out of the car.

I walked around my property, looking, remembering. Though it made no sense, the house already looked sad.

You know how places get when they're empty . . .

I took a quick look at the pond. The fish were still there. They swam up to greet me and I obliged with food.

"See you guys," I said, and left, wondering how many would survive.

11

I made it to Benedict a few minutes later.

The black van and the unmarked were gone. Two of the three garage doors were open and I saw Robin inside, wearing work clothes and goggles, standing behind her lathe.

She saw me coming and turned off the machine. A gold BMW coupe was parked in the third garage. The rest of the space was a near duplicate of the Venice shop.

"Looks like you're all set up," I said.

She pushed her goggles up on her forehead. "This isn't too bad, actually, as long as I leave the door open for ventilation. How come you're back so soon?"

"No one home."

"Flake out on you?"

"It looks like they're gone for a while."

"Moved out?"

"Must be the week for it."

"How could you tell?"

"Two days' mail in the box and her husband's business was padlocked."

"Considerate of her to let you know."

"Etiquette isn't her strong suit. She wasn't thrilled about my evaluation in the first place, though I thought we were making progress. She probably took the girls out of state—maybe Hawaii.

When I spoke to her yesterday she made a crack about a Honolulu vacation. Or Mexico. Her husband may have family there. . . . I'd better call the judge."

"We set up an office for you in one of the bedrooms," she said, leaning over and pecking my cheek. "Gave you the one with the best view, plus there's a Hockney on the wall—two guys showering." She smiled. "Poor Milo—he was a little embarrassed about it—started muttering about the 'atmosphere.' Almost apologizing. After all he did to help us. I sat him down and we had a good talk."

"About what?"

"Stuff—the meaning of life. I told him you could handle the *atmosphere*."

"What he say to that?"

"Just grunted and rubbed his face the way he does. Then I made coffee and told him if he ever learned to play an instrument I'd build one for him."

"Safe offer," I said.

"Maybe not. When we were talking, it came up that he used to play the accordion when he was a kid. And he sings—have you ever heard him?"

"No."

"Well, he sang for me this afternoon. After some prodding. Did an old Irish folk song—and guess what? He's got a really nice voice."

"Basso profundo?"

"*Tenor*, of all things. He used to be in the church choir when he was a little boy."

I smiled. "That's a little hard to picture."

"There's probably a lot about him you don't know."

"Probably," I said. "Each year I get in touch with more of my ignorance. . . . Speaking of grunts, where's our guest?"

"Sleeping in the service porch. I tried keeping him here while I worked, but he kept charging the machines—he was ready to take on the bandsaw when I got him out of here and locked him in."

"Tough love, huh? Did he do his little strangulation routine?"

"Oh, sure," she said. She put her hand around her throat and made a gagging sound. "I yelled at him to be quiet and he stopped."

"Poor guy. He probably thought you were going to be his salvation."

She grinned. "I may be sultry and sensual, but I ain't easy."

I let the dog loose, gave him time to pee outside, and took him into my new office. A chrome-and-glass-topped desk was pushed up against one wall. My papers and books were piled neatly on a black velour couch. The view was fantastic, but after a few minutes I stopped noticing it.

I phoned superior court, got Steve Huff in his chambers, and told him about Evelyn Rodriguez's no-show.

"Maybe she just forgot," he said. "Denial, avoidance, whatever."

"I think there's a good chance she's gone, Steve." I described Roddy Rodriguez's locked yard.

"Sounds like it," he said. "There goes another one."

"Can't say that I blame her. When I saw her two days ago, she really opened up about the girls' problems. They're having plenty of them. And Donald wrote me a letter—no remorse, just tooting his own horn as a good dad."

"Wrote you a *letter*?"

"His lawyer's been calling me, too."

"Any intimidation?"

I hesitated. "No, just nagging."

"Too bad. No law against that . . . no, can't say that I blame her either, Alex—off the record. Do you want to wait and try again, or just write up your report now—document all the crap she told you?"

"What's the difference?"

"The difference is how quickly you want to get paid versus how much lead time you want to give her, if she *has* hightailed it. Once you put it in writing and I receive it, I'm obligated to send it over to Bucklear. Even with reasonable delays he gets it in a couple of weeks or so, then *he* files paper and gets warrants out on her."

"A murderer gets warrants on a grandmother taking her grandkids out of town? Do we file that under 'I for irony' or 'N for nuts'?"

"Do I take that to mean you'll wait?"

"How much lead time can I give her?"

"A reasonable period. Consistent with typical medical-psychological practice."

"Meaning??"

"Meaning what shrinks normally do. Three, four, even five weeks wouldn't chafe any hides—you guys are notorious for being sloppy about your paperwork. You might even stretch it to six or seven—but you never heard that from me. In fact, we never had this talk, did we?"

"Judge who?" I said.

"Attaboy—oops, bailiff's buzzing me, time to be Solomonic again, bye-bye." I put the phone down. The bulldog placed his paws on my knees and tried to get up on my lap. I lifted him and he settled on me like a warm hunk of clay. At *least* thirty pounds.

The Hockney was right in front of me. Great painting. As was the Thomas Hart Benton drawing on the opposite wall—a mural study depicting hypermuscular workmen cheerfully constructing a WPA dam.

I looked at both of them for a while and wondered what Robin and Milo had talked about. The dog stayed as motionless as a little furry Buddha. I rubbed his head and his jowls and he licked my hand. A boy and his dog . . . I realized I hadn't gotten the number for the bulldog club, yet. Almost five p.m. Too late to call the AKC.

I'd do it tomorrow morning.

Denial, avoidance, whatever.

That night I slept fitfully. Friday morning at eight I phoned North Carolina and got an address for the French Bulldog Club of America, in Rahway, New Jersey. A post office box. No phone number was available.

At eight-ten, I called the Rodriguez house. A phone company recording said that line had been disconnected. I pictured Evelyn and the girls barreling over a dirt road in Baja, Rodriguez following in his truck. Or maybe the four of them, wandering through Waikiki with glazed tourists' eyes. If only they knew how much we had in common now . . .

I began unpacking books. At eight thirty-five, the doorbell rang and Milo appeared on one of the TV monitors, tapping a foot and carrying a white bag.

"Breakfast," he said, as I let him in. "I already gave Ms. Castagna hers. God, that woman works—what've you been doing?"

"Getting organized."

"Sleep okay?"

"Great," I lied. "Thanks a lot for setting us up."

He looked around. "How's the office?"

"Perfect."

"Great view, huh?"

"To die for."

We went into the kitchen and he took some onion rolls and two Styrofoam cups of coffee out of the bag.

We sat at a blue granite table. He said, "What's your schedule like today?"

"It's pretty open now that the Wallace thing's on hold. Looks like Grandma decided to take matters into her own hands."

I recounted what I'd found in Sunland.

He said, "They're probably better off. If you feel like taking on a little assignment, I've got one for you."

"What?"

"Go over to the Mental Health Center and talk to Ms. Jean Jeffers. I finally got through to her—she actually called me back last night, which I thought was pretty cool for a bureaucrat. Better attitude than I expected, too. Down to earth. Not that she shouldn't cooperate, after what happened to Becky. I told her we'd come across some harassment crimes—didn't go into specifics—that we had reason to believe might be coming from one of her patients. Someone we also had reason to believe was a buddy of Hewitt's. Mentioning *his* name got her going—she went on about how Becky's murder had traumatized all of them. Still sounds pretty shook up."

He tore an onion roll into three pieces, placed the segments on the table like monte cards, picked one up, and ate it.

"Anyway, I asked her if she knew who Hewitt hung out with and she said no. Then I asked her if I could look at her patient roster, and she said she wanted to help but no—the confidentiality thing. So I threw Tarasoff at her, hoping she didn't know the law that well. But she did: no specific threat against a specific victim, no Tarasoff obligation. At *that* point, I played my trump card: told her the department had a consultant doing some profiling work for us on psycho crimes—a genuine 'pee aitch dee' who respected confidentiality and would be discreet, and I gave her your name in case maybe she heard of you. And guess what, she thought she had. Especially after I told her you were semi-famous."

"Hoo-hah."

"Hoo-hah to the max. She said she couldn't promise anything, but she'd be willing to at least talk to you. Maybe there'd be some way to work something out. The more we talked, the friendlier she got. My feeling is she wants to help but is afraid of being burned by more publicity. So be gentle with her."

"No brass knucks," I said. "How much do I tell her?"

He ate another piece of roll. "As little as possible."

"When can she see me?"

"This afternoon. Here's the number." He took a scrap of paper out of his pocket, gave it to me, and stood.

"Where you going?" I said.

"Over the hill. Van Nuys. Try to find out what I can about who cut up Myra Paprock five years ago."

After he was gone, I called in for messages—still nothing from Shirley Rosenblatt in New York—then wrote a letter to the bulldog club informing them I'd found what might possibly be a member's pet. At nine-thirty, I phoned Jean Jeffers and was put through to her secretary, who sounded as if she'd been expecting me. An appointment with Ms. Jeffers was available in an hour if I was free.

I grabbed a roll, put on a tie, and left.

The center was in a block of cheerless, pastel-colored apartments, in a quiet part of West L.A. not far from Santa Monica. An old, working-class district, near an industrial park whose galloping expansion had been choked off by hard times. Constructus interruptus had left its mark all over the neighborhood—half-framed buildings, empty lots dug out for foundations and left as dry sumps, pigeon-specked FOR SALE signs, boarded-up windows on condemned prewar bungalows.

The clinic was the only charming bit of architecture in sight. Its front windows were barred, but boxes filled with begonias hung from the iron. The spot on the sidewalk where Dorsey Hewitt had fallen dead was clean. But for a couple of trash-

choked shopping carts in front, it could have been a private sani-
tarium.

A generous lot next door was two-thirds empty and marked
EMPLOYEES ONLY. NO PATIENT PARKING. I decided a consultant qualified
as someone's employee, and parked there.

I made my way back to the front of the building, passing the
section of wall that had been obsessed upon by the TV camera. A
cement cornerstone etched with names of forgotten politicos
stated that the building had been dedicated as a veterans clinic in
1919. The door Hewitt had come out of was just to the right, unmarked and locked—two locks, each almost as large as the one
sealing Roddy Rodriguez's brickyard.

The main entrance was dead center, through a squat arch
leading to a courtyard with an empty fountain. A loggia to the
right of the fountain—the path Hewitt would have taken to get to
the unmarked door—was sectioned off by thick steel mesh that
looked brand-new. An open hallway on the opposite side led me
around the fountain to glass-paned doors.

A blue-uniformed guard stood behind the doors, tall, old,
black, chewing gum. He looked me over and unlatched one of the
doors, then pointed to a metal detector to his left—one of those
walk-through airport things. I set it off and had to give the guard
my keys before passing silently.

"Go 'head," he said, handing them back.

I walked up to a reception desk. A young black woman sat
behind more mesh. "Can I help you?"

"Dr. Delaware for Ms. Jeffers."

"One minute." She got on the phone. Behind her were three
other women at desks, typing and talking into receivers. The windows behind them were barred. Through the bars, I saw trucks,
cars, and shadows—the gray, graffitied walls of an alley.

I was standing in a small, unfurnished area painted light
green and broken only by a single door to the right. Claustropho-
bic. It reminded me of the sally port at the county jail and I wondered how a paranoid schizophrenic or someone in crisis would
handle it. How easy it would be for someone with a muddled
psyche to make it from the no-parking lot, through the metal detector, to this holding cell.

The receptionist said, "Okay, she's all the way down at the
end," and pressed a button. The door buzzed—not quite as loudly

as the one at the pawnshop, but just as obnoxiously—and I opened it and stepped into a very long, cream-colored hall marked by lots of doors. Thick, gray carpeting covered the floor. The light was very bright.

Most of the doors were blank, a few were labeled THERAPY, and even fewer bore slide-in signs with people's names on them. The cream paint smelled fresh; how many coats had it taken to cover up the blood?

The corridor was silent except for my footsteps—the kind of womblike damping that comes only from real soundproofing. As I made my way to the end, a door on the left opened, spilling out people but no noise.

Three people, two women and a man, poorly dressed and shuffling. Not a group; each walked alone. The man was lantern-jawed and stooped, the women heavy and red-faced, with cracked swollen legs and stringy hair. All of them looked down at the carpet as they passed me. They grasped small white pieces of paper, "Rx" stamped at the top.

The room they'd exited was classroom-sized and crowded with another thirty or so people queued up before a metal desk. A young man sat at the desk, talked briefly to each person who stood before him, then filled out a prescription blank and handed it over with a smile. The people in line scuffed forward as automatically as cans on a conveyor belt. Some of them held out their hands in anticipation before they got to the doctor. None of them left without paper, none seemed cheered.

I resumed walking. The door at the end had a slide-in that said JEAN JEFFERS, MSW, LCSW. DIRECTOR.

Inside was a five-by-five secretarial area occupied by a young, full-faced, Asian woman. Her desk was barely big enough to hold a PC and a blotter. The wall behind her was so narrow that a dark, mock wood door almost filled it. A radio on an end table played soft rock almost inaudibly. A nameplate in front of the computer said MARY CHIN.

She said, "Dr. Delaware? Go right in, Jean will see you."

"Thank you."

She began to open the door. A woman caught it from the other side and pulled it all the way back. Forty-five or so, tall and blond. She wore a crimson shirtdress gathered at the waist by a wide, white belt.

"Doctor? I'm Jean." She held out her hand. Almost as big as mine, lanolin soft. The left one bore a ruby solitaire ring over a broad, gold wedding band.

More white in her teardrop earrings and a mock ivory bracelet around one wrist. A sensible-looking watch encircled the other.

She had a strong frame and carried no extra fat. The belt showed off a firm waist. Her face was long, lightly tanned, with soft, generous features. Only her upper lip had been skimped upon by nature—not much more than a pencil line. Its mate was full and glossed. Dark blue eyes studied me from under black lashes. Gold-framed half-glasses hung from a white cord around her neck. Her hair was frosted almost white at the tips, clipped short in back and layered back at the sides. Pure utility except for a thick, Veronica Lake flap in front. It swooped to the right, almost hiding her right eye. A handsome woman.

She flipped her hair and smiled.

"Thanks for seeing me," I said.

"Of course, doctor. Please have a seat."

Her office was the standard twelve-by-twelve setup, with a real wood desk, two upholstered armchairs, a three-drawer double file, a nearly empty bookcase, and some paintings of seagulls. On the desk were a pen, a memo pad, and a short stack of file folders.

A photo in a standup frame was centered on one of the shelves—she and a nice-looking, heavyset man about her age, the two of them in Hawaiian shirts and bedecked with leis. Social work diplomas made out to Jean Marie LaPorte were propped on another shelf, all from California colleges. I scanned the dates. If she'd graduated college at twenty-two, she was exactly forty-five.

"You're a clinical psychologist, right?" she said, sitting behind the desk.

I took one of the chairs. "Yes."

"You know, when Detective Sturgis mentioned your name I thought I recognized it, though I still can't figure out from where."

She smiled again. I returned it.

She said, "How does a psychologist come to be a police consultant?"

"By accident, really. Several years ago I was treating some children who'd been abused at a day-care center. I ended up testifying in court and getting involved in the legal system. One thing led to another."

"Day-care center—the man who took pictures? The one involved with that horrible molesters' club?"

I nodded.

"Well, that must be where I remember your name from. You were quite a hero, weren't you?"

"Not really. I did my job."

"Well," she said, sitting forward and pushing hair out of her eyes, "I'm sure you're being modest. Child abuse is so—to tell you the truth, I couldn't work with it myself. Which may sound funny considering what we deal with here. But children—" She shook her head. "It would be too hard for me to find any sympathy for the abusers even if they were once victims themselves."

"I know what you mean."

"To me that's the lowest—violating a child's trust. How do you manage to deal with it?"

"It wasn't easy," I said. "I saw myself as the child's ally and tried to do whatever helped."

"Tried? You don't do abuse work anymore?"

"Occasionally, when it comes up as part of a custody case. Mostly I consult the court on trauma and divorce issues."

"Do you do any therapy at all?"

"Not much."

"Me, neither." She sat back. "My main goal in school was to become a therapist, but I can't remember the last time I actually did any real therapy."

She smiled again and shook her head. The wave of hair covered her eyes and she flipped it back—a curiously adolescent mannerism.

"Anyway," she said, "about what Detective Sturgis wants, I just don't know how I can really help. I really need to safeguard our people's confidentiality—despite what happened to Becky." She folded her lips inward, lowered her eyes, and shook her head.

I said, "It must have been terrifying."

"It happened too *quickly* to be terrifying—the *terrifying* part didn't hit me until after it was over—seeing her . . . what he . . . now I really know what they mean by posttraumatic stress. No substitute for direct experience, huh?"

She pressed the skinny upper lip with one finger, as if keeping it still.

"No one knew what he was doing to her. I was right here, going about my business the whole time he was—the treatment rooms are totally soundproofed. He—" She removed her finger. A white pressure circle dotted her lip, then slowly faded.

"Then I heard noise from the hall," she said. "That horrible screaming—he just kept *screaming.*"

" 'Bad love,' " I said.

Her mouth remained open. The blue eyes dulled for a second. "Yes . . . he . . . I went out to Mary's office and she wasn't there, so I opened the door to the hall and saw him. Screaming, waving it—the knife—*splashing* blood, the wall—he saw me—I saw his eyes settle on me—focusing—and he kept screaming. I slammed the door, shoved Mary's desk up against it, and ran back into my office. Slammed *that* door and blocked *it.* I hid behind my chair the whole time it was . . . it wasn't till later that I found out he'd grabbed Adeline." She wiped her eyes. "I'm sorry, you don't need to hear this."

"No, no, please."

She glanced at her message pad. Blank. Picking up the pen, she wrote something on it.

"No, that's it—I've told it so many times . . . no one knows how long he—if she suffered for a long time. That's the one thing I *can* hope. That she didn't. The thought of her trapped in there with him . . ." She shook her head and touched her temples. "They soundproofed the rooms back in the sixties, when this place was a Vietnam veterans' counseling center. We sure don't need it."

"Why's that?"

"Because *no one* does much therapy around here."

She took a deep breath and slapped her hands lightly on the desk. "Life goes on, right? Would you like something to drink? We've got a coffee machine in the other wing. I can have Mary go get some."

"No, thanks."

"Lucky choice." Smile. "It's actually pretty vile."

"How come no one does much therapy?" I said. "Too disturbed a population?"

"Too disturbed, too poor, too many of them. They need food and shelter and to stop hearing voices. The preferred treatment is Thorazine. And Haldol and lithium and Tegretol and whatever else chases the demons away. Counseling would be a nice luxury, but with our caseload it ends up being a very low priority. Not to mention funding. That's why we don't have any psychologists on our staff, just caseworkers, and most of them are SWAs—assistants. Like Becky."

"On the way in I saw a doctor giving out prescriptions."

"That's right," she said. "It's Friday, isn't it? That's Dr. Wintell, our once-a-week psychiatrist. He's just out of his residency, a real nice kid. But when his practice builds up, he'll be out of here like all the others."

"If no one does therapy, what was Becky doing with Hewitt in the therapy room?"

"I didn't say we never talk to our people, just that we don't do much insight work. Sometimes we get cramped for space and the workers use the treatment rooms to do their paperwork. Basically, all of us use what's on hand. As to what Becky was doing with him, it could have been anything. Giving him a voucher for an SRO hotel, telling him where to get deloused. Then again, maybe she *was* trying to get into his head—she was that kind of person."

"What kind is that?"

"An optimist. Idealistic. Most of us start out that way, don't we?"

I nodded. "Did Hewitt have a history of violence?"

"None that was listed in our files. He'd been arrested just a few weeks before for theft and was due to stand trial—maybe she was counseling him about that. There was *nothing* on paper that would have warned us. And even if he was violent, there's a good chance the information would never have gotten to us, with all the red tape."

She put down her pen and looked at me. Flipped her hair. "The truth is, he was exactly like so many others who come in and out of here—there's still no way to know."

She picked up one of the folders.

"This is his file. The police confiscated it and returned it, so I guess it's not confidential anymore."

Inside were only two sheets, one clipped to each of the covers. The first was an intake form listing Dorsey Hewitt's age as thirty-one and his address as "none." Under REASON FOR REFERRAL someone had written "multiple social problems." Under DIAGNOSIS: "prob. chron. schiz." The rest of the categories—PROGNOSIS, FAMILY SUPPORT, MEDICAL HISTORY, OTHER PSYCH. TREATMENT—had been left blank. Nothing about "bad love."

At the bottom of the form were notations of referral for food stamps. The signature read, "R. Basille, SWA."

The facing page was white and smooth, marked only with the notation, "Will follow as needed, R.B., SWA." The date was eight weeks prior to the murder. I handed the folder back.

"Not much," I said.

She gave a sad smile. "Paperwork wasn't Becky's forte."

"So you have no idea how many times she actually saw him?"

"Guess that doesn't say much for my administrative skills, does it? But I'm not one of those people who believes in riding the staff, checking out every little picayune detail. I try to find the best people I can, motivate them, and give them room to move. Generally it works out. With Becky . . ."

She threw up her hands. "She was a doll, a really sweet person. Not much for rules and regulations, but so what?"

She shook her head. "We'd talked about it—helping her get her paperwork in on time. She promised to try, but to tell the truth, I didn't harbor much hope. And I didn't care. Because she was productive where it counted—getting on the phone all day with agencies and arguing for every last penny for her cases. She stayed late, did whatever it took to help them. Who knows? Maybe she was going that extra mile for Hewitt."

She picked up the phone. "Mary? Coffee, please. . . . No, just one."

Putting it down, she said, "The *real* horror is that it could happen again. We have a steel corral now, to direct them out onto the street after they get their meds. The county finally sent us a guard and the detector, but you tell me how to predict which of them is going to blow."

"We're not very good prophets under the best of circumstances."

"No, we're not. Hundreds of people file in here each week, for meds and vouchers. We've *got* to let them in. We're the court of last resort. Any of them could be another Hewitt. Even if we wanted to lock them up, we couldn't. The state hospitals that haven't been shut down are filled to capacity—I don't know what your theory is about psychosis, but mine is that most psychotics are born with it—it's biological, like any other illness. But instead of treating them, we demonize them or idealize them, and they get caught in the squeeze between the do-gooders who think they should be allowed to run free and the skinflints who think all they need is to pull themselves up by the bootstraps."

"I know," I said. "When I was in grad school the whole community psych thing was in full bloom—schizophrenia as an alternative lifestyle, liberating patients from the back wards and empowering them to take over their own treatment."

"Empowering." She laughed without opening her mouth.

"I had a professor who was a fanatic on the subject," I said. "Studied the mental health system in Belgium or somewhere and wrote a book on it. He had us do a paper on deinstitutionalization. The more I researched it, the less feasible it seemed. I started to wonder what would happen to psychotics who needed medication and couldn't be counted upon to take it. He handed the paper back with one comment, 'Medication is mind control,' and gave me a C-minus."

"Well, I give you an A. Some of our patients can't be counted upon to feed themselves, let alone calibrate dosage. In my opinion, deinstitutionalization's the major culprit in the homeless problem. Sure, some street people are working folks who hit the skids, but at least thirty or forty percent are severely mentally debilitated. They belong in hospitals, not under some freeway. And now with all the weird street drugs out there, the old cliché that the mentally ill aren't violent just isn't true anymore. Each year it gets uglier and uglier, Dr. Delaware. I pray there won't be another Hewitt, but I don't count on it."

"Do you try at all to identify which patients are violent?"

"If we have police records, we take them seriously, but like I said, that's rare. We've got to be our own police here. If someone goes around making threats, we call security. But most of them are quiet. Hewitt was. Didn't really relate to anyone else that I'm aware of—that's why we're probably not going to be much help to Detective Sturgis. What exactly is he after, anyway?"

"Apparently, he suspects Hewitt had a friend who may be harassing some people, and he's trying to find out if the friend was a patient here."

"Well, after Sturgis called me I asked some of the other workers if they'd seen Hewitt with anyone, and none of them had. The only one who might have known was Becky."

"Is she the only one who worked with him?"

She nodded.

"How long had she been working here?"

"A little over a year. She got her assistantship from junior college last summer and applied right afterward. One of those second careers—she'd worked as a secretary for a while, decided to go back to school in order to do something socially important—her words."

Her eyes flickered and her mouth set—the lower lip compressing and making her look older.

"Such a sweet girl," she said. She shook her head, then looked at me. "You know—I just thought of something. Hewitt's attorney—the one defending him on that theft thing? *He* might know if Hewitt had any friends. I think I've got his name tucked away somewhere—hold on."

She went to the file, opened the middle drawer, and began flipping. "Just one second, so much junk in here. . . . He called me—the attorney—after Becky's murder. Wanting to know if there was anything he could do. I think he wanted to talk—to get his own guilt off his chest. I didn't have time for . . . ah, here we go."

She pulled out a piece of cardboard stapled with business cards. Working a staple free with her fingernails, she removed a card and gave it to me.

Cheap white paper, green letters.

Andrew Coburg
Attorney-at-Law
The Human Interest Law Center
1912 Lincoln Avenue
Venice, California

"Human interest law," I said.

"I think it's one of those storefront things."

"Thanks," I said, pocketing the card. "I'll pass it along to Detective Sturgis."

The door opened and Mary came in with the coffee.

Jean Jeffers thanked her and told her to tell someone named Amy that she'd be ready to see her in a minute.

When the door closed, she began stirring her coffee.

"Well," she said, "it was nice talking to you. Sorry I couldn't do more."

"Thanks for your time," I said. "Is there anyone else I could talk to who might be able to help?"

"No one I can think of."

"What about the woman he took hostage?"

"Adeline? Now there's a *really* sad story. She'd transferred over here a month before from a center in South Central because she had high blood pressure and wanted a safer environment."

She threw up her hands again and gave a sour laugh.

"Any particular reason Hewitt grabbed *her*?" I said.

"You mean did she know him?"

"Yes."

She shook her head. The hair flap obscured her eye and she left it there. "Just pure bad luck. She happened to be sitting at a desk in the hall, working, just as he was running out, and he grabbed her."

She walked me to the door. People kept coming out of the psychiatrist's office. She looked at them.

"How can you ever know someone like that, anyway?" she said. "When you get down to it, how can you ever really know anyone?"

12

I decided to drive to Andrew Coburg's office and tender an appeal to his human interest. Getting onto Pico, I drove to Lincoln and headed south into Venice.

The Human Interest Law Center turned out, indeed, to be a storefront—one of three set into an old mustard-colored, one-story building. The brick facade was chipped. Next door was a liquor store advertising screwtop wine on special. The other side was vacant. On the window was painted DELI *** LUNCH & DINNER.

The law office window was papered with wrinkled aluminum foil. An American flag hung over the doorway. Printed on one of the white stripes was KNOW YOUR RIGHTS.

The door was closed but unlocked. As I pushed it open a bell tinkled, but no one came out to greet me. In front of me was a particle-board partition. A black arrow pointed left and hand-painted signs said WELCOME! and BIENVENIDOS! A mass of noise—voices, phone rings, clicking typewriter keys—came from the other side.

I followed the arrow around the partition to a single large room, long and narrow. The walls were gray-white and crowded with bulletin boards and posters, the ceiling a high, dark nest of ductwork, electrical wiring, and stammering fluorescent tubes.

No secretary or receptionist. Eight or nine mismatched desks were spread around the room, each equipped with a black dial phone, a typewriter, and a facing chair. Behind each chair was a

U-shaped construction of PVC tubing. White muslin curtains hung from the frame—the kind used for mock privacy in hospitals. Some of the curtains were drawn, others were open. Shoes and cuffs were visible beneath the hems of the drawn drapes.

Young people sat behind the desks, talking into phones or to people in the chairs. The clients were mostly black or Hispanic. Some looked asleep. One of them—an old man of indeterminate race—held a terrier mutt on his lap. A few small children wandered around looking lost.

The desk nearest to me was occupied by a dark-haired man wearing a green plaid suit jacket, white shirt, and bolo tie. He needed a shave, his hair was greased, and his face was as sharp as an icepick. Though the phone receiver was cradled under his chin, he didn't appear to be talking or listening, and his eyes drifted over to me.

"What can I do for you?"

"I'm looking for Andrew Coburg."

"Back there." Making a small, meaningless movement with his head. "But I think he's with someone."

"Which desk?" I said.

He put the phone down, swiveled, and pointed to a station in the center of the room. Drapes drawn. Dirty sneakers and an inch of hairy shin below the hem of the muslin.

"Okay if I wait?"

"Sure. You an attorney?"

"No."

"Sure, wait." He picked up the phone and began dialing laboriously. Someone must have answered, because he said, "Yeah, hi, it's Hank, over at H.I. Yeah, me too—yeah." Laughter. "Listen, what about that *nolo* we talked about? Go and check—yeah, I think so. Yeah."

I stood against the partition and read the posters. One featured a bald eagle on crutches and said HEAL OUR SYSTEM. Another was printed in Spanish—something to do with *immigración* and *liberación*.

The sharp-faced man started talking in lawyer's jargon, jabbing the air with a pen and laughing intermittently. He was still on the phone when the curtains at Andrew Coburg's station parted. An emaciated man wearing a filthy cableknit sweater and cutoff shorts got up. He was bearded and had matted hair, and my chest tightened when I saw him because he could have been

Dorsey Hewitt's brother. Then I realized I was seeing the brother-hood of poverty and madness.

He and Coburg shook hands and he left, eyes half closed. As he passed me I backed away from the stench. He passed close to the man named Hank, too, but the lawyer didn't notice, kept talking and laughing.

Coburg was still standing. He wiped his hands on his pants, yawned and stretched. Early thirties, six one, two hundred. Pear shaped, fair haired, arms slightly too short for his long-waisted body. His hair was brass colored, worn full at the sides with no sideburns. He had a soft face, fine features, and rosy cheeks, had probably been a beautiful baby.

He wore a chambray work shirt with the sleeves rolled to the elbows, loosened paisley tie five years too narrow, rumpled khakis, saddle shoes. The laces on one shoe were untied.

Stretching again, he sat, picked up his phone, and began dialing. Most of the other lawyers were on the phone now. The room sounded like a giant switchboard.

I walked over to him. His eyebrows rose as I sat down, but he didn't show any signs of annoyance. Probably used to walk-ins.

He said, "Listen, gotta go," into the phone. "What's that? Fine —I accept that, just as long as we have a clear understanding, okay? What? . . . No, I've got someone here. Okay. Bye. Cheers."

He hung up and said, "Hi, how can I help you?" in a pleasant voice. His tie was clipped with an unusual bit of jewelry: red guitar pick glued to a silver bar.

I told him who I was and that I was trying to locate any friends of Dorsey Hewitt.

"Dorsey. One of my triumphs," he said, all the pleasantness gone. He sat back, crossed his legs. "So what paper do you work for?"

"I'm a psychologist. Just like I said."

He smiled. "Really?"

I smiled back. "Scout's honor."

"And a police consultant, too."

"That's right."

"You don't mind if I see some ID, do you?"

I showed him my psych license, my med school faculty card, and my old LAPD consultant's tag.

"The police," he said, as if he still couldn't believe it. "Is that a problem for you?"

"In what way?"

"Working with the police mentality? All that intolerance—the authoritarianism."

"Not really," I said. "Police officers vary, like anyone else."

"That hasn't been my experience," he said. There was a jar of licorice sticks near his typewriter. He took one and held out the container.

"No, thanks."

"High blood pressure?"

"No."

"Licorice raises it," he said, chewing. "Mine tends to be low. I'm not saying they're intrinsically bad—the police. I'm sure most of them start out as okay human beings. But the job corrupts—too much power, too little accountability."

"I guess the same could be said for doctors and lawyers."

He smiled again. "That's no comfort." The smile stayed on his face, but it began to look out of place. "So. Why does a police consultant need to know anything about Dorsey's *friends*?"

I gave him the same explanation I'd offered Jean Jeffers.

Midway through, his phone rang. He picked it up, said, "What? Okay, sure. . . . Hi, Bill, what is it? What? *What*? You've got to be kidding! No walkie, no talkie—I *mean* it. This is a bull-squat misdemeanor we're talking abou—I don't care what else he's—okay, you do that. Good idea. Go ahead. *Talk* to him and get back to me. Bye."

He put the phone down. "Where were we? Oh, yeah, harassment. What kind?"

"I don't know all the details."

He pulled his head back and squinted. His neck was thick, but soft. His short arms folded over his abdomen and didn't move. "Cops ask you to consult but don't let you in on the details? Typical. *I* wouldn't take the gig."

Not seeing any way out of it, I said, "Someone's been sending people harassing tapes with what may be Hewitt's voice on them —screaming 'bad love'—the same thing he screamed after he murdered Becky Basille."

Coburg thought for a minute. "So? Someone taped him off the TV. No shortage of strange souls out there. Keeps both of us busy."

"Maybe," I said. "But the police think it's worth looking into."

"Who's getting these tapes?"

"That I don't know."

"Must be someone important for the cops to go to all this trouble."

I shrugged. "You could ask them." I recited Milo's name and number. He didn't bother to write it down.

Taking another licorice stick from the jar, he said, "Tapes. So what's the big deal?"

"The police are wondering if Hewitt might have had a close friend—someone influenced by what he did. Someone with the same dangerous tendencies."

"Influenced?" He looked puzzled. "What, some kind of harassment club? Street people going after the good citizenry?"

"Hewitt wasn't exactly harmless."

He began twisting the licorice stick. "Actually, he was. He was *surprisingly* harmless when he took his medicine. On one of his good days, you might have met him and found him a nice guy."

"Was he off his medicine when he committed the murder?"

"That's what the coroner says. Too much alcohol, not enough Thorazine. Given the biochemistry, he must have stopped eating pills a week or so before."

"Why?"

"Who knows? I doubt it was a conscious decision—'hmm, guess I won't take my meds this morning and let's see how the day goes.' More likely he ran out, tried to get a refill, and ran into such a hassle he gave up. Then, as he got crazier and crazier, he probably forgot all about the pills and why he was taking them in the first place. Happens all the time to people at the bottom. Every detail of daily living's a struggle for them, but they're expected to remember appointments, fill out forms, wait in line, follow a schedule."

"I know," I said. "I've been to the center. Wondered how the patients coped."

"Not well is how they cope. Even when they play by the rules they get turned away—mean old Mr. Recession. Do you have any idea how hard it is for a sick person without money to get help in this city?"

"Sure do," I said. "I spent ten years at Western Pediatric Medical Center."

"Over in Hollywood?"

I nodded.

"Okay," he said, "so you *do* know. Not that I'm glossing over what Dorsey did—that poor girl, every attorney's nightmare, I still lose sleep thinking about it. But he was a victim, too—as sappy and knee-jerk as that sounds. He should have been taken care of, not forced to fend for himself."

"Institutionalized?"

His eyes turned angry. I noticed their color for the first time: very pale brown, almost tan.

"Taken *care* of. Not *jailed*—oh, hell, even jail wouldn't have been bad if that would have meant treatment. But it never does."

"Had he been psychotic for a long time?"

"I don't know. He wasn't someone you just sat down and had a chat with—so tell me your life history, pal. Most of the time he was somewhere else."

"Where was he from, originally?"

"Oklahoma, I think. But he'd been in L.A. for years."

"Living on the street?"

"Since he was a kid."

"Any family?"

"None that I know of."

He took hold of the licorice, touched it to his lip, and used his other hand to caress his tie. Somewhere else, himself.

When he touched his phone I knew he was ready to break off the conversation.

"What kind of music do you play?" I glanced at the guitar-pick clasp.

"What? Oh, this? I just noodle around on weekends."

"Me, too. I worked my way through college playing guitar."

"Yeah? Guess lots of guys did." He pulled the front end of the tie down and looked at the ceiling. I felt his interest continue to slip.

"What do you do mostly, electric or acoustic?"

"Lately I've been getting into electric." Smile. "So what's this? Gaining rapport with the subject? Got to hand it to you. At least you didn't get into the usual police-prosecutor rap—guilt-tripping me for what Dorsey did, asking me how can I live with myself defending scum."

"That's because I don't have a problem with that," I said. "It's a good system and you're an important part of it—and no, I'm not patronizing you."

He held out his hands. "Whoa."

I smiled.

"Actually, it's an *okay* system," he said. "I'll bet if you met the Founding Fathers, you wouldn't think they were such great guys. Slaveowners, fat cats, and they sure didn't think much of women and kids."

The phone rang again. He took the call while gnawing on the remains of the licorice, talking lawyerese, bartering some defendant's future, never raising his voice.

When he hung up, he said, "We try to make the system work for the people the Founding Fathers didn't care about."

"Who funds you?"

"Grants, donations—interested in contributing?"

"I'll think about it."

He grinned. "Sure you will. Either way, we'll get by—bad salaries, no expense accounts. That's why most of these people'll be gone by next year—soon as they start thinking home equity and German cars."

"What about you?"

He laughed. "Me? I'm a veteran. Five years and thriving. Because it's a heck of a lot more satisfying than drawing up wills or defending polluters."

He turned serious, looked away from me.

"Sure it gets ugly," he said, as if responding to a question. "What Dorsey did was as ugly as it gets." Eye flicker. "Jesus, what a . . . it was a tragedy. How else can you put it? A goddamn stupid tragedy. I know I couldn't have done anything differently, but it shouldn't have happened—it just stinks, but what can you do when society keeps lowering itself to the brutal denominator? Dorsey'd never shown me any signs of violence. *Nothing.* I was serious when I said you would have liked him. Most of the time he was pleasant—soft-spoken, passive. One of my easier clients, actually. A little paranoid, but it was always low key, he never got aggressive with it."

"What kind of delusions did he have?"

"The usual. Voices in his head telling him to do stuff—cross the street six times one day, drink tomato juice the next—I don't remember exactly."

"Did the voices make him angry?"

"They annoyed him, but no, I wouldn't call it anger. It was as if he accepted the voices as being a part of him. I see that a lot in the long-timers. They're used to it, deal with it. Nothing aggressive or hostile, that's for sure."

"As long as he took his medication."

"I assumed he was taking it because he was always okay with me."

"How well did you know him?"

"I wouldn't call it knowing. I did some basic legal stuff for him."

"When did you first meet him?"

He looked up at the ductwork again. "Let's see . . . it would have to be around a year ago."

"Walk-in?"

"No, he was referred by the court."

"What kind of theft were you defending him on?"

Smile. "Cops didn't tell you?"

"I don't get involved in more than I need to."

"Smart. *Theft* is an overstatement. He lifted a bottle of gin from a liquor store, and a couple of sticks of beef jerky. Did it in plain sight of the clerk and got busted. I'm sure he didn't even mean it. Clerk nearly broke his arm restraining him."

"What defense were you planning?"

"What do you think?"

"Plea bargain."

"What else? He had no prior record other than petty stuff. The way the jails are crowded it would have been a slam-dunk."

He sat up and inserted five fingers into his thick hair. Massaging his scalp, he said, "Gritz."

"Pardon me?"

"It's a name. Gritz."

"As in hominy?"

"With a 'z.' The closest I can come to someone who might be called Dorsey's friend."

"First name or last?"

"Don't know. He came by here a couple of times with Dorsey. Another homeless guy. The only reason I know his name is because I noticed him hanging around over there"—pointing to the partition—"asked Dorsey who he was and Dorsey said 'Gritz.' First thing I said was what you just did: 'As in hominy?' That went right over Dorsey's head, and I tried to explain it. Spelled 'grits', told him what they were, asked him if it was a last name or a first name. He said no, it was a *name* and it was spelled with a 'z.' He spelled it for me. Really slowly—he always talked slow. 'G-R-I-T-Z.' Like it was profound. For all I know he was making it up."

"Did he tend to do that?"

"He was schizophrenic—what do you think?"

"Did he ever mention the term 'bad love' to you?"

He shook his head. "First time I heard about that was from the police. Asking me why Dorsey had screamed it—as if I'd know."

Pushing himself away from the desk, he wheeled back in his chair, then sat up. "And that's about all she wrote."

"Can you describe this Gritz fellow?"

He thought. "It was a while ago . . . about the same age as Dorsey—though with street people you can't really tell. Shorter than Dorsey, I think." He looked at his watch. "There's a call I've got to make."

I got up and thanked him for his time.

He waved it off and picked up the phone.

"Any idea where this Gritz might be located?" I said, as he dialed.

"Nope."

"Where did Dorsey hang out?"

"Wherever he could—and I'm not being flip. When it was warm, he liked to go down by the beach—Pacific Palisades Park, all up and down the beaches on PCH. When it cooled down, I was able to get him into a shelter or an SRO a couple of times, but he actually preferred sleeping outdoors—lots of times he bunked down in Little Calcutta."

"Where's that?"

"Freeway overpass, West L.A."

"Which freeway?"

"San Diego, just past Sepulveda. Never saw it?"

I shook my head.

He shook his, too, smiled, and put down the phone. "The invisible city . . . there used to be these little hovels there called Komfy Kort—built God knows when, for Mexican workers doing the day-labor pickup thing on Sawtelle."

"Those I remember," I said.

"Did you happen to notice they're not there anymore? City tore them down a few years ago and the street people moved onto the property. Nothing to tear down with *them*, so what could the city do but keep chasing them out? And what with voodoo economics taking hold, *that* became too expensive. So the city let them stay."

"Little Calcutta."

"Yeah, it's a great little suburb—you look like a West Side kind of guy—live anywhere near there?"

"Not that far."

"Go by and take a look, if you can spare the time. See who your neighbors are."

13

I drove east to the overpass Coburg had described. The freeway formed a concrete ceiling over a fenced dirt lot, an arcing canopy of surprising grace supported by columns that would have challenged Samson. The shade it cast was cool and gray. Even with my windows closed I could hear the roar of unseen cars.

The lot was empty and the dirt looked fresh. No tents or bedrolls, no signs of habitation.

I pulled over across the street, in front of a self-storage facility the size of an army base, and idled the Seville.

Little Calcutta. The fresh dirt suggested a bulldozer party. Maybe the city had finally cleared it.

I drove farther, slowly, past Exposition Boulevard. The west side of the street was lined with apartment buildings, the freeway concealed by ivied slopes. A few more empty spots peeked behind the usual chain link. A couple of overturned shopping carts made me stop and peer into the shadows.

Nothing.

I cruised several more blocks, until the freeway twisted out of sight. Then I turned around.

As I neared Exposition again, I spied something shiny and huge—a white-metal mountain, some sort of factory or plant. Giant canisters, duodenal twists of pipe, five-story ladders, valves that hinted at monstrous pressure.

Running parallel to the machine works was a blackened length of railroad track. Bordering the rails was a desert-pale table of sand.

Twenty years in L.A., and I'd never noticed it before.

Invisible city.

I headed toward the tracks, getting close enough to read a small red-and-blue sign on one of the giant towers. AVALON GRAVEL AND ASPHALT.

As I prepared to reverse direction again, I noticed another fenced lot catercorner to the plant—darker, almost blackened by the freeway, blocked from street view by green-gray shrubs. The chain-link fence was obscured by sections of bowed, graffitied plywood, the wood nearly blotted out by the hieroglyphics of rage.

Pulling to the curb, I turned off the engine and got out. The air smelled of dust and spoiled milk. The plant was as still as a mural.

The only other vehicle in sight was the burnt-out chassis of something two-doored, with a crushed roof. My Seville was old and in need of a paint job, but here it looked like a royal coach.

I crossed the empty street over to the plywooded fence and looked through an unblocked section of link. Shapes began forming in the darkness, materializing through the metal diamonds like holograms.

An overturned chair bleeding stuffing and springs.

An empty lineman's spool stripped of wire and cracked down the middle.

Food wrappers. Something green and shredded that might once have been a sleeping bag. And always the overhead roar, constant as breath.

Then movement—something on the ground, shifting, rolling. But it was submerged deeply in the shadows and I couldn't tell if it was human, or even real.

I looked up and down the fence, searching for an entrance to the lot, had to walk a ways until I found it: a square hatch cut into the link, held in place with rusty baling wire.

Prying the wires loose took a while and hurt my fingers. Finally, I bent the flap back, squatted, and passed through, retying one wire from the other side. Making my way across the soft dirt, my nostrils full of shit smell, I dodged chunks of concrete, Styrofoam food containers, lumps of things that didn't bear further inspection. No bottles or cans—probably because they were recyclable and redeemable. Let's hear it for green power.

But nothing green here. Just blacks, grays, browns. Perfect camouflage for a covert world.

A vile smell overcame even the excremental stench. Hearing the buzz of flies, I looked down at a cat's carcass that was so fresh the maggots hadn't yet homesteaded, and gave it a wide berth. Onward, past an old blanket, clumps of newspaper so sodden they looked like printed bread dough . . . no people that I could see, no movement. Where had the movement come from?

I arrived at the spot where I thought the thing had rolled, toward the back of the covered lot, just a few feet from the inner angle of a canted concrete wall.

Standing again, I focused. Waited. Felt my back itch.

Saw it again.

Movement. Hair. Hands. Someone lying rolled up in a sheet —several sheets, a mummy wrap of frayed bed linens. Twitchy movements below.

Lovemaking? No. No room for two people in the swaddle.

I walked toward it slowly, making sure I approached head-on, not wanting to startle.

My shoes kicked something hard. The impact was inaudible over the roar, but the figure in the sheeting sat up.

A young, dark Latina, bare shouldered. Soft shoulders, a large vaccine crater on one arm.

She stared at me, pressing the sheets up to her chest, long hair wild and sticky looking.

Her mouth was open, her face round and plain, scared and baffled.

And humiliated.

The sheet dropped a bit and I saw that she was naked. Something dark and urgent snuffled at her breast—a small head.

A baby. The rest of it concealed by the filthy cotton.

I backed away, smiled, held up my hand in greeting.

The young mother's face was electric with fear.

The baby kept suckling and she placed one hand over its tiny skull.

Near her feet was a small cardboard box. I got down and looked inside. Disposable diapers, new and used. More flies. A can of condensed milk and a rusty opener. A nearly empty bag of potato chips, a pair of rubber sandals, and a pacifier.

The woman tried to nourish her baby while rolling away from me, unraveling more of the sheets and exposing a mottled thigh.

As I started to turn away, the look in her eyes changed from fear to recognition and then to another type of fear.

I whipped around and found myself face-to-face with a man.

A boy, actually, seventeen or eighteen. Also Latin, small and flimsily built, with a fuzz mustache and a sloping chin so weak it seemed part of his skinny neck. His eyes were downslanted and frantic. His mouth hung open; a lot of his teeth were gone. He had on a torn, checked flannel shirt, stretched-out doubleknit pants, and unlaced sneakers. His ankles were black with dirt.

His hands trembled around an iron bar.

I stepped away. He hesitated, then came toward me.

A high sound pierced the freeway din.

The woman screaming.

Startled, the boy looked at her and I moved in, grabbed the bar, and twisted it out of his grip. The inertia threw him backwards onto the ground so easily that I felt like a bully.

He stayed there, looking up at me, shielding his face with one hand, ready to be beaten.

The woman was up, tripping out of the sheets, naked, the baby left squalling on the dirt. Her belly was pendulous and stretchmarked, her breasts limp as a crone's, though she couldn't have been much older than twenty.

I threw the bar as far as I could and held out both hands in what I hoped was a gesture of peace.

The two of them looked at me. Now I felt like a bad parent.

The baby was openmouthed with rage, clawing the air and kicking. I pointed to it.

The woman rushed over and picked it up. Realizing she was naked, she crouched and hung her head.

The chinless boy's hands were still shaking. I tried another smile and his eyes drooped, tugged down by despair.

I took out my wallet, removed a ten, walked over to the woman and held it out to her.

She didn't move.

I put the bill in the cardboard box. Went back to the boy, took out another ten and showed it to him.

More of that same hesitation he'd shown before coming at me with the bar. Then he took a step, biting his lip and teetering like a high-wire artist, and snatched the money.

Holding out yet another bill, I headed for the place where I'd broken through the fence. Checking my back as I trotted through the muck.

After a few steps the boy started following me. I picked up the pace and he tried to catch up, but couldn't. Walking was an effort for him. His mouth was open and his limbs looked rubbery. I wondered when he'd last eaten.

I made it to the flap, untied the wire and walked out to the sidewalk. He came through several moments later, rubbing his eyes.

The light hurt my pupils. He appeared to be in agony.

He finally stopped rubbing. I said, *"Habla inglés?"*

"I'm from Tucson, man," he said, in unaccented English.

His hands were fisted, but the tremor and his small bones mocked his fighter's stance. He started to cough, dry and wheezing. Tried to bring up phlegm and couldn't.

"Didn't mean to scare you," I said.

He was looking at the money. I extended my arm and he snatched the bill and crammed it under his waistband. The pants were much too big for him and held together with a red plastic belt. One of his sneakers was patched with cellophane tape. As his hand balled up around the bill, I saw that the pinkie of his left hand was missing.

"Gimme more," he said.

I didn't say anything.

"Gimme more. But she won' fuck you, anyway."

"I don't want her to."

He flinched. Thought a moment. "I won', neither."

"I'm not interested in that, either."

He frowned, put a finger inside his mouth and rubbed his gums.

I gave a quick look around, saw no one, and took out a fourth ten.

"Whu'?" he said, yanking his hand free and making a grab for it.

Holding it out of reach, I said, "Is that Little Calcutta?"

"Huh?"

"The place we just were. Is that Little Calcutta?"

"Maybe."

"Maybe?"

"Yeah." He coughed some more, hit his chest with the four-fingered hand.

"How many people live there?"

"I dunno."

"Are there others in there right now? People I didn't see?"
He considered his answer. Shook his head.

"Are there ever others?"

"Sometimes."

"Where are they now?"

"Around." He looked at the money, worked his tongue against his cheek, and came closer.

"She fucks you, it's twenty bucks."

I put the bill in my pocket.

"Hey!" he said, as if I'd cheated at a game.

"I don't want to fuck anyone," I said. "I just want some information. Answer my questions and you'll get paid, okay?"

"Why, man?"

"Because I'm a curious guy."

"Cop?"

"No."

He flexed his shoulders and rubbed his gums some more. When he removed his hand, the fingers were bloody.

"Is the baby yours?" I said.

"Thas what you wanna know?"

"Is it?"

"I dunno."

"It needs to be looked at by a doctor."

"I dunno."

"Is she your woman?"

He smiled. "Sometimes."

"What's your name?"

"Terminator Three." Glaring. Challenging me to mock him.

"Okay," I said. "Are there more people in there?"

"I told you, man. Not now, just at night."

"They come back at night?"

"Yuh."

"Every night?"

He looked at me as if I were stupid. Shook his head slowly. "Some nights—it changes places, I dunno."

"It moves from place to place?"

"Yeah."

Tent City as a concept. Some New Wave journalist would have a ball with it.

"What about a guy named Gritz?"

"Huh?"

"Gritz." I began the description Coburg had given me, and to my surprise he broke in: "Yeah."

"You know him?"

"I seen him."

"Does he live there?"

The hand went back into his mouth. He fiddled, twisted, pulled out a tooth and grinned. The root was inky with decay. He spit blood onto the pavement and wiped his mouth with his sleeve.

"Does Gritz hang out here?"

He didn't hear me, was looking at the tooth, fascinated. I repeated the question. He kept staring, finally dropped the tooth into his pocket.

"Not no more," he said.

"When's the last time you saw him?"

"Dunno."

"Days? Weeks?"

"Dunno."

He reached out to touch the sleeve of my jacket. Fifteen-year-old Harris Tweed. The cuffs were starting to fuzz.

I stepped back.

"Wool?" he said.

"Yeah."

He licked his lips.

"What do you know about Gritz?"

"Nuthin'."

"But you definitely know him?"

"I seen him around."

"When's the last time you saw him around?"

He closed his eyes. Opened them. "A week."

"A week definitely, or a week maybe?"

"I think—I dunno, man."

"Any idea where he is now?"

"To get rich."

"To get rich?"

"Yeah, that's what he said—he was drinking and partying, you know. And singing—sometimes he liked to sing—and he was singing about hey, man, I'm gonna get rich soon. Gonna get me a car and a boat—that kind of shit."

"Did he say how he was going to get rich?"

"Nah." A hint of threat sharpened his eyes. Fatigue wiped it out. He slumped.

"He didn't say how?" I repeated.

"No, man. He wuz partying and singing—he was nuts. That's *it*, man."

"Is Gritz a first name or a last name?"

"*Dunno*, man." He coughed, hit his chest, wheezed, "Fuck."

"If I told you to see a doctor, you'd shine me on, wouldn't you?"

Gap-toothed grin. "You gonna pay me to go?"

"What if you had a disease you could give to her—or the baby?"

"Gimme more money." Holding out a hand again.

"The baby needs to see a doctor."

"Gimme more money."

"Who'd Gritz hang out with?"

"No one."

"No one at all?"

"I dunno, man. Gimme more money."

"What about a guy named Hewitt?"

"Huh?"

"A guy named Dorsey Hewitt? Ever see Gritz with him?"

I described Hewitt. The boy stared—not that much blanker than his general demeanor, but enough to tell me his ignorance was real.

"Hewitt," I repeated.

"Don' know the dude."

"How long have you been hanging out here?"

"Hunerd years." Phlegmy laugh.

"Hewitt killed a woman. It was on the news."

"Don't got cable."

"A social worker named Rebecca Basille—at the Westside Mental Health Center?"

"Yeah, I heard something."

"What?"

Grin. "Music. In my head." He tapped one ear and smiled. "It's like rock and soul, man. The def cool no-fool."

I sighed involuntarily.

He brightened, latching on to my frustration like a buzzard on carrion. "Gimme *money*, man." Cough. *"Gimme."*

"Anything else you want to tell me?"

"Yeah."

Tapping one foot. Waiting for the straight man.

"What?" I said.

"The baby's mine." Smile. His remaining teeth were pink with fresh blood.

"Congratulations."

"Got a cigarette?"

"I don't smoke."

"Then gimme *money*. I aks around for you, man. You come back and I tell you everything I aksed."

I counted what I had in my wallet.

Two twenties and three singles. Gave him all of it. The jacket, too.

14

He scrambled back through the fence and disappeared. I hung around until his footsteps died, then walked back to the car. The air had cooled—sudden shifts were becoming the rule this autumn —and a soft wind from the east was nudging scraps of garbage off the sidewalk.

I gassed up the Seville at a station on Olympic and used the pay phone to get the number of the nearest Social Services office. After being put on hold several times and transferred from bureaucrat to bureaucrat, I managed to reach a supervisor and tell her about the infant living under the freeway.

"Was the baby being mistreated, sir?"

"No."

"Did the baby look malnourished?"

"Actually, no, but—"

"Were there bruises or scars anywhere visible on the baby's body or other signs of abuse?"

"Nothing," I said. "The mother was caring for the baby, but they're living in filthy conditions out there. And the boy who might be the baby's father has a cough that sounds tubercular."

"Was the *baby* coughing?"

"Not yet."

"For a tuberculosis investigation, you'd have to call public health. Ask for a communicable disease officer."

"There's nothing you can do?"

"Doesn't sound like there's anything we should be doing, sir."

"How 'bout getting the baby some shelter?"

"They'd have to ask, sir."

"The baby would?" ˉ

"The legal guardians. We don't just go out looking for people."

Click.

The dial tone was as loud as the freeway. I felt nuts. How did the certifiable psychotics handle it?

I wanted to call Robin. Then I realized I hadn't memorized my new phone number, didn't even know the name of the house's owner. I called Milo. He was at his desk and gave me the seven digits, then said, "Before you hang up, I just got through with Myra Paprock's file. She wasn't a therapist. Real estate agent, killed on the job. Showing a house and somebody cut her, robbed her, raped her, and wrote 'bad love' on the wall with her lipstick."

"Oh, Jesus."

"Yeah. In the photos, the lipstick looks like blood."

"Real estate agent," I said. "That's sometimes a second career. Maybe she worked as some kind of therapist first."

"If she did it's not down here in the file, and the Van Nuys guys seem to have done a pretty thorough job. Plus Shipler—the beating victim—wasn't a shrink, either, so I don't see any obvious mental health connection here."

"What did he do?"

"Janitor. Night custodian at Jefferson High. I haven't gotten his file yet, but I had a records clerk over at Central give me the basics."

"Was he killed on the job, too?"

"Nope, in the comfort of his own home."

"Where'd he live?"

"Budlong Avenue—South L.A."

"Black?"

"Yeah."

"What happened to him?"

"Pounded to mush and the house was trashed."

"Robbery?"

"Doubtful. His stereo, TV, and some jewelry were left behind."

"What, then? Someone looking for something?"

"Or someone got really angry. I want to read the whole file—got a call in for it."

"Real estate agent and janitor," I said. "Doesn't make any sense. Any connection between them?"

"Other than 'bad love' on the wall, there doesn't seem to be any. Nothing matches. She was thirty-five, he was sixty-one. He was killed early morning—right after he finished work on the nightshift—and she got it in the middle of the day. She was stabbed, he was clubbed. There were even differences in what the killer used to write 'bad love.' Shipler's was done in molasses from his fridge."

"In both cases the killer was opportunistic—used something of the victim's."

"Weapons, too," he said. "She was killed with a kitchen knife from the house she was showing, Shipler with a fireplace poker that was identified as his. So?"

"I don't know, maybe it indicates some kind of power thing—dominance over the victims—turning the victims against themselves. Like using my tree branch on the koi. Were there any bondage or S&M overtones to either murder?"

"Paprock's bra was wrapped around her neck, but the coroner said it was done when she was already dead. Far as I can tell there were no sexual overtones at all to Shipler."

"Still," I said, "the message was important. It must mean something to the killer."

"I'm sure it does," he said, without enthusiasm.

"Did Shipler live alone?"

"Yeah, divorced."

"What about Paprock?"

"No match there, either. Married, two kids."

"If nothing was taken from Shipler's house," I said, "what was the assumed motive?"

"A gang thing—there was lots of activity in Shipler's neighborhood, even back then. Lots more, now. Like you said before, a trashed house could mean someone looking for something. Central figured dope. Figured Shipler was involved on some level and 'bad love' was some sort of gangbanger slogan they hadn't heard of yet. They checked it out with the CRASH detail and *they* hadn't heard of it, but new stuff comes up all the time."

"Did Shipler turn out to be involved in gangs or dope?"

"Far as I can tell, he had no record, but plenty of scrotes slip through the cracks. In terms of there being no burglary, Southwest figured it was punks panicking and leaving before they could take anything. Which is consistent with gang wannabees—new recruits out on a virgin adventure."

"An initiation thing?"

"Yeah, they start 'em young. Automatics in the diapers. Speaking of which, I caught my little truant bastards on the Palms robbery—thirteen and fifteen. No doubt they'll get referred for some kind of therapy. Want a referral?"

"No, thanks."

"Cynic."

"Was there gang activity where Paprock was killed?"

"A little, on the fringes. It's mostly working-class tough— north end of Van Nuys. No one made the gang assumption in that one, but maybe if Van Nuys had talked to Southwest, they would have. Neither of them knew about the other case—still don't."

"Going to tell them?" I said.

"First I'm gonna read Shipler's file thoroughly, see what I can pull out of it. Then, yeah, I'll have to tell them, do the old network blah blah. Both cases are real cold—be interesting to see what kind of responses I get. Hopefully the whole thing won't deteriorate into endless memories. Though if 'bad love' shows up anywhere in *Stoumen's* file, we've got interstate blah blah."

"Hear from Seattle, yet?"

"Very briefly. They're sending down records—it'll probably take a week or so. Both detectives on that one are retired and unavailable. Probable translation: burnouts gone fishing. If anything provocative comes up in the file, I'll bug 'em anyway."

"What about the FBI records on other 'bad love' murders?"

"Not yet. *Them* gears grind slowly."

"A real estate agent, a janitor, and 'bad love,' " I said. "I still think it has something to do with that conference. Or de Bosch himself—Paprock and Shipler could have been his patients."

"So why would someone kill them?"

"Maybe it's another patient, mad about something."

"Then what's *your* connection?"

"I don't know. . . . Nothing makes sense, dammit."

"You learn anything from Jeffers?"

"No one at the center remembers Hewitt having any friends.

But she referred me to Hewitt's lawyer and he gave me a name and possible address." I described my encounter with the people under the freeway.

"Gritz," he said. "As in hominy."

"With a 'z.' Could be a first name or a last, or just a nickname."

"I'll run it through."

"The kid I spoke to said he's been gone about a week. He also said Gritz was talking and singing about getting rich."

"Singing?"

"That's what he said."

"Oh those romantic hoboes, strumming around the campfire."

"Maybe Gritz had some kind of job lined up, or maybe it's baloney. The kid could very well have been putting me on. For what it's worth, he said he'd ask around, I should come back later."

"Getting rich," he said. "*Everyone* talks and sings about it. That Calcutta place might be the dregs, but it's still L.A."

"True," I said. "But wouldn't it be interesting if Gritz really did expect to get paid for something—like killing my koi, and other nasties."

"Hitman on a fish? So who's doing the hiring?"

"The anonymous bad guy—I know, it's a ridiculous idea."

"At this point nothing's ridiculous, Alex, but if someone was looking to hire a nighttime skulker, would they choose a homeless nutcase?"

"True. . . . Maybe what Gritz was hired for was to scream on tape—to imitate Hewitt because he knew what Hewitt sounded like."

"Imitate?" he said. "Those voice tracks sounded identical to me, Alex. Though we may never be able to verify it. I talked to the voiceprint guy over at the sheriff's, and screams *are* useless, legally. In order to make a match that can be used in court, you need two samples, minimum of twenty words on each and the exact same phrases. Even then, it gets challenged a lot and thrown out."

"What about for nonadmissible comparison?"

"Matching screams is still an iffy business. It's words that have unique characteristics. I asked the sheriff to give a listen anyway. He said he's backlogged but would try to get to it eventually. . . . Why would someone want to imitate Hewitt?"

"I don't know—I can't help but think the tape's part of a ritual. Something ceremonial that means something only to the killer."

"What about the kid on the tape?"

"Could be a homeless kid—someone from Little Calcutta or some place like it. Living down there could explain the robot quality of the voice—despair. You should have seen it, Milo. The boy's teeth were rotting, he had a tubercular cough. The girl was naked, wrapped up in a sheet, trying to feed the baby. If I'd offered enough money, I probably could have *bought* the baby."

"I've seen it," he said softly.

"I know you have. I have too. It's all around. But I haven't really let it register for a while."

"What're you gonna do, solve everyone's problems? Plenty of your own to deal with, for the time being. You get names on the freeway people?"

"Not the girl. *He* calls himself Terminator Three."

He laughed. "No one else down there besides them and the baby?"

"No one I could see, and I was flashing ten-dollar bills."

"Real smart, Alex."

"I watched my back."

"Yeah."

"The kid said the place fills up at night. I could go back after dark and see if anyone else knows Gritz."

"You're really in the mood to get your throat cut, aren't you?"

"If I had a macho cop with me I'd be safe, right?"

"Don't count on it. . . . Yeah, okay, it's probably a waste of time, but that makes me feel *right* at home."

Robin was still working in the garage, hunched over her bench, wielding shiny sharp things that resembled dental picks. Her hair was tied up and her goggles were lodged in her curls. Under her overalls, her T-shirt was tightened by perspiration. She said, "Hi, doll," as her hands continued to move. The dog was at her feet and he stood and licked my hand as I looked over Robin's shoulder.

A tiny rectangle of abalone was clamped to a padded section of the bench. The edges were beveled and the corners were inlaid with bits of ivory and gold wire. She'd traced the shell with minuscule curlicue shapes, cut out some of them, and was in the process of excising another.

"Beautiful," I said. "Fretboard inlay?"

"Uh-huh. Thanks." She blew away dust and cleaned the edge of a pick with a fingernail.

"You do root canal, too?"

She laughed and hunched lower. The tools clicked as she carved out a speck of shell. "Kind of baroque for my taste, but it's for a stockbroker who wants a showpiece for his wall."

She worked some more, finally put the tools down, wiped her forehead, and wiggled her fingers. "Enough for one day, I'm cramping up."

"Everything okay?" I rubbed her neck.

"Nice and quiet. How about you?"

"Not bad."

I kissed her. The wind got stronger and drier, ruffling the cypress trees and shooting a cold stream through the open garage. Robin unclamped the abalone, and put it in her pocket. Her arms were goosebumped. I put mine around them and the two of us headed for the house. By the time we got to the door, the wind was whipping the trees and stirring the dust, causing the bulldog to blink and sniff.

"Santa Ana?" she said.

"Too cold. Probably the tail end of something arctic."

"Brr," she said, unlocking the door. "Leave your jacket in the car?"

I shook my head. We went inside.

"You were wearing one, weren't you?" she said, rubbing her hands together. "That baggy brown tweed."

Artist's eye.

"Yup."

"Did you lose it?"

"Not exactly."

"Not exactly?"

"I gave it away."

She laughed. "You what?"

"No big deal. It was fraying."

"Who'd you give it to?"

I told her about Little Calcutta. She listened with her hands on her hips, shaking her head, and went into the kitchen to wash her hands. When she came back, her head was still moving from side to side.

"I know, I know," I said. "It was a bleeding-heart reflex, but they really were pitiful—it was a cheap old thing, anyway."

"You wore it the first time we went out. I never liked it."

"You didn't?"

"Nope. Too philosophy prof."

"Why didn't you tell me?"

She shrugged. "It wasn't that important."

"Snoring, poor taste in haberdashery. What else don't you like that you haven't informed me about?"

"Nothing. Now that you've ditched the coat, you're perfect."

She ruffled my hair, walked to the French doors, and looked out at the mountains. They were shimmering, denuded in patches, where the foliage was brushed back like blow-dried hair. The pool water was choppy, the surface gritty with leaves and dirt.

Robin loosened her hair. I hung back and kept looking at her.

Perfect female statuary, rock-still against the turbulence.

She unsnapped one overall strap, then the other, letting the baggy denim collapse around her feet, and stood there in T-shirt and panties.

Half turning, hands on hips, she looked back at me. "How 'bout giving *me* something, big boy?" she said, in a Mae West voice.

The dog grumbled. Robin cracked up. "Quiet, you! You're wrecking my timing."

"Now it feels like a home," she said, snuggling under the covers. "Though I do prefer our little love nest, be it ever so humble. So what'd you find out today?"

My second summation of the day. I did it quickly, adding what Milo'd told me about the murders and leaving out the gross pathology. Even sanitized, it was bad, and she turned quiet.

I rubbed her lower back, allowing my hand to linger on swells and dimples. Her body loosened, but only for a moment.

"You're sure you've never heard of those other two people?" she said, stilling my hand.

"I'm sure. And there doesn't even seem to be any connection between the two of *them*. The woman was a white real estate agent, the man a black janitor. He was twenty-six years older, they lived on opposite ends of the city, were killed in different ways. Nothing in common but 'bad love.' Maybe they were patients of de Bosch."

"They couldn't be old patients of *yours*?"

"No way," I said. "I've been through every one of my case files. To be honest, I don't see the patient angle as too likely, period. If someone has a hangup with de Bosch, why go after the people he treated?"

"What about group therapy, Alex? Things can get rough in groups, can't they? People lashing out at one another? Maybe someone got dumped on badly and never forgot it."

"I guess it's possible," I said, sitting up. "A good therapist always tries to keep a handle on the group's emotional climate, but things can get out of control. And sometimes there's no way to know someone's feeling victimized. Once, at the hospital, I had to calm down the father of a kid with a bone tumor who brought a loaded pistol onto the ward. When I finally got him to open up, it came out that he'd been boiling for weeks. But there was no warning at all—till then he'd been a really easygoing guy."

"There you go," she said. "So maybe some patient of de Bosch's sat there and took it and never told anyone. Finally, years later, he decided to get even."

"But what kind of therapy group would bring together a real estate agent from the valley and a black janitor?"

"I don't know—maybe *they* weren't the patients, maybe their kids were. A parents' group for problem kids—de Bosch was basically a *child* therapist, wasn't he?"

I nodded, trying to imagine it. "Shipler was a lot older than Paprock—I suppose she could have been a young mother and he an old father."

We heard scratching and thumping at the door. I got up and opened it and the dog bounded in. He headed straight for Robin's side of the bed, stood on his hind legs, put his paws on the mattress, and began snorting. She lifted him up and he rewarded her with lusty licks.

"Settle down," she said. "Uh-oh—look, he's getting excited."

"Without testicles, yet. See the effect you have on men?"

"But of *course*." She batted her lashes at me, turned back to the dog, and finally got him to lie still by kneading the folds of flesh around his jowls. He lapsed into sleep with an ease that I envied. But when I leaned over to kiss her, he opened his eyes, snuffled, and insinuated himself between us, curling atop the covers and licking his paws.

I said, "Maybe Milo can get hold of Paprock's and Shipler's medical histories, see if de Bosch's name or the Corrective School appears on them. Sometimes people conceal psych treatment, but with the cost, it's more likely there's some kind of insurance record. I'll ask him when I see him tonight."

"What's tonight?"

"We were planning on going back to the freeway, try to talk to more of the homeless people in order to get a handle on this Gritz character."

"Is it safe going back there?"

"I'll have Milo with me. Whether or not it's productive remains to be seen."

"All right," she said uneasily. "If you want it to be productive, why don't you stop at a market and get those people some food?"

"Good idea. You're full of them today, aren't you?"

"Motivation," she said. She turned serious, reached up and held my face in both of her hands. "I want this to be over. Please take care of yourself."

"Promise." We managed to maintain a convoluted embrace despite the dog.

I fell asleep, smelling perfume and kibble. When I woke up my stomach was sour and my feet were sore. Inhaling and letting out the air, I sat up and cleared my eyes.

"What is it?" Robin mumbled, her back to me.

"Just thinking."

"About what?" She rolled over and faced me.

"Someone in a therapy group, getting wounded and keeping it inside all these years."

She touched my face.

"What the hell do I have to do with it?" I said. "Am I just a name on a damned brochure, or did I hurt someone without ever knowing it?"

15

I heard the unhealthy-sounding engine from inside the house. Milo's Fiat, reduced to a squat little toy on the monitor.

I went outside. The wind had stopped. The car expelled a plume of smoke, then convulsed. It didn't look as if it would survive the evening.

"Figured it would blend in where we're going," he said, getting out. He carried a large, white plastic bag and was wearing work clothes. The bag smelled of garlic and meat.

"More food?" I said.

"Sandwiches—Italian. Just consider me your official LAPD delivery boy."

Robin was back in the garage, working under a funnel of fluorescence. The dog was there, too, and he charged us, heading straight for the bag.

Milo lifted it out of reach. "Sit. Stay—better yet, go away."

The dog snorted once, turned his back on us, and sank to his haunches.

Milo said, "Well, one out of three ain't bad." He waved at Robin. She raised a hand and put down her tools.

"She looks right at home," he said. "How 'bout you, Nick Danger?"

"I'm fine. Anything on Gritz in the records?"

Before he could answer, Robin came over.

"He's brought us dinner," I said.

"What a prince." She kissed his cheek. "Are you hungry right now?"

"Not really," he said, touching his gut and looking down at the ground. "Had a little appetizer while I waited."

"Good for you," she said. "Growing boy."

"Growing the wrong way."

"You're fine, Milo. You've got *presence*." She patted his shoulder. From the way her fingers were flexing I knew she was eager to get back to her bench. I was itchy, too, thinking of the freeway people. The dog continued to sulk.

"How 'bout you, hon?" she said to me. The dog came over, thinking—or pretending—it was meant for him.

"I can wait."

"Me, too. So let me stick this in the fridge and when you guys get back, we'll chow down."

"Sounds good." Milo gave her the bag. The dog tried to lick it and she said, "Relax, I've got a Milk-Bone for you."

Above the roofline, the sky was black and empty. Lights from the houses across the canyon seemed a continent away.

"You'll be okay?" I said.

"I'll be fine. Go." She gave me a quick kiss and a small shove.

Milo and I headed for the Fiat. The dog watched us drive away.

The sound of the gate clanking shut made me feel better about leaving her up there. Milo coasted to Benedict, shifted to first, then upward, squeezing as much speed as possible out of the little car. Shifting roughly, big hands nearly covering the top of the steering wheel. As we headed south, I said, "Anything on Gritz?"

"One possible citation—thank God it's an unusual name. Lyle Edward, male white, thirty-four years old, five six, one thirty, I forget the color of his eyes."

"Coburg said he was shorter than Hewitt."

He nodded. "Bunch of drunk and disorderlies from back when we still bothered with those, possession of narcotics, couple of shoplifting busts, nothing heavy."

"When did he come to L.A.?"

"First arrest was fourteen years ago. The computer gives him no known address, no parole officer, either. He got probation for some of his naughties, lived at county jail for the others, and paid his debt in full."

"Any mention of mental illness?"

"There wouldn't be unless he was classified as a mentally disordered sex offender or committed some other kind of violent psycho crime."

"I'll call Jean Jeffers Monday, see if I can find out if he ever got treated at the center."

"Meanwhile, we can talk to the offrampers, for what it's worth. All he is is a name, so far."

"Robin suggested we should bring them food. Increase the rapport."

He shrugged. "Why not. There's a minimarket over on Olympic."

We drove a bit more. He frowned and rubbed his face with one hand.

"Something the matter?" I said.

"Nah . . . just the usual. Justice got raped again—my truant scumbags. The old lady died this afternoon."

"I'm sorry. Does that make it murder?"

He pumped his gas pedal leg. "It makes it *shit*. She had badly clogged arteries and a big tumor growing in her colon. Autopsy said it was just a matter of time. That, her age, and the fact that the kids never actually touched her means the DA's office doesn't want to bother to prove it was an unnatural death. Once they hospitalized her, she was never well enough to get even a deathbed declaration, and without her testimony, there's not much of a case against the little bastards even for robbery. So they probably get a stern lecture and walk. Wanna make a bet by the time they start shaving, someone else'll be dead?"

He got to Sunset and joined the smooth, fast traffic flowing west from Beverly Hills. Amid the Teutonic tanks and cigarillo sports jobs, the Fiat looked like a mistake. A Mercedes cut in front of us and Milo swore viciously.

I said, "You could give him a ticket."

"Don't tempt me."

A mile later, I said, "Robin came up with a possible link between Paprock and Shipler. Both could have been in group therapy with de Bosch. Treatment for themselves, or some kind of parent's group to talk about problem kids. The killer could also have been in the group, gotten treated roughly—or thought he had—and developed a grudge."

"Group therapy . . ."

"Some kind of common problem—what else would draw two people from such different backgrounds to de Bosch?"

"Interesting . . . but if it was a parent's group, de Bosch didn't run it. He died in eighty, and Paprock's kids are six and seven years old now. So they weren't alive when he was. In fact, at the time Myra died, they were only babies. So what kind of problems could they have had?"

"Maybe it was a child-rearing program. Or some kind of chronic illness support group. And are you sure Paprock was only married once?"

"According to her file she was."

"Okay," I said. "So maybe *Katarina* was the therapist. Or someone else at the school—maybe the killer believes in collective guilt. Or it could have been an *adult* treatment group. Child therapists don't always limit themselves to kids."

"Fine. But now we're back to the same old question: what's *your* link?"

"Has to be the conference. The killer's gotten severely paranoid—let his rage get out of control. To him, anyone associated with de Bosch is guilty, and where better to start than a bunch of therapists paying public homage to the old man? Maybe Stoumen's hit-and-run was no accident."

"What? Major-league mass murder? The killer's going after patients *and* therapists?"

"I don't know—I'm just grasping."

He heard the frustration in my voice. "It's okay, keep grasping. Doesn't cost the taxpayers a dime. For all I know we're dealing with something so crazy it'll never make sense."

We rode for a while. Then he said, "De Bosch's clinic was private, expensive. How could a janitor like Shipler afford getting treatment there?"

"Sometimes private clinics treat a few hardship cases. Or maybe Shipler had good health insurance through the school system. What about Paprock? Did she have money?"

"Nothing huge, as far as I can tell. Husband worked as a car salesman."

"Can you get hold of their insurance records?"

"If they had any, and haven't been destroyed."

I thought of two motherless grade-school children and said, "How old, exactly, were Paprock's children at the time of her murder?"

"Don't remember exactly—little."

"Who raised them?"

"I assume the husband."

"Is he still in town?"

"Don't know that either, yet."

"If he is, maybe he'll be willing to talk about her, tell us if she was ever a therapy patient at de Bosch's clinic."

He hooked a finger toward the rear seat. "Got the file right there. Check out the address."

I swung around toward the darkened seat and saw a file box.

"Right on top," he said. "The brown one."

Colors were indistinguishable in the darkness, but I reached over, groped around, and came up with a folder. Opening it, I squinted.

"There's a penlight in the glove compartment."

I tried to open the compartment, but it was stuck. Milo leaned across and slammed it with his fist. The door dropped open and papers slid to the floor. I stuffed them back in and finally found the light. Its skinny beam fell on a page of crime-scene photos stapled to the right-hand page. Lots of pink and red. Writing on a wall: a closeup of "bad love" in big, red block letters that matched the blood on the floor . . . neat lettering . . . a bloody thing below.

I turned to the facing page. The name of Myra Paprock's widower was midway through the intake data.

"Ralph Martin Paprock," I said. "Valley Vista Cadillac. The home address is in North Hollywood."

"I'll run it through DMV, see if he's still around."

I said, "I need to keep looking for the other conference people to warn them."

"Sure, but if you can't tell them who and why, what does that leave? 'Dear Sir or Madam, this is to inform you you might be bludgeoned, stabbed, or run over by an unidentified, revenge-crazed psycho?"

"Maybe one of them can tell me the who and why. And I

know I'd have liked to have been warned. The problem is finding them. None of them are working or living where they were at the time of the conference. And the woman I thought might be Rosenblatt's wife hasn't returned any of my calls."

Another stretch of silence.

"You're wondering," he said, "if they've been visited, too."

"It did cross my mind. Katarina's not been listed in the APA directory for five years. She could have just stopped paying dues, but it doesn't seem like her to just drop out of psychology and close up the school. She was ambitious, very much taken with carrying on her father's work."

"Well," he said, "it should be easy enough to check tax rolls and Social Security records on all of them, find out who's breathing and who ain't."

He reached Hilgard and turned left, passing the campus of the university where I'd jumped through academic hoops for so many years.

"So many people gone," I said. "Now the Wallace girls. It's as if everyone's folding up their tents and escaping."

"Hey," he said, "maybe they know something we don't."

The strip-mall at Olympic and Westwood was dark except for the flagrant white glare from the minimart. The store was quiet, with a turbaned Pakistani drinking Gatorade behind the counter.

We stocked up on overpriced bread, canned soup, lunch meat, cereal, and milk. The Pakistani eyed us unpleasantly as he tallied up the total. He wore a company shirt printed repetitively with the name of the mart's parent company in lawn green. The nametag pinned to his breast pocket was blank.

Milo reached for his wallet. I got mine out first and handed the clerk cash. He continued to look unhappy.

"Whatsamatter?" said Milo. "Too much cholesterol in our diet?"

The clerk pursed his lips and glanced up at the video camera above the door. The machine's cyclops eye was sweeping the store slowly. The screen below filled with milky gray images.

We followed his gaze to the dairy case. An unkempt man stood in front of it, not moving, staring at cartons of Half-and-Half. I hadn't noticed him while shopping and wondered where he'd come from.

Milo eyed him for a long moment, then turned back to the clerk.

"Yeah, police work's strenuous," he said in a loud voice. "Got to shovel in those calories in order to catch the bad guys."

He laughed even louder. It sounded almost mad.

The man at the dairy case twitched and half turned. He glared at us for a second, then returned to studying the cream.

He was gaunt and hairy, wearing a dirt-blackened army jacket, jeans, and beach sandals. His hands shook and one clouded eye had to be blind.

Another member of Dorsey Hewitt's extended family.

He slapped the back of his neck with one hand, turned again, tried to match Milo's stare.

Milo gave a salute. "Evening, pal."

The man didn't move for a second. Then he shoved his hands into his pockets and left the store, sandals slapping the vinyl floor.

The clerk watched him go. The cash register gave a computer burp and expelled a receipt. The clerk tore off the tape and dropped it into one of the half-dozen bags we'd filled.

"Got a box for all this?" said Milo.

"No, sir," said the clerk.

"What about in back?"

Shrug.

We carried the food out. The gaunt man was at the far end of the lot, kicking asphalt and walking from store to store, staring at black glass.

"Hey," Milo called out. No response. He repeated it, pulled a cereal variety pack out of one of the bags and waved it over his head.

The man straightened, looked toward us, but didn't approach. Milo walked ten feet from him and underhanded the cereal.

The man shot his arms out, missed the catch, sank to his knees, and retrieved it. Milo was heading back to the car and didn't see the look on the man's face. Confusion, distrust, then a spark of gratitude that fizzled just short of ignition.

The gaunt man hobbled off into the darkness, fingers ripping at the plastic wrapping, sprinkling cereal onto the pavement.

Milo said, "Let's get the hell out of here." We got into the Fiat and he drove around toward the back of the mall where three dumpsters sat. Several empty cartons were piled up loosely against the bins, most of them torn beyond utility. We finally found a couple that looked and smelled relatively clean, put the bags in them, and stashed the food in back of the car, next to Myra Paprock's homicide file.

A sliver of moon was barely visible behind a cloud-veil, and the sky looked dirty. The freeway was a stain topped with light and noise. After we rounded Exposition, Little Calcutta continued to elude us—the darkness and the plywood barrier concealed the lot totally. But the place on the sidewalk where I'd talked to Terminator Three was just within the light of an ailing street lamp and I was able to point it out to Milo.

We got out and found gaps in the plywood. Through them, blue tongues quivered—thin, gaseous alcohol flames.

"Sterno," I said.

Milo said, "Frugal gourmets."

I took him to the spot along the fence where I'd unhinged the makeshift hatch a few hours before. Extra wires had been added since then, rusty and rough, wound too tightly to unravel by hand.

Milo took a Swiss army knife out of his trouser pocket and flipped out a tiny pliers-like tool. Twisting and snipping, he managed to free the hatch.

We went back to the car, took out the boxes of groceries, and stepped through. Blue lights began extinguishing, as if we'd brought a hard wind.

Milo reached into his trousers again and pulled out the penlight I'd used in the car. I'd replaced it in the glove compartment and hadn't seen him pocket it.

He removed something from one of the grocery bags and shined the light on it. Plastic-wrapped bologna slices.

He held it up and shouted, "Food!"

Barely audible over the freeway. Fires continued to go out.

Training his beam more directly on the bologna, he waved the meat back and forth. The package and the hand that held it seemed suspended in midair, a special effect.

When nothing happened for several more seconds, he placed the meat on the ground, making sure to keep the penlight trained on it, then removed more groceries from his bag and spread them out on the dirt. Walking backward, toward the hatch, he created a snaky trail of food that led out to the sidewalk.

"Goddamn Hansel and Gretel," he muttered, then he slipped back out.

I followed him. He was standing against the Fiat, had emptied one bag and crumpled it and was tossing it from hand to hand.

As we stood there and waited, cars rocketed overhead and the concrete hummed. Milo lit up a bad panatela and blew short-lived smoke rings.

A few minutes later, he stubbed out his cigar and jammed it between his fingers. Walking back to the hatch, he stuck his head through, didn't move for a second, then beckoned me to follow him through.

We stopped just a few feet from the hatch and he aimed the penlight upward, highlighting movement about fifteen feet up.

Frantic, choppy, a scramble of arms.

Squinting, I managed to make out human forms. Down on their knees, scooping and snatching, just as the man at the minimart had done.

Within seconds they were gone and the food had vanished. Milo cupped his hands around his mouth and shouted over the freeway: "Lots more, folks."

Nothing.

He clicked his light off and we retreated to the other side of the fence again.

It seemed like a game—a futile one. But he looked at ease.

He began emptying another bag, placing food on the streetlit patch of sidewalk, just out of reach of the hatch. Then he returned to the car, sat on the rear deck causing the springs to groan, and relit his cigar.

Luring and trapping—*enjoying* the hunt.

More time passed. Milo's eyes kept shifting to the fence, then leaving it. His expression didn't change, the cigar tilted as he bit down on it.

Then he stayed on the fence.

A large, dark hand was reaching out, straining to grab a loaf of white bread.

Milo went over and kicked the package away and the hand drew back.

"Sorry," said Milo. "No grain without pain."

He took his badge out and shoved it at the hatch.

"Just talk, that's it," he said.

Nothing.

Sighing, he picked up the bread, tossed it through the hatch. Picking up a can of soup, he wiggled it.

"Make it a balanced meal, pal."

A moment later, a pair of unlaced sneakers appeared in the opening. Above them, the frayed cuffs of greasy-looking plaid pants and the bottom seam of an army blanket.

The head above the cloth remained unseen, shielded by darkness.

Milo held the soup can between thumb and forefinger. New Orleans Gourmet Gumbo.

"Lots more where this came from," he said. "Just for answering a few questions, no hassles."

One plaid leg angled forward through the opening. A sneaker hit the pavement, then the other.

A man emerged into the streetlight, wincing.

He had the blanket wrapped around him to the knees, covering his head like a monk's cowl and shrouding most of his face.

What showed of the skin was black and grainy. The man took an awkward step, as if testing the integrity of the sidewalk, and the blanket dropped a bit. His skull was big and half bald, above a long, bony face that looked caved in. His beard was a kinky gray rash, his skin cracked and caked. Fifty or sixty or seventy. A battered nose so flat it almost merged with his crushed cheeks, spreading like melted tar. His eyes squinted and watered and didn't stop moving.

He had the white bread in his hand and was looking at the soup.

Milo tried to give it to him.

The man hesitated, working his jaws. His eyes were quieter now.

"Know what a gift horse is?" said Milo.

The man swallowed. Drawing his blanket around himself, he squeezed the bread so hard the loaf turned into a figure eight.

I went over to him and said, "We just want to talk, that's it."

He looked into my eyes. His were jaundiced and clogged with blood vessels, but something shone through—maybe intelligence, maybe just suspicion. He smelled of vomit and alcohol belch and breath mints, and his lips were as loose as a mastiff's. I worked hard at standing my ground.

Milo came up behind me and covered some of the stench with

cigar smoke. He put the soup up against the man's chest. The man looked at it and finally took it, but continued to stare at me.

"You are not police." His voice was surprisingly clear. "You are definitely not police."

"True," I said. "But he is."

The man glanced at Milo and smiled. Rubbing the part of the blanket that covered his abdomen, he shoved both hands under it, secreting the bread and the soup.

"A few questions, friend," said Milo. "Simple stuff."

"Nothing in life is simple," said the man.

Milo hooked a thumb at the bags on the sidewalk. "A philosopher. There's enough there to feed you and your friends—have a nice little party."

The man shook his head. "It could be poison."

"Why the hell would it be poison?"

Smile. "Why not? The world's poison. A while back someone gave someone a present and it was full of poison and someone died."

"Where'd this happen?"

"Mars."

"Seriously."

"Venus."

"Okay," said Milo, blowing smoke. "Suit yourself, we'll ask our questions elsewhere."

The man licked his lips. "Go ahead. I've got the virus, makes no difference to me."

"The virus, huh?" said Milo.

"Don't believe me, you can kiss me."

The man flicked his tongue. The blanket fell to his shoulders. Underneath, he wore a greasy Bush-Quayle T-shirt. His neck and shoulders were emaciated.

"I'll pass," said Milo.

The man laughed. "Bet you will—now what? Gonna beat it *out* of me?"

"Beat what out of you?"

"Whatever you want. You've got the power."

"Nah," said Milo. "This is the new LAPD. We're New Age sensitive guys."

The man laughed. His breath was hot and emetic. "Bearshit. You'll always be savages—got to be to keep order."

Milo said, "Have a nice day," and began to turn.

"What do you want to know, anyway?"

"Anything about a citizen named Lyle Edward Gritz," said Milo. "You know him?"

"Like a brother."

"That so?"

"Yup," said the man. "Unfortunately, this day and age, families deteriorating and all, that means not well at all."

Milo looked over at the hatch. "He in there now?"

"Nope."

"See him recently?"

"Nope."

"But he did hang out here."

"From time to time."

"When was the last time?"

The man ignored the question and began staring at me again.

"What *are* you?" he said. "Some kind of journalist riding along?"

"He's a doctor," said Milo.

"Oh yeah?" Smile. "Got any penicillin? Things get pretty infectious down here. Amoxicillin, erythromycin, tetracycline—anything to zap those little cocci boogers?"

I said, "I'm a psychologist."

"Ooh," said the man, as if wounded. He closed his eyes and shook his head. When he opened them they were dry and focused. "Then you're not worth a damn to me—pardon my linguistics."

"Gritz," said Milo. "Can you tell me anything about him?"

The man appeared to be contemplating. "White trash, juicehead, low IQ. But able-bodied. He had no excuse ending up down here. Not that I do—you probably think I was some kind of white collar overachiever, don't you? 'Cause I'm black and I know grammar."

Smiling.

I smiled back.

"Wrong," he said. "I collected *garbage*. Professionally. City of Compton. Good pay, you wear your gloves, it's fine, terrific benefits. My mistake was leaving and starting my own business. Vinyl flooring. I did good work, had six people working for me. Did fine until business slumped and I let the dope comfort me."

He produced one arm from under the blanket. Raised it and let the sleeve fall back from a bony forearm. The underside of the limb was knotted with scars and abscesses, keloidal and bunched, raw in spots.

"This is a fresh one," he said, eyeing a scab near his wrist. "Got off just before sundown. I waive my rights, why don't you take me in, give me a bunk for the night?"

"Not my thing," said Milo.

"Not your thing?" The man laughed. "What are you, some kind of liberal?"

Milo looked at him and smoked.

The man put his arm back. "Well, at least get me a *real* doctor, so I can get hold of some methadone."

"What about the county?"

"County ran out. Can't even get antibiotics from the county."

"Well," said Milo, "I can give you a lift to an emergency room if you want."

The man laughed again, scornfully. "For what? Wait around all night with gunshots and heart attacks? I've got no active diagnosis—just the virus, no symptoms yet. So all they'll do is keep me waiting. Jail's better—they process you faster."

"Here," said Milo, dipping into his pocket for his wallet. He took out some bills and handed them to the man. "Find a room, keep the change."

The man gave a warm, broad smile and tucked the money under his blanket. "That's real nice, Mr. Policeman. You made this po', unfortunate, homeless individual's evening."

Milo said, "Was Gritz into dope, too?"

"Just juice. Like I said, white trash. Him and his hillbilly singing."

"He liked to sing?"

"All the time, this yodely white-trash voice. Wanted to be Elvis."

"Any talent?"

The man shrugged.

"Did he ever get violent with anyone?"

"Not that I saw."

"What else can you tell me about him?"

"Not much. Sticks to himself—we all do. This is Little Calcutta, not some hippie commune."

"He ever hang out with anyone?"

"Not that I saw."

"How about Dorsey Hewitt?"

The man's lips pursed. "Hewitt, Hewitt . . . the one that did that caseworker?"

"You knew him?"

"No, I read the paper—when that fool did that, I was worried. Backlash. Citizens coming down here and taking it out on all us po' unfortunates."

"You never met Hewitt?"

"Nope."

"Don't know if he and Gritz were buddies?"

"How would I know that if I never met him?"

"Someone told us Gritz talked about getting rich."

"Sure, he always did, the fool. Gonna cut a record. Gonna be the next Elvis. Pour a bottle down his gullet and he was number one on the charts."

The man turned to me. "What do you think my diagnosis is?"

"Don't know you well enough," I said.

"They—the interns over at County—said I had an affective disease—severe mood swings. Then they cut off my methadone."

He clicked his teeth together and waited for me to comment. When I didn't, he said, "Supposedly I was using stuff to self-medicate—being my own psychiatrist." He laughed. "Bearshit. I used it to be *happy*."

Milo said, "Back on track: what else do you know about Gritz?"

"That's it." Smile. "Do I still get to keep the money?"

"Is Terminator Three still here?" I said.

"Who?"

"A kid from Arizona. Missing pinkie, bad cough. He has a girlfriend and a baby."

"Oh yeah, Wayne. He's calling himself *that*, now?" Laughter. "Nah, they all packed up this afternoon. Like I said, people come and go—speaking of which . . ."

He hooded himself with the blanket and, keeping his eyes on us, began edging toward the fence.

"What about your room for the night?" said Milo.

The man stopped and looked back. "Nah, I'll camp out tonight. Fresh air." Grin.

Milo laughed a little bit with him, then eyed the food. "What about all this?"

The man scrutinized the groceries. "Yeah, I'll take some of that Gatorade. The Pepsi, too."

He picked up the beverages and stashed them under the blanket.

"That's it?" said Milo.

"On a diet," said the man. "You want, you can bring the rest of it inside. I'm sure someone'll take it off your hands."

The hooded man led us through the darkness, walking unsteadily but without hesitation, like a well-practiced blind man.

Milo and I stumbled and fought to keep our balance, hauling boxes with only the skimpy guidance of the penlight beam.

As we progressed, I sensed human presence—the heat of fear. Then the petrol sweetness of Sterno.

Urine. Shit. Tobacco. Mildew.

The ammonia of fresh semen.

The hooded man stopped and pointed to the ground.

We put the boxes down and a blue flame ignited. Then another.

The concrete wall came into focus, in front of it bedrolls, piles of newspaper. Bodies and faces blue-lit by the flames.

"Suppertime, chillun'," shouted the man, over the noise of the freeway. Then he was gone.

More lights.

Ten or so people appeared, faceless, sexless, huddled like storm victims.

Milo took something out of the box and held it out. A hand reached out and snatched it. More people collected around us, blue tinted, rabbity, openmouthed with expectation.

Milo leaned forward, moving his mouth around his cigar. What he said made some of the people bolt. Others stayed to listen, and a few talked back.

He distributed more food. I joined in, feeling hands brush against mine. Finally our boxes were empty and we stood, alone.

Milo swung the penlight around the lot, exposing cloth heaps, lean-tos, people eating.

The hooded black man, sitting with his back up against the freeway wall, plaid legs splayed. One naked arm stretched out over a skinny thigh, bound at the biceps by a coil of something elastic.

A beautiful smile on his face, a needle buried deep in his flesh.

Milo snapped his head away and lowered the beam.

"C'mon," he said, loud enough for me to hear.

He headed west rather than back toward Beverly Hills, saying, "Well, that was a big goddamn zero."

"None of them had anything to say?"

"The consensus, for what it's worth, is that Lyle Gritz hasn't been seen for a week or two and that it's no big deal, he drifts in and out. He did, indeed, mouth off a bit about getting rich before he split, but they've all heard that before."

"The next Elvis."

He nodded. "Music fantasies, not fish murder. I pressed for details and one of them claimed to have seen him get into someone's car a week or so ago—across the street, over at the cement yard. But that same person seemed rather addled and had absolutely no clue as to make, model, color, or any other distinguishing details. And I'm not sure he didn't just say it because I was pushing. I'll see if Gritz's name shows up on any recent arrest files. You can ask Jeffers if he was ever a patient at the center. If he was, maybe you can get her to point you in any direction he may have gone. But even if we do find him, I'm not convinced it means a damn thing. Now you up for a little rest-stop? I'm still smelling that hellhole."

He drove to a cocktail lounge on Wilshire, in the drab part of Santa Monica. Neon highball glass above a quilted door. I'd never been there, but the way he pulled into the parking lot told me he knew it well.

Inside, the place wasn't much brighter than the overpass. We washed our hands in the men's room and took stools at the bar. The decor was red vinyl and nicotine. The resident rummies seemed to be elderly and listless. A few looked dead asleep. The jukebox helped things along with low-volume Vic Damone.

Milo scooped up a handful of bar nuts and fed his face. Ordered a double Chivas and didn't comment when I asked for a Coke.

"Where's the phone?" I said.

He pointed to a corner.

I called Robin. "How's it going?"

"Not bad," she said. "The other man in my life and I are cuddled up watching a sitcom."

"Funny?"

"I don't think so, and he's not laughing—just drooling. Any progress?"

"Not really, but we did give away lots of food."

"Well," she said, "good deeds don't hurt. Coming home?"

"Milo wanted to stop for a drink. Depending on his mood, I may need to drive him home. Go ahead and eat without us."

"Okay. . . . I'll leave a light in the window and a bone in your dish."

16

Though Milo seemed coherent by the time we reached Benedict Canyon, I suggested he sack out in one of the bedrooms, and he agreed without protest. When I awoke Saturday morning at seven, he was gone and the bed he'd slept in was in perfect order.

At nine, my pond maintenance people called to confirm they'd be moving the fish at two p.m.

Robin and I had breakfast, then I drove to the biomed library.

I looked up Wilbert Harrison in the psychiatric section of the *Directory of Medical Specialists*. His most recent listing was ten years old—an address on Signal Street in Ojai, no phone number. I copied it down and read his bio.

Medical education at Columbia University and the Menninger Clinic, a fellowship in social anthropology at UC Santa Barbara and a clinical appointment at the de Bosch Institute and Corrective School.

The anthro training was interesting, suggesting interests that stretched beyond private practice. But he'd had no academic appointments and his fields of specialty were psychoanalysis and the treatment of impaired physicians and health professionals. His birthdate made him sixty-five. Old enough to have retired—the move to Ojai from Beverly Hills and the lack of a phone listing implied a yearning for the quiet life.

I flipped forward to the R's and found Harvey Rosenblatt's

citation, complete with the NYU affiliation and an office on East Sixty-fifth Street in Manhattan. Same address as the Shirley I'd been trying to reach. Had she ignored my call because they were no longer together—divorced? Or something worse?

I read on. Rosenblatt had graduated from NYU, done his clinical training at Bellevue, the Robert Evanston Hale Psychoanalytic Institute in Manhattan, and Southwick Hospital in England. Fields of specialty, psychoanalysis and psychoanalytic psychotherapy. Fifty-eight years old.

He was listed in the next volume of the directory, too. I worked my way forward in time, until his name no longer appeared.

Four years ago.

Right between the Paprock and Shipler murders.

You're wondering if they've been visited, too.

One way to check: like most house organs, the *Journal of the American Medical Association* ran obituaries each month. I went up to the stacks and retrieved bound copies, four and five years old for Rosenblatt, ten and eleven for Harrison.

There were no notices on either psychiatrist. But maybe they hadn't bothered to join the AMA.

I consulted the *American Journal of Psychiatry*. Nothing there, either. Perhaps neither man had been a member of the specialty guild.

Bound copies of the *American Psychological Association Directory* were just a few aisles over. The five-year-old listing on Katarina de Bosch that I'd found in my volume at home was indeed her last.

No death notice on her, either.

So maybe I was working myself up for nothing.

I thought of another possible way to locate addresses—bylines in scientific publications. The *Index Medicus* and *Psychological Abstracts* revealed that Katarina had coauthored a couple of articles with her father, but nothing since his death. One of them had to do with child rearing and contained a reference to "bad love":

The process of mother-child bonding forms the foundation for all intimate relationships, and disruptions in this process plant the seed of psychopathology in later life. Good love—the nurturant, altruistic, psychosocial "suckling" by the mother/parenting figure, contributes to the child's sense of security and, hence, molds his ability to form stable attachments. Bad love—the abuse of parental authority—creates cynicism, alienation, hostility, and, in the worst cases, violent acting-out that is the child's attempt to seek retribution from the breast that has failed him.

Retribution. The abuse of parental authority. Someone had been failed. Someone was seeking revenge.

I checked for articles by Harrison and Rosenblatt. Neither had published a word.

No great surprise, most practitioners never get into print. But it still seemed odd that I couldn't locate any of them.

One therapist to go: the social worker, Mitchell Lerner.

He'd been last counted a member in good standing of the national social work organization six years ago. I made a note of his office address on Laurel Canyon and the accompanying phone number. BA from Cal State Northridge, MSW from Berkeley, clinical training at San Francisco General Hospital, followed by two years as a staff social worker at the Corrective School.

Another disciple. Under specialties he'd listed family therapy and substance abuse.

Not hoping for much, I took the stairs back up to the stacks and pulled out six- and seven-year-old bound volumes of the social work journal.

No obits on him either, but a paragraph headed "Suspensions" just below the death notices in a December issue caught my eye. A list followed. Thirteen clinical social workers dropped by the organization because of ethics violations. Dead center among the names, "Lerner, Mitchell A."

No details were given about his or any of the others' sins. The State Board of Behavioral Science Examiners was closed for the weekend, so I jotted down the date he'd been expelled and made a note to call first thing Monday morning.

Figuring I'd learned as much as I could from books, I left the library. Back at the house on Benedict, Robin was working and the dog looked bored. He followed me into the house and slavered as I fixed myself a sandwich. I did some paperwork and shared my lunch with him, and he tagged along as I walked outside to the Seville.

"Where to?" said Robin.

"The house. I want to make sure the fish get transferred okay."

She gave a doubtful look but said nothing.

"There'll be plenty of people around," I said.

She nodded and looked over at the car. The dog was pawing the front bumper. It made her smile.

"Someone's in a traveling mood. Why don't you take him along?"

"Sure, but pond drainage isn't his thing—the water phobia."

"Why don't you try some therapy with him?"

"Why not?" I said. "This could be the start of a whole new career."

The four-man crew had arrived early, and when I got there the pond was half empty, the waterfall switched off, and the fish transferred to aerated, blue vats that sat in the bed of a pickup truck. Workers uprooted plants and bagged them, shoveled gravel, and checked the air lines to the vats.

I checked in with the crew boss, a skinny brown kid with blond Rasta locks and a dyed white chin beard. The dog kept his distance, but followed me as I went up to the terrace to pick up two days' worth of mail.

Lots of stuff, most of it routine. The exception was a long white envelope.

Cheap paper that I'd seen before.

SHERMAN BUCKLEAR, ATTORNEY-AT-LAW above a return address in Simi Valley.

Inside was a letter informing me that Petitioner Donald Dell Wallace had good reason to believe that I had knowledge of the whereabouts of said petitioner's legal offspring, Chondra Nicolette Wallace and Tiffani Starr Wallace and was demanding that I pass along said information to said petitioner's attorney, without delay, so that said petitioner's legal rights would not be abridged.

The rest consisted of threats in legalese. I put the letter back in the envelope and pocketed it. The dog was scratching at the front door.

"Nostalgic already?" I unlocked the door and he ran ahead of me, straight into the kitchen. Straight to the refrigerator.

Milo's spiritual son.

Scratch, scratch, pant, pant.

I realized that, in all the haste of moving, I'd forgotten to remove the perishables from the fridge.

I did a quick visual survey of the shelves, spilled out milk and dumped cheese that had turned and fruit that was beginning to brown. Putting the unspoiled food in a bag, I thought of the people under the freeway.

Some meatloaf remained in a plastic container. It smelled okay and the dog looked as if he'd seen the messiah.

"Okay, okay." I put it in a bowl and set it down before him, bagged the good fruits and vegetables and brought them down to the car.

The pond crew was finishing up. The koi in the truck all seemed to be swimming fine.

The crew boss said, "Okay, we've got the sump running, it'll take another hour or so to drain off. You want us to wait, we can, but you're paying us by the hour, so you can stick around and turn it off yourself."

"No problem," I said, glancing at the truck. "Take care of them."

"Sure. When do you think you'll be wanting 'em back?"

"Don't know yet."

"Some kind of long vacation?"

"Something like that."

"Cool." He handed me a bill and got behind the wheel of the truck. A moment later, they were gone and all I heard was the slow gurgle of draining water.

I sat down on the bank of what was now a muddy hole, waiting and watching the level drop. The heat and the quiet combined to lull me, and I wasn't sure how long I'd been there when someone said, "Hey."

I jerked up, groggily.

A man stood in the gateway, holding a tire iron.

Late twenties or early thirties, heavy growth of dark stubble, thick black Fu Manchu that drooped to his chin.

He had on greasy jeans and Wellington boots with chains, a black T-shirt under a heavy black leather vest. Black, thinning hair, gold hoop earring, steel chains around his neck. Big tattooed arms. Big, hard belly, bowlegs. Maybe six one, two hundred.

Red-rimmed eyes.

At Sunny's Sun Valley, next door to Rodriguez's masonry yard, he'd been wearing a black cap that said CAT.

The muscular guy at the bar who hadn't said much.

He whistled once and came closer. Let one hand drop from the iron. Lowered the metal, swung it parallel to his leg in a slow, small arc and came a few steps closer. Looked at my face. His wore a slow, lazy smile of recognition.

"Retaining wall, huh?"

"What do you want?"

"Donald's kids, man." Deep slurry voice. He sounded as if he'd come straight from the bar.

"They're not here."

"Where, man?"

"I don't know."

The iron arc widened.

I said, "Why would I know?"

"You were lookin' for the little brown brother, man. Maybe you found him."

"I didn't."

"Maybe you *did*, man." Stepping forward. Just a few feet away, now. Lots of missing teeth. Mustache clogged with dandruff. An angry pus pimple had erupted under his left eye. The tattoos were badly done, a green-blue riot of female torsos, bloody blades, and Gothic lettering.

I said, "I already got a letter from Wallace's lawyer—"

"Fuck *that*." He came within swinging range, smelling like the bottom of a clothes hamper that needed emptying.

I backed up. Not much room to maneuver. Behind me was shrubbery—hedges and the maple tree whose branch had been used to skewer the koi.

"You're not helping Donald Dell," I said. "This won't look good for him."

"Who gives a fuck, man? You're off the case."

He swung the iron listlessly, pointing downward and hitting the dirt. Looking at the pond just for a second, then back at me. I searched the area for possible weapons.

Slim pickings: oversized polyethylene bags left behind by the pond crew. Lengths of rubber hosing. A couple of sheets of scummy filter screen. Maybe the koi net. Six feet of stout oak handle below a steel-mesh cup—but it was out of reach.

"Since when?" I said.

"*What?*"

"Since when am I off the case?"

"Since we said so, man."

"The Iron Priests?"

"Where're the kids, man?"

"I told you. I don't know."

He shook his head and advanced. "Don't get hurt over it, man. It's just a job, what the fuck."

"You like fish?" I said.

"Huh?"

"Fish. Finny creatures. Seafood. Piscinoids."

"Hey, ma—"

"You like to sneak around, spearing 'em? Breaking branches off trees and doing the old rotisserie bit?"

"*What?*"

"You've been here before, haven't you? Sportfishing carp, you sick fuck."

Confusion tugged at his face, zipping it up into something peevish and tight and offering a hint of what he'd look like on the off-chance he made it to old age. Then anger took its place—a brattish resentment—and he lifted the iron and took a poke at my middle.

I danced away.

"Hey," he said, annoyed. He jabbed again, missed. Sloshed, but not enough to stagger, and there was force in his movements. "Here, chickie chick." He laughed.

I kept moving away from his blows, managed to get up on the rock rim of the pond. The stones were slick with algae and I used my arms for balance. That made him laugh some more. He shouted, came after me, clumsy and slow. Caught up in the game as if it were what he'd come for.

He began making barnyard clucks.

I split my focus between the iron and his eyes. Readying myself for the chance to use surprise and his own weight against him. If I missed, my hand would get shattered.

"Boom, boom, boom," he said. "Chickie-chick."

"C'mon, stupid," I said.

His face puffed up and reddened. Two-handing the iron, he made a sudden swing for my knees.

I jumped back, stumbled, pitched forward onto the pond rim, breaking my fall with my palms.

The iron landed on rock and clanged. He raised it high over his head.

The next sounds came from behind him.

Deep bark.

Angry snorts.

He wheeled toward them, holding the iron in front of his own chest in instinctive defense. Just in time to see the bulldog racing toward him, a little black bullet, its teeth bared in a pearly grimace.

Just in time for me to spring to my feet and throw my arms around his front.

Not enough force to knock him over, but I got my hands on the ends of the iron and slammed it hard into his rib cage. Something cracked.

He said, "Ohh," sounding curiously girlish. Buckled. Bent.

The dog was on him now, fixing his teeth on denim leg, shaking his head from side to side, growling and spraying spit.

The man's back was pushing against me. I pressed up on the iron, sharply, forcing it under his chin. Got it against his Adam's apple and pulled in steadily until he made gagging noises and started to loosen his grip.

I held on. Finally, he dropped his arms and let his full weight fall against me. Struggling to remain on my feet, I let him sink to the ground, hoping I hadn't destroyed his larynx but not torturing myself over it.

The dog stayed on him, grunting and eating denim.

The man sank to the dirt. I felt for a pulse. Nice and steady, and he was already starting to move and groan.

I looked for something to bind him. The polyethylene bags. Telling the dog, "Stay," I ran to get them. I tied them together, managed to fashion two thick, plastic ropes and used one to secure his hands behind his back, the other his legs.

The dog had stepped back to watch me, head cocked. I said, "You did great, Spike, but you don't get to eat this one. How about sirloin instead—it's higher grade."

The man opened his eyes. Tried to speak but produced only a retching cough. The front of his neck was swollen, and a deep blue bruise that matched his tattooes was starting to blossom.

The dog padded over to him.

The man's eyes sparked. He turned his head away and grimaced in pain.

I said, "Stay, Spike. No blood."

The dog looked up at me with soft eyes that I hoped wouldn't betray him.

The man coughed and choked.

The dog's nostrils opened and shut. Saliva dripped from his maw and he growled.

"Good boy, Spike," I said. "Watch him for a sec, and if he gives you any problems, you're allowed to rip out his throat for an appetizer."

17

"What an idiot," said Milo, putting his notepad away. "His name's Hurley Keffler and he's got a sheet, but not much of one. More of a bad guy wannabee. We found his bike parked down the road. He claims he wasn't stalking you, got here just as the pond people drove away and decided to have a talk."

"Just one of those impulsive weekend jaunts, huh?"

"Yeah."

We were up on the landing, watching the police cars drive away. The dog watched, too, sticking his flat face through the slats of the railing, ears pricked.

"I found a letter from the Wallaces' lawyer in my mailbox," I said. "He wanted to know where the girls were and threatened me with legal action if I didn't tell him. Looks like the Priests decided not to wait."

"It might not be an official Priest mission," he said. "Just Keffler having a few too many and deciding to improvise. His dinky record, he's probably low man in the gang, trying to impress the hairy brothers."

"What are you booking him on?"

"ADW, trespassing, DUI if his blood alcohol's high enough to prove he drove over here soused. If the Priests go his bail, he'll probably be out within a few days. I'll have a talk with them, tell them to lock him in the house. What a clown."

He chuckled. "Bet your little chokehold didn't do much for his powers of comprehension, either. What'd you use, one of those karate things I'm always ribbing you about?"

"Actually," I said, bending and patting the dog's muscular neck, "*he* gets the credit. Pulled a sneak attack from the back that allowed me to jump Keffler. Plus he overcame his water phobia— ran right up to the pond."

"No kidding?" Smile. "Okay, I'll put him up for sainthood." He bent, too, and rubbed the dog behind the ears. "Congrats, St. Doggus, you're a K-9 hero."

The driver of one of the black-and-whites looked up at us and Milo waved him on.

"Good boy," I said to the dog.

"Seeing as he's saved your kneecaps, Alex, don't you think he deserves a real name? My vote's still for Rover."

"When I was trying to intimidate Keffler, I called him Spike."

"Very manly."

"Only problem is," I said, "he's already got a name—some-one's bound to come get him. What a drag. I'm getting kind of attached to him."

"What?" He elbowed my ribs, gently. "We're afraid of getting hurt, so we don't reach out for intimacy? Give him a goddamn name, Alex. *Empower* him so he can fulfill his dogly potential."

I laughed and rubbed the dog some more. He panted and put his head against my leg.

"Keffler's not the one who killed the koi," I said. "When I mentioned it, he fuzzed over completely."

"Probably," he said. "That tree branch was too subtle for the Priests. They would have taken out all the fish and mashed 'em up, maybe eaten them and left the bones."

"Back to our 'bad love' fiend," I said. "Anything new on Lyle Gritz?"

"Not yet."

"I was over at the library this morning, checking out the pro-fessional directories. No current listings on Rosenblatt or Katarina de Bosch. Harrison moved to Ojai and has no phone number, which sounds like retirement—and the social worker, Lerner, was suspended from the social work organization for an ethics viola-tion."

"What kind of violation?"

"The directory didn't say."

"What's it usually mean? Sleeping with a patient?"

"That's the most common, but it could also be financial she-nanigans, betrayal of confidentiality, or a personal problem, like drug or alcohol addiction."

He rested his arms on the top of the railing. The squad cars were gone now. My pond was a dry hole and the sump pump was sucking air. I went down to the garden, dog at my heels, and turned it off.

When I got back, Milo said, "If Lerner was a bad boy, *he* could have done something that pissed off a patient."

"Sure," I said. "I looked up de Bosch's writings on 'bad love.' Specifically, it refers to abuse of parental authority leading to alienation, cynicism, and, in extreme cases, violence. De Bosch actually used the term 'retribution.' But, pardon the whining, I still don't know what the hell *I* could have done."

"Why don't you try to get in touch with Harrison in Ojai, see if he has any idea what's going on? If his number's unlisted, I can get it for you."

"Okay," I said. "And Harrison may be a good source for another reason. When therapists are suspended, they're usually required to get therapy. One of Harrison's specialties was treating impaired therapists. Wouldn't it be interesting if he treated Lerner? It's not that farfetched—Lerner turning to someone he knew. Get me that number right now and I'll call."

He went to his car and got on the radio. Returned ten minutes later and said, "No listing at all, even though the address is still on the tax roles. Can you spare the time for a little drive? Ojai's nice this time of year. Cute little shops, antiques, whatever. Take the lovely Miss C for a cruise up the coast, combine business with pleasure."

"Get out of town for a while?"

He shrugged.

"Okay," I said. "And Ojai's close to Santa Barbara—I can extend my trip. De Bosch's school is defunct, but it might be interesting to see if any of the neighbors remember it. Maybe there was some kind of scandal, something that closed it down and left someone with a long-term grudge."

"Sure, snoop around. If Robin can stand it, who am I to try and stop you?"

He slapped my back. "I'm off."

"Where to?"

"A little more research on Paprock and Shipler."

"Anything new?"

"Nope. I'm planning to drop in on Paprock's husband tomorrow. He's still a car salesman at the Cadillac place, and Sunday's a good day for those guys."

"I'll go with you."

"Thought you were cruising to Ojai."

"Monday," I said. "Monday's a good day for psychologists."

"Oh, yeah? Why's that?"

"Blue day for everyone else. We get to concentrate on other people's problems and forget our own."

I went back into the house and looked through the freezer. In our haste to move, we hadn't emptied it, and there were several steaks in the top compartment. I took out a choice-cut rib eye and put it in the oven to broil. The dog's eyes were glued to my every move. As the aroma of broiling meat filled the kitchen, his nose started to go crazy and he got down on the floor in a supplicatory posture.

"Restrain the caballos," I said. "All good things come to those who salivate."

I petted him and called my service for messages. Only one, from Jean Jeffers. The clinic director had called at eleven a.m. leaving an 818 return number.

"Did she say what it was about?" I asked the operator.

"No, just to call her, doctor."

I did and got an answering tape with a friendly-sounding male voice backgrounded by Neil Diamond. I was starting to leave a message when Jean's voice broke in.

"Hi, thanks for calling back."

"Hi, what's up?"

I thought I heard her sigh. "I've got some . . . I think it would be best if we met personally."

"Something about Hewitt?"

"Somethi—I'm sorry, I'd rather just talk about it in person, if you don't mind."

"Sure. Where and when would you like to meet?"

"Tomorrow would be okay for me."

"Tomorrow's fine."

"Great," she said. "Where do you live?"

"West L.A."

"I'm in Studio City, but I don't mind coming over the hill on the weekend."

"I can come out to the valley."

"No, actually, I like to come out when it's not for work. Never get a chance to enjoy the city. Whereabouts in West L.A.?"

"Near Beverly Hills."

"Okay . . . how about Amanda's, it's a little place on Beverly Drive."

"What time?"

"Say one p.m.?"

"One it is."

Nervous laughter. "I know this must seem strange coming out of the blue, but maybe . . . oh, let's just talk about it tomorrow."

I gave the dog a few bites of steak, wrapped the rest in plastic, and pocketed it. Then we drove to the pet store, where I let him sniff around the food bags. He lingered at some stuff that claimed to be scientifically formulated. Organic ingredients. Twice the cost of any of the others.

"You earned it," I said, and I purchased ten pounds along with several packets of assorted canine snacks.

Going home, he munched happily on a bacon-flavored pretzel.

"*Bon appetit*, Spike," I said. "Your real name's probably something like Pierre de Cordon Bleu."

Back at the house on Benedict Canyon, I found Robin reading in the living room. I told her what had happened with Hurley Keffler and she listened, quiet and resigned, as if I were a delinquent child with no hope of rehabilitation.

"What a good friend you turned out to be," she said to the dog. He jumped up on the couch and put his head in her lap.

"So what are they going to do with him—this Keffler?"

"He'll be in jail for a while."

"How long's a while?"

"Probably not long. His gang's likely to make his bail."

"And then?"

"And then he'll be out, but he won't know this address."

"Okay."

"Want to take a drive up to Ojai and Santa Barbara, next couple of days?"

"Business or pleasure?"

"Both." I told her about Lerner and Harrison, my wanting to speak to the Corrective School's neighbors.

"Love to, but I really shouldn't, Alex. Too much work down here."

"Sure?"

"I am, hon. Sorry." She touched my face. "There's so much piled up, and even though I've got all my gear set up, it feels different here—I'm working slower, need to get back on the track."

"I'm really putting you through it, aren't I?"

"No," she said, smiling and mussing my hair. "You're the one being put through."

The smile lingered and grew into a soft laugh.

"What's funny?" I said.

"The way men think. As if our going through some stress together would be putting me *through* it. I'm worried about you, but I'm glad to be here with you—to be part of it. Putting me *through* it means something totally different."

"Such as?"

"Constantly diminishing me—condescending to me, dismissing my opinions. Anything that would make me question my worth. Do those kinds of things to a woman and she may stay with you, but she'll never think the same of you."

"Oh."

"Oh," she said, laughing and hugging me. "Pretty profound, huh? Are you mad at me for not wanting to go to Ojai?"

"No, just disappointed."

"You go anyway. Promise to be careful?"

"I promise."

"Good," she said. "That's important."

18

We had dinner at an Indian place near Beverly Hills' eastern border with L.A., washing the meal down with clove tea and driving home feeling good. Robin went to run a bath and I phoned Milo at home and told him about Jean's call.

"She has something to tell me but wouldn't elaborate over the phone—sounded nervous. My guess is she found something about Hewitt that scares her. I'm meeting her at one, and I'll ask her about Gritz. When were you planning to see Ralph Paprock?"

"Right around then."

"Care to make it earlier?"

"Dealership won't be open. I suppose we could catch him just as he comes in."

"I'll pick you up."

Sunday morning I drove to West Hollywood. Milo's and Rick's place was a small, perfectly kept Spanish house at the end of one of those short, obscure streets that hide in the grotesque shadow of the Design Center's blue-green mass. Cedars-Sinai was within walking distance. Sometimes Rick jogged to work. Today, he hadn't: the white Porsche was gone.

Milo was waiting outside. The small front lawn had been replaced by ground cover and the flowers were blooming bright orange.

He saw me looking at it and said, "Drought resistant," as he got into the car. "That 'environmental designer' I told you about. Guy would upholster the world in cactus if he could."

I took Laurel Canyon up into the Valley, passing stilt-box houses and postmodern cabins, the decaying Palladian estate where Houdini had done tricks for Jean Harlow. A governor had once lived right around there. None of the magic had rubbed off.

At Ventura, I turned left and traveled two miles to Valley Vista Cadillac. The showroom was fronted by twenty-foot slabs of plate glass and bordered by a huge outdoor lot. Banners were strung on high-tension wire. The lights were off, but morning sun managed to get in and bounce off the sparkling bodies of brand-new coupes and sedans. The cars out on the lot were blinding.

A trim black man in a well-cut navy suit stood next to a smoke-gray Seville. When he saw us get out of my seventy-nine, he went over to the front door and unlocked it, even though business hours hadn't begun. When Milo and I stepped in, his hand was out and his smile was blooming brighter than Milo's lawn.

He had a perfectly trimmed pencil mustache and a pin-collar shirt as white as an avalanche. Off to the side of the showroom, beyond the cars, was a warren of cubicles, and I could hear someone talking on the phone. The cars were spotless and perfectly detailed. The whole place smelled of leather and rubber and conspicuous consumption. My car had smelled that way once, even though I'd bought it used. Someone had told me the fragrance came in aerosol cans.

"That's a classic you've got," said the man, looking through the window.

"Been good to me," I said.

"Keep it and garage it, that's what I'd do. One of these days you'll see it appreciate, like money in the bank. Meanwhile, you can be driving something new for every day. Good lines this year, don't you think?"

"Very nice."

"Got those foreign deals beat hands down. Get folks in to actually test drive, they see that. You a lawyer?"

"Psychologist."

He gave an uncertain smile and I found a business card in my hand.

John Allbright
Sales Executive

"Got a real good suspension this year, too," he said. "With all due respect to your classic, I think you'll find it a whole other world, drive-wise. Great sound system, too, if you go for the Bose option and—"

"We're looking for Ralph Paprock," said Milo.

Allbright looked at him. Squinted. Put his hand to his mouth and compressed his smile manually.

"Ralph," he said. "Sure. Ralph's over there."

Pointing to the cubicles, he walked away fast, ending up in a glass corner, where he lit up a cigarette and stared out at the lot.

The first two compartments were empty. Ralph Paprock sat behind a desk in the third. He was in his late forties, narrow and tan, with sparse gray-blond hair on top and a bit more of it on the sides, combed over his ears. His double-breasted suit was the same cut as Allbright's, olive green, just a bit too bright. His shirt was cream with a long-point collar, his tie crowded with parrots and palm trees.

He was hunched over some papers. The tip of his tongue protruded from the corner of his narrow mouth. The pen in his right hand tapped his blotter very fast. His nails were shiny.

When Milo cleared his throat, the tongue zipped in and an eager grin took hold of Paprock's face. Despite the smile, his face was tired, the muscles loose and droopy. His eyes were small and amber. The suit gave them a khaki tint.

"Gentlemen. How can I help you?"

Milo said, "Mr. Paprock, I'm Detective Sturgis, Los Angeles police," and handed him a card.

The look that took hold of the salesman next—*What are you hitting me with this time?*—made me feel lousy. We had nothing to offer him and plenty to take.

He put his pen down.

I caught a side view of a photo on his desk, propped up next to a mug printed with the Cadillac crest. Two round-faced, fair-haired children. The younger one, a girl, was smiling, but the boy seemed to be on the verge of tears. Behind them hovered a woman of around seventy with butterfly glasses and cold-waved white hair. She resembled Paprock, but she had a stronger jaw.

Milo said, "Sorry to bother you, Mr. Paprock, but we've come across another homicide that might be related to your wife's and wondered if we could ask you a few questions."

"Another—a *new* one?" said Paprock. "I didn't see anything on the news."

"Not exactly, sir. This crime occurred three years ago—"

"Three years ago? Three *years* and you've just come *across* it? Did you finally get him?"

"No, sir."

"Jesus." Paprock's hands were flat on the desk and his forehead had erupted in sweat. He wiped it with the back of one hand. "Just what I need to start off the week."

There were two chairs facing his desk. He stared at them but didn't say anything else.

Milo motioned me into the office and closed the door behind us. There was very little standing room. Paprock held a hand out to the chairs and we sat. A certificate behind the desk said he'd been a prizewinning salesman. The date was three summers ago.

"Who's the other victim?" he said.

"A man named Rodney Shipler."

"A man?"

"Yes, sir."

"A man—I don't understand."

"You don't recognize the name?"

"No. And if it was a man, what makes you think it has anything to do with my Myra?"

"The words 'bad love' were written at the crime scene."

" 'Bad love,' " said Paprock. "I used to dream about that. Make up different meanings for it. But still . . ."

He closed his eyes, opened them, took a bottle out of his desk drawer. Enteric aspirin. Popping a couple of tablets, he dropped the bottle into his breast pocket, behind the colored handkerchief.

"What kind of meanings?" said Milo.

Paprock looked at him. "Crazy stuff—trying to figure out what the hell it meant. I don't remember. What's the difference?"

He began moving his hands around, stirring the air very quickly, as if searching for something to grab. "Was there any—some sign of—was this Shipler . . . what I'm getting at is, was there something sexual?"

"No, sir."

Paprock said, " 'Cause that's what *they* told me they thought it might mean. The first cops. Some psychotic thing—using—sex in a bad way, some sort of sex nut. A pervert *bragging* about what he did—bad love."

Nothing like that had been in Myra Paprock's file.

Milo nodded.

"A man," said Paprock. "So what are you *telling* me? The first cops had it all *wrong*? They went and looked for the *wrong* thing?"

"We don't really know much at all at this point, sir. Just that someone wrote 'bad love' at the scene of Mr. Shipler's homicide."

"Shipler." Paprock squinted. "You're opening the whole thing up again, 'cause of him?"

"We're taking a look at the facts, Mr. Paprock."

Paprock closed his eyes, opened them, and took a deep breath. "My Myra was taken *apart*. I had to identify her. To you that kind of thing's probably old hat, but . . ." Shake of the head.

"It's never old hat, sir."

Paprock gave him a doubtful look. "After I did it—identified her—it took me a long time to be able to remember her the way she used to be . . . even now . . . the first cops said whoever— did those things to her, did them after she was dead." Alarm brightened his eyes. "They were right about *that*, weren't they?"

"Yes, sir."

Paprock's hands gripped the edge of his desk and he wheeled forward. "Tell me the truth, detective—I *mean* it. I don't want to think of her suffering, but if—no, forget it, don't tell me a damn thing, I don't *want* to know."

"She didn't suffer, sir. The only thing new is Mr. Shipler's murder."

More sweat. Another wipe.

"Afterwards," said Paprock. "After I identified her—I had to go tell my kids. The older one, anyway—the little one was just a baby. Actually, the older one wasn't much more than a baby, either, but he was asking for her, I had to tell him something."

He knocked the knuckles of both hands together. Shook his head, tapped the desk.

"It took a helluva long time to get it set in my mind—what had happened. When I went to tell my boy, all I could think of was what I'd seen in the morgue—imagining her . . . and here he is asking for Mommy. 'Mommy, Mommy'—he was two and a half. I told him Mommy got sick and went to sleep forever. When his sister got old enough, I gave *him* the job of telling *her*. They're great kids, my mother's been helping me take care of them, she's close to eighty and they don't give her any problems. So who needs to change that? Who needs Myra's name in the papers and digging it all up? There was a time, finding out who did it was *all* that mattered to me, but I got over that. What's the difference, anyway? She's not coming back, right?"

I nodded. Milo didn't move.

Paprock touched his brow and opened his eyes wide, as if exercising the lids.

"That it?" he said.

"Just a few questions about your wife's background," said Milo.

"Her *background*?"

"Her work background, Mr. Paprock. Before she became a real estate agent, did she do anything else?"

"Why?"

"Just collecting facts, sir."

"She worked for a bank, okay? What kind of work did this Shipler do?"

"He was a janitor. What bank did she work for?"

"Trust Federal, over in Encino. She was a loan officer—that's how I met her. We used to channel our car loans through there and one day I went down there on a big fleet sale and she was at the loan desk."

Milo took out his notepad and wrote.

"She would have probably made vice president," said Paprock. "She was smart. But she wanted to work for herself, had enough of bureaucracies. So she studied for her broker's license at night, then quit. Was doing real well, lots of sales . . ."

He looked off to one side, fixing his gaze on a poster. Two perfect-looking, tennis-clad people getting into a turquoise Coupe de Ville with diamond-bright wire wheels. Behind the car, the marble-and-glass facade of a resort hotel. Crystal chandelier. Perfect-looking doorman smiling at them.

"Bureaucracies," said Milo. "Did she deal with any others before the bank?"

"Yeah," said Paprock, still turned away. "She taught school—but that was before I met her."

"Here in L.A.?"

"No, up near Santa Barbara—Goleta."

"Goleta," said Milo. "Do you remember the name of the school?"

Paprock faced us again. "Some public school—why? What does her work have to do with anything?"

"Maybe nothing, sir, but please bear with me. Did she ever teach in L.A.?"

"Not to my knowledge. By the time she moved down here, she was fed up with teaching."

"Why's that?"

"The whole situation—kids not interested in learning, lousy pay—what's to like about it?"

"A public school," I said.

"Yeah."

Milo said, "What subjects did she teach?"

"All of them, I guess. She taught fifth grade, or maybe it was fourth, I dunno. In elementary school, you teach all the subjects, right? We never really had any detailed discussions about it."

"Did she teach anywhere before Goleta?" said Milo.

"Not as far as I know. I think that was her first job out of school."

"When would that be?"

"Let's see, she graduated at twenty-two, she'd be forty this May." He winced. "So that would have been, what, eighteen years ago. I think she taught maybe four or five years, then she switched to banking."

He looked at the poster again and wiped his forehead.

Milo closed his pad. The sound made Paprock jump. His eyes met Milo's. Milo gave as gentle a smile as I'd ever seen him muster. "Thanks for your time, Mr. Paprock. Is there anything else you want to tell us?"

"Sure," said Paprock. "I want to tell you to find the filthy fuck who killed my wife and put me in a room with him." He rubbed his eyes. Made two fists and opened them and gave a sick smile. "Fat chance."

Milo and I stood. A second later, Paprock rose, too. He was medium-sized, slightly round-backed, almost dainty.

He patted his chest, removed the aspirin bottle from his breast pocket and passed it from hand to hand. Walking around the desk, he pushed the door open and held it for us. No sign of John Allbright or anyone else. Paprock walked us through the showroom, touching the flanks of a gold Eldorado in passing.

"Whyncha buy a car, as long as you're here?" he said. Then he colored through his tan and stopped.

Milo held out his hand.

Paprock shook it, then mine.

We thanked him again for his time.

"Look," he said, "what I said before—about not wanting to know? That was bullshit. I still think about her. I got married again, it lasted three months, my kids hated the bitch. Myra was . . . special. The kids, someday they're gonna have to know. I'll handle it. I can handle it. You find something, you tell me, okay? You find *anything*, you tell me."

I headed for Coldwater Canyon and the drive back to the city.

"Public school near Santa Barbara," I said. "Lousy pay, so maybe she moonlighted at a local private place."

"A reasonable assumption," said Milo. He lowered the Seville's passenger window, lit up a bad cigar, and blew smoke out at the hot valley air. The city was digging up Ventura Boulevard and sawhorses blocked one lane. Bad traffic usually made Milo curse. This time he kept quiet, puffing and thinking.

I said, "Shipler was a school janitor. Maybe he worked at de Bosch's school, too. That could be our connection: they were both staffers, not patients."

"Twenty years ago. . . . Wonder how long the school district keeps records. I'll check, see if Shipler transferred down from Santa Barbara."

"More reasons for me to drive up there," I said.

"When are you doing it?"

"Tomorrow. Robin can't make it—all for the best. Between trying to find remnants of the school and looking for Wilbert Harrison in Ojai, it won't be a pleasure trip."

"Those other guys—the therapists at the symposium—they worked at the school, too, right?"

"Harrison and Lerner did. But not Rosenblatt—he trained with de Bosch in England. I'm not sure about Stoumen, but he was a contemporary of de Bosch, and Katarina asked him to speak, so there was probably some kind of relationship."

"So, one way or the other, it all boils down to de Bosch. . . . Anyone seen as being close to him is fair game for this nut. . . . Bad love—destroying a kid's sense of trust, huh?"

"That's the concept."

I reached Coldwater and started the climb. He drew on his cigar and said, "Paprock was right about his wife. You saw the pictures—she *was* taken apart."

"Poor guy," I said. "Walking wounded."

"What I told him, about her being dead when she was raped? True. But she suffered, Alex. Sixty-four stab wounds and plenty of them landed before she died. That kind of revenge—rage? Someone must have gotten fucked up big-time."

19

I made it to Beverly Hills with five minutes to spare for my one o'clock with Jean Jeffers. Parking was a problem and I had to use a city lot two blocks down from Amanda's, waiting at the curb as a contemplative valet decided whether or not to put up the FULL sign.

He finally let me in, and I arrived at the restaurant five minutes late. The place was jammed and it reeked of Parmesan cheese. A hostess was calling out names from a clipboarded list and walking the chosen across a deliberately cracked white marble floor. The tables were marble, too, and a gray faux-marble treatment had been given to the walls. The crypt look, nice and cold, but the room was hot with impatience and I had to elbow my way through a cranky crowd.

I looked around and saw Jean already seated at a table near the back, next to the south wall of the restaurant. She waved. The man next to her looked at me but didn't move.

I recalled him as the heavyset fellow from the photo in her office, a little heavier, a little grayer. In the picture, he and Jean had been wearing leis and matching Hawaiian shirts. Today, they'd kept the Bobbsey twins thing going with a white linen dress for her, white linen shirt for him, and matching yellow golf sweaters.

I waved back and went over. They had half-empty coffee cups

in front of them and pieces of buttered olive bread on their bread plates. The man had an executive haircut and an executive face. Great shave, sunburnt neck, blue eyes, the skin around them slightly bagged.

Jean rose a little as I sat down. He didn't, though his expression was friendly enough.

"This is my husband, Dick Jeffers. Dick, Dr. Alex Delaware."

"Doctor."

"Mr. Jeffers."

He smiled as he shot out his arm. "Dick."

"Alex."

"Fair enough."

I sat down across from them. Both their yellow sweaters had crossed tennis-racquet logos. His bore a small, gold Masonic pin.

"Well," said Jean, "some crowd. Hope the food's good."

"Beverly Hills," said her husband. "The good life."

She smiled at him, looked down at her lap. A large, white purse sat there and one of her arms was around it.

Dick Jeffers said, "Guess I'll be going, Jeanie. Nice to meet you, doctor."

"Same here."

"Okay, honey," said Jean.

Cheek pecks, then Jeffers stood. He seemed to lose balance for a second, caught himself by resting one palm on the table. Jean looked away from him as he straightened. He shoved the chair back with the rear of his thighs and gave me a wink. Then he walked off, limping noticeably.

Jean said, "He has one leg, just got a brand new prosthesis and it's taking a while getting used to." It sounded like something she'd said many times before.

I said, "That can be tough. Years ago, I worked with children with missing limbs."

"Did you?" she said. "Well, Dick lost his in an auto accident."

Pain in her eyes. I said, "Recently?"

"Oh, no, several years ago. Before anyone really appreciated the value of seat belts. He was driving a convertible, was unbelted, got hit from behind and thrown out. Another car ran over his leg."

"Terrible."

"Thank God he wasn't killed. I met him when he was in

rehab. I was doing a rotation at Rancho Los Amigos and he was there for a couple of months. He made a great adjustment to his appliance—always had until it started bothering him a few months ago. He'll get used to the new one. He's a good guy, very determined."

I smiled.

"So," she said, "how are you?"

"Fine. And intrigued."

"By?"

"Your call."

"Oh." The sheet of hair fell over her eye. She let it stay there. "Well, I didn't mean to be overly dramatic, it's just—" She looked around. "Why don't we order first, and then we can talk about it."

We read the menu. Someone in the kitchen had a thing for balsamic vinegar.

When she said, "Well, I know what *I* want," I waved over a waiter. Asian kid, around nineteen, with a waist-length ponytail and ten stud earrings rimming the outer cartilage of his left ear. It hurt to look at him and I stared at the table as Jean ordered an *insalata* something or other. I asked for linguine marinara and an iced tea. Ruined Ear came back quickly with the drink and a refill of her coffee.

When he left, she said, "So you live pretty close to here?"

"Not far."

"For a while Dick and I thought about moving over the hill, but then prices started to go crazy."

"They've slid quite a bit recently."

"Not enough." She smiled. "Not that I'm complaining. Dick's an aerospace engineer and he does well, but you never know when the government's going to cancel a project. The place we've got in Studio City is really pretty nice." She looked at her watch. "He's probably over at Rudnicks now. He likes to shop there for sweaters."

"He's not having lunch?"

"What I need to talk to you about is confidential. Dick understands that. So why did I bring him with me, right? To be honest, it's because I'm still shaky. Still haven't gotten used to being alone."

"I don't blame you."

"Don't you think I should be past it by now?"

"I probably wouldn't be."

"That's a very nice thing to say."

"It's the truth."

Another smile. She reached over and touched my hand, just for a second. Then back to her coffee cup.

"I'm *sleeping* a little better," she said, "but still far from perfect. In the beginning I'd be up all night, heart pounding away, nauseated. Now I can *get* to sleep, but sometimes I still wake up all in a knot. Sometimes the thought of going to work makes me just want to crawl back in bed. Dick works in Westchester near the airport, so sometimes we take one car and he drops me off and picks me up. I guess I've become pretty dependent on him."

She gave a small smile. The unspoken message: *for a change.*

"Meanwhile, I'm telling the staff and the patients there's nothing to worry about. Nothing like consistency."

Ear brought the food.

"This looks yum," she said, pushing her fork around in her salad bowl. But she didn't eat, and one arm stayed around her purse.

I tried a little linguine. Memories of school lunch.

She nibbled on a piece of lettuce. Dabbed at her mouth. Looked around. Unsnapped the purse.

"You have to promise me to keep this absolutely confidential," she said. "At least where you got it from, okay?"

"Does it relate to Hewitt?"

"In a way. Mostly—it's nothing that can help Detective Sturgis—not that I can see, anyway. I shouldn't even be showing it to you. But people are being harassed and I know what it's like to feel besieged. So if this does lead anywhere, please keep me out of it—please?"

"All right," I said.

"Thank you." She inhaled, shoved her hand into the purse, and drew out a legal-sized envelope. White, clean, unmarked. She held on to it. The paper made her nails look especially red.

"Remember how sketchy Becky's notes on Hewitt were?" she said. "How I made excuses for her, saying she'd been a good therapist but not big on paperwork? Well, it bothered me more than I let on. Even for Becky that was cursory—I guess I just didn't want to deal with anything related to her murder. But after you left, I kept thinking about it and went looking to see if she'd taken any other notes that had somehow been misfiled. With all the up-heaval right after, housekeeping wasn't exactly a high priority. I didn't find anything, so I asked Mary, my secretary. She said all Becky's active charts had been distributed to other caseworkers, but it was possible some of her inactive files might have ended up in our storage room. So she and I took some time on Friday and looked around for a few hours, and sure enough, stuck in a corner was a box with Becky's initials on it—'RB.' Who knows how it got there. Inside was junk that had been removed from her desk—pens, paper clips, whatever. Underneath all that, was this."

Her hand shook slightly as she handed me the envelope.

I removed the contents. Three sheets of horizontal-ruled chart paper, slightly grimy and bearing deep fold marks, each partially filled with typed notations.

The first was dated six months ago:

Saw DH today. Still hearing vces, but meds seem to hlp. Still dealing w strss of strt-life. Came in with G, both strssd.

BB, SWA

Three weeks later:

D lots better. Snstv, too. Just meds, or me? Ha ha. Maybe some hope?

BB, SWA

Then:

D showing feelngs, more and more. Tlking lots, too. Very good! Yeah, thrpy! Success! But keep limits.

BB, SWA

D cohrnt—hr brshed, totally clean! But still late. Talk re childhd, etc. Some p-c, but approp. G there, waiting. A bit hostl? Jealous? Follow.

BB

D a diff prsn. Open, vrbal, affectnt. Still late. A bit more p-c. Approp? Set lmts? Talk to JJ? Wrth the progrss? Yes!

BB

D late, but less—15 min. Some anx. Hrng vcs? Denies, says strss, alchl—drnkng with G. Talked re G, re rel bet D and G. Some anx, defens, but also opn-mind. More p-c, but ok, relieves anx. O.K.

BB

D looking hppy. Vry vrbl, no angr, no hrng vcs. G not there. Conflct bet G and D? P-c, tried to kss, no hostil when I say no. Good! Approp soc sklls! Rah rah!

BB

The final note was dated three weeks before Becky's murder:

D early—positv change! Yeah! G waits in hall. Definit hostil. Rel bet D and G straind? Re me? D's growth a stress on G? More p-c. Kss, but quick. Much affectn. Talk re this. Boundaries, lmts, etc. D a little down, but dealt w it, approp.

BB

" 'P-c,' " I said, putting the papers down.

"Physical contact," she said, miserably. "I went over and over it and it's the only thing that makes sense."

I reread the notes. "I think you're right."

"Hewitt was getting attached to her. Progressively more physical."

She shuddered. "Look at the last one. She let him *kiss* her. She must have totally lost control of the situation. I had no idea—she never told me."

"She obviously thought of telling you—'talk to JJ?' "

"But she didn't follow through. Look what she wrote right after that."

I read out loud: " 'Worth the progress? Yes!' Sounds like she convinced herself she was helping him."

"She convinced herself she knew what she was *doing*." She shook her head and looked down at the table. "My God."

"Beginner's euphoria," I said.

"She was such a sweet thing—so naive. I should have kept a closer eye on her. Maybe if I had, it could've been prevented." She pushed her salad away. Her hair hung in a sheet. Her head rested in her hands and I heard her sigh.

I said, "Hewitt was psychotic, Jean. Who knows what set him off."

She looked up. "Letting him *kiss* her sure didn't help! She talks about setting limits, but he probably saw it as rejection, what with his paranoia!"

She'd allowed her voice to climb. The man at the next table looked up from his cappuccino. Jean smiled at him, picked up her napkin, and wiped her face.

I scanned the notes again. *Yeah, therapy! Rah rah!*

She held out her hand. "I need them back."

I gave her the papers and she slipped them back in the envelope.

I said, "What are you going to do with them?"

"Destroy them. Can you just imagine what the media would do with it? Blaming Becky, turning the whole thing into something sleazy? Please, Alex, keep it to yourself. I don't want to see Becky victimized a second time." She flipped her hair again. "Also, to be perfectly honest, I don't want to be blamed for not supervising her."

"It took guts for you to show it to me," I said.

"Guts?" She laughed softly. "Stupidity, maybe, but for some reason I trust you—I don't even know why I did show it to you—getting it off my chest, I guess."

She put the envelope in her purse and shook her head again.

"How could she have let it *happen*? She talks about *him* trying to touch her and kiss her, but what I got between the lines was her developing some sort of feelings for *him*. All that *p-cing*, as if it was a cute little game. Don't you agree?"

"Fondness for him definitely comes across," I said. "Whether or not it was sexual, I don't know."

"Even if it was plain *affection*, it was irrational. The man was psychotic, couldn't even keep himself *clean*. And this *G* person she keeps mentioning, I still have no idea who *that* is. Probably Hewitt's girlfriend—some other psychotic he met on the street and dragged in with him. Becky was getting herself involved in a love triangle with *psychotics*, for God's sake. How could she? She was naive, but she was bright—how could she have shown such poor judgment?"

"She probably didn't think she was doing anything wrong, Jean. Otherwise, why would she have kept notes?"

"But if she thought what she was doing was okay, why not keep those notes right in Hewitt's chart?"

"Good point," I said.

"It's a mess. I should have supervised her more closely. I should have been more in touch. . . . I just can't understand how she could have let him get that close to her."

"Countertransference," I said. "Happens all the time."

"With someone like that?"

"Prison therapists get attached to convicts. Who knows what causes attraction?"

"*I* should have known."

"No sense blaming yourself. No matter how closely you supervise someone, you can't be with them twenty-four hours a day. She was trained, Jean. It was up to her to tell you."

"I *tried* to supervise her. I made appointments, but she broke more than she kept. Still, I could have clamped down further—I should've. If I'd had any *idea* . . . she never gave a *hint*. Always had a smile on her face, like one of those kids who works at Disneyland."

"She *was* happy," I said. "She thought she was curing him."

"Yup. What a mess . . . I probably showed it to you because you were sympathetic and I'm still so uptight over what happened . . . I thought I could talk to you."

"You can."

"I appreciate that," she said wearily, "but let's be honest. What good will more talking do? Becky's dead and I'm going to have to live with the fact that I might have been able to prevent it."

"I don't see it that way. You did all you could."

"You're sweet." She looked at my hand, as if ready to touch it again. But she didn't move and her eyes shifted to her salad.

"Happy lunch," she said glumly.

"Jean, it's possible the notes might be relevant to Detective Sturgis."

"How?"

" 'G' may not be a woman."

"You *know* who it is?" This time her hand did move. Covering mine, taking hold of my fingers. Ice cold.

"That lawyer whose card you gave me—Andrew Coburg? I went over to see him and he told me Hewitt had a friend named Gritz. Lyle Edward Gritz."

No reaction.

I said, "Gritz is a heavy drinker, and he has a criminal record. He and Hewitt hung out together, and now no one can find him. A week or two ago, Gritz told some street people he expected to get rich, then he disappeared."

"Get rich? How?"

"He didn't say, though in the past he'd talked about becoming a recording star. For all I know, it was drunk talk and has nothing to do with Becky. But if 'G' does refer to him, it indicates tension between him and Becky."

"Gritz," she said. "I assumed G was a woman. Are you saying Hewitt and this Gritz had something homosexual going on and Becky stepped in the middle of it? Oh, God, it just keeps getting worse, doesn't it?"

"Maybe there was nothing sexual between Gritz and Hewitt. Just a close friendship that Becky intruded upon."

"Maybe . . ." She pulled out the envelope, removed the notes, ran her finger down the page, and read. "Yes, I see what you mean. Once you think of G as a man you don't have to see it that way at all. Just friendship. . . . But whatever the reason, Becky felt G was hostile to her."

"She was getting between them," I said. "The whole therapy process was challenging whatever Hewitt had with Gritz. How did Becky phrase it in that last note?"

"Let me see—here it is: 'Relationship between D and G strained. Me? D's growth?' Yes, I see what you mean. Then right after that, she mentions another p-c—the session where he actually kissed her. . . . You know, you could read this and feel almost as if she was seducing him." She crumpled the notes. "God, what a travesty—why are you interested in this Gritz? You think he could be the one harassing people?"

"It's possible."

"Why? What else has he done criminally?"

"I'm not sure of the details, but the harassment involved the words 'bad love'—"

"What Hewitt screamed . . . Does that actually *mean* something? What's going *on*?"

Her fingers had become laced with mine. I looked at them and she pulled away and fooled with her hair. The flap covered one eye. The exposed one was alive with fear.

I said, "I don't know, Jean. But given the notes, I have to wonder if Gritz played a role in getting Hewitt to murder Becky."

"Played a *role*? How?"

"By working on Hewitt's paranoia—telling Hewitt things about Becky. If he was a close friend, he'd know which buttons to push."

"Oh, God," she said. "And now he's missing . . . it's not over, is it?"

"Maybe it is. This is all conjecture, Jean. But finding Gritz would help clear it up. Any chance he was a patient at the center?"

"The name doesn't ring a bell . . . bad love . . . I thought Hewitt was just raving, now you're saying maybe he was reacting to something that had gone on between him and Becky? That he killed her because she rejected him."

"Could be," I said. "I found a reference to 'bad love' in the psych literature. It's a term coined by a psychoanalyst named Andres de Bosch."

She stared at me, nodded slowly. "I think I've heard of him. What did he say about it?"

"He used it to describe poor child rearing—a parent betraying a child's trust. Building up faith and then destroying it. In extreme cases, he theorized, it could lead to violence. If you consider the therapist-patient relationship similar to child rearing, the same theory could be applied to cases of transference gone really bad. Hewitt may have heard about 'bad love' somewhere—probably from another therapist or even from Gritz. When he felt Becky had rejected him, he fell apart, became a betrayed child—and lashed out violently."

"Betrayed child?" she said. "You're saying his killing her was a *tantrum*?"

"A tantrum heated to the boiling point by Hewitt's delusions. And by his failure to take his medication. Who knows, Gritz may have convinced him not to take it."

"Gritz," she said. "How do you spell it?"

I told her. "Be good to know if he was one of your patients."

"I'll comb the files first thing tomorrow, take that damned storage room *apart* if I have to. If he's anywhere in there, I'll call you right away. We need to know for our own safety."

"I'll be out of town tomorrow. You can leave a message with my service."

"All day tomorrow?" A touch of panic in her voice.

I nodded. "Santa Barbara and back."

"I love Santa Barbara. It's gorgeous. Taking some vacation time?"

"De Bosch used to have a clinic and a school up there. I'm going to try and find out if Hewitt or Gritz were ever patients."

"I'll let you know if he was ours. Call me back, okay? Let me know what you find."

"Sure."

She looked at her salad again. "I can't eat."

I waved Ear over and got the bill.

She said, "No, I invited *you*," and tried to take it, but she didn't put up much of a fight and I ended up paying.

She stashed the notes in her purse and glanced at her watch. "Dick's not coming back for another half an hour."

"I can wait."

"No, I won't keep you. But I wouldn't mind some fresh air. I'll walk you to your car."

Just outside the restaurant she paused to button her sweater and smooth her hair. The first time, the buttons were out of line and she had to redo them.

We walked to the city lot without speaking. She looked in shop windows but seemed uninterested in the wares they displayed. Waiting until I'd redeemed the keys from the attendant, she accompanied me to the Seville.

"Thanks," I said, shaking her hand. I opened the driver's door.

She said, "What I said before still stands, right? About keeping all this quiet?"

"Of course."

"It's nothing Detective Sturgis could ever use, anyway," she said. "Legally speaking—what does it really prove?"

"Just that people are fallible."

"Oh, boy, are they."

I got into the car. She leaned in through the window.

"You're more than just a consultant on this, aren't you?"

"What makes you say that?"

"Your passion. Consultants don't go this far."

I smiled. "I take my work seriously."

She moved her head back, as if I'd blown garlic in her face.

"So do I," she said. "Sometimes I wish I didn't."

20

Monday morning at nine, I set out for Ojai, taking the 405 to the 101 and making it to the strawberry fields of Camarillo in less than an hour. Migrant workers stooped in the stubby, green rows. The crop became blue cabbage and the air turned bitter. Kissy-face billboards boosted housing developments and home equity loans.

Just past the Ventura County Fairgrounds, I turned onto 33 north, speeding by an oil refinery that resembled a giant junkyard. Another few miles of trailer parks and mower rental sheds and things got pretty: two lanes draped by eucalyptus, black mountains off to the northwest, the peaks flesh colored where the sun hit.

The town of Ojai was a quarter of an hour farther, announced by a bike and equestrian trail, orange groves, and signs directing the motorist to the Ojai Palm Spa, the Humanos Theosophic Institute, Marmalade Hot Springs. To the south were the clean, green slopes of a country club. The cars were good-looking and so were the people.

Ojai proper was quiet and slow moving, with one traffic light. The main drag was Ojai Avenue, lined with the kind of low-rise, neo-Spanish architecture that usually means tight zoning laws. Unrestricted parking, plenty of spaces. Tans and smiles, natural fibers and good posture.

On the left side of the avenue, a colonnaded, tile-roofed building was filled with storefronts. Native American art and antiques, body wraps and herbal facials, a Little Olde Tea Shoppe. Across the street was an old theater, freshly adobed. Playing tonight: *Leningrad Cowboys.*

I had my Ventura County Thomas Guide on the passenger seat, but I didn't need it. Signal was a couple of intersections up, and 800 north meant a left turn.

Big trees and small houses, residential lots alternating with olive groves. A drainage ditch paved with fieldstones ran alongside the left side of the street, spanned every few yards by one-stride foot bridges. Wilbert Harrison's address was near the top, one of the last houses before open fields took over.

It was a shingle-roofed wooden cottage painted an odd purplish-red and nearly hidden behind unruly snarls of agave cactus. The purple was vivid and it shone through the agave's sawtooth leaves like a wound. Atop a steep dirt driveway, a Chevy station wagon was parked up against a single garage. Four stone steps led up to the front porch. The screen door was shut, but the wooden one behind it was wide open.

I knocked on the frame while looking into a small, dark living room, plank floored and crowded with old furniture, shawls, throw pillows, an upright piano. A bay window was lined with dusty bottles.

Chamber music came from another room.

I knocked louder.

"One minute." The music turned off and a man appeared from a doorway to the right.

Short. Chubby as in his old picture and white haired. He had on a polyester jumpsuit the same purplish-red as the house. Some of the furniture was upholstered that color, too.

He opened the screen door and gave me a curious but friendly look. His eyes were gray, but they picked up magenta accents from his surroundings. There was a softness to his face, but no weakness.

"Dr. Harrison?"

"Yes, I'm Bert Harrison." His voice was a clear baritone. The jumpsuit was zipped in the front and had large, floppy lapels. Short-sleeved, it exposed white, freckled arms. His face was freckled, too, and I noticed reddish-blond tints in his white hair. He wore a pinkie ring set with a violet cabochon, and a bolo tie with leather thongs held together by a big, shapeless purple rock. Sandals on his feet, no socks.

"My name is Alex Delaware. I'm a clinical psychologist from Los Angeles and I wondered if I could talk to you about Andres de Bosch and 'bad love.' "

The eyes didn't change shape or hue, but they became more focused.

He said, "I know you. We've met somewhere."

"Nineteen seventy-nine," I said. "There was a conference at Western Pediatric Medical Center on de Bosch's work. You presented a paper and I was a co-chair, but we never actually met."

"Yes," he said, smiling. "You were there as the hospital's representative, but your heart wasn't in it."

"You *remember* that?"

"Distinctly. The entire conference had that flavor—ambivalence all around. You were very young—you wore a beard then, didn't you?"

"Yes," I said, amazed.

"The beginnings of old age," he said, still smiling. "Distant memories become clearer, but I can't remember where I put my keys."

"I'm still impressed, doctor."

"I remember the beard vividly, perhaps because I have trouble growing one. And your voice. Full of stress. Just as it is right now. Well, come in, let's take care of it. Coffee or tea?"

There was a small kitchen beyond the living room and a door that led to a single bedroom. The little I could see of the sleeping chamber was purple and book-lined.

The kitchen table was birch, not more than four feet long. The counters were old white tile trimmed with purple-red bullnoses.

He fixed instant coffee for both of us and we sat. The scale of the table put us close together, elbows nearly touching.

"In answer to your unasked question," he said, whitening his coffee with lots of cream, then adding three spoonfuls of sugar, "it's the only color I can see. A rare genetic condition. Everything else in my world is gray, so I do what I can to brighten it."

"Makes sense," I said.

"Now that that's out of the way, tell me what's on your mind

concerning Andres and 'bad love'—that was the title of the conference, wasn't it."

"Yes. You don't seem surprised that I just popped in."

"Oh, I am. But I like surprises—anything that breaks up routine has the ability to freshen our lives."

"This may not be a pleasant surprise, Dr. Harrison. You may
be in danger."

His expression didn't change. "How so?"

I told him about the "bad love" tape, my revenge theory, the
possible links to Dorsey Hewitt and Lyle Gritz.

"And you think one of these men may have been a former
patient of Andres's?"

"It's possible. Hewitt was thirty-three when he died, and
Gritz is a year older, so either of them could have been his patient
as a child. Hewitt killed one psychotherapist, perhaps under
Gritz's influence, and Gritz is still out there, possibly still trying to
even scores."

"What would he be trying to avenge?"

"Some kind of mistreatment—by de Bosch himself or a disciple. Something had happened at the school."

No response.

I said, "Real or imagined. Hewitt was a paranoid schizophrenic. I don't know Gritz's diagnosis, but he may be delusional,
as well. The two of them could have influenced each other's pathology."

"Symbiotic psychosis?"

"Or at least shared delusions—playing on each other's paranoia."

He blinked hard. "Tapes, calls . . . no, I haven't experienced
anything like that. And the name of this person who giggled over
the phone was Silk?"

I nodded.

"Hmm. And what role do you think the conference played?"

"It may have triggered something—I really don't know, but
it's my only link to de Bosch. I felt an obligation to tell you because one of the other speakers—Dr. Stoumen—was killed last
year, and I haven't been able to loca—"

"Grant?" he said, leaning forward close enough for me to
smell the mint on his breath. "I heard he died in an auto accident."

"A hit-and-run accident. While attending a conference. He

stepped off the curb and was knocked down by a car. It was never solved, Dr. Harrison. The police put it down to Dr. Stoumen's old age—poor vision, faulty hearing."

"A conference," he said. "Poor Grant—he was a nice man."

"Did he ever work at the school?"

"He did occasional consultations. Coming up summers for a week or two, combining vacation with business. Hit-and-run . . ." He shook his head.

"And as I was saying, I can't locate any of the other speakers or co-chairs."

"You've located me."

"You're the only one, Dr. Harrison."

"Bert, please. Just out of curiosity, how did you find me?"

"From the *Directory of Medical Specialists*."

"Oh. I suppose I forgot to cancel it." He looked troubled.

"I didn't want to impose on your privacy, but—"

"No, no, that's fine. You're here for my own good . . . and, to tell the truth, I welcome visitors. After thirty years in practice, it's nice to talk to people rather than just listen."

"Do you know where any of the others are? Katarina de Bosch, Mitchell Lerner, Harvey Rosenblatt."

"Katarina is just up the coast, in Santa Barbara."

"She's still there?"

"I haven't heard that she's moved."

"Do you have her address?"

"And her phone number. Here, let me call it for you."

He reached over, pulled a crimson rotary phone from the counter, and put it on the table. As he dialed I wrote down the number on the phone. Then he held the receiver to his ear for a while, before putting it down.

"No answer," he said.

"When's the last time you saw her?"

He thought. "I suppose about a year or so. By coincidence. I was in a bookstore in Santa Barbara and ran into her, browsing."

"Psychology?"

He smiled. "No, fiction, actually. She was in the science-fiction section. Would you like her address?"

"Please."

He wrote it down and gave it to me. Shoreline Drive.

"The ocean side," he said, "just up from the marina."

I remembered the slide Katarina had shown. Blue skies behind a wheelchair. The ocean.

"Did she live there with her father?" I said.

"Since the two of them came to California."

"She was very attached to him, wasn't she?"

"She worshiped him." He continued to look preoccupied.

"Did she ever marry?"

He shook his head.

"When did the school close?" I said.

"Not long after Andres died—eighty-one, I believe."

"Katarina didn't want to keep it going?"

He put his hands around his coffee cup. He had hammer
thumbs and his other digits were short. "You'd have to ask her
about that."

"Does she do any kind of psychological work now?"

"Not to my knowledge."

"Early retirement?"

He shrugged and drank. Put his cup down and touched the
stone of his bolo tie. Something bothering him.

I said, "I only met her twice, but I don't see her as someone
with hobbies, Bert."

He smiled. "You encountered the force of her personality."

"She was the reason I was at the conference against my will.
She pulled strings with the chief of staff."

"That was Katarina," he said. "Life as target practice: set your
sights, aim, and shoot. She pressured me to speak, too."

"You were reluctant?"

"Yes, but let's get back to Grant for a moment. Hit-and-run
isn't really the same as premeditated murder."

"Maybe I'm wrong, but I still can't find anyone who was up
on that dais."

He grabbed the cup with both hands. "I can tell you about
Mitch—Mitchell Lerner. He's dead. Also the result of an accident.
Hiking. Down in Mexico—Acapulco. He fell from a high cliff."

"When?"

"Two years ago."

One year before Stoumen, one year after Rodney Shipler. Fill
in the gaps. . . .

". . . the time," he was saying, "I had no reason to assume it
was anything but an accident. Especially in view of it being a fall."

"Why's that?"

He worked his jaws and his hands went flat on the table. His mouth twisted a couple of times. Anxiety and something else—dentures.

"Mitchell had occasional balance problems," he said.

"Alcohol?"

He stared at me.

"I know about his suspension," I said.

"I'm sorry, I can't talk any more about him."

"Meaning he was your patient—your bio mentioned your specialties. Impaired therapists."

Silence that served as affirmation. Then he said, "He was trying to ease his way back into work. The trip to Mexico was part of that. He was attending a conference there."

He put his finger in his mouth and fooled with his bridgework.

"Well," he said, smiling, "I don't go to conferences anymore, so maybe I'm safe."

"Does the name Myra Paprock mean anything to you?"

He shook his head. "Who is she?"

"A woman who was murdered five years ago. The words 'bad love' were scrawled at the murder scene in her lipstick. And the police have found one other killing where the phrase was written. A man named Rodney Shipler, beaten to death *three* years ago."

"No," he said, "I don't know him, either. Are they therapists?"

"No."

"Then what would they have to do with the conference?"

"Nothing that I know of, but maybe they had something to do with de Bosch. Myra Paprock was working as a real estate agent at the time, but before that she was a teacher in Goleta. Maybe she moonlighted at the Corrective School. This was before she married, so her surname would have been something other than Paprock."

"Myra," he said, rubbing his lip. "There *was* a Myra who taught there when I was consulting. A young woman, just out of college . . . blond, pretty . . . a little . . ." He closed his eyes. "Myra . . . Myra . . . what was her name—Myra *Evans*, I think. Yes, I'm pretty sure that's what it was. Myra Evans. And now you're saying she was murdered . . ."

"What else were you going to say about her, Bert?"

"Excuse me?"

"You just said she was blond, pretty, and something else."

"Nothing, really," he said. "I just remembered her as being a little hard. Nothing pathologic—the dogmatism of youth."

"Was she rough on the kids?"

"Abusive? I never saw it. It wasn't that kind of place—Andres's force of personality was enough to maintain a certain level of . . . order."

"What was Myra's method for maintaining order?"

"Lots of rules. One of those everything-by-the-rules types. No shades of gray."

"Was Dr. Stoumen like that too?"

"Grant was . . . orthodox. He liked his rules. But he was an extremely gentle person, somewhat shy."

"And Lerner?"

"Anything but rigid. *Lack* of discipline was his problem."

"Harvey Rosenblatt?"

"Don't know him at all. Never met him before the conference."

"So you never saw Myra Evans come down too hard on a child?"

"No . . . I barely remember her—these are just impressions, they may be faulty."

"I doubt it."

He moved his jaws from side to side. "All these murders. You actually think . . ." Shaking his head.

I said, "How important was the concept of 'bad love' to de Bosch's philosophy?"

"I'd say it was fairly central," he said. "Andres was very concerned with justice—he saw achieving consistency in our world as a prime motive. Saw many symptoms as attempts to accomplish that."

"The search for order."

Nod. "And good love."

"When did you become disillusioned about him?"

He looked pained.

I held my gaze and said, "You said Katarina pressured you to speak at the symposium. Why would a faithful student have to be pressured?"

He got up, turned his back on me, and rested his palms on the counter. A little man in ridiculous clothing, trying to bring color to his world.

"I really wasn't that close to him," he said. "After I began my anthropology studies, I wasn't around much." Taking a couple of steps, he wiped the counter with one stubby hand.

"Your own search for consistency?"

He stiffened but didn't turn.

"Racism," he said. "I heard Andres making remarks."

"About who?"

"Blacks, Mexicans."

"Were there black and Mexican children at the school?"

"Yes, but he didn't malign them. It was the workers—hired laborers. There was acreage behind the school. Andres hired people down on lower State Street to come clear the weeds every month or so."

"What did you hear him say about them?"

"The usual garbage—that they were lazy, stupid. Genetically inferior. He called the blacks one half-step up from apes, said the Mexicans weren't much better."

"He said this to your face?"

Hesitation. "No. To Katarina. I overheard it."

I said, "She didn't disagree with him, did she?"

He turned around. "She *never* disagreed with him."

"How did you happen to overhear their conversation?"

"I wasn't eavesdropping," he said. "That would almost have been better. I walked in on the middle of the conversation and Andres didn't bother to interrupt himself. That really troubled me —the fact that he thought I would laugh along with it. And it wasn't just once—I heard him say those things several times. Almost taunting me. I didn't respond. He was my teacher and I became a worm."

He returned to his chair, slumping a bit.

I said, "Did Katarina respond at all to his remarks?"

"She laughed. . . . I was disgusted. Lord knows I'm no paragon of virtue, I've done my share of pretending to listen to patients when my mind was elsewhere. Pretending to care. Been married five times, never longer than twenty-six months. When I finally achieved enough insight to realize I should stop making women's lives miserable, I opted for the solitary life. Drew plenty of blood along the way, so I don't put myself up on any moral pedestal. But I *have* always prided myself on tolerance—I'm sure part of it is personal. I was born with multiple anomalies. Other things besides the lack of color vision."

He looked away, as if considering his choices. Held out his short fingers and waved them. Pointing at his mouth, he said, "I'm completely edentulous. Born without adult teeth. My right foot has three toes, the left one is clubbed. I'm unable to sire children and one of my kidneys atrophied when I was three. Most of my childhood was spent in bed due to severe skin rashes and a hole in the ventricular septum of my heart. So I guess I'm a little sensitive to discrimination. But I didn't speak up, just left the school."

I nodded. "Did de Bosch's intolerance come out in other ways?"

"No, that's the thing. On a day-to-day basis, he was extremely liberal. *Publicly*, he was liberal—took in minority patients, most of them charity cases, and seemed to treat them as well as the others. And in his writings, he was *brilliantly* tolerant. Have you ever read his essay on the Nazis?"

"No."

"Brilliant," he repeated. "He composed it while fighting in the French Resistance. Taking the bastards' own pseudo-theories of racial superiority and throwing it all back in their faces with good, sound science. That was one of the things that attracted me to him when I was a resident. The *combination* of social conscience and psychoanalysis. Too many analysts live in a twelve-foot-square world—the office as universe, rich people on the couch, summers in Vienna. I wanted more."

"Is that why you studied anthropology?"

"I wanted to learn about other cultures. And Andres supported me in that. Told me it would make me a better therapist. He *was* a great mentor, Alex. That's why it was so crushing to hear him sneer at those field hands—like seeing one's father in a disgusting light. I swallowed it in silence several times. Finally, I resigned and left town."

"For Beverly Hills?"

"I did a year of research in Chile, then caved in and returned to my own twelve-foot-square world."

"Did you tell him why you were leaving?"

"No, just that I was unhappy, but he understood." He shook his head. "He was an intimidating man. I was a coward."

"It had to take force of personality to dominate Katarina."

"Oh, yes, and he did dominate her . . . after I returned from Chile, he called me just once. We had a frosty conversation, and that was that."

"But Katarina wanted you at the conference anyway."

"She wanted me because I was part of his past—the glory years. By then he was a vegetable and she was *resurrecting* him. She brought me pictures of him in his wheelchair. 'You abandoned him once, Bert. Don't do it again.' Guilt's a great motivator."

He looked away. Worked his jaws.

"I don't see any obvious tie-in," I said, "but Rodney Shipler, the man who was beaten to death, was black. At the time of his murder, he was a school janitor in L.A. Do you have any memory of him at all?"

"No, that name isn't familiar." He looked back at me. Edgy—guilty?

"What is it, Bert?"

"What's what?"

"Something's on your mind." I smiled. "Your face is full of stress."

He smiled back and sighed. "Something came into my mind. Your Mr. Silk. Probably irrelevant."

"Something about Lerner?"

"No, no, this is something that happened after the 'bad love' conference—soon after, a couple of days, I believe." He closed his eyes and rubbed his forehead, as if coaxing forth memories.

"Yes, it was two or three days," he said, working his jaws again. "I received a call in my office. After hours. I was on my way out and I picked up the phone before the answering service could get to it. A man was on the other end, very agitated, very angry. A young man—or at least he sounded young. He said he'd sat through my speech at the conference and wanted to make an appointment. Wanted to go into long-term psychoanalysis with me. But the way he said it—hostile, almost sarcastic—brought my guard up, and I asked him what kinds of problems he was experiencing. He said there were many—too many to go into over the phone and that my speech had reminded him of them. I asked him how, but he wouldn't say. His voice was *saturated* with stress —real suffering. He demanded to know if I was going to help him. I said, of course, I'd stay late and see him right away."

"You considered it a crisis?"

"At the least, a borderline crisis—there was real pain in his voice. An ego highly at risk. And," he smiled, "I had no pressing engagements other than dinner with one of my wives—the third one, I think. You can see why I was such a poor matrimonial prospect. . . . Anyway, to my surprise, he said no, right now wasn't a good time for him, but he could come in the next evening. Standoffish, all of a sudden. As if *I'd* come on too strong for *him*. I was a bit taken aback, but you know patients—the resistance, the ambivalence."

I nodded.

He said, "So we made an appointment for the following afternoon. But he never showed up. The phone number he'd given me was out of order and he wasn't listed in any local phone books. I thought it odd, but after all, odd is our business, isn't it? I thought about it for a while, then I forgot about it. Until today. His being at the conference . . . all that anger." Shrug. "I don't know."

"Was his name Silk?"

"This is the part I hesitate about, Alex. He never became my patient, formally, but in a sense he was. Because he asked for help and I counseled him over the phone—or at least I attempted to."

"There was no formal treatment, Bert. I don't see any problem, legally."

"That's not the point. Morally, it's an issue—moral issues transcend the law." He slapped his own wrist and smiled. "Gawd, doesn't that sound self-righteous."

"There *is* a moral issue," I said. "But weigh it against the alternatives. Two definite murders. Three if you include Grant Stoumen. Maybe four, if someone pushed Mitchell Lerner off that cliff. Myra Paprock was raped, as well. Taken apart physically. She left two small children. I just met her husband. He still hasn't healed."

"You're quite good at guilt yourself, young man."

"Whatever works, Bert. How's that for a moral stance?"

He smiled. "No doubt you're a practical therapist. . . . No his name wasn't Silk. Another type of fabric. That's what made me think of it. Merino." He spelled it out.

"First name?"

"He didn't give one. Called himself 'Mister.' Mr. Merino. It sounded pretentious in someone so young. Awful insecurity."

"Can you pinpoint his age?"

"Twenties—early twenties would be my guess. He had a young man's impetuousness. Poor impulse control to call like that and make demands. But he was stressed, and stress causes regression, so maybe he was older."

"When was the Corrective School established?"

"Nineteen sixty-two."

"So if he was in his twenties in seventy-nine, he could easily have been a patient. Or one of the field hands—Merino's an Hispanic name."

"Or someone with no connection to the school at all," he said. "What if he was just someone with deep-seated problems who sat in on the conference and reacted to it for one reason or another?"

"Could be," I said, calculating silently: Dorsey Hewitt would have been around eighteen in 1979. Lyle Gritz, a year older.

"All right," I said, "thanks for telling me, and I won't give out the information unless it's essential. Is there anything else you remember that might help?"

"No, I don't think so. Thank *you*. For warning me."

He looked around his small house with longing. I knew the feeling.

"Do you have a place to go?" I said.

Nod. "There are always places. New adventures."

He walked me to my car. The heat had turned up a bit and the air was thick with honeybees.

"Off to Santa Barbara now?" he said.

"Yes."

"Give Katarina my best when you see her. The easiest way is Highway 150. Pick it up just out of town and take it all the way. It's no more than a half-hour drive."

"Thanks."

We shook hands.

"One more thing, Bert?"

"Yes?"

"Mitchell Lerner's problems. Could they have resulted in any way from his work at the school—or did they *cause* problems there?"

"I don't know," he said. "He never spoke about the school. He was a *very* closed person—highly defensive."

"So you did ask him about it?"

"I asked him about every element of his past. He refused to talk about anything but his drinking. And even then, just in terms of getting rid of a bad habit. In his own work, he despised behaviorism, but when it came to his therapy, he wanted to be reconditioned. Overnight. Something short term and discreet—hypnosis, whatever."

"You're an analyst. Why did he come to you?"

"Safety of the familiar." He smiled. "And I've been known to be pragmatic from time to time."

"If he was so resistant, why'd he bother to go into therapy in the first place?"

"As a condition of his probation. The social work ethics committee demanded it, because it had affected his work—missed appointments, failure to submit insurance forms so his patients could recover. I'm afraid he acted the same way as a patient. Not showing up, very unreliable."

"How long did you see him?"

"Obviously, not long enough."

21

There seemed little doubt that Myra Evans and Myra Paprock were the same person. And that her murder and the deaths of others were related to de Bosch and his school.

Silk. Merino.

The conference putting someone in touch with his problems . . . some sort of trauma.

Bad love.

Taken apart.

A child's voice chanting.

I felt a sudden stab of panic about leaving Robin alone, stopped in the center of Ojai, and called her from a pay phone. No answer. The Benedict number had been channeled through my answering service, and on the fifth ring an operator picked up.

I asked her if Robin had left word where she was going.

"No, she didn't, doctor. Would you like your messages?"

"Please."

"Just one, actually, from a Mr. Sturgis. He called to say Van Nuys will be getting to your tape soon—got a broken stereo, Dr. Delaware?"

"Nothing that simple," I said.

"Well, you know how it is, doctor. They keep making things more complicated so people have to feel stupid."

*   *   *

I picked up 150 a few miles out of town and headed northwest on two curving lanes. Lake Casitas meandered parallel to the highway, massive and gray under a listless sun. The land side was mostly avocado groves, gold tipped with new growth. Halfway to Santa Barbara, the road reconnected with 101 and I traveled the last twelve miles at freeway speed.

I kept thinking about what Harrison had told me about de Bosch's racism and wondered what I'd tell Katarina when I found her, how I'd approach her.

I got off the highway without an answer, bought gas, and called the number Harrison had given me. No answer. Deciding to delay confrontation for a while, I looked through my Thomas Guide for the site where the Corrective School had once been. Near the border with Montecito, several miles closer than Shoreline Drive—an omen.

It turned out to be a straight, shady street lined with gated properties. The eucalyptus here grew huge, but the trees looked dried out, almost dessicated. Despite the fire risk, shake roofs were in abundance. So were Mercedes.

The exact address corresponded to a new-looking tract behind high stone walls. A sign advertised six custom homes. What I could see of them was massive and cream colored.

Across the way was a pink and brown Tudor mansion with a sign out in front that said THE BANCROFT SCHOOL. A semicircular gravel drive girdled the building. A black Lincoln was parked under a spreading live oak.

A man got out of the car. Midsixties—old enough to remember. I drove across the road, pulled up next to his driver's side, and lowered my window.

His expression wasn't friendly. He was big and powerful looking, dressed in tweeds and a light blue sweater vest despite the heat, and he had very white, very straight hair and knocked-about features. A leather briefcase—an old one with a brass clasp —dangled from one hand. The leather had been freshly oiled—I could smell it. Several pens were clasped to his breast pocket. He looked the Seville over with narrow, dark eyes, then had a go at my face.

"Excuse me," I said, "was the Corrective School once across the street?"

Scowl. "That's right." He turned to leave.

"How long has it been gone?"

"Quite a while. Why?"

"I just had a few questions about it."

He put his briefcase down and peered into the car. "Are you an . . . alumnus?"

"No."

He looked relieved.

"Do alumni come back frequently?" I said.

"No, not frequently, but . . . you do know what kind of school it was."

"Troubled children."

"A bad lot. We were never happy with it—we were here first, you know. My father broke ground thirty years before *they* came."

"Really."

"We were here before most of the houses. This was all agricultural back then."

"Did the students from the Corrective School cause problems?"

"And what's your interest in that?"

"I'm a psychologist," I said, and gave him a card. "I'm doing some consulting to the Los Angeles Police Department, and there's some evidence one of the alumni is involved in something unpleasant."

"Something unpleasant. Well, that's not much of a surprise, is it?" He scowled again. His eyebrows were bushy, low-set, and still dark, giving him a look of perpetual annoyance. "What kind of unpleasantness?"

"I'm sorry but I can't go into detail—is it Mr. Bancroft?"

"It certainly is." He produced a card of his own, white, heavy stock, a heraldic shield in one corner.

The Bancroft School
Est. 1933 by Col. C. H. Bancroft (Ret.)

"Building Scholarship and Character"

Condon H. Bancroft, Jr., B.A., M.A., Headmaster

"By unpleasant do you mean criminal?" he said.

"It's possible."

He gave a knowing nod.

I said, "Why did the place close down?"

"He died—the Frenchman—and no one was left to run it. It's an art, education."

"Didn't he have a daughter?"

His eyebrows arched. "She offered me the place, but I turned her down. Error on my part—I should have done it for the land alone. Now they've come and built *those*." He cast a glare at the stone wall.

"They?"

"Some sort of foreign group. Asians, of course. She offered me all of it, lock, stock. But she wanted an outlandish amount of money and refused to negotiate. For *them*, money's no object."

"She's still here in town, isn't she?"

"She's in Santa *Barbara*," he said.

I wondered where he thought he was, then I answered my own question: Montecito wannabee.

"This unpleasantness," he said. "It isn't anything that would —*impinge* upon my school, is it? I don't want publicity, the police traipsing around."

"Did de Bosch's students ever impinge?"

"No, because I made sure they didn't. For all practical purposes, this property line was as impermeable as the Berlin Wall." He drew a line in the gravel with the toe of one wingtip. "Some of them had been to reform school. Fire setters, bullies, truants—all sorts of miscreants."

"Must have been difficult being this close."

"No, it wasn't *difficult*," he reprimanded. "If they chanced to wander, I sent them hopping right back."

"So you never had any problems?"

"Noise was a problem. There was always too much noise. The only *untoward* thing occurred after they were gone. One of them showed up and made quite a nuisance of himself." Smile. "His condition didn't speak well of the Frenchman's methods."

"What condition was that?"

"A *tramp*," he said. "Unwashed, uncombed, high on drugs— his eyes had that look."

"How do you know he was an alumnus?"

"Because he told me he was. Said it in those words: 'I'm an alumnus.' As if that should have impressed me."

"How long ago was this?"

"Quite a while—let's see, I was interviewing the Crummer boy. The youngest one, and he applied around . . . ten years ago."

"And how old was this tramp?"

"Twenties. A real churl. He barged right into my office, past my secretary. I was interviewing young Crummer and his parents —a fine family, the elder boys had attended Bancroft quite successfully. The scene *he* created dissuaded them from sending the youngest lad here."

"What did he want?"

"*Where* was the school? *What* had happened to it? Raising his voice and creating a scene—poor Mrs. Crummer. I thought I'd have to call the police, but I was finally able to convince him to leave by telling him the Frenchman was long dead."

"That satisfied him?"

The eyebrows dipped. "I don't know *what* it did to him but he left. Lucky for him—I'd had my fill." A big fist shook. "He was insane—*must* have been on drugs."

"Can you describe him?"

"Dirty, uncombed—what's the difference? And he didn't have a car, he walked away on foot—I watched him. Probably on his way to the highway. God help anyone who picked him up."

He watched me leave, too, standing with his arms folded across his chest as I drove away. I realized I hadn't heard or seen any children at his school.

Bullies and fire setters. A tramp in his twenties.

Trying to dig up the past.

The same man who'd called Harrison?

Merino.

Silk. A thing for fabrics.

Hewitt and Gritz, two tramps who would have been in their twenties back then.

Myra Paprock was killed five years ago. Two years after that, Shipler. Then Lerner. Then Stoumen. Was Rosenblatt still alive?

Katarina was, just a few miles up this beautiful road. That gave us something in common.

I was ready to talk to her.

*   *   *

Cabrillo Boulevard swept up past the ocean, cleansed of the weekend tourist swarm and the bad sidewalk art. The wharf looked depopulated and its far end disappeared in a bank of fog. A few cyclists pumped in the bike lane and joggers and speed walkers chased immortality. I passed the big new hotels that commandeered the prime ocean views and the motels that followed them like afterthoughts. Passed a small seafood place where Robin and I had eaten shrimp and drunk beer. People were eating there now, laughing, tan.

Santa Barbara was a beautiful place, but sometimes it spooked me. Too much psychic space between the haves and the have-nots and not enough geography. A walk up State Street took you from welfare hotels and mean bars to custom jewelers, custom tailors, and two-bucks-a-scoop ice cream. The fringes of Isla Vista and Goleta were as hard as any inner city, but Montecito was still a place where people ate cake. Sometimes the tension seemed murderous.

I pictured Andres de Bosch trolling lower State for day laborers. His daughter listening and laughing as he dehumanized those he'd found. . . .

Cabrillo climbed higher and emptied of pedestrians, and I caught an eyeful of endless Pacific. Sailboats were out in force at the marina, most of them floundering as they searched for a tailwind. Nearer to the horizon, fishing scows sat, still as artist's models. The boulevard flattened once again, turned into Shoreline and got residential. I began checking the numbers on the curb.

Most of the houses were fifties rancheros, several of them in renovation. I remembered the neighborhood as well planted. Today, lots of the plants were gone, and the ones that remained looked discouraged. The drought had come hard to this town kissed by salt water.

The lawns were suffering the most, most of them dead or dying. A few were vivid green—too green.

Spray paint.

Santa Barbara, trying to free itself from dependence on Sierra snowpack, had declared mandatory rationing long before L.A. Now the town was returning to desert, but the addiction to emerald was hard to shake.

I reached Katarina's house. Older than its neighbors and considerably smaller, a pale blue, English country cottage with two turrets, a slate roof that needed mending, and a big dirt expanse in front. A privet hedge rimmed the plot, uneven, and picked apart in spots. What had once been a rose garden was now a collection of trellised sticks.

An old-fashioned wire-link gate was fastened across an asphalt driveway, but as I pulled up I could see it was unlocked. I got out and pushed it open and walked up the drive. The asphalt was old and cracked, stretching a hundred feet to the tail end of a small, Japanese car.

Drapes whited all the windows of the house. The front door was paneled oak, its varnish bubbling, a NEIGHBORHOOD WATCH sticker affixed just below the lion's head knocker. Below that was another one, bearing the name of an alarm company.

I rang the bell. Waited. Did it again. Waited some more. Used the lion. Nothing.

No one was around. I could hear the ocean.

I went around the side, past the little white car and a high-peaked garage with sagging swivel doors left half open. The back-yard was twice the size of the front plot and denuded. The borders with its neighbors were obscured by thick plantings of dead citrus and dead avocado. On the ground were shapeless patches of life-less shrubbery. Even the weeds were struggling.

But a couple of giant pines toward the back had survived nicely, their roots deep enough to tap into groundwater. Their trunks yearned for the ragged cliff that overlooked the beach. Through their boughs, the ocean was gray lacquer. The property was at least a hundred feet up, but the tide was a drum roll, loud enough to block out every other sound.

I looked at the rear of the house. Buttoned up and curtained. Near the cliff was an old redwood table and two chairs, guano specked and faded to ash. But half of the table was covered with a white tablecloth, and on the cloth were a cup and saucer and a plate.

I walked over. Coffee dregs in the cup, crumbs on the plate, and an orange smear that looked like ossified marmalade.

The ocean grumbled and seabirds shrieked in response. I walked to the edge of the cliff. To the spot where Katarina had photographed her father, slumped in his wheelchair.

Dry dirt. No fence, easy fall. I peered over and a splinter of vertigo pierced my chest. When it subsided, I looked over again. The hillside was gouged with erosion—giant fingermarks that traced a dead drop down to the rocky beach.

The gulls screamed again—a reprimand that reminded me I was trespassing.

The coffee and crumbs said Katarina was in town. Probably gone out for an errand.

I could wait here, but the more efficient thing would be to call Milo and catch him up on Becky Basille's notes, Harrison, and Bancroft.

As I started to leave, I passed the garage once again and saw the rear end of another car, parked in front of the little white sedan. Bigger and darker—black. The distinctive vertical slash taillights of a Buick Electra. Same car I'd seen at the front of the hospital, in seventy-nine.

Something near the rear tire.

Fingers. White and thin. A hand, the top speckled by an eczematous rash.

No, another kind of speckling.

Darker than eczema.

She was lying on the cement floor, faceup, parallel to the Buick, nearly concealed under the chassis. The other hand was over her head, palm exposed, gouged with deep cuts. Tendons looped from some of the wounds, limp as tired elastic bands.

Defense cuts.

She had on a pink housedress under a white terry cloth robe. The robe was splayed open and the dress was pushed up past her waist, nearly reaching her chin. Her feet were bare, the soles grimed by garage dirt. Her eyeglasses were a few feet away, one of the sidepieces twisted nearly off, one of the lenses cracked.

Her neck was cut, too, but most of the damage had been done to her abdomen. It was black and red—ripped apart, a jumble of viscera—but oddly bloated.

The vertigo returned. I wheeled around, then checked my back. I faced the body again and felt myself grow weirdly calm. Time slowed and an internal rush and roar filled my head, as if the ocean had been transplanted there.

Something missing. Where was the inevitable message?

I forced myself to look for red letters.

Searching for two words . . . nothing. Nothing in the garage but the car and Katarina and a small metal workbench off to one side, backed by a pegboard panel.

A workbench like Robin's, but cluttered with paint cans, tools, gluepots, jars of shellac. Hanging from the pegboard, hooks bearing hammers, gouges, chisels—one of the chisel hooks empty.

A knife on the table, its blade glazed red.

Birchwood handle. Wide tapered blade. Everything glazed . . . the bench stained, but no words, just a spatter of stains.

Old paint blotches. New ones. All mixed in with the telltale red-brown.

Dribs and droplets but no proclamation.

Something white underneath the handle of the killing tool.

A scrap of paper. Not white—almost white, beige. A nice, classy shade of ecru.

Business card.

Confident-looking brown letters said:

SDI, Inc.
9817 Wilshire Boulevard
Suite 1233
Beverly Hills, CA 90212

Something else.

In the upper right.

Tiny.

Hand printed by ballpoint.

Printed neatly, the characters identical to the lettering on my tape package.

So much pressure on the pen that the stiff paper had been torn through in spots.

BL!

22

I ran down the driveway, threw myself into the car, and sped down to the marina. There was a pay phone on the boat moorings, near some trash cans. The stench was welcome.

I tried Robin again. Still no answer.

A detective at West L.A. Robbery-Homicide said, "He's not in."

"It's an emergency."

"Sorry, don't know where he is."

"Maybe he's out in his car," I said. "Could you try radioing him?"

His voice hardened: "Who is this?"

"Assistant Chief Murchison," I said without thinking, marveling at the ease of the lie.

Second of silence. Something that might have been a gulp. "One moment, sir."

Thirty seconds later: "Sturgis."

"It's me, Milo—"

Pause.

"Alex," I said.

"You palmed yourself off as *Murchison*?"

"Katarina's dead. I just found her body." I gave him the details, describing the crime scene in a rapid word storm. The card with the "bad love" message.

"Same printing as the package the tape came in."

"SDI," he said.

"It's right there in Beverly Hills. Maybe he chose to use it for the message for a reason."

"SDI . . . sure as hell not the Strategic Defense Initiative."

"Could you check on Robin? I know the place is secure, but the killer's picking up speed, and the idea of her being alone up there . . . I tried calling her twice, but she's not in."

"Probably went out to do some shopping, but I'll stop by."

"Thanks. What do I do now? I haven't even called the local police yet."

"Where are you?"

"Pay phone, a few minutes from the house."

"Okay, go back there. Stay away from the actual crime scene and just wait. I'll call Santa Barbara PD, tell 'em you're kosher, then I'll head up there myself—what time is it?—three-thirty . . . I should be there by six, the latest."

I waited near the cliff, as far from the garage as I could be. Staring at the ocean, inhaling brine, and trying to make sense of things.

Two young uniforms showed up first. One stayed with the body and the other took a superficial report from me—name, rank, serial number, time and place—listening courteously and just a bit suspiciously.

Twenty minutes later, a pair of detectives arrived. One was a woman named Sarah Grayson, tall, slim, attractive, in her forties. Her eyes were slightly slanted, colored an even brown. They moved slowly but frequently. Taking things in. Reserving judgment.

Her partner was a big, heavy man named Steen, with a bushy dark mustache and not much hair on top. He went straight into the garage and left me to Grayson.

Somehow we'd ended up back near the cliff edge. I told her tape recorder everything I knew, and she listened without interruption. Then she pointed at the water and said, "There's a seal flipping around out there."

I followed her arm and made out a small black dot, ten

breaststrokes from the tideline, cutting a perpendicular line through the breakwaters.

"Or a sea lion," she said. "Those are the ones with the ears, right?"

I shrugged.

"Let's go over it again, doctor."

When I finished, she said, "So you were looking for Dr. de Bosch to warn her about this revenge nut?"

"That, and I wanted to find out if she could tell me anything about why he's *out* for revenge."

"And you think it has something to do with this school?"

"She and her father ran it. It's the only thing I can come up with."

"What was the exact name of the school?" she said.

"The de Bosch Institute and Corrective School. It closed in eighty-one."

"And you thought she'd know what happened because she was the owner's daughter."

I nodded and looked at the rear of the house. "There could be records in there. Therapy notes, something about an incident that traumatized one of the students enough to set him off years later."

"What kind of students went to this school?"

"Emotionally disturbed. Mr. Bancroft, the owner of the school across the street, described them as antisocial—fire setters, truants, and other miscreants."

She smiled. "I know Mr. Bancroft. So when do you think this traumatic episode might have occurred?"

"Some time before nineteen seventy-nine."

"Because of that conference?"

"That's right."

She thought for a while. "And how long was the school around?"

"From nineteen sixty-two to eighty-one."

"Well, that's verifiable," she said, more to herself than to me. "Maybe if there was a trauma we'll have a record of it. Assuming something happened."

"What do you mean?"

"You just told me you think this guy's crazy, doctor—this supposed avenger." She kept her eyes on me and turned one of her earrings. "So maybe he cooked it all up in his head."

"Maybe, but being psychotic doesn't mean being totally delusional—most psychotics have periods of lucidity. And psychotics
can be traumatized, too. Plus, he might not even be psychotic. Just
extremely disturbed."

She smiled again. "You sound like an expert witness. Cautious."

"I've been to court."

"I know—Detective Sturgis told me. And I discussed you
with Judge Stephen Huff, too, just to play it safe."

"You know Steve?"

"Know him well. I used to work juvenile down in L.A. Steve
was handling that kind of thing, back then. I know Milo, too. You
keep good company, doctor."

She looked at the house. "This victim down in L.A.—Ms.
Paprock. You think she taught at the school?"

"Yes. Under the name of Evans. Myra Evans. Her day job was
with the public school system in Goleta. There might still be
records of that. And the male victim, Rodney Shipler, worked as a
school janitor in L.A., so he may have had a similar job up here."

"Shipler," she said, still looking at the house. "Whereabouts
in L.A. do you practice?"

"Westside."

"Child counseling?"

"I do mostly forensic work now. Custody evaluations, injury
cases."

"Custody—*that* can get mean." She turned her earring again.
"Well, we'll go and look around in the house soon as the tech
team and the coroner come and okay it."

She gazed at the ocean some more, brought her eyes back to
the redwood table, and lingered on the coffee cup.

"Having her breakfast," she said. "The dregs still haven't so-
lidified, so my guess is this is from this morning."

I nodded. "That's why I thought she was home. But if she
was eating out here and he surprised her, wouldn't the house be
open? Look how sealed up it looks. And why didn't anyone hear
her scream?"

Holding up a finger, she slung her purse over her shoulder
and went to the garage. She and Steen came out a few minutes
later. He was holding a metal tape measure and a camera, listening to her and nodding.

She took something out of her purse. Surgical gloves. After shaking them out, she donned them and tried a rear door. It opened. She stuck her head inside for a moment, then drew it back.

Another conference with Steen.

Back to me.

"What's in there?" I said.

"Total mess," she said, wrinkling her nose.

"Another body?"

"Not that I can see so far. . . . Look, doctor, it's going to take a long time to get things sorted out here. Why don't you just try to relax until Detective Sturgis gets here? Sorry you can't sit on these chairs, but if you don't mind the grass, get yourself a place over on that side." Indicating the south end of the yard. "I already checked it for footprints and it's okay—ah, look, there's another sea lion. It's real pretty up here, isn't it?"

Milo made it by five forty-eight. I'd staked out a position in a corner of the yard, and he walked straight to it after talking to Grayson.

"Robin was still out when I checked," he said. "Her truck and her purse were gone and so was the dog, and she'd written down something on the fridge pad about salad, so she probably went shopping. I saw absolutely nothing wrong. Don't worry."

"Maybe she should stay with you."

"Why?"

"I'm not safe to be around."

He looked at me. "Okay, sure, if it helps your peace of mind. But we'll *keep* you safe."

He put a hand on my shoulder for a moment, then entered the garage and stayed there for twenty minutes or so. The coroner had come and gone and so had the body, and the technicians were still working, dusting and peeking and making casts. I watched them until Milo came out.

"Let's go," he said.

"Where?"

"Out of here."

"They don't need me anymore?"

"Did you tell Sally everything you know?"

"Yup."

"Then let's go."

We left, passing the garage. Steen was on his knees by a chalk body outline, talking into a tape recorder. Sarah Grayson was standing near him, writing in a notepad. She saw me and waved, then returned to her work.

"Nice lady," I said, as we walked away.

"She was one of Central Juvey's best investigators, used to be married to one of the watch commanders—real asshole, mean drunk. Rumor had it he was rough on her and the kids."

"Physically rough?"

He shrugged. "I never saw bruises, but he had a vicious temper. Finally, they got divorced, and a couple of months later he came over to her place, raising a ruckus, and ended up shooting himself in the foot and losing a toe." Smile. "Whole big investigation. Afterward, Sally moved up here and the asshole retired on disability and packed out to Idaho."

"In the foot," I said. "Not exactly a marksman."

He smiled again. "Actually, he was a crack shot, had once been a range instructor. A lot of people found it hard to believe he'd done it to himself, but you know how it is with chronic alcohol abuse. All that loss of *muscle* control. No telling."

We reached the street. Santa Barbara police cars were parked at the curb, sandwiching the Seville. Neighbors were pressing up against the crime scene tape, and a TV van was driving up. I looked in vain for Milo's Fiat or an unmarked.

"Where's your car?"

"Back in L.A. I took a chopper."

"To where?"

"The airport."

"How'd you get here from there?"

"Santa Barb uniform picked me up."

"Status," I said. "Hoo-hah."

"Yeah," he said. "Sally used to live in Mar Vista. I was the detective on her ex's toe job."

"Oh."

"Yeah. Oh. Now *you* drive me. Let's split before the press leeches start sucking."

*   *   *

I headed down Cabrillo. He said, "Are you too wiped out or grossed out to eat?"

"I haven't eaten since breakfast. I can probably hold something down, or at least watch you."

"Voyeur—this looks okay, pull in." He pointed to a small seafood place tucked next to one of the beach motels. Inside was a scattering of oilcloth-draped tables with abalone-shell ashtrays, sawdust floors, netted walls, a live bar, and a self-order counter. The special of the day was salmon and chips. Both Milo and I ordered it, took a number, and sat down at a window table. We tried to look through the traffic at the water. A young waitress inquired if we wanted anything to drink, brought us two beers, and left us alone.

I called Robin again, using a phone at the back, next to a cigarette machine. Still out. When I got back to the table, Milo was wiping foam from his upper lip.

"Katarina was pregnant," he said. "Coroner actually found the fetus hanging out of her."

"God," I said, remembering the mess and the bloated abdomen. "How far along was she?"

"Five to six months. Coroner could tell it was a boy."

I tried to push aside my revulsion. "Harrison said she never married and she lived alone. Who could the father have been?"

"Probably some med student with a Mensa membership. SDI stands for Seminal Depository and Inventory."

"A sperm bank?"

"This particular one claims to screen its donors for both brains and brawn."

"Designer babies," I said. "Yeah, I can see Katarina going for something like that. Artificial insemination would give her total control over the child rearing, no emotional entanglements. . . . At five months she'd probably be showing. That's why the killer concentrated on her belly—focused his anger there. Wiping out de Bosch's line."

He frowned.

I said, "Maybe the sperm bank's card was chosen for the message for that same reason. The way it was pinned under the murder weapon was deliberate—setting the scene. It's all a big ritual for him."

The waitress brought the food. A look at our faces erased the smile on hers.

I said, "He's trying to obliterate everything associated with de Bosch. And once again, he used a weapon he found on hand. Turning the victim against herself—insult *and* injury. Trying to reverse what he thinks was done to him. But he must have brought another weapon with him, to intimidate her."

"His fists could have been all he needed for that. Lots of bruises around her eyes."

"Did he hit her hard enough to knock her out?"

"Hard to tell without an autopsy, but Sally said the coroner didn't think so."

"If she was conscious, why didn't anyone hear her scream?"

"Sometimes people don't scream," he said. "Lots of times they freeze and can't get a sound out. Or the head blows could have stunned her. Even if she did scream, it might not have helped. Neighbors on both sides are away, and the ocean blocks out lots of sound to begin with."

"What about other neighbors? Didn't anyone see someone enter the property?"

"No one's come forward yet. Sally and Steen are gonna do a door-to-door canvass."

"Sally said the house was a mess. Did she mean poor housekeeping or a toss?"

"A toss. There was overturned furniture, ripped upholstery."

"Rage," I said. "Or he could have been looking for old school records. Something that might incriminate him."

"Getting rid of the evidence? He's been bumping off people for years, why start covering now?"

"Maybe he's getting more nervous."

"My experience is just the opposite," he said. "Killers acquire a taste for it, enjoy it more and more and get careless."

"Hope he did get careless and you find something in there."

"It'll take a couple of days to do a thorough workover."

"From the outside, the place looked sealed up. If I hadn't seen the breakfast dishes, I would have assumed Katarina was out of town. The killer must have closed the drapes after he killed her, then tossed in peace."

"Like you said, it's a ritual, something he sets up carefully."

"So, we're not dealing with a raving psychotic. Everything

that's happened is too calculated for a schizophrenic: traveling around to conventions, simulating accidents. Skewering my fish. Taping Hewitt screaming. Stalking, delaying gratification for years. This is calculated cruelty, Milo. Some kind of psychopath. Becky's notes mean we have to look at Gritz carefully. If he's Silk-Merino, his street-bum-alkie thing may be a disguise. The perfect disguise, when you think about it, Milo. The homeless are every-where, part of the scenery. To most of us they all look alike. I remember seeing a guy at Coburg's office. He looked so similar to Hewitt it startled me. All Bancroft really remembered about his intruder, besides age, was dirt and hair."

He thought. "How many years ago did Bancroft say this guy barged in?"

"Around ten. The guy was in his twenties, so he'd be in his thirties now, which would fit Gritz. Bert Harrison's Mr. Merino fits that time frame, too. Both Merino and Bancroft's tramp were agitated. Merino talked about the conference putting him in touch with his problems. A few years later, the tramp returned to his old school, causing a scene, trying to dig up his past. So it could be the same guy, or maybe there are lots of Corrective School alumni wandering around, trying to put their lives together. Whatever the case, something *happened* there, Milo. Bancroft called the school's students miscreants and fire setters. He denied there'd been any major problems that he couldn't handle, but he could have been lying."

"Well," he said, "local records can be checked, and Sally'll be talking to Bancroft again, see if she can get more details."

"Good luck to her. He doesn't suffer the middle class lightly."

He smiled and lifted his glass. "That's okay. Sally doesn't suffer assholes lightly."

He drank some beer but didn't touch his food. I looked at mine. It appeared well prepared but had all the appeal of fried lint.

I said, "Myra Paprock taught school here during the late sixties to the midseventies, so that's probably the time frame we're looking at. Lyle Gritz would have been around ten or eleven. Harrison remembers Myra as being young and very dogmatic. So maybe she got heavy-handed with discipline. Something a child could perceive as bad love. Shipler could have worked there, too, as a janitor. Got involved, somehow, in whatever happened. And most of the conference speakers were on staff then, too. I've got the exact dates in my notes back home. Let's finish up here, get back to L.A., and check."

"You check," he said. "I'll be staying up here for a day or two, working with Sally and Bill Steen. Leave messages at her desk." He gave me a business card.

I said, "The killer's been accelerating his pace. One year between victims, now only a few months between Stoumen and Katarina."

"Unless there are other victims we don't know about."

"True. I still can't find Harvey Rosenblatt, and his wife hasn't returned my call. Maybe she's a widow who just doesn't want to deal with it. But I've got to keep trying. If Rosenblatt's alive, I need to warn him—need to warn Harrison, too. Let me call him right now and tell him about Katarina."

I returned to the pay phone and dialed Ojai while reading the warning label on the cigarette machine. No answer, no tape. I hoped it was because Harrison's self-preservation instincts were sharp. The little man would make an easy, crimson target.

When I returned to the table, Milo still hadn't eaten.

"Gone," I said. "Maybe hiding already. He said he had somewhere to go."

"I'll ask an Ojai cop to stop by. What about Becky Basille? How do you fit her into this? Hewitt screaming 'bad love,' the killer taping Hewitt?"

"Maybe Hewitt was a Corrective School alumnus, too. Or maybe the killer indoctrinated Hewitt about bad love. If G is our guy, Becky's notes imply a close relationship of some kind between him and Hewitt. If I'm right about the killer not being psychotic, he'd have been the more put-together partner—the dominant one. Able to push Hewitt's buttons, feed Hewitt's paranoia, get him off his medication, and turn him against his therapist. Because of *his* hatred of therapists. Plus, he had another reason to hate Becky: Hewitt was getting attached to her."

Milo began cutting salmon with his fork. Stopped and ran his hand over his face. "I'm still looking for Mr. Gritz. Pulled his complete sheet and it's all minor league."

"He told the Calcutta folks he was going to get rich. Could there be some kind of profit motive to these murders?"

"Maybe he was just bragging. Psychopaths do that." He

looked at his food and shoved his plate away. "Who'm I kidding?"

"The kid on the tape," I said. "Any record of Gritz having children?"

He shook his head.

"The chant," I said. " 'Bad love, bad love, don't give me the bad love.' *Sounds* like something an abused kid might say. Having a child recite it could be part of the ritual. Reliving the past, using de Bosch's own terminology. God only knows what else he's done, trying to work through his pain."

He took out his wallet, pulled out cash, and put it on the table. Tried to catch the waitress's attention, but her back was to us.

"Milo," I said, "Becky might still be a link. She could have talked to someone about Hewitt and G."

"Like who?"

"A relative, a friend. Did she have a boyfriend?"

"You're saying she broke confidentiality?"

"She was a beginner, and we already know she wasn't that careful."

"Don't know about any boyfriend," he said. "But why would she not tell Jeffers, then go and gab to a layperson?"

"Because telling Jeffers would have meant getting pulled off Hewitt's case. And she could have talked without feeling she was breaching confidentiality. Leaving out names. But she might have said something to someone that can give us a lead."

"The only member of her family I ever met was her mother, and that was just once, to listen to her cry."

"A mother can be a confidante."

He looked at me. "After that picnic with Paprock's husband, you'd be willing to do another exhumation?"

"What else do we have going?"

He pushed food around his plate. "She was a nice person— the mother. What approach would you take with her?"

"Straight and narrow. Hewitt had a friend who may be involved in other killings. Someone whose name starts with G. Did Becky ever talk about him?"

He caught the waitress's eye and waved her over. She smiled and held up a finger, finished reciting the specials to a couple across the room.

"She lives near Park LaBrea," he said. "Near the art museum. Ramona or Rowena, something like that. I think she's in the book. Though she may have unlisted it after the murder. If she did, call me at Sally's and I'll get it for you."

He looked at our untouched plates, took a toothpick from a can on the table, and poked at his incisors.

"Got your message about the sheriff," I said. "When does he plan to get to the tape?"

"Next couple of days, unless some emergency comes up. Don't know what it'll accomplish, but at least we'll feel scientific."

"Speaking of science," I said, "any estimates yet about when Katarina was killed?"

"Coroner's initial guess is anywhere from eight to twenty hours before you found her."

"Eight's more likely. The coffee dregs were still moist. If I'd gotten there a little earlier I might have—"

"Gotten hurt yourself." He leaned forward. "Forget the rescue fantasies, Alex."

My head hurt and so did my eyes. I rubbed them and drank water.

The waitress came over and looked at our uneaten meals.

"Is something wrong?"

"No," said Milo. "Something just came up and we've gotta run."

"I can doggy-bag it for you."

"No, that's okay." He handed her the cash.

She frowned. "Oka-ay, I'll be back with your change, sir."

"Keep it."

Her smile was as wide as the beach. *Thank* you, sir—we're offering a complimentary custard dessert, today."

Milo patted his gut. "Maybe another time."

"You're sure, sir? They're real good." She touched his arm, briefly. *"Really."*

"Okay," he said, "you twisted my arm. Pack a couple to go."

"Right away, sir."

She ran off and came back seconds later with a paper bag printed with the face of a happy-looking hound and the words FOR BOWSER. Milo carried it and we left the restaurant and headed for the Seville. As I got in the car, I realized he wasn't with me and I turned back to see him standing over a skinny, barechested kid of around eighteen. The kid was sitting on the breezeway in front of the motel and holding a shirt-cardboard sign that said, WILL WORK FOR FOOD. His tan was intense, his cheeks were sunken, and his hair was a greasy umbrella.

Milo gave him the bag. The kid said something. Milo looked angry, but he reached into his wallet and handed the kid something green.

Then he got in the passenger seat and growled: "Take me to work."

23

The scene in the garage stayed with me during the drive back to L.A. Bad traffic just past Thousand Oaks had me sitting still, Katarina's mangled body filling my head. I listened to the Seville idle, thought about pain and vengeance and Robin all alone up on Benedict Canyon. Mr. Silk, whoever he was, had won a partial victory.

Things finally got moving again. I escaped 101, made it to 405 and had a clear sail to Sunset. I was heading up Benedict shortly after nine-thirty when I noticed two red dots floating ahead of me.

Brake lights. A car stopped.

It seemed to be paused right in front of the narrow road that led to my adopted home, though from this distance, I couldn't be sure. I put on speed, but before I got there, the lights dimmed and the car was gone, traveling too fast for me to catch up.

Probably nothing, but I was stumbling along the thin line between paranoia and caution and my heart was pounding. I waited. Everything stayed silent. I drove up to the white gate, slipped the cardkey in the slot, and raced up the cypress-lined driveway.

The house was lit from within, the garage shut. I approached the front door, wet with sweat, turned the key, and stepped inside, chest bursting.

Robin was stretched out on a sofa reading a design magazine.

The bulldog was wedged between her legs, head nestled in her lap, trapdoor mouth open and snoring.

"Beauty and the Beast," I said, but my voice was weak.

She looked up, smiled, and held out her hand. The dog opened one eye, then let the lid drop.

"Been shopping all afternoon?" I said, taking off my jacket. "I tried calling a bunch of times."

"Uh-huh," she said. "Lots of errands. . . . What's the matter, Alex?"

I told her what I'd found on Shoreline Drive.

"Oh, no!" She propped herself on her elbows. The dog grumbled awake, but he stayed down. "You came so close to walking in on it."

I sat down. As she squeezed my hand, I recounted what I'd found and what I'd learned from Bert Harrison and Condon Bancroft. She listened with her fingers at her mouth.

"Whoever's behind this is relentless," I said. "I want you to move somewhere else temporarily."

She sat up completely. *"What?"*

"Just for a while. I'm not safe to be around."

"We moved so you *would* be, Alex. How could anyone know you're here?"

Thinking of the brake lights, I said, "I'm sure no one does, but I just want to be careful. I spoke to Milo. You can move into his place. Just till things ease up."

"It's not necessary, Alex."

The dog was completely awake now, shifting his glance from Robin to me, his brow wrinkles deeper. The confusion and fear of a kid watching his parents fight.

"Just temporarily," I said.

"Temporarily? If this person's done everything you think he has, he waits years! So what kind of temporary are we talking about here?"

I had no answer.

She said, "No. No way, Alex, I won't leave you. To hell with him—he can't do that to us."

"Robin, she was pregnant. I saw what he did to her."

"No," she said, eyes brimming. "Please. I don't want to hear about it."

"Okay," I said.

She pitched forward as if falling and grabbed my shoulders with both hands. Pulling me closer, she held on tight, as if still off balance. Her cheek was up against mine and her breath was in my ear, hot and quick.

"It's okay," I said. "We'll work it out."

She squeezed me. "Oh, Alex, let's just move to another planet."

The dog jumped from the couch to the floor, sat down and stared at us. Whistling noises came from his compressed nostrils, but his eyes were clear and active, almost human.

"Hey, Spike," I said, reaching over. "He been good?"

"The best."

The affection in her voice made his ears go up. He trotted up to the edge of the couch and rested his flews on her knee. She caressed his head and he lifted his chin and gave her palm a long, wet tongue swipe.

"You could take *him* with you," I said. "You'd have *constant* masculine attention."

"Put it out of your mind, Alex." Her nails dug into my back. "We probably won't have him much longer, anyway. I got a call this morning from a group called French Bulldog Rescue. Very sweet lady over in Burbank—you wrote to the national club and they forwarded it to her. She's putting out feelers, says these little guys are almost never intentionally abandoned, so it's just a matter of time before the owners call to claim him."

"No one's reported him missing so far?"

"No, but don't get your hopes up. She's got a pretty good communication network, seems pretty sure she'll find his owner. She offered to come by and take him off our hands, but I said we'd care for him in the meantime."

The dog was looking up at me expectantly. I rested my hand on his head and he made a low, satisfied noise.

Robin said, "Now I know how foster parents feel." She grabbed a handful of soft chin and kissed it. Her shorts had rolled high on her thighs and she tugged them down. "Have you had dinner yet?"

"No."

"I bought stuff—chilies rellenos, enchiladas. Even got a six-pack of Corona, so we could pretend we were party animals. It's a little late now to start a whole feast, but I can put something together if you're hungry."

"Don't bother, I'll make a sandwich."

"No, *let* me, Alex. I need something to do with my hands. Afterward we can get in bed with the crossword and some really bad TV and who knows what else."

"Who knows?" I said, drawing her to me.

We turned off the lights around midnight. I fell away easily, but I woke up feeling as if I'd been drained of body fluids.

I endured breakfast, feeding the dog bits of scrambled egg and making conversation with Robin until the two of them went to the garage.

As soon as I was alone, I called Dr. Shirley Rosenblatt in Manhattan and got the same taped message. I repeated my pitch, told her it was more urgent than ever, and asked her to get in touch as soon as possible. When no callback had come in by the time I'd finished showering, shaving, and dressing, I phoned Jean Jeffers. She was out for the day—some kind of meeting downtown—and hadn't left word with her secretary about Lyle Gritz. Remembering her eagerness to look for him, I figured she'd come up empty.

Information had no listing for a Ramona or Rowena Basille, but there was a "Basille, R." on 618 South Hauser Street. Right near Park LaBrea.

An older woman's voice answered, "Hello."

"Mrs. Basille?"

"This is Rolanda, who're you?" Scratchy timbre, the midwestern tones I'd grown up with.

"My name's Alex Delaware. I'm a psychologist, consulting to the Los Angeles Police Department—"

"Yes?" Rise in pitch.

"Sorry to be bothering you—"

"What is it? What's happened?"

"Nothing, Mrs. Basille. I was just wondering if I could ask you a few questions."

"About Becky?"

"About someone Becky might have known."

"Who?"

"A friend of Dorsey Hewitt's."

The name made her groan. "What friend? Who? I don't understand."

"A man named Lyle Gritz—"

"What about him? What's going on?"

"Have you ever heard of him?"

"No, never. What's this got to do with Rebecca?"

"Nothing directly, Mrs. Basille, but Gritz may have been involved in some other crimes. He may also have used the names Silk or Merino."

"What kind of crimes? Murders?"

"Yes."

"I don't understand. Why's a psychologist calling—that's what you said you were, right? Psychologist, psychiatrist?"

"Psychologist."

"If there's murders involved, why aren't the police calling?"

"It's not an official investigation, yet."

Pause. "Okay, who are you, buster? Some sleazy tabloid writer? I've already been through that, and let me tell you what you can—"

"I'm not a reporter," I said. "I'm who I said I was, Mrs. Basille. If you'd like to verify it, you can call Detective Milo Sturgis at West L.A. detectives. He gave me your name—"

"Sturgis," she said.

"He handled the investigation of Becky's case."

"Which one was that—oh yeah, the big one . . . yeah, he tried to be nice. But where does he come off giving you my name? What are you doing, some kind of psychological *study*? Want to make me a guinea pig?"

"No, nothing like that—"

"What, then?"

There seemed no choice. "My involvement's a lot more personal, Mrs. Basille. I'm a potential victim."

"A vic—of who, this Gritch?"

"Gritz. Lyle Edward Gritz. Or Silk or—"

"Never heard of any of those."

"There's evidence he's been murdering psychotherapists—several of them over a five-year period."

"Oh, no."

"The latest occurred yesterday, in Santa Barbara. A woman named Katarina de Bosch."

"Yester—oh, goodness." Her voice changed—lower, softer, still perplexed. "And now you think he's out for *you*?"

"Yes."

"Why?"

"He may have a thing against psychotherapists. He leaves a message at the crime scene. The words 'bad love'—"

"That's the same thing that scum yelled out!"

"That's why we think there may be a connection. Last week, I received a tape with someone chanting 'bad love.' As well as a sample of Hewitt screaming. Shortly after that, I got a crank phone call, then someone snuck onto my property and did damage."

"What are you *saying*? That Rebecca was *part* of something?"

"I really don't know, Mrs. Basille."

"But maybe that's what it *was*? Someone *else* was involved in my Becky's . . ."

A loud bang percussed in my ear. A few seconds later: "Dropped the phone, you still there?"

"Yes."

"So what're you saying? This Gritz could have been involved in hurting my baby?"

"I wish I could tell you, Mrs. Basille. Gritz and Hewitt were friends, so it's possible Gritz had some influence on Hewitt. But there's no evidence—"

"Bad *love*," she said. "No one was ever able to explain to me what it meant."

"It's a psychological term coined by Katarina de Bosch's father—Dr. Andres de Bosch."

"Debauch?"

"De Bosch. He was a psychologist who ran a remedial school up in Santa Barbara."

No reaction.

I said, "Lyle Gritz may have been a patient there. For all I know, Hewitt may have been also. Did Rebecca ever mention anything related to any of this?"

"No . . . God in heaven . . . I think I'm going to be sick."

"I'm truly sorry, Mrs.—"

"What'd you say your name was?"

"Alex Delaware."

"Give me your phone number."

I did.

"Okay," she said, "I'm calling that Sturgis right now and checking you out."

"He's in Santa Barbara. You can reach him at the police department there." I fished around, retrieved Sarah Grayson's card, and read off the number.

She hung up without comment.

Ten minutes later, my service put her through.

"He wasn't in," she said, "but I spoke to a woman cop who said you're for real. So, okay, I'm sorry for what you're going through—once you been through it you get sorry a *lot* for other people. Okay, what can I do for you?"

"I was just wondering if Becky ever talked about her work. Said anything that might help find Gritz and clear this up."

"Talked? Yeah, she talked. She loved her . . . hold on . . . my stomach . . . hold on, I thought I was okay, but now I feel like I have to throw up again—let me go do that, and then I'll call you back—no, forget that, I hate the phone. Phone rings now, my heart starts going like it's going to explode—you want to come down and see me it's okay. Let me see what you look like, I hate the phone."

"How about I come to your house?"

"Sure—no, forget it. The place is depressing. I never was a homemaker, now I don't do a darn thing. Why don't you meet me over in Hancock Park? Not the neighborhood, the actual park—know where it is?"

"Over by the tar pits."

"Yeah, meet me on the Sixth Street side, behind the museums. There's a shady area, some benches. What're you gonna wear?"

"Jeans and a white shirt."

"Fine. I'll be wearing—no, this is wrinkled, gotta change it—I'll be wearing a . . . green blouse. Green with a white collar. Just look for an ugly old woman with a green blouse and a crappy disposition."

The blouse was grass green. She was sitting under a thatch of mismatched trees, on a bench facing the rolling lawn that separated the County Art Museum from the dinosaur depository George Page had built with Mission Pack money. At the end of the lawn the tar pits were an oily black sump behind wrought iron pickets. Through the fence, plaster mastodons reared and glared at the traffic on Wilshire Boulevard. Tar leaked through the entire park, seeping up in random spots, and I just missed stepping in a bubbling pool as I made my way toward Rolanda Basille.

Her back was to Sixth Street, but I had a three-quarter view of her body. Around sixty-five. Her collar was a snowy Peter Pan job, her slacks olive wool, much too heavy for the weather. She had hair dyed as black as the tar, cut in a flapper bob with eyebrow-length bangs. Her face was crinkled and small. Arthritic hands curled in her lap. Red tennis shoes covered her feet, over white socks, folded over once. A big, green plastic purse hung from her shoulder. If she weighed a hundred pounds, it was after Thanksgiving dinner.

The ground was covered with dry leaves and I made noise as I approached. She kept gazing out at the lawn and didn't look back. Children were playing there, mobile dots on an emerald screen, but I wasn't sure she saw them.

The random trees had been trimmed to form a canopy, and the shadows they cast were absolute. Several other benches were scattered nearby, most of them empty. A black man slept on one, a paper bag next to his head. Two women of Rolanda Basille's approximate age sat on another, strumming guitars and singing.

I walked in front of her.

She barely looked up, then slapped the bench.

I sat down. Music drifted over from the two guitarists. Some sort of folk song, a foreign language.

"The Stepne sisters," she said, sticking out her tongue. "They're here all the time. They stink. Did you ever see a picture of my daughter?"

"Just in the paper."

"That wasn't a flattering one." She opened the big purse, searched for a while, and took out a medium-sized envelope. Withdrawing three color photographs, she handed them to me.

Professional portraits, passable quality. Rebecca Basille sitting in a white wicker chair, posed three different ways in front of a mountain-stream backdrop, wearing a powder-blue dress and pearls. Big smile. Terrific teeth. Very pretty; soft, curvy build, soft arms, a trifle heavy. The dress was low-cut and showed some cleavage. Her brown hair was shiny and long and iron-curled at the ends, her eyes full of humor and just a bit of apprehension, as if she'd been sitting for a long time and had doubts about the outcome.

"Very lovely," I said.

"She was beautiful," said Rolanda. "Inside and out."

She held out her hand and I returned the photos. After she'd replaced them in the purse, she said, "I just wanted you to see the person she was, though even these don't do it. She didn't like having her picture taken—used to be chubby when she was little. Her face was always gorgeous."

I nodded.

She said, "There was a wounded bird within five miles, Becky'd find it and bring it home. Shoeboxes and cotton balls and eyedroppers. She tried to save anything—*bugs*—those little gray curly things?"

"Potato bugs?"

"Those. Moths, ladybugs, whatever, she'd save 'em. When she was *real* little she went through this stage of not wanting anyone to cut the lawn because she thought it hurt the grass."

She tried to smile, but her lips got away from her and began trembling. She covered them with one hand.

"You see what I'm saying?" she said, finally.

"I do."

"She never changed. In school, she went straight for the outcasts—anyone who was different, or hurting—the retarded kids, harelips, you name it. Sometimes I think she was *attracted* to hurt."

Another forage in the purse. She found red-framed sunglasses and put them on. Given the ambient shade, they must have blacked out the world.

I said, "I can see why she went into social work."

"Exactly. I always figured she would do something like that, always told her nursing or social work would be perfect for her. But of course when you tell them, they do something else. So it took her a while to know what she wanted. She didn't want to go to college, did some waitressing, some file clerking, secretarial. My other kids were different. Real driven. Got a boy practicing orthopedic medicine in Reno, and my older girl works in a bank in St. Louis—assistant vice president."

"Was Becky the youngest?"

She nodded. "Nine years between her and Kathy, eleven between her and Carl. She was—I was forty-one when I had her, and her father was five years older than me. He walked out on us right after she was born. Left me high and dry with three kids. Sugar diabetic, and he refused to stop drinking. He started losing feeling in his feet, then the eyes started going. Finally, they began cutting pieces off of him and he decided with no toes and one arm it was time to be a swinging bachelor—crazy, huh?"

She shook her head.

"He moved to Tahoe, didn't last long after that," she said. "Becky was two when he died. We hadn't heard from him all that time, suddenly the government started sending me his veteran's benefits. . . . You think that's what made her so vulnerable? No —what do you people call it?—father role model?"

"How was Becky vulnerable?" I said.

"Too trusting." She touched her collar, smoothed out an invisible wrinkle. "She went straight for the losers. Believed every cock-and-bull story."

"What kind of losers?"

"More wounded birds. Guys she thought she could fix. She wanted to fix the world."

Her hands began to shake and she shoved them under her purse. The Stepne sisters were singing louder. She said: "Shut up."

"Did the losers mistreat her?"

"Losers," she said, as if she hadn't heard. "The great poet with no poems to show for it, living off welfare. Bunch of musicians, so-called. Not men. Little boys. I nagged her all the time, all the dead-ends she was choosing. In the end, none of that mattered a whit, did it?"

She lifted her sunglasses and wiped an eye with one finger. Putting the shades back, she said, "You don't need to hear this, you've got your own problems."

I saw faint reflections of myself in her black lenses, distorted and tense.

"You seem like a nice young fellow, listening to me go on like this. Ever save any bugs yourself?"

"Maybe a couple of times."

She smiled. "Bet it was more than a couple. Bet you punched those holes in the top of the jars so the bugs could breathe, right? Bet your mother loved that, too, all those creepy things in the house."

I laughed.

"I'm right, aren't I? *I* should be a psychologist."

"It does bring back certain memories," I said.

"Sure," she said. "Out to save the world, all of you. You married?"

"No."

"A fellow like you, same attitude as my Becky, you would

have been okay for her. You could have saved the world together. But to be honest, she probably wouldn't have gone for you—no offense, you're just too . . . put-together. That's a compliment, believe me." She patted my knee. Frowned. "I'm sorry for what you're going through. And be sure to take good care of yourself. Something happens to you, your mother's going to die, over and over. You'll be gone but she'll be left dying every *day*—understand?"

The hand on my knee clawed.

I nodded.

"Something happens to you, your mother's going to lie in bed and think about you, over and over and over. Wondering how much you suffered. Wondering what you were *thinking* when it happened to you—*why* it happened to her kid and not someone else's. Do you understand what I'm saying?"

"I do."

"So be careful."

"That's why I'm here," I said. "To protect myself."

She whipped off the sunglasses. Her eyes were so raw the whites looked brown. "Gritz—no, she never said a word about anyone named that. Or Silk or Merino."

"Did she ever talk about Hewitt?"

"No, not really." She seemed to be deliberating. I didn't move or speak.

The raw eyes moistened. "She mentioned him once—maybe a week or two before. Said she was treating this really crazy person and thought she was helping him. She said it respectfully—this poor, sick fellow that she really wanted to help. Schizophrenic, whatever—hearing voices. No one else had been able to help him, but she thought she could. He was starting to trust her."

She spat on the ground.

"She mentioned him by name?"

"No. She made a point of not talking about any of them by name. Big point of following the rules."

Remembering Becky's sketchy notes and lack of follow-through with Jean, I said, "A real stickler, huh?"

"That was Becky. Back when she was in grade school, her teachers always said they wished they had a classroom full of Beckys. Even with her loser boyfriends, she always stayed on the straight and narrow, not using drugs, nothing. That's why they wouldn't . . ."

She shook her head. Put her glasses back on and showed me the back of her head. Between thin strands of dyed hair, her neck was liver-spotted and loose-skinned.

I said, "Why they wouldn't what?"

No answer for a moment.

Then: "They wouldn't stick with her—*they* always left *her*. Can you beat that? The ones who were going to get divorced, always went back to their wives. The ones who were on the wagon, always fell off. And left *her*. She was *ten* times the human being any of them were, but *they* always walked out on *her*, can you beat that?"

"They were the unstable ones," I said.

"Exactly. Dead-end losers. What she needed was someone with high standards, but she wasn't attracted to that—only the broken ones."

"Was she in a relationship at the time she died?"

"I don't know—probably. The last time I saw her—couple of days before she stopped by to give me some laundry—I asked her how her social life was and she refused to talk about it. What that usually meant was she was involved with someone she knew I'd nag her about. I got upset with her—we didn't talk much. How was I supposed to know it was the last time and I should have enjoyed every minute I had with her?"

Her shoulders bowed and quivered.

I touched one of them and she sat up suddenly.

"Enough of this—I hate this moping around. That's why I quit that survivor's group your friend Sturgis recommended. Too much self-pity. Meanwhile, I haven't done a damn thing for you."

My head was full of assumptions and guesses. Learning of Becky's attraction to losers had firmed up the suspicions left by her notes. I smiled and said, "It's been good talking to you."

"Good talking to you, too. Do I get a bill?"

"No, the first hour's free."

"Well, look at that. Handsome, a Caddy, and a sense of humor to boot—you do pretty well, don't you? Financially."

"I do okay."

"Modesty—bet you do better than okay. That's what I wanted for Becky. Security. I told her, what are you wasting your time for, doing dirty work for the county? Finish up your degree, get some kind of license, open up an office in Beverly Hills and treat fat people or those women who starve themselves. Make some *money*.

No crime in that, right? But she wouldn't hear of it, wanted to do *important* work. With people who were really *needy*."

She shook her head.

"Saving the bugs," she said, almost inaudibly. "She thought she was dealing with those potato thingies, but a scorpion got into the jar."

24

Her description of Becky as a stickler for the rules didn't fit with Jean Jeffers' recollections. A mother's vision could be overly rosy, but she'd been frank about Becky's chronic attraction to losers.

Had Becky finally been attracted to the ultimate loser? How loose had things gotten between her and Hewitt?

And what twisted dynamic bound the two of them to G?

Bad love.

Blaming the victim bothered me, but revenge seemed to be the fuel that powered the killer's engine, and I had to wonder if Becky had been a target of something other than random psychosis.

I drove home straining to make sense of it. No strange vehicles within a hundred yards of the gate, and last night's anxiety seemed silly. Robin was working, looking preoccupied and content, and the dog was chewing a nylon bone.

"Milo just called from Santa Barbara," she said. "The number's on the kitchen counter."

I went into the house, found an 805 exchange that wasn't Sally Grayson's, and punched it. A voice answered, "Records."

"Dr. Delaware returning Detective Sturgis's call."

"One minute."

I waited five.

"Sturgis."

"Hi. Just got through talking to Becky's mother. Becky never mentioned anyone by name, but she did talk about helping a poor unfortunate psychotic who could very well have been Hewitt."

"No mention of Gritz?"

"Nor of Silk or Merino. One thing that was interesting, though: she said Becky liked to mend broken wings and had a penchant for losers—guys who involved her in dead-end relationships. If you think of Hewitt as the ultimate loser, it supports what we suspected about things getting unprofessional between them. Having said all that, I don't know that it *leads* us anywhere."

"Well, we're not doing much better here. No school records at Katarina's house, so either she never kept them or the killer made off with them. We do have confirmation that Myra Evans was Myra Paprock, but it's a no-go on Rodney Shipler. His tax records show him working for the L.A. Unified School District for thirty years—right after he got out of the Army. Never up here—and I verified it with the S.B. district. No connection at all to the de Bosch school."

"What about summer vacations?" I said. "School personnel sometimes take part-time jobs during the off-season."

"Summers he worked in L.A."

"How long was he in the Army?"

"Fifteen years—staff sergeant, most of it over in the Philippines. Honorable discharge, no blots on his record."

"He made somebody mad."

"It doesn't look like it was someone at the school. In fact, we can't find any records of *anything* fishy happening out at the school. No fires or felonies or anything anybody would want to avenge, Alex. Just a few complaints about noise from Bancroft and one vehicular accident that did occur when Myra Evans was teaching there—May of seventy-three—but it was clearly an accident. One of the students stole a school truck and took a joyride. Made it up to the Riviera district and spun off a mountain road. He died, Santa Barbara PD investigated, found no foul play."

"How old was the student?"

"Fifteen."

"Vehicular accident off a mountain road," I said. "Grant Stoumen was hit by a car and Mitchell Lerner was pushed off a mountain."

"That's a little abstract, Alex."

"Maybe not, if matching things—achieving consistency—is part of the killer's fantasy."

Pause. "You'd know more about that than I would, but why focus on the school when we've got a victim with no connection to it? No obvious connection to de Bosch, period."

"Shipler could have been connected to the symposium."

"How? A janitor with a side interest in psychology, or did he sweep up afterward?"

"Maybe it's the race angle somehow. Shipler was black and de Bosch was a covert bigot."

"Why would someone pissed off about *racism* beat a *black* man to death?"

"I don't know . . . but I'm sure de Bosch is at the core of this. The school, the conference—all of it. Merino told Harrison the conference set off something in him—maybe it was seeing de Bosch lauded publicly, when he knew the truth to be otherwise."

"Maybe, but so far the school's got a clean record."

"Bancroft seemed to think it was a hotbed of antisocial behavior."

"Bancroft isn't your most reliable witness. Sally says he's been known to hit the bottle pretty hard, and his world view's somewhat to the right of the Klan. Compared to his old man, he's a pussycat. The two of them had a special thing for de Bosch because de Bosch overbid Bancroft Senior for the land the school was built on. When de Bosch broke ground in sixty-two, they tried to mobilize the neighbors against it—disturbed kids running amok. But no one went along with it because the Bancrofts had alienated everyone over the years."

"The neighbors didn't mind a school for problem kids?"

"There were some worries, but the lot being vacant bothered them more. Vagrants used to come off the highway, light fires, toss trash, make a mess. Bancroft Senior had dickered with the owner for years, making offers, withdrawing them. De Bosch's school was an improvement as far as the neighborhood was concerned. Real quiet, no problems."

"Except for a fifteen-year-old kid in a stolen truck."

"One incident in twenty years, Alex. Considering that de Bosch dealt with emotionally disturbed kids, wouldn't you say that's pretty good?"

"I'd say it's excellent," I said. "Exemplary. And one way to keep things so tidy is through firm discipline. *Very* firm discipline."

He sighed. "Sure, it's possible. But if de Bosch was running a torture chamber, wouldn't there be complaints?"

"Five dead people is a complaint."

"Okay. But if you want a hostility motive, look at Bancroft. He had a *hard-on* for de Bosch for over twenty years. But that doesn't mean he ran around the country murdering everyone associated with him."

"Maybe he *should* be looked into."

"He will be," he said wearily. "He's *being* looked into. Meanwhile, you be careful and sit tight. I'm sorry, Alex, I wish the goddamn pieces had fit together neatly, but it's turning out to be messy."

"Just like real life," I said. "Anything new on Katarina?"

"Coroner still can't decide if she was conscious or unconscious after those blows to the face. Her baby was, indeed, a twenty-two-week-old normal male, Caucasian. I called the sperm bank, they wouldn't even verify she was a customer. Sally and I can probably pry some information loose, eventually. Meanwhile, is Robin coming to us? Rick says no problem except for Rover— excuse me, Spike. Dog allergy. But if Robin really wants to take the pooch with her, he can put himself on antihistamines."

"He won't need to," I said. "Robin insists on staying with me."

"Must be your charm . . . well, don't sweat it, I'm sure you're safe."

"Hope so." I told him about the brake lights the previous night.

"Just lights, nothing funny?"

"Just lights. And then the car drove off."

"What time was this?"

"Nine forty-five or so."

"Any other cars around?"

"Quite a few."

"Sounds like nothing. If you see anything funny, call Beverly Hills PD—they protect their citizenry."

"I will. Thanks for everything. . . . The kid who went off the mountain, did he have a name?"

"Still on that, huh?" He gave a small laugh. "His name was Delmar Parker and he originally came from New Orleans."

"What was he being treated for at the school?"

"Don't know, there's no complete police report, because the case was closed and filed. We're working from summary cards at the coroner's office and lucky to find *them*. . . . Let's see . . . name, date, age, cause of death—multiple traumas and internal injuries—place of birth, N'Awleens . . . parent or guardian—here it is—the mother . . . Marie A. Parker."

"Any address?"

"No. Why? You want to dig up *another* one?"

"No," I said. "I don't *want* to dig up anything, believe me. I'm just grasping, Milo."

Silence. "Okay, I'll try, but don't count on it. It was a long time ago. People move. People die."

I pretended everything was normal. Robin and I ate lunch out by the pool. The sky was clear and beautiful, bracing itself for a smog cloud heading over from the east.

Lifestyles of the rich and fearful.

Terror and anger still gnawed at my spine, but I thought of the people under the freeway and knew I had it damned good.

The phone rang. My service operator said, "There's a long-distance call for you, Dr. Delaware. From New York, a Mr. Rosenblatt."

"Mister, not doctor?"

"Mister's what he said."

"Okay," I said. "Put him on."

She did, but no one answered my hello. A few seconds later a young woman with an all-business voice clicked in and said, "Schechter, Mohl, and Trimmer. Who are you holding for?"

"Mr. Rosenblatt."

"One moment."

A few seconds later a young voice said, "This is Mr. Rosenblatt."

"This is Dr. Delaware."

Throat clear. "Dr. Delaware, my name is Joshua Rosenblatt, I'm a practicing attorney here in New York and I'm calling to ask you to stop phoning my mother, Dr. Shirley Rosenblatt."

"I've been phoning because I was concerned about your father—"

"Then you have nothing to be concerned about."

"He's all right?"

Silence.

I said, "Is he all right?"

"No. I wouldn't say that." Pause. "My father's deceased."

I felt myself deflate. "I'm sorry."

"Be that as it may, Dr. Delaware—"

"When did it happen? Was it four years ago?"

Long silence. Throat clear. "I really don't want to get into this, doctor."

"Was it made to look like an accident?" I said. "Some kind of fall? Something to do with a vehicle? Were the words 'bad love' left anywhere at his death scene?"

"Doctor," he began, but his voice broke on the second syllable and he blurted: "We've been through enough, already. At this point, there's no need to rake it up."

"I'm in danger," I said. "Maybe from the same person who killed your father."

"What!"

"I called because I was trying to *warn* your father and I'm so sorry it's too late. I only met him once, but I liked him. He seemed like a really decent guy."

Long pause. "When did you meet him?" he said, softly.

"In nineteen seventy-nine, here in Los Angeles. He and I co-chaired a mental health symposium called 'Good Love/Bad Love, Strategies in a Changing World.' A tribute to a teacher of your father's named Andres de Bosch."

No response.

"Mr. Rosenblatt?"

"None of this makes any sense."

"You were with him on that trip," I said. "Don't you remember?"

"I went on lots of trips with my father."

"I know," I said. "He told me. He talked about you quite a bit. Said you were his youngest. You liked hot dogs and video games—he wanted to take you to Disneyland, but the park closed early in the fall, so I suggested he take you to the Santa Monica pier. Did you go?"

"Hot dogs." His voice sounded weak. "So what? What's the point?"

"I think that trip had something to do with his death."

"No, no, that's crazy—no. Back in seventy-nine?"

"Some kind of long-term revenge plot," I said. "Something to do with Andres de Bosch. The person who murdered your father has killed other people. At least five others, maybe more."

I gave him names, dates, places.

He said, "I don't know any of those people. This is crazy. This is really insane."

"Yes, it is, but it's all true. And I may be next. I need to talk to your mother. The killer may have presented himself to your father as a patient—lured him that way. If she's still got your father's old appointment books, it could—"

"No, she has nothing. Leave her out of this."

"My life's at stake. Why won't your mother just talk to me? Why'd she have you call me instead of calling herself?"

"Because she can't," he said angrily. "Can't talk to anyone. She had a stroke a month ago and her speech was severely affected. It just came back a few weeks ago, but she's still weak."

"I'm sorry, but—"

"Listen, I'm sorry, too. For what *you're* going through. But at this point, I just don't see what I can do for you."

"Your mother's talking now."

"Yes, but she's weak. Really weak. And to have her talk about my father. . . . She just started rehab and she's making progress, Dr. Delaware. I can't have her interrogated."

"You never told her I called?"

"I'm taking care of her. It calls for decisions."

"I understand," I said. "But I don't want to interrogate her, I just want to talk to her. A few questions. At her pace—I can fly out to New York, if that'll help, and do it face-to-face. As many sessions as she needs. Go as slowly as she needs."

"You'd *do* that? Fly out here?"

"What choice do I have?"

I heard him blow out breath. "Even so," he said. "Her talking about Dad—no, it's too risky. I'm sorry, but I have to hold firm."

"I'll work with her doctors, Mr. Rosenblatt. Clear my questions with them and with you. I've done hospital work for years. I understand illness and recovery."

"What makes you think she knows anything that could help you?"

"At this point she's my last hope, Mr. Rosenblatt. The creep who's after me is picking up his pace. He murdered someone in Santa Barbara yesterday—de Bosch's daughter. She was pregnant. He cut her up, made it a point to go after the fetus."

"Oh, God."

"He's stalking me," I said. "To tell the truth, I'd be safer in New York than here. One way or the other, I may come out."

Another exhalation. "I doubt she can help you, but I'll ask."

"I really apprecia—"

"Don't thank me yet. I'm not promising anything. And fax your credentials to me, so I can check them out. Include two verifiable references."

"No problem," I said. "And if your mother won't speak to me, please ask her if she knows anything about the term 'bad love.' And did your father report anything unusual about the nineteen seventy-nine conference. You can also throw out some names: Lyle Gritz, Dorsey Hewitt, Silk, Merino."

"Who're they?"

"Hewitt's a definite killer—murdered a therapist out here and was shot by the police. Gritz was his friend, may have been an accomplice. He may also be the one who killed your father. Silk and Merino are possible aliases."

"Fake names?" he said. "This is so bizarre."

"One more thing," I said. "There's an LAPD detective working the case out here, named Milo Sturgis. I'm going to inform him of your father's murder and he'll be contacting the New York police and asking for records."

"That won't help you," he said. "Believe me."

25

Milo was no longer at Records, and Sally Grayson's number was picked up by a male detective who hadn't seen her all morning and had no idea who Milo was. I left a message, and wondered why Joshua Rosenblatt had been so sure the police couldn't help.

My offer to go to New York had been impulsive—probably an escape reflex—but maybe something would come out of my talk with Shirley Rosenblatt.

I'd leave as soon as possible; Robin would *have* to move out now.

I looked out at the pool, still as a slab of turquoise. A few leaves floated on top.

Who cleaned it? How often?

I didn't know much about this place.

Didn't know when I'd be able to leave it.

I got up, ready to drive into Beverly Hills to find a fax service. Just as I put my wallet in my pants pocket, the phone rang and my service operator said, "A Mr. Bucklear wants to talk to you, doctor."

"Put him on."

Click.

"Doctor? Sherman Bucklear."

"Hello."

"Have you received my correspondence?"

"Yes, I have."

"I haven't received any reply, doctor."

"Didn't know there was anything to reply to."

"I have reason to believe you have knowledge of the where-abouts—"

"I don't."

"Can you prove that?"

"Do I have to?"

Pause. "Doctor, we can go about this civilly or things can get complicated."

"Complicate away, Sherman."

"Now, wait a sec—"

I hung up. It felt great to be petty. Before I could put down the phone, the service patched in again with a call from New York.

"Dr. Delaware? Josh Rosenblatt, again. My mother's willing to talk to you but I've got to warn you, she can't handle much— just a few minutes at a time. I haven't discussed any details with her. All she knows is you knew my father and think he was murdered. She may have nothing to tell you. You may end up wasting your time."

"I'll take the chance. When would you like me there?"

"What's today? Tuesday . . . Friday's bad and she needs her weekends for total bedrest—Thursday, I guess."

"If I can catch a flight tonight, how about tomorrow?"

"Tomorrow . . . I guess so. But it'll have to be in the after-noon. Mornings she has her therapy, then she naps. Come to my office first—500 Fifth Avenue. Schechter, Mohl, and Trimmer. The thirty-third floor. Have you faxed me your credentials yet?"

"Just on my way out to do it."

"Good, because that'll be a prerequisite. Send me something with a picture, too. If everything checks out, I'll see you, say, two-thirty."

I found a quick-print place on Cañon Drive and faxed my documents to New York. Returning home, I postponed telling Robin and called an airline, booking myself a ten p.m. flight out of LAX. I asked the ticket agent about hotels.

She said, "Midtown? I really don't know, sir, but you might try the Middleton. The executives from our company stay there, but it's expensive. Of course, everything in New York is unless you want a real dive."

I thanked her and phoned the hotel. A very bored-sounding man took my credit card number, then grudgingly agreed to give me a single room for two hundred and twenty dollars a night. When he quoted the price, he suppressed a yawn.

I told Robin about Rosenblatt first.

She shook her head, took hold of my hand.

"Four years ago," I said. "Another gap filled in."

"How'd he die?"

"The son didn't go into any details. But if the killer's being consistent, it was probably something to do with a car or a fall."

"All those people. My God." Pressing my hand up against her cheek, she closed her eyes. The smell of glue hung in the garage, along with coffee and dust and the sound of the dog's breathing.

I felt him nosing up against my leg. Looked down at his wide, flat face. He blinked a couple of times and licked my hand.

I told Robin of my plan to fly east and offered to have her come with me.

She said, "There'd be no point to it, would there?"

"It's not going to be a vacation, just more digging up people's misery. I'm starting to feel like a ghoul."

She looked off, at her tools and her molds.

"Only time I've been in New York was a family trip. We went all the way up to Niagara Falls, Mom and Dad squabbling the whole time."

"I haven't been there, myself, since grad school."

She nodded, touched my biceps, rubbed it. "You have to go— things are getting uglier and uglier here. When are you leaving?"

"I was thinking tonight."

"I'll take you to the airport. When will you be coming home, so I can pick you up?"

"Depends on what I find—probably within a day or two."

"Do you have a place to stay?"

"I found a hotel."

"A hotel," she said. "You, alone in some room . . ." She shook her head.

"Could you please stay with Milo and Rick while I'm gone? I know it's disruptive and unnecessary, but I'd have a lot more peace of mind."

She touched my face again. "You haven't had much of that lately, have you? Sure, why not."

I tried a couple more times to reach Milo without success. Wanting to get Robin settled as soon as possible, I phoned his house. Rick was there and I told him we'd be coming over.

"We'll take good care of her, Alex. I'm really sorry for all this crap you've been going through. I'm sure the big guy will get to the bottom of it."

"I'm sure he will, too. Will the dog be a problem?"

"No, I don't think so. Milo tells me he's pretty cute."

"Milo never expressed any affection for him in my presence."

"Does that surprise you?"

"No," I said.

He laughed.

"Are you badly allergic, Rick?"

"Don't know, never had a dog. But don't worry, I'll pick up some Seldane in the ER, or write myself a scrip. Speaking of which, I have to head over to Cedars pretty soon. When were you planning on coming?"

"This evening. Any idea when Milo'll be back?"

"Your guess is as good as mine. . . . Tell you what, I'll leave a key in back of the house. There're two sago palms growing up against the rear wall—you haven't been here since we reland-scaped, have you?"

"Just to pick up Milo."

"Came out great, our water consumption's way down . . . the sago palms—do you know what they are?"

"Squat things with leaves that look like fan blades?"

"Exactly. I'll leave the key under the branches of the smaller one—the one on the right. Milo would kill me if he knew." More laughter. "We have a new alarm code, too—he changes it every couple of months."

He rattled off five numbers. I copied them down and thanked him again.

"Pleasure," he said. "This should be fun, we've never had a pet."

*   *   *

I packed my carry-on and Robin packed hers. We took the dog for a walk around the property and played with him, and finally he got sleepy. We left him resting and drove into town for an early dinner, taking Robin's truck. Cholesterol palace on South Beverly Drive: thick steaks and home-fried potatoes served in lumberjack portions at prices no lumberjack could afford. The food looked great and smelled great, and my taste buds told me it probably tasted great, too. But somewhere along the line the circuitry between my tongue and my brain fizzed and I found myself chewing mechanically, forcing meat down a dry, tight throat.

At seven, we cleaned the house on Benedict, picked up the dog, locked up, and drove over to West Hollywood. The key was where Rick had said it would be, placed on the ground precisely at the middle of the palm's corrugated trunk. The rest of the yard was desert-pale and composed, drought-tolerant plants spread expertly around the tiny space. The walls were higher and topped with ragged stone.

Inside, the place was different, too: whitewashed hardwood floors, big leather chairs, glass tables, gray fabric walls. The guest room was pine. An old iron bed was freshly made and turned down. A single white rose rested on the pillow and a bar of Swiss chocolate was on a dish on the nightstand.

"How sweet," said Robin, picking up the flower and twirling it. She looked around. "This is like a great little inn."

Sheets of newspaper were spread on the floor next to the bed. On them were a white ceramic bowl filled with water, a plastic-wrapped hunk of cheddar cheese, and a shirt cardboard lettered in fountain pen, in Rick's perfect, surgeon's hand: POOCH'S CORNER.

The dog went straight for the cheese—nosing it and having trouble with the concept of see-through plastic. I unwrapped it and fed it to him in bits.

We let him explore the yard for a while, then went back inside. "Every time I come here, they've done something else," Robin said.

"*They?* I don't think so, Rob."

"True. You know, sometimes I have trouble imagining Milo living here."

"I bet he loves it. Refuge from all the ugliness, someone else to worry about the details for a change."

"You're probably right—we can all use a refuge, can't we?"

At eight, she drove me to LAX. The place had been rebuilt a few years ago, for the Olympics, and was a lot more manageable, but incoming arteries were still clogged and we waited to enter the departure lanes.

The whole city had been freshened up for the games, more energy and creativity mustered during one summer than the brain-dead mayor and the piss-and-moan city council had come up with in two decades. Now they were back to their old apathy-and-sleaze routine, and the city was rotting wherever the rich didn't live.

Robin pulled up to the curb. The dog couldn't enter the terminal, so we said our good-byes right there, and feeling lost and edgy, I entered the building.

The main hall was a painfully bright temple of transition. People looked either bone weary or jumpy. Security clearance was slow because the western-garbed man in front of me kept setting off the metal detector. Finally, someone figured out it was due to the metal shanks in his snakeskin boots, and we started moving again.

I made it to the gate by nine-fifteen. Got my boarding pass, waited a half hour, then stood in line and finally got to my seat. The plane began taxiing at ten-ten, then stopped. We sat on the runway for a while and finally lifted off. A couple of thousand feet up, L.A. was still a giant circuit board. Then a cloud bank. Then darkness.

I slept on and off for most of the flight, woke varnished in sweat.

Kennedy was crowded and hostile. I lugged my carry-on past the hordes at the baggage carousels and picked up a cab at the curb. The car smelled of boiled cabbage and was plastered with no-smoking signs in English, Spanish, and Japanese. The driver had an unpronounceable name and he wore a blue tank top and a white ski hat. The hat was rolled triple so the edge created a brim. It resembled a soft bowler.

I said, "The Middleton Hotel, on West Fifty-second Street."

He grunted something and drove off, very slowly. The little I saw of Queens from the highway was low-rise and old, bricks and chrome and graffiti. But when we got on the Queensboro Bridge, the water was calm and lovely and the skyline of Manhattan loomed with threat and promise.

The Middleton was twenty stories of black granite sandwiched between office buildings that dwarfed it. The doorman looked ready for retirement and the lobby was shabby, elegant, and empty.

My room was on the tenth floor, small as a death row cell, filled with colonial furniture and sealed by blackout drapes. Clean and well ordered, but it smelled of mildew and roach killer. A dead quail-hunt print hung over the bed. The air-conditioner was a heavy-metal instrument. Street noise made it up this far with little loss of volume.

No rose on my pillow.

Unpacking, I changed into shorts and a T-shirt, ordered a three-dollar English muffin and five-dollar eggs, then punched the operator's 0 and asked for a wakeup call at one. The food came surprisingly quickly and, even more amazing, was tasty.

When I finished, I put the tray on a glass-topped bureau, pulled back the covers, and got into bed. The TV remote was bolted to the nightstand. A cardboard guide listed thirty or so cable stations. The last choice was an early morning public access show featuring a dull, pudgy nude man interviewing dull, nude women. He had narrow, womanish shoulders and a very hairy body.

"Okay, Velvet," he said, leering. "So . . . what do you do for, uh . . . fun?"

A painfully thin blond with a beak nose and frizzy hair touched a nipple and said, "Macramé."

I switched off the set.

Lights out. The blackout drapes did their job well.

My heart was as dark as the room.

26

I beat the wakeup call by more than an hour. After showering, shaving, and dressing, I drew open the drapes on a view of the red-brick building across the street. Men in white shirts and ties were framed in its windows, sitting at desks, talking into phones, and stabbing the air with pens. Down below, the streets were clogged with double-parked cars. Horns blatted. Someone was using a compression drill. Even through the sealed windows I could smell the city.

I phoned Robin at just past nine L.A. time. We told each other we were fine and chatted for a while before she put Milo on.

"Talk about bicoastal," he said. "Expedition or escape?"

"Bit of both, I guess. Thanks for taking care of the lady and the tramp."

"Pleasure. Got a little more info on Mr. Gritz. Traced him to a small town in Georgia and just got finished talking to the police chief. Seems Lyle was a weird kid. Acted goofy, walked funny, mumbled a lot, didn't have any friends. Out of school more than he was in, never learned to read properly or speak clearly. His home life was predictably bad, too. No father on the scene, and he and his mother lived in a trailer on the outskirts of town. He started drinking, slid straight into trouble. Shoplifting, theft, vandalism. Once in a while he'd get into a fight with someone bigger and stronger than himself and come out the loser. Chief said he locked him up plenty, but he didn't seem to care, jail was as good as his home, or better. He used to sit in his cell and rock and talk to himself, as if he was in his own world."

"Sounds more like the early signs of schizophrenia than a developing psychopath," I said. "Onset during adolescence fits the schizophrenic pattern, too. What *doesn't* fit is the kind of calculated thing we're dealing with. Does this sound like a guy who could blend in at medical conferences? Delay gratification long enough to plot murders years in advance?"

"Not really. But maybe he changed when he grew up, got smoother."

"Mr. Silk," I said.

"Maybe he's a good faker. Always was. Faked looking nuts, even back then—psychopaths do that all the time, right?"

"They do," I said. "But did this police chief sound like someone easily fooled?"

"No. He said the kid was nuts but had one thing going for him. Musical talent. Taught himself to play guitar and mandolin and banjo and a bunch of other instruments."

"The next Elvis."

"Yeah. And for a while people thought he might actually make something of himself. Then one day, he just left town and no one heard from him again."

"How long ago was this?"

"Nineteen-seventy."

"So he was only twelve. Any idea why he left?"

"Chief had just busted him for drunk and disorderly again, gave him the usual lecture, then added a few bucks for him to get some new clothes and a haircut. Figured maybe if the kid looked better he'd act better. Lyle walked out of the police station and headed straight for the train depot. Police chief later found he used the money to buy a one-way ticket to Atlanta."

"Twelve years old," I said. "He could have kept traveling and ended up in Santa Barbara, been taken in by de Bosch as a charity case—de Bosch liked to put forth the humanitarian image, publicly."

"Wish I could get hold of school records. No one seems to have any. Not the city or the county."

"What about federal? If de Bosch applied for government funding for the charity cases, there might be some kind of documentation."

"Don't know how long those agencies hold on to their

records, but I'll check. So far I'm drawing a blank on this bastard. First time he shows up in California is an arrest nine years ago. No NCIC record prior to that, so that's over a decade between his leaving Georgia and the beginnings of his West Coast life of crime. If he got busted for petty stuff in other small towns, it might very well not have been entered into the national computer. But still, you'd expect something. He's a bad egg, where the hell was he all that time?"

"How about in a mental institution?" I said. "Twelve years old, out on his own. God knows what could have happened to him out on the street. He might have suffered a mental breakdown and got put away. Or, if he was at the school the same time as Delmar Parker, maybe he observed Delmar's death and broke down over that."

"Big assumption, he and Delmar knowing each other."

"It is, but there are some factors that might point in that direction: he and Delmar were around the same age, both were Southern boys a long way from home. Maybe Gritz finally made a friend. Maybe he even had something to do with Delmar stealing the truck. If he did and escaped death but saw Delmar die, that could have pulled the rug out from under him, psychologically."

"So now he's blaming the school and de Bosch and everyone associated with it? Sure, why not? I just wish we could push it past theory. Place Gritz in Santa Barbara, let alone the school, let alone knowing the Parker kid, et cetera, et cetera."

"Any luck finding Parker's mother?"

"She doesn't live in New Orleans, and I haven't been able to find any other relatives. So where does this Silk-Merino thing come in? Why would a Southern boy pick himself a Latino alias?"

"Merino's a type of wool," I said. "Or a sheep—the flock following the shepherd, and getting misled?"

"Baaa," he said. "When are you planning to see Rosenblatt's kid?"

"Couple of hours."

"Good luck. And don't worry, everything here's cool. Ms. Castagna lends a nice touch to the place, maybe we'll keep her."

"No, I don't think so."

"Sure," he said, chuckling. "Why not? Woman's touch and all that. Hell, we can keep the beast, too. Put up a picket fence around the lawn. One big happy family."

*   *   *

New York was as clear as an etching, all corners and windows, vanishing rooflines, skinny strips of blue sky.

I walked to the law firm, heading south on Fifth Avenue, swept along in the midtown tide, comforted, somehow, by the forced intimacy.

The shop windows were as glossy as diamonds. People wearing business faces hurtled toward the next obligation. Three-card monte players shouted invitations, took quick profit, then vaporized into the crowd. Street vendors hawked silly toys, cheap watches, tourist maps, and paperback books stripped of their covers. The homeless squatted in doorways, leaned against buildings. Bearing crudely lettered signs and paper cups, their hands out, their eyes leeched of expectation. So many more of them than in L.A. but yet they seemed to belong, part of the city's rhythm.

Five Hundred Fifth Avenue was a six-hundred-foot limestone tower, the lobby an arena of marble and granite. I arrived with an hour to spare and walked back outside, wondering what to do with the time. I bought a hot dog from a pushcart, ate it watching the throng. Then I spotted the main branch of the public library, just across Forty-second Street, and made my way up the broad, stone stairs.

After a bit of asking and wandering, I located the periodicals room. The hour went fast as I checked four-year-old New York newspapers for obituaries on Harvey Rosenblatt. Nothing.

I thought of the psychiatrist's kind, open manner. The loving way he'd spoken about his wife and children.

A teenaged boy who'd liked hot dogs. The taste of mine was still on my lips, sour and warm.

My thoughts shifted to a twelve-year-old, leaving town on a one-way ticket to Atlanta.

Life had sneak attacked both of them, but Josh Rosenblatt had been much more heavily armed for the ambush. I left to see how well he'd survived.

Schechter, Mohl, and Trimmer's decorator had gone for Tradition: carved, riff-oak panels with laundry-sharp creases, layers of heavy moldings, voluptuous plaster work, wool rugs over herringbone floors. The receptionist's desk was a huge, walnut antique. The receptionist was pure contemporary: midtwenties, white-blonde, *Vogue* face, hair tied back tight enough to pucker her hairline, breasts sharp enough to make an embrace dangerous.

She checked a ledger and said, "Have a seat and Mr. Rosenblatt will be right with you."

I waited twenty minutes until the door to the inner offices opened and a tall, good-looking young man stepped into the reception area.

I knew he was twenty-seven, but he looked like a college student. His face was long and grave under dark, wavy hair, nose narrow and full, his chin strong and dimpled. He wore a pin-striped charcoal suit, white tab shirt, and red and pearl tie. Pearl pocket handkerchief, quadruple pointed, tassled black loafers, gold Phi Beta Kappa pin in his lapel. Intense brown eyes and a golf tan. If law started to bore him, he could always pose for the Brooks Brothers catalogue.

"Dr. Delaware, Josh Rosenblatt."

No smile. One arm out. Bone-crusher handshake.

I followed him through a quarter acre of secretaries, file cabinets, and computers to a broad wall of doors. His was just off to the left. His name in brass, on polished oak.

His office wasn't much bigger than my hotel cubicle, but one wall was glass and it offered a falcon's lair view of the city. On the wall were two degrees from Columbia, his Phi Beta Kappa certificate, and a lacrosse stick mounted diagonally. A gym bag sat in one corner. Documents were piled up everywhere, including on one of the straight-backed side chairs facing the desk. I took the empty chair. He removed his jacket and tossed it on the desk. Very broad shoulders, powerful chest, outsize hands.

He sat down amid the clutter, shuffled papers while studying me.

"What kind of law do you practice?" I said.

"Business."

"Do you litigate?"

"Only when I need to get a taxi—no, I'm one of the behind-the-scenes guys. Mole in a suit."

He drummed the desk with his palm a few times. Kept staring at me. Put his hands down flat.

"Same face as your picture," he said. "I'd expected someone older—closer to . . . Dad's age."

"I appreciate your taking the time. Having someone you love murdered—"

"He wasn't murdered," he said, almost barking. "Not officially, anyway. *Officially*, he committed *suicide*, though the rabbi filed it as an accident so he could be buried with his parents."

"Suicide?"

"You met my dad—did he seem like an unhappy person?"

"On the contrary."

"Damn *right* on the contrary." His face reddened. "He *loved* life—really knew how to have fun. We used to kid him that he never really grew up. That's what made him a good psychiatrist. He was such a happy guy, other psychiatrists used to make *jokes* about it. Harvey Rosenblatt, the only well-adjusted shrink in New York."

He got up, looked down on me.

"He was *never* depressed—the least moody person I ever met. And he was a great father. Never played shrink with us at home. Just a dad. He played ball with me even though he was no good at it. Couldn't change a lightbulb, but no matter what he was doing, he'd put it aside to listen to you. And we knew it—all three of us. We saw what other fathers were like and we *appreciated* him. We never believed he killed himself, but they kept saying it, the goddamn police. 'The evidence is clear.' Over and over, like a broken record."

He cursed and slapped the desk. "They're a bureaucracy just like everything else in this city. They went from point A to point B, found C and said, good night, time to punch the clock and go home. So we hired a private investigator—someone the firm had used—and all *he* did was go over the same territory the police had covered, say the same damn thing. So I guess I should be happy you're here, telling me we weren't nuts."

"How did they say it happened?" I said. "A car crash or some kind of fall?"

He pulled his head back as if avoiding a punch. Glared at me. Began loosening his tie, then thought better of it and tugged it up against his throat, even tighter. Picking up his jacket, he flipped it over his shoulder.

"Let's get the hell out of here."

"You in shape?" he said, looking me up and down.

"Decent."

"Twenty blocks do you in?"

I shook my head.

He pressed forward into the throng, heading uptown. I jogged to catch up, watching him manipulate the sidewalk like an Indy driver, swaying into openings, stepping off the curb when that was the fastest way to go. Swinging his arms and looking straight ahead, sharp-eyed, watchful, self-defensive. I started to notice lots of other people with that same look. Thousands of people running the urban gauntlet.

I expected him to stop at Sixty-fifth Street, but he kept going to Sixty-seventh. Turning east, he led me up two blocks and stopped in front of a red-brick building, eight floors high, plain and flat, set between two ornate graystones. On the ground floor were medical offices. The town house on the right housed a French restaurant with a long black awning lettered in gold at street level. A couple of limousines were parked at the curb.

He pointed upward. "That's where it happened. An apartment on the top floor, and yeah, they said he jumped."

"Whose apartment was it?"

He kept staring up. Then down at the pavement. Directly in front of us, a dermatologist's window was fronted by a boxful of geraniums. Josh seemed to study the flowers. When he faced me, pain had immobilized his face.

"It's my mother's story," he said.

Shirley and Harvey Rosenblatt had worked where they lived, in a narrow brownstone with a gated entry. Three stories, more geraniums, a maple with an iron trunk guard surviving at the curb.

Josh produced a ring of keys and used one key to open the gate. The lobby ceiling was coffered walnut, the floor was covered in tiny black-and-white hexagonal tiles backed by etched glass double doors and a brass elevator. The walls were freshly painted beige. A potted palm stood in one corner. Another was occupied by a Louis XIV chair.

Three brass mailboxes were bolted to the north wall. Number 1 said, ROSENBLATT. Josh unlocked it and drew out a stack of envelopes before unlatching the glass doors. Behind it was a smaller vestibule, dark paneled and gloomy. Soup and powdered-cleanser smells. Two more walnut doors, one unmarked, with a mezuzah nailed to the post, the other bearing a brass plaque that said SHIRLEY M. ROSENBLATT, PH.D., P.C. The faint outline of where another sign had been glued was visible just above.

Josh unlocked the plain one and held it open for me. I stepped into a narrow entry hall lined with framed Daumier prints. To my left was a bentwood hall tree from which hung a single raincoat.

A gray tabby cat came from nowhere and padded toward us on the parquet floor.

Josh stepped in front of me and said, "Hey, Leo."

The cat stopped, arched its tail, relaxed it, and walked up to him. He dropped his hand. The cat's tongue darted. When it saw me, its yellow eyes slitted.

Josh said, "It's okay, Leo. I guess." He scooped up the cat, held it to his chest, and told me, "This way."

The hall emptied into a small sitting room. To the right was a dining room furnished with mock Chippendale, to the left a tiny kitchen, white and spotless. Though the shades were up on every window, the view was a brownstone six feet away, leaving the entire apartment dark and denlike. Simple furniture, not much of it. Some paintings, nothing flashy or expensive. Everything perfectly in place. I knew one way Josh had rebelled.

Beyond the sitting room was another living area, slightly larger, more casual. TV, easy chairs, a spinet piano, three walls of bookshelves filled with hardbacks and family photos. The fourth was bisected by an arched door that Josh opened.

"Hello?" Josh said, sticking his head through. The cat fussed and he let it down. It studied me, finally disappeared behind a sofa.

The sound of another door opening. Josh stepped back as a black woman in a white nurse's uniform came out. In her forties, she had a round face, a stocky but shapely figure, and bright eyes.

"Hello, Mr. Rosenblatt." West Indian accent.

"Selena," he said, taking her hand. "How is she?"

"Everything is *perfect*. She had a generous breakfast and a nice long nap. Robbie was here at ten, and they did almost the full hour of exercise."

"Good. Is she up now?"

"Yes." The nurse's eyes shifted to me. "She's been waiting for you."

"This is Dr. Delaware."

"Hello, doctor. Selena Limberton."

"Hello." We shook hands. Josh said, "Have you had your lunch break yet?"

"No," said the nurse.

"Now would be a good time."

They talked a bit more, about medicines and exercises, and I studied the family portraits, settling on one that showed Harvey Rosenblatt in a dark three-piece suit, beaming in the midst of his brood. Josh around eighteen, with long, unruly hair, a fuzzy mustache, and black-rimmed eyeglasses. Next to him, a beautiful girl with a long, graceful face and sculpted cheekbones, maybe two or three years older. The same dark eyes as her brother. The oldest child was a young man in his midtwenties who resembled Josh, but thick necked and heavier, with cruder features, curly hair, and a full, dark beard that mimicked his father's.

Shirley Rosenblatt was tiny, fair, and blue-eyed, her blond hair cut very short, her smile full but frail even in health. Her shoulders weren't much wider than those of a child. It was hard to imagine her birthing the robust trio.

Mrs. Limberton said, "All righty, then, I'll be back in an hour —where's Leo?"

Josh looked around.

I said, "I think he's hiding behind the couch."

The nurse went over, bent, and lifted the cat. His body was limp. Nuzzling him, she said, "I'll bring you back some chicken if you behave." The cat blinked. She set him down on the couch and he curled up, eyes open and watchful.

Josh said, "Did you feed the fish?"

She smiled. "Yes. Everything's taken care of. Now you don't worry yourself about any more details, she's going to be fine. Nice meeting you, doctor. Bye-bye."

The door closed. Josh frowned.

"Don't worry?" he said. "I went to school to learn how to worry."

27

Another small room, this one yellow, the windows misted by lace curtains.

Shirley Rosenblatt looked better than I had expected, propped up in a hospital bed and covered to the waist with a white comforter. Her hair was still blond, though dyed lighter, and she'd grown it out a little. Her delicate face had remained pretty.

A wicker bed tray was pushed into one corner. To one side of the bed was a cane chair and a pine dresser topped by perfume bottles. Opposite that stood a large saltwater aquarium on a teakwood base. The water bubbled silently. Gorgeous fish glided through a miniature coral reef.

Josh kissed his mother's forehead. She smiled and took hold of his hand. Her fingers barely stretched the width. The comforter dropped a couple of inches. She was wearing a flannel nightgown, buttoned to the neck and fastened with a bow. On her nightstand was a collection of pill bottles, a stack of magazines, and a coil-spring hand-grip exerciser.

Josh held onto her hand. She smiled up at him, then turned the smile on me. Gentle blue eyes. None of her children had gotten them.

Josh said, "Here's the mail. Want me to open it?"

She shook her head and reached out. He put the stack on her lap, but she left it there and continued to look at me.

"This is Dr. Delaware," he said.

I said, "Alex Delaware." But I didn't hold out my hand because I didn't want to dislodge his. "Thanks for seeing me, Dr. Rosenblatt."

"Shirley." Her voice was very weak and talking seemed a great effort, but the word came out clearly. She blinked a couple of times. Her right shoulder was lower than her left and her right eyelid bagged a bit.

She kissed Joshua's hand. Slowly, she said, "You can go, hon."

He looked at me, then back at her. "Sure?"

Nod.

"Okay, but I'm coming back in half an hour. I already let Mrs. Limberton go to lunch and I don't want you alone for too long."

"It's okay. She doesn't eat long."

"I'll make sure she stays all afternoon until I get here—probably not before seven-thirty. I have paperwork. Is that okay, or do you want to eat earlier?"

"Seven-thirty is fine, honey."

"Chinese?"

She nodded and smiled, let go of his hand.

"I can also get Thai if you want," he said. "That place on Fifty-sixth."

"Anything," she said. "As long as it's with you." She reached up with both hands and he bent for a hug.

After he straightened, she said, "Bye, sweets."

"Bye. Take care of yourself."

One final look at me, and then he was gone.

She pushed a button and propped herself up higher. Took a breath and said, "I'm blessed. Working with kids . . . my own turned out great."

"I'm sure it wasn't an accident."

She shrugged. The higher shoulder made it all the way through the gesture. "I don't know . . . so much is chance."

She pointed to the cane chair.

I pulled it up close and sat down.

"You're a child therapist, too?"

I nodded.

She took a long time to touch her lip. Another while to tap her brow. "I think I've seen your name on articles . . . anxiety?"

"Years ago."

"Nice to meet you." Her voice faded. I leaned closer.

"Stroke," she said and tried to shrug again.

I said, "Josh told me."

She looked surprised, then amused. "He hasn't told many people. Protecting me. Sweet. All my kids are. But Josh lives at home, we see more of each other . . ."

"Where are the others?"

"Sarah's in Boston. Teaches pediatrics at Tufts. David's a biologist at the National Cancer Institute in Washington."

"Three for three," I said.

She smiled and looked at the fish tank. "Batting a thousand . . . Harvey liked baseball. You only met him once?"

"Yes." I told her where and when.

"Harvey," she said, savoring the word, "was the nicest man I've ever known. *My* mother used to say don't marry for looks or money, both can disappear fast, so marry for nice."

"Good advice."

"Are you married?"

"Not yet."

"Do you have someone?"

"Yes. And she's very nice."

"Good." She began laughing. Very little sound came out, but her face was animated. Managing to raise one hand, she touched her chest. "Forget the Ph.D. I'm just a Jewish mother."

"Maybe the two aren't all that different."

"No. They are. Therapists don't judge, right? Or at least we pretend we don't. Mothers are always judging."

She tried to lift an envelope from the mail stack. Got hold of a corner and fumbled.

"Tell me," she said, letting go, "about my husband."

I began, including the other murders but leaving out the savagery. When I reached the part about "bad love" and my revenge theory, her eyes started blinking rapidly and I was afraid I'd caused some sort of stress reaction. But when I paused, she said, "Go on," and as I did, she seemed to sit up straighter and taller, and a cool, analytic light sharpened her eyes.

The therapist in her driving out the patient.

I'd been there. Now I was on the couch, opening myself up to this tiny, crippled woman.

When I was finished, she looked at the dresser and said, "Open that middle drawer and take out the file."

I found a black-and-white marbled box with a snap latch resting atop neatly folded sweaters. As I started to hand it to her, she said, "Open it."

I sat down beside her and unlatched the box. Inside were documents, a thick sheaf of them. On top was Harvey Rosenblatt's medical license.

"Go on," she said.

I began leafing. Psychiatric board certification. Internship and residency papers. A certificate from the Robert Evanston Hale Psychoanalytic Institute in Manhattan. Another from Southwick Hospital. A six-year-old letter from the dean of the NYU medical school reaffirming Rosenblatt's appointment as associate clinical professor of psychiatry. An honorable discharge from the Navy, where he'd served as a flight surgeon aboard an aircraft carrier. A couple of life insurance policies, one issued by the American Psychiatric Association. So he had been a member—the absence of an obituary was probably due to shame about suicide. As I came to his last will and testament, Shirley Rosenblatt looked away.

Death certificate. Burial forms.

I heard her say, "Should be next."

Next was a stapled collection of photocopied sheets. The face sheet was white. Handwritten on it was "Investig. Info."

I removed it from the box. She sank back against the pillows and I saw that she was breathing hard. When I began to read, she closed her eyes.

Page two was a police report. The writer was one Detective Salvatore J. Giordano, 19th Precinct, Borough of Manhattan, City of New York. In his

opinion, and supported by subsequently entered Medical Examiner's Report, Case #1453331, Deceased Victim Rosenblatt, H. A., white male, age 59, expired as the consequence of a rapid downward descent from diagrammed window B, master bedroom, of said address on E. 67 St., and subsequent extreme bodily contact with pavement in front of said address.

Descent process was most probably self-induced, as
D. Victim's blood alcohol was not elevated and there is
no lab evidence of drug-induced accident and no signs of
coerced egress enforced on Deceased Victim on the part
of another as well as no skidmarks on the carpeting of
said address or defense marks on window sills, and, in
summary, no evidence of the presence of any other individual at said address. Of further note is the presence of
Drinking Glass A (see diagram) and Apparatus B (see
diagram) conforming to method operandus of the "East
Side Burglar."

An aerial diagram at the bottom of the page illustrated the
locations of doors, windows, and furniture in the room where
Harvey Rosenblatt had spent his last moments.

A bed, two nightstands, two dressers—one marked "Low,"
the other "High"—a television set, something marked "antique,"
and a magazine rack. On one of the nightstands were written
"Glass A" and "Apparatus B (lockpicks, files, and keys)." Arrows
marked the window from which the psychiatrist had leaped.

The next paragraph identified the apartment as an eighth-
floor, five-room unit in a co-op building. At the time of Rosenblatt's jump, the owners and sole occupants, Mr. and Mrs.
Malcolm J. Rulerad, he a banker, she an attorney, were away in
Europe on a three-week vacation. Neither had ever met

deceased Victim Rosenblatt and both witnesses state un-
equivocally that they have no idea how D.V. gained ingress to said domicile. However, the burglary apparatus
recovered from a bathroom of said domicile indicates
Breaking and Entering, and the fact that the day doorman, Mr. William P. O'Donnell, states he never saw D.
Victim enter the building's main lobby, indicates a
stealthy ingress by D. Victim. Furthermore, Drinking
Glass A, subsequently identified by Mrs. Rulerad as coming from her kitchen, was full of a dark liquid, subsequently identified as Diet Pepsi-Cola, a drink favored by
Mrs. M. Rulerad, and this is in conformity with the
method operandus of three prior B and E burglaries
within a six-block radius, previously attributed to the

"East Side Burglar," in which soft drinks were displayed in a partially drunk status. Though D. Victim's wife denies a criminal history on the part of D. Victim, who she says was a psychiatrist, physical evidence indicates a "secret life" on the part of D. Victim and a possible motive: guilt over said secret life due to D. Victim being a psychiatrist and outward "solid citizen" and finally coming to grips with this unrespectable secret.

Next came a half page follow-up by Detective Giordano, dated a week later:

> Case #1453331, Rosenblatt, H. Requested permission from D. Victim's wife to search home premises on E. 65 St. due to search for evidence related to D. Victim's death. Said search effected 4/17/85 at 3:23 P.M. to 5:17 P.M. in company of Det. B. Wildebrandt and Officer J. McGovern. Home and office premises of D. Victim searched in presence of D. Victim's wife, Shirley Rosenblatt. No contraband from previous "East Side Burglaries" found. Permission requested to read D. Victim's psychiatric files for possible patient/fence connection, refused by S. Rosenblatt. Will consult with Chief of Dets. A. M. Talisiani.

The following page was typed on a different machine and signed by Detective Lewis S. Jackson, 19th Precinct. The date was four weeks later.

> Conf. on Det. Giordano's case, #1453331, H. A. Rosenblatt. Det. Giordano on med. leave. D. Victim's wife, Shirley Rosenblatt, and son, Joshua Rosenblatt, requested meeting to review case. Wanting "progress" report. Met with them at Pcnct. Told of disposition. Very angry, said they were "deceived" as to purpose of home search. Son stated he is an attorney, knows "people." He and mother convinced hom., not sui. Stated D.V. not depressed, never depressed, not "criminal." Further stated "there was some sort of setup." Further stated D.V. had talked to wife, prior to death, about "upsetting case that could be related to what happened to my dad," but when asked

for details, said he didn't know because D.V. was psychiatrist and kept secrets because of "ethics." When told
nothing more could be done based on available evidence,
son became even more irate and threatened to "go above
you to get some action." Conversation reported to Chief
of Dets. A. M. Talisiani.

The final two pages consisted of a letter on heavy white bond,
dated one and a half months later.

COMSAC INVESTIGATIVE SERVICES
513 Fifth Avenue
Suite 3463
New York, NY 10110

June 30, 1985

Dr. Shirley Rosenblatt
c/o J. Rosenblatt, Esq.
Schechter, Mohl, and Trimmer
500 Fifth Avenue
Suite 3300
New York, NY 10110

Dear Dr. Rosenblatt:
    Pursuant to your request, we have reviewed data and materials
relevant to the unfortunate death of your husband, including but
not limited to detailed inspection of all case reports, forensic reports,
and laboratory analyses. We have also interviewed police personnel
involved in this case.

    Personal inspection of the premises where aforesaid unfortunate
death took place was not fully accomplished because the owners of
the apartment in question, Mr. and Mrs. Malcolm J. Rulerad, did
not grant permission to our staff to enter and inspect. However, we
do feel that we have accrued enough data with which to evaluate
your case and we regret to inform you that we see no reason to
doubt the conclusions of the police department in this matter. Fur-
thermore, in view of the specific details of this case, we do not advise
any further investigation into this matter.

Please feel free to get in touch if there are any questions concerning this matter.

Respectfully yours,
Robert D. Sugrue
Senior Investigator and Supervisor

INVOICE FOR SERVICES RENDERED

Twenty-two (22) hours at
Sixty-Five (65) Dollars per Hour: $1430.00

Minus 10% Professional Discount to
Schechter, Mohl, and Trimmer, Attys: $1287.00

Please Remit This Sum

I put down the file.

Shirley Rosenblatt's eyes were wide open and moist.

"The second death," she said. "Like killing him again." Shake of head. "Four years . . . but it's still—that's why Josh is so angry. No resolution. Now, you come . . ."

"I'm—"

"No." She managed to place a finger over her mouth. Dropped it and smiled. "Good. The truth outs."

Wider smile, a different meaning behind it.

"Harvey as a burglar," she said. "It's almost funny. And I'm not in prolonged denial. I lived with him for thirty-one years."

Sounding resolute, but she looked to me for confirmation, anyway.

I nodded.

She shook her head. "So how did he get in that apartment, right? That's what they kept asking me, and I didn't know what to tell them."

"He was lured there," I said. "Probably under the guise of a patient call. Someone he thought he could help."

"Harvey," she said softly. She closed her eyes. Opened them. "The police kept saying suicide. Over and over. . . . Because Harvey was a psychiatrist, one of them—the chief of detectives—Talisiani—told me everyone knew psychiatrists had a high suicide rate. Then he told me to consider myself lucky that they weren't pursuing it further. That if they did, everything would come out."

" 'In view of the specific details of this case,' " I said.

"That's the private one, right? Comsac. At least the police were a lot more . . . direct. Talisiani told me if we made waves Harvey's name would be dragged through the slime. The whole family would be permanently coated with 'slime.' He seemed *offended* that we didn't want him to close the case. As if we were criminals. Everyone made us feel that way . . . and now you're coming and telling me we were right."

She managed to press her palms together. "Thank you."

She slumped back on the pillow and breathed hard through dry lips. Tears filled her eyes, overflowed, and began draining down her cheeks. I wiped them with a tissue. Her lower body still hadn't moved.

"I'm so sad," she whispered. "Thinking about it, again . . . picturing it. But I'm glad you've come. You've . . . validated me —us. I'm only sorry you have to go through this pain. You really think it's something to do with Andres?"

"I do."

"Harvey never said anything."

I said, "The upsetting case Josh told Detective Jackson about—"

"A few weeks before . . ." Two deep breaths. "We were lunching, Harvey and I. We had lunch almost every day. He was upset. He was rarely upset—such an even man . . . he said it was a case. A patient he'd just talked to, he'd found it very disillusioning."

She turned toward me and her face was quaking.

"Disillusioned about Andres?" I said.

"He didn't mention Andres's name . . . didn't give me any details."

"Nothing at all?"

"Harvey and I never talked about cases. We made that rule right at the beginning of our marriage . . . two therapists . . . it's so easy to slip. You tell yourself it's . . . okay, it's professional consultation. And then you let loose more details than you need to. And then names slip out . . . and then you're talking about patients to your therapist friends at cocktail parties." She shook her head. "Rules are best."

"But Harvey must have told you something to make you suspect a connection to his death."

"No," she said sadly. "We really didn't suspect . . . we were just . . . grasping. Looking for anything out of the ordinary. So the police would see Harvey didn't . . . the whole thing was so . . . psychotic. Harvey in a stranger's apartment."

Remembered shame colored her face.

I said, "The owners of the apartment—the Rulerads. Harvey didn't know them?"

"They were mean people. Cold. I called the wife and begged her to let the private detective in to look. I even apologized—for what I don't know. She told me I was lucky she wasn't suing me for Harvey's break-in and hung up."

She closed her eyes for a long time and didn't move. I wondered if she'd fallen asleep.

Then she said, "Harvey was so affected . . . by this patient. *That's* what made me suspect. Cases never got to him. To be disillusioned . . . Andres? It doesn't make sense."

"De Bosch was his teacher, wasn't he? If Harvey learned something terrible about him, that could have disillusioned him."

Slow, sad nod.

I said, "How close was their relationship?"

"Teacher and student close. Harvey admired Andres, though he thought he was a little . . . authoritarian."

"Authoritarian in what way?"

"Dogmatic—when he was convinced he was right. Harvey thought it ironic, since Andres had fought so hard against the Nazis . . . wrote so passionately for democracy . . . yet his personal style could be so . . ."

"Dictatorial?"

"At times. But Harvey still admired him. For who he was, what he'd done. Saving those French children from the Vichy government, his work on child development. And he *was* a good teacher. Once in a while I sat in on seminars. Andres holding court —like a don. He could talk for hours and keep you interested . . . lots of jokes. Tying everything in with punchlines. Sometimes he brought children in from the wards. He had a gift—they opened up to him."

"What about Katarina?" I said. "Harvey told me she sat in, too."

"She did . . . just a child, herself—a teenager, but she spoke up as if she was a peer. And now she's . . . and those other people—how can this be!"

"Sometimes authoritarianism can go too far," I said.

Her cheeks shook. Then her mouth turned up in a tiny, disturbing smile. "Yes, I suppose nothing's what it seems, is it? Patients have been telling me that for thirty years and I've been nodding and saying, yes, I know . . . I really didn't know . . ."

"Did you ever go back into Harvey's files? To try to figure which patient had upset him?"

Long stare. Guilty nod.

"He kept tapes," she said. "He didn't like writing—arthritis—so he taped. I wouldn't let the police listen to them . . . protecting the patients. But later, I began playing them for myself . . . I gave myself an excuse. For their own good—I was responsible for them, until they found another permanent therapist. Had to call them, to notify them . . . so I needed to know them." Downcast eyes. "Flimsy . . . I listened anyway. Months of sessions, Harvey's voice . . . sometimes I couldn't stand it. But there was nothing that would have disillusioned him. All his patients were like old friends. He hadn't taken on any new ones for two years."

"None at all?"

She shook her head. "Harvey was an old-fashioned analyst. The couch, free association, long-term, intensive work. The same fifteen people, three to five times a week."

"Even an old patient might have told him something disillusioning."

"No," she said, "there was nothing like that in any of the sessions. And none of his old patients brought him to harm. They all loved him."

"What did you do with the tapes?"

Rather than answer, she said, "He was gentle, accepting. He helped those people. They were all crushed."

"Did you pick any of them up as patients?"

"No . . . I was in no shape to work. Not for a long time. Even my own patients . . ." She attempted another shrug. "Things fell apart for a while . . . so many people let down. That's why I didn't pursue his death. For my kids and for his patients—his extended family. For me. I couldn't have us dragged through the slime. Do you understand?"

"Of course." I asked her again what she'd done with the tapes.

"I destroyed them," she said, as if hearing the question for the first time. "Smashed the cassettes with a hammer . . . one by one

. . . what a mess . . . threw it all away." She smiled. "Cathar-
sis?"

I said, "Did Harvey attend any conventions just before his
death? Any psychiatric meetings or seminars on child welfare?"

"No. Why?"

"Because professional meetings may set the killer off. Two of
the other therapists were murdered at conventions. And the de
Bosch symposium where I met Harvey may have triggered the
killings in the first place."

"No," she said. "No, he didn't attend anything. He'd sworn
off conventions. Sworn off academia. Gave up his appointment at
NYU so he could concentrate on his patients and his family and
getting in shape—his father had died young of a heart attack. Harvey had reached that age, confronted his own mortality. He was
starting to work out. Trimming the fat from his diet and his life—
that's a quote. . . . He said he wanted to be around for me and
the kids for a long, long time."

Grimacing, she lifted her hand, with effort, and let it drop
upon mine. Her palm was soft and cold. Her eyes aimed at the
fish tank and stayed there.

"Is there anything else you can tell me?" I said. "Anything at
all?"

She thought for a long time. "No . . . I'm sorry, I wish there
was."

"Thanks for seeing me," I said. Her hand weighed a ton.

"Please let me know," she said, keeping it there. "Whatever
you find."

"I will."

"How long will you be in New York?"

"I think I'll try to head back this evening."

"If you need a place to stay, you're welcome here . . . if you
don't mind a pull-out couch."

"That's very kind," I said, "but I need to be getting back."

"Your nice woman?"

"And my home." Whatever that meant.

Grimacing, she exerted barely tangible pressure upon my
hand. Giving *me* comfort.

We heard the door close, then footsteps. Josh came in, holding
Leo, the cat. He looked at our hands and his eyebrows dipped.

"You okay?" he said to his mother.

"Yes, honey. Dr. Delaware's been helpful. It's good you brought him."

"Helpful how?"

"He validated us . . . about Dad."

"Great," said Josh, putting the cat down. "Meanwhile, you're not getting enough rest."

Her lower lip dropped.

"Enough exertion, Mom," he said. *"Please.* You have to rest."

"I'm okay, honey. Really."

I felt a small tug atop my hand, not much more than a muscle twitch. Lifting her hand and placing it on the bedcovers, I stood.

Josh walked around the other side of the bed and began straightening the covers. "You *really* need to rest, Mom. The doctor said rest is the most important thing."

"I know . . . I'm sorry . . . I will, Josh."

"Good."

She made a gulping sound. Tears clouded the gentle blue eyes.

"Oh, Mom," he cried out, sounding ten years old.

"It's okay, honey."

"No, no, I'm being an asshole, I'm sorry, it's been a really tough day."

"Tell me about it, baby."

"Believe me, you don't want to hear it."

"Yes, I do. Tell me."

He sat down next to her. I slipped out the door and saw myself out of the apartment.

28

I reserved a seat on the next flight back to L.A., threw clothes in my bag, and told Milo and Rick's message machine my arrival time. Checking out of the Middleton, I flagged a taxi to Kennedy.

A fire on Queens Boulevard slowed things down and it took an hour and three quarters to reach the airport. When I got to the check-in counter, I learned my flight had been delayed for thirty-five minutes. Pay TVs were attached to some of the seats, and travelers stared at their screens as if some kind of truth was being broadcast.

I found a terminal lounge that looked half decent and downed a leathery corned beef sandwich and a club soda while eavesdropping on a group of salesmen. Their truths were simple: the economy sucked and women didn't know what the hell they wanted.

I returned to the departure area, found a free TV, and fed it quarters. A local station was broadcasting the news and that seemed about as good as it was going to get.

Potholes in the Bronx. Condom handouts in the public schools. The mayor fighting with the city council as the city accrued crushing debt. That made me feel right at home.

A few more local stories, and then the anchorwoman said, "Nationally, government statistics show a decline in consumer spending, and a Senate subcommittee is investigating charges of influence peddling by another of the President's sons. And in California, officials at Folsom Prison report that a lockdown has apparently been successful in averting riots in the wake of what is believed to have been a racially motivated double murder at that maximum-security facility. Early this morning, two inmates, both believed to have been associates of a white supremacist gang, were stabbed to death by unknown inmates suspected of belonging to the Nuestra Raza, a Mexican gang. The dead men, identified as Rennard Russell Haupt and Donald Dell Wallace, were both serving sentences for murder. A prison investigation into the killings continues . . ."

Nuestra Raza. NR forever. The tattoos on Roddy Rodriguez's hands. . . .

I thought of Rodriguez's masonry yard, shut down, cleaned out, and padlocked. The flight from the house on McVine prepared well in advance.

Evelyn had entertained me in her backyard, as her husband's homeboys honed their shanks.

Making an appointment for Wednesday, then going into the house with her husband and changing it to Thursday.

Twenty-four more hours for getaway.

Hurley Keffler's debacle at my house made sense now, as did Sherman Bucklear's nagging. Prison rumblings had probably told the Iron Priests what was brewing. Locating Rodriguez might have forestalled the hit or, if the deed had already been done, given the Priests instant payback.

Payback.

The same old stupid cycle of violence.

Burglary tools and a quick shove out a eight-story window.

A corpse on a garage floor, a little boy baby never to be.

Two little girls on the run.

Were Chondra and Tiffani in some Mexican border town, being tutored in Fugitive 1A with more care than they'd ever been taught to read or write?

Or maybe Evelyn had taken them somewhere they could blend in. On the surface. But, suckled on violence, they'd always be different. Unable to understand why, years later, they gravitated toward cruel, violent men.

Static dripped out of the speakers—a barely comprehensible

voice announcing something about boarding. I got up and took my place in line. Six thousand miles in less than twenty-four hours. My mind and my legs ached. I wondered if Shirley Rosenblatt would ever be able to walk again.

Soon, I'd be three time zones away from her problems and a lot closer to my own.

The flight got in just before midnight. The terminal was deserted and Robin was waiting outside the automatic doors.

"You look exhausted," she said, as we walked to her truck.

"I've felt perkier."

"Well, I've got some news that might perk you up. Milo called just before I left to pick you up. Something about the tape. I was just out the door and he was running, too, but he says he learned something important."

"The sheriff who was working on it must have picked up something. Where's Milo now?"

"Out on some assignment. He said he'd be home when we got there."

"Which home?"

The question threw her. "Oh—Milo's house. He and Rick took really good care of us. And home is where the heart is, right?"

I slept in the car. We pulled up at Milo's house at twelve-forty. He was waiting in the living room, wearing a gray polo shirt and jeans. A cup of coffee was in front of him, next to a portable tape recorder. The dog snored at his feet, but woke up when we came in, gave out a few desultory licks, then collapsed again.

"Welcome home, boys and girls."

I put my bags down. "Did you hear about Donald Dell?"

Milo nodded.

"What?" said Robin.

I told her.

She said, "Oh . . ."

Milo said, "Nuestra Raza. Could be the father-in-law."

"That's what I figured. It's probably why Evelyn post-

poned her appointment with me. Rodriguez told her they had to
leave Wednesday. And why Hurley Keffler hassled me—where is
he?"

"Still in. I found a few traffic warrants and had one of the
jailers lose his paperwork—just another few days, but every little
bit helps."

Robin said, "It never ends."

"It's all right," I said. "There's no reason for the Priests to
bother us."

"True," said Milo, too quickly. "They and the Raza boys will
be concentrating on each other now. That's their main game: my
turn to die, your turn to die."

"Lovely," said Robin.

"I had some Foothill guys drop in on them after Keffler's
bust," he said, "but I'll see if I can arrange another visit.
Don't worry about them, Rob. Really. They're the least of our
problems."

"As opposed to?"

He looked at the tape recorder.

We sat down. He punched a button.

The child's voice came on.

> Bad love bad love.
> Don't give me the bad love.

I looked at him. He held up a finger.

> Bad love bad love.
> Don't give me the bad love . . .

Same flat tones, but this time the voice was that of a man.

Ordinary, middle-pitched, male voice. Nothing remarkable
about the accent or the timbre.

The child's voice transformed—some kind of electronic manipulation?

Something familiar about the voice . . . but I couldn't
place it.

Someone I'd met a long time ago? In 1979?

The room was silent, except for the dog's breathing.

Milo turned the recorder off and looked at me. "Ring any bells?"

I said, "There's something about it, but I don't know what it is."

"The kid's voice was phony. What you just heard might be the real bad guy. No bells, huh?"

"Let me hear it again."

Rewind. Play.

"Again," I said.

This time, I listened with my eyes closed, squinting so hard the lids felt welded together.

Listening to someone who hated me.

Nothing registered.

Robin and Milo studied my face as if it were some great wonder. My head hurt badly.

"No," I said. "I still can't pinpoint it—I can't even be sure I've actually heard it."

Robin touched my shoulder. Milo's face was blank, but his eyes showed disappointment.

I glanced at the recorder and nodded.

He rewound again.

This time the voice seemed even more distant—as if my memory was spiraling away from me. As if I'd missed my chance.

"Goddammit," I said. The dog's eyes opened. He trotted over to me and nuzzled my hand. I rubbed his head, looked at Milo. "One more time."

Robin said, "You're tired. Why don't we try again in the morning?"

"Just once more," I said.

Rewind. Play.

The voice.

Completely foreign now. Mocking me.

I buried my face in my hands. Robin's hands on my neck were an abstract comfort—I appreciated the sentiment but couldn't relax.

"What did you mean *might* be the bad guy?" I asked Milo.

"Sheriff's scientific guess. He tuned it down from the kid's voice using a preset frequency."

"How can he be sure the kid's voice was altered in the first place?"

"Because his machines told him so. He came across it by accident—working on the screams—which, incidentally, he's ninety-nine percent positive are Hewitt's. Then he got to the kid chanting and something bothered him about it—the evenness of the voice."

"The robot quality," I said.

"Yeah. But he didn't assume brainwashing or anything else psychological. He's a techno-dude, so he analyzed the sound waves and saw something fishy with the cycle-to-cycle amplitude—the changes in pitch within each sound wave. Real human voices shimmer and jitter. This didn't, so he knew the tape had been messed with electronically, probably using a pitch shifter. It's a gizmo that samples a sound and changes the frequency. Tune up, you've got Alvin and the Chipmunks; tune down, you're James Earl Jones."

"Hi-tech bad guy," I said.

"Not really. The basic machines are pretty cheap. People attach them to phones—women living alone wanting to sound like Joe Testosterone. They're also used for recording music—creating automatic harmonies. A singer lays down a vocal track, then creates a harmony and overdubs it, instant Everly Brothers."

"Sure," said Robin. "Shifters are used all the time. I've seen them interfaced with amps so guitarists can do multiple tracks."

"Lyle Gritz," I said. "The next Elvis. . . . How'd the sheriff know which frequency to tune down to?"

"He assumed we were dealing with a male bad guy using a relatively cheap shifter because nowadays the better machines *can* be programmed to include jitter. The cheap ones usually come with two, maybe three standard settings: tune up to kid, tune down to adult, sometimes there's an intermediate setting for adult female. By computing the pitch difference, he worked backwards and tuned down. But if our guy's some sort of acoustics nut with fancy equipment, there may be other things he's done to alter his voice and what you heard may be nowhere near his real voice."

"It may not even be his voice that he altered. He could have shifted someone else's."

"That, too. But you think you might have heard him before."

"That was my first impression. But I don't know. I don't trust my judgment anymore."

"Well," he said, "at least we know there's no actual kid involved."

"Thank God for that. Okay, leave the tape with me. I'll work with it tomorrow, see if anything clicks."

"The screams being Hewitt, what does 'ninety-nine percent' mean?"

"It means the sheriff'll get up on the stand and testify it's highly probable to the best of his professional knowledge. Only trouble is, we need to get someone on trial first."

"So I was right, this isn't some homeless guy. He'd need a place to keep his equipment."

He shrugged. "Maybe he's got a secret den somewhere and that's where he's hiding out right now. I had talks about Gritz with detectives at other substations. If the scrote's still lurking around, we'll hook him."

"He is," I said. "He hasn't completed his homework."

I told Milo what I'd learned in New York.

He said, "Pseudo-burglary? Sounds hokey."

"New York cops didn't think so. It matched some previous break-ins in the neighborhood: jimmied locks, people on vacation, a glass of soda left on the bedroom nightstand. Soda from the victim's kitchen. Sound familiar?"

"Were any of the other burglaries in the papers?"

"I don't know."

"If they were, all we've probably got is a copycat. If they weren't, maybe our killer has a burglary sideline. Why don't you get a hold of some four-year-old papers and find out. I'll phone New York and see if Gritz's name or Silk-Merino's shows up on their blotters around the time of Rosenblatt's fall."

"He's been pretty careful about keeping his nose clean so far."

"It doesn't have to be a major felony, Alex. Son of Sam got busted on a parking ticket. Lots of cases get solved that way, the stupid stuff."

"Okay," I said. "I'll hit the library soon as it opens."

He picked up his cup and drank. "So what's Rosenblatt's motive for jumping supposed to have been?"

"Guilt. Coming to grips with his secret criminal identity."

He scowled. "What, he's standing there, about to glom jewelry, and he suddenly gets a guilt flash? Sounds like horseshit to me."

"The family thought so, too, but the New York police seemed convinced. They told the widow if she pressed the issue, everyone's name would be dragged through the slime. A private investigator she hired told her the same thing, more tactfully."

I gave him names and he jotted them down.

Looking into his coffee, he said, "You want, there's still some in the pot."

"No, thanks."

Robin said, "Another fall—just like the other two."

"Delmar Parker's run off the mountain," I said. "That has to be the connection. The killer was traumatized in a major way and is trying to get even. We've got to find out more about the accident."

Milo said, "I still haven't had any luck locating Delmar's mother. And none of the Santa Barbara papers covered the crash."

"Out of all those Corrective School alumni," I said, "someone's got to know."

"Still no files, anywhere. Sally and the gang pried up Katarina's floorboards. And we can't find any records, yet, of de Bosch applying for government funds."

Over the rim of his cup, his face was heavy and beat. He ran his hand over it.

"It bothers me," he said. "Rosenblatt—an experienced psychiatrist—meeting someone in a strange apartment like that."

"He was experienced, but he had a soft heart. The killer could have lured him there with a cry for help."

"That's not exactly standard operating shrink procedure, is it? Was Rosenblatt some kind of avant-garde guy, believed in on-the-scene treatment?"

"His wife said he was an orthodox analyst."

"Those guys *never* leave the office, right? Need their couches and their little notebooks."

"True, but she also said he'd been very upset by something that had happened in a session recently. Disillusioned. It's a reasonable bet it had something to do with de Bosch. Something that shook him up enough to meet the killer out of the office. He could have believed he was going to the killer's home—the killer could have given him a good rationale for meeting there. Like a disability that kept him homebound—maybe even bedridden. The window Rosenblatt went out of was in a bedroom."

"Phony cripple," he said, nodding. "Then Rosenblatt goes to

the window and the bad guy jumps up, shoves him out . . . very cold. And the wife had no idea what disillusioned him enough to make a house call?"

"She tried to find out. Broke her own rules and listened to his therapy tapes. But there was nothing out of the ordinary in them."

"This disillusioning thing definitely happened during a session?"

"That's what he told her."

"So maybe the session where he died wasn't the first with the killer. So why wasn't the first session on tape?"

"Maybe Rosenblatt didn't take his recorder with him. Or the patient requested no taping. Rosenblatt would have complied. Or maybe the session was recorded and the tape got destroyed."

"A stranger's bedroom—that has almost a sexual flavor to it, don't you think?"

I nodded. "The ritual."

"Who owned the place?"

"A couple named Rulerad. They said they'd never heard of Harvey Rosenblatt. Shirley said they were pretty hostile to her. Refused access to the private detective and threatened to sue her."

"Can't really blame them, can you? Come home and find out someone broke into your place and used it for a swan dive. Was Rosenblatt the type to be a soft touch for a sob story?"

"Definitely. He probably got the same kind of call Bert Harrison did and responded to it. And died because of it."

Milo said, "So why did the killer keep his appointment with Rosenblatt but not with Harrison? Why, now that I'm thinking about it, was Harrison let off the hook completely? *He* worked for de Bosch, *he* spoke at that goddamn conference, too. So how come everyone else in that boat is sunk or sinking and *he's* on shore drinking piña coladas?"

"I don't know."

"I mean, that's funny, don't you think, Alex? That break in the pattern—maybe I should learn a little more about Harrison."

"Maybe," I said, feeling sick. "Wouldn't *that* be something. There I was, sitting across the table from him—trying to protect him . . . he treated Mitch Lerner. He knew where Katarina lived . . . hard to believe. He seemed like such a sweet guy."

"Any idea where he's gone?"

I shook my head. "But he's not exactly unobtrusive with those purple clothes."

"Purple clothes?" said Robin.

"He says it's the only color he can see."

"Another weird one," said Milo. "What is it about your profession?"

"Ask the killer," I said. "He's got strong opinions on the subject."

29

We spent the night at Milo's. After he left for work, I stayed and listened to the tape another dozen times.

The chanting man sounded like an accountant tallying up a sum.

That maddening hint of familiarity, but nothing jelled.

We returned to Benedict Canyon, where Robin took the dog to the garage and I called in for messages. One from Jean Jeffers—*No record of Mr. G*—and a request to phone Judge Stephen Huff.

I reached him in his chambers.

"Hi, Alex. I assume you heard."

"Is there anything I should know other than what's been on the news?"

"They're pretty positive who did it, but can't prove it yet. Two Mexican gang members—they're figuring some kind of drug war."

"That's probably it," I said.

"Well, that's one way to settle a case. Any word from the grandmother?"

"Not a one."

"Better off—the kids, I mean. Away from all of this—don't you think?"

"Depends on what environment they've been placed into."

"Oh, sure. Absolutely. Well, thanks for your help. Onward toward justice."

*   *   *

Several more tries at the tape, then I left for the Beverly Hills library.

I scoured four- and five-year-old editions of New York dailies all morning, reading very slowly and carefully, but finding no record of any "East Side Burglar."

No great surprise: the 19th Precinct serviced a high-priced zip code, and its inhabitants probably despised getting their names anywhere in the paper other than the society pages. The people who *owned* the papers and broadcast the news probably lived in the 19th. The rest of the city would know exactly what they wanted it to.

Lack of coverage still didn't mean Rosenblatt's killer had committed the earlier break-ins. Local residents might be aware of the burglaries, and a local could know who was on vacation and for how long. But the idea of a 19th Precinct resident owning burglary tools and robbing from his neighbors seemed less than likely. So Mr. Silk probably had burgled before. Ritualistically.

The same attempt to use what was at hand, to master and dominate the victim.

Bad love.

Myra Evans Paprock.

Rodney Shipler.

Katarina.

Only at those three scenes had the words been left behind.

Three bloody, undisguised murders. No attempt made to present them as anything else.

Stoumen, Lerner, and Rosenblatt, on the other hand, had been dispatched as phony accidents.

Two classes of victims . . . two kinds of revenge?

Butchery for the laypeople, falls for the therapists.

But *Katarina* had been a therapist . . .

Then I realized that at the time of Mr. Silk's trauma—sometime before seventy-nine, probably closer to seventy-three, the year Delmar Parker had gone off the mountain—she hadn't yet graduated. In her early twenties, still a grad student.

Two patterns . . . part of some elaborate rage-lust fantasy that a sane mind could never hope to understand?

And where did Becky Basille fit in?

Two killers . . .

I remembered the clean, bustling street where Harvey Rosenblatt had landed: French restaurants, flower boxes, and limos.

How long had it taken the poor man to realize what the swift, sharp shove at the small of his back meant?

I hoped he hadn't. Hoped, against logic, that he'd felt nothing but the Icarus-pleasure of pure flight.

A fall, always a fall.

Delmar Parker. Had to be.

Avenging an abused child?

Surely if de Bosch had been abusive, someone would remember.

Why hadn't anyone spoken out after all these years?

But no big puzzle there: without proof, who would believe them? And why rake up the dirt around a dead man's grave if it meant stirring up one's own childhood demons?

Still, *someone* had to know what happened to the boy in the stolen truck, and why it had set off a killer.

I sat there for a long time, staring at tiny, microfilmed words.

Corrective School alumni . . . how to get hold of them. Then I thought of one. Someone I'd never met, a name I'd never even learned.

A problem child whose treatment had given Katarina the leash to put around my neck.

I returned the microfilm spools and rushed to the pay phones in the library's lobby, trying to figure out who to call.

Western Pediatric, the late seventies . . .

The hospital had undergone a massive financial and professional overhaul during the past year. So many people gone.

But one notable one had returned.

Reuben Eagle had been chief resident when I'd started as a staff psychologist. He'd taken a professorship at the U's med school, a gifted teacher, specializing in medical education. The new Western Peds board had just wooed him back as general pediatrics division head. I'd just seen his picture in the hospital newsletter: the same tortoiseshell spectacles, the light brown hair thinner, grayer, the lean, ruddy outdoorsman's face adorned by a trimmed, graying beard.

His secretary said he was out on the wards and I asked her to page him. He answered a few moments later, saying, "Rube Eagle," in a soft, pleasant voice.

"Rube, it's Alex Delaware."

"Alex—wow, this is a surprise."

"How're things going?"

"Not bad, how about you?"

"Hanging in. Listen, Rube, I need a small favor. I'm trying to locate one of Henry Bork's daughters and I was wondering if you had any idea how to reach her."

"Which daughter? Henry and Mo had a bunch—three or four, I think."

"The youngest. She had learning problems, was sent to a remedial school in Santa Barbara around seventy-six or seventy-seven. She'd be around twenty-eight or twenty-nine now."

"That would have to be Meredith," he said. "*Her* I remember because one year Henry had the interns' party at his house and she was there—very good-looking, a real flirt. I thought she was older and ended up talking to her. Then someone warned me and I split fast."

"Warned you about her age?"

"That and her problems. Supposedly a wild kid. I remember hearing something about institutionalization. Apparently she really put Henry and Mo through it—did you know he died?"

"Yes," I said.

"Ben Wardley, too. And Milt Chenier . . . how come you're looking for Meredith?"

"Long story, Rube. It has to do with the school she was sent to."

"What about it?"

"Things may have happened there."

"Happened? *Another* mess?" He sounded more sad than surprised.

"It's possible."

"Anything I should know about?"

"Not unless you had something to do with the school—the Corrective School, founded by a psychologist named Andres de Bosch."

"Nope," he said. "Well, I hope you clear it up. And as far as Meredith's concerned, I think she still lives in L.A. Something to do with the film business."

"Is her name still Bork?"

"Hmm, don't know—if you'd like I can call Mo and find out. She's still pretty involved with the hospital—I can tell her I'm putting a mailing list together or something."

"I'd really appreciate that, Rube."

"Stay on the line, I'll see if I can get her."

I waited for fifteen minutes with the speaker to my mouth. Pretending to look busy each time someone came by to use the phone. Finally, Rube came back on the line.

"Alex?"

"Still here."

"Yes, Meredith's in L.A. She has her own public relations firm. I don't know if she ever married, but she still goes by Bork."

He gave me the address and phone number and I thanked him again.

"Sure bet . . . another mess. Too bad. How'd you get involved, Alex? Through a patient?"

"No," I said. "Someone sent me a message."

Bork and Hoffman Public Relations, 8845 Wilshire Boulevard, Suite 304.

The eastern edge of Beverly Hills. A five-minute ride from the library.

The receptionist said, "Ms. Bork is on another line."

"I'll hold."

"And what was the name again?"

"Dr. Alex Delaware. I worked with her father at Western Pediatric Medical Center."

"One moment, sir."

A few minutes later: "Sir? Ms. Bork will be right with you." Then, a smoky female voice: "Meredith Bork."

I introduced myself.

She said, "I specialize in the entertainment industries, doctor —movies, theater. We do a few doctors when they write books. Have you written a book?"

"No—"

"Just want to beef up your practice, a little press exposure? Good idea in today's economy, but it's not our thing. Sorry. I'll be happy to give you the name of someone who does medical publicity, though—"

"Thanks, but I'm not looking for a publicist."

"Oh?"

"Ms. Bork, I'm sorry to bother you, but what I'm after is some information about Andres de Bosch and the Corrective School, in Santa Barbara."

Silence.

"Ms. Bork?"

"This is for *real*?"

"Some suspicions have come up about mistreatment at the school. Things that happened during the early seventies. An accident involving a boy named Delmar Parker."

No answer.

"May, nineteen seventy-three," I said. "Delmar Parker went off a mountain road and died. Do you remember hearing anything about him? Or anything about mistreatment?"

"This is too much," she said. "Why the fuck is this any of *your* business?"

"I work as a consultant to the police."

"The *police* are investigating the school?"

"They're doing a preliminary investigation."

Harsh laughter. "You're putting me on."

"No." I gave her Milo as a reference.

She said, "Okay, so? What makes you think I even went to this school?"

"I worked at Western Pediatric Medical Center when your father was chief of staff and—"

"Word got around. Oh, I'll just bet it did. Jesus."

"Ms. Bork, I'm really sorry—"

"I'll just bet it did . . . the Corrective School." Another angry laugh. "Finally."

Silence.

"After all these years. What a trip . . . the Corrective School. For bad little children in need of correction. Yeah, I was corrected, all right. I was corrected up the ying-yang."

"Were you mistreated?"

"Mistreated?" Peals of laughter so loud I backed away from the receiver. "How delicately put, doctor. Are you a delicate man? One of those sensitive guys really tuned in to people's feelings?"

"I try."

"Well, goody for you—I'm sorry, this *is* serious, isn't it. My problem—always was. Not taking things seriously. Not being *ma-*

ture. Being mature's a drag, isn't it, doc? I fucking refuse. That's why I work in entertainment. Nobody in entertainment's grown up. Why do *you* do what *you* do?"

"Fame and fortune," I said.

She laughed, harder and louder. "Psychologists, psychiatrists, I've known a shitload of them . . . how do I know you're for real —hey, this isn't some gag, is it? Did *Ron* put you up to this?"

"Who's Ron?"

"Another sensitive guy."

"Don't know him."

"I'll bet."

"I'd be happy to show you credentials."

"Sure, slip them through the phone."

"Want me to fax them?"

"Nah . . . what's the diff? So what do you really want?"

"Just to talk to you a bit about the school."

"Good old school. School days, cruel days . . . hold on . . ." Click. Silence. Click. "Where are you calling from?"

"Not far from your office."

"What, the pay phone downstairs, like in the movies?"

"Mile away. I can be there in five minutes."

"How convenient. No, I don't want to bring my personal shit into the office. Meet me at Cafe Mocha in an hour, or forget it. Know where it is?"

"No."

"Wilshire near Crescent Heights. Tacky little strip mall on the . . . southeast corner. Great coffee, people pretending to be *artistes*. I'll be in a booth near the back. If you're late, I won't wait around."

The restaurant was a narrow storefront blocked by blue ging-ham curtains. Pine tables and booths, half of them empty. Sacks of coffee stood on the floor near the entrance, listing like melting snowmen. A few desperate-looking types sat far from one another, poring over screenplays.

Meredith Bork was in the last booth, her back to the wall, a mug in her left hand. A big, beautiful, dark-haired woman sitting high and straight. The moment I walked in, her eyes were on me and they didn't waver as I approached.

Her hair was true black and shiny, brushed straight back from her head and worn loose around her shoulders. Her face was olive tinted like Robin's, just a bit rounder than oval, with wide, full lips, a straight, narrow nose, and a perfect chin. Perfect cheekbones, too, below huge gray-blue eyes. Silver-blue nail polish to match her silk blouse. Two buttons undone, freckled chest, an inch of cleavage. Strong, square shoulders, lots of bracelets around surprisingly slender wrists. Lots of gold, all over. Even in the weak light, she sparkled.

She said, "Great. You're cute. I allow you to sit."

She put the mug down next to a plate bearing an oversized muffin.

"Fiber," she said. "The religion of the nineties."

A waitress came over and informed me the coffee of the day was Ethiopian. I said that was fine and received my own mug.

"Ethiopian," said Meredith Bork. "They're starving over there, aren't they? But they're exporting designer beans? Don't you think that's weird?"

"Someone always does okay," I said. "No matter how bad things get."

"How true, how true." She smiled. "I like this guy. Perfect mixture of sincerity and cynicism. *Lots* of women love it, right? You probably use it to get laid, then get bored and leave them weeping, right?"

I laughed involuntarily. "No."

"No, you don't get *laid*, or no, you don't get *bored*?"

"No, I'm not into conning women."

"Gay?"

"No."

"What's your problem, then?"

"Are we discussing that?"

"Why not?" Giant smile. Capped teeth. "You want to discuss *my* problems, jocko, fair is fair."

I raised my cup to my lips.

"How's the java?" she said. "Those starving Ethiopians know how to grow 'em?"

"Very good."

"I'm *so* veddy glad. Mine's Colombian. My regular fix. I keep hoping there'll be a packaging error and I'll get a little snort mixed in with the grind."

She rubbed her nose and winked, leaned forward, and showed more chest. A black lace bra cut into soft, freckled flesh. She wore a perfume I'd never smelled before. Lots of grass, lots of flowers, a bit of her own perspiration.

She giggled. "No, I'm just joshing you, Mr.—sorry, *Doctor* No Con. I know how touchy you healer types are about that. Daddy always had a *bovine* when someone called him mister."

"Alex is fine."

"Alex. The Great. *Are* you great? Wanna *fuck and suck*?"

Before my mouth could close, she said, "But seriously, folks."

Her smile was still on high beam and her breasts were still pushing forward. But she'd reddened and the muscles beneath one of the lovely cheekbones were twitching.

She said, "What a tasteless thing to say, right? Stupid, too, in the virus era. So let's forget about stripping off my *clothes* and concentrate on stripping my *psyche*, right?"

"Meredith—"

"That's the name, don't wear it out." Her hand brushed against the mug and a few droplets of coffee spilled on the table.

"Shit," she said, grabbing a napkin and blotting. "Now you've *really* got me spazzing."

"We don't need to talk about you, personally," I said. "Just about the school."

"Not talk about *me*? That's my favorite *topic*, Alex, the sincere shrink. I've spent Godknowshowmuch money talking to your ilk about *me*. They all pretended to be utterly fascinated, least you can do is fake it, too."

I sat back and smiled.

"I don't *like* you," she said. "Way too agreeable. Can you get a hard-on on demand—no, scratch that, no more dirty talk. This is going to be a platonic, asexual, antiseptic discussion . . . the Corrective School. How I spent my summer vacation by Meredith Spill-the-Coffee Bork."

"Were you there for only one summer?"

"It was enough, believe me."

The waitress came over and asked if we wanted anything else.

"No, dear, we're in love, we don't need anything else," said Meredith, waving her away. A wine list was propped between the salt and pepper shakers. She pulled it out and studied it. Moving her lips. Tiny droplets had formed over them. Her smooth, brown brow puckered.

She put the list down and wiped the sweat from her mouth.

"Caught me," she said. "Dyslexic. Not illiterate—I probably know more about what's going on than your average asshole senator. But it takes effort—little tricks so the words make sense." Another huge smile. "That's why I like to work with Hollywood assholes. *None* of them read."

"Is the dyslexia why you went to the Corrective School?"

"I didn't *go, Alex.* I was sent. And no, that wasn't the official reason. The official reason was I was *acting out.* One of you guys' quaint little terms for being a naughty girl—do you want to know how?"

"If you'd like to tell me."

"Of course I would, I'm an exhibitionist. No, scratch that. What's it your business?" She moistened her lips and smiled. "Suffice it to say I learned about cocks when I was much too young to appreciate them." She held out her mug to me, as if it were a microphone. "And why was that, Contestant Number One? Why, for the washer-dryer and the trip to Hawaii, did a sweet young thing from Sierra Madre besmirch herself?"

I didn't speak.

"Buzz," she said. "Sorry, Number One, that's not quick enough. The correct answer is: poor self-esteem. Twentieth-century root of all evil, right? I was fourteen and could barely read, so instead, I learned to give dynamite blow jobs."

I looked down at my coffee.

"Oh, look, I've *embarrassed* him—don't worry, I'm okay. Damn proud of my blow jobs. You work with what you've got." Her grin was huge but hard to gauge.

"One fateful morning, Mommy discovered strange, yucky stains on my junior high prom dress. Mommy consulted with learned Doctor Daddy and the two of them threw a joint shit-fit. The day school ended I was shipped off to the wild and woolly hills of Santa Barbara. Little brown uniforms, ugly shoes, girls' bunks separated from the boys' bunks by a scuzzy vegetable garden. Dr. Botch stroking his little goatee and telling us this could turn out to be the best summer we ever had."

She hid her mouth behind her mug, broke off a piece of muffin, and let it crumble between her fingers.

"I couldn't read, so they sent me to Buchenwald-on-the-Pacific. There's juvenile justice for you."

"Did de Bosch ever diagnose your dyslexia?" I said.

"You kidding? All he did was throw this Freudian shit at me: I was frustrated because Mommy had Daddy and I wanted him. So I was trying to be a woman, rather than a girl—acting *out*—in order to *displace* her."

She laughed. "Believe me, I *knew* what I wanted, and it wasn't *Daddy*. It was lean, young, well-hung bodies and James Dean faces. And I had the power to get it all back then. I believed in myself until Botch botched me up."

All at once her face changed, loosening and paling. She put the mug down hard, shook her hair like a wet puppy, and rubbed her temples.

"What did he do to you?" I said.

"Tore my soul out," she said glibly. But as she spoke she brought strands of hair forward and hid her face.

Long silence.

"Shit," she said finally. "This is harder than I thought it would be. How did he mess me up? Subtly. Nothing he could go to jail for, darling. So tell your police pals to go back to giving parking tickets, you'll never pin him. Besides, he must be ancient by now. Who's going to drag a poor old fart into court?"

"He's dead."

The hair fell away. Her eyes were very still. "Oh . . . well, that's okay by me, pal. Was it long and painful, by any chance?"

"He killed himself. He'd been sick for a while. Multiple strokes."

"Killed himself how?"

"Pills."

"When?"

"Nineteen-eighty."

The eyes tightened. "Eighty? So what's all this b.s. about an investigation?"

Her arm shot forward and she grabbed my wrist. Big, *strong* woman. "Fess up, psych-man: Who are you and what's all this really about?"

A few heads turned. She let go of my arm.

I pulled out ID, showed it to her, and said, "I've told you the truth, and what it's about is revenge."

I summarized the "bad love" murders, throwing out names of victims.

When I finished, she was smiling.

"Well, I'm sorry for those others, but . . ."

"But what?"

"Bad love," she said. "Turning his own crap against him. I like that."

"Bad love was something he *did*?"

"Oh, yeah," she said, through clenched jaws. "Bad love meant you were a worthless piece of shit who deserved to be mistreated. Bad *love* for bad little *children*—like psychological acupuncture, these tiny little needles, jabbing, twisting."

Her wrists rotated. Jewelry flashed. "But no scars. No, we didn't want to leave any marks on the beautiful little children."

"What did he actually do?"

"He *bounced* us. Good love one day, bad love the next. Publicly—when we were all together, in the lunch room, at an assembly—he was Joe Jolly. When visitors came, too. Joe Jolly. Laughing, telling jokes, lots of jokes. Tousling our hair, joining in our games—he was old but athletic. Used to like to play tether ball. When someone hurt their hand on the knob, he'd make a big show of cuddling them and kissing the boo-boo. Mister Compassionate—*Doctor* Compassionate. Telling us we were the most beautiful children in the world, the school was the most beautiful school, the teachers the most beautiful teachers. The goddamn *vegetable* garden was beautiful, even though the stuff we planted always came out stringy and we had to eat it anyway. We were one big happy, global family, a real sixties kind of thing—sometimes he even wore these puka shells around his neck, over his pukey tie."

"That was good love," I said.

She nodded and gave a small, ugly laugh. "One big family—but if you got on his bad side—if you acted *out*, then he gave you a *private* session. And all of a sudden you weren't beautiful anymore, all of a sudden the world turned *real* ugly."

She sniffed and used her napkin to wipe her nose. Thinking of her Colombian coffee comment, I wondered if she'd fortified herself for our appointment. She cut me off midthought:

"Don't worry, it's not nasal candy, it's plain old emotion. And the emotion I feel for that bastard, even with his being dead, is pure hatred. Isn't that amazing—after all these years? I'm surprising *myself* with how much I hate him. Because he *made* me hate *myself*—it took years to get out from under his fucking bad love."

"The private sessions," I said.

"*Real* private . . . he hit me where it counted. I didn't need anyone tearing down my self-esteem—I was already fucked up enough, not able to read at thirteen. Everyone blaming me, me blaming myself . . . my sisters were all A students. I got D's. I was a premature baby. Difficult labor. Must have affected my brain—the dyslexia, my other prob—"

She threw up her hands and fluttered her fingers.

"So now it's out," she said, smiling. "I have yet *another* problem. Want a shot at that diagnosis, Contestant Number One?"

I shook my head.

"Not a gambler? Oh, well, there's no reason I should be ashamed, it's all chemistry—that was my point, wasn't it? Bipolar affective disorder. Your basic, garden variety manic-depressive maniac. You tell people you're manic and they say, oh yeah, I'm feeling really manic, too. And you say, no, no, no, this is different. This is *real*, my little pretties."

"Are you on lithium?"

Nod. "Unless the work piles up and I need the extra push. I finally found a psychiatrist who knew what the hell he was doing. All the others were ignorant assholes like Dr. Botch. Analyzing me, blaming me. Botch nearly convinced me I *did* want to fuck Daddy. He *totally* convinced me I was *bad*."

"With bad love?"

She stood suddenly and snatched up her purse. She was six feet tall, with a tiny waist, narrow hips, and long legs under a charcoal-colored silk miniskirt. The skirt had ridden up, revealing sleek thigh. If she realized it, she didn't choose to fix it.

"He's worried I'm leaving." She laughed. "Mellow out, son. Just going to pee."

She made an abrupt about-face and sashayed toward the rear of the restaurant. A few moments later, I got up and verified that the restrooms were back there, and the only exit a grimy gray door with a bar across it marked EMERGENCY.

She returned a few minutes later, hair fluffed, eyes puffy but freshly shadowed. Sitting down, she nudged my shin with a toe and gave a weak smile. Waving for the waitress, she got a refill and drank half the cup, taking long, silent swallows.

Looking ready to choke. My therapeutic impulse was to pat her hand. I resisted it.

"Bad love," she said softly. "Little rooms. Little locked cells. Bare bulbs—or sometimes he'd just light a candle. Candles *we* made in crafts. *Beautiful* candles—actually they were ugly pieces of shit, with this really disgusting scent. Nothing in the cell but two chairs. He'd sit opposite you, your knees almost touching. Nothing between you. Then he'd stare at you for a long time. A *long* time. Then he'd start talking in this low, relaxed voice—like it was just a chat, like it was just two people having a nice, civil conversation. And at first you'd think you were getting away easy, he'd sound so pleasant. Smiling, playing with that stupid little beard or his puka shells."

She said, "Shit," and drank coffee.

"What did he talk about?"

"He'd start off lecturing about human nature. How everyone had good parts of their character and bad parts and the difference between the successful people and the unsuccessful people was which part you used. And that we kids were there because we were using too much bad part and not enough good part. Because we'd gotten warped somehow—*damaged* was the way he put it— from wanting to sleep with our mommies and our daddies. But how everyone else at the school was now doing great. *Everyone except you, young lady, is controlling their impulses and learning to use the good part. They* are going to be okay. *They* deserve good love and are going to have *happy* lives."

She closed her eyes. Took a deep breath. Funneled her lips into a pinhole and blew air out through it.

"Then he'd stop. To let it all sink in. And stare some more. And get even closer. His breath always stank of cabbage . . . the room was so small the smell filled it—*he* filled it. He wasn't a big man, but in there he was *huge*. You felt like an ant, about to be crushed—like the room was running out of air and you were going to strangle . . . the way he stared—his eyes were like drills. And the look—when you got the bad love. After the soft talk was through. This hatred—letting you know you were scum.

" '*You,*' he'd say. And then he'd repeat it. '*You, you, you.*' And then it would start—*you* were the only one who wasn't doing good. *You* couldn't control your impulses, *you* weren't trying—*you* were acting just like an animal. A dirty, filthy animal—a *vermin* animal. That was a favorite of his. Vermin animals—in his creepy

Inspector Clouseau accent. *Vermeen aneemals*. Then he'd start calling you other names. Fool, idiot, weakling, moron, savage, excrement. No curse words, just one insult after another, sometimes in French. Saying them so quietly you could barely hear them. But you had to hear them because there was nothing else to hear in that room. Just the wax dripping, sometimes a plumbing pipe would rumble, but mostly it was silent. You *had* to listen."

A lost look came into her eyes. She shifted as far from me as the booth would allow. When she spoke again, her voice was even softer, but deeper, almost masculine.

"You are acting like vermin animal, young lady. You are going to live like vermin animal and you will end up dying like vermin animal. And then he'd go into these detailed descriptions of how vermin lived and died and how no one loved them and gave them good love because they didn't deserve it and how the only thing they deserved was bad love and filth and humiliation."

She reached for her mug. Her hand shook and she braced it with the other one before raising the coffee to her lips.

"He'd keep going like that. Don't ask me how long because I don't know—it felt like years. *Chanting.* Over and over and over. You *will* get the bad love, you *will* get the bad love . . . pain, and suffering and loneliness that would never end—prison, where people will rape you and cut you and tie you up so you can't move. Horrible diseases you will get—he'd go into the symptoms. Talk about the loneliness, how you'd always be alone. Like a corpse left out in the desert to dry. Like a piece of dirt on some cold, distant planet—he was full of analogies, Dr. B. was, *playing* loneliness like an instrument. *Your life will be as empty and dark as this room we are sitting in, young lady. Your entire future will be desolate. No good love from anyone—no good love, just bad love, filth, and degradation. Because that is what bad children deserve. A cold, lonely world for children who act like vermin animals.* Then he'd show photos. Dead bodies, concentration camp stuff. *This is how you will end up!"*

She shifted closer.

"He'd just *chant* it," she said, touching my cuff. "Like some priest . . . throwing out these images. Not giving you a chance to speak. He made you feel you were the only bad person in a beautiful world—a shit smear on silk. And you believed him. You believed everyone was changing for the better, learning to control themselves. Everyone was on his side, you were the *only* piece of shit."

"Cutting you off," I said, "so you wouldn't confide in the other kids."

"It worked; I never confided in anyone. Later, when I was out of there—*years* later—I realized it was stupid, I couldn't have been the only one. I'd seen other kids go into the rooms—it seems so ridiculously logical now. But back then, I couldn't—he kept focusing me in on *myself*. On the bad parts of me. The *vermin animal* parts."

"You were isolated right from the beginning. New environment, new routine."

"Exactly!" she said, squeezing my arm. "I was scared *shitless*. My parents never told me where we were going, just shoved me in the car and tossed in a suitcase. The whole ride up there, they wouldn't speak to me. When we got there, they drove through the gates, dumped me in the office, left me there and drove away. Later I found out that's what he instructed them to do. Have a happy summer, Meredith . . ."

Her eyes got wet. "I'd just repeated seventh grade. Finally faked enough to barely pass and was looking forward to a vacation. I thought summer would be the beach and Lake Arrowhead —we had a cabin, always went there as a family. They dumped me and went without me . . . no apologies, no explanation. I thought I'd died and gone to hell—sitting in that office, all those brown uniforms, no one talking to me. Then *he* came out, smiling like a clown, saying, what a pretty girl you are, telling me to come with him, *he'd* be taking care of me. I thought: what a jerk, no problem putting it over on him. The first time I stepped out of line, he let it pass. The second time, he pulled me into a room and bad-loved me. I walked out of there in a semi-coma . . . blitzed, wasted—it's hard to explain, but it was almost like dying. Like bad dope—I felt I was on a rocky island in the middle of a storm. This crazy, black, roaring sea, with sharks all around . . . no escape, him working on my bad parts—chewing me *up*!"

"What a nightmare," I said.

"The first week I hardly slept or ate. Lost ten pounds. The worst part was that you believed him. He had a way of taking over your head—like he was sitting in your skull, scraping away at your brain. You really felt you were shit and belonged in hell."

"None of the kids *ever* talked to each other?"

"Maybe some did, I didn't. Maybe I could've, I don't know—I sure didn't *feel* I could. Everyone walking around smiling, saying how great Dr. B. was. Such a *beautiful* guy. You found yourself saying it, too, mouthing along without thinking, like one of those dumb camp songs. There was this—this *feverish* atmosphere to the place. Grinning idiots. Like a cult. You felt if you spoke out against him, someone would pour poison Kool-Aid down your throat."

"Was physical punishment ever part of bad love?"

"Once in a while—usually a slap, a pinch, nothing that hurt too much. It was mostly the humiliation—the surprise. When he *wanted* to hurt you, he'd poke you in the elbow or the shoulder. Flick his finger on the bone. He knew all the spots . . . nothing that would leave a scar, not that anyone would have believed us, anyway. Who were we? Truants, fuckups, rejects. Even *now*, would I be credible? Four abortions, Valium, Librium, Thorazine, Elavil, lithium? All the other things I've done? Wouldn't some lawyer dig that up and put *me* on trial? Wouldn't I be a piece of *shit* all over again?"

"Probably."

Her smile was rich with disgust. "I'm *jazzed* that he's dead—doubly jazzed he did it to himself—his turn for humiliation."

She looked up at the ceiling.

"What is it?" I said.

"Killing himself—do you think he could have felt some guilt?"

"With what you've told me, it's hard to imagine."

"Yeah. You're probably right . . . yeah, he slapped me plenty of times, but the pain was *welcome*. 'Cause when he was getting *physical*, he wasn't *talking*. His voice. His *words*. He could reach into your center and squeeze the life out of you . . . did you know he used to write columns in magazines—humane child rearing? People sent in problems and he'd offer fucking *solutions*?"

I sighed.

"Yes," she said. "My sad, sad story—such pathos." Looking around the restaurant, she cupped one ear. "Any daytime-serial people listening? Got a bitchin' script for you."

"You never told anyone?"

"Not until you, dear." Smile. "Aren't you flattered? All those shrinks and you're the *very* first—why, you've deflowered me—busted my psychological *cherry*!"

"Interesting way to put it."

"But fitting, right? Therapy's just like fucking—you open yourself up to a stranger and hope for the best."

I said, "You said you saw other kids going into the rooms. Were they taken by other people, or just de Bosch?"

"Mostly by him, sometimes by that creepy daughter of his. *I* always got personal attention from the big cheese—Daddy's social position and all that."

"Katarina was involved in treatment? When exactly were you there?"

"Seventy-six."

"She was only twenty-three. Still a student."

Shrug. "Everyone treated her as if she was a shrink. What she was was a real *bitch*. Walking around with this smug look on her face—Daddy was the king and she was the princess. Now there's one dutiful daughter who really *did* want to fuck Papa."

"Did you have any direct dealings with her?"

"Other than a sneer in the hall? No."

"What about other staffers? Did you see any of them doing private sessions?"

"No."

"None of those names I mentioned rang a bell?"

She gave a pained look. "It all blurs—I've been through changes, my whole *life* until a few years ago is a blur."

"Can I go over those names again?"

"Sure, why not." She picked up her cup and drank.

"Grant Stoumen."

Headshake.

"Mitchell Lerner."

"Maybe . . . that one's a little familiar, but I have no face to go with it."

I gave her some time to think.

She said, "Nope."

"Harvey Rosenblatt."

"Uh-uh."

"Wilbert Harrison."

"No."

"He's a little man who wears purple all the time."

"Does he ride a pink elephant?" Grin.

"Myra Evans."

Eyeblink. Frown.

I repeated the name.

"You used another name before," she said. "Myra something hyphenated."

"Evans-Paprock—Paprock was her married name."

"Evans." Another smile, not at all happy. "Myra Evans— Myra the Bitch. She was a teacher, right? A little blond with a tight butt and an attitude—am I right?"

I nodded.

"Yeah," she said. "Myra the Bitch. She was assigned to tread where others had failed. Like teaching *moi* how to read. She kept drilling me, harassing me, forcing me to do stupid exercises that didn't do a fucking bit of good because the words stayed all scrambled. When I got something wrong, she'd clap her hands together and say *no* in this loud voice. Like training a dog. Telling me I was stupid, a moron, not paying attention—she used to clamp her hands on my face and force me to look into her eyes."

She placed her hands on my cheeks and pressed them together, hard. Her palms were wet and her mouth was parted. She brought me forward and I thought she might kiss me. Instead, she said, "Pay attention! Listen, you moron!" in a grating voice.

I suppressed the impulse to twist free. That instant of confinement drove my empathy up another notch.

"Pay *attention*! Stop *wandering*, stupid! This is *important*! You need to *learn* this! If you don't pay *attention*, you can't *learn*!"

She squeezed harder. Let go. Smiled again. "Breath mints— that was her smell. Isn't it funny how you remember the smells? Mints, but her breath was still shitty. She thought she was hot. Kinda young, little miniskirts, big boobs . . . maybe she was letting Dr. B. slip it to her."

"Why do you say that?"

"Because of the way she acted around him. Looks. Following him around. She reported directly to him. One thing you could count on, after a difficult session with Miss Bitch, you'd soon be seeing Dr. Botch for candles and needle twisting. So she got murdered, huh?"

"Very nastily."

"Too bad." She pouted, then smiled. "See, I can be a hypocrite, too. It's called acting, I work with people who do it for a living—we all do, actually, don't we?"

"What about Rodney Shipler? Does that name mean anything to you?"

"Nope."

"Delmar Parker—the boy I told you about over the phone."

"Yeah, the truck. That's how I knew you were for real. He was before my time."

"May seventy-three. You heard about it?"

"I heard about it from *Botch*. Boy, did I."

"During a bad love session?"

Nod. "The wages of sin. I'd committed some major felony—I think it was not wearing underwear, or something. Or maybe he caught me with a boy—I don't remember. He said I was a *vermeen aneemal* and stupid, then gave me this whole spiel about a *vermeen aneemal* boy who'd received the ultimate punishment for *his* stupidity. 'Death, young lady. Death.' "

"What did he say happened?"

"The kid stole a truck, ran it off the road, and got killed. Proof positive of what happened to *vermeen aneemal* moron children. Botch had a good time with it—making fun of the kid, laughing a lot, as if it were just a big joke. *'Do you comprehend, you bad, styupid girl? A boy so styupid, he steals a truck even though he doesn't know how to drive? Ha ha ha. A boy so styupid he virtually choreographs his own death? Ha ha ha.'* "

"He used that word? 'Choreograph'?"

"Yes," she said, looking surprised. "I believe he actually did."

"What else did he say about the accident?"

"Disgusting details—that was part of bad love. Grossing you out. He had a ball with this one. How they didn't find the boy right away and when they did there were maggots in his mouth and crawling in and out of his eyes—*'He is being eaten by maggots, my dear Meredith. Feasted upon. Consumed. And the animals have feasted upon him, too. Chewed away most of his face—it is a real mess— just like your character, styupid Meredith. You are not listening, you are not concentrating, you bad, styupid girl. We are trying to mold you into something decent but you refuse to cooperate. Think, Meredith. Think of that styupid boy. The bad love he received from the maggots. That is what happens when vermeen aneemals don't change their ways.'* "

She gave a hard, dry laugh and dabbed her nose again.

"That might not be an exact quote, but it's pretty damn close. He also got into this whole racist rap—said the kid in the truck was black. 'A *savage*, Meredith. A jungle *native*. Why would you want to imitate the savages when there's a world of *civilization* out there?' On top of everything else, he's a racist, too. Even without the rap, you could tell. The looks he gave the minority kids."

"Were there a lot of minority kids?"

She shook her head. "Just a few. Tokens, probably—part of the public image. In public he was Mr. Liberal—pictures of Martin Luther King and Gandhi and the Kennedys all over the place. Like I said, it's all acting—the world is a fucking stage."

She placed her hands flat on the table, looking ready to get up again.

"A couple more names," I said. "Silk."

Headshake.

"Merino."

"What is this, a fabric show? Uh-uh."

"Lyle Gritz?"

"Grits and toast," she said. "Nope. How many people have gotten bumped off, anyway?"

"Lots. I'm on the list, too."

Her eyes rounded. "You? Why?"

"I co-chaired a symposium on de Bosch's work. At Western Peds."

"Why?" she said coldly. "Were you a fan?"

"No. Actually, your father requested it of me."

"Requested it, huh? What approach did he take? Squeezing your balls or kissing your ass?"

"Squeezing. He did it as a favor to Katarina."

"Symposium, huh? Gee thanks, *Dad*. The man tortures me, so you throw him a party—when did this take place?"

"Seventy-nine."

She thought. "Seventy-nine—I was in Boston in seventy-nine. Catholic girls' school, even though we weren't Catholic . . . a symposium." She laughed.

"You never told your parents anything that happened at the Corrective School?"

"Nothing—I was too numb, and they wouldn't have listened, anyway. After that summer, I didn't talk to anyone, just went along, like some robot. They handed Botch a naughty *acting-out* girl and got back this compliant little zombie. They thought it was a miracle *cure*. Years later, they were still saying it was the best decision they ever made. I'd just stare at them, want to kill them, keep my feelings all inside."

The pale eyes were wet.

"How long did you stay that way?" I said softly.

"I don't know—months, years—like I said, it blurs. All I know is it took a real long time to get back to my true self, get smart enough to mess around and cover my tracks. No sticky stains on the clothes."

She licked her lips and grinned. A tear dripped down one cheek. She wiped it away angrily.

"When I was eighteen, I told them 'fuck you' and left—ran away with a guy who came to unclog the toilet."

"Sounds like you've done pretty well since."

"How kind of you to say so, dear—oh yeah, it's been a blast. PR's a bullshit business, so I'm perfect for it. Throwing parties, setting up promos. Feeding rumors to the idiot press. Well, the show must go on. Ciao. It was real, stud."

She stood and nearly ran out of the restaurant.

I put money on the table and followed her, caught up as she was getting into a red Mustang convertible. The car looked new, but there were dings and dents all along the driver's side.

"Uh-uh, no more," she said, starting the engine. "You get a quickie mind-fuck for your ten bucks, and that's it."

"Just wanted to thank you," I said.

"Polite, too," she said. "I *really* don't like you."

30

Robin said, "Bad love. The hypocrisy."

"The bastard coins a phrase to describe poor child rearing, but has his own private meaning for it."

"Victimizing little kids." Her hands tightened around the handle of a wood rasp. The blade caught on a piece of rosewood, and she pulled it free and put it down.

"And," I said, "if this woman's experience was typical, the victimization was perfectly legal. De Bosch didn't sexually molest anyone, and none of the physical things he did would fall under any child-abuse statutes but Sweden's."

"Not the poking and slapping?"

"No bruises, no case, and usually you need deep wounds and broken bones to get anywhere legally. Corporal punishment's still allowed in many schools. Back then, it was accepted procedure. And there's never been any law against mind control or psychological abuse—how can you pin down the criteria? Basically, de Bosch behaved like a really rotten parent, and that's no crime."

She shook her head. "And no one ever said anything."

"Maybe some of the children did, but I doubt anyone believed them. These were problem kids. Their credibility was low and their parents were angry. In some cases de Bosch was probably the court of last resort. This woman came back to her family traumatized but perfectly compliant. They never suspected the summer at the school was anything but successful."

"Some success."

"We're talking ultrahigh levels of parental frustration, Rob. Even if what de Bosch did had come to light and some parents had pulled their kids out, I'll bet you others would have rushed to enroll theirs. De Bosch's victims never had any legal recourse. Now, one of them's evening the score his own way."

"The same old chain," she said. "Victims and victimizers."

"The thing that bothers me, though, is why the killer didn't strike out against de Bosch, only the disciples. Unless de Bosch died before the killer was old enough—or assertive enough—to put together a revenge plot."

"Or crazy enough."

"That, too. If I'm right about the killer being directly traumatized by Delmar Parker's accident, we're talking about someone who was a student at the school in 1973. De Bosch died seven years later, so the killer may still have been a kid. Felons that young rarely commit carefully planned crimes. They're more into impulsive stuff. Another thing that could have stopped him from getting de Bosch was being locked up. Jail or a mental institution. That fits with our Mr. Gritz—the ten years unaccounted for between his leaving Georgia and getting arrested here."

"More frustration," she said.

"Exactly. Not being able to punish de Bosch directly could have heated him up even further. The first murder occurred five years ago. Myra Paprock. Maybe that was the year he was released. Myra would have been a good target for him. A trusted disciple, dictatorial."

"Makes sense," she said, looking down at her workbench and arranging some files, "if de Bosch really killed himself. But what if he was murdered and made to look like a suicide?"

"I don't think so," I said. "His death was too peaceful—overdose of medication. Why would the killer butcher subordinates and allow the boss to get off so easy? And a ritual approach—one that fulfilled a psychological need—would have meant leaving the best for last, not starting with de Bosch first and working backwards."

"Best for last," she said, in a tremulous voice. "So where do you fit in?"

"The only thing I can think of is that damned symposium."

She started to switch off her tools. The dog tagged after her, stopping each time she did, looking up, as if seeking approval.

"Alex," she said, removing her apron, "if de Bosch did commit suicide, do you think it could have been due to remorse? It doesn't mean much, but it would be nice to think of him having some self-doubts."

"The woman asked me the same thing. I'd have liked to say yes—*she'd* have loved to *hear* it, but she wouldn't have bought it. The man she described didn't sound very conscience laden. My guess is his motivation was just what the papers printed: despondence over ill health. The slides his daughter flashed at the symposium showed a physical wreck."

"A wrecker," she said.

"Yeah. Who knows how many kids he messed up over the years?"

The dog heard the tension in my voice and cocked his head. I petted him and said, "So who's the higher life-form, anyway, bub?"

Robin picked up a broom and began to sweep wood shavings.

"Any other calls?" I said, holding the dustpan for her.

"Uh-uh." She finished and wiped her hands. We stepped out of the garage and she pulled down the door. The mountains across the canyon were clear and greening. Drought-starved shoots, trying for another season.

All at once the big, low house seemed more foreign than ever. We went inside. The furniture looked strange.

In the bedroom, Robin unbuttoned her work shirt and I unsnapped her bra and cupped her breasts. They were warm and heavy in my palms and as I touched her, she arched her back. Then she stepped away from me and crossed her arms over her chest.

"Let's get out of here, Alex—out of the city."

"Sure," I said, looking over at the dog, head-butting the bedcovers. "Do we take him with us?"

"I'm not talking summer vacation, just dinner. Somewhere far enough to feel *different*. He'll be fine. We'll leave food and water, the air-conditioning on, give him a couple of chew-bones."

"Okay, where would you like to go?"

Her smile was barren. "Normally I'd say Santa Barbara."

I forced myself to laugh. "How about the other direction—Laguna Beach?"

"Laguna would be peachy." She came over and placed

my hands on her hips. "Remember that place with the ocean view?"

"Yeah," I said. "Calamari and pictures of weeping clowns— wonder if it's still in business?"

"If it isn't, there'll be someplace else. The main thing is we get away."

We left at seven-thirty, to avoid the freeway jam, taking the truck because the gas tank was fuller. I drove, enjoying the height and the heft and the power. A tape Robin had picked up at Mc-Cabe's was in the deck: a teenager named Allison Krause, singing bluegrass in a voice as sweet and clear as first love and running off fiddle solos that had the wondrous ease of the prodigy.

I hadn't called Milo to tell him about Meredith.

Another scumbag, he'd say, world-weary. Then he'd rub his face . . .

I thought of the man on the tape, chanting like a child, re-living his past. . . .

Bad thoughts intruding.

I felt Robin tighten up. Her fingers had been tapping my thigh in time with the music, now they stopped. I squeezed them. Strummed the fingertips, let my hand wander to her small, hard waist as the truck roared in the fast lane.

She had on black leotards under a short denim skirt. Her hair was tied up, showing off her neck, smooth as cream. A man with a functioning brain would have thanked God for sitting next to her.

I pressed my cheek against hers. Let my shoulders drop and bobbed my head to the music. Not fooling her, but she knew I was trying and she put her hand high on my thigh.

A babe and a truck and the open road.

By the time I reached Long Beach, it started to feel real.

Laguna was quieter and darker than I remembered, the art fair over, nearly all the tourist traps and galleries closed.

The place with the squid and clowns was no longer in busi-ness; a karaoke bar had taken its place—people getting slogged on margaritas and pretending to be Righteous Brothers. The painful sounds made their way to the sidewalk.

We found a pleasant-looking cafe farther up the street, ate huge, cold salads, decent swordfish, and excellent Chilean sea bass with french fries and coleslaw, and drank a bit of wine, then strong black coffee.

Walking it off, we went far enough past the commercial zone to get an ocean glimpse of our own. The water was a thousand miles of black beyond a white thread of sand. The waves rolled drunkenly, sending up ice chips of spray and an occasional roar that sounded like applause. We held hands so tightly our fingers ached, grabbed at each other, and kissed until our tongues throbbed.

Barely enough light to see Robin's dark eyes, narrowing.

She bit my lower lip and I knew some of it was passion, the rest, anger. I kissed her behind her ear and we embraced for a long time, then we returned to the truck and drove north, out of town.

"Don't get on the freeway," she said. "Drive awhile."

I got onto Laguna Canyon Road, went for several miles, and made a random turn onto an unmarked strip that corkscrewed up into the mountains.

No talk or music. Her hands on me as she cried out her tension. We passed a pottery studio, its wooden sign barely lit by a dusty bulb. A glimpse of chicken-wire fencing. A couple of horse ranches, an unmarked shack. Then nothing for a long time and the road dead-ended at brush.

Crickets and shadows, the ocean nowhere in sight.

I put the truck in reverse. Robin stopped me and turned off the engine.

We locked eyes and kissed, fumbling with each other's clothing.

Stripped completely naked, we held each other, shivering, knitting our limbs. Breathing into one another, fighting for oblivion.

The ride back was slow and silent, and I managed to keep reality at bay till we got off the freeway. Robin slept, as she had since we'd crossed the L.A. county line, low in the seat, half smiling.

It was one forty-two in the morning and Sunset was nearly

bare of cars. The familiar eastward cruise was solitary and peaceful. As I approached the Beverly Glen intersection, I prepared to shoot through the green light. Then wailing sirens sounded from somewhere I couldn't pinpoint, surrounding me, growing louder.

I slowed and stopped. Robin was startled, sitting up just as flashing red lights popped out from around the bend and the sirens became unbearable. A hook-and-ladder came at us from the east, bearing down; for an instant I felt trapped. Then the fire engine made a sharp right turn, northward, onto the Glen, followed closely by another fire truck, then another smaller unit. A cherry-topped sedan brought up the rear as the sirens tapered off to a distant whistle.

Robin was clutching the armrest. Her eyes were gigantic, as if the lids had been stapled back.

We looked at each other.

I turned left and followed the shrieking caravan.

A hundred yards in I could smell it. A pot left too long on the stove, overlaid with gasoline.

I put on speed, just able to see the fire car's taillights. Hoping the company would continue on up, toward Mulholland and beyond. But they hooked west.

Up an old bridle path that led up to a solitary property.

Robin held her head and moaned as I floored the truck. Coming to my street, I sped up the slope. The road was blocked by the newly arrived fire trucks and I had to pull over and park.

Work lights were scattered about, highlighting the firefighters' yellow hats. Lots of movement, but the night blocked out the details.

Robin and I jumped out and began running up the hill. The burnt stench was stronger now, the sky a black, camouflaging host for the plumes of dark smoke that shot upward in greasy gray spirals. I could feel the fire—the caustic heat—better than I could see it. My body was drenched with sweat. I was cold to the marrow.

The firefighters were uncoiling hoses and shouting, too busy to notice us.

What had once been my pond gate was charcoal. The carport had collapsed and the entire right side of my house was smoldering. The back of the building was haloed in orange. Tongues of fire licked the sky. Sparks jumped and died, wood crackled and crashed.

A tall firefighter handed a hose to another man and pulled off his gloves. He saw us and came forward, gesturing us back.

We walked toward him.

"It's our house," I said.

The look of pity on his face cut me deeply. He was black, with a big jaw and wide, dark mustache. "Sorry, folks—we're working hard on it, got here as quick as we could from the Mulholland substation. Reinforcements just came in from Beverly Hills."

Robin said, "Is it all gone?"

He removed his hat and wiped his forehead, exhaling. "It wasn't as of a few minutes ago, ma'am, and we've controlled it— you should start to see that smoke turn white real soon."

"How bad is it?"

He hesitated. "To be frank, ma'am, you've suffered some serious structural damage all along the rear. What with the drought and all that wood siding—your roof's half gone, must have been pretty dry up there. What was it, ceramic tile?"

"Some sort of tile," I said. "It came with the house, I don't know."

"Those old roofs . . . give thanks it wasn't wood shingle, that would have been like a pile of kindling."

Robin was looking at him but she wasn't listening to him. He bit his lip, started to place a hand on her shoulder, but stopped himself. Putting his glove back on, he turned to me.

"If the wind doesn't do squirrely things, we should be able to save some of it. Get you in there soon as possible to start taking a look."

Robin started to cry.

The fireman said, "I'm real sorry, ma'am—if you need a blanket, we've got some in the truck."

"No," she said. "What happened?"

"Don't know exactly, yet—why don't you talk to the captain —that gentleman over there? Captain Gillespie. He should be able to help you."

After pointing to a medium-sized man up near the carport, he ran off. We made our way to the captain. His back was to us and I tapped him on the shoulder. He turned quickly, looking ready to snap. One look at us shut his mouth. He was in his fifties and had a deeply scored face that was almost a perfect square.

Tugging at his chin strap: "Owners?"

Two nods.

"Sorry, folks—out for the night?"

More nods. I felt encased in sand. Movement was an ordeal.

"Well, we've been at it for about half an hour, and I think we got to it relatively fast after ignition. Luckily, someone driving up the Glen smelled it and phoned it in on cellular. We've got most of the really hot spots out. Look for white smoke soon, Mr.—?"

"Alex Delaware. This is Robin Castagna."

"Ron Gillespie, Mr. Delaware. Are you the legal owners or tenants?"

"Owners."

Another pitying look. A whooshing sound came from the house. He glanced over his shoulder, then looked back.

"We should be able to save at least half of it, but our water does some damage, too." He looked back again. Something creased his brow. "One minute." Jogging over to a group of new arrivals, he pointed at my flaming roof and spread his arms like a preacher.

When he came back, he said, "You folks want something to drink? C'mon, let's get away from the heat."

We followed him down the road a bit. The house was still in sight. Some of the smoke had startened to lighten, pluming upward like an earthborn cloud.

He pulled a canteen out of his jacket and held it out to us.

Robin shook her head.

I said, "No, thanks."

Gillespie opened the bottle and drank. Screwing the cap back on, he said, "Do you know of anyone who'd want to do this to you?"

"Why?"

He stared at me. "Usually, people say no."

"There is someone," I said. "I don't know who—it's a long story—there's a police detective you can talk to."

I gave him Milo's name and he wrote it down.

"I'd better call him now," he said. "Our arson investigators will be in on it too. This is an obvious intentional, we've got three discrete points of origin and we found a gasoline can out back that's probably the accelerant—looks like the bastard didn't even try to hide it."

"No," I said. "He wouldn't want to do that."

He stared at me again. I looked back without focusing.

Gillespie said, "I'll go call that detective now."

31

Milo spent a few seconds of silent comfort with us, then he huddled with Gillespie.

The fire went out, sending off columns of white smoke. Some time after—I still don't know how long—Robin and I were able to tour the damage, accompanied by a fireman with a flashlight who looked out for our safety but hung back, diplomatically, as we stumbled and cursed in the dark.

The garden and the rear half of the house were a total loss, the air still hot and bitter. The front rooms were sodden and putrid, ash filled, already moldering. I ran my hand along scorched furniture, fingered hot dust, looked at ruined art and decimated keepsakes, TV and stereo equipment that had blistered and burst. After a while it got too difficult. I pulled the paintings and prints that looked intact off the wall and made a neat stack. Short stack. My Bellows boxing print seemed to have come out okay, but the frame was blackened around the edges.

Robin was across the living room when I said, "I've got to get out of here."

She gave a dull nod—more of a bow. We carried the art out and took it to the truck.

Beyond the vehicles, Milo and Gillespie were still conferring and a third man had joined them—young, chubby, balding, with bristly red hair. He held a pad and his writing hand was busy.

"Drew Seaver," he said, holding out the other one. "Fire Department arson investigator. Detective Sturgis has been filling me in—sounds like you've really been through it. I'll have some questions for you, but they can wait a couple of days."

Milo told him, "I'll get you whatever you need."

"Fine," said Seaver. "What's your insurance situation, doctor?"

As if cued, Captain Gillespie said, "Better be getting back—good luck, folks."

When he was gone, Seaver repeated his insurance question.

I said, "I never really checked the details. I'm up to date on my premiums."

"Well, that's good. Those insurance guys are real sonofa's, believe me. Dot your 'i' wrong and they'll find a way not to pay you. You need any help with justification, just have 'em call me."

He handed me his card. "That and a statement from Detective Sturgis should handle it."

"What needs to be handled?" said Robin. "What do we need to justify?"

Seaver picked at his chin. His lips were thick, pink, and soft looking, with a natural turndown that made him look sad.

"Arson fires tend to be self-generated, Mrs. Delaware. In lots of cases, anyway. Like I said, insurance companies'll do anything not to pay up. First thing they're going to be assuming is you're behind this."

"Then fuck 'em," said Milo. To us: "Don't sweat it, I'll handle it."

Seaver said, "Okay . . . well, better be looking around some more." Cracking a brief smile, he left.

Milo's hair was ragged, his eyes electric. He had on a shirt and tie, but the tie was crooked and his collar was loosened. In the darkness his acne-scarred face looked like moonscape. His hand moved over it rapidly and repeatedly—almost ticlike.

"It's okay," said Robin.

"No, no," he said. "Uh-uh, don't comfort me—you're the victims—goddamn protect and serve—some protection. I know it sounds like a crock but we *are* gonna get him—one fucking way or the other, he's history. We'll get free of this."

The three of us walked back to the truck. Milo's unmarked was parked behind it. None of us looked back.

The firefighters' lights were going out, one by one, as some of the trucks pulled away. Sunrise was several hours away. Without the bulbs and the flames, the night seemed hollow, just a thin membrane holding back the void.

"Wanna go back with me?" said Milo.

"No," I said. "I can handle it."

Robin stood on tiptoes and kissed his cheek.

"I found out what de Bosch's sin was," I said. I told him of Meredith Bork's experience.

"You stab me, I stab you," he said. "No fucking excuse."

"Can we be sure this wasn't the Iron Priests?"

"We can't be sure of anything," he said furiously. "But a thousand to one it's not them. No offense, but you're just not important enough to them—they want Raza blood. No, this was our bad love buddy—remember Bancroft's comment about firesetters at the school?"

"You told me there was no record of any fires there."

"Yeah . . . the kids behaved themselves there. It's when they graduated that the problems started."

I drove, but I felt as if I was being towed. Each segment of white line diminished me. Across the cab of the truck, Robin wept, unable to stop, finally surrendering to deep, wracking sobs.

I was beyond tears.

Just as I crossed into Beverly Hills, she took a sucking breath and pressed fisted hands together.

"Oh, well," she said, "I always wanted to redecorate."

I must have laughed, because my throat hurt and I heard two voices chuckling hysterically.

"What style should we choose?" I said. "Phoenix Rococo?"

Benedict Canyon appeared. Red light. I stopped. My eyes felt acid washed.

"It was a crummy little place anyway," she said. "No, it wasn't, it was a beautiful little place—oh, Alex!"

I pulled her to me. Her body felt heavy but boneless.

Green light. My brain said go, but my foot was slow to follow. Trying not to think of everything I'd lost—and everything yet to lose—I managed to complete the left turn and began a solitary crawl up Benedict.

Home temporary home.

The dog would run out to greet us. I felt inadequate for the role of animal buddy. For anything.

I drove up to the white gate. It took a long time to find the card key, even longer to slip it in the slot. Moving the truck up the drive, I counted cypress trees in an effort to settle my mind on something.

I parked next to the Seville and we got out.

The dog didn't rush out to greet us.

I fumbled with the key to the front door. Turned it. As I walked through the door, something cold and hard pressed against my left temple and a hand reached around and clapped me hard on the right side of my head.

Immobilizing my skull.

"Hello, doctor," said a voice from a chant. "Welcome to Bad Love."

32

He said, "Don't move or speak, pardon the cliché."

The pressure on my temple was intense. Strong fingers dug into my cheek.

"Good," he said. "Obedient. You must have been a good student."

Dig.

"*Were* you?"

"I was okay."

"Such modesty—you were a lot *better* than okay. Your fourth-grade teacher, Mrs. Lyndon, said you were one of the best students she ever had—do you remember Mrs. Lyndon?"

Squeeze and shake.

"Yes."

"She remembers you . . . such a *good* little boy . . . keep being good: hands on head."

As my fingers touched my hair, the lights went on.

One of the couches was out of place, pushed closer to the coffee table. There were drinks and plates on the coffee table. A glass of something brown. The bag of taco chips Robin had bought a couple of days ago was open, crumbs scattered on the table.

Making himself comfortable.

Knowing we'd be gone for a while but would come back, nowhere else to go.

Because he'd used the fire to flush me out. Used the time to prepare the scene.

The ritual.

Choreographing death.

Firesetters and felons . . .

I considered how to get at him. Felt the pressure, saw only dark sleeve. Where was Robin?

"Forward march," he said, but he continued to hold me still.

Footsteps on marble. Someone walked into my line of sight, holding Robin the same way.

Tall. Bulky black sweater. Baggy black slacks. Black ski mask with eye holes. Shiny eyes, the color indeterminate at this distance. He towered over Robin, gripping her face and forcing her eyes up at the ceiling. Her neck was stretched, exposed.

I gave an involuntary start, and the hand gripped my head harder.

Imprisoning it.

I knew where they'd learned that.

Bumping and scratching from the back of the house. The dog tied out there, behind drapes that had been drawn over the French doors.

Something else at Robin's head besides a hand. Automatic pistol, small, chrome plated.

Bump, scratch.

The voice behind me laughed.

"Great attack dog . . . some tight security you've got here. Alarm system with an obvious home run, one snip and bye-bye. Fancy electric gate a dwarf could climb over, and a cute little closed-circuit TV to announce your arrival."

More laughter. The tall man with Robin didn't move or make a sound.

Two types of killing. Two killers. . . .

My captor said, "Okay, campers."

The tall man shifted his free hand from Robin's face to the small of her back and began propelling her down the hallway toward the bedrooms.

Swinging his hips. Effeminate.

Walking the way Robin walked.

A woman? A tall woman with strong shoulders . . .

I'd talked to a tall, angry woman this afternoon.

A Corrective School alumna with plenty of reason to hate.

I really don't like you.

I'd called Meredith out of the blue, yet she'd been willing to talk to me—too eager.

And she had a special reason to feel rage over the Western Peds symposium.

Thanks, Dad.

I'd just stare at them, want to kill them, keep my feelings all inside.

Alone with Robin, now. Her appetites and anger . . .

"Forward march, fool." The gun stayed in place as the hand moved from my face. No more pressure, but his touch lingered like phantom pain.

A sharp prod to my kidneys as he shoved me farther into the room. Onto a couch. As I bounced, my hands left my head.

His foot met my shin and pain burned through my leg.

"Back up—up, up, up!"

I complied, waiting to be tied or restrained.

But he let me stay there, hands on head, and sat down facing me, just out of reach.

I saw the gun first. Another automatic—bigger than Meredith's. Dull black, a dark wooden grip. Freshly oiled; I could smell it.

He looked tall too. Long waist, and long legs that he planted firmly on the marble. A little narrow in the shoulders. Arms a bit short. Navy blue sweatshirt with a designer logo. Black jeans, black leather, high-top athletic shoes that looked spanking new.

The chic thing to wear for homicide—the avenger reads *GQ*.

His mask had a mouth cutout. A sharklike smile filled the hole.

The dog scratched some more.

Under the mask, his forehead moved.

He crossed his legs, keeping the big black gun a couple of feet from the center of my chest. Breathing fast, but his arm was stable.

Using his free hand, he reached up and began rolling his mask up, doing it deftly, so that his eyes never moved from mine and his gun arm never faltered.

Doing it slowly.

The wool peeled away like a snake's molt, exposing a soft, unremarkable face with fine features.

Rosy cheeks. The hair brass colored, thinning, worn thicker at the sides, now matted by the mask.

Andrew Coburg.

The storefront lawyer's smile was wide, wet—impish.

A surprise-party smile.

He twirled the mask and tossed it over his shoulder. "Voilà."

I struggled to make sense of it—Coburg directing me to Gritz. Misdirecting me. Careful researcher . . . Mrs. Lyndon . . .

"I really *like* this place," he said. "Despite all the queer art. Nice, crisp, cruel, L.A. ambience. Much better than that little yuppie log cabin of yours. And *cliff*side—talk about perfect. Not to mention your little friend's *truck*—unbelievable. Couldn't have set it up better myself."

He winked. "Almost makes you believe in God, doesn't it? Fate, karma, predestination, collective unconscious—choose your dogma . . . do you have any idea what I'm talking about?"

"Delmar Parker," I said.

The dead boy's name blotted out his smile.

"I'm talking about consonance," he said. "Making it *right*."

"But Delmar has something to do with it, doesn't he? Something beyond bad love."

He uncrossed his legs. The gun made a small arc. "What do you know about bad love, you pretentious yuppie prick?"

The gun arm was board rigid. Then it began vibrating. He looked at it for just a second. Laughed, as if trying to erase his outburst.

Scratch, bump. The dog was throwing himself hard against the glass.

Coburg snickered. "Little *pit* puppy. Maybe after it's over I'll take him home with me."

Smiling but sweating. The rosy cheeks deep with color.

Trying to keep my face neutral, I strained to hear sounds from the bedrooms. Nothing.

"So you think you know about bad love," said Coburg.

"Meredith told me about it," I said.

His brow tightened and mottled.

The dog kept scraping. The old-man whining sound filtered through the glass. Coburg gave a disgusted look.

"You don't know anything," he said.

"So tell me."

"Shut your mouth." The gun arm shot forward again.

I didn't move.

He said, "You don't know a *tenth* of it. Don't flatter yourself with empathy, *fuck* your empathy."

The dog bumped some more. Coburg's eyes flattened.

"Maybe I'll just shoot it . . . skin it and gut it . . . how good can a shrink's dog be, anyway? How many shrinks does it take to change a lightbulb? None. They're all dead."

He laughed a bit more. Wiped sweat from his nose. I concentrated on the gun arm. It remained firmly in place, as if cut off from the rest of him.

"Do you know what *my* sin was?" he said. "The great transgression that bought me a ticket to hell?"

Ticket to hell. Meredith had called the school the same thing.

I shook my head. My armpits were aching, my fingers turning numb.

He said, "Enuresis. When I was a kid I used to piss my bed." He laughed.

"They treated me as if I *liked* it," he said. "Mumsy and Evil Stepdaddy. As if I liked clammy sheets and that litter-box smell. They were *convinced* I was doing it on purpose, so they beat me. So I got more nervous and pissed gallons. So then what did they do?"

Looking at me, waiting.

"They beat you some more."

"Bingo. *And* washed my dick with lye soap and all sorts of other wonderful stuff."

Still smiling, but his cheeks were scarlet. His hair was plastered to his forehead, his shoulders hunched under the designer sweatshirt.

My first thought, seeing those rosy cheeks, had been: *a beautiful baby.*

"So I started to do other things," he said. "Really naughty things. Could anyone blame me? Being tortured for something that I had no control over?"

I shook my head again. For a split second I felt my agreement meant something to him. Then a distracted look came into his eyes. The gun arm pushed forward and the black-metal barrel edged closer to my heart.

"What's the current lowdown on enuresis, anyway?" he said. "Do you pricks still tell parents it's a mental disease?"

"It's genetic," I said. "Related to sleep patterns. Generally it goes away by itself."

"You don't treat it anymore?"

"Sometimes behavior therapy is used."

"*You* ever treat kids for it?"

"When they want to be treated."

"Sure," he grinned. "You're a real humanitarian." The grin died. "So what were you doing making speeches—paying homage to *Hitler?*"

"I—"

"Shut up." The gun jabbed my chest. "That was rhetorical, don't speak unless you're spoken to . . . sleep patterns, huh? You quacks weren't saying that back when I was getting beaten with a strap. You had all sorts of other voodoo theories back then—one of your fellow quacks told Mumsy and Evil that I was screwed up sexually. Another said I was seriously depressed and needed to be hospitalized. And one genius told them I was doing it because I was angry about their marriage. Which was true. But I wasn't *pissing* because of it. *That* one they bought. Evil really got into expressing *his* anger. Big financial man, spiffy dresser—he had a whole collection of fancy belts. Lizard, alligator, calfskin, all with nice sharp buckles. One day I went to school with an especially nice collection of welts on my arm. A teacher started asking questions and the next thing I knew I was on a plane with dear old Mumsy to sunny California. Go west, little bad boy."

He let his free hand drop to his lap. His eyes looked tired and his shoulders rounded.

The dog was still throwing himself against the glass.

Coburg stared straight at me.

I said, "How old were you when they put you in the school?"

The gun jabbed again, forcing me backward against the couch. All at once his face was up against mine, breathing licorice. I could see dried mucus in his nostrils. He spat. His saliva was cold and thick as it oozed down the side of my face.

"I'm not *there*, yet," he said, between barely moving lips. "Why don't you shut up and let me *tell* it?"

Breathing hard and fast. I made myself look into his eyes, feeling the gun without seeing it. My pulse thundered in my ears. The spit continued its downward trail. Reaching my chin. Dripping onto my shirt.

He looked repulsed, struck out, slapping me and wiping me simultaneously. Wiped his hand on the seat cushion.

"They didn't *put* me there right away. They put me in another dungeon first. Right across the street—can you believe that, two hellholes on the same street—what was it, zoned H1 for hell? A real shithole run by a nincompoop alkie, but expensive as hell, so, of course, Mumsy thought it was good, the woman was always such an *arriviste*."

I tried to look like a fascinated student . . . still no sounds from the bedrooms.

Coburg said, "A nincompoop. Not even a challenge. A book of matches and some notebook paper." Smile.

Firesetters and truants . . . Bancroft hadn't said the fire was at *his* school.

"Poor Mumsy was *stymied*, out on the next plane, the poor thing. This wonderful look of *hopelessness* on her face—and she such an educated woman. Crying as we waited for our taxi—I thought I'd finally scored a point. Then *he* walked over. From across the street. This *goatish* thing in a black suit and cheap shoes. Taking Mummy's hand, telling her he'd heard what had happened, tsk-tsking and letting her cry some more about her bad little boy. Then telling her *his* school could handle those kinds of things. Guaranteed. All the while tousling my hair—twelve years old and he was tousling my fucking hair. His hand stank of cabbage and bay rum."

The gun hand wavered a bit . . . not enough.

Scratch, bump.

"Mummy was *thrilled*—she knew him from his magazine articles. A famous man willing to tame her wild child." His free hand fluttered. "The cab came and she sent it off empty."

The gun withdrew far enough for me to see its black snout, dark against his white knuckles.

Two hellholes on the same street. De Bosch exploiting Bancroft's failures. An alumnus of both schools, coming back years later, a tramp . . . the clean-cut face in front of me bore no street scars. But sometimes the wounds that healed weren't the important ones.

"Across the street I went. Mummy signed some papers and left me alone with Hitler. He smiled at me and said, 'Andrew, little Andrew. We have the same name, let's be friends.' Me saying, 'Fuck you, old goat.' He smiled again and patted my head. Took me down a long dark hall, shoved me into a cell, and locked it. I cried all night. When they let me out for lunch, I snuck into the kitchen and found matches."

A wistful look came into his eyes.

"How thorough was I tonight? Did I leave anything standing at Casa del Shrinko?"

I remained silent.

The gun poked me. "*Did* I?"

"Not much."

"Good. It's a shoddy world, thoroughness is so rare a quality. You personify shoddiness. You were as easy to get to as a sardine in a can. All of you were—tell me, why are psychotherapists such a passive, *helpless* bunch? Why are you all such absolute *wimps—talking* about life rather than *doing* anything?"

I didn't answer.

He said, "You really are, you know. Such an *unimpressive* group. Stripped of your jargon, you're noth—if that dog of yours doesn't shut up, I'm going to kill him—better yet, I'll make *you* kill him. Make you *eat* him—we can grill him on that barbecue you've got out back. A nice little *hot* dog—that would be justice, wouldn't it—making you confront your own cruelty? Give you a taste of *empathy?*"

"Why don't we just let him go?" I said. "He's not mine, just a stray I took in."

"How kind of you." Jab. My breastbone felt inflamed.

I said, "Why don't we let my friend go, too? She hasn't seen your faces."

He smiled and settled back a bit.

"Shoddiness," he said. "That's the big problem. Phony science, false premises, false promises. You pretend to help people but you just mind-fuck them."

He leaned forward. "How do you manage to live with yourself, knowing you're a phony?"

Jab. "Answer me."

"I've helped people."

"How? With voodoo? With bad love?"

Trying to keep the whine out of *my* voice, I said, "I had nothing to do with de Bosch except for that symposium."

"*Except* for? *Except* for! That's like Eichmann saying he had nothing to do with Hitler *except* for getting those trains to the camps. That symposium was a public *love fest*, you asshole! You stood up there and canonized him! He tortured children and you *canonized* him!"

"I didn't know."

"Yeah, you and all the other good Germans."

He spat at me again. The knuckles of his gun hand were tiny cauliflowers. Sweat popped at his hairline.

"That's *it*?" he said. "That's your *excuse*—'I didn't *know*'? *Pathetic*. Just like all the others. For a bunch of supposedly educated people, you can't even *plead* for yourselves effectively. No class. *Delmar* had more class in his little finger than the lot of you put together, and he was *retarded*. Not that it stopped them from bad-loving him day in and day out."

He shook his head and flung sweat. I saw his index finger move up and down the trigger. The painful, hungry look on his face made my bowels churn. But then it was gone and he was smiling again.

"Retarded," he said, as if enjoying the word. "Fourteen, but he was more like a seven-year-old. I was twelve, but I ended up being his big brother. He was the only one in the place who'd talk to me—beware the dangerous pyromaniac—Hitler warned them all against having anything to do with me. I was completely shunned except by Delmar. He couldn't think clearly, but he had a heart of gold. Hitler took him in for the publicity—poor little Negro retardo helped by the great white doctor. When visitors came, he always had his hand on Delmar's woolly little head. But Delmar was no great success. Delmar couldn't remember rules or learn how to read and write. So when there were no visitors around, he kept bad-loving him, over and over. And when that didn't work, they sent in the she-beast."

"Myra Evans?"

"No, not her, you idiot. She was the *bitch*, I'm talking about the *beast*—Dr. *Daughter*. Kill-Me *Kate*—thank you, I already have."

High-pitched laughter. The gun moved back some more and I stared into its single, black eye.

The dog began scratching again, but Coburg didn't notice.

"When the *beast* finished with Delmar, he was drooling and crapping his pants and banging his head against the wall."

"What did she do to him?"

"What did she *do*? She did a number on his *head*. And other parts of his body."

"She molested him?"

His free hand touched his cheek and he arched his eyebrows.

"Such *shock*, the poor man is *shocked*! Yeah, she *molested* him, you idiot. In ways that *hurt*. He'd come back from sessions with her crying and *holding* himself. Crawl into bed, weeping. I had the room next door. I'd pick the lock and sneak him something to drink. When I asked him what the matter was, he wouldn't tell me. Not for weeks. Then he finally did. I didn't know much about sex, period, let alone ugly things. He pulled down his pants and showed me the marks. Dried blood all over his shorts. *That* was my introduction to the birds and the bees. It *altered* me, it altered me."

His lips vibrated and he swallowed hard a couple of times. The gun arm like steel.

The glass door vibrated.

"So he took the truck," I said. "To escape what she was doing to him."

"*We* took it. I knew how to drive because Evil had a farm in Connecti—a summer place, lots of trucks and tractors. One of the farmhands taught me. Planning the break was hard because Delmar had trouble remembering details. We had a bunch of false starts. Finally we made it out, late at night, everyone asleep. Delmar was scared. I had to drag him."

The gun barrel made tiny arcs.

"I had no idea which way to go, so I just drove. The roads kept getting curvier. Delmar was scared out of his mind, crying for his mama. I'm telling him everything's okay—but some idiot left sawhorses in the middle of the road—a ditch, no warning lights. We skidded . . . off the road . . . I yelled for Delmar to jump free, tried to *pull* him out, but he was too heavy—then my door flipped open and I was thrown out. Delmar . . ."

He licked his lips and breathed with forced deliberation. His finger tapped the trigger.

"Boom. Kaboom," he said. "Life is so tenuous, isn't it?"

He looked winded, dripping perspiration. The big smile on his face was forced.

"He . . . it took me two hours to walk back to hell. My clothes were torn and I'd twisted my ankle. It was a miracle—I was alive. Meant for something. I managed to crawl into bed . . . my teeth were chattering so loud I was sure everyone would wake up. It took a while till the commotion began. Talking, footsteps, lights going on. Then Hitler came stomping into my room, tore the covers off me, and stared at me—foaming at the mouth. I looked right back at him. This crazy look came into his eyes and he lifted his hands—like he was ready to claw me. I stared right back at him and pulled my pud. And he just let his arms drop. Walked out. Never spoke to me again. I was locked in my room for three days. On the fourth day, Mummy came and picked me up. Go east, young victor."

"So you won," I said.

"Oh, yeah," he said. "I was the conquering hero." Jab. "My victory bought me more dungeons. More sadists, pills, and needles. That's what your places are about, whether you call them hospitals or jails or *schools*. Killing the *spirit*."

I remembered the flash of anger he'd shown in his office, when we'd talked about Dorsey Hewitt.

He should have been taken care of . . .

Institutionalized?

Taken care of. Not jailed—oh, hell, even jail wouldn't have been bad if that would have meant treatment. But it never does.

"But you got past that," I said. "You made it through law school, you're helping other people."

He laughed and the gun retreated an inch or two.

"Don't patronize me, you fuck. Yeah, let's hear it for higher education. You know where I learned my torts and jurisprudence? The library at Rahway State Prison. Filing *appeals* for myself and the other wretches. *That's* where I learned the law was written by the oppressors to benefit the oppressors. But like fire, you could learn to use it. Make it *work* for you."

He laughed again and wiped his forehead. "The only bars I ever passed, were the ones on my *cell*. For five years, I've been going up against yuppie careerist assholes from Harvard and Stanford and kicking their asses in court. I've had judges compliment my work."

"Five years," I said. "Right after Myra."

"Right *before*." He grinned. "The bitch was a gift to myself. I'd just gotten the gig at the center. Gave myself two gifts. The bitch and a new guitar—black Les Paul Special. You remember my guitar, don't you? All that rapport-building crap you slung at me in my office?"

The guitar-pick tiepin . . .

What do you do mostly, electric or acoustic?

Lately I've been getting into electric.

Special effects, too. Phase shifters . . .

He grinned and raised his free hand as if for a high-five. "Hey, bro, let's jam and cut a record."

"Is that the offer you gave Lyle Gritz?"

The grin shrank.

"A human decoy," I said. "To throw me off the track?"

He jabbed me hard with the gun and slapped my face with his free hand. "Shut up and stop *controlling,* or I'll do you right here and make your little friend in there clean it up. Keep those fucking hands up—up!"

I felt spit hit my cheek again and roll over my lips. Silence from the bedroom. The dog's struggles had become background noise.

"Say you're sorry," he said, "for trying to control."

"I'm sorry."

He reached over and patted my cheek. Almost tenderly.

"The bitch," he said wistfully. "She was *given* to me. Served on a plate with parsley and new potatoes."

The gun wavered, then straightened. He crossed his legs. The soles of his shoes were unmarked except for a few bits of gravel stuck in the treads.

"Karma," he said. "I was living out in the valley, nice little bachelor pad in Van Nuys. Driving home on a Sunday. These flags out at the curb. Open house for sale. When I was a kid, I liked other people's houses—anything better than my own. I got good at getting *into* other people's houses. This one looked like it might have a few souvenirs, so I stopped to check it out. I ring the bell. The real estate agent comes to the door and right away she's giving me her pitch. Da *da,* da *da,* da *da,* da *da.*

"But I'm not hearing a word she's saying. I'm looking at her face and it's the *bitch.* Some wrinkles, her boobs are sagging, but there's no doubt about it. She's shaking my hand, talking about pride of ownership, owner will carry. And it hits me: this is no accident. This is *karma.* All these years I'd been thinking about justice. All those nights I lay in bed thinking about getting Hitler, but the fuck beat me to it."

He grimaced, as if stung. "I thought I'd put *that* behind me, then I looked into the bitch's eyes and realized I hadn't. And she made it so easy—playing *her* part. Turning her back and walking right in front of me. Open invitation."

He coughed. Cleared his throat. The gun bumped against my sternum.

"Everything was perfect—no one around. I locked all the doors without her noticing, she's too busy giving me her spiel. When we reached an inner bathroom with no windows, I hit her. And did her. She fell apart as if she was made of nothing. At first it was messy. Then it got easier. Like a good riff, the rhythm."

He talked on for a long while, slipping into a drone, like a surgeon dictating operating-room notes. Giving me details I didn't want to hear. I tuned out, listening to the dog thump and bark, listening for sounds from the bedrooms that never came.

Silence. Sighing. He said, "I found my life's work."

"Rodney Shipler," I said. "He didn't work at the school, did he? Was he a relative of Delmar's?"

"Father. In name only."

"What was his crime?"

"Complicity. Delmar's mom was dead, Shipler was the only member of Delmar's family I could find. Delmar told me his dad was named Rodney and he worked for the L.A. schools—I thought he was a teacher. Finally I located him over in South Central. A janitor. This tired old asshole, big and fat, living by himself, drinking whiskey out of a Dixie cup. I told him I was a lawyer and I knew what really happened to his son. Said we could sue, class action—even after the bitch, I was still trying to work within the system. He sat there drinking and listening, then asked me could I guarantee him a lot of money in his pocket. I told him no, money wasn't the issue. The publicity would expose Hitler for what he'd really been. Delmar would be a hero."

Jab. "Shipler poured himself another cup and told me he didn't give a shit about that. Said Delmar's mom had been some whore he'd met in Manila who wasn't worth the time of day. Said Delmar had been a fool and a troublemaker from day one. I tried to reason with him—show him the importance of exposing Hitler. He told me to get the hell out. Tried to push me out."

Coburg's eyes flared. The gun seemed fused to his hand.

"Another good German. He tried to push me out—real bully, but I taught him about justice. After that, I knew the only way was swift punishment—the system wasn't set up to do the job."

I said, "One form of punishment for the underlings, another for the high command."

"Exactly. Fair is fair." He smiled. "Finally *someone* catches on.

Mrs. Lyndon was *right*, you *are* a clever piece of work. I told her I was a reporter, doing a story on you. She was so happy to help . . . her little A student." The gun tickled my ribs. "You deserve something for paying attention—maybe I'll knock you unconscious before I roll you over the cliff outside. Such a perfect setup . . ." Head cock toward the front door. "Would you like that?"

Before I could answer: "Just *kidding*! Your eyes will be taped *open*, you'll experience every *second* of hell, just like I did."

He laughed. Droned some more, describing how he'd beaten Rodney Shipler to death, blow by blow.

When he was through, I said, "Katarina was high command also. Why'd you wait so long for her?"

Trying to buy time with questions—but to what end? A longer ordeal for Robin—why was it so quiet in there?

My eyes shifted downward. The damn gun arm wasn't moving.

He said, "Why do you think, clever boy? Saving the best for last—and you messed me up royal. *You* were supposed to go before *her*, but then you started snooping around, sending your queer police buddy snooping, so I had to do her out of sequence. . . . I'm pissed at you for that. Maybe I'll put your girlfriend on the *barbecue*. Make you watch that with your eyelids taped open."

Smiling. Sighing. "Still, she-beast got done, and what's done is done . . . do you know how she handled her fate? Total *passivity*. Just like the *rest* of you." Jab. "What kind of person would want to spend his life just sitting there listening—not *doing* anything?"

He laughed.

"She got down on her knees and begged. Her she-beast throat got all clogged up like a toilet full of shit. . . . She was eating breakfast, I just strolled in, put this gun to her head, said 'bad love, she-beast.' And she just fell apart."

Shaking his head, as if still not believing. Slight shift of the gun.

"Not an ounce of fight. No fun. I had to stand her up and order her to make a run for it. Kicked her *butt* to get her to move. Even with that, all she could do was stumble into the garage and get down on her knees again. *Then* she snapped out of her trance. *Then* she started begging. Crying, pointing to her stomach, telling

me she's pregnant, please have pity on my baby. Like *she* had pity
. . . then she pulled a card out of her pocket, trying to prove it to
me. A sperm bank. Which makes sense, who would have *done*
her?" Laughter. "Like that was a reason. Saving her beastly fetus.
Au contraire, that was the best reason of *all* to *do* her. Kill Hitler's
seed."

Another shake of the head. "Unbelievable. She bloodies Delmar's shorts and thinks that's a good reason. . . . She started to
tell me she was on my side, she'd helped me, killing *him*."

"She killed her father?"

"She claimed she OD'ed him on pills. Like she'd gotten some
insight. But I knew she did it as a favor to *him*. Putting him out of
his misery. Making sure *I'd* never get to him. Giving me *another*
reason to do her hard and long, she's blabbing and just digging
herself deeper." Smile. "I made sure to do the baby first. Pulled it
out, still attached to her, showed it to her and put it back in her."

The dog's struggles seemed to be weakening; I thought I
heard him whimper.

Coburg said, "You messed up my order, but that's okay, I'll
get creative. You and your little friend will be an adequate final
act."

"What about the others?" I said, fighting to keep my voice
even. Fighting to focus my own rage. "Why'd you choose the order you did?"

"I keep telling you, I didn't choose *anything*. The pattern constructed itself. I put your names into a hat and drew them out,
eeny-meeny—all the meanies."

"The names of the people who spoke at the symposium."

Nod. "All you good Germans. I'd been thinking about all of
you for years—even before doing the bitch."

"You were there," I said. "Listening to us."

"Sitting in a back row, taking it all in."

"You were a kid. How'd you come to be there?"

"More karma. I was nineteen, living in Hollywood and crash-
ing at a halfway house on Serrano."

Just a few blocks from Western Peds.

". . . taking a walk on Sunset and I saw this program board
out in front. Psychiatric symposium, tomorrow morning."

Tensing up, he waved the gun, arm dipping for just one second, then snapping back into place, the barrel touching my shirt.

"*His* name . . . I went in and picked up a brochure at the

information desk. Shaved and showered and put on my best clothes and just walked in. And watched all you hypocritical bastards get up there and say what a *pioneer* he'd been. Child *advocate*. Gifted *teacher*. The she-beast and her home movies. Everyone smiling and applauding—I could barely sit there without screaming—I should have screamed. Should have gotten up and told all of you what you really were. But I was young, no confidence. So instead, I went out that night and hurt *myself*. Which bought me another dungeon. *Lots* of time to think and get my *focus*. I'd cut out your pictures. Pasted them on a piece of paper. Kept the paper in a box. Along with other important things. I've lived with you assholes longer than most people stay married."

"Why was Dr. Harrison spared?"

He stared at me, as if I'd said something stupid. "Because he *listened*. Right after the Hitler canonization, I called him and told him it had bothered me. And he *listened*. I could tell he was taking me seriously. He made an appointment to speak to me. I was going to show up, but something came up—another dungeon."

"Why'd you tell him your name was Merino? Why'd you tell *me* you were Mr. Silk?"

Wrinkled forehead. "You spoke to Harrison? Maybe I'll visit him after all."

A sick feeling flooded me. "He doesn't know anyth—"

"Don't fret, fool, I'm fair, always have been. I gave all of you the same chance I gave Harrison. But the rest of you flunked."

"You never called me," I said.

Smile. "November thirtieth, nineteen seventy-nine. Two p.m. I have a written record of it. Your snotty secretary insisted you only treated children and couldn't see me."

"She wasn't supposed to screen—I never knew."

"That's an *excuse*? When the troops fuck up, the general's culpable. And it was a chance you didn't even deserve—a lot more than I got, or Delmar, or any of the other *loved* ones. You muffed it, bro."

"But Rosenblatt," I said. "He *did* see you."

"He was the *biggest* hypocrite. Pretending to understand—the soft voice, the phony *empathy*. Then he revealed his true colors. Quizzing me, trying to get into *my* head." Coburg put on an unctuous look: " 'I'm hearing a lot of pain . . . one thing you might consider is talking about this more.' " Fury compressed the light brown eyes. "The phony bastard wanted to give me *psychoanalysis* to deal with my *conflicts*. Hundred-buck-an-hour *couch work* as a cure for political oppression because he couldn't accept the fact that he'd worshiped Hitler. He sat there and *pretended* to hear, but he didn't believe me. Just wanted to mess with my head—the worst one of all, bye-bye birdie."

He made a shoving motion with his free hand and smiled.

I said, "How'd you get him to see you outside his office?"

"I told him I was bedridden. Crippled by something Hitler had done. *That* piqued his interest, he came right over that evening, with his kind looks and his beard and his bad tweed suit—it was hot but he needed his little shrink costume. The whole time he was there, I stayed in bed. The second time, also. I had him bring me a drink . . . . serving *me*. It was a really muggy day, the window was *wide* open for air. Tissue box on the ledge—karma. I pretended to sneeze and asked him to get me a tissue." Shove. "Fly away, hypocrite bird."

Other people's houses. A financial man . . . A farm in Connecticut. Did that mean an apartment in New York City? And her such an educated woman.

She a lawyer, he a banker.

I said, "The apartment belonged to your mother and stepfather."

He shook his head joyfully. "Clever little Alex. Mrs. Lyndon would be so proud. . . . Mummy and Evil were in Europe, so I decided to crash at the old homestead. Rosenblatt's office two blocks away . . . karma. Eight floors up, have a nice flight."

Mr. and Mrs. Malcolm J. Rulerad. Cold people, Shirley Rosenblatt had said. Unwilling to let a private investigator search their place. Guarding more than privacy? How much had they known?

"You left burglar tools behind," I said. "Did you need them to get in, or were you just setting it up as another East Side burglary?"

He tried to mask his surprise with a slow, languid smile. "My, my, we *have* been busy. No, I had a key. One keeps looking for home sweet home. The big Brady Bunch in the sky . . ."

"Stoumen and Lerner," I said. "Did they meet with you?"

"No," he said, suddenly angry again. "Stoumen's excuse was that he was retired. Another flunky shutting me out, did I want to speak to the doctor on call—you people really don't know how to delegate authority properly. And Lerner made an appointment but didn't show up, the rude bastard."

The unreliability Harrison had spoken of: *it had affected his work—missed appointments.*

"So you tracked them down at conferences—how'd you get hold of the membership lists?"

"Some of us are thorough—Mrs. Lyndon would have liked me, too—what a kindly old bag, all that midwestern salt-of-the-earth friendliness. Research is *such* fun, maybe I'll visit *her* in person someday."

"Did Meredith help you get the lists?" I said. "Was she doing publicity for the conventions?"

Pursed lips. Tense brow. The hand wavered. "Meredith . . . ah, yes, dear *Meredith*. She's been a great help—now, stop asking stupid questions and get down on your knees—keep those hands up—keep them up!"

Moving as slowly as I could, I got off the couch and kneeled, trying to keep a fix on the gun.

Silence, then another impact that shook the glass.

"The dog's definitely chops and steaks," he said.

The gun touched the crown of my head. He ruffled my hair with the barrel and I knew he was remembering.

The weapon pressed down on me, harder, as if boring into my skull. All I could see were his shoes, the bottoms of his jeans. A grout seam between two marble tiles.

"Say you're sorry," he said.

"Sorry."

"Louder."

"*Sorry.*"

"Personalize it—'I'm sorry, Andrew.' "

"I'm sorry, Andrew."

"More sincerity."

"I'm sorry, Andrew."

He made me repeat it six times, then he sighed. "I guess that's as good as it's going to get. How are you feeling right now?"

"I've been better."

Chuckle. "I'll bet you have—stand up slowly—*slowly*. Slo-o-o-wly. Keep those hands up—hands on head—Simon says."

He stepped back, the gun trained on my head. Behind me was the couch. Chairs all around. An upholstered prison, nowhere to go . . . a run for it would be suicide, leaving Robin to deal with his frustration. . . .

The dog throwing himself, harder . . .

I was upright now. He stepped closer. We came face-to-face. Licorice and rage, lowering the gun and pushing it against my navel. Then up at my throat. Then down again.

Playing.

Choreography.

"I see it," he said. "Behind your eyes—the fear—you *know* where you're going, don't you?"

I said nothing.

"Don't you?"

"Where am I going?"

"Straight to hell. One-way ticket."

The gun nudged my groin. Moved up to my throat again. Pressed against my heart. Back down to my crotch.

Taking on a rhythm—the musician in him . . . moving his hips.

I was altered . . .

Groin. Heart. Groin.

He poked my crotch and laughed. When he raised the gun again, I exploded, chopping the gun wrist with my right hand as I stabbed at his eye with the stiffened fingertips of my left.

The gun fired as he lost balance.

He landed on his side, the gun still laced between his fingers. I stomped on his wrist. His free hand was clamped over his face. When he pulled it free and grabbed at my leg, his eye was shut, bleeding.

I stomped again and again. He roared with pain. The gun hand was limp, but the weapon remained entangled. He struggled to lift it and aim. I dropped my knee full force on his arm, got hold of the hand, tugging, twisting, finally freeing the automatic.

My turn to aim. My hands were numb. I had trouble bending my fingers around the trigger. He slid across the carpet on his back, kicking out randomly, holding his eye. Blood ran over his hand. His escape was blocked by a sofa. Flailing and kicking—he looked at me.

No—*behind* me.

He screamed, "Do it!" as I ducked and wheeled, facing the hallway.

The smaller gun in my face. A woman's hand behind it. Red nails. Coburg shouting, "Do it! Do it! Do it!" Starting to get up.

I dropped to the floor just as the little gun went off.

More gunshots. Hollow pops, softer than the black pistol's thunder.

Coburg on me. We rolled. I struck out with the black gun and caught the side of his head. He fell back, soundlessly, landed on his back. Not moving.

Where was the silver gun? Arcing toward me again from across the room. Two red-nailed hands starting to squeeze.

I dove behind the couch.

Pop! The fabric puckered and gobbets of stuffing flew inches from my face.

I pressed myself flush to the marble.

Pop! Pop, pop!

Heavy breathing—gasping—but whose I couldn't tell.

Pop!

A dull noise from my back, then the windchime song of shattered glass. Scampering feet.

A small, black blur raced past me toward Meredith.

Hooking my arm around the couch, I fired the big black automatic blindly, trying to aim well above dog level. The recoil drove me backward. Something crashed.

Barks and growls and female screams.

I scuttled to the opposite side of the couch, squeezed the trigger, waited for return fire.

More screams. Footsteps. Human. Getting distant.

I hazarded a look around the couch, saw her heading for the front door, silver gun dangling like a purse.

Coburg still down.

Where was the dog?

Meredith was almost at the door now. The bolt was thrown—she was having trouble with it.

I rushed her, pointing the black gun, feeling the trigger's heavy action start to give.

Swift justice.

Screaming "Stop!" I fired into a wall.

She obeyed. Held onto the silver gun.

"Drop it, drop it!"

The gun fell to the floor and skidded away.

She said, "I'm sorry, I didn't want to—he made me."

"Turn around."

She did. I yanked off her mask.

Her face was trembling, but she tossed her hair in a gesture more suited for a teenager.

Blond hair.

My hand was still compressing the trigger. I forced myself not to move.

Jean Jeffers said, "He made me," and glanced at Coburg. He remained openmouthed and inert, and her eyes died. She tried tears.

"You rescued me," she said. "Thanks."

"What'd you do with Robin?"

"She's fine—I promise. She's in there—go see."

"Step out in front of me."

"Sure, but this is silly, Alex. He made me—he's crazy—we're on the same side, Alex."

Another look at Coburg.

His chest wasn't moving.

Keeping the black gun on Jeffers, I stooped and pocketed the silver one. Maintaining a clear view of her, I managed to pull a large, upholstered chair over the bottom half of Coburg's body. Not worth much, but it would have to do for the moment.

I walked Jeffers back to the bedroom. The door was closed. The dog stood on his hind legs, scratching at it, gouging the paint. An acetone stink came from the other side. Familiar . . .

"Open it," I said.

She did.

Robin was spreadeagled on the bed, hands and feet tied to the posts with nylon fishing line, duct tape over her mouth, a bandana over her eyes. On the nightstand were the spool of line, scissors, nail polish, a box of tissues, and Robin's manicure set.

Nail polish remover—the acetone.

A used emery board. Jeffers had passed the time by doing her nails.

She said, "Let me free her, right now."

I pocketed the scissors and let her, using her hands. She worked clumsily, the dog up on the bed, growling at her, circling Robin, licking Robin's face. Specks of blood dappled his fur. Diamond glints of broken glass . . . Robin sat up and rubbed her wrists and looked at me, stunned.

I motioned her off the bed and gave her the silver gun. Shoved Jeffers down on it, belly down, hands behind her back.

"Did she hurt you?" I said.

Jeffers said, "Of course I didn't."

Robin shook her head.

Jeffers' red nails were so fresh they still looked wet.

She said, "Can we please—"

Robin tied her up quickly. Then we returned to the living room. Coburg's head where I'd hit him was huge, soft, eggplant-purple. He was starting to move a bit but hadn't regained consciousness.

Robin trussed him expertly, those good, strong hands.

The dog was at my feet, panting. I got down and inspected him. He licked my hands. Licked the gun.

Superficial cuts, no sign he was suffering. Robin picked the glass out of his fur and lifted him, kissing him, cradling him like a baby.

I picked up the phone.

33

Three days later, I waited for Milo at a place named Angela's, across the street from the West L.A. stationhouse. The front was a coffee shop. In back was a cocktail lounge where detectives, lawyers, bailbondsmen, and felons drank and worked on their lung tumors.

I took a booth at the rear of the lounge, drinking coffee and trying to concentrate on the morning paper. Nothing yet on the "bad love" murders, orders of the brass till it got sorted out. Coburg was in the hospital, and Milo had been virtually sequestered with Jean Jeffers at the county jail.

When he showed up, fifteen minutes late, a woman was with him, thirties, black. The two of them stood in the doorway of the lounge, outlined by hazy gray light.

Adeline Potthurst, the social worker I'd seen on film, Dorsey Hewitt's knife up against her throat.

She looked older and heavier. A big white purse was clutched in front of her, like a fig leaf.

Milo said something to her. She glanced over at me and replied. A bit more conversation, then they shook hands and she left.

He came over and slid into the booth. "Remember her? She's talking to me."

"She have anything interesting to say?"

He smiled, lit up a cigar, and added to the pollution. "Oh, yeah."

Before he could elaborate, a waitress arrived and took his Diet Coke order.

When she left, he said, "Lots happening. I've got New York records placing Coburg in Manhattan during all the East Side break-ins up till the day after Rosenblatt's death: busted for shop-lifting, he was arrested in Times Square two days before the first burglary, went to court the day he shoved Rosenblatt out the win-dow, but his attorney got a continuance. Records listed his address as some dive near Times Square."

"So he celebrated with murder."

He nodded grimly. "Jivin' Jean finally opened up—her attor-ney convinced her to sell out Coburg for a reduced plea to acces-sory. Names, dates, places, she's puttin' on a good show."

"What's her connection to de Bosch?"

"She says none," he said. "Claims the revenge thing was all Coburg's game, she didn't really know what he was up to. She says she met him at a mental health convention—advocacy for the homeless. Struck up a conversation at the bar and found they had lots in common."

"Social worker encounters public interest lawyer," I said. "A couple of idealists, huh?"

"God help us." He loosened his tie.

"Coburg probably went to lots of conventions. With his phony law degree and his public-interest persona, he would have fit right in. Meanwhile, he's looking for de Bosch disciples. *And* trying to undo his past. Symbolically. All those years he spent in institutions. Now he's in the power role, hobnobbing with ther-apists. He was like a little kid, thinking magically. Pretending he could make it all go away."

"We're still trying to unravel his travel schedule, place him and Jeffers together at least once: Acapulco, the week Mitchell Ler-ner was killed. Jeffers admits going along for the weekend—she presented a paper—but claims to know nothing about Lerner. She also admits using her position to get Coburg shrink mailing lists, but says she thought he just wanted to use them in order to adver-tise the law center."

"How does she explain trussing up Robin and taking potshots at me?"

He grinned. "What do you think?"

"The Devil made her do it."

"You bet. As their relationship developed, Coburg began to dominate her psychologically and physically. She'd started to have some suspicions about him, but was too afraid to back away from him."

"Does physically mean sexually?"

"She says there was some of that, but mostly she claims he used mind control, threats, and intimidation to get into her head. Kind of a mini-Manson thing: poor, vulnerable woman taken in by psychopathic Svengali. She says the night he announced he was going to get you, she didn't want any part of it. But Coburg threatened to tell her husband the two of them had been screwing for five years, and when that didn't work, he flat out said he'd kill her."

"How does she explain being so vulnerable?"

"Because she'd been abused as a kid. She says that was what drew her to Coburg—their mutual experiences. At first, their relationship was platonic. Lunch, talking about work, Coburg helping some of her clients out of legal jams, she helping *him* get social services for his. Eventually, it got more personal, but still no sex. Then one day, Coburg took her to his apartment, cooked lunch, had a heart to heart and told her all the shit he'd been through as a kid. She told him she had, too, and they ended up having this big emotional scene—cathartic, she called it. *Then* they went to bed and the whole relationship started taking another turn."

"Five years," I said. "That's when the murders began. . . . Who does she say abused her?"

"Daddy. She's free and easy with the ugly details, but it'll be impossible to verify—both parents and her only sibling, a brother, are dead."

"Natural causes?"

"We're looking into it."

"Convenient," I said. "Everyone's a victim. I guess she could be telling the truth about being abused. First time I met her she told me violating a child's trust was the lowest, she could never work with abuse cases. Then again, she could have been toying with me—she and Coburg got off on playing games."

"Even if it's true, it doesn't change the fact that she's a psychopathic witch. *Couple* of goddamn psychopaths—there's your two pathologies scenario."

"The bond between them couldn't be that deep. It didn't take long for her to sell him out."

"Honor among scumbags." His drink came and he cooled his hands on the glass.

I said, "So what about Becky? What does Jean say the link was between her and Coburg?"

"She claims to have no idea what his motive was, there." He smiled. "And guess what? He didn't have one, other than making Jean happy."

"Becky was *Jean's* thing?"

"You bet. And that's what I'm gonna get her on. All her cooperation on the other murders isn't going to help her there, because I've got independent info on a motive: Becky and Dick Jeffers were having an affair. For six months."

"How'd you find that out?"

"From the newly talkative Ms. Adeline Potthurst. Adeline saw Becky and Dick Jeffers together, sneaking off during a Christmas party at the center. Kissing passionately, his hand up her skirt."

"Not very discreet."

"Apparently Becky and Dick weren't—he used to come by to pick up Jean and end up talking to Becky, body language all over the place. The affair was semipublic knowledge at the center—I checked it out with some of the other workers and they confirm it."

"Meaning Jean knew."

"Jean knew because Dickie told her. I had a chat with him this morning—guy's a basket case—and he admitted everything. Six months of illicit passion. Said he was planning to leave Jean for Becky, and he let Jean know it."

"How'd she react?"

"Calmly. They had a nice chat and she told him she loved him, was committed to him, please give it some thought, let's get some counseling, et cetera."

"Did they?"

"No. A month later, Becky's dead. And there's no reason for anyone to make a connection—a nut hacking her up. The way I see it, it's just like you said: Jean and Coburg searched for a nut who could be *manipulated* to hack her up and came up with Hewitt—both of them had ties to him."

"What was Jeffers' tie?"

"She was his therapist before transferring him to Becky—supposedly because of a heavy workload."

"She told me Becky was the only therapist he had."

"Adeline says no, Jeffers definitely treated him. And Mary Chin, Jeffers' secretary, confirms it. Twice-a-week sessions, sometimes more, for at least three or four months before Becky took over. We can't find any therapy notes—no doubt Jeffers destroyed them—but that only makes it look worse for her."

I said, "She made a point of telling me she didn't do therapy anymore—another mind game . . . why didn't the fact that she was working with Hewitt ever come out after Becky's murder?"

The hand went over his face. "We didn't ask, and no one volunteered. Why would they? Everyone saw it as psycho kills girl. And we killed the psycho. No one suspected a damn thing—none of the staffers at the center or Dick Jeffers. He's pretty freaked out now. Coming to grips with the monster he's been living with. Says he's willing to testify against her—whether or not he sticks with that remains to be seen."

"An affair," I said. "So goddamned mundane. Jean sleeps with Coburg for five years, but Becky gets the death penalty . . . typical psychopathic thinking, the ego out of control: you hurt me, I kill you."

"Yeah," he said, drinking and licking his lips. "So tell me, specifically, how would you get a nut like Hewitt to kill?"

"I'd pick someone with strong paranoid tendencies whose fantasies got violent when he was off his medicine. Then I'd *get* him off his medicine, either by convincing him to stop taking it or by substituting a placebo, and try to get as much control as I could over his psyche as he deteriorated. Maybe use some age-regression techniques—hypnosis or free association, bring him back to his childhood—get him to confront the helplessness of childhood. To *feel* it. The pain, the rage."

"The screams," he said.

I nodded. "That's probably why they taped him. They got him to scream out his pain, played it back for him—you remember how hard it was to listen to. Can you imagine a schizophrenic dealing with that? Meanwhile, they're also teaching him about bad love, evil shrinks—indoctrinating him, telling him he's been a victim. And insinuating *Becky* into the delusion, as a major-league evil shrink—the purveyor of bad love. They continue to increase his paranoia by praising him for it. Convincing him he's some kind of soldier on a mission: get Becky. Then they transfer him to her. But I'll bet Jean continued to see him on the side. Prepping him, directing him. Backed up by Coburg—another authority figure for Hewitt. And the beauty of it is even if Hewitt hadn't been killed at the scene and had talked, who would have believed him? He was crazy."

"That's about the way I had it," he said. "But hearing you organize it that way helps."

"It's not hard evidence."

"I know, but the circumstantial case is building up, bit by bit. The DA's going to let Coburg's attorney know how extensively Jeffers is ratting him out, then offer a deal: no death penalty in return for Coburg ratting on Jeffers over Becky. My bet is Coburg takes it. We'll get both of them."

"Poor Becky."

"Yeah. Guess how she and Dick got started? Jean had Becky over for dinner, supervisor-student rapport and all that. Eyes across the fried chicken, a couple of knee nudges. Next day Becky and Dick are at a motel."

"Mrs. Basille said she thought Becky had a new beau. Becky wouldn't talk about it, which led Mrs. Basille to suspect it was someone she wouldn't have approved of—what she called a loser. Becky'd gone with married men before—guys who promised to get divorced but never did. Dick was *exactly* her type—married *and* disabled."

"What does disabled have to do with it?"

"Becky had a thing for guys with problems. Wounded birds. Jeffers' missing leg meshed nicely with that."

"He's missing a leg? That's what the limp is?"

"He wears a prosthesis. Becky's dad was diabetic. Lost some of *his* limbs."

"Jesus." He smoked. "So maybe there is something to this psychology stuff, huh?"

I thought about Becky Basille, trapped in a locked room with a madman. "Everything Jean and Coburg *did* was part of the ritual. Like forging Becky's therapy notes and scripting them to make it seem Becky was having an affair with *Hewitt*. In addition to diverting us, once more, to Gritz, it added insult to injury by humiliating Becky. As if that could undo the humiliation Becky'd caused Jean."

He stubbed out his cigar. "Speaking of Gritz, I think I found him. Once I realized Coburg and Jeffers were probably using him as a distraction, I figured the poor sucker's life expectancy wasn't too great and started to call around at morgues. Long Beach has someone who fits his description perfectly. Multiple stab wounds and ligature around the neck—a guitar string."

"The next Elvis. I'd check Coburg's guitar case."

"Del Hardy already did. Coburg's got a bunch of guitars. And a phase shifter and other recording stuff. In one of the cases was a set of brand-new strings. Missing the low E. The other interesting things that came up were a man's shirt too small to be Coburg's, torn up and used for a rag, still stinking of booze. And an old Corrective School attendance roster with nineteen seventy-three ripped out."

"Small shirt," I said. "Gritz was a little man."

He nodded. "And a client of the law center. Coburg had gotten *him* off a theft thing, too, couple of months ago."

"Any indication he ever knew Hewitt?"

"No."

"Poor guy," I said. "They probably lured him with notions of being a recording star—let him play with the guitars and the gizmos, make a demo. That's why he talked about getting rich. Then they killed him and used him as a red herring. No family connections, the perfect victim. Where was the body found?"

"Near the harbor. Naked, no ID, quite a bit worse for wear. He'd been in one of their coolers with a John Doe toe tag. They figure he's been dead anywhere from four days to a week."

"Right around the time you called Jeffers and asked her to speak to me. You said she thought she recognized my name. When I got there she pretended it was because of the Casa de los Niños case. But she knew it from Coburg's hit list—it must have shocked them, their next victim in their face, like that. Your making the connection between the 'bad love' tape and what happened to Becky. Someone else might have backed off, but clearing the list just meant too much to Coburg—he couldn't let go of it. So he and Jean decided to stay on track and use Gritz as extra insurance.

Jeffers sends me to Coburg, Coburg just happens to remember Gritz was Hewitt's friend and directs me to Little Calcutta. Then, just in case we still weren't biting, Jeffers produces the therapy notes with all those references to 'G.' Maybe I should have wondered—Jeffers made such a big deal about Becky being a lousy note taker, then magically these appear. Mrs. Basille said Becky was a real stickler for the rules, but I figured she was just out of touch."

"There was no way to know," he said. "These people are from another planet."

"That lunch with Jeffers," I said, feeling suddenly chilled. "She sat across from me—touching my hand, letting loose the tears. Bringing Dick along was another ritual: Becky vanquished, Jean was showing off her spoils. After we were finished eating, she insisted on walking me to my car. Stood on the sidewalk, misbuttoned her sweater, and had to redo it. Probably a signal to Coburg, waiting somewhere across the street. She stayed with me all the way to the Seville—tagging the car for Coburg. He followed me up to Benedict and learned where I was hiding out."

He shook his head. "We hadn'ta caught them, they'd probably run for office."

"At lunch, I told Jeffers that I was going to Santa Barbara the next day to talk to Katarina. That got them worried I'd learn something—maybe even bring back the school roster. So they were forced to break sequence—Coburg beat me up there and killed Katarina before me. And tossed the house. Any idea why Coburg called himself Silk and Merino?"

"I asked the asshole. He didn't answer, just smiled that creepy smile. I started to walk out and then he said, 'Look it up.' So I did. In the dictionary. 'Coburg' is an old English word for imitation silk or wool. . . . Enough of this, my head's splitting. . . . How are you and Robin doing?"

"We've been able to go back to the house."

"Anything left?"

"Mostly ashes."

He shook his head. "I'm sorry, Alex."

I said, "We'll survive—we're surviving. And living in the shop's not bad—the smallness is actually kind of comforting."

"Insurance company jerking you around?"

"As predicted."

"Let me know if I can do anything."

"I will."

"And when you're ready for a contractor, I've got a possible for you—ex-cop, does nice work relatively cheap."

"Thanks," I said. "Thanks for everything—and sorry about the rental house. I'm sure your banker didn't expect bullet holes in his walls. Tell him to send me the bill."

"Don't worry about it. It's the most exciting thing's ever happened to him."

I smiled. He looked away.

"Shootout at the Beverly Hills corral," he said. "I should have been there."

"How could you have known?"

"Knowing's my job."

"You offered to drive us home, I turned you down."

"I shouldn't have listened to you."

"Come on, Milo. You did everything you could. To paraphrase a friend of mine: 'Don't flog yourself.' "

He frowned, tilted his glass, poured ice down his gullet, and crunched. "How's Rov—Spike?"

"A few surface cuts. The vet said bulldogs have high pain thresholds. A throwback to when they were used for baiting."

"Right through the glass." He shook his head. "Little maniac must have taken a running start and gone ballistic. Talk about devotion."

"You see it from time to time," I said. Then I ordered him another Coke.

34

I drove back to Venice. The shop was empty and Robin had left a note on her workbench:

11:45 a.m. Had to run to the lumberyard. Back at 2. Pls. call Mrs. Braithwaite. Says she's Spike's owner.

Pacific Palisades exchange. I phoned it before the disappointment could sink in.

A middle-aged female voice said, "Hello?"

"Mrs. Braithwaite? Dr. Delaware returning your call."

"Oh, doctor! Thank you for calling, and thank you for caring for our little Barry! Is he all right?"

"Perfect. He's a great dog," I said.

"Yes, he is. We were so worried, starting to give up hope."

"Well, he's in the pink."

"That's wonderful!"

"I guess you'd like to come by to get him. He should be back by two."

Hesitation. "Oh, certainly. Two it is."

I busied myself with the phone. Calling Shirley Rosenblatt and having a half-hour talk with her. Calling Bert Harrison, then the insurance company, where I dealt with some truly vile individuals.

I thought about the Wallace girls for a while, then remembered another little girl, the one who'd lost her boxer—Karen Alnord. I had no record of her number. All my papers were gone. Where had she lived—Reseda. On Cohasset.

I got the number from information. A woman answered and I asked for Karen.

"She's at school." Brilliant, Delaware. "Who's this?"

I gave her my name. "She called me about her boxer. I was just wondering if you found him."

"Yes, we have," she said edgily.

"Great. Thanks."

"For what?"

"Good news."

Mrs. Braithwaite showed up at one forty-five. She was short, thin, and sixtyish, with an upswept, tightly waved, tapioca-colored hairdo, sun wrinkles, and narrow brown eyes behind pearloid-framed glasses. Her maroon I. Magnin suit would have fetched top dollar at a vintage boutique, and her pearls were real. She carried a bag that matched the suit and wore a bejeweled American flag lapel pin.

She looked around the shop, confused.

"Robin's place of business," I said. "We're in between houses —planning some construction."

"Well, good luck on that. I've been through it, and one meets such an unsavory element."

"Can I offer you something to drink?"

"No, thank you."

I pulled up a chair for her. She remained standing and opened her handbag. Taking out a check, she tried to give it to me.

Ten dollars.

"No, no," I said.

"Oh, doctor, I insist."

"It's not necessary."

"But the expenses—I know how Barry eats."

"He's earned his way." I smiled. "Charming fellow."

"Yes, isn't he?" she said, but with a curious lack of passion. "Are you sure I can't reimburse you?"

"Give it to charity."

She thought. "All right, that's a good idea. Planned Parenthood always needs help."

She sat down. I repeated my drink offer and she said, "It's really not necessary, but iced tea would be fine if you have it."

As I fixed the drink, she inspected the shop some more.

When I gave her the glass, she thanked me again and sipped daintily.

"Does your wife fix violins?"

"A few. Mostly guitars and mandolins. She fixes and makes them."

"My father played the violin—quite well, actually. We went to the Bowl every summer to hear Jascha Heifetz play. Back when you could still enjoy a civilized drive through Hollywood. He taught at USC—Heifetz did, not Father. Though Father was an alumnus. So is my son. He's in marketing."

I smiled.

"May I ask what kind of doctor you are?"

"Psychologist."

Sip. "And where did you find Barry?"

"He showed up at my house."

"Where's that, doctor?"

"Just off Beverly Glen."

"South of Sunset, or north?"

"A mile and a half north."

"How odd . . . well, thank heavens for good samaritans. It's so nice to have one's faith in human nature restored."

"How did you find me, Mrs. Braithwaite?"

"From Mae Josephs at Frenchie Rescue—we were in Palm Desert and didn't get her message until today."

The door opened and Robin came in, carrying a bag and holding the dog by the leash.

"Barry!" said Mrs. Braithwaite. She got off the chair. The dog trotted straight to her and licked her hand.

"Barry, Barry, little Barry. You've had quite an adventure, haven't you!"

She petted him.

He licked her some more, then turned around, stared at me, and cocked his head.

"You look wonderful, Barry," said Mrs. Braithwaite. To us: "He looks *wonderful*, thank you so much."

"Our pleasure," said Robin. "He's a great little guy."

"Yes, he is—*aren't* you, Barrymore? Such a *sweet* boy, even with your snoring—did he snore?"

"Loud and clear," said Robin. Smiling, but her eyes had that pretears look I knew so well. I took her hand. She squeezed mine and began emptying the bag. Ebony bridge blanks.

The dog padded back over to us and propped his forelegs on Robin's thigh. She rubbed him under the chin. He pressed his little head to her leg.

"Mother loved that. The snoring. Barry was actually Mother's —she kept English bulldogs and Frenchies for over fifty years. Did quite a bit of breeding and showing in her day. And obedience training."

"Did she perimeter train him?" I said. "To avoid water?"

"Oh, of course. She trained all her dogs. She had lily ponds and a big pool, and the poor things sink like stones. Then her back started to go and the English were too heavy for her to carry, so she kept only Frenchies. Then she got too weak even for the Frenchies. Barry was her last little boy. She imported him three years ago. Flew him all the way from Holland."

A linen hankie came out of the handbag. She took off her glasses and dabbed at her eyes.

"Mother passed away three weeks ago. She'd been ill for a while and Barry was her faithful companion—weren't you, sweetie?"

She reached out her hand. The dog settled on all fours but remained next to Robin.

Mrs. Braithwaite dabbed some more. "He stayed in bed with her, barked for the nurse when she started to—I do believe he was the reason she kept going as long as she did. But of course, in— when she—the last time we had to call the paramedics, *such* terror and commotion. Barry must have slipped out. I didn't realize it until later. . . ."

"Where did your mother live?" I said.

"Little Holmby. Just off Comstock, south of the boulevard."

Two miles from my house.

She said, "He managed to cross Sunset—all that traffic." Dab. "Poor little *boy*, if anything had *happened* to you!"

"Well," said Robin, "thank God he made it."

"Yes. I see that—you've made a nice little home for him, haven't you?"

"We tried."

"Yes, yes, I can see that . . . yes . . . would you like to have him?"

Robin's mouth dropped open. She looked at me.

I said, "You don't want him?"

"It's not a matter of that, doctor. I *adore* animals, but my husband doesn't. Or rather, *they* don't like *him*. Allergies. Severe ones. Dogs, cats, horses—anything with fur sets him off and he swells up like a balloon. As is, I'm going to have to take a bubble bath the moment I get home, or Monty will be wheezing the moment he sees me."

She pulled something else out of the purse and gave it to me.

An AKC pedigree sheet for "Van Der Legyh's Lionel Barrymore On Stage." A family tree that put mine to shame.

Mrs. Braithwaite said, "Isn't that noble?"

"Very."

Robin said, "We'd love to take him."

"Good. I was hoping you were nice people."

Smiling, but she took another dubious look around the shop. "He likes his liver snaps and his sausage sticks. Cheese, as well, of course. Though he doesn't seem to have any affection for Edam— isn't that odd, his being Dutch?"

Robin said, "We'll support him in the lifestyle to which he's become accustomed."

"Ye-ess . . ." She glanced furtively around the shop. "I'm sure he'll love your *new* home—will it be in the same location?"

"Absolutely," I said, scooping up the dog and rubbing his tummy. "We've been happy there."

35

It came in a plain white envelope.

Pressed into my hand as I walked out the shop's side door, Spike heeling.

I looked up to see Ruthanne Wallace's kid sister, Bonnie. Tight jeans tucked into cowboy boots, white blouse, no bra, nipples assertive.

She winked at me, tickled my palm with her finger, and ran to the curb. A dark blue Chevy Caprice with chrome wheels and black windows was idling there, blowing smoke. She jumped in, slammed the door, and the car sped off.

No postmark on the envelope, no lettering. Too thin to have anything in it but paper.

I slit it open with my fingernail.

A piece of notebook paper, torn evenly in half.

A note on the first:

Dear doctor.

I am fine. I am happy. Thank you for try to help us. Jesus loves you.

Tiffani.

A drawing on the second. Blue skies, golden sun, green grass, red flowers.

A girl sitting in what looked like an aboveground swimming pool. Fat droplets of water scattering, the girl's face a perfect circle bisected by a crescent-shaped smile.

A signature in the lower right corner: Chondra W.

A title next to the sun:

HAVING FUN.

"Sounds like a good idea," I said to Spike.

Snort, snort.